HER FATHER'S DAUGHTER

"You do not have to work so hard."

"I do, Franz," Katherine told her husband firmly. "I most certainly do!"

"Why? Because of your father?"

"What does he have to do with this?"

"You are trying to prove that you can make as big an impact in the world as he did."

"That's preposterous," Katherine responded coldly.

A minute passed in silence. Then, "Katherine, I am sorry."

Franz's arms snaked around her. Still angry, she ignored his overtures. But some of that anger was now directed inward, because Franz had touched raw nerves. If she'd been working on the *Express* or the *Mail,* it would have been a job, nothing more. Working for her father was different. She had to prove something, not to her father, but to her co-workers. She had to work twice as hard, achieve twice the results, just to be their equal.

And maybe . . . just maybe . . . she was trying to prove something to herself as well. That she was her father's daughter in more ways than just the color of her eyes . . .

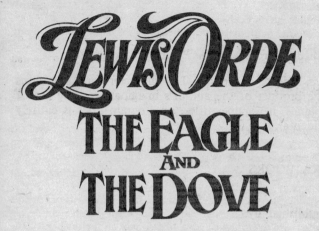

LEWIS ORDE

THE EAGLE
AND
THE DOVE

ZEBRA BOOKS
KENSINGTON PUBLISHING CORP.

Published in hardcover as *The Proprietor's Daughter.*

ZEBRA BOOKS

are published by

Kensington Publishing Corp.
475 Park Avenue South
New York, NY 10016

First Zebra Books printing: December, 1989

Printed in the United States of America

For Collie,
who told me that an even-money winner
is always better than a 50–1 loser.
No sounder advice on life could any father
give his son.

1

Katherine Kassler felt her husband stir beside her in the king-sized brass bed, and she knew it was ten minutes before six. Franz Kassler had a mental clock that unfailingly tugged him from sleep at precisely the same time each morning. Winter or summer, rain or shine, early or late to bed the previous night: it did not matter. At exactly ten minutes before six, even before the housekeeper had stumbled out of bed, Franz was awake and ready for his morning run over London's Hampstead Heath.

The weight on the mattress moved as Franz lifted the quilt, swung his legs over the side, and stood up. Katherine cracked one eye open, focusing slowly in the dimness of the June dawn. Married six years, she still found enormous pleasure in looking at the body of her German-born husband. Tall, fair, athletic, he had a physique that was muscular without being grotesque. Like some mythical Greek god on Mount Olympus, Katherine always thought. But then again, those Greek gods on Olympus should have been so lucky!

Through one barely open eye, Katherine followed her husband's every move as he walked across the sand-colored Wilton. Sliding back a mirrored closet door, he pulled out a gray track suit. As he slipped into it, first the top and then the bottom, Katherine felt a twinge of regret at being deprived of her view. That disappointment lasted for barely a second, until an enjoyable notion took its place. My husband — Katherine pressed her thighs together in an involuntary gesture of anticipation — is one of those rare men who look better without any clothes on at all. My husband is the kind of man who makes tailors throw away their cutting shears, in absolute despair, because no matter what magic they perform with cloth and padding, they can never hope to improve on what nature has bestowed on him in the first place.

Franz began to turn around. Katherine snapped shut the open eye, assuming the pose of sleep. It was best to watch when Franz did not realize he was under observation. But Franz's light blue eyes danced with laughter, as though he understood exactly what had been happening while his back was turned. He leaned over the bed to kiss his apparently sleeping wife on the cheek before leaving the room and pulling the door shut behind himself.

Katherine opened both eyes. The room was growing brighter with each passing second. She lay back, hands clasped behind her head. She could never understand how Franz found such reward in running. He swore that breathing in deep lungfuls of crisp morning air and pumping oxygen through his bloodstream tuned his mind to cope with the coming day. Katherine was the opposite. She preferred to lie in and stare at the ceiling while she planned her day. Only after Franz had returned from the Heath, and had put in another twenty minutes of vigorous exercise, would she get up, as prepared to face the world as he was.

She listened for sounds of the front door closing, the slap of Franz's Pumas on the ground. Instead, her own bedroom door flew open. Two pajama-clad, fair-haired children, a boy of five and a girl of three, exploded into the room.

"Happy birthday, Mummy!"

Henry reached his mother first. Clutched in his hands was a brightly colored sheet of paper. "Look what I made for you! A birthday card, and I painted it!"

Katherine took the card from her son. "It's lovely, thank you very much." As she studied it—a house, a tree, a blue sky with a yellow sun, and a stick woman she assumed was meant to be herself—chubby arms were flung around her neck. A mumbled birthday wish and a wet, sucking kiss announced Joanne's arrival on the bed.

Katherine leaned back against the headboard of thick brass rails, an arm around each child. She glanced toward the open door. In the hallway stood Franz. Instead of beginning his run, he had been priming the children to celebrate their mother's twenty-sixth birthday.

"Happy birthday," Franz called out. "Do you not think you should get up and enjoy it?"

Katherine plucked the pillow from behind her head and flung it at him. He ducked, laughed, and disappeared. A minute later, Katherine heard the front door close.

"Do you like my birthday card?" Henry asked.

"I love it, darling. Did you really do it by yourself?"

The boy nodded solemnly, blue eyes large and round as he acknowledged the magnitude of his deed. Katherine kissed him and his sister, then she clapped her hands. "Both of you go out and play now. I want to get up."

She watched the children chase each other across the room. The door slammed; excited squeals erupted in the hall. Then came a new sound. A woman's voice, singsong but full of authority. Katherine smiled. The children might take liberties with her and

9

Franz, but they toed the line when facing Edna Griffiths, the middle-aged housekeeper who had been with the family for two years.

When the noise subsided, Katherine got up. She walked into the *en suite* bathroom, shivering as the soles of her feet came in contact with the pale beige Italian marble floor. After stepping out of her filmy nightgown, she entered the shower stall, pulled closed the glass door, and turned the water full on. The last vestiges of sleep departed in a blast of ice-cold water.

Refreshed by the shower, Katherine wrapped herself in a terrycloth robe and sat at her dressing table, inspecting her reflection while she ran a brush through thick, shoulder-length blond hair. She liked what she saw. Clear-complexioned, a straight nose set between wide-spaced eyes. Her father's eyes, vivid blue, capable of expressing any emotion. A facial shape that could not quite make up its mind, oval until it reached the chin, and then just a hint of squareness. Her father's chin, determined. She was, all in all, her father's daughter, and Katherine regarded that as the finest compliment she could ever ask for.

Hair still damp, she made her way down to the breakfast room. Decorated country-style, with oak floor and beamed ceiling, the breakfast room overlooked a back garden that was a jungle of shrubs and trees and uncut grass; both Franz and Katherine maintained that children could never have fun in a carefully cultivated garden. Henry and Joanne, now washed and dressed, were sitting at the pine table. Edna Griffiths, a large bustling woman with salt-and-pepper hair pulled back into a functional bun, placed dishes full of cereal in front of them, with the ever-optimistic admonition not to make a mess.

"Kettle's on, Mrs. Kassler," the housekeeper said. "Tea'll be up in a couple of minutes."

"Thank you." This early in the morning, Katherine

had to concentrate to understand the housekeeper. Despite having left her native Swansea twenty years earlier, Edna still possessed a lilting brogue. Instead of speaking sentences, she had a tendency to chant them. Caught between Franz's clipped German accent and the housekeeper's musical Welsh voice, Katherine sometimes felt that she was trapped in the middle of an amateur dramatics production.

Franz returned to the house as Katherine was sipping a cup of tea. Red-faced, skin glistening with perspiration, he entered the breakfast room and stood next to Katherine. "Happy birthday again," he said, and bent down to kiss her.

"If you genuinely wanted me to have a really happy birthday, you would have let me sleep," she complained lightly.

"If I had let you sleep, you would have slept through this." From a pocket in the track suit top, Franz withdrew a small square box.

Watched closely by the children, Katherine opened the box. Inside was a diamond eternity ring. She swung around. "It's beautiful—" she began, before realizing that Franz was no longer there. She could only hear the hammering of his feet as he took the stairs two at a time on his way to the top floor of the three-story house. There were times, Katherine decided, when he had to be the most unromantic swine in the entire world! And those times were always in the morning, when exercise was king.

Katherine waited for fifteen minutes before following Franz up to the top floor. Originally, the sixty-year-old house had contained six bedrooms, four on the second floor, and two on the third. When Katherine and Franz had bought the house six years earlier, they'd had it renovated from the ground up. The work had included gutting the two top bedrooms to create one large game room. Inside was a snooker table and an assortment of exercise equipment:

11

weights, a rowing machine, and a section of bars affixed to one wall.

Reaching the top of the stairs, Katherine heard explosive bursts of breath as Franz pushed himself through the final part of his rigorous daily fitness program. Katherine swung back the door. Franz had discarded the track suit. In black shorts and a white West German soccer shirt — Katherine had made him a gift of a dozen such shirts after West Germany had won the World Cup two years earlier, in 1974 — Franz was lying on a padded gymnasium mat, feet hooked beneath the bottom rung of the wall bars, hands clasped behind his neck as he executed sit-ups. Veins popped in his temples each time he swung his torso up and forward.

"For God's sake, enough already!" Katherine cried out. "You'll do yourself an injury."

"Another twenty!" Franz gasped. "Do you — nineteen, eighteen, seventeen — like the ring?"

"I love it. But I love you more. It hurts me to see you torture yourself like this."

"Not torture! Eleven . . . ten . . . nine . . . !" Franz finished the count and lay back, chest rising and falling like an angry ocean. "Every mile I run, every sit-up I do, adds to my life expectancy. I do not do this for myself. I do it for you, for the children."

"I know you do." Katherine walked to where Franz lay and knelt beside him. Her hair covered his face as she lowered her lips onto his. She found the heat and sweat exciting, like a horse steaming after a gallant race. Katherine could always sympathize with that.

Franz reached up. His hands snaked beneath the terry robe. "If only I had known."

"If only you had known what?"

"That you were waiting for me like this."

"What would you have done?"

"I would have run faster, to be back here sooner."

Katherine stood up, walked to the door and locked

12

it. Turning around, she shrugged herself out of the robe and lay down beside Franz on the padded mat. "I think I'm out of shape. May I join your fitness class?"

"What do you want your exercises to achieve?"

Katherine pulled Franz's West German soccer shirt over his head and tossed it into a corner of the room. "I am looking," she whispered as the tips of her fingers dug tantalizingly beneath the waistband of Franz's shorts, "for an exercise that will give me internal satisfaction."

Franz arched his back and wriggled out of his shorts. "I think I have the very thing you are seeking."

"Oh?" Katherine returned to being the instigator. She kissed Franz's eyebrows, so white as to be almost invisible. Her right hand traced a pattern across his flat stomach, fingernails catching in hair. "Tell me about it."

"It is similar to a push-up," Franz said. He lifted his head just enough to touch his lips to Katherine's right breast, caress the swollen nipple with his tongue. "But you need a partner because you would look very foolish doing it by yourself. Specifically, you need a partner with whom you are in love."

How could she have thought him unromantic? "I love you," she whispered.

"Even hot and sweaty?"

"Especially hot and sweaty!"

Franz began to laugh. Katherine cut off the noise by covering his mouth with her own. It was all she could do to stop giggling as well. Moments like this, stealing away from the rest of the household to make love, were to be treasured.

She sat astride him, balancing, eyes closed, senses seeking that plane of ecstasy. She felt his hands on her shoulders, drawing her down. Their faces touched, and then, with a swift, practiced movement, they rolled over. Katherine's legs wrapped themselves

13

around Franz, her heels dug into him, a rider urging greater effort from her mount. She held him with her arms, with her legs, with her body, and in one gigantic, throbbing spasm, she enveloped his climax within her own.

"Was that a better birthday present than the ring?"

"You bet it was!" she replied, and gently bit his ear.

Fifty minutes passed before they returned downstairs. Franz wore a double-breasted suit, while Katherine was dressed in a gabardine navy pleated skirt with matching jacket, and a cream silk blouse. She bought half a dozen such suits at a time from Harrods, varying the colors and fabrics, but always staying within set style parameters. Fashionable yet businesslike—that was the way she liked to dress for work.

The breakfast room was empty, the children playing in the garden. On the pine table lay the two newspapers that were delivered to the house. Franz lifted the distinctively pink *Financial Times*. Katherine eagerly flicked through the pages of the *Daily Eagle*.

"Are you in there today?" Franz asked.

Katherine's answer was to fold back the newspaper to the Monday's women's section. There was her picture at the top of a feature about a home in Highgate for battered women. Franz read the story as though he were going over a company report, eyes lifting important words and phrases from each paragraph before darting on to the next.

"Poor women, to go through so much."

"That's because they don't have husbands like you."

Franz accepted the compliment with a warm smile. He leaned forward to kiss Katherine gently on the lips, and told her that he would see her that evening.

Katherine followed him to the front door, watching as he climbed into a silver Jaguar sedan and swung out of the driveway, heading for his office in Hayes, near London Airport. Soon after, Katherine left the house, carrying a slim leather attaché case in preference to a handbag. The diamond eternity ring shone brightly from the same finger on which she wore her wedding and engagement rings. She drove her white Triumph Stag as far as Chalk Farm station, taking the underground from there into town. At Tottenham Court Road, instead of changing trains, she rode the escalator to the street. She was early. The weather, for once, was marvelous. She would walk the remaining mile or so.

The warm early morning sun matched the glow inside Katherine. She passed Holborn station, turned down Kingsway and cut through Lincoln's Inn Fields. There was something to be said for starting the day the way she had started it with Franz. A broad grin spread across Katherine's face, happy and stupid and glad to be alive. She bit it back before the people she passed could question her sanity. But what did they know? Had they commenced their day on such a wonderful note? Katherine doubted it, certainly so if the gloomy Monday-morning expressions on their faces were any barometer of how they felt.

She reached Fleet Street to find it at a standstill. Newspaper trucks grumbled in place, the household names emblazoned on their sides now preaching solely to the converted. Buses and taxis disgorged passengers who preferred to get out and walk. Car drivers, unable to do otherwise, simply sat and waited. Only motorcycles moved, jockeying their way through the narrowest of gaps with a defiant roar.

After picking her way through the stagnant sea of traffic, Katherine paused to look down the length of Fleet Street to where it ended at Ludgate Circus, with its imposing backdrop of St. Paul's Cathedral. No matter how many times she had seen it, this view of the world's most famous newspaper street never ceased to thrill her, never failed to instill in her a sense of wonder that she was a part of it. She loved this street like no other place in the entire world.

She turned into Bouverie Street. Above a doorway, in raised white letters, was the legend: Eagle Newspapers Limited. On either side of the door was a title: *Daily Eagle, Sunday Eagle*. Not as grandiose an entrance as that of the *Telegraph* or the *Express*, Katherine could not help thinking, but then the *Daily Eagle* had been publishing for only eleven years, and its Sunday version for five years less. A moment or two when compared with the longevity of Fleet Street's more illustrious denizens.

Entering the building, Katherine came face-to-face with an enlarged, framed copy of the *Daily Eagle*'s first front page. A proud banner in red and black, a lead story about the 1965 Rhodesian independence crisis. Katherine had been fifteen then, a schoolgirl, but she recalled that first issue as clearly as if it had been printed only yesterday, for it had signified the moment when she had decided to become a journalist herself, a writer who would one day work on the *Daily Eagle*.

Heels clicking loudly on the marble floor, she crossed the foyer to one of the two elevators. An elderly man with World War II combat ribbons pinned to his black uniform jacket touched a hand to his lined forehead in a greeting reminiscent of a military salute.

"You're looking very lovely today, miss. Does this old soldier's heart good to see you."

"Thank you, Archie. You're looking very smart yourself." She watched him spin a shining steel wheel, and the elevator began to rise slowly. Katherine had a soft spot for Archie Waters. A retired army sergeant, he had been with Eagle Newspapers since the very first day. His bristling short hair had turned whiter in eleven years, but his back was as straight as it had ever been, and his skin glowed with a just-scrubbed freshness.

"Beautiful day out there, isn't it, Miss Eagles?" Archie ventured. "Makes you think we might even be blessed with a summer this year."

"I wouldn't be that optimistic. Come Wimbledon fortnight and we'll be eating our strawberries and cream beneath umbrellas, just like we always seem to do."

Katherine no longer tried to correct the elevator operator about her name. When she had started work eight years earlier, she had been Miss Eagles. But two years after that, she had married Franz and she'd been Katherine Kassler ever since. Katherine Kassler on her byline and on her paycheck. Katherine Kassler to everyone except Archie Waters. Perhaps Archie found Eagles easier. After all, it was the same as the newspaper company which employed him, just as it was the same as the man who owned the company. Roland Eagles, Katherine's father.

As the elevator crept level with the second floor, Archie said: "That story you wrote in today's paper, Miss Eagles. Made me good and mad, it did."

Katherine was not surprised to hear Archie comment about the women's section; the elderly man read every word of every page while he waited for his elevator to be summoned. "What do you think should be done about it, Archie?"

"Bring back the birch," he answered immediately. "That's the only thing bullies understand, a good taste of what they give out. Think twice before they ever laid a hand on some poor woman again, I can tell you."

The elevator wheezed to a halt at the third floor. Archie started to slide back the door, then stopped. He looked uncertainly at Katherine. "Do you think you could spare me a few minutes later on, Miss Eagles? I need some advice."

17

Katherine was puzzled. What advice could she possibly give a man like Archie? "Let me do a couple of things first."

Archie slid the door fully open, and Katherine stepped out into the *Daily Eagle*'s editorial offices. The smaller editorial staff of the *Sunday Eagle* was housed on the second floor. The two newspapers shared advertising and circulation staff, and printing facilities, but editorial remained independent. Nodding, smiling, and saying, "Good morning," she made her way past blocks of desks belonging to news and sports writers, business writers, and industrial specialists. She considered Archie Waters's comments again. One thing stuck in her mind—what she'd written had made him good and mad. If she could make an old soldier good and mad, then she must be doing her job well. Especially when she was writing about women who were the complete opposite to herself, a woman who had known only wealth and comfort.

The knowledge that she could transcend such a gap filled Katherine with satisfaction. Another young woman with a similar background might have been content to write society pieces, little puffs about a life-style that only one percent of the country gave a damn about. Not Katherine. To her, being a journalist was more important than flattering the egos of the select few. She wanted to write about real people, about the other ninety-nine percent, with such warmth and feeling that her readers would care enough about their problems to demand change. To do so, she was not about to let a privileged background stand in her way.

She reached that area of the editorial floor allocated to the staff of the *Daily Eagle*'s women's pages. Katherine assumed she was the first to arrive, until she saw the door to Erica Bentley's office closed, with a large "Do Not Disturb" sign hanging from the handle. Erica, who edited the women's section, was Katherine's immediate boss. Through the window, Katherine could see her hunched over her desk, making notations on sheets of paper. Only then did Katherine remember that Erica had a budget meeting scheduled for later that morning; she was revving up to fight for more money for her department.

Katherine's own desk was by a small, grimy window overlooking Fleet Street. She dropped her attaché case to the floor and sat down, glancing at the half-dozen messages tucked into the platen of her typewriter. As she assigned priorities, the telephone rang. She lifted the receiver.

"Happy birthday, Kathy," the caller greeted her.

No one but Katherine's father ever called her by the familiar Kathy. No one else ever dared, not even Franz. She loathed the diminutive version of her name, except when her father used it. Over the years, he had made it something special, an esoteric code of love between father and daughter. "You must have eyes everywhere," she told him. "I just this instant got to my desk."

"I'm supposed to have eyes everywhere. I have to know what time my staff gets in."

Katherine swung around to look over the editorial floor. Was her father there, on another line, laughing as he witnessed her confusion? No. Roland Eagles would be calling from his office on the fifth floor of the Adler's department store on Regent Street, where he could gaze through his picture window at the Café Royal, and then down the sweeping curve of Regency architecture to Piccadilly Circus and the statue of Eros.

"The children know it's your birthday?" Roland asked.

Katherine could hear the pleasure in her father's voice as he spoke of his grandchildren. "Henry presented me with a card he'd painted. Joanne gave me a

19

big, wet kiss."

"I envy you," Roland told his daughter. "Nothing's as sweet as a little girl's big wet kiss. I should know — you gave me plenty."

"Daddy, you're embarrassing me."

"I don't mean to, Kathy. What did Franz give you?"

"A beautiful diamond eternity ring. And . . . "

"And . . . ?"

"Nothing." Katherine bit her bottom lip, and touched a hand to her burning cheek. "I was thinking aloud."

"What time will you be over for dinner tonight?"

"Seven-thirty."

"Look forward to seeing you then, Kathy."

Before the connection was broken, Katherine blew a kiss into the mouthpiece. Sharing her birthday with her father was a tradition. The occasion was as important for Roland as it was for her. Not even a guaranteed exclusive on the Second Coming would stop her from keeping that date.

Katherine spent much of the morning catching up on correspondence. When she finished, just after eleven, she remembered her promise to Archie Waters. She walked across the editorial floor and summoned the elevator. "Got time for a cup of tea?" she asked Archie.

Archie accompanied Katherine to a small canteen on the fourth floor. They took cups of tea to a table in the corner. Archie lit a pipe, puffed on it for a few moments, then asked: "What do you know about Islington?"

"It's in North London, and it's become quite fashionable. It's in demand because it's close to the City and the West End." Katherine recalled that Archie lived in Islington. How did he, with his old-fashioned values, feel about his neighborhood changing from working-class to chic, his comfortable pubs being transformed into trendy bars, and his cafés to restaurants with French and Italian names? The affluent young moved in, altered the character of an area, and no one ever seemed to care about the people whose lives they changed.

"Property values have gone up in leaps and bounds," Archie said. "That's fine for homeowners, but people paying rent—people like me—are left holding the short end of the stick."

"What do you want my advice about? Changing neighborhoods?"

"No. Landlords harassing tenants. I live in a block of flats called Cadmus Court, which is on the edge of Islington's *desirable* section. The owners of the building, a mob called Cadmus Property Company, want to do the flats up, then sell them off for a nice profit."

"How many flats are there at Cadmus Court?"

"Sixteen. Four floors, four flats on each. Some three bedrooms, some two. Six months ago, all the flats were occupied. By working people, like me. Cadmus Property Company paid off ten of the tenants. Gave them five hundred pounds each to clear out and find somewhere else to live."

"Five hundred pounds? That won't go far." Katherine bit her tongue immediately; it might not seem a fortune to her, but it was a far from paltry sum for a man like Archie.

"It was enough to get ten of the tenants to leave. The rest of us said no. So the offer was increased to seven hundred and fifty pounds. Two more families left. Then the owners changed tactics. The carrot hadn't worked, so they turned to the stick. Garbage was dumped in the hallways, things broke down and weren't fixed. An empty flat was let to the biggest bunch of rowdies you ever saw. They were only there for a month, but it seemed like a year. Loud parties every night, carryings on like you wouldn't believe.

21

Enough for three more tenants to pack up and leave. Now I'm the only tenant left."

"Wait a minute," Katherine said. "Are you saying the rowdies were placed in the building by the owners? Just to cause a disturbance?"

"Of course they were. When Cadmus Property Company is paying folk to leave, why would they accept new tenants?"

"It's just you and your grandson, right?"

"That's right. Brian. He's sixteen. My son died when the boy was young. His mother was a no-good trollop. Didn't care about the boy at all, only about having a good time. So my wife and me, we brought him up like he was our own. Now, of course, with my wife gone these past eighteen months, it's just me." Archie let out a long sigh and gazed absently at his pipe. "As if life's not tough enough, I've got my landlord trying to kick me out on the street. Now they've started decorating the empty flats. Until late each night they work. It's impossible to get any sleep."

"There are laws to protect tenants from unscrupulous landlords, Archie. Why don't you go to the police?"

"The police?" Archie's look of derision left Katherine with little doubt about his opinions of the police. "Those useless buggers couldn't find their way out of a cul-de-sac in broad daylight. I thought, Miss Eagles, that maybe you could write about it in the paper, like you wrote about that shelter today."

"Accuse the owners of breaking every landlord-tenant act in the book?" Katherine shook her head. "No, Archie, all that might do is leave us open for a libel suit." Which my father, she added silently, would eventually have to settle.

"Miss Eagles, I've lived in Cadmus Court for fifteen years, ever since I got out of the army, and long before the present owners had the building. I'd have

22

an awful time finding any place half as good. I just can't afford to move, certainly not when I've got my grandson to consider."

Mention of the elevator man's grandson tipped the balance for Katherine. Despite the shake of her head only moments earlier, she'd been trying to find a way to help the elderly man. The odds were stacked against him, and Katherine had inherited her father's affection for a gutsy underdog. Now she was certain she had to help him. The cross he's carried all these years, bringing up his late son's child. Doing it alone for the past eighteen months. Katherine knew she would never be able to look him in the eye unless she helped.

"Leave it with me, Archie. I'll see what I can do."

Katherine returned to her desk, knowing that she would have to talk to Erica Bentley about it. Erica was her boss; even the owner's daughter went through a chain of command.

Erica returned at one-fifteen. "Meetings," she muttered disparagingly when she saw Katherine. "That's all anyone ever does around this bloody place. Had lunch yet, or are you demonstrating how conscientious you are by working through it?"

They rode the elevator to ground level, and walked west along Fleet Street. They presented a study in contrasts. Eleven years older than Katherine, Erica was a tall, willowy woman who could have made herself look quite attractive. She had chosen not to, wearing heavy glasses that accentuated the thinness of her face, and flowing dresses that wrapped themselves around her spare frame like a flag twisted around its pole on a windy day. It was as though she were flaunting a sign proclaiming that whatever she had achieved had been done on talent and hard work alone. Next to Erica, Katherine, in her well-cut suit and heavy silk blouse, looked every inch the fashionable businesswoman.

23

The relationship between the two women was also unusual. Erica was placed in the odd position of supervising the proprietor's daughter, although Katherine had pointedly never made any fuss over the family connection to Eagle Newspapers. When she had commenced working at the *Daily Eagle* in 1968, she'd followed the same route taken by any newcomer: running errands and doing odd jobs.

Only once during those early days had anyone poked fun at Katherine for her pedigree. In February 1969, a show-business writer noted for his acerbic wit had called Katherine to his desk. "Would you run over to the Theatre Royal in Drury Lane and pick up my comps for *Mame?* If," he added as Katherine turned to leave on the errand, "that isn't too demeaning a task for our owner's precious little ray of sunshine?"

Katherine swung around, eyes as cold and hard as sapphires. "Don't you bloody well patronize me!" she snapped in a voice that cut clear across the editorial department.

Leaving the show-business writer with a scarlet face, Katherine marched tight-lipped across the suddenly silent floor. As she reached the elevator, a sports writer called out, "Winner by first-round knockout, and still champion of editorial, Katherine knock-your-block-off Eagles!" It was all Katherine could do to keep from exploding with laughter until the elevator door had closed behind her.

After a year at the *Daily Eagle*, Katherine had moved as a junior reporter to the women's section, to work for Erica. Between 1971 and 1973, Katherine took a leave to begin her family. When she returned to work, she resumed her former professional relationship with Erica, and from it a firm friendship had grown. Both Erica and her veterinarian husband, Cliff Bentley, were keen riders. They lived on a small farm near Farnham, an hour south of London on the

24

Surrey-Hampshire border, and were members of a local hunt. Katherine had been an avid horse lover from the moment she had first been treated to a pony ride at Regent's Park Zoo. At least once a month, Katherine, Franz, and the children would spend a day with Erica and Cliff Bentley at the farm. Those days were of special importance to Katherine for the closeness they provided with her two young children. Balancing motherhood and a career was no simple feat, especially when that career entailed occasional evening work. On the weekends, she had the opportunity to amend for her absences.

The two women entered an Italian restaurant. After the waiter had taken their orders, Erica said, "I've heard a lot of very positive response to that article on the women's shelter. Good social-minded reporting."

Katherine spotted her opening. "Archie Waters thought highly of it as well. Said that the story"—Katherine stiffened her back, thrust out her chest, and affected the elderly man's slight Cockney accent—"had made him good and mad. Buggers should be birched!"

Erica gave a dry chuckle. "Archie, our arbiter of good journalistic taste. But then again, maybe he's not so wrong."

"Poor devil's got a ton of trouble at home. Enough to make him tug on my arm and ask for some help."

"Tell me about it."

Katherine did. Over lunch, she told Erica everything. How Archie had brought up his own grandson, the harassment and upheaval he now faced. "I can see you're itching to write the story," Erica said at last. "And if you include as much passion as you used in telling me the tale, you'll have our entire readership in tears. Only that kind of story is not in my bailiwick. I can't say yea or nay on it. All I can do is pass the idea on to Gerry Waller."

Katherine was satisifed with that. Gerald Waller,

the *Daily Eagle*'s editor, was always stressing the importance of having plenty of human interest in the newspaper. Waller had probably been one of those at the budget meeting who had praised the story in that morning's edition.

As they drank coffee, Erica asked, "Made any plans for New Year's Eve yet?"

"A bit in the future, isn't it?"

"Cliff's idea, actually. Why don't you all spend it at the farm, and then you and Franz can be our guests for the New Year's Day foxhunt meet. It's ceremonial, really. Get dressed up in full regalia, assemble in the village square, have a picture taken for the local newspaper. Or are you" — she gave Katherine a look filled with suspicion — "one of those holier-than-thou nasties who opposes foxhunting?"

"Do you ever catch any?"

Erica shook her head. "We drag hunt, lay our own trail for the hounds. That way, there's always a scent to follow, so no one's disappointed. We get a good run for our money, plus we can dictate where the hounds run. No farms, no main roads, and no damned railway lines. Besides, you don't really think my veterinarian husband would belong if we killed foxes, do you?"

"I was wondering about that."

"We still get picketed by the real antihunt fanatics, though. They're against the very principle of hunting. They can't accept that we're just having harmless fun. Too bad."

"Yes, it is," Katherine agreed. "I'll pencil the date in my diary now."

Half an hour after returning from lunch, Katherine received a summons from Sally Roberts, editorial director of Eagle Newspapers. Katherine took just enough time to run a brush through her hair, then she took the elevator to the fifth and top floor—the group's executive floor.

Sally Roberts's office was unlike any other on the top floor. The rest had somber paneling, dark carpet, the forbidding appearance of an exclusive men's club. Sally's was painted in pastel shades. The carpet had a bright pattern, and the furniture was modern. The ambience was Sally's statement that the group had a woman on its board.

When Katherine entered, Sally was wiping the leaves of a rubber tree plant that stood in a brass bucket by the window.

"Ah, the birthday girl," Sally greeted her. "Having a good one?"

"Not bad." Of all people, Katherine thought, Sally Roberts was the one guaranteed to remember her birthday.

Sally sat behind a large mahogany desk. Her dress was a dark green which almost matched the color of her eyes. Katherine had noticed Sally favored that particular shade, because it also complemented the auburn of her wavy hair.

As Katherine settled on the sofa facing Sally's desk, Gerald Waller entered the office. Like Sally, the editor of the *Daily Eagle* was in his early fifties, but he could have passed for forty. No gray streaked his dark brown hair, his face was barely lined, and he lacked even the suggestion of a paunch. The youthful appearance, though, was more than offset by his conservative sartorial tastes, which had caused Erica Bentley to once scathingly remark that Waller owned the world's most comprehensive collection of dark blue suits and white shirts. Katherine liked and respected Waller. He was a hands-on editor, who got himself involved with almost every story.

"Sally . . . Katherine . . ." Waller greeted both women before sitting down and lighting a cigarette.

"Erica mentioned your lunchtime conversation,"

Sally said to Katherine. "Archie's troubles. What do you have in mind?"

Katherine knew she was being asked to sell her idea. "Learn for myself if there's a story. See this harassment firsthand."

"Live with Archie?" Waller asked incredulously.

Katherine nodded. "Just for some of the time. Pretend to be his niece, come up from the country to find work in London." She recognized doubt on Waller's face, and knew exactly what was passing through his mind. Waller was editor—God, Jehovah, Jesus Christ, and Allah all rolled up into one. But in this particular instance, Katherine's father paid God's salary, provided Him with a new Rover sedan each year, contributed to a generous pension plan, and never queried His expenses. The possibility of placing Katherine in even the slightest danger gave Waller cause for concern.

Katherine pressed on. "Only I could pull this off. No one else on the editorial staff has the special rapport I have with Archie. He's like a grandfather figure to me."

Waller wavered. "I don't know, Katherine. Erica says she can spare you, but I just don't know."

"With the victim working for Eagle Newspapers, you'll be able to run the *Daily Eagle* name on every line of the story."

Waller gave a sudden grin, which accentuated the boyishness of his face. "You just persuaded me, Katherine. Make your arrangements to adopt Archie as an uncle, and I'll make certain that you have a photographer nearby at all times. The biggest and strongest we have on staff. But just be careful, all right?"

"I promise."

Waller glanced at his watch and excused himself. As he left the office, Sally's secretary entered and placed a green folder on her desk. Sally pushed it across to Katherine, saying, "This will give you a start, some research on Cadmus Property Company."

"You knew Gerry Waller would approve my idea?"

"I never doubted that you'd know how to get around him."

Katherine opened the folder, read aloud the pertinent details. "Cadmus Property Company's run by a man named Nigel Hawtrey. . . . Archie Waters's block of flats was the first property they bought, back in 1970, and the company's name derives from that initial purchase. . . . Since then, they've acquired five more properties in London. . . . All like Cadmus Court, nice blocks at one time but dilapidated when purchased, so picked up quite cheaply. . . . And all are buildings in areas tipped to be on the upswing." Katherine closed the folder and dropped it onto the desk. "So they can do more of what they're doing to Archie."

"Unless something's done about it," Sally said.

"Did you ever do this kind of investigative reporting in your day, Sally?"

"In my day?" Sally burst out laughing. "I'm still enjoying my day, young lady. I'm only fifty-four, so please don't have me drawing my pension just yet."

"You know what I mean—when you were writing, instead of sitting comfortably on the top floor."

"I did my share. Only in those days, during the war and the bad times afterwards, it was known as muckraking."

Katherine glanced at Sally's left hand. The fingers were devoid of jewelry. Sally had been married twice. A divorce had finished the second, the war had put an untimely end to the first. "Well . . . " Katherine stood up. "I suppose I should start getting into the role of Archie's niece. Do you think I could be his niece from Swansea or Cardiff, somewhere in Wales?"

Sally appeared mystified. "Why Wales?"

29

"Thanks to my housekeeper, I now do a wonderfully authentic Welsh accent. Want to hear?"

Sally waved a hand of dismissal. "Spare me that, please. Get out of here and rake some muck."

2

At five-thirty that evening, Katherine left the newspaper building to join the homeward surge of people on the underground. She took the train to Chalk Farm, where she had left her sports car, and from there battled rush-hour traffic for the remaining few miles home.

She drove without thinking, moving forward or stopping as conditions dictated. Her mind was still at work, locked into that meeting about Cadmus Court. Two words kept surfacing. Special rapport. She had claimed to share such a bond with Archie Waters—that was why she alone would be able to do justice to the story. To a degree, she did. Yet she knew that if a special rapport did exist between herself and anyone else at Eagle Newspapers, that person was Sally Roberts.

At one period or another during Katherine's life, Sally had acted as older sister, favorite aunt, best friend, and fairy godmother. In all probability, although Katherine could not recall it, Sally had changed her and powdered her bottom as well. It seemed she had always been there, with sound advice, a restraining touch, and just occasionally a firm hand to shove Katherine toward a certain objec-

31

tive. Sally had performed many of the same roles for Katherine's father. Plus one other. Twenty-nine years earlier, Sally had been Roland Eagles's lover.

Ahead of Katherine, a traffic light changed to amber. She debated going through until she spotted a police car tucked down a side street. She stopped, applied the handbrake, and continued her train of thought. Sally and Roland Eagles had met in November 1947, on a train from Aldershot to London. In those days, Sally had been a reporter on the now-defunct London *Evening Mercury,* and Roland . . . well, Katherine supposed it was true to say that her father had been between careers. Only hours before meeting Sally, he had exchanged his British army uniform and captain's pips for civilian clothes.

Roland had entered the army in 1940, on his sixteenth birthday. He had lied about his age because he was desperate to join the fight. Only two days earlier, his parents and younger brother and sister had been killed during a German air raid on the Kent coastal town of Margate. When a crippled Heinkel had jettisoned its bomb load along the street where the Eagles family lived, Roland's childhood had come to a savage end.

It had been a happy childhood, marred for Roland by only one thing: the black void that existed between Roland's father and his family. Roland's mother was Catholic, and his Jewish father had incurred the wrath of his own well-to-do family by falling in love with her. The final split had come when Roland's father had married the girl, changed his name to Eagles, and moved from London to the coast. After that, neither side had attempted to make contact. Katherine recalled her father describing the speedy burial service for his family. How he had carried two separate hatreds that day, each screaming for vengeance: one against the men who had caused his family to perish; the other against his father's family, who did not even know his father was dead. Didn't even know that Roland existed!

The traffic light turned green, and Katherine pressed the accelerator to the floor, enjoying the brief stretch of clear road. Her father had avenged himself, all right, for the loss of his family. Awarded the Military Medal *and* the Military Cross—bravery both as a corporal at El Alamein and a lieutenant at Normandy. When he left the army in November 1947, though, he still had one piece of unfinished business. He no longer hated his father's family because he had come to realize that some of the blame must rest with his own father's unforgiving attitude. Roland just wanted to meet them. Not knock on their door and introduce himself like some outcast begging for admittance. First, he wanted to make a name for himself in a country that was recovering from a long and costly war. And then he wanted to meet his father's wealthy family as an equal.

Starting with nothing more than a bankrupt electrical company saved from receivership, Roland had created a retail empire called the Eagles Group. Department stores in Britain, Europe, and the United States. And finally the newspaper group; the dream of every self-made man, to be a press baron. And Sally Roberts had been with him every step of the way, from a lover to friend, and finally employee. No, that wasn't strictly true, Katherine told herself. Sally had never been an employee of Roland Eagles; she had always been his peer.

Katherine considered how strongly the Eagles Group had affected her own life. It was through the group she had met Franz. In the beginning of 1967, Katherine had been vacationing with her father in Monte Carlo. Also at Monte Carlo was a German industrialist named Heinrich Kassler, who was accompanied by his son. Roland and Heinrich Kassler

33

were long-time business associates, who shared a fascination for games of chance. While the two men had amused themselves at the gambling tables, a sixteen-year-old English girl had fallen in love with a German boy of twenty.

For three and a half years, the romance had been kept alive through letters, telephone calls, occasional visits. Then, in 1970, everything changed. The older Kassler asked Roland if he could find Franz a job in London with the Eagles Group; the experience of working in another country, he claimed, would do the young man good. From Katherine, Roland learned the real reason behind the request. Franz had been in trouble, arrested during a Vietnam demonstration outside an American air base. The resultant publicity had severely embarrassed his father. While Roland wavered, Katherine pressured. At last, Roland gave Franz a position in operations, the day-to-day running of the stores.

Within three months of Franz's coming to England, shortly after Katherine's twentieth birthday, they were married. As if to cement the union, Roland sold Heinrich Kassler some of his holdings in the Eagles Group. It was more than a sentimental gesture, however, because it gave Roland the capital to buy back and own privately Eagle Newspapers Limited and a group of department stores based in London's Regent Street, with branches in Manchester and Edinburgh. The department stores had been taken over by the Eagles Group ten years earlier, after Roland had organized a raid on the shares. His aim, he had said at the time, was to use the three prestigious stores to head up what was then a diverse group of shops with little apparent cohesion or direction. In truth, he acquired the stores because of their name, Adler's. The same name Roland's father had rejected so many years earlier, during the split with his family. Roland had introduced himself to his father's family as an equal—by mounting a share raid on what should have been his birthright.

Heinrich Kassler's death in an automobile accident three years after the wedding brought home to Roland that it was time to take things easier. He relinquished his chairmanship of the Eagles Group, sold his shares, and concentrated on running the newspaper group and the Adler's department stores. Both were businesses, Katherine knew, which ran themselves adequately without any help from her father. She often wondered how much he really missed the furious pace of the business life he'd known. . . .

When she arrived home at six-thirty, she found Edna Griffiths preparing Henry and Joanne for bed. "Mr. Kassler telephoned half an hour ago," Edna told Katherine. "Said he'd be stuck in a meeting until late, and would you go on alone to your father? He'll meet you there."

After a quick shower, Katherine put on jeans and a robin's egg blue cashmere roll-neck sweater. Traffic was lighter when she left the house. She could drive the Stag as its designers had intended it to be driven: top down, wind buffeting her face and lifting her hair. She drove the same way she handled a horse, with an easy confidence that, in a less competent person, would have bordered on the reckless. She passed through Stanmore, on London's northwest fringe, and accelerated hard up the long hill leading from the village. Her father's home was at the very top, opposite the common where the local cricket team played on summer weekends.

Drawing level with the common, Katherine swung left to pass between the red-brick pillars marking the entrance to Roland Eagles's home. She doubted that her father had ever once, during his twelve years in the house, wandered across the road to watch a cricket match. He had no interest at all in sport,

35

except for horse racing. Even then, it was not the beauty of the animals that excited him, as it did his daughter, but the opportunity to gamble. To test his skill. How many times had Katherine argued with her father over that . . . ! She recalled once screaming at him in childish fury that God had not created horses for men to bet money on! To which Roland, straight-faced, had teasingly replied: "You're perfectly right. God put them on earth so mankind could have glue."

She stopped in front of the house and switched off the engine. The front door opened and Roland stood framed in the doorway, a tall man with thinning silver hair and a round face dominated by eyes that were every bit as blue as his daughter's. He wore a dark gray single-breasted suit which, although simple in style, was exquisitely tailored. The suit, like almost every piece of clothing Roland wore, came from H. Huntsman and Sons, in Savile Row.

Katherine climbed out of the car, ran toward her father and kissed him on the cheek. Roland held her close for several seconds before gently pushing her back to arm's length so he could study her face. "Look at you—little Kathy, all grown up."

"How does it feel to have a daughter of twenty-six?"

"Old. Ancient. Venerable. Antique."

"That's all?"

"Give me a minute to check the thesaurus, come up with a few more similes."

"Synonyms," Katherine corrected him. "A simile is a figure of speech which likens one object to another, while a synonym—"

Roland placed a finger on his daughter's mouth. "I don't need to know the difference between similies and synonyms. I hire people like you to know for me."

Katherine stepped back, hands on hips. "You're

like all employers — you think your money can buy everything."

"As opposed to journalists, who think they're the only ones in the entire world fit to make moral judgments?"

Katherine laughed and kissed her father again. She entered the house, walking through the large reception hall into the drawing room with its comfortable floral-print chairs and sofas. In front of the bay window was a Victorian-style rocking horse. Pinned to its head was a card with Katherine's name.

"Is that really for me?" She moved closer to inspect the horse. It was fifty-two inches at the head, dappled gray with white mane and tails and tan leather upholstery. "Or is it for Henry and Joanne? Your subtle way of spoiling them even more under the guise of giving me a present."

"Does it really matter?"

"No." She mounted the horse sidesaddle. It could go up to the game room, where the children would be able to ride it to their heart's content. Just as long as Franz was not going through his morning exercise routine — and she was not with him!

She slid off the horse as the drawing room's double doors opened. A thin man in his late middle years, wearing a black jacket and gray striped trousers, entered the room. "Miss Katherine, how nice to see-you."

"Thank you, Mr. Parsons. Are you and Mrs. Parsons well?" Arthur Parsons and his wife, Peg, had been with Roland for twelve years. At fourteen, Katherine had felt uncomfortable calling them by their given names. Now, grown up, habit precluded familiarity.

"Very well, thank you." Parsons turned to Roland. "Dinner will be ready whenever you desire, sir."

"Half an hour or so. We're waiting for my son-in-law."

"As you wish, sir."

Parsons withdrew, closing the doors behind him. Katherine walked across the room to the fireplace. The mantelpiece was bare except for a clock and a framed black-and-white photograph. She took the picture to the bay window, which looked out over a colorful rose garden.

"You know, other than your hair going gray and . . . well, sort of thin, you've hardly changed in the last twenty-seven years."

"I believe I've just been damned with faint praise," Roland said as he joined Katherine at the window. The photograph showed him sitting at a table in a London nightclub. Next to him was a young woman with jet-black hair and dark, lively eyes. The light of the photographer's flashbulb was bright in their faces, and they shared a slightly startled look, as if they somehow understood that they would soon be the standard-bearers of youth and romance in an age of austerity and ration books.

The young woman was Catarina Luisa María Menéndez, the eighteen-year-old daughter of Nicanor Menéndez, the Argentine Ambassador to the Court of St. James's. Catarina and Roland were in love and wanted to marry, but the ambassador refused to give his consent to such a match. Nicanor Menéndez had brought his only daughter to England for her to meet a suitor of quality, a man from a long-established, well-connected family: he had not intended her to be swept off her feet by a sharp-witted, half-Jewish adventurer.

After failing to change the ambassador's mind, the lovers eloped on New Year's Day 1950, fleeing to Scotland, where the age of consent was lower and Catarina could marry without her father's blessing.

Soon, the need for their haste became obvious. Catarina was expecting a baby, but it was a pregnancy she was fated to complete in tragic circumstances. A month short of full term, she and Roland were involved in a car accident. Catarina's head hit the dashboard. She lost consciousness. Doctors diagnosed a massive cerebral hemorrhage, caused by the bursting of an aneurysm at the base of Catarina's brain. Her condition deteriorated, and Roland was faced with a terrifying choice—try to save the child and almost certainly lose the mother, or continue fighting for the mother and probably lose both. Staring numbly at the doctors, he forced his mouth to form the words "Save the child."

Half an hour after the baby girl was delivered through cesarean section, Catarina died.

Roland gave his daughter two names: Katherine after her mother, and Elizabeth after his own mother. He would have more children, in relationships that were doomed not to last. A son and daughter by a woman with whom he lived for several years and who eventually married someone else; another son, by his second wife, a Frenchwoman, who took the boy to live in Paris after the marriage collapsed. But he would never feel as close to them as he did to Katherine. She meant so much more to him than any other child ever could. She was the living link to Catarina, the fruit of what he was certain would forever remain the single great love of his life. And the black-and-white photograph he kept on the drawing-room mantelpiece was his favorite pictorial memory of the time with Catarina. Their relationship had still been carefree then. Her father, unaware of the depth of their feeling, had not yet tried to terminate it.

"Every time I've ever made a wish," Katherine said, "it's been the same one—that she were still here."

"Your wishes echoed mine." Roland wrapped an arm around his daughter's shoulders and squeezed fondly. "You and your mother would have got on like a house on fire, provided you both saw eye-to-eye on everything. She had a will of iron. Death was the only foe she couldn't get the better of."

Katherine rested her head against her father's arm. She understood how full of contrasts this day was for him. The happiness of his daughter's birthday coupled with the anguish generated by the anniversary of his wife's death.

"The only thing that stopped me from throwing a rope over the nearest tree that day," Roland murmured, "was you."

Katherine shuddered. "Please don't talk like that."

"Kathy, darling, you saved my life. If you hadn't been there, if I hadn't had you to worry about . . ." His voice trailed away as another scene was triggered by this day. The memory of a final confrontation with Ambassador Menéndez, the two men fighting in a court of law over the right to bring up Katherine. Roland had won custody of his daughter by beating down the ambassador's charge that he was an unfit father, and then he'd continued to show what a loving father he was by raising the most beautiful and talented daughter any man could possibly want.

At last, Katherine replaced the picture on the mantelpiece. She had inherited none of her mother's gypsy looks. Her own fairness, Roland had told her, came from his mother. Too bad there were no photographs for Katherine to see, to compare; they had all been destroyed when the house had been bombed.

Franz arrived a few minutes before eight. They sat down to eat, Roland at the head of the long table in the dining room, his daughter and son-in-law on either side of him. Arthur Parsons formally served the meal of vichyssoise and poached salmon, which his wife had prepared.

"What's the latest news from the house I built?" Roland asked his son-in-law.

Franz chuckled at Roland's description of the Eagles Group. He might have resigned as chairman three years earlier and sold his shares, but he could never forget that he had been the driving force behind the success of the corporation which still carried his name. Franz kept Roland abreast of all developments before they reached the financial pages. "We are contemplating some further expansion in the States."

"The Biwell shops?" Roland asked, referring to a chain of discount appliance stores along the East Coast.

"Yes. The opportunity has arisen to acquire a similar group of stores in the Midwest. Sometime in the near future, we shall be meeting with our American lawyers."

Katherine glanced at her father, saw the gleam in his eyes. "You wish you were a part of it, don't you?"

"Do I?" Roland seemed amused by his daughter's assumption.

"I can see you do. You're sitting there with your tongue hanging out at the very mention of a major takeover. You miss the life, don't you? What you're left with isn't enough."

Roland set down his knife and fork and looked along the length of the table to the French windows leading out to an immaculately maintained back garden. "What I have now—the three Adler's stores and Eagle Newspapers Limited—runs itself very well. I might attend meetings, spend time in offices, but I'm not really necessary to the workings of those companies. I make the motions, that's all. It's like"—he looked from one young face to the other, uncertain that they would be able to understand—"when a child grows up. A father is still a father, but what function does he really have to perform? He can advise, perhaps, but his child is an adult now

41

and no longer really needs any help."

"You sound like an echo of Sally earlier today," Katherine said. "I referred to the way things had been during her day, and she jumped down my throat. Seems I was trying to retire her before she was good and ready. Now you're regretting having retired yourself."

"The scourge of the middle-aged," Roland joked. "Constantly searching for proof of one's usefulness."

"I've got a way for you to be useful." Without mentioning that she would be spending time at Archie Waters's home, Katherine spoke of the assignment she'd taken on. "Before I left the office tonight, I did some research on Cadmus Property Company, the building's owners. I'd guessed that they'd be some small and nasty firm looking for a fast killing, but it turns out that they're owned by one very big and very respectable corporation, Saxon Holdings."

Roland whistled in surprise. "The *Wunderkind* . . . that was John Saxon's nickname when he started Saxon Holdings fifteen years ago. Made himself a millionaire by the time he was twenty-five. Moved property around like he was playing Monopoly. Whatever he bought, he always had another buyer for—at a much better price. His secret in those days was buying without ever risking a penny of his own money. Now, of course, he buys for the longer term."

"What's John Saxon like, as a person?"

"I only met him once, ten years ago. We sat together on some government panel. As I recall, he was exactly what you'd expect a *Wunderkind* to be. Effusive, charming, perfectly capable of selling freezers in Alaska during January, and central heating in the Congo during the middle of August." Roland paused while Arthur Parsons removed the dinner plates and refilled the wineglasses from a bottle of Meursault. "From that one meeting, I don't think I'm really qualified to say what John Saxon's like. But I can certainly tell you what he is *not* like. He is not the kind of man to harass a tenant who's probably paying minimal rent to begin with. Saxon Holdings, Kathy, owns commercial property on the best streets. Luxury residential buildings in Mayfair and Knightsbridge. I would not have thought they'd own a rundown block of flats in some place like Islington. But even if they do, they are not going to risk their good reputation by criminally driving out tenants just to turn a fast profit. Be very careful before you link a man like John Saxon with such a thing."

"Do you think it could be happening without Saxon knowing?" Franz asked.

Roland considered the question. "I suppose it's possible. The brigadier doesn't always know what every corporal in the brigade is up to."

Katherine and Franz left the house at ten-thirty. After kissing her father good night, she held onto him and asked: "What are you going to do now, Daddy? Sit in the front room and remember?"

Roland gave his daughter a patient smile. "Can you think of a better way to commemorate this particular day? Kathy, I loved your mother more than I ever loved any woman, and she loved me just as passionately. Because of that, I believe that on this day each year, we can communicate with each other, reach out beyond whatever physical boundaries normally limit us and make contact."

Katherine blinked back a tear. It tore right through her to know that after twenty-six years her father remained as devoted to her mother as he had ever been. "Will you give her my love?"

"I always do, darling." Roland helped his daughter into the open sports car. "And she always sends you hers."

Franz's Jaguar followed the Triumph Stag down the hill and through the village. After two traffic circles, the road widened into a divided highway. Franz accelerated. The luxury sedan glided past the sports car and pulled back into the inside lane. Katherine flashed her lights, and Franz responded with a clenched-fist victory salute.

Katherine bit her lower lip. She glanced over her shoulder, changed down, and pulled out. The tachometer needle swung toward the red zone. When she changed up again, the Jaguar was once more positioned comfortably in her rearview mirror. Even her gesture of triumph was more dramatic—with no roof to impede it, her thrusting fist soared up toward the stars.

They played leapfrog all the way home. Overtaking, cutting in front of each other, flashing headlights, waving fists, and laughing. Katherine knew she should have been cold with the roof down and the wind roaring past her ears, but excitement lent warmth to her body.

Franz reached home first. Katherine came in right on his tail. They clambered out of their cars and embraced. "Thank God the police were busy elsewhere," Katherine said. "Otherwise we'd both have spent the night in jail."

Still hugging each other, they entered the house. Belatedly, Katherine remembered the lateness of the hour. She raised a finger to her lips, and with exaggeratedly cautious steps they climbed the stairs. In their own room, Franz collapsed backwards onto the bed, arms outstretched, chest heaving with laughter. Katherine fell face-down on top of him.

"You drive the same way you make love," she told him "Like a wild man."

"I did not notice you observing speed limits." He lifted his face to kiss her.

"You make me so happy," she said.

"Not half as happy as you have made me."

They undressed and made love, exploring with sensations of wonder and surprise, feeling pleasure that after six years there was nothing false or automatic about their movements, nothing jaded about their passion for each other.

Afterwards, as they lay spoon-in-spoon, hovering between wakefulness and slumber, Katherine said, "Remember that assignment I mentioned I was working on?"

"The building owned by the company of the *Wunderkind?*"

"I'm going to be staying there, a few hours every night. From early evening until around midnight."

Franz's body stiffened. "What is the point of that?"

"To get a firsthand feel for what's going on."

"How many nights will you be doing this?"

"As long as necessary."

"And the children? Who is supposed to look after the children while you get this feel for what is going on?"

Katherine turned around to face Franz in the darkness. Although his voice was low, she sensed his displeasure. Franz had many traits that could be considered old-fashioned. In many areas, Katherine was old-fashioned herself. Except when it came to a woman having a career of her own. There, she and Franz differed totally. He could never understand that a woman would actually *want* to work. He believed that a married woman should work only if financial circumstances dictated it, and then the husband should be ashamed of himself for failing to be an adequate provider.

"We have a very capable housekeeper," Katherine said slowly. "Edna will look after the children for the few evenings I won't be here."

"Edna is not the children's mother. She was hired

to run the house, not substitute for you."

"Damn it, Franz! Do I complain about those times you work late—even the times you have to go away? Do I accuse you of being a lousy father because of it?"

"The work I do is important."

"What do you think mine is—a hobby? I help people with my work; what's more important than that?"

"But you do not need to do it."

"I do, Franz. I most certainly do!"

"Why? Because of your father?"

"What does he have to do with this?"

"You are trying to prove yourself."

"What's that supposed to mean?"

"You are trying to prove that you can make as big an impact in the world as he did."

"That's preposterous," Katherine responded before turning around again, presenting her back to Franz. She had nothing to prove where her father was concerned. She was his daughter, not his son. Only sons had to fight their way out of their father's shadow, like Franz had done in Germany. Embarrassing his father's establishment values by joining Vietnam demonstrations outside American bases. Only Katherine would not bring that up, because Franz's father was dead, and you let the dead rest.

A minute passed where no word was spoken, no sound made. Then, "Katherine, I am sorry."

Franz's arms snaked around her. She felt his body pressing, a growing hardness. Still angry, she ignored his overtures. But some of that anger was now directed inward, because Franz had touched raw nerves. If she'd been working on the *Express*, the *Mail*, or—God forbid!—Murdoch's *Sun*, it would have been a job, nothing more. She would have completed her work professionally, and gone home in the evening. Working for her father was different.

She had to prove something, not to her father but to her coworkers. She had to work twice as hard, achieve twice the results, just to be their equal. Nobody ever commented on the relationship—at least, not since seven years earlier when she'd put the show-business writer firmly in his place—but she knew that she was under constant scrutiny for any sign of nepotism.

And maybe . . . just maybe . . . she was trying to prove something to herself as well. That she was her father's daughter in more ways than just the color of her eyes and the shape of her jaw.

3

Katherine began the assignment two days later, on the Wednesday. She left the *Daily Eagle* early that evening in the company of Archie Waters. Her car and any jewelry she customarily wore were back at home in Hampstead, along with her real identity. She was now Archie's niece, up from Southend on the Essex coast, staying with her uncle while she found work in London. She wore a cotton print dress, low-heeled shoes, and a raincoat, which had been purchased at Marks and Spencer in Oxford Street. Even her hair was styled differently, pulled back in a ponytail that made her look barely twenty years old.

Cadmus Court was a squat four-story building backing onto a small park. The approach from the main road was along a short street lined with neat attached houses, each boasting its own carefully groomed postage stamp of a garden. The effect of brightness and order was destroyed as Katherine drew close to Cadmus Court. The outside of the building was a dirty gray, badly in need of paint. Shrubbery was overgrown. The double gates leading to the small forecourt were hanging off their hinges. Beyond the gates were parked two battered, rusty vans.

"Builders," Archie explained as he walked across the forecourt. "Vans belong to the builders." Even as he spoke, Katherine heard the high-pitched shriek of a power saw from somewhere within the building.

Archie's home was on the second floor. Katherine followed him up a flight of stairs and then picked her way along a narrow hallway strewn with building materials and garbage. Two young men in overalls came through the doorway of an empty apartment, struggling with an old bathtub. They dumped it right in front of Archie, forcing him to maneuver awkwardly around the obstacle.

"Better watch where you're going, grandpa," one of the men said. "Bath's big enough to see, isn't it?" Then, noticing Katherine, the builder rolled his eyes and whistled. Katherine saw Archie's face whiten with barely suppressed fury. Twenty years earlier, he would have dulled the freshness of these two men by quick-marching them around the parade ground under full pack for a couple of hours. Now he was an elderly man who could do little but accept their insolence.

Archie rang the bell at the next apartment. The door was opened by a boy in his middle teens.

"This is my grandson, Brian."

Katherine said "Hello" and smiled, trying hard not to show how put off she was by the first sight of Archie's grandson. He was a clone of ten thousand other youths. Same clothes: jeans, sleeveless sweater over a striped shirt, heavy welted shoes. Same surly expression stamped across his face. The same belligerent challenge in his dark brown eyes.

Archie's voice was sharp. "Brian, where's your manners? Invite the lady in; take her coat."

Scowling, Brian held out his hand. Katherine gave him her coat and entered. Archie showed her around—two bedrooms, large living and dining

49

rooms, a bright kitchen overlooking the park at the rear of the building. He was particularly proud of a varnished display case affixed to the living-room wall. In it were decorations from Archie's military service in World War II, Malaya, Korea, and Cyprus.

Katherine ate with Archie and his grandson the pork chops the old man prepared. She was not surprised that Archie could cook; he did everything else. The instant the meal was finished, Brian pushed himself back from the table, stood up, and turned around. Archie rapped on the table with the pipe he had been about to light. "Haven't you forgotten something, young man?"

"Excuse me, please," The request was forced, the words spoken grudgingly.

"That's better." Archie watched the boy leave the room. A minute later, the front door slammed.

Archie allowed Katherine to help him clean up, then they sat in the living room. "Is Brian still at school?" Katherine asked.

"Until next month, when the term ends."

"What will he do then?"

"I'll ask around the newspaper for him. He rides a moped, so maybe there'll be an opening for a messenger. Keep him out of trouble, at least." Archie drew on his pipe and trickled smoke from his mouth. "You have to understand, Miss Eagles, he's not really a bad lad, but he's taken to hanging around with a rotten mob. This crowd he meets up with at the football games every week. The ones who start all the trouble, the fights. Skinheads they used to call themselves—"

"We still use that name," Katherine said, referring to the press. In popular-newspaper parlance, the word *skinhead* had become synonymous with soccer hooliganism.

"Well, since they stopped practically shaving their

heads, grew their hair a bit, the skinhead name's died," Archie said. "That's what Brian tells me. But they still all dress the same, like they're in some kind of uniform."

Just then, a tremendous hammering erupted. The common wall between the living room and the adjacent apartment shuddered. Archie leaped from his chair just in time to grab the display case full of military decorations before it crashed to the floor. "The builders," he said unnecessarily, "reminding us that they're hard at work."

"And by some chance, they have to work right next door to the only occupied flat." Katherine jotted down shorthand symbols on a small pad. "I'd like a picture of you saving that display case, and one of the junk in the hallway. Our photographer's sitting twenty yards up the street in his car."

The builders left shortly after eleven o'clock, and silence descended. Katherine summoned the *Eagle* photographer, a burly man named Sid Hall, who, coincidentally, happened to be a judo black belt. Under Katherine's direction, Hall photographed the litter in the hallway and Archie saving the display case. Earlier, the photographer had taken exterior shots to show the building's neglected state.

At midnight, Hall drove Katherine home. She found Franz occupying an armchair in the library. Next to him, on a mahogany side table, rested a pile of business reports. "Staying up late to work?" Katherine asked as she kissed him. "Or to check that your wife's still in one piece?"

"A little of both." He ran his eyes over her, as if to make certain she was really unharmed. "You look like a schoolgirl, with your hair like that, and in those clothes. A schoolgirl should not be out so late."

"I had good protection." She described Sid Hall, the *Eagle*'s picture-taking *judoka*. On the way upstairs, she told Franz what had happened that night, breaking into the story only to look in on Henry and Joanne, and plant a kiss on the forehead of each sleeping child.

As they settled in bed, Katherine gave Franz the most gentle of kisses, nothing more than a brush of her lips against his, followed by the words "Thanks for keeping a light burning in the window."

He returned the kiss. "Do you really think I could go to bed without knowing you were all right?"

They fell asleep in a better humor than they had done two nights earlier.

Katherine found Sid Hall's photographs on her desk when she arrived at the office the next morning. She carried them to a meeting that afternoon with Gerald Waller and Sally Roberts.

"Not bad for a night's work," Waller said as he sifted through the pictures. "What's next on the agenda?"

"Get the other side of the story."

"How do you propose doing that?" Sally asked. "By seeing the man who runs the management company? What was his name?"

"Hawtrey. Nigel Hawtrey. Of course I'm not going to visit him. I'd give away the fact that I'm working on a story if I did. Instead, I'll make him come to me."

That evening, Katherine again made the journey to Islington with Archie Waters. The noise from the next apartment provided a steady accompaniment to the evening meal. It seemed to increase as Archie watched television with his grandson, who had stayed in. By nine-thirty, the noise had reached a crescendo, a frenzy of hammering that shook the walls.

Katherine removed a slip of paper from her purse. "Archie, ring this number. It's the home of Nigel Hawtrey, the managing director of Cadmus Property

Company."

"How did you get that? It's ex-directory."

"Power of the press." She swore she spotted a flicker of interest in Brian's dark eyes. It was the first positive sign she had seen from the boy.

Archie dialed the number. "Mr. Hawtrey! This is Archie Waters from Cadmus Court!" He had to yell to make himself heard over the noise from next door. "I want you to listen to something!" He dragged the telephone over to the front door, flung it open, and thrust the receiver out into the hallway. The noise, if it were at all possible, seemed even louder out there. "Do you hear that, Mr. Hawtrey? That's what I've got to put up with at nine-thirty at night. If I can't get any peace and quiet then, by damn, neither will you!"

Ten minutes later, on Katherine's instructions, Archie dialed the number again. "Mr. Hawtrey, it's still as noisy as ever!" Once more he held the receiver out in the hallway. "The moment your men stop disturbing me, I'll stop disturbing you."

When Archie telephoned a third time, there was no answer. Either Nigel Hawtrey was refusing to lift the receiver, or, as Katherine hoped, he was on his way to Cadmus Court.

After thirty minutes, the noise from the next apartment ceased. The heavy silence that followed was broken at last by a loud, authoritative knock on the front door. Archie pulled it back. Outside stood a tall, fat man in his late thirties. An open-necked shirt, blue sportcoat, and black trousers strained to contain his girth. His curly brown hair was tangled, and his watery blue eyes blinked rapidly from behind horn-rimmed glasses.

"How the bloody hell did you get my phone number?"

"That's my business!" Archie replied with equal vehemence. "I just wanted you to hear the racket I

53

have to live with."

Nigel Hawtrey squeezed through the doorway to tower over Archie. He took no notice of Katherine and Brian, who stood behind the elderly man. "Don't blame me for your troubles, Mr. Waters. You're your own worst enemy. Whatever's happened here, you brought it on your own head."

"How's that?"

"You had the opportunity to move out and be paid for it. You decided not to. That was your prerogative, but now you can't blame me for trying to make a profit on this building. I want to knock it into shape, then sell it. The other tenants saw the sense of getting out, but you, the old soldier, you had to dig in, didn't you? Fine, if you want to carry on living here, paying a tiny portion of the true rental value, go right ahead. But you're going to have to put up with a little inconvenience now and then."

"A little inconvenience?" Katherine echoed. "Any dictionary worth its sale would define this as harassment."

Hawtrey's eyes darted past Archie to Katherine. "And who would you be—some do-gooder from the Citizen's Advice Bureau?"

"I'm Mr. Waters's niece. I'm living with my uncle while I find a job in London."

"His niece, eh? Well let me tell you something about your uncle. It's him who's harassing me. Lives here for next to nothing and expects roses, too." Hawtrey swung back to Archie. "If you want to speak to me again, you call me during office hours, *at* my office. You ever call me at home again, and you'll find out what harassment is!" He spun around and left. Within a minute, the noise from the next apartment picked up again. It did not cease until after midnight, as if the builders had been told to work even longer hours. A little extra aggravation for the Cadmus Court holdout . . .

Late Thursday night, long after Katherine had been taken back to Hampstead by Sid Hall, a lone marksman stood in the park behind Cadmus Court and flung rocks through every rear-facing window of Archie Waters's home. The first missile crashed through the window of Brian's bedroom, showering the boy with glass as he lay in bed. The next went through Archie's bedroom window. A third shattered the kitchen window, and a fourth and fifth accounted for the bathroom and toilet. No other apartment suffered damage. Whoever threw the rocks was very familiar with the layout of the building.

Sid Hall rushed to Islington the following morning to take photographs of the damage. That same afternoon, clutching an envelope full of barely dry prints, Katherine took a taxi from Fleet Street to St. James's Square, between Piccadilly and Pall Mall. The taxi set her down on the south side of the square. Through a revolving door, she entered a modern six-story building which proclaimed itself, in gold-colored block capitals, to be Saxon House. The first five floors were leased to a variety of tenants: an advertising agency, a public relations firm, accountants, quantity surveyors, publishers, importers. Katherine punched the elevator button for the sixth floor, where Saxon Holdings had its head office.

The elevator halted. She stepped out into a reception area, facing a desk at which sat a stern-faced, gray-haired woman. The wall behind the desk displayed pictures of the company's many properties. Katherine recognized several of the buildings. What had her father said? Commercial property on the best streets, luxury residential buildings in Mayfair and Knightsbridge. It made no sense for a top company like this to be involved with a place like Cadmus Court. Or with a fat bully like Nigel

Hawtrey!

"May I help you?" the receptionist asked.

"I'd like to see Mr. Saxon."

"Your name?"

She took Archie's surname. "Katherine Waters."

The receptionist checked a large desk diary. "You don't have an appointment, do you? I'm sorry, but Mr. Saxon is a very busy man. If you'd like to leave a message for him—"

Katherine cut the woman off by dropping the envelope full of photographs onto her desk. "Just make sure he sees these. They're pictures of damage done to the home of my uncle, Archie Waters, who's a tenant in Cadmus Court, a building owned by one of Mr. Saxon's companies. You can also tell Mr. Saxon that the damage was authorized by the man who runs the company for him, Nigel Hawtrey." She swung around, walked to the elevator and jabbed the button. The elevator arrived immediately. As the door closed, Katherine saw the receptionist scurrying from her desk, the envelope in her hand.

Katherine left the elevator at the ground floor and headed for the revolving door. She noticed the doorman sitting at his desk, talking on the telephone. As she neared the door, the man put down the receiver and chased after her.

"Miss Waters!" Katherine stopped and turned around. "Mr. Saxon would like to see you. Would you please go back upstairs?"

"Thank you." She returned to the elevator. This time, when it opened on the top floor, the receptionist was not at her desk. She was standing by the elevator door, waiting for Katherine.

"Please come with me, Miss Waters." The woman's tone was as unctuous now as it had been abrasive before. She led Katherine through a long corridor flanked by glass-fronted offices. They reached a heavy oak door. The receptionist opened it. "Mr. Saxon, we managed to catch the young lady."

Katherine entered the office. John Saxon, standing by open French windows that led out to a narrow wrought-iron balcony, was gazing down at St. James's Square. Katherine remained in the center of the large office, wondering when the man would acknowledge her presence.

At last, he turned around. "I was hoping it would be you."

"I beg your pardon?" She began to feel flustered.

"Come here." Saxon took her arm and propelled her to the balcony. "My front garden, that's how I think of St. James's Square. When I'm not busy, I like to stand on the balcony and look out over my front garden, especially at this time of year when everything's so green. Wonderful sight, isn't it?"

Saxon continued talking as Katherine looked down. "Those are plane trees in the square, very tall. And that equestrian statue of William the Third, erected in 1807, you know." He lifted his hand to indicate buildings. "The architectural mix describes London's history. Those Georgian town houses on the north and west sides of the square, the nineteenth- and twentieth-century buildings on the other two sides. It's a *Who's Who* of London, the people who've lived here. Why, number ten St. James's Square alone has been the residence of three prime ministers, William Pitt, Edward Stanley, and Gladstone."

Katherine finally found her voice. "Thank you for the history lesson, but that is not the reason I came to see you."

Saxon seemed not to hear. "A couple of minutes ago, I saw a taxi stop. A blond woman, holding a large envelope, got out." Still holding Katherine's arm, he guided her to his desk, where Sid Hall's pictures were spread out. "Then, when these were

57

given to me, left here by a young and very angry blond, I just put two and two together and figured it had to be you."

Katherine freed herself of Saxon's grip. She had time to take stock of him now. She judged him to be in his late thirties or early forties, not quite six feet tall, and slim enough to look like a clotheshorse for the lightweight tan suit he wore. Light brown hair was parted high on the right side, and his brown eyes had a hint of warmth and humor in them, as if he were enjoying some private joke. Perhaps he was, Katherine reflected. Having seen her climb from the taxi, he'd been proven right about her identity. He was allowed to smile at that, to congratulate himself for his perception.

"Is that the only reason you sent the doorman after me? Because you . . . you . . ."

"Fancied you?" Saxon suggested as he sat on a leather couch by the windows. "Can you think of a better reason?"

"Yes, I most certainly can. Like sending the door-man after me because you were ashamed of the disgusting treatment meted out to my uncle by one of your companies."

"I'm sorry to disappoint you, Miss Waters, but I'm not ashamed of anything. It is preposterous to believe that Mr. Hawtrey of Cadmus Property Company could be responsible for the damage depicted in those photographs."

"Take my word for it—he was."

"Oh, for heaven's sake!" Saxon gave Katherine a hint that temper lay just below sophistication. "Those windows look out onto a park. Any drunk on his way home from the pub could have done it. Any little delinquent who likes to hear the sound of breaking glass could have been responsible."

"Then how do you explain why only my uncle's windows were hit? The only occupied flat in the building."

"Maybe someone has a grudge against your uncle."

"Yes, your Mr. Hawtrey. And what about the other harassment to which my uncle has been subjected?"

Saxon went to his desk and flicked the switch on the intercom. Moments later, a young woman entered the office and gave Saxon a file. Scanning through it, he asked Katherine: "What harassment are we talking about?"

"Garbage in the hallways. Breakdowns that weren't fixed. Renting to rowdy tenants. And now builders who work next door until midnight."

"The garbage in the hallways . . . it's an open building, Miss Waters; anyone can walk in and vandalize the place. Breakdowns are always rectified as soon as it's humanly possible. The noisy tenants were evicted after we had complaints, and as quickly as the legal processes allowed us to perform the eviction. And as for builders working late, Mr. Hawtrey is under instructions to have Cadmus Court renovated and on the market at the earliest possible time."

Katherine was about to argue that breakdowns had not always been fixed. She was about to ask why, when tenants had been paid to leave, an apartment had been let to a crowd of troublemakers. But Saxon cut her off with an imperious wave of the hand.

"The board of directors of Saxon Holdings has the utmost faith in Mr. Hawtrey's ability to get the job done. And to get it done within the confines of law and decency."

The humorous glint in Saxon's eyes was a mirage, Katherine decided. "Thank you for seeing me, Mr. Saxon. Our meeting has been an enlightening experience."

She left Saxon House thinking deeply about the man after whom it was named. John Saxon was every bit as charming as her father had said he was. She'd seen that in the first few minutes when he had talked so knowingly, and so lovingly, of St. James's Square. He was a man to whom historical surroundings were important. He was proud to be a part of them. Proud, she thought, to be English. But that charm served only to camouflage a heart of ice.

Or did it? What about her father's other comment: the brigadier not knowing what every corporal in the brigade was up to? Was it possible that Saxon did not know the truth about Hawtrey? She hoped that was the case, because, for some reason, she did not want Saxon to be involved in anything so despicable.

By Friday evening, all the broken windows had been replaced. Katherine had little doubt that her visit to John Saxon had prompted the hasty repair.

Friday and Saturday evening at Cadmus Court passed without incident. Brian went out on his moped both nights, each time returning as his grandfather was escorting Katherine to Sid Hall's car. Katherine questioned how much longer she would be able to justify monopolizing the staff photographer. Nothing was happening. Even the renovation noise had been toned down, and the builders ceased work at six each evening. Had she, by seeing Saxon, killed her own story?

On Sunday, Katherine and Franz took the children to Erica and Cliff Bentley's farm. Katherine went out of her way to compensate Henry and Joanne for her absences. While the other three adults rode, Katherine remained with the children, balancing them carefully on a chestnut pony. By the time they returned home in the late afternoon, Katherine knew that the children had forgiven her for any neglect they might have felt. More important, she had squared her own conscience.

In the evening, as she traveled to Islington to resume the role of Archie Waters's niece, she made up her mind to end the assignment that night. Realistically, she had finished it by going to see John Saxon. She had put him in the picture, and he had corrected the problem. . . .

There were times when a newspaper did not need to print a story to settle a matter, she explained to Archie, after informing him of her decision. "I didn't even have to tell Mr. Saxon that I was with the *Eagle* to make him act. He may have defended Hawtrey, for appearance's sake, but he took swift action, didn't he? Your windows were repaired the same day, and for the past couple of nights there has been no noise."

"What do you think'll happen in the end, Miss Eagles?"

There, Katherine was stumped. Would the building be sold with a sitting tenant, thereby lowering its value? Or would Archie eventually find himself in court, on the wrong end of an eviction suit?

Katherine's fifth and final evening at Cadmus Court was not a complete loss. Brian remained home that night. For the first time he seemed communicative, dropping the pose of swaggering toughness; it was as if he had finally decided to accept Katherine and show approval for her efforts.

"What's working on a newspaper like?" he asked Katherine out of the blue.

"I enjoy it."

"What do you enjoy, seeing your name in print?"

"Helping people like your grandfather. Seeing my name in print lost its gloss a long time ago." It was a lie, but Katherine forgave herself; the thrill of seeing her byline would never diminish. "Did your grandfather mention that he'd ask at the newspaper if there's a job for you?"

"He's talked about it a few times."

"Would you like to work there?"

"I guess it's all right. Got to work somewhere, haven't I?"

"It helps if you like where you work."

"Job satisfaction, eh?" he asked with a grin. Then he surprised Katherine by saying: "I thought you were some stuck-up, toffee-nosed bit when I first saw you. But you helped my grandpa. Thanks."

Katherine felt like asking Brian whether she'd helped him as well; after all, he also lived in Cadmus Court. But she could guess how he would reply: Brian Waters did not need any stuck-up, toffee-nosed bit to help him out, thank you very much!

At ten-thirty, Katherine prepared to leave. Archie walked her downstairs. The forecourt light had gone out, and that end of the street was in darkness. The closest illumination came from the rectangle of brightness that was the living-room window of Archie's home.

"Like the blackout during the war," Archie murmured. "Let's just hope we can find your photographer's car."

Clutching Archie's arm, Katherine stumbled across the forecourt. She passed through the gate and came abreast of the alley leading behind Cadmus Court to the park. Nervously, she glanced into the mouth of the alley. It was as black as pitch; all the devils of hell could be lurking down there, and she would never know. She walked more quickly. Her eyes were playing tricks, conjuring up two shadowy forms that detached themselves from the inky blackness and lunged at her and Archie.

She heard a grunt of surprise and pain as something hard cracked across Archie's head. As he staggered back, a fist smacked Katherine a glancing blow in the face. Stars exploded inside her head. She lashed out wildly, fingers curved, nails raking the air like talons. And then, with every ounce of strength she possessed, she screamed.

A car door slammed. Katherine heard feet pounding, saw a blur of motion. The man who had hit her seemed to fly. Arms and legs flailing, he defied gravity for a second before smashing into a wall and sliding to the ground. The second man turned to run. A hand grabbed his shoulder and swung him around. A foot hooked his leg. An abrupt shift of weight and he went down.

"You all right, Katherine?" Sid Hall asked.

"I . . . I think so." She touched just above her left cheek, where the blow had landed. "What about Archie?"

The photographer produced a small flashlight and shone the beam around. Archie was struggling to his feet. Blood trickled down the side of his face from a cut above his ear. "I'm fine, Miss Eagles. Thick skull."

Sid Hall directed the beam downward. On the ground were two men. One had raw grooves down his face where Katherine's nails had found a target. "Know them?" the photographer asked.

"Well enough," Archie answered.

"They're the two men," Katherine said, "who were working on the flat next to Archie."

Above the pain in her face, she felt disappointed at being so wrong about John Saxon. He had not rectified the situation at all. He'd just waited a couple of days and then increased the stakes, exchanged harassment for physical intimidation to rid Cadmus Court of its last troublesome tenant.

Too bad, Katherine thought. But what could you really expect of a man conceited enough to consider St. James's Square his own front garden?

* * *

Katherine arrived home at two-thirty, after Sid Hall had driven both her and Archie to the hospital casualty department. Franz was waiting up when she entered the house. She had telephoned him from the hospital to tell him there had been some trouble and to assure him that she was all right. Nonetheless, he was expecting the worst.

"What in God's name happened to you?" he demanded when he saw her partly closed left eye and the growing bruise. "Your face looks like it was used as a punching bag."

"It was." She told him what had happened. "Archie's taking a couple of days off—he got a nasty crack on the head—but I'll be all right to go in tomorrow."

"Perhaps you should take some time off as well. It seems that you have given more than enough for your job already."

By morning, the eye was far worse, almost completely closed and surrounded by a livid purple bruise. Katherine would not let the children into the bedroom, fearing they would be frightened by the sight of her. When she came downstairs, she was wearing a large pair of black glasses to hide the bruise.

"I have a headache, darling," she explained after Henry had asked why she had on dark glasses.

"Will you tell your father the same lie?" Franz wanted to know, once Henry had left the room.

"We'll worry about that when it happens, won't we?"

Katherine got to Fleet Street just after midday. Crossing the lobby of the Eagle building, she came face-to-face with Erica Bentley, who was on her way out to lunch. The *Daily Eagle*'s women's editor threw her arms around Katherine's neck and hugged her tightly. "Jesus, but I've been worried sick ever since I heard what happened to you last night. Sid Hall told me. I tried phoning you—"

"I know." Katherine had not wanted to speak to anyone that morning. Edna Griffiths had taken the calls. "Didn't the housekeeper tell you I was all right?"

"Yes, but I want to see for myself." Erica whistled as she lifted Katherine's dark glasses to check the damage. "If I were you, kid, I'd put in for hazard-ous-duty pay."

Reaching her desk, Katherine found a note from Gerald Waller's secretary asking her to see the editor the moment she arrived. She knocked on his perpet-ually half-open door and entered. After ascertaining that Katherine was all right, Waller handed her the photographs Sid Hall had taken the previous night: the two men on the ground, before Hall had turned them over to the police; Archie Waters, with the flash picking out the trickle of blood from the cut above his ear; and Katherine, dazed as she touched her eye.

"You look like you don't know what day of the week it is."

"Neither would you, if someone had just jumped out of a dark alley and stuck his fist in your eye."

"*Touché*. Instead of this," Waller said, "I'd prefer that we used a picture of you sitting at your type-writer."

"You don't want a picture of me at all. I'm writing the story, not starring in it."

"But you are. You starred in it as Archie's niece. It's great: concerned journalist involves herself—"

"And gets a black eye in the process."

"That," Waller said, assuming his strict, no-non-sense editor's tone, "is the way I want it. A picture of you and your black eye, sitting at your typewriter, bashing out the exposé. If you'll pardon my choice of verbs."

65

Katherine returned to her desk and began to write the story, switching from her customary taut news style to a subjective first person. She typed away busily, every so often glancing at Sid Hall's photographs — in case her spirit flagged, she could always look at pictorial proof of what she had been through.

4

The Cadmus Court story ran the next day, a full page with liberal photographic coverage, including one of Katherine sitting at her typewriter, swollen eye plainly visible. Nigel Hawtrey was depicted as an ogre, a landlord who hired builders to double as strong-arm men. John Saxon was described as either a willing accomplice to Hawtrey's criminal acts, or, to give him the benefit of any possible doubt, a property magnate so involved in his own importance that he was unable to see what was happening beyond the edge of his shiny desk.

Katherine was still wearing the dark glasses when she went to work on Tuesday. She found Archie Waters already back on the job; one day of idleness was sufficient for the old soldier. She smiled at him, and asked, "See yourself in the paper, Archie?" Then, noticing the sour expression on his face, her smile waned. "What's the matter?"

"I took your father up to the top floor fifteen minutes ago, Miss Eagles. Looked fit to be tied, he did."

"I see." Katherine had wondered how her father would react when he saw the story. Now she knew. Fit to be tied. She could not remember the last time she had seen him angry. Roland Eagles had remarkable control of his temper; perhaps that was one of the reasons he had been so successful in life, having rarely allowed his clarity of thought to be blurred by violent emotion.

The elevator stopped at the third floor. As Katherine stepped out, some of the editorial staff began a chorus of "For she's a jolly good fellow." She responded with a half-hearted wave. Knowing her father was in the building had taken the edge off her triumph.

"Katherine!" Erica's voice came from her small office.

"I know—my father's upstairs. And in a foul mood."

"He's biting Sally Roberts's head off at the minute."

"I'll go up there."

"I didn't hear anything about your presence being required at this particular moment."

"All the more reason I should be there."

Katherine rode up to the fifth floor. Marching right past Sally's secretary, she opened the office door and walked in. Sally and Roland faced each other across the desk. It was obvious they had been arguing, and now, having run out of harsh words to say to each other, were saying nothing at all. The silence in the room was oppressive. It reminded Katherine of standing beneath a huge cloud, waiting for the rain to fall.

Both Sally and Roland were surprised by Katherine's abrupt and unannounced entrance. She tried to dispel some of the gloom by greeting her father with a bright and cheerful "Good morning. What brings you to Fleet Street?"

Roland glared at her. "Take off those ridiculous glasses. I want to see exactly what happened to you."

She removed the glasses. "It's nothing that won't

go away."

Roland, his eyes a dark and angry blue, turned from Katherine to Sally. "You had no right to allow my daughter to involve herself in an assignment where she could receive an injury like that."

"It was not my business," Sally answered evenly. "It was Gerry Waller's concern. He is the editor. He makes all the decisions regarding what goes into the newspaper."

"Then we'll wait until he gets here."

"He doesn't come in until midday," Katherine said.

"I rang his home in Chelsea half an hour ago. If he is at all interested in continuing his association with Eagle Newspapers, he will be here very soon, mark my words."

Katherine started to open her mouth in protest, then closed it again on a signal from Sally. Before any more was said, they would wait for the *Daily Eagle*'s editor.

Gerald Waller arrived fifteen minutes later. "What's the big panic all about?" he wanted to know. "Did World War Three break out without the *Eagle* knowing of it?"

The sarcasm was deflected right over Roland's head by his anger. "How dare you place my daughter in danger?"

"And how dare *you* question the way I run this newspaper?" Waller fired back. Any earlier doubts he might have harbored about exposing Katherine to possible peril were of no consequence now. Not when his position was being challenged. "You appointed me as editor. You appear to have been quite satisfied with my performance for the past eleven years, but if you want to start criticizing my decisions now, go ahead and sack me and appoint yourself in my place. I will not remain on a newspaper when my integrity is compromised."

"Damn your integrity! Surely I am entitled to expect that you will have the common sense not to allow my daughter into a situation where she might be harmed." Roland had known he would receive a fierce argument. Journalists resent intrusions into their odd little world, and Waller was no exception. As editor, he would zealously protect every responsibility that went with the title. Roland could influence the political platform of his newspapers by filling the upper-level positions with people who agreed with his own moderate views, but he could not interfere editorially. Not unless he wanted a knock-down, drag-out brawl. Which was precisely what he had now.

"If I treated Katherine as your daughter, and not as just another member of editorial, I would have a revolution on my hands. Not from other staff, but from Katherine herself."

Katherine interposed herself into the confrontation. "You knew about the story," she reminded her father. "We talked about it on my birthday, over dinner at your house."

"I know. But you never mentioned anything about sticking yourself in the firing line, or getting injured."

"This"—Katherine pointed at her eye—"is not an injury. It's a medal, a badge of courage. It proves I've paid my dues."

"Paid them most handsomely," Sally said. "Good crusading journalism. Our sales will be up today." She turned to Roland. "Katherine was never forced into doing anything she didn't want to do."

"She was the person best suited for this assignment," Waller added. "That was why she got it. Whether or not she is related to the proprietor of this newspaper is beside the point."

"Yes, but—" Roland had been taken aback by Katherine's presence; it had removed some of the sting from his anger. Now, surprise had turned to astonishment at the way she had aligned herself with Waller and Sally. To fight her own father! Damned journalists—they all stuck together. Blood might be thicker than water, but it was certainly thinner than printers' ink.

Sally's telephone rang. She lifted the receiver, spoke for a few seconds, then looked directly at Katherine. "You might have some more dues to pay. John Saxon's downstairs, wanting to speak to you."

"I'll see him with you," Roland offered.

"No, you will not," Waller contradicted. "Mr. Saxon is undoubtedly here about a story one of *my* people wrote, not about a story *your* daughter wrote. If anyone will be with Katherine, it will be me. As editor. She does not need her father holding her hand at this particular moment."

Roland's eyes glowed. "I will not be there as her father. I will be there as proprietor. As publisher."

"Roland." Sally spoke his name softly. Not as employee to boss, but as long-standing friend to friend. "Stay out of it. If legal proceedings are involved, you'll hear soon enough."

"Come on, Katherine," Waller said. "Let's learn from Mr. Saxon the names of his solicitors."

Katherine followed the editor out of his office. As she passed her father, she felt a moment of sympathy. He seemed so lost. He had come to the newspaper looking for a fight, but he had not expected his own daughter to side against him. Katherine believed she understood what was really bothering him. Over dinner on her birthday, she had accused him of being like a man without arms. She had not realized then just how accurate the remark had been. After a life full of meeting challenges, her father was questioning his existence.

Inside the office, Roland stood in the center of the floor, gazing at Sally. "Sometimes I tend to forget that Kathy's all grown up with a mind of her own. I still get the urge to be a father and make sure none of the other children play too rough."

Sally walked up to Roland, brushed a dust mote from the jacket of his dark gray pinstripe suit, and kissed him on the lips. "Don't ever lose that urge, Roland Eagles. Just try to keep it a little more beneath the surface, that's all."

Katherine accompanied Gerald Waller to the editor's office. Two minutes later, John Saxon was shown in. Katherine introduced the two men, after which Saxon said to her, "Perhaps you'd like to introduce yourself as well. Obviously, you're not a young woman called Katherine Waters, whose Uncle Archie lives at Cadmus Court. Incidentally, was that the good Mr. Waters who just brought me up here in the lift?"

"It was. And my real name is Katherine Kassler."

"I know. Your father owns this newspaper, doesn't he? I should have guessed last week that you were not who you claimed to be. No tenant would have brought photographs like you did. Certainly not such professional prints."

"Mr. Saxon, if you came here to admit I fooled you," Katherine said, "I already know I did."

Quite abruptly, Saxon's tone changed. From brusque, sure of himself, it became soft. "I came to apologize. To tell you that I'm sorry I ever doubted your word. It's just that Nigel Hawtrey had been with the company for a long time. I had the utmost faith in him. The utmost misplaced faith, as it now turns out."

"What's happened to him?"

"He's gone. Paid off. We've had a complete personnel purge at the company he controlled."

"What was Hawtrey's motive in terrorizing the

72

tenants the way he did?" Waller asked.

"The oldest one in the world. Greed. Nigel ran a small company for us, which specialized in buying up speculative properties, buildings in improving areas. The idea was to hold the properties until maximum appreciation had been achieved, do them up, and sell them. The moment a deal went through, Nigel saw a large bonus." Saxon looked toward Katherine. "Did you mean that about me? So wrapped up in my own importance, I can't see past the end of my desk?"

"If I wrote it, Mr. Saxon, I must have meant it."

Saxon nodded slowly. "I suppose I asked for it."

"You most certainly did. However"—Katherine glanced at Waller—"it wouldn't do any harm to write a short follow-up piece, would it? Show how the *Eagle* made things happen."

"Thank you," Saxon said. "After today, your readers must think I'm a hard-hearted ass. I'd appreciate the opportunity to show them that I can do the right thing. I would also like you to formally introduce me to Archie Waters. I think my company owes him something."

Katherine left Waller's office with John Saxon. She introduced him to Archie Waters, and in the time it took for the elevator to descend from the editorial floor to the lobby, Saxon had promised to make it all up. Cadmus Property Company would no longer try to sell the building. It would be kept and managed properly. And Archie's home would be completely redecorated.

"I'm not such a heartless devil after all, am I?" Saxon asked as Katherine saw him to the door of the Eagle building.

"You sound as though you're seeking your own approval."

"I already have that. I was looking for yours."

Katherine stared at Saxon and wondered how

much it had taken for him to make the journey from St. James's Square. He had that warmth in his eyes, yet she felt he was a man who did not really give a damn whether people approved of him or not.

"I'm still waiting for an answer."

Katherine put into words her thoughts from Sunday night. "I don't think I could ever wholeheartedly approve of a man who claims that St. James's Square is his own front garden."

To her surprise, Saxon burst out laughing. "I knew that went down like a lead balloon the moment I said it. I was holding your arm at the time, and I could feel it turn to wood." They reached the street. Moments later, a maroon Rolls Royce Silver Shadow drew up. Before the uniformed chauffeur could help, Saxon opened the rear door and jumped in. Katherine watched until the Rolls turned the corner and was lost to sight.

The following morning, she arrived at work to find one dozen long-stemmed red roses on her desk. The accompanying card was unsigned, and bore the simple message: "From my own front garden."

An hour later, John Saxon telephoned. "Were my roses delivered?"

"They were. I was about to telephone and thank you."

"Demonstrate your gratitude by having lunch with me."

"I'm afraid that's quite impossible."

"Not today. I wouldn't dream of asking you at such short notice. Tomorrow, sometime next week, even."

"That's also out of the question."

A short pause from Saxon's end of the line was followed by "I understand. You must be very busy."

"I'm afraid so. Between working on a newspaper and looking after two small children and one large husband, I don't have much time left for anything else."

Saxon chuckled. "Whatever attributes you might possess, subtlety is most assuredly not one of them. But you make your point very clearly. Goodbye."

In St. James's Square, Saxon replaced the receiver. And at the *Daily Eagle,* Katherine remained staring at the telephone, confused, knowing she had done the correct thing in turning down the invitation, but wondering — just wondering — what an hour or two over lunch with John Saxon would have been like.

She was crazy, she told herself. She loved Franz, loved him more than anything else in the world. How could she possibly be frightened that her feelings for him might be compromised by a lunch date with another man?

The story on Cadmus Court aroused a wave of reaction. Some of it amused Katherine, like the left-wing tenants' group which made a big show of presenting her with a plaque acclaiming her effort and sacrifice on behalf of the working class. The very next day, the president of the group telephoned to request the plaque's immediate return. The group's members had not realized that Katherine's father owned the newspaper; the awards were meant for workers, not for bosses.

Another approach, made by local Labour Party officials, was received more seriously. Was Katherine interested in being a candidate for the next borough election? A young woman who combined family life with a highly visible career would be a sure draw among young women voters. Katherine declined, but not before expressing how flattered she felt. She was not a politically minded person. Not for her could there be blind allegiance, a vote for the party rather than for the man or the issue. It was another area in which she emulated her father. He had always stressed that good flourished in both major political parties, but the farther left you went in Labour, and the farther right you traveled among Conservatives, the wilder the lunatics and bigots became. Sanity prevailed only in the Labour right wing and the Conservative left, the crossover point of common sense and common decency.

The most tantalizing response of all came from within the *Daily Eagle*. Erica Bentley broke the news in an offhand manner over lunch at the Cheshire Cheese toward the end of July. "I should never have let you take that assignment at Cadmus Court, you know. Now I've gone and lost one of my best people."

"Thanks for the compliment, but I'm not going anywhere."

"Oh yes, you are. To your own column, you're going."

"What?"

"You heard me. You're about to be offered a brand new column, a platform where you can wield a gleaming broadsword on behalf of readers who've been given the short end of the stick. Of course, if you're not interested, I'm sure Gerry Waller won't force it on you."

The news became official two days later. The column would be called "Satisfaction Guaranteed!" and Katherine, so Sally Roberts promised, "would be able to rake all the muck she could find."

"Satisfaction Guaranteed!" would debut in the last week of September. Advertisements ran in both the *Daily* and *Sunday Eagle;* spots were scheduled for commercial television. Katherine saw her own face staring back at her from billboards, a portrait shot worked into a caricature of Don Quixote tilting at a row of windmills. Each time she saw one of the advertisements, a thrill swept over her. It was all she could do to refrain from stopping people in the street and telling them that they'd better buy a paper when her first column came out.

Three weeks later, Katherine was dithering over which topic to use for the column's launch. She had narrowed the choice down to three: a blind woman threatened with eviction from an old-age home because her newly acquired guide dog violated a no-pets rule, a dry cleaner claiming that he and fellow merchants were being shaken down by council garbage collectors who refused to make regular pickups unless they were tipped, and an accusation of police harassment by a black youth club.

Katherine took her work home, asking the housekeeper which subject she ought to use. Edna Griffiths gave the question careful consideration. "You've covered rotten landlords already, and as for those colored kids and their club—"

"You think I should do the council dustmen," Katherine cut in quickly, before Edna could air even a mild prejudice.

"Yes, do the dustmen," the housekeeper agreed. "Do them good and proper, lazy good-for-nothings. Drop garbage all over the yard for fifty-one weeks of the year, they do. Then comes Our Lord's birthday, they turn up with their compliments-of-the-season smiles and their grubby hands stretched out for a Christmas present."

Katherine laughed. She would wait until Franz got home, to ask his opinion as well. He would be late tonight, having spent the day in Amsterdam, at a department store owned by the Eagles Group. Katherine did not mind Franz's occasional day trips to Europe. They were really no different from any other day. She heard him leave the house in the morning for his run over the heath, and at night she went to sleep in his arms—just like always. The only trips she disliked were those he made to the United States, when he would be away for three or four days.

Franz arrived home at nine-thirty. He never returned from even a simple day trip without bringing gifts. This time, he had a Dutch-girl doll for Joanne and a toy car for Henry. To Katherine, he gave a tall box. She opened it. Inside was a model windmill, with battery-powered wooden blades.

"Now you have the real thing to tilt at," Franz told her.

She kissed him and promised to put the windmill on her desk as a reminder of her new position. When she asked Franz which topic she should use for her first column, he agreed with the housekeeper's choice. "Get to the bottom of the story about the dustmen who are extorting money from the merchants. Your readers will be able to sympathize with it. Everyone hates the dustmen. If you feel you really must do something about the black youth club, wait until 'Satisfaction Guaranteed!' is more established and you can afford to go into a subject with which your readers might not be so sympathetic."

Katherine saw the sense of Franz's suggestion, the financial sense of it. Going after the garbage crews would have wider appeal than questioning police behavior against black youths. Later, after building up readership loyalty, she could air more urgent social issues.

Sometimes it was good for a principled writer to share her bed with a hard-headed pragmatist, who appreciated that every business had two functions to perform: to give a service, and to make a profit.

The new position entitled Katherine to her own office and a pair of assistants. She selected two junior reporters in their early twenties, Heather Harvey, a chubby girl with curly black hair and lively brown eyes, and Derek Simon, a tall young man with thinning sandy hair over a very high forehead.

Together, they soon wrapped up the garbage extortion story. They spoke to the merchants involved. Posing as shop clerks, they watched garbage collections being made. Sid Hall joined them, using a telephoto lens to capture pictures of the truck driver being handed money by each shop owner before any trash would be loaded. The driver always offered a reason for wanting payment. Many of the merchants were simply told that their level of garbage exceeded the council limit, whatever that was; no one seemed too certain. For the dry-cleaning shop, the driver used his imagination. Exhaust ducts from the machines were near where the garbage was stacked. The dustmen had to risk inhaling dangerous chemicals; they were entitled to a hefty tip.

Finally, Katherine visited the council offices with Sid Hall. For once, the photographer carried no evidence of his trade, although one pocket of his loud Prince of Wales check sportcoat bulged strangely.

"Are you aware" Katherine asked the supervisor, "that one of your garbage crews is operating an extortion racket?"

The supervisor, a dry, officious man, sprang to the defense of his department. "That is a preposterous accusation! Preposterous *and* slanderous!"

"Look at these, and tell me that again." Katherine spread half a dozen photographs across the man's desk. Each one showed the truck driver accepting his payoff. As the supervisor's mouth dropped in amazement, Sid Hall pulled a pocket camera with a built-in flash from his jacket pocket, whipped it up to eye level, and pressed the shutter button.

It was the picture of the shocked supervisor that topped Katherine's first column. Beneath it was the headline "Why Is This Man Gaping?" At the bottom of the column were the photographs that had so stunned him. In between was the story of how a group of merchants, fed up with complaining to the council about irregularities in the garbage collection, had called in the *Daily Eagle* to have their Satisfaction Guaranteed!

Katherine celebrated at lunchtime, champagne in plastic glasses passed around the editorial floor. The telephone had been ringing all morning with readers who had problems that needed solving; there would be no shortage of topics for the new column.

"Enjoy your triumph while you can," Gerald Waller advised Katherine. "Glory is like today's headline—very fleeting. Tomorrow, everyone will be after your blood."

"Especially a group of dustmen." But she doubted it. The men had not been fired; they'd been disciplined, whatever that meant. Katherine suspected that dismissal would involve a clash with whatever union guarded their interests, and before you knew where you were, every municipal worker in the country would be out on strike.

Erica came up and kissed her. "Taught you well, didn't I?"

"You did." Erica's sentiments were identical to those of Sally Roberts, who had come down earlier from the executive floor to offer congratulations. Katherine had learned plenty from each woman.

"Got a big evening all planned?" Erica asked.

"Just an early night to recover from all this excitement."

"What? You're not painting the town red with Franz?"

"He's not here. He had to fly to Chicago yesterday."

"Oh, that's marvelous. Your big day, and he clears off."

"He's working on some acquisition over there. It sounds so easy, buying a bunch of stores, but there's so much more to it than just the transfer of some deed. All the people involved—"

"I'll make sure to tell him what a loyal wife you are. He disappears for your big moment, and you won't hear a bad word said about him."

Katherine turned away to look at the model windmill on her desk. Someone had flicked the switch, and the blades were revolving lazily. Everyone had been a part of her triumphant moment . . . her father, who had sent a congratulatory telegram, and her fellow journalists, who had gathered for this small party on the editorial floor, and had treated her exactly as she wanted to be treated—as one of their own. Everyone had shared this moment with her except Franz, who had popped the surprise three days earlier that he would be flying to Chicago.

"Can't you put it off?" she had pleaded. "You know what happens this week."

"I know. But, Katherine, your first column will be a success whether I am here or not."

"That's not the point."

"Katherine, there is nothing I can do about it. I am not the only person involved. I cannot ask for meetings to be put off for a few days because my wife's new column is appearing."

He had left instructions with his secretary to send a huge display of flowers and a card to Katherine at the *Daily Eagle,* but it was not the same. Katherine wanted him here to share this moment with her. She didn't want his flowers, his card, his good wishes, and his absence!

Sensing Katherine's bitterness, Erica switched sides. "Your man's got an important job to do. You shouldn't be so upset just because he's not here."

"What makes you think I'm upset?"

"I'm women's editor . . . I know these things,"

Erica answered, nodding sagely. "What about Franz's work in Chicago? Once this deal goes through, he's going to want to celebrate, isn't he? So how do you think he's going to feel with you not being there to celebrate with him because you had your first column?"

"For someone who talks in riddles," Katherine said with a wan smile, "you occasionally make a lot of sense."

"That's better. Now have a good time."

Katherine did, her mood lifted by the talk with Erica. She had not completely forgiven Franz for being away, but she was not going to let his absence ruin the day.

She left the office just after six o'clock. Walking along Fleet Street, close to the curb, she heard her name being called. She turned around as a moped slid to a halt beside her.

"Want to jump up behind me and go for a ride?" Brian Waters asked, lifting the visor of his crash helmet.

"Is this how you normally pick up girls?" When Brian nodded, Katherine asked, "What are you doing on Fleet Street?"

"My job's here, isn't it? I started work with Mercury Messengers a few weeks ago."

Katherine nodded, remembering Archie Waters mentioning that he had found Brian a job with the messenger company owned by Eagle Newspapers; in all the excitement of getting the column off the ground, it had slipped her mind. "Are you enjoying it?"

"Yeah, it's all right. 'Bye then." Revving the moped's tiny engine, he sped away.

Katherine watched him weave in and out of the stagnant rush hour. Cheeky little devil, asking if she wanted a ride. His grandfather would have a fit if he knew. So would her own father. Sixteen-year-old messenger boys were not supposed to speak that way to the boss's daughter.

Katherine arrived at work the following morning to find another bunch of long-stemmed red roses in her office. Even before she flicked open the accompanying envelope and looked at the card, she knew who had sent them.

"Well done," she read aloud, "for putting our slothful council workers in their place."

"Beg your pardon?" said Derek Simon, who had followed her into the office.

"Talking to myself. Did you see who brought these?"

"They were sent up from the front desk."

Katherine waited for Derek to leave the office before dialing the number of Saxon Holdings. When she was through to John Saxon, she asked, "Are these also from your front garden?"

"No. I'm learning humility. I no longer claim St. James's Square as my own private property."

"I'm glad I had such a positive effect on you.".

"I enjoyed your first column. I'd like to discuss it."

"Go ahead."

"Over lunch."

"You don't give up easily, do you?"

"Not even when informed about small children and large husbands."

Large, inconsiderate husbands, Katherine thought, who disappear when you want them around to be part of something really special. Bed had been a particularly solitary place last night. As if to emphasize his absence, Franz had telephoned just as Katherine was turning out the bedside light. He had asked how the first column had been accepted, and she'd told him about the small party. At last, they had said good night, blowing kisses across some four thousand miles of space and cable. And Katherine had gone to sleep wondering how sincere Franz's interest really was. After all, deep down he did not believe women should work. Was that why he had made no special effort to be with Katherine on her big day?

In his office overlooking St. James's Square, John Saxon decided that the long pause was indecision on Katherine's part. She was weakening, and he was ready to take advantage of it. From the moment he'd first seen Katherine in his office, Saxon had been charmed by her freshness. Then, when he'd learned her true identity—had seen the other, businesslike, side of her—his interest had increased. The large husband and two small children did not concern him. When he wanted something, he viewed obstacles only as hindrances to be overcome. "What harm can there possibly be in a short business lunch?" he asked Katherine. "I'm sure you have them all the time."

"All right, Mr. Saxon. A business lunch. Let's make it for today, my diary's empty." Katherine heard her own voice and felt shocked by the words. She had never meant to accept Saxon's offer. She had intended to push him off as she had done the last time. But some inner control had taken over her tongue. Curiosity—and, perhaps, a way to get back at Franz?—had superseded caution.

At one o'clock, Katherine stood outside the Eagle building, eyes seeking the distinctive maroon Rolls Royce. Instead, a black taxi drew up. The rear door swung open. Inside, sitting so deeply in the shadow that he was almost unrecognizable, was John Saxon. Katherine climbed in.

"I was expecting your Rolls."

"The Roller's too noticeable. I thought you'd prefer to be seen getting into something of a more anonymous nature."

The taxi driver moved away before Katherine was fully settled, and she slid across the seat into Saxon's arms. "No need to throw yourself at me," he cautioned.

Katherine felt her face reddening. Suddenly, she was wishing that she were back in her office, or having lunch with Erica. "Don't worry, it won't happen again."

She barely spoke a word during the journey across the Thames to the Anchor, an eighteenth-century riverside public house and restaurant that enjoyed historic ties with the old Globe Theatre and Samuel Johnson. Once inside, though, gazing at ancient oak beams and the minstrels' gallery, Katherine began to relax. Drinks came. They ordered food, specialties of the house—roast ribs for Saxon, lamb chops for Katherine.

"I have a sudden urge to start quoting Dr. Johnson," she said, staring past Saxon's head to a picture of the famous writer. "What was it now? 'When a man is tired of London, he is tired of life—' "

" 'For London has all that life can afford.' " Saxon nodded and smiled. "My own favorite is . . . 'When a man knows he is to be hanged in a fortnight, it concentrates his mind wonderfully.' "

"That's a little too morbid for my taste. I much prefer"—Katherine immersed herself fully into the game—" 'It is better to live rich than to die rich.' "

" 'Too few people do," Saxon said in agreement. "There's also one the good doctor wrote especially for you."

"What was that?"

" 'No man but a blockhead ever wrote except for money.' "

Katherine repeated the sentence, thought it over carefully. "It's sexist as all hell, but I'll accept it."

Once the meal was served, Katherine guided the

conversation down a more serious path. "My father told me you used to move property around as though you were playing Monopoly."

"Did he now? When did he tell you this?"

"When I began working on the Cadmus Court story. He also warned me to be very careful about linking your name with tenant harassment. Most specifically" — she suddenly wanted to pass on the compliment — "he said you were not the kind of man to be involved in something so reprehensible."

Saxon sat back, his face reflecting pleasure. "Thank him for me. You know, your father was once a big hero of mine."

"Oh? How was that?"

"When he eloped with your mother. That Argentine girl, she was your mother, wasn't she?"

"Yes. Catarina Menéndez."

"The ambassador's daughter. I was thirteen then. Your father and mother were front-page news. The whole country was being turned upside down to find them."

"You have the advantage of me," Katherine admitted. "I don't remember any of it."

"No, but if you had been there, you'd have been as thrilled as the rest of us."

"The rest of us?"

"Britain's fed-up, disgruntled youth. It was nineteen fifty. All we knew was bomb sites and ration books. And then along came your father and that wonderful elopement. Something else was on the front page for a change. Something bright and happy and cheerful. All of us, we hated that Argentine Ambassador Menéndez for trying to put a stop to it. He was one of the older generation, the world-wreckers who had given us those bomb sites and ration books."

"You're talking about my grandfather."

"What is he to you? After your mother died, he

wanted to take you away from your father and bring you up in Argentina. I followed the court case in the newspapers, how your grandfather tried to brand your father as being unfit to care for a child." Saxon's voice dropped when he added: "I'm very glad he failed."

"Why?" Katherine recalled her first opinions of Saxon. "Were you happy to see an Argentine lose to an Englishman?"

"Partly that. But mostly because if your grandfather had won his case, you'd be having lunch on the River Plate right now with some dark and handsome hidalgo. Instead, you're having lunch on the Thames with me."

While Katherine smiled at the comment, she wondered whether Saxon knew that the rift between her father and his Argentine father-in-law had lasted right up to the moment of her wedding with Franz. Although there had been no communication for twenty years, Roland, as a courtesy, had sent Menéndez an invitation. The former ambassador had turned it down, only to arrive unexpectedly at Claridge's toward the end of the wedding ball. At the very last, he had given Katherine an envelope containing a check for a million dollars. When she'd protested that she could not possibly accept such a gift, her father had insisted that she take it. The sheer size of the gift, he'd explained, was her Argentine grandfather's way of squaring accounts, of making peace with himself for having neglected his granddaughter all these years. Her father had been right, of course. . . .

"You really do know a lot about my father, my family," she told Saxon. "Tell me something about yourself."

"Why?" A grin accompanied the challenge. Katherine had noticed that the expression appeared often on his face. It was an attractive grin, full of cheer and just a hint of mischief.

"Old newspaper habit, getting background information about prominent people in case something important happens to them. They might be included in the New Year's Honours List—"

"Or they might die." The grin came again, with devilment as its main ingredient. "All right, background. I'm forty years old. I grew up in Streatham, South London. Grammar school education, no fancy public school. Left when I was sixteen, and went to work for an estate agent—learning a reputable business. Two years later, the army grabbed me. I was twenty when I finished my national service and went back to the estate agent, but after a while I wanted bigger things. The estate agent was on the ground floor of a four-story office building. Above was an office-machine repair shop that had been there for donkey's years. It was for sale. I borrowed the money to buy it, not because I wanted to fix typewriters, but because I happened to know that the inventory included the lease of the building. I paid rent for the entire building, which wasn't much, but it enabled me to charge everyone else as much as I could."

Katherine did not want to hear how millions were made. Perhaps it was because she'd been born into wealth, but she had never found the accumulation of it very interesting. "Tell me about your personal life. Where do you live?"

"I have a house in town, Marble Arch. That's where I spend my weeks."

"And your weekends?"

"Oxfordshire. Fifteen of the most beautiful acres you've ever seen near Henley-on-Thames, with four hundred feet of river frontage. As for my marital status—"

"I didn't ask."

"But you were about to. I'm divorced. For six

years now, the same length of time I was married."

Katherine knew it was none of her business, but some instinct prompted her to ask, "What went wrong?"

"I've never seen that kind of information included in any knighthood story or obituary."

"There has to be a first sometime."

"To be honest, I was giving too much time to work, and not enough to Deidre—that was my wife. I kept telling her that I was building a business, that she had to be patient. Deidre told me I should be building a marriage. I guess I never realized you had to keep working on a marriage once the honeymoon was over."

Saxon's admission of failure touched a chord within Katherine. He was a self-made man with a streak of arrogance, to which, she supposed, he was entitled. But the touch of regret at things he had missed made him extremely human.

She glanced down at the gold Patek Philippe on her wrist, shocked to see it was already two-thirty. "I have to get back to my office."

"The owner's daughter has to punch a clock?"

"I never think of myself in that capacity."

They rode a cab back to Fleet Street. Instead of having the driver stop right outside the Eagle building, Saxon instructed the man to park fifty yards away. Katherine stepped out and looked back into the cab.

"Thank you for lunch. I enjoyed exchanging Dr. Johnson quotes with you."

"Lunch was rushed. We could enjoy a leisurely dinner more."

Katherine knew she should close the door gently but firmly in Saxon's face and walk away. Instead, she stood there, saying, "I don't think that would be a very good idea."

"A dinner date," Saxon continued, as though

Katherine had not spoken. His eyes fixed themselves on her customary suit, charcoal gray today, with an ice-blue silk blouse. "A dinner date where you can exchange those business outfits you always wear for something glamorous. Then we can behave like two adults who aren't ashamed to admit being attracted to each other."

"Am I attracted to you?"

"If you weren't, you'd never have met me for lunch."

The confidence in his voice annoyed Katherine. "Good afternoon, Mr. Saxon." Very formally, she held out her hand to be shaken before walking away.

For a dozen steps, she felt his eyes burning into her back like twin laser beams. She willed herself to continue walking steadily toward the Eagle building, where she would feel so much safer. But, damn it, she *was* attracted to him! Even if she wasn't too certain why. Was it his strength of personality, or was it because he was so different from Franz? So English, while Franz was so cosmopolitan.

At the very last moment, as she stepped into the shadow of the Eagle building entrance, her determination wilted. She could not stop from looking back. No supernatural force transformed her into a pillar of salt, but she caught a glimpse of John Saxon sitting in the taxi, gazing at her with a self-assured smile.

Katherine returned to her office wishing she could turn back the clock to that morning. She would never acknowledge the roses. She would let him call her to see if she had received them. Then *she* would have the advantage. He would not be able to lead so naturally into asking her to lunch, and she would have been spared the confusion she felt now.

By the time Franz returned from Chicago, two days later, Katherine had managed to rationalize the entire episode. It was flirting, nothing more. Everyone flirted. Men and women working together in an office, passengers on a train, total strangers. Eye contact, a couple of words. There was nothing harmful in it. Besides, if Franz had not been away during this particular week, it would never have happened!

"Do you ever flirt with your secretary?" she asked Franz in bed on the night he had returned from Chicago.

"Katherine, you have seen my secretary. She is fifty years old and formidable. Why do you ask?"

Katherine lied. "It's just that most of the men at the paper seem to flirt with most of the women, and I was worried whether I could trust you."

Franz gave a doleful sigh. "Trust me. The last time I flirted with anyone was in Monte Carlo ten years ago. I am still paying for that flirtation."

"You rotten devil! But I trust you anyway." Rolling over to snuggle closer to Franz, Katherine pushed John Saxon clean out of her mind.

5

From the moment of its launch, "Satisfaction Guaranteed!" was one of the hottest items on Fleet Street. There was no shortage of subjects for Katherine and her two assistants to cover. The column featured everything from the quality of care at a nursing home — after the family of an elderly resident had taken its case to the *Daily Eagle* as a last resort to helping a young couple through a jungle of bureaucratic nonsense when they wanted to adopt an orphaned Lebanese child. The final strip of red tape was removed from that case the week before Christmas, and the *Eagle*'s December 24 front page showed the joyous couple with their newly adopted child. "Our Christmas Present," declared the headline. Damp eyes and lumps in throats were not confined to the *Eagle*'s readers; there were several cases among its staff.

In those first three months, Katherine was featured in three women's magazines, asked to speak at two conferences, and invited to take part in a weekly television series on consumer rights. If nothing else, the television appearances made her alter her style of dress. "Seventy percent of the country is still watching black and white," Erica Bentley told her. "You wear those suits, and only the thirty percent with color sets will realize you've got different clothes on each time you appear. The other seventy percent, well, they're going to think you've only got one item in your entire wardrobe."

Katherine took the hint. She went out and bought a new image for her television appearances: high-fashion clothing in colorful, patterned fabrics. *Daily Eagle* editor Gerald Waller's conservative sensibilities were appalled the first time he saw Katherine on television; he sent her a tongue-in-cheek memo which proclaimed that if she ever turned up for work at the *Eagle* dressed like that, he would instruct the doorman to refuse her entrance. There was no way, though, that Waller could argue, even jokingly, with the sharp jump in circulation, most of which was directly attributable to "Satisfaction Guaranteed!" On Christmas Eve, he sent out another memo, thanking the column's staff for their efforts; to Katherine, he presented a gold-plated etching of her first column.

On Christmas Day, the entire Kassler household rose early. A Christmas tree stood in the library, with much of the space beneath it taken up by two gifts—a bicycle with training wheels for Henry and a tricycle for Joanne. Dressed warmly, the children wheeled the gifts into the front garden, where they rode around the gravel driveway, while Katherine watched and Franz took photographs with the Leica hanging from his neck.

After locking the gate to make sure the children did not ride out into the street, Franz and Katherine returned to the library. The Christmas tree seemed barren with the removal of the two largest presents. Katherine handed Franz a small, square box containing a pair of gold cuff links from Asprey in New Bond Street. In return, he have her a three-rope pearl choker with a sapphire clasp. As they kissed and wished each other a merry Christmas, they could hear the children's laughter from outside.

Shortly before noon, the family left for Roland Eagles's home on Stanmore Common. In the back of Franz's Jaguar, between the two children, sat Edna Griffiths, as much a part of the family as if she were tied by blood. Christmas, traditionally hosted by Roland, was a very close affair. No friends, just a family gathering which also included Sally Roberts, who drove out from her apartment in Mayfair's Curzon Street.

Sally was there when the Kasslers arrived, her red Fiat sports car parked in front of the house. Shoulders were hugged, cheeks and lips kissed, more gifts exchanged.

"For you." Katherine offered her father a large package.

Roland opened it to find a mahogany and box-wood chest containing fifty Davidoff cigars. "Thank you, darling. And in return . . ." He lifted a flat shape from beneath the tree and presented it to Katherine.

"Painting?" she asked. Roland nodded. Katherine untied string, peeled back corrugated paper. She sucked in her breath when she saw the hunt scene painted by Augustus John. "It's wonderful." She passed the painting to Franz before throwing her arms around Roland's neck.

"You're going hunting with Erica and Cliff Bentley next week, aren't you?" Sally asked.

"Not hunting exactly," Franz answered. "Just the New Year's Day meet. A ceremonial parade, nothing more."

"That must be like getting all dressed up and having nowhere to go," Sally said. "Still, I suppose it's better than chasing some poor fox all over the countryside."

Arthur Parsons appeared, black jacket and gray

94

striped trousers immaculately pressed, to offer drinks on a silver tray. Twenty minutes later, he asked everyone to take their places in the dining room.

"Mrs. Parsons has outdone herself this year," Roland announced as Parsons poured champagne into Waterford flutes.

"Something's been smelling absolutely fantastic ever since I arrived," Sally added. "What is it?"

Parsons's face wore a smile of quiet pride. "A French Christmas meal, Miss Roberts. Pâté de foie gras, followed by soured cream oysters, then truffled young turkey with mushroom and Madeira sauce. And for dessert, a chestnut and chocolate Christmas cake." Parsons set down the champagne bottle and stood surveying the table for a moment. "The French call it *Le Reveillon,* eaten on Christmas Eve, after they return from church. Mrs. Parsons decided to make it for Christmas Day because, quite frankly, whatever the French do, the British can always improve upon." He bowed slightly, turned around, and walked out of the dining room to an enthusiastic round of applause.

Two hours later, when the meal was finished, applause rang out for the chef. Peg Parsons came into the dining room, a short, dumpy woman whose body was covered by a huge white apron that stretched from her neck to below her knees.

"A triumph, Mrs. Parsons!" Roland declared. "Now we're all going to have to walk over the common to work off the calories."

Roland lit one of the Davidoff cigars given to him by Katherine and Franz. Wearing an old sheepskin coat, he led the way out of the house, across the road, and onto the common. Katherine was glad to see that her father and Sally were walking the same way as Franz and herself, arm in arm, as comfortable together as if they were a matching pair.

A brisk wind was blowing across the common, yet Katherine, wrapped up in a suede jacket identical to that worn by Franz, was delightfully warm. A good year was coming to an end. Perhaps the most fulfilling year of her life. And she was certain that an even better year beckoned.

Katherine took the following week off from work to spend with her children. In a whirlwind rush of activity, she took Henry and Joanne to Regent's Park Zoo, where they spent a day gaping at the animals; then to the Tower of London, to see the Crown Jewels; to Madame Tussaud's and the Planetarium on Marylebone Road; and finally to a brace of pantomime favorites—*Dick Whittington* and *Cinderella*.

In the children's eyes, the only outing to compare with the pantomimes was lunch with their grandfather, in the restaurant on the fifth floor of the main Adler's department store on Regent Street. Katherine took Henry and Joanne there before the matinée performance of *Cinderella*. The restaurant was full of bargain hunters, who flooded into the West End this time of year for the seasonal sales; a long line of hungry people waited to be seated. But in one corner, overlooking Regent Street, was a solitary table for four with a reserved sign. "As important as the store's customers are," Roland said, as he sat down with his guests, "my daughter and grandchildren come first."

"Especially your grandchildren," Katherine countered.

"Only because they're easier to please."

By the time the week was over, Katherine was physically and mentally exhausted. Running all over town with two active children, she told herself, could do that to a person. But then again, she'd enjoyed every single minute of it. As well as repaying the children for the times she had not been there during the year, she had more than amply recompensed herself as well.

The farm owned by Erica and Cliff Bentley wasn't much as far as farms went. Not in size, anyway, its land having been sold off over the years in separate parcels, until only fifteen acres remained. The beauty of it lay in the farmhouse, a fully restored, spacious residence dating from the middle of the eighteenth century.

It was in the farmhouse that the Kassler family welcomed in the new year. For Joanne and Henry, a year died and a year was born while they slept upstairs in one of the guest bedrooms. For Katherine and Franz, the transformation took place as they stood in the farmhouse's drawing room, warmed by a fire roaring in a brick and copper hearth, and listening to an old grandfather clock wind itself up with much whirring and wheezing to strike twelve.

As the first chime reverberated through the paneled room, Cliff Bentley solemnly raised a glass that bubbled with champagne. He was a stout man, three inches shorter than his wife, with a wide, perfectly round bald spot in the center of his head. At first glance, he could have been mistaken for an accountant or a lawyer, a member of a dry and dusty profession. Veterinarian, somehow, seemed too exciting for him. But his mild appearance concealed a healthy love of the outdoors and a robust, irreverent sense of humor.

"To a wonderful 1977," Cliff intoned solemnly as the grandfather clock's final chime died away. "May it make us even happier than its predecessor did."

Standing next to Katherine, Franz said: "Is there anything that could make you happier in 1977?"

97

Katherine thought it over. "Maybe just one thing."

"What is that?"

"I'd like you to be home the next time I have something special to celebrate."

Franz gave her a quizzical look but said nothing. Only later, when they went upstairs to bed, did he bring up the subject. "All this time, have you been angry about my not being here in September?"

"Subconsciously, I must have been. That remark about you being home came out all by itself," Katherine explained. "I never meant to say it."

Embarrassed that she should have brought up the hurt again, she murmured something about seeing that the children were all right. She tiptoed down the hallway to the room that Henry and Joanne shared for the night. After standing in the doorway for a minute, watching as they slept soundly, she returned to Franz. She found him sitting on the edge of the huge four-poster bed that seemed so in character with the farmhouse's atmosphere. He was wearing his shirt and underpants, and had one foot up in the air as he peeled off a sock. Katherine started to laugh.

"What is so funny? You left here angry—at yourself, at me, I do not know—and you return amused."

"You look like Tom Jones."

"The singer?"

"No, the character Albert Finney played in the film. You look just like him, sitting half naked on the edge of that four-poster." Katherine stared down at the floor for a moment, then lifted her gaze to meet Franz's clear blue eyes. "About before, I'm sorry I made that remark. Believe me, there's nothing in the world that could make me any happier than I am already."

Franz let the apology pass. "I saw *Tom Jones,* and I remember that Mr. Jones spent most of his time doing this. . . ."

Laughing, he tried to wrestle Katherine onto the bed. She darted away. As he reached out for her, she dived across the bed to the other side. Franz followed, grabbing her around the waist in a rugby tackle which sent her crashing to the floor with a bang that echoed around the room.

Moments later, a bell rang sharply. Sitting on the floor, Katherine and Franz stared at each other. The ringing came again, and their eyes traveled to a bedside table. On it was a white telephone.

"It can't possibly be for us," Katherine said. "It must be for Cliff. Probably a dire emergency"—she giggled—"some cat or dog that drank too much to welcome in the new year."

The telephone rang four more times. At last, Franz lifted the receiver and breathed a wary "Hello?" Cliff Bentley's voice boomed out of the earpiece. "Having a spot of bother getting accustomed to the bed, old boy?"

Franz gulped; his face turned scarlet. "No, Cliff, no. It was Katherine. She . . . tripped over a loose piece of carpet, that is all."

"All right then. If you need anything, our bedroom's on the ground floor. Right *beneath* your room. Good night."

After replacing the receiver, Franz looked toward Katherine, who was clutching her stomach with one hand and pointing to the floor with the other. Franz's eyes followed the pointing finger, all the way down to polished chestnut floorboards, with not a scrap of carpet to be seen!

Franz arose at his normal time on New Year's Day. Moving carefully to avoid disturbing Katherine, he slipped out of bed and stood by the window that overlooked the farm. Two miles away, bathed in the faint glow of the moon, was the sleepy Hampshire village. In some of the houses, tiny squares of light glimmered. As his eyes grew accustomed to the grayness, Franz could just discern the steeple of the church in the center of the village.

He opened the window a fraction, welcoming the cold air that forced its way in. It drove the remnants of sleep from his brain and made him wish he was out there running, hearing the frost crackle beneath his shoes. But he had made a promise to Katherine. Just this once, while they stayed at the Bentley farm, he would forgo his daily exercise routine.

Turning from the window, he saw Katherine sitting up in bed. "How long have you been awake?"

"From the moment you lowered the temperature in here by fifty degrees. I am absolutely frozen, you inconsiderate oaf. Close that window and come back to bed, where all civilized people belong on New Year's Day."

Franz returned to bed, but could not fall asleep again. Accustomed to rising early, he found it hard to break the routine. He simply lay there, listening to Katherine's rhythmic breathing, feeling her warm body next to his own.

By eight o'clock, the house was alive with activity. Edna Griffiths worked in the kitchen, helping Erica make breakfast, while Katherine prepared the children for the day. Their only riding would be in the Jaguar, driven into the village by Edna, but they would not feel left out. Katherine had bought them hunting outfits so they would be miniature replicas of their parents.

Following breakfast, the adults gathered in front of the drawing-room fire. Both Franz and Cliff wore tweed jackets and hard bowler hats. Erica and Katherine wore black jackets with velvet trim, and velvet-covered hard hunting caps. Four gleaming pairs of riding boots reflected flame from the fire, four pairs of breeches shone with a pristine cleanliness.

Cliff passed out glasses, pouring a tot of Scotch into each. "To keep in the warmth and drive out the cold."

Frost was still on the ground when they went outside; a weak sun shone from between light, scattered clouds. Four horses were saddled: a large gray Irish cob for Franz, medium-weight gray geldings for Katherine and Erica, and a chestnut gelding for Cliff. Watching the adults prepare to mount, the children clamored to sit up on a horse. Katherine balanced Joanne on top of the gentle cob, while Erica held Henry on one of the gray geldings.

Once the children were put into the Jaguar, Edna drove off toward the village. Franz was the first to mount, towering above the others. Katherine had to squint as she looked up at him. Framed by a wintry sun, he cut a haughty figure, back erect, reins gripped easily but firmly in his hand.

"We should take a picture of you," Katherine said, as she mounted her gray gelding and drew close to Franz. "You belong on the cover of *Horse and Hound* or *Tailor and Cutter.*"

The others mounted. Erica rode alongside Franz, while Katherine followed with Cliff. They left the farm and rode sedately toward the assembly point, just outside the village. Thirty riders were already there, some resplendent in scarlet jackets, others in tweed or black. The riders formed into a long column of twos to begin the procession through the village. Cottage doors and windows opened as they passed, and villagers called out greetings. Katherine waved back, enjoying this moment of tradition. She saw Franz, riding in front of her, doff his bowler hat to one elderly woman who stood by the roadside to watch the hunt pass.

In the center of the village was a cobblestoned square. The church stood there as did a dozen shops, shuttered for the day. Only the King's Arms

101

was open, ready with a warm welcome for the holiday trade. In front of the public house, a sizable crowd had gathered; village locals mixed with townspeople curious to see the customs of country life. Henry and Joanne, holding on to Edna Griffiths's hands, stood at the very front of the crowd. Recognizing their parents, they began to jump up and down excitedly, and it was only with difficulty that Edna restrained them from breaking free and rushing over to the horses.

The hunt assembled in front of the King's Arms. The landlord emerged, bearing a tankard, which he handed up to the white-haired master of the hunt. A photographer from a local newspaper stepped forward to take a picture. As the master raised the tankard to his mouth, a disturbance broke out at the rear of the crowd. A dozen men and women, some waving placards that called for an end to hunting, pushed forward.

"Ignore them," Cliff advised, as Katherine swung around in the saddle to see what the noise was all about.

"Are they dangerous?" she asked, worried more for the children and the housekeeper than for herself.

"Nuisance value, that's all."

In front, Erica turned around. "If we had the hounds out, those idiots would try to ruin the dogs' sense of smell by waving aniseed-soaked rags in front of them."

On cue, the dozen protestors began to chant. "Murderers! Murderers! Murderers!" Which then changed to another slogan, three words rattled out in staccato fashion. "Ban the hunt! Ban the hunt! Ban the hunt!"

The master of the hunt raised himself in the saddle to look down at the protesters. "Why don't you cretins find something useful to do?"

"We are doing something useful!" a man yelled back. "We're stopping Hitlers like you from butchering helpless animals."

"We do not butcher anything! We drag hunt!"

The master's argument was drowned out by a chorus of jeers. A woman in a blue duffel coat, face hidden by the hood, shouted, "Liar! Liar!"

The chant was instantly taken up by the other protesters. Katherine watched the master's face grow as red as his jacket. His hands trembled as they held the reins, and she knew he was exerting every ounce of willpower to hold himself back. He raised a hand, the signal to depart. Horses began to move. The situation appeared under control. Then the woman in the blue duffel coat made a throwing motion. A firecracker arced through the air, exploding with a sharp report in the center of the hunt.

Several horses shied away in terror. More fireworks followed as the protesters followed the woman's lead. Katherine saw one land close to her own gelding. She pulled back on the reins to steady the horse. As it swung around, she spotted Edna Griffiths dragging the children away from the front of the crowd. Right next to them was the woman in the blue duffel coat. Even as Katherine looked, the woman raised her arm again.

Katherine's eyes remained fixed on the firework, from the moment it left the woman's hand, until it landed directly beneath the large gray Irish cob.

"Franz!"

Katherine screamed her husband's name in warning at the very instant the firework exploded. The cob reared up on its hind legs like a circus horse. Franz lost his grip on the reins. His feet slipped out of the stirrups and he tumbled backwards. The protective bowler hat skittered away into the forest of horse's legs as Franz's neck and shoulders slammed sickeningly into the cobblestones.

Leaping from her own horse, Katherine ran to where Franz lay. She cradled his head in her hands. Blood matted his blond hair. His face was terrifyingly white, drained of its normal vibrant color. His eyes were fixed open, staring but unseeing. His breathing was ragged.

A hand touched Katherine's shoulder. She looked up to see Cliff. He helped her stand, then passed her to Erica, who held her tightly. Cliff knelt down beside Franz, the veterinarian filling in as doctor. There was nothing he could do.

Erica maintained a steady patter of conversation to occupy Katherine's mind. "Edna took the children back to the farm. She thought it was best to keep them out of the cold. That's all you need, isn't it? The children coming down with a cold."

"Franz . . . ?" Katherine tried to turn her head. She saw the members of the hunt standing around awkwardly, mingling with the villagers. Where were the antihunt protesters whose wild actions had led to this tragedy? Where was the woman in the blue duffel coat?

An ambulance arrived. Franz was loaded into it. Katherine elected to ride with him. Before the door closed, she called out to Erica to telephone her father. Then she sat down for the long ride to the hospital.

Roland Eagles enjoyed a quiet New Year's Eve with Sally Roberts at her apartment. After dinner, they went out for an arm-in-arm walk, Sally snuggled up in a full-length mink coat, which had been Roland's Christmas gift to her, and Roland equally warm in a new cashmere coat, which had been completed by Huntsman only the previous week, his Christmas present to himself.

Eventually, they stood outside an imposing Regency house in Mount Street. A small brass plaque announced the existence of a private club named Kendall's. Roland had been a member for many years.

"Why?" Sally asked in mild protest, "did I just know that we would somehow wind up here?"

"Because you're psychic, and inordinately clever," Roland answered. "A few spins of the wheel, that's all."

"And what will I do while you gamble?"

"Stand by to bring me bundles of luck, of course. Just like you always do."

Once inside Kendall's, after Roland had signed Sally in as his guest, they were transported through time to an earlier, more elegant era. Ornate crystal chandeliers hung from high vaulted ceilings; deep carpet muffled footsteps. Among the paintings on the wall were two Constables and a Gainsborough, depicting calm, pastoral English scenes of a bygone age, and a Hogarth with its satirical glimpse of eighteenth-century England. Even the hum of conversation around the roulette, blackjack, and chemin-de-fer tables was muted, as though club members were not engaged in gambling, but in holy worship.

While Sally watched, Roland played roulette, swinging for half an hour on the pendulum of profit and loss. At one point he was ahead by two thousand pounds. When he decided to quit, he was behind by four hundred pounds.

"You didn't bring me any luck," Roland chided Sally lightly as they walked back to her apartment.

"I most certainly did. Unfortunately, it was all bad." She snaked her arm through his and kissed him. "Sorry."

"That's all right. Just to show how magnanimous I am, I shall not hold you totally responsible."

"Big of you. Hardly an auspicious way to begin

the new year, though, dropping four hundred pounds."

"We're still in 1976," Roland reminded her. "I was just washing out any bad luck with the old year. Like casting my sins into the river, the way orthodox Jews do on their New Year."

"Feeling for your roots?" Sally teased. "I never thought you were the superstitious kind, Roland Eagles."

"Show me a gambler who's not superstitious, and I'll show you a gambler with no heart."

They reached Sally's apartment at ten minutes before midnight. She made hot chocolate, and as a clock chimed in the new year, they toasted each other with heavy mugs.

"To a year free of typographical errors," Sally said.

"And a year free of libel suits," Roland responded.

"We'll do our best." Sally was amused at the recent change in Roland's attitude toward Eagle Newspapers. Ever since Katherine's assignment at Cadmus Court, and the subsequent attack on her, Roland had become much more interested in the workings of his small newspaper group. Instead of being satisfied with simply reading through the minutes of editorial and advertising meetings, he now attended them. His contributions to the meetings had been significant, as Sally had always known they would be, should he ever decide to become fully involved. He had suggested that the *Daily Eagle*'s business page be enlarged to a special pull-out section each Monday. The expansion, which had occurred the first week of December, had brought about a notable increase in advertising for banking services and share offerings.

At twelve-thirty, when Roland asked Sally to telephone for a taxi to take him home, she offered to drive him instead. He thanked her, but said no. "I don't want you on the roads tonight. Not everyone welcomed in the new year as judiciously as we did, with hot chocolate."

Sally did not argue. She made the call, then, while they waited for the taxi, she said, "You know, it's about time you rejoined the twentieth century and started driving for yourself again."

"Cars have changed too much since I last drove. I'm not sure I'd know what to do anymore, so stop trying to get an old dog to learn new tricks."

"We're not talking about a dog; we're talking about you. Make a New Year's resolution to book into a driving school."

"I don't think so. I like being chauffeured around."

"That's not the truth, and you know it," Sally argued, totally unconvinced by Roland's claim. They had discussed this countless times in the past twenty-six years, and she had never managed to shift Roland's position. Twenty-six years had passed since Roland had sat behind the wheel of a car—that June day in 1950 when Catarina had died.

Sally knew the accident had not been Roland's fault. He had lost control of the car only after braking sharply to avoid hitting a pedestrian who had stepped out right in front of him. Nor had the accident been fully to blame for his young wife's death. The aneurysm that had caused the massive cerebral hemorrhage might have been congenital; doctors had assured Roland that it could have ruptured at any time. Only it had chosen to rupture when Catarina had hit her head on the dashboard, during an accident where Roland was at the wheel. Because of that tragic fluke of timing, Roland had never stopped blaming himself.

Part of his self-punishment was refusing to drive. At first, with the memory of the accident so fresh,

Roland had been unable to sit in the driver's seat. As time had passed, he had become accustomed to being driven here and there. For many years he had employed a personal assistant-cum-chauffeur, until the man had retired eighteen months earlier. Now, a company driver picked Roland up in the morning and took him home at night. If he needed to go out when the driver was unavailable, he could always take a taxi or call on Arthur Parsons. In the garage of the house was an old Bentley, which had been used by the chauffeur. Among Parsons's responsibilities was seeing that the Bentley was maintained and ready for use should Roland need to go somewhere.

When the taxi arrived, Sally walked down to the street with Roland. He kissed her good night, wished her a happy New Year again, and climbed into the taxi. As it moved away, he looked back at Sally standing in the road, waving. He waved in response, feeling tired in a contented sort of way.

Roland spent the entire journey leaning back, eyes half-closed, congratulating himself for being one of the luckiest men alive. He had endured his share of heartache—who had not?—but he'd had the good times as well. And who was to say that tragedy did not carry its own silver lining? It made you appreciate life's sweet triumphs even more. For a moment, he pitied those people who had never known anything but happiness. Such people were unable to appreciate their own good luck. Like being born rich. A man who'd never had to struggle for money could never fully understand just how nice it was to have it.

Most important, Roland knew he was fortunate enough to be loved by two particularly wonderful and fascinating women. His daughter . . . and his editorial director. He grinned as he recalled Katherine standing up to him in Sally's office, pointing to her black eye and calling it a badge of courage. The girl had her mother's fire, no doubt at that.

Any man could count himself damned lucky if he found one good woman to love him. Including Catarina, Roland had found three.

On New Year's Day, Roland indulged himself by sleeping late. It was after nine when he arose. The large house was silent. Arthur and Peg Parsons, who had the day off, had driven out to Cambridge to visit friends. Over a cup of coffee, Roland glanced through the morning paper. The day stretched out ahead like a vacation. Completely alone, with no plans other than doing absolutely nothing. Tomorrow, Sunday, he would be busy enough, when Katherine and Franz brought the children over for the afternoon. Today he would just relax.

Wrapped up in a sheepskin coat, he took a long walk across the common, nodding to people he passed, wishing total strangers a happy New Year. How should he spend this day relaxing? He knew. He'd sit by the television all afternoon and watch the racing. But first, he would go down to the village and invest some money at the local betting shop. Such a personal involvement would make the racing far more enjoyable.

The walk down the long, steep hill was invigorating. He made his bets and returned home, striding up the hill with the energy of a man half his age. While his legs remained so firm, he would not miss the convenience of a car at all.

At midday, he settled down in front of the television, pad and pencil ready on the arm of the chair to compute his winnings. After all, if you couldn't ride the wave of blind optimism on New Year's Day, when could you?

Ten minutes later, he had forgotten all about an afternoon of racing. That was when Erica Bentley telephoned to say Franz had been taken to the hospital following a riding accident.

Katherine presented an odd figure in the hospital waiting room, riding boots, breeches, and black jacket contrasting vividly with the sterile white surroundings. The hard hunting cap was still perched on her blond hair, and she paced agitatedly from one side of the small room to the other, slapping her right thigh every so often with the leather gloves she had worn to the meet.

When Franz had been taken from the ambulance, Katherine had tried to follow. As doors closed in her face, a nursing sister had taken her by the arm and gently guided her into the waiting room. "The moment the doctors learn anything, they'll let you know," the sister promised. "Now why don't you just sit down here and try not to worry? I'll bring you a nice cup of tea."

That had been forty-five minutes earlier. The tea was still where the sister had set it down, untouched and cold, the surface congealed. Katherine had been unable to drink it; her stomach felt like a nest of icy vipers.

An hour after the ambulance reached the hospital, Cliff Bentley arrived, like Katherine still wearing his riding outfit. He began to apologize for taking so long—"I had to be sure that Erica, your housekeeper, and the children got back to the farm safely"—but Katherine brushed it aside. She wanted to know only one thing: "Did you manage to reach my father?"

"Erica did. He's on his way here."

Katherine breathed a sigh of relief. From Roland, she would draw the strength necessary to face this ordeal.

"Any word yet on Franz's condition?" Cliff asked.

"Nothing."

Cliff nodded and tried to keep a glum expression from his round face. He might be only a veterinarian, a man accustomed to treating the maladies of farm animals and domestic pets, but he was sure that his initial off-the-cuff diagnosis, made while Franz lay on the cobblestoned street, was correct. The young man had broken his neck. That was why Cliff had moved Katherine away; the last thing he needed was motion of any kind.

When Roland arrived, he was not alone. Sally Roberts had driven him to the hospital. Roland had never realized how difficult it was to find a taxi on New Year's Day. He had telephoned cab ranks and car-hire companies without success. At last, praying desperately that the telephone would not ring unanswered, he had called the apartment in Mayfair. He had caught Sally drying herself after a bath. Ten minutes later, hurriedly dressed in slacks, a thick woolen sweater, and a leather jacket, with her damp auburn hair tucked into a warm angora cap, Sally was driving north toward Roland's home.

Katherine rushed into her father's arms the moment he stepped into the small waiting room. His embrace soothed her frayed nerves, and by the time he asked if she knew anything about Franz's condition, she was very close to being in total control of herself.

"Erica mentioned something about a demonstration causing the accident," Roland said.

"Anti–blood sport fanatics," Katherine replied. "Their protest turned vicious. . . ." Cliff Bentley listened in amazement as Katherine described the incident. Moments earlier she'd been on edge, like a caged animal. Now, so close to Roland Eagles, she seemed as cool and smooth as marble. Erica had often told her husband that a special relationship existed between father and daughter, but Cliff had never witnessed it until this moment.

111

Even as Cliff pondered the change, Katherine turned to him. "I'll be all right now. Thank you for coming."

Cliff sensed that the family had closed ranks in its crisis. Sally Roberts was obviously a part of that family, but he was not. "Any message for your housekeeper?"

"Tell her to drive the children home and do whatever she can to keep them from missing their father. I'll telephone her there the moment I hear anything."

When Cliff left to return to the farm, Katherine sat down, her father on one side, Sally on the other. "You know," she said quietly, "I saw that woman raise her arm to throw the firework. If I had called out a moment earlier, Franz might have been able to anticipate, to maneuver the cob away. He's a skillful rider; he could have reacted in time."

"Don't you mean," Sally countered, "that if some criminally insane idiot had not thrown a firework, it would never have happened? The accident had nothing to do with you, Katherine, so you can get that crazy notion right out of your mind."

Roland looked across his daughter's head to Sally, knowing her words had been intended as much for him as for Katherine. The sense of *déjà vu* was overpowering. Was this what Katherine had inherited from him, what he had willed her as a legacy? Tragedy?

A doctor entered the waiting room, an elderly man with thin gray hair and a gentle, sympathetic face. "Mrs. Kassler, I'm afraid I have some difficult news for you."

"Yes?" A little of the calmness disappeared. Katherine's face became strained, skin stretched over bone. One hand grasped her father's hand, the other slipped through Sally's arm.

"Your husband has suffered fractures of the sixth and seventh cervical vertebrae. He's paralyzed from below his shoulders to his toes. He has the slightest use of his arms, that is all. He cannot push them out from himself, but if they are held out for him, he can pull them back."

As Katherine sat staring at the doctor, Roland asked, "Will this paralysis be permanent?"

"At this moment, it is impossible to tell. Our major concern at the present time is performing an operation to straighten the damaged vertebrae and relieve pressure on the spinal cord. Perhaps Mrs. Kassler would leave a telephone number where she can be—"

"We'll wait," Katherine said firmly.

The doctor left. Around the three people in the waiting room, the hospital carried on its normal routine. Visiting time came, and people thronged the hospital's wide corridors. Nursing shifts changed. Sally went out, returning with tea and sandwiches from a nearby restaurant. Later, Roland went for a walk, needing the crisp evening air to clear his head. While out, he bought a newspaper. Three of the five horses he'd bet on had won; the other two had both placed. He could not have cared had all five selections fallen at the first fence.

Katherine never moved from the waiting room, except to visit the washroom. She presented a picture of primness, a rider in a show waiting for her turn to impress the panel of judges.

Close to midnight, the same doctor returned to the three people in the small waiting room. His face appeared longer now, his eyes tired. "The operation is over. Your husband's condition is as satisfactory as can be expected."

"The paralysis? If he should recover movement—more than just being able to pull his arms toward himself—how long would it take?"

"Anywhere from two months to, perhaps, several years."

"May I see him?"

"He is sedated. He will not even know you're there."

"I just want to see for myself what's happened."

The doctor nodded. "For a minute, that's all." He led her away, leaving Roland alone with Sally.

Katherine returned five minutes later. The coolness had completely deserted her. Her face was drawn and ashen, her shoulders stooped. Whatever she had seen had shocked her self-control to pieces.

Roland put his arm around her shoulders. "We'll take you back to Hampstead. I'll stay with you tonight."

Katherine remained silent until she was in Sally's sports car, sitting on the bench seat in the back. Only as they cleared the hospital grounds did she begin to speak, and then in a voice so low, so filled with horror and disgust, that Roland and Sally had to strain to hear her words.

"They allowed me to look at Franz through a window. They wouldn't let me into his room, just through this window. He was all covered up, except for his head. I could only see his head. It was shaved, and these *things* were sticking out of his skull. Tongs, with weights attached to them to keep his neck in traction. They must have drilled . . . holes . . . in . . . his . . . skull to insert them."

Roland started to say something. Sally touched his arm and motioned for him to remain quiet. Let Katherine carry on speaking, let her spill everything out and feel better for it.

"He was on a high bed," Katherine continued, "his head below the rest of his body. The doctor told me it was Franz, but I couldn't recognize him. Tongs . . ." She enunciated the word with loathing. "Just like you'd use to pick up a piece of ice."

Then, leaving that vision imprinted clearly in everyone's imagination, Katherine lapsed back into

114

silence, saying not another word until Sally pulled into the driveway of the Hampstead house. Franz's Jaguar was there, driven back from the farm by Edna Griffiths. The only light in the house shone from the hallway. The bedrooms were in darkness. Katherine remembered that she had not telephoned the housekeeper as she had promised to do. Now it was early morning; tired of waiting, Edna had gone to sleep.

"You don't have to stay with me," Katherine told her father as he helped her from Sally's car. "I'll be fine."

"Are you certain?" Roland did not relish the prospect of leaving Katherine by herself on such a night.

"I am not alone," Katherine said. "Edna's here."

"And personally," Sally broke in, "I could not think of a broader, more staunch shoulder to lean on. Get back in the car, Roland. I'll take you to Stanmore."

Katherine kissed her father good night. After watching the car pull away, she let herself into the house, welcoming the echoing quietness. She was grateful to Sally. As much as her father wanted to keep her company on this night, so Katherine wanted just as much to be on her own. To think, and to wonder what would happen next.

She climbed the stairs, and looked in on the children. Both slept peacefully. Whatever memories they had of their father's fall were not disturbing their sleep. Tomorrow, Katherine would talk to them, explain that their father had been hurt, that he would not be coming home for some time. But he would be all right eventually. He'd be back, getting up at ten minutes to six every morning for his run over Hampstead Heath, his athletic shoes slapping against the concrete in a steady, comforting cadence. God . . . she hoped he would!

From looking in on the children, Katherine went to her own room. Sitting on the edge of the brass bed, she lifted a hand to remove the hard, velvet-covered hunting cap. A dull throbbing ache pressed against her skull, but it was nothing compared to what Franz must be suffering. The thought of those dreadful tongs sticking out of his head made Katherine shiver.

A creaking noise came from above, as though someone's foot had found a bad floorboard in the recreation room. What was up there? A ghost? Franz's spirit? His body confined in a hospital, but his spirit free to roam? She left the bedroom, took the stairs to the third floor, and turned on the light. The recreation room was empty, of course, the creaking noise nothing more than the monologue of an old house in winter as wood contracted with the cold.

She looked around at the wall bars, the weights, the rowing machine. When would they be used again? And by whom? A man with a broken neck did not need such things.

Two months to several years, that's what the doctor had said. If Franz recovered the ability to move, to walk, it could take anywhere from two months to several years. And if he did not recover?

Katherine's mind went back exactly ten years in time, to those first few days of 1967. A short vacation in Monte Carlo, a few days her father had stolen from his full business diary because he did not see enough of his daughter. She'd been out walking. A tall, blond young man had approached. Franz had seen Katherine at the hotel. He wanted to know if he could meet her at that night's dance. She had told him, very properly, that she would have to ask her father first.

They had met that night; they'd danced and fallen in love. And then they'd parted, returning to their different countries. Letters . . . visits by Franz to London, by Roland and Katherine to the mountain-chalet vacation home of Franz's family. And then, in 1970, the request by Franz's father for Roland to find a position for his son in England.

Katherine recalled telling her father the real reason for the request, Franz's trouble in Germany. She remembered Roland's face as he considered the information, stern at first, then softening when he said, "All right, I'll offer Franz a job in store operations, the same as he's doing for his father. But, Kathy, if he gets involved in anti-American demonstrations here, and drags you along, I won't wait for the Home Office to deport him. I'll kick him out of the country myself."

Roland's concern had been unfounded. Within minutes of being collected at Heathrow Airport, sitting in the back of the chauffeured Bentley with Katherine, Franz made it abundantly clear that his demonstration days were over. "When I protested in Germany," he told Roland, "it was not so much against the Americans as against my father's generation. They led us into a terrible war, and they still govern our country. I was protesting what my father's generation left us as a legacy — a divided country, and the reputation of being the birthplace of some of the most heinous acts known to man."

Katherine's memory formed the picture of her father turning away, unable to match Franz's blazing intensity. Later, Roland had said to his daughter, "No wonder you always rushed down to greet the postman each morning. Franz's letters must have read straight from the heart."

Franz had found a furnished apartment in town. He saw Katherine almost every evening. Dinner, a movie, dancing, or sometimes just a drive or a walk. No matter what time Franz brought her home, though, Roland would always be waiting up. Like an anxious mother hen, Katherine thought with a half smile.

When Franz had been in London for three weeks, Katherine had taken him to the wedding of a family friend. After the party, they had gone to Franz's apartment. Katherine had returned home that night just before dawn. As she crossed the hall toward the stairs, her father's voice—coming from the doorway of the drawing room—had stopped her.

"Kathy."

She turned around.

"Where did you go with Franz?"

"To a jazz club. Then for a walk on the Embankment."

"You must have frozen."

"Franz had his arm around me."

"I should hope so."

She started up the stairs again, halted, and swung around. "I can't lie to you. We went back to Franz's."

"Do you love him?"

"I think so."

"That's not good enough, Kathy. I knew I loved your mother when I was with her the first time."

A week later, Katherine had told Roland that she and Franz wanted to live together. The memory of that particular moment turned the half smile on Katherine's face into a broad grin. It had been one of the infrequent times she had seen her father stuck for words. At last, he had spoken to both her and Franz. Formally, over dinner at the house. After ascertaining that Franz and Katherine did, indeed, love each other, he had said, "If you're both so certain that living together is right, then go the whole damned hog and get married! If I am to be blessed with grandchildren, I would like it to be while I'm still fit enough to push a carriage. And I would like to have a son-in-law as well. . . ."

The grin faded abruptly as Katherine's memory flashed across the intervening years, jarring to a halt twenty-four hours earlier. New Year's Eve at the Bentley farm. What was it she had told Franz? What would make her happier? "I'd like you to be home the next time I have something special to celebrate." That was it. Nothing harmful or malicious about that, just a little wish that her husband would be home when she had a big event to shout about.

Satan must have eavesdropped on that conversation, because Katherine's wish had been granted. But not in the way that she would ever have wanted it to be fulfilled.

Most probably, Franz would be home the next time she had something to celebrate.

In a . . .

Her mind struggled to form the words, to include an obscenity she would never normally dream of using. But on this first obscene day of the new year, it somehow seemed so horribly fitting.

Franz would be home, all right. Sitting there in a fucking wheelchair!

6

The time immediately following the new year comprised the most agonizing period of Katherine's life. Four days after the accident, when it seemed that nothing worse could possibly happen, Franz contracted pneumonia. A tracheotomy was performed, a tube inserted into his throat to bring up the mucus congesting his lungs before he drowned in his own fluids; another tube was inserted in his nostrils to drain water from his stomach. Each evening, when Katherine left the hospital after visiting Franz, she wondered if she would ever see him again.

Even after the lung infection cleared, the throat tube remained in place because Franz's cough reflex was not powerful enough to assure keeping the bronchial passage clear. Every time Katherine saw the tube, she was reminded that a broken neck was just the start; the illnesses that attended such an injury, and the enforced immobility that went with it, could be just as terrifying.

The first signs of improvement came after six weeks, when Franz was able to straighten his arms and move his wrists. Physiotherapy began, limited exercises where his hands were strapped to a bar above the bed so he could strengthen his arms by lifting himself. A panoramic mirror was fitted to the bar, allowing Franz to see what was happening around him. Finally, a television set was brought in, angled so he could watch it from his supine position.

In Katherine's eyes, the television was the best therapy of all. When she arrived at the hospital each afternoon, Franz seemed a little more cheerful. The television kept him in contact with the outside world. He discussed news events with Katherine, and for the first time since the accident, he seemed truly optimistic. Instead of saying, "*If* I walk again," he used the word *when*. It was a good time, Katherine believed, to broach a subject she had so far kept to herself.

"Henry and Joanne keep asking when they can visit you. Do you feel up to seeing them?"

"Of course." Franz looked in the mirror at the photograph on the bedside table. It was one he had taken on Christmas Day, of Henry and Joanne on their new bicycles. "When will you bring them?"

"This coming Saturday."

For the rest of the week, Katherine and the children eagerly anticipated the special visit. But when she took Henry and Joanne to see their father on Saturday afternoon, Franz's room was in darkness. Leaving the children in the corridor, Katherine entered the room. The blinds were drawn, the television was nowhere in sight. Franz lay on the bed, eyes screwed shut, his face a painful grimace.

"Franz . . . ? The children are outside."

"Take them away."

Stunned, Katherine could only say, "But you said you wanted to see them."

"Take them away. I do not want them to see what I have become. A cripple, that is all I am. A useless cripple." Then, in a pitifully pleading voice, as though speaking directly to God, he asked, "Why could the horse have not fallen on me?"

From a doctor, Katherine learned what had happened. Franz had been watching a Saturday-afternoon sports program. He had seen a race, athletes pounding around a track, running as he had once loved to run. Then he had looked in the mirror at his own legs—those limbs which had no movement, no feeling—and he had summoned the nurse to remove the television and draw the blinds.

Katherine returned to the room. "You'll run again," she told Franz. "Once you're better, you'll go running over the heath, just like you did before."

"Do you still not understand? I have broken my neck. I will be crippled until the day I die."

Katherine rushed from the room, collected Henry and Joanne, and drove them home without them seeing their father. She spent the entire journey fighting back tears. As long as Franz had believed he would recover, she had held the same conviction. Now that his faith had been shattered, her own optimism lay in ruins.

From that moment, Franz underwent a personality change. He seemed to care little for what happened to him. He was neither encouraged when the strength in his arms showed marginal improvement, nor disappointed when it became obvious that he would never regain any body use below his arms. He accepted the rehabilitative process with a stoic fatalism. It was as though, doctors told Katherine, he was doing the therapists a favor by submitting himself to it.

His moods fluctuated. Sometimes when Katherine visited, he was receptive, asking about Henry and Joanne, about the house, even about the newspaper. Abruptly, his mood would shift. Just as Katherine felt it might be a good time to ask if he wanted the children to visit, Franz's tolerance level would flash to the other end of the scale, and he would demand to be left alone.

"Go! Leave me!" he would snap. "I do not need your pity!"

"I'm not here because I pity you. I'm here because I love you, and for no other reason."

"Love me?" He gave a dry croak of a laugh. "How can anyone in their right mind" — he gestured helplessly at his legs — "love something like this?"

"Stop feeling so full of self-pity. A lot of other people who broke their necks didn't live to complain about it."

Grim humor glinted in Franz's blue eyes. "Who? Murderers who were hanged?"

Eight months after the accident, Franz began to spend weekends at home, Saturday morning to Sunday afternoon. The visits, accompanied by an attendant named Jimmy Phillips, were to reacquaint Franz with living in a house. To accustom him to being with his family again; with whole, healthy people, and not with other patients whose physical disabilities he shared.

The house had been altered from the day that Franz had last seen it, when he, Katherine, the children, and Edna Griffiths had left to spend New Year's Eve at the Bentley farm. Ground-floor doorways had been widened to allow access to a wheelchair; ramps had been fitted over steps. It seemed to Franz that everywhere he looked, he saw a reminder that he was crippled. Even the library at the front of the house, where he had brought home work from the office, had been altered. It was now a bedroom. The bathroom that adjoined it was fitted with the bars and supports that a handicapped person would need.

The weekend visits gave the children their first opportunity to see their father. No matter how sweetly Katherine had coated the pill of rejection — inventing stories about infections in the hospital that she did not want Henry and Joanne catching; even an excuse, the one time they had accompanied their mother to the hospital, about Franz being too tired to see them — they had been badly hurt. On that first visit home, before Franz was lifted from the car by Jimmy Phillips, Katherine told him exactly how she wanted him to behave.

"Franz, today's a big day for everyone. Inside, there's a welcome-home party all set out. Henry and Joanne have presents for you. They've been looking forward to today for weeks. Please don't let them see the face I've seen at the hospital."

Before Franz could answer, Jimmy Phillips spoke up. "Don't you worry about a thing, Mrs. Kassler. All the way here, your husband's been talking about nothing else but seeing his kids. And you, of course."

Katherine smiled. She liked the attendant, a cheerful, middleaged cockney who had once dreamed of a boxing career in the heavyweight division. Despite his ponderous size and fearsome looks — shaggy dark hair, and a nose that appeared to have been broken at least a dozen times — Jimmy Phillips was one of the most gentle men Katherine had ever known. He had been recommended by a nursing agency to care for Franz once he returned home. With just enough strength in his hands and arms to lift a fork or spoon, Franz would need constant attention.

Katherine stood aside as the attendant lifted Franz from the front passenger seat as easily as if he were a baby and placed him in the wheelchair. "Isn't that right, Mr. Kassler, what I just told Mrs. Kassler?"

Katherine saw Franz move his head in answer to the question. Phillips pushed the wheelchair up the steep ramp leading to the front door. As the ramp leveled out into the entrance hall of the house, Franz saw "Welcome" banners suspended from the ceiling. Shining gold stars and silver tinsel drifted in the breeze. His eyes filled with tears when he saw the waiting people. His father-in-law and Sally Roberts. The Bentleys. Edna Griffiths. And standing in front of them all, his son and daughter, Henry and Joanne. How could he possibly have denied them the right to visit him?

Smiling, he slowly held out his hands to them. They rushed forward, flung their arms around his neck — gently, as their mother had instructed them — and kissed him. But at the very moment of contact, Franz felt a backing-off. He told himself that he understood. The children had not seen him for eight months. They were wary, a little afraid. And who could blame them? Adults realized the changes that sickness could make upon a man, but children did not possess the wisdom of older heads. They could only compare what was with what had been. Their father had been a fit and happy man, who took great pride in his physical ability. The man they had been told to greet was a mere shadow of such a person, a white-faced, crippled specter.

The smile remained etched on Franz's face, but agonizing pain swept through him.

Six more weekend visits followed. Then, at the beginning of November, exactly ten months after the accident, Franz came home for good.

While Franz had been away, Katherine had divided her life into two compartments: the harsh world of reality, and the less stressful world of make-believe.

Reality was visiting Franz every afternoon, searching desperately for any sign of physical improvement and a corresponding improvement in his mental state. Make-believe was carrying on life as normally as possible, fulfilling her functions as both a mother of two young children and a woman with a blossoming career. The only way she could successfully accomplish that was by acting as if nothing was wrong.

Initially, she had felt callous, and perhaps a trifle guilty. After all, what right did she have to continue with her own life, to find enjoyment in her work — even to laugh — while Franz lay in a hospital bed? Slowly, those feelings had yielded to a pragmatic appraisal of the situation, which she summed up by asking out loud, each time she felt herself falling apart, "How on earth will Franz be helped if I allow my own life to collapse because I'm sick with worry over him?" The answer she gave herself each time was obvious. "He won't be helped at all, you idiot, so get a grip on yourself and carry on!"

The dual role became a part of Katherine's life. She altered her day, rising at six each morning to spend time with the children as Franz had always done. At work, she gave greater responsibility to Heather and Derek, her two assistants on "Satisfaction Guaranteed!" When Katherine left the Eagle building early each afternoon to visit Franz, she was certain that the column was in the most capable of hands.

Franz's return to the house in Hampstead erased the line between reality and make-believe, and brought Katherine's carefully constructed world crashing down. It was no longer possible to pretend that nothing was wrong when Franz was present in the house, when he was sleeping downstairs, and when he was being bathed and dressed each morning by Jimmy Phillips, who was now as much a part of the household as Edna Griffiths was.

Along with his damaged body and his wheelchair, Franz brought tension home with him.

Katherine saw it in the children. They were quieter, less rambunctious, especially at mealtimes, when Franz was helped to the table by Phillips. Henry and Joanne would stare at their plates, unwilling to look at the man opposite them. They acted like normal children, Katherine noticed, only on those days when Phillips drove Franz to the hospital for routine therapy. Then they would play in the jungle of a back garden, or in the house, as carefree as two young children were supposed to be, until they heard the crunch of the Jaguar's wide tires on the gravel of the driveway, saw Phillips remove the collapsible wheelchair from the trunk of the car, and lift Franz into it. The abnormal quietness would then return, and with it the refusal to look into the face of the man who was their father. Franz, aware of his children's confusion, and not wishing to disturb them even more by forcing them to acknowledge him, withdrew.

After six weeks, Katherine's nerves were on edge. It was close to Christmas. Instead of seasonal joy, the house was full of fear and distrust. The next time Franz was taken to the hospital for therapy, Katherine called the children into the breakfast room and asked why they were rebuffing their father.

"He isn't like our daddy used to be," Henry answered. "He frightens us now."

Despite the high-pitched voice, Katherine could not help marveling how adult her son sounded. "Why should you be frightened of him? Because he's in a wheelchair? Now that's silly, isn't it?"

"Our daddy would never frighten us," Henry said defiantly.

Katherine turned to Joanne. Less self-assured than her brother, the four-year-old girl just nodded in agreement. And Katherine wondered what was more to blame for the alienation between children and father—Franz's injury itself, or his refusal to let the children see him in the hospital? During the eight months from the accident to his first visit home, had Franz and his children become strangers?

That evening, after Henry and Joanne had gone to

bed, and while Edna Griffiths was busy in the kitchen, Katherine decided to discuss the situation with Franz. She found him in the television room, watching a movie with Jimmy Phillips.

"Franz, can we talk?"

"Of course."

"Privately, Franz."

"Excuse me," Phillips said, and walked to the door before Franz could ask him to leave. Katherine took the seat Phillips had vacated, next to the straight-backed, heavily padded armchair in which Franz sat. A plaid blanket was stretched over his legs, as though to ward off a bothersome draft. But there were no gaps in the walls or windows of the television room for any draft to find its way through, and Katherine knew that the blanket was there only to hide Franz's legs from his eyes.

"What do you want to talk about?" Franz asked.

"About you and the children. You're complete strangers to each other. Franz, it has to be you who makes the first move."

Franz's eyes turned damp. "Katherine, you will never know how much I want to make that move. But they rejected me once—"

"When?"

"That first time I came home for the weekend. I could feel their rejection when they rushed up to kiss me and give me their presents. At the last moment, they held back, and it was like someone had stuck a knife in me."

"Franz, you have to try again."

"Do you understand what it feels like to have your own children frightened of you?"

"It's because they don't know you. You were away for eight months before you first came home. Ten months altogether, and in all that time you would not let them see you in the hospital."

Franz blinked away tears. "Katherine, how do

Henry and Joanne remember me?"

"As you were, of course."

"Perhaps it is best that way. Children should always think of their father as strong. Not like this."

"All I'm asking is that you try." She stood up, then stooped to kiss him. He turned his face slightly, so that her lips met his cheek. Ever since his return home, he'd offered her his cheek. Perhaps the children were not the only strangers in his life; his wife merited that title, too.

She walked toward the door. As she reached it, she turned around. "When I said I wanted to talk to you, why didn't you ask Jimmy to leave immediately?"

"Because I wanted him here."

"Why?" she asked although she was certain that she already knew the answer.

"Jimmy Phillips knows me as I am now. You, the children, your father, everyone else . . . you all knew me as I was. I feel most comfortable with Jimmy, because he cannot make comparisons."

Katherine went to the kitchen, where she found Phillips sampling some of the fruitcake Edna Griffiths had just baked. The housekeeper stood waiting for the attendant's words of approval. When they came, her huge, round face beamed with happiness. Katherine noticed that Edna's hair was no longer in a tidy bun. It was down, resting on her shoulders. And she was wearing makeup; just a touch of lipstick, a trace of eye shadow, a little color in her cheeks, nothing more. But it was the first time Katherine had seen the housekeeper use any cosmetics.

"You can go back to Mr. Kassler now," Katherine told Phillips.

The attendant returned to the television room with a tray bearing two cups of tea and some fruitcake.

Katherine waited until Phillips had helped Franz

129

into bed in the converted ground-floor room before she went upstairs. She lay quietly, staring up at the ceiling, her mind a meeting place for a thousand jumbled thoughts. There was a surreptitious air of romance in the house. Edna Griffiths, the long-established housekeeper, and the newly arrived Jimmy Phillips, who had become a part of the household as Franz's full-time attendant. When had that relationship started? And why, Katherine asked herself, did she feel jealous of the middle-aged couple for the little bit of happiness they had found to share?

It wasn't romance as Katherine had known it with Franz, a fiery, passionate love affair. This was quiet, refined, limited to a word of approval over a piece of cake, and gratitude that such approval had been forthcoming. God . . . she smiled at the notion of Edna and Phillips making love as she and Franz had made love. That was like thinking such thoughts about one's parents — surely they didn't do things like that! Yet whatever the housekeeper and Phillips shared, it was more than what had passed between Katherine and Franz for a year now; or what, barring a miracle, would ever pass between them again.

She stretched out in the bed, closing her eyes, and recalling how it had been. Franz next to her, hard, muscular, assertive, and, simultaneously, so gentle and caring. Her skin caught fire, burning the satin sheets that caressed it. She pressed her thighs together, stretched her arms to clasp the brass rails of the headboard in a rigid grip. And then, as memory alone drove her to the point of climax, she wondered whether or not she still loved Franz. Or was that love now tinged with pity? She did not honestly know. Her hands released the rails, and she let out her breath in a long, tired sigh.

Before sleep came, she considered the newest

member of the household. No wonder Jimmy Phillips's pugilistic career had been a flop—he was too easygoing, too likable. Katherine liked him. Edna certainly did. The children as well, because he frequently found the time to play with them. Most of all, Franz liked him, felt most comfortable with him, because Phillips had never known Franz when he had been whole. He'd always known him as a handicapped man, so he couldn't make comparisons.

And everyone, Katherine thought, as she rolled over and buried her face in the pillow, knew that comparisons were odious.

Christmas was the most miserable holiday Katherine had ever known, a complete reversal of previous years' joy. The trappings of the season were all there—the tree, the gifts, the visit to her father's home for lunch—but all feeling was missing. Franz, Katherine saw, did his best to communicate with his son and daughter. He had been out with Jimmy Phillips to buy presents, a talking doll with several changes of clothes for Joanne, and a large toy truck for Henry. Even at Katherine's prodding, the children received the gifts with little more than a cool courtesy; they displayed none of the enthusiasm and love that small children normally show for a parent.

The traditional Christmas Day journey to Stanmore Common was a crowded one. Phillips drove the Jaguar, while Franz sat strapped into the front passenger seat. Katherine and Edna Griffiths shared an overflowing backseat with the children. When the family arrived at Roland Eagles's home, the children rushed into the house, making straight for the Christmas tree in the drawing room. When they found the toys Roland had bought for them, their affection was overwhelming. He stooped to let them

131

kiss him. At that exact moment, Franz was wheeled into the room. Katherine caught the expression on his face—wretchedness, with just a trace of anger that life had treated him so unfairly—before he replaced it with a bland mask.

The Christmas meal was another of Peg Parsons's culinary masterpieces—traditionally English this year, smoked salmon, a hearty soup, turkey with spicy stuffing, and roast potatoes—but Katherine kept her attention on Franz, who sat opposite her. Bracketed by Phillips and Sally Roberts, he barely touched any of the food that was placed in front of him. It came as no surprise to Katherine when, just as Arthur Parsons prepared to serve the Christmas pudding, Franz said, "I really do not feel well. Would you think me very rude if I asked to be excused?" Without waiting for an answer, he turned to Phillips. "Please take me home."

Katherine started to stand as though she, too, would leave. Roland's voice carried along the table. "Sit down, Kathy, there's a good girl. Mr. Parsons will drive you, Edna, and the children home later on."

Katherine watched Franz and Phillips leave. She heard the trunk lid slamming on the collapsed wheelchair, the chatter of an engine starting. Cries of excitement distracted her. In the Christmas pudding, Henry and Joanne had each discovered an old gold sovereign, which Roland had bought just for this occasion. The noise of the children was something new, and suddenly Katherine understood just why Franz had chosen that particular moment to leave. The children would never be able to enjoy themselves while sitting at the same table. He was their father, and he loved them too much to spoil their Christmas.

After the meal, Sally suggested that Roland and Katherine accompany her on a walk across the common. Before they'd gone a hundred yards, Katherine learned that the walk wasn't just to work off calories.

"Katherine, Gerry Waller's been muttering complaints about 'Satisfaction Guaranteed!' in my ear," Sally said.

"What kind of complaints?" Katherine's voice, honed with an edge of defensiveness, was sharper than she'd intended it to be. "Why hasn't he made them to me?"

"Because you're never there, and that's part of the reason he's complaining. The column's going downhill in a hurry. You're pushing too much onto your assistants' shoulders. They're too inexperienced to handle it, and they're certainly not being paid enough to carry that kind of responsibility."

Roland took over from Sally. "Kathy, while Franz was away, you were terrific. You soldiered on just like I did after your mother, God rest her soul, passed away. But now that he's home, you're beginning to fall to pieces. I saw the way you jumped up before, when Franz said he wanted to go home. You were ready to go as well, take the children with you, and spoil everyone's day. Maybe you think that because you're Franz's wife, you also have to be his full-time nurse. He has an attendant, Kathy, and Jimmy seems like a very capable person. Franz doesn't need you tailoring your life to suit his needs. The best thing you can do — for yourself, for Franz, for everyone and everything you come in contact with — is to remember that you have other obligations."

When Katherine answered, the sharp edge in her voice was even more noticeable. "That's ridiculous. Any problems I have at home stay there. I carry my weight at the *Eagle* just as well as anyone else does."

When Roland opened his mouth to respond, Sally touched his arm. Never mind right or wrong; tem-

133

pers were becoming frayed on both sides. Christmas Day was not the time for a family argument, into which Sally knew she would be drawn. "All right, Katherine, enough said. It's important that you should know what's going through Gerry Waller's mind these days, that's all."

"Tell Gerry that he's got nothing to worry about."

When Katherine returned to work, she carried her personal Christmas mood with her. Not comfort and joy, but tidings of anger. For once, she barely acknowledged Archie Waters's cheerful greeting as she boarded his elevator. Even Erica Bentley's bright "Good morning, having a nice Christmas?" was met with nothing more than a grimace. It struck Katherine that a coolness had grown between her and Erica during recent weeks. Although Katherine had not ridden since the accident—she'd been too busy to even think about pleasure—the two women had remained close friends. Until . . . until Franz had come home, and destroyed the protective cocoon of reality and make-believe that I'd managed to build up, Katherine thought.

When Gerald Waller arrived in his office, he found Katherine waiting. "How dare you complain to other people about the manner in which I conduct myself? If there's something you don't like about the way I'm working, you tell me. Don't embarrass me by telling everyone else."

Waller leaned back in his chair and let Katherine blow off steam. Finally, he said, "I wasn't trying to embarrass you. I was merely trying to do you a favor, by getting someone close to you to drop a word of advice in your ear."

"And they did just that. Now how about telling *me* exactly why you're unhappy about my column?"

"Your two assistants, Derek Simon and Heather

Harvey, are extremely capable for what they are—a couple of young and very enthusiastic reporters. They're also very inexperienced. They have to be told; they have to be led. During the past couple of months, you've let them lead themselves. Two good stories were messed up because of their inexperience—the jewelry insurance fraud, and the travel agency that was illegally holding on to deposits."

"Wait a minute, Gerry. Criminal prosecution has resulted in the jewelry fraud. And it was our investigation, the original tip to us, that led to police action."

"Damn the police! I'm only interested in the *Eagle*. Your assistants were too inexperienced to handle these stories on their own, so two good exclusives were lost to 'Satisfaction Guaranteed!' and to this newspaper. That's all I care about."

"What about the stories that did come through?"

Waller gave a deprecating wave of the hand. "Small stuff. A little old lady cheated out of a couple of pounds, a man in trouble with his local council because he built a wall an inch too high. Not even worth bothering about. Katherine, when we started 'Satisfaction Guaranteed!,' it was a high flyer. Now it's staggering along like a punch-drunk fighter. You've got to make up your mind whether you're going to give the proper effort to continue with it. If not, well, maybe we can find better use for the space."

The suggestion that "Satisfaction Guaranteed" could be heading for the spike was a shock to Katherine. It was all so sudden. Although she had taken liberties with her working habits, she didn't think she had put the column at risk. Obviously she had. Maybe not while Franz was in the hospital, but ever since he'd come home. Damn it! Everything had gone wrong since Franz had come home.

When she emerged from Waller's office, it was

already lunchtime. She invited Derek and Heather out to eat, taking them by taxi to London's Chinese area, just north of Leicester Square. Over barbecued lamb, she said, "Gerry Waller's threatening to close us down."

"Does it have anything to do with the two stories that got away from us?" Derek wanted to know.

"Some. It also has to do with the quality of the stories that did not get away from us. They were nothing stories, certainly not the kind of help-the-public exposés the column was built on. It isn't your fault, though. It's all mine. I got myself too involved with my troubles at home. I let things slip. Now we have to come back with a real blockbuster. What"— she paused for a moment, because the question she was about to ask demonstrated exactly how far out of touch with her own department she really was— "do we have cooking?"

Heather's answer prompted a feeling of relief. "We think we've got something good. A man named Tony Burgess contacted us the other day. Trouble with a car."

Derek took up the story. "The car belongs to Burgess's wife, a woman named Angela. It needed some work done, and Burgess claims that the dealer—a company called Skrone Motors, where the car was purchased two years ago—charged for the work and never did it."

Katherine knew of Skrone Motors, a large dealership with branches on both sides of the Thames. Good, when you wanted to make a name for yourself—or, in her own case, remake that name—you didn't pick a fight with a mouse. You slapped your gauntlet across a lion's face. "Sounds promising. One of you set up a meeting with the Burgesses."

Derek made the appointment for that evening. Katherine called home and told Edna Griffiths that she would be late. Were the children and Franz all right? It occurred to her as she replaced the receiver that she had lumped Franz together with Henry and Joanne. Was that how she looked on him now — not as a husband, but as another child who needed caring for?

While Heather remained in the office, searching through the files for information on Skrone Motors, Katherine and Derek drove to the North London suburb of Finchley, where the Burgess family lived. Tony Burgess, a short, stocky man in a gray flannel suit, was waiting for them. He led them into the garage, where a yellow MG Midget was raised up on axle stands.

"The clutch of my wife's Midget was slipping," he told Katherine and Derek. "I took it to Skrone's for a new clutch. It worked fine for three months, the length of the warranty, then it started to slip again."

"How many miles had been done in that time?" Derek asked.

"About a thousand. I couldn't understand why a clutch would go again so quickly, so I looked at it myself."

"Are you a mechanic?" Katherine wanted to know.

"I'm an engineer. Technical director of a security company, burglar and fire alarms, et cetera." Leading the two journalists to a workbench, he picked up a circular object, about the size of a dinner plate, with a hole in the center and four springs. "This is what I found inside my wife's Midget. A very, very used clutch. There's no way one thousand miles could have worn the linings this badly. I think Skrone's just found some way to adjust the blasted clutch to make it stop slipping, and then they charged us for installing a brand new one. According to me, that's robbery."

Katherine watched Derek take a closer look at the clutch plate, and nod his head. "I assume you've been back to Skrone's. What did they say?"

"Denied it, of course. Claimed any parts their men had installed were new. You try telling me that's new."

"Have you tried any other means of solving this problem?"

"Like what?"

"Isn't there some overseeing body, some trade committee to regulate garages?"

Burgess laughed. "That's like having the thieves police the thieves. No, I came to your newspaper because I figured that was the only way I'd ever get any satisfaction. That's what you call yourselves, isn't it?"

Skrone Motors had been founded twenty-eight years earlier in Northwest London by a man named Edward Skrone. Operating on a lot the size of an average backyard, he had bought and sold used cars of any make or vintage. Now he owned flourishing dealerships in Colindale, Harrow, and Surbiton.

Skrone was a tall, portly man, with a mop of pure white hair. Although in his sixties, he still liked to get out on the selling floor. Which was why he was strolling around the Colindale showroom early in the morning when a white Triumph Stag wheeled onto the lot, and a blond woman wearing a fur-lined leather coat and brown boots climbed out. A burly, dark-haired man remained sitting in the passenger seat.

Like a true gentleman, Skrone swung the showroom door open before Katherine could reach for the handle. "Exceptional car, the Stag. How long have you had it, Miss . . . ?"

"Mrs. Mrs. Katherine Kassler. And I'm not here to buy a car or sell one. I'm looking for Mr. Edward Skrone."

"You have found him. How may I be of service?"

"I'm from the *Daily Eagle,* Mr. Skrone. Specifically, the 'Satisfaction Guaranteed!' column. May we speak in private?"

"Of course." Skrone led the way to his glass-walled office at the center of the showroom.

"I'm here on behalf of customers of yours, Mr. Skrone. Tony Burgess and his wife. They claim—"

Skrone's courtly manner disappeared. His voice turned hard. "I know exactly what they claim."

"And what do you have to say?"

"Only that I am amazed that a newspaper of the *Daily Eagle*'s stature would even give credence to such trash."

"Did your service department simply adjust a clutch while claiming to have replaced it?"

Skrone drew himself up to his full height. "Madam, I will not dignify that question with a reply. Please leave." He ushered Katherine from the office to the front door. As he held it open for her, he said, "You would do well to remember that Skrone Motors is a regular and generous advertiser in both the *Daily Eagle* and the *Sunday Eagle.* If you persist with this, I will have to reevaluate my company's advertising strategy."

"Don't threaten me, Mr. Skrone. Eagle Newspapers places more value on the truth than it does on advertising revenue. Besides, didn't your service department have some similar trouble three or four years ago?" Heather had done her work well. The young reporter had stayed at the newspaper until after twelve the previous night, digging up any dirt there was to know about Skrone Motors. She had come up with a scandal from 1974, when the service department had made a habit of charging for genuine replacement electrical parts while using reconditioned units.

"Whatever happened then is history, Mrs. Kassler. It was a mistake on the part of my *former* service

139

manager, who was dismissed the instant I learned what he had been doing. Any profits went into his pocket, not mine. Good day to you."

Skrone stepped outside the showroom, as if to be certain that his visitor left. Katherine signaled with her right hand. The passenger door of the Triumph Stag popped open and Sid Hall jumped out, camera aimed at the showroom door. The photograph he took was of Skrone escorting Katherine from the premises.

"Pompous ass," Katherine muttered as she started the Stag's engine. "Have that picture developed right away, Sid. I've got a meeting with the editor at noon."

Sid Hall had the print on Katherine's desk by eleven-thirty. Skrone had his arm raised, finger pointing. Katherine took the photograph to her meeting with Gerald Waller.

"Who is this gentleman telling you never to darken his doorstep again?" Waller asked.

"That's Edward Skrone, chairman of Skrone Motors. They got into trouble a few years back for misrepresentation, billing customers for new parts while using reconditioned parts. Seems like they're up to their old tricks again."

Waller lit a cigarette and listened closely to Katherine's story. When she finished, he remained silent for a few seconds before saying, "Tell me one thing—where's the satisfaction?"

"We haven't got it yet, but we will."

"Your next column is scheduled for Monday, which means you have to finish it by Friday, two days from now. How sure are you of having it wrapped up by then?" Stubbing out the cigarette in a heavy crystal ashtray, Waller added in a softer tone, "You need something really outstanding this time, Katherine."

"You don't have to remind me that the last couple

140

haven't been exactly earth-shattering. Besides, even if we don't get Skrone's to make good by press time, we can still print the story, can't we? Both sides."

"What both sides? From what you've told me, Edward Skrone hasn't admitted or denied a thing. He's refused to comment."

"Which means . . . ? Edward Skrone is just doing what gangsters always do in American films—refusing to answer on the grounds that he might drop himself right in it." Katherine gazed expectantly at the editor. "Gerry, we've got a report from two unbiased, independent mechanics. Both say that it's impossible for a clutch to wear that badly in just one thousand miles. Besides, Skrone Motors has a history of pulling fast ones."

"Skrone Motors also has a history of advertising."

"Mr. Waller!" All of Katherine's disapproval came out in the formal use of his surname. "I'd expect to hear that kind of reasoning from our advertising staff, but not from you."

"I know, I know. I should feel ashamed of myself. And I promise you I will do—the moment the price of a newspaper covers the cost of getting it out onto the street. All I'm asking you to do is proceed with caution."

Katherine left Waller's office recalling her father's advice when she had gone after John Saxon over what was happening at Cadmus Court. Roland Eagle's advice had been the same as Waller's. Use caution. And just look what had happened there! The story had turned out to be her big break. By the time she reached her own office, she was regarding Waller's advice as a lucky omen.

She traveled home that night in a rare bright mood. After tucking in the children with a good-night kiss, Katherine came downstairs to find Jimmy Phillips helping the housekeeper load plates into the dishwasher.

"Would you two like to go out tonight? See a film?"

"What about Mr. Kassler?" Phillips asked.

"I'll be able to take care of him."

After Phillips and Edna had left, Katherine entered the television room. Franz was sitting in his armchair, the plaid blanket covering his legs. "Where is Jimmy?" he asked.

"He and Edna went out to see a film."

"Which one?"

"They hadn't decided yet. What are you watching?"

"A documentary on Africa."

"I have a better idea. Why don't I just turn off the set?" Before Franz could argue, Katherine walked to the television, and flicked the switch. Then she settled herself in the chair next to Franz. "I'd like to talk to you."

"About what?"

"About a lot of things. Do you realize that we haven't talked properly—just the two of us alone—for a year? I don't know anything about you anymore, and you certainly know nothing about me. We're strangers who just happen to share a house."

"We have been married almost eight years—what do you mean we're strangers?"

"I married a man filled with fire. Whatever he did, whether it was something as noble and romantic as supporting a cause, or as simple as reading a book, he did it with intensity. With passion. That man loved me the same way. Not with just his body, but with all of his heart." She felt his hand move beneath her own, a frightened creature trying to escape from a trap. She held him tightly, refusing to let go.

"This stranger with whom you share the house . . . he is filled with ice, is that it?"

"How else would you describe him? He is so cold

he will not even sit at the dinner table with his children."

Franz blinked, and for an instant Katherine felt regret. That last blow had been several feet below his belt, but, damn it, she was going to draw him out from the wall he'd built to hide behind.

"Remember that first time we made love? At your place, just after you'd come to London. You drove me back to my father's home shortly before dawn—"

"Your father was waiting up."

Katherine saw the trace of a smile flicker across Franz's face. "And you ran away, didn't you? You drove off down the hill as fast as you could, while I had to face the music alone."

"Katherine, if there had been the slightest possibility of your father being harsh with you, do you seriously believe I would have left you alone?"

"Of course not. Tell me, do you still feel the same way for me, Franz? Do you still love me?"

"I will always love you, Katherine. But you know I am no good for you anymore. Not like this." He forced a gentle smile onto his face. "Did you request Jimmy and Edna to go out for the evening, so we could be alone?"

"Yes. I wanted to get to know you again. I wanted to smash down the wall you've been building up ever since the accident. I know you erected it to protect yourself, but you're hurting your children, and you're hurting me. I don't like sharing my home with a stranger, Franz. Please make the effort to become a part of this family again, because I can't exist with the way things are right now. Forget about protecting yourself. Nothing can possibly harm you more than you've been harmed already. Having Henry and Joanne reject you can't hurt as much as breaking your neck all over again. Just keep trying, because eventually they will accept you."

7

On Thursday, Katherine doggedly pursued Edward Skrone. She telephoned his main dealership at Colindale, only to be told that he had just left to visit his company's Harrow showroom. The first three times she tried the Harrow number, she was informed that Skrone had not arrived. The fourth time, the receptionist told her that she had just missed him. The chairman had been and gone in a matter of minutes.

"Where will I be able to reach him?" Katherine asked.

"He has a lunch appointment, after which he'll be driving to Surbiton." The girl sounded bored, and Katherine could imagine her sitting at a desk, filing her nails as she spoke. "He won't get there until midafternoon."

"Could you give me the telephone number?"

"I could," the receptionist answered, "but I don't think there's really any point. When I told Mr. Skrone you'd phoned, he expressly said that he did not wish to speak to you." With that, she hung up.

Katherine was in a quandary. She had until five o'clock the following afternoon. If the column was not ready to go to press by then, an advertisement, or some innocuous filler, would be dropped into the space "Satisfaction Guaranteed!" traditionally occupied. That would probably signify the kiss of death for the column, and Katherine would have no one to blame but herself.

She lay awake until late that night, turning the problem over in her mind, but it was not until the following morning, as she stood beneath the shower, that the solution came. So simple that she could not understand how she had failed to grasp it before. It was an either-or situation, and either way she could not lose.

At nine-thirty, she was once more at the main showroom of Skrone Motors. Edward Skrone saw the white Stag drive onto the lot. Having failed to respond to Katherine's calls, he had been expecting a personal visit.

"Good morning, Mrs. Kassler. And where are you hiding your photographer this time?"

"I no longer require his services. Despite your threats about cutting advertising, my column on Skrone Motors and the Burgesses will appear on Monday. I haven't written the final story yet because, quite frankly, its contents are up to you."

"Oh, and what is that supposed to mean?"

"I'm giving you a choice, Mr. Skrone. Either we have a happy ending, where Skrone Motors does the work properly on Angela Burgess's car—"

"For which you, of course, will take full credit."

"Or we print all the details as we know them, and the column ends with a loud challenge to you to put the matter right. That is"—Katherine gave Skrone a cool smile—"after our readers have been reminded that this isn't really the first time strange goings-on have occurred within your service department."

"Mrs. Kassler, publish whatever you wish. I could not care less. But before you print a word, just make certain your newspaper carries adequate libel insur-

145

ance."

"If I were you, Mr. Skrone, I wouldn't worry about the *Eagle*'s libel insurance: I'd be more concerned about other dissatisfied customers of this company popping out of the woodwork once my column is printed!"

Forty minutes later, Katherine was channeling all of her energy into a furious burst of typing. Standing behind her, watching, were Derek Simon and Heather Harvey.

"Well?" Katherine asked, as she typed the final word and tore the sheet of paper from the platen. "Does that put Mr. Edward pompous Skrone in his place or not?"

"Only if that place happens to be six feet under," Derek answered. "You've absolutely buried the poor man."

"Which is precisely what he deserves." Feeling pleased with herself, and more than a little relieved that she had come through with the story, Katherine sent the column on its way.

Early in the afternoon, Edward Skrone telephoned her. Heather took the call and, at Katherine's prompting, said she was at lunch.

Skrone made five more calls that afternoon. Each time, while Katherine listened in, Heather had an excuse ready. A sixth and final call came at five-fifteen, just as Katherine was preparing to go home. This time, Heather told Skrone that Katherine had already left for the weekend.

"Could you give me her home number?"

"I could," answered Heather, who had been carefully rehearsed by Katherine in case this particular scenario should occur. "But there really isn't any point in doing so. When I passed on your earlier messages, Mrs. Kassler specifically said she did not wish to speak to you."

* * *

After dinner that evening, Katherine told Franz about the Skrone story. "I'm looking forward to Monday," she said, "because that's when 'Satisfaction Guaranteed!' gets back on track."

"I prefer to anticipate tomorrow."

"Why?"

"Jimmy and I went shopping this afternoon." He turned to the attendant. "Jimmy, show Mrs. Kassler what we bought."

Jimmy went outside to the car. He returned carrying a radio-controlled scale model of a World War II Spitfire. Attaching the five-foot wings to the fuselage, he held up the graceful aircraft for Katherine to see.

"Are we going to the park tomorrow?" Katherine asked.

"Yes," Franz answered. "We are going to have a family outing at the park."

Later that evening, Phillips went out with Edna. Katherine remained in the television room with Franz. The purchase of the model aircraft, and the plans he had made for flying it with the children, loosened the reserve he had built up. He found it easy, for the first time, to talk about his feelings.

"In the hospital, while I was lying there," he whispered, "I used to wonder what good I would be to you. In my mind, I asked you a thousand times if you wanted to divorce me, but I could never find the courage to ask you out loud. In case . . . in case you said yes."

The confession shocked Katherine so much that she was unable to speak for a minute. Divorce? The very idea was abhorrent. She had been brought up in her mother's religion, as a Catholic. Roland Eagles had once told her how Catarina had made him promise that, should she die, their children would be raised as Catholics. It was some kind of premonition, Roland explained, a foreboding of death experienced before Catarina was even pregnant. He had made the promise, and after her death, he had honored it. Although he followed no particular religion himself, Roland had made certain that Katherine was denied nothing. What she did when she grew up and followed her own mind was her business, but Roland saw to it that she was baptized into the faith of her mother, and that she underwent Confirmation and First Communion when the time came.

It was not her Catholic upbringing alone that made Katherine feel so stunned at the thought of divorce. Her own definition of right and wrong made it detestable. The marriage vows she had exchanged with Franz eight years before were so much more than mere clichés. In sickness and in health, to Katherine's way of thinking, meant just that.

"Did you really think I'd desert you just because you aren't able to do some of the things you could do before the accident?" she asked him.

"I did not say desert. I used the word *divorce.*"

"Sometimes the two words can be interchangeable."

Franz looked away, unable to hold Katherine's candid gaze. Somehow, she made him feel ashamed of himself for having even considered that she would be interested in divorcing him. In deserting him.

"Hey . . ." Katherine touched Franz's arm, forcing him to turn back to her. "Do you need a pilot's license to operate that model plane?"

A smile lit Franz's face as he remembered the happiness he had planned for this weekend.

Franz's plans were almost thwarted by the weather. It rained all day Saturday, and all Sunday morning. It was not until Sunday afternoon that the clouds finally broke. Warmed by a hearty lunch of country vegetable soup and shepherd's pie, the family traveled in the Jaguar to a nearby park. Jimmy Phillips started the engine of the model Spitfire. When it was buzzing fiercely, he hand-launched it into the light breeze.

Franz's limited hand movements prevented him from operating the controls. Phillips performed the job, turning the Spitfire in graceful circles. When the fuel supply ran out, he glided the aircraft to a smooth landing on the tarmac of the parking lot where they had assembled.

"Would you like to fly it?" Phillips asked Henry. The boy nodded. Once the Spitfire was airborne again, Phillips squatted beside Henry. Guided by the attendant's hands, Henry operated the controls.

"Left," Phillips urged, and the Spitfire passed over their heads at a hundred feet.

"Climb, make it climb now." The Spitfire pointed its nose at the cold gray sky, and grew smaller in their vision. "Level. Level it out." Phillips made Henry's hands perform the correct motions on the controls. The Spitfire cruised steadily for a few seconds, then it began to descend, the propeller still.

While Phillips refueled the aircraft, Katherine spoke to the children. "Are you enjoying yourselves?"

"Did you see how I made it fly?" Henry's question was followed immediately by a demand from Joanne that she also fly the plane.

"I asked if you were enjoying yourselves." When the children nodded, Katherine added, "Don't you think you should thank your father? He bought the plane for you."

The children's excitement was replaced by perplexity. Katherine noticed how Henry, especially, kept looking from the Spitfire to Franz's face. When Franz smiled, Henry gave the faintest uncertain smile in return. A few more flights, Katherine

149

thought, and the gap between father and children would disappear completely.

"Chocks away!" Phillips called out as he tightened the compression screw on the small engine. The noise increased to buzz-saw pitch, and Phillips launched the Spitfire once more.

"How about making it loop the loop?" Katherine called out.

Squatting once more beside Henry, Phillips pushed the boy's hands in the right direction. High above them, the Spitfire looped over onto its back, fell into a steep dive, and leveled out. "Again!" Henry cried excitedly, and pushed at the controls before Phillips had a chance to guide him.

The Spitfire climbed once more. Instead of looping over onto its back and beginning the dive, it sideslipped. Phillips grabbed at the controls, but it was already too late. The plane continued to slip for a few seconds, its propeller biting the air in vain. One wing dipped, the other lifted. The nose dropped down. While Phillips frantically worked the controls, the model Spitfire plunged toward the group of people on the ground.

Katherine's scream rose above the buzzing of the engine. "Jimmy, do something! For God's sake, the bloody thing's coming straight for us!"

At the very last moment, when the plane was only forty yards above the ground, Phillips managed to regain some control. The nose lifted. The steep dive leveled out. The Spitfire flashed over their heads toward the park perimeter, and the houses and trees beyond it. Phillips's further frantic manipulation of the controls achieved nothing. Engine still racing, the Spitfire smashed into the trees.

Henry was off like a flash of lightning, running toward the park entrance, only fifty yards away, and yelling, "I'll get it! I'll get it!" Before anyone could gather their wits, he was halfway to the entrance.

"Henry!" Katherine shouted. "Come back here!"

As she started to run after him, Jimmy Phillips plunged past her. "Stop him, for God's sake!" Katherine called out. "Stop him before he reaches the road!"

Phillips did not waste breath replying. Arms pumping like pistons, he sprinted after the young boy. Caring only for the model aircraft, and totally oblivious to the consternation behind him, Henry left the park and ran across the road toward the trees where the Spitfire had crashed. Seconds later, Phillips came through the gate like an express train. Above the beating of his own heart, he could hear another sound, the growling of a heavy engine. Henry was halfway across the road, stopping, turning, freezing into immobility like a rabbit hypnotized by a car's headlights. Bearing down on him was a furniture truck, wheels skidding on the greasy road surface as the driver stamped on his brakes.

Another noise drilled its way through Phillips's head: Katherine's shriek of horror when she reached the park gate and saw what was happening. The shriek acted on Phillips like a whip to a horse. Without thinking of his own safety, he charged across the road. A horn blasted. The truck's engine roared in his ears. He flung himself at the statue that was Henry. The truck rumbled past, its driver turning the air blue with profanity as he checked in his mirror to ensure he had hit no one.

Phillips sat in the gutter, looking down at the boy imprisoned in his arms. Katherine raced across the road and knelt beside them. "Thank you, thank you" was all she could say, and it would never be enough to express the gratitude she felt toward Jimmy Phillips. She had no doubt that his bravery had saved her son from being crushed to death beneath the truck. She sat on the curb and took Henry in her arms. He began to cry, complaining

151

that his left arm hurt. When Katherine touched it, he yelled in pain. Careful not to disturb his injured arm, she held him to her. She did not even notice the people who came out of nearby houses to learn what all the fuss was about.

"I'll see to Mr. Kassler and Joanne," Phillips said.

Katherine nodded. In the excitement, she had forgotten her husband and daughter. Concerned people from the houses asked if they could be of help. Still shocked, Katherine could do nothing but shake her head and hug her son. Heavy rain began to fall. By the time someone thought to bring an umbrella from one of the houses, mother and son were soaked right through.

As Phillips returned in the Jaguar, with Franz beside him and Joanne in the back, an ambulance arrived. "You go with Henry to the hospital, Mrs. Kassler. I'll take Mr. Kassler and Joanne home."

A man in a black uniform lifted Henry into the ambulance. Before Katherine followed, she locked eyes with Franz. His face was white and waxen. His shoulders and head were trembling, and though he tried to speak, no words came out.

"I'll telephone from the hospital when there's news," Katherine promised. She climbed into the ambulance and sat down next to Henry, holding his right hand as the vehicle moved off.

Katherine telephoned home from the hospital forty-five minutes later to tell Phillips that Henry had broken his left arm. When she asked how Franz was, the attendant answered that he had not spoken a word since returning from the park; he was just sitting in the television room, staring at the wall.

A taxi brought Henry and Katherine home two hours later. Henry's left arm was in a cast. While Edna Griffiths made a fuss over Henry, Katherine went into the television room. Franz was exactly as Phillips had described him over the telephone: pale-faced, staring numbly at the wall.

"Franz . . ." Katherine took the seat next to him. "Henry's all right; a broken arm, that was all. In a few weeks the cast will be off . . ."

Slowly Franz turned his head toward her. "I tried, Katherine. I tried to be friends with my children again, and you saw what happened. It almost cost Henry his life. If it had not been for Jimmy, Henry would have been killed."

"It wasn't your fault, Franz. You didn't tell Henry to run after the plane."

"But if I had not bought the plane in the first place—"

"Stop it, Franz! That's a ridiculous thing to say." She grabbed his arm, and he turned away, staring once more at the wall, alone in the world of guilt he had created for himself.

Katherine watched him for fully a minute before leaving the room. Whatever good Franz had done by the purchase of the model aircraft had been more than shattered by Henry's wild enthusiasm. Something deep within Franz had been smashed at the same time. Trapped within his crippled body, his brain no longer functioned clearly. His reasoning was as broken as his spine. He could not cope with setbacks. All he could do was sit and stare and try to block out the world.

Had she been too quick to reject his offer of divorce? Too quick, too considerate, and too damned righteous? In that moment, as she left the room, the truth hit her. Her love for Franz was based on memory and pity. And they were a lousy basis for any kind of relationship.

"Mrs. Kassler . . ." Edna stood in front of Katherine, blocking her progress along the hall. "I really do think you should get out of those wet clothes before you catch your death."

For the first time, Katherine took notice of her

own condition. Her hair was plastered to her head, and her clothes were sticking to her. The insides of her thighs were starting to chafe where wet denim had rubbed. "I'll have a hot shower and change into some dry clothes." She looked past the housekeeper. "Where is Henry?"

"He's in the breakfast room. With Jimmy. Joanne's there as well, making a big fuss of her brother."

"Would you stay with the children, please? Give them something to eat or drink, whatever they want. I'd rather Jimmy kept Mr. Kassler company at the moment."

"Is there something wrong?"

"No. I just don't want Mr. Kassler to be left on his own." She ran up the stairs, thinking that there was no need for the housekeeper to know that Katherine was concerned about her husband's mental equilibrium.

She remained under the steaming shower until the water began to run cool. Feeling a thousand percent better, she wrapped herself in a terry-cloth robe and lifted the receiver of the bedside telephone. The number she dialed was that of her father. Arthur Parsons answered, telling Katherine that he had just returned from driving Roland into town.

"He was having dinner with Miss Roberts. After that, he said he might visit Kendall's Club in Mount Street."

"Thank you, Mr. Parsons." She glanced at the clock next to the telephone. It was coming up to seven. She dialed a Mayfair number. "Sally, it's Katherine. Is my father there?"

"Yes, he is. Everything all right?"

Katherine avoided answering the question by asking Sally to call Roland to the telephone. Moments later, Katherine heard her father's voice. "Kathy, what is it?"

154

"Henry had an accident, but thank the Lord it's a lot less bad than it might have been." Concisely, she told the story of the boy running into the street, and Jimmy Phillips saving him, in all probability, from being killed. "It isn't Henry I need to talk to you about."

"Is it Franz?"

"Yes."

It never occurred to Roland to ask Katherine whether it could wait until the following morning. If his daughter needed him, he was always available. "Come over here. I'm sure Sally cooked enough to feed an extra mouth."

"I'm really not hungry. I'll drop by at nine o'clock."

"All right, Kathy, we'll be waiting for you."

Wearing a fur-lined leather coat over jeans and a cashmere sweater, Katherine left the house at eight-thirty. The night air was freezing, but she drove with the Triumph's roof folded back. She needed to blow away the cobwebs and think clearly, because she had reached a point of no return in her life with Franz.

"You look like you could do with a hot cup of something" was Sally's greeting as she opened the door of her apartment. She took Katherine's coat and led her through to the living room. It was furnished in a modern style, leather-covered couches and chairs, side tables made of wood and glass. Roland stood by the window overlooking Curzon Street, hands clasped behind his back. When Katherine entered, he swung around.

"Did you really drive all the way here with the top down?" When Katherine nodded, Roland added, "Now I know you're crazy, but I love you all the same." He walked across the room to hug her. "What's all this about Franz?"

Sally pushed him away. "Let the poor girl thaw out first, for God's sake. Sit down, Katherine. Don't

answer any questions until you're good and ready."
Sally guided Katherine into one of the chairs, then
went off to the kitchen, returning a minute later
with a steaming cup of chocolate. Katherine accepted it gratefully, noticing that her father and
Sally were drinking the same. Was that a sign of
getting older, a cup of hot chocolate instead of an
after-dinner liqueur?

"Take your time, Kathy," Roland said. "Just tell us
at your own pace what's gone wrong."

Katherine found herself pouring out months of
bottled-up anguish. Her own inability to handle the
situation since Franz's return, the tension in the
house, Franz's suggestion of divorce, and her immediate rejection of it. And, finally, that afternoon at
the park. "I think Franz was troubled before . . . I
know he was; he couldn't cope mentally with being
handicapped. He was always talking about people
who knew him before, how they made comparisons.
Then he had this moment of closeness with the
children, only to see it swing around so suddenly.
The reverse has absolutely destroyed him, and in
some bizarre way he thinks he's to blame because he
bought the damned plane in the first place. Jimmy
Phillips has been sitting with Franz for the past
couple of hours, and Franz hasn't spoken a word to
him. He just sits there, staring at nothing."

"Are you having second thoughts about rejecting
the idea of divorce?" Sally asked.

"How could I leave him?" Katherine wanted to
know. "He can't fend for himself. It's like having a
third child in the house, even more dependent than
the other two."

"Whatever arrangements were made, he would
have the best care available," Roland assured her.
"Don't tie yourself up with blame. You've done
everything in your power to help, but you also have
to think about yourself, Joanne, and Henry."

Roland took a deep breath and plunged on. "Kathy, darling, if you did not harbor any reservations about divorce, you wouldn't be human. You'd have a heart of stone, and I would not want to see that particular personality trait in any daughter of mine."

Sally waited a few seconds before saying, "The fact that you've actually discussed divorce as an option means you've just overcome an enormous psychological hurdle, Katherine. Now that you admit the possibility of divorce exists, you can take however long you need to reach the right decision about it."

Despite feeling emotionally drawn after the rigors of the day, Katherine laughed. "Spoken like a true women's page editor. Sally, you would have made a wonderful advice-to-the-lovelorn columnist."

Katherine left for home soon after. It had only been a short talk, yet her mind was much clearer now. Her father's support and Sally's no-nonsense advice had opened possibilities. They had referred to divorce as an option, a move she could make whenever she deemed it necessary. Because she now understood that such an option was available, she could take her time in reaching a decision. And making sure it was the right decision!

The house was quiet when she returned. The light in Franz's downstairs bedroom was out. The top-floor room where Phillips lived was also in darkness. The dramatic excitement of the day had exhausted everyone, including herself. She fell asleep within five minutes of resting her head on the pillow.

When she awakened the following morning, her throat was raw, her limbs ached, and her head felt filled with cement. She forced herself out of bed, cursing her stupidity with every painful moment. Standing around for hours in rain-soaked clothes, and then driving to Sally's home on a winter's night with the roof down — she deserved every germ she'd encouraged.

Downstairs, she avoided everyone as best she could, taking a cup of tea to one corner of the breakfast room. Edna, the children, and Phillips wisely kept their distance. When she asked, in a croaking voice, about Franz, Phillips answered that he had requested breakfast in his room; appetite, if not sociability, had returned.

She left the house at nine o'clock, driving as usual to Chalk Farm Station. As she entered the station, she remembered that she had not even looked at the copy of the *Daily Eagle* that was delivered to the house. She bought one from the newsstand, flicking through it as the elevator dropped her from street level to the bowels of the station.

By the time the train came, her mood was much brighter. The column about Skrone Motors was a cracker, and "Satisfaction Guaranteed!" was right back on form.

When she entered the elevator in the Eagle building, Archie Waters greeted her with a salute. "Enjoyed your column, Miss Eagles. Another villain gets his comeuppance at your hands."

She crossed the editorial floor, listening to the babble of voices, the ringing of telephones, the erratic clattering of typewriters. After the topsy-turvy weekend she had just experienced, Katherine welcomed the familiar commotion. Reaching her office, she found Heather Harvey and Derek Simon waiting.

"Telephone's been ringing ever since we got in," Derek said. "People who want to speak to you with possible leads."

"Keep taking the calls, will you? The only person I'll speak to is Gerry Waller, when he gets in, because I want to hear from him just how good we look today." Hanging a "Do Not Disturb" sign on the door handle, Katherine shut herself away from the rest of the newspaper.

She spent the morning doing paperwork. Budget allocations were being made soon, and she wanted her little department to get its fair share. She heard the telephone ring, and each time one of her assistants answered. No one bothered her until just after midday, when Heather knocked on the office door.

"Mr. Waller's on the telephone."

"Thank you." Katherine lifted the receiver, ready to enjoy her moment of triumph, certain it would go a long way toward removing some of the sting from the weekend's events. "Good morning, Gerry. Have you seen the column yet?"

"I most certainly have. And now I'd like to see you."

"As long as you don't mind me coughing and sneezing."

"I'll take you any way you wish to come, Katherine. Just make it right now, please."

She replaced the receiver, stood up, and straightened her skirt. "Back in a few minutes," she told Heather and Derek. As she made the lengthy journey to the editor's office, she could not help wondering why his voice had sounded so strained.

To Katherine's surprise, the door to Waller's office was closed. The editor's secretary told her to go right in. Katherine knocked, opened the door, and entered. Waller was not alone. He had two visitors: a stocky fair-haired man with a ginger handlebar moustache, whom Katherine did not know, and a tall man with a head full of snowy white hair, whom she most certainly did know. Edward Skrone.

"Katherine . . ." Waller rose from behind his desk. "Mr. Skrone you know. The other gentleman is Horace—"

"Grimley," said the fair-haired man, standing up. "I am Horace Grimley, Mr. Skrone's solicitor."

"Solicitor?"

"Precisely, madam. Mr. Skrone feels he had been grossly libeled by yourself and by Eagle Newspapers Limited."

"What do you have to say, Katherine?" Waller asked.

"In what manner does Mr. Skrone feel he has been libeled?"

"In the entire context of the scurrilous article which appears in today's edition of the *Daily Eagle*. It is a pack of lies from the first line to the last."

"In your opinion," Katherine added.

At last, the chairman of Skrone Motors spoke. "On what did you base your allegations against my firm, Mrs. Kassler?"

"You know what I based them on. Tony Burgess. On what he showed me—the work your company did, or didn't do, to his car."

"While he was telling and showing you all this, did he happen to mention his previous connection to Skrone Motors?"

Anxiety worried Katherine's stomach as she said, "What previous connection?"

Grimley took over. "Mr. Burgess is the technical director of a security company that, eighteen months ago, did some work for Skrone Motors. A complete burglar alarm system. Which, unfortunately, failed the very first time it was tested. Thieves broke in one weekend and made away with some twenty thousand pounds that was in the safe. Skrone Motors had an independent agency check the alarm system. It had failed because it was installed improperly."

As the solicitor paused, Skrone picked up the baton. "We demanded that Mr. Burgess's company remove the faulty system, repay us the money we had invested in it, and offer some compensation for our losses. Not all of it, you understand, was covered by insurance. This they did, but only after legal maneuvers." Skrone inclined his head toward Grimley, who gave a smug smile. "Mr. Burgess, whose fault the failure was, came out of the whole affair with rather a lot of egg on his face. He threatened to get his own back, and he used you to do so."

"How?" Katherine asked, although she could guess the answer.

"He and his wife bought the MG Midget from Skrone Motors, perhaps a year before his company installed the alarm system. A few months ago, the Midget needed a clutch. Claiming that hard feelings no longer existed, Mr. Burgess brought the car to us, and we carried out the necessary work. I can assure you, Mrs. Kassler, that my company put in a new clutch. I would bet every penny I own that Mr. Burgess then replaced that brand-new clutch with some worn-out clutch he had found in a breaker's yard, and used your 'Satisfaction Guaranteed!' column, and your own gullibility, Mrs. Kassler, to make Skrone Motors look bad."

"The *Daily Eagle* has not been a newspaper in this unfortunate affair," Grimley added. "It has simply been the means of one man's twisted vengeance against another. I am afraid that we cannot allow that situation to pass uncorrected."

Stunned by the entire revelation, Katherine demanded of Skrone, "Then why, in God's name, did you say nothing about this to me at the time?"

"Mrs. Kassler, you walked into my showroom with your mind already made up. You had swallowed Mr. Burgess's story, hook, line, and sinker, and you were looking for a fight. When you asked for my comments, your manner was so ungracious and hostile that I felt you had already tried and convicted me. So, damn you, I thought, I'd let you carry on."

"Carry on until the story came out in print, where we all look terrible?"

"I tried to stop you once more. On Friday. I called your office a number of times. At first, I was given the royal runaround. Finally, when I asked for your home number, after being told that you had left for the weekend, I was informed in a very snooty manner that there was no point in ringing you at home because you wouldn't speak to me anyway. So, I thought: you publish, and you be damned."

Katherine turned to Waller. "What can we do about Burgess?"

"Burgess doesn't matter. Our concern is to clear this up."

"We will take action against Mr. Burgess, you can be assured of that," Grimley promised. "However, we would like to come to some amicable arrangement with Eagle Newspapers. I have already discussed this with Mr. Skrone, and we agree that ample compensation would be a correction—written by your staff, and approved by us—of the same size as the original article. Your newspaper did, after all, carry the story in good faith. The only malice was contained in Mrs. Kassler's attitude."

The two men left. Katherine remained standing in front of Waller's desk, feeling like some naughty child on a trip to the headmaster's study. Waller looked at her through the smoke of a freshly lit cigarette. "If this is the last we hear of this particular incident," he said slowly, "then I think we can count ourselves very lucky. A correction is a cheap price to pay for what could have been a very nasty situation. Do you agree?"

"Yes." Katherine felt she had to say more. "Gerry, if you choose to dismiss me, I'm certain that my father wouldn't interfere. He hired you to run the newspaper, as I heard you remind him once before."

Waller smiled at that. "I'm not going to dismiss you. But I can assure you that today's 'Satisfaction Guaranteed!' will be the very last."

"What about my two assistants, Derek Simon and Heather Harvey? This had nothing to do with them."

"They'll be offered other positions."

"And me? Do I go back to working with Erica Bentley?"

Waller shook his head. "Erica already has a full staff. I had planned to transfer you to news."

Being responsible to Lawrie Stimkin, the *Eagle*'s news editor, was a blow to Katherine. Stimkin, a middle-aged bachelor, was known by the *Eagle*'s female staff members as Fleet Street's leading male chauvinist pig. "If I elect not to take the job?"

"Then you may resign. Please let me know by five o'clock."

Katherine walked back to her office in a daze. She took Derek and Heather out to lunch, and told them what had happened. When she returned, she found a message from Sally Roberts, asking her to come up to the executive floor.

"What do you intend doing?" Sally asked her.

"I'm staying, of course."

"As a news reporter?"

"Sally, from that day in 1965 when my father launched the *Eagle,* it was my burning ambition to work on it. Nothing is going to drive me away from this place, not even the loss of my little empire."

"You might have to take some pretty hard ribbing."

"I can live with it. Has anyone spoken to my father?"

"I did, after Gerry Waller spoke to you. Your father agreed with the action Gerry took. He was grateful to get out of this without an expensive libel action. He also told me that he was hoping you'd do exactly as you're planning to do—stick it out as a news reporter, and not resign. Just don't let Lawrie Stimkin wear you down. He's driven more than one woman reporter out of the building."

"Like I said, Sally, nothing is going to chase me

out of here. When I do eventually leave the *Eagle,* it will be because it's time to move on. Not because someone has driven me to it."

8

Katherine did not take up her new position immediately. Owed vacation time, she decided to exchange the gloom of an English winter for the sunshine of Tenerife, in the Canary Islands. She booked airline flights and week-long hotel reservations for the entire household, confident that the change of scenery would benefit everyone. A week in the sun would help Henry's arm to heal quicker. It would certainly pick up her own spirits, and it might even lift the veil of depression that had settled over Franz. When she broke the news to Franz, however, he told her that he was not interested in leaving London for a week.

"You go," he said. "Take the children with you and enjoy yourselves. I am quite content to stay here."

"And do what?" Stare into space? she wondered; watch whatever's on the television?

"I have to go to the hospital for therapy."

Katherine felt he was using that as an excuse. He did not want to go away with her and the children because he believed his broken body imposed on them. Like any loving husband and father, he wanted only what was best for his family; perversely, he felt that his absence from their lives fell into that category. It seemed that nothing could shake the despondency that imprisoned him. Even the counseling he received at the hospital had little effect, and when Katherine had suggested he seek other help, he had refused to listen to her.

She changed the reservations, and flew to Tenerife with Henry and Joanne. While the children played on the beach and cavorted in the water, with Henry's cast protected by a plastic bag, Katherine sat back and tried to come to terms with what had happened to her life.

Not long ago, she'd been very proud of having a marriage and a career that were both successful. Pride had certainly gone before a fall. Now, the marriage was wallowing like a rudderless ship, and the career had been switched from the main line to a local track. She understood that there was nothing to be done about the marriage, not until Franz found a way out of his depression, but there was plenty she could do about the career. All she had to do was prove that she was the best news reporter on the *Eagle,* and while she was doing that, she'd keep eyes and ears open for other opportunities.

For the first few days in Tenerife, the children never mentioned their father. On the day before they were due to fly home, Henry asked, "Will Daddy ever be able to walk again?"

"I don't know, darling."

"I broke my arm, and the doctor said it would be as good as new. Why can't Daddy's neck be as good as new?"

Katherine lifted Henry up. "Necks are a lot more complicated than arms."

"Will he always be so angry?"

"He isn't angry," Katherine answered. "He's sad." But she understood where Henry saw anger in his father's frustration at being so dependent on others.

Both children bought gifts for their father. He accepted them graciously and asked Henry and Joanne if they'd had a nice time in Tenerife. Then the curtain fell again, and Franz withdrew behind it. . . .

Wearing a golden tan, and with her hair bleached even lighter by the Tenerife sun, Katherine turned up for her first day on the *Eagle*'s news desk. Lawrie Stimkin was waiting for her. He summoned her into his glass-fronted office—much larger than the one Katherine had used until her demotion—and gave her the same welcoming speech he issued to everyone.

"Welcome to the best bloody news department on all of Fleet Street," Stimkin growled in a heavy Scottish brogue. Fifty years old, he had left his native Glasgow twenty-eight years earlier to find newspaper fame in London. He had brought with him all the negative stereotypical characteristics of a Scot. He was notoriously cheap with a penny, always finding an excuse to disappear when his turn came to buy a round of drinks. He was dour in looks—possessing a long, lugubrious face with sunken brown eyes—and he was dour in nature, never joining in the laughter that greeted some ribald joke.

"I want nothing fancy, nothing funny. Remember, we're reporters here, not fiction writers. Double- and triple-check all facts and names. And if I see one story from you that uses *prior to* instead of *before,* or *conflagration* instead of *fire,* you'll be out on Fleet Street before you can sing 'God Save the Queen.' Do I make myself clear, Kathy?"

She let the "Kathy" pass. This time. "I'm familiar with Eagle style. I'm not exactly a newcomer to the company."

Stimkin glared at her, so neat and professional-looking. His own clothes—wrinkled sportcoat and trousers—looked positively shabby by comparison. "There's one thing I need to know." The deeply set eyes took on a gleam of humor. "Are you one of those women who burst into tears if a single word of their copy's changed? Or are you the daddy's-little-darling type, who'll go running to her father because she thinks her words are too precious to be edited?"

Katherine stared right back, refusing to yield in this battle of wills. She guessed that Stimkin viewed her as a natural enemy, because she came from a background totally different from his own. His father had been a dockworker and union official on Clydeside; his two brothers, a teacher and an engineer, were members of the Communist Party. Stimkin's own political views were not so vehement, but Katherine guessed he detested nepotism. This was a part of the ribbing that Sally Roberts had told her to expect. You didn't give up a shiny new Mercedes for a secondhand Volkswagen without other Volkswagen owners making comments.

"Well, Kathy? Will you go running to your father?"

Katherine understood that this was her moment of truth. She could either cave in now, or she could make the stand she had vowed to make. "My name is Katherine. If you call me Kathy one more time, I am going to plant this"—she tapped the pointed toe of her dark brown boot on the parquet floor—"where it will transform you from a bass-baritone into a coloratura soprano."

All humor disappeared instantly from Stimkin's eyes. "See?" Katherine said. "I've just answered your question. I don't need to run to my father, because I'm perfectly capable of fighting my own battles. And for your further information, I do not burst into tears when copy of mine is edited—professionally!"

Katherine soon learned that the pace of the news desk was ten times faster than that of anything on which she had worked before. Lawrie Stimkin ran his reporters ragged. In her first day alone, Katherine's assignments varied from interviewing a minor Hollywood celebrity who was staying at the Connaught, to covering a student demonstration at a college, topped off by reporting on a traffic accident. When she went home that evening, she was ready to drop. But the very next morning, when she came down for breakfast, her first act was to pick up the delivered copy of the *Eagle*. The only story of hers that was carried concerned the student demonstration. Her photograph, which had always accompanied her columns, was missing, and the subject matter was not what she would have chosen. But a byline was a byline, all the same.

Stimkin kept her so busy that it wasn't until her second week on the news desk that she found time to meet Erica Bentley for lunch. As they sat down in the restaurant, Erica said, "This is the first lunch we've had since Franz came home. Where have you been hiding?"

"Hiding? Nowhere. I've just been forsaking old friends. I'm sorry, and now can we change the subject?"

"All right. How do you like your new job?"

"I don't get to stand around and gather dust, that's for sure. This morning, I had to interview some duchess whose husband had just run off with the maid. She bit my head off, demanded to know why newspapers couldn't concentrate on the misfortunes of the poor . . . why we had to bother *decent* people. And this afternoon, I'm supposed to cover the opening of some strip club in Soho, where the strippers are men."

"Be sure to let me see the pictures."

Katherine grimaced. "To tell you the truth, Erica, I wish I was back working for you. Writing about women's subjects was more fun than covering traffic accidents. Only Gerry said your department was full."

"That's not exactly true. Gerry did talk to me about you, but I didn't think it would do your career any good to come back to the women's pages."

"Why on earth not?"

"You can't go back in life, Katherine. If you can get

past the fact that Lawrie Stimkin gets out of the wrong side of bed every morning, you'll find that working for him will give you another perspective on this business. Believe me when I say it will help you grow professionally."

"I've picked up a few pointers from him already. But I certainly wouldn't let him know that."

"Has he given you any trouble?"

"He tried to. I told him if he didn't quit, I'd kick him where it would make him a soprano."

Erica roared with laughter. "Good for you. You're probably the first person who ever stood up to him."

After lunch, as they walked back to the Eagle building, Erica touched Katherine's arm. "You haven't been out to the farm for more than a year. Is it because of the accident?"

"Yes. I used to love horses, Erica. The first piece of mail that was ever addressed to me was a copy of *Horse and Hound*. But now, all horses make me think of is that hideous day."

Erica nodded understandingly. "Just remember, when things get too hectic here, or too depressing at home, there's always a place where peace and sanity prevail."

"Thanks, Erica. I will remember that. One weekend, when it gets a bit warmer, I'll bring Henry and Joanne out for the day."

After Katherine had been on news for two weeks, Lawrie Stimkin called her into his office. He was wearing the same rumpled sportcoat and creased trousers he always seemed to wear. Wondering whether he had any other clothes, Katherine smiled.

"Something funny?" Stimkin asked.

"Just remembering an amusing thing that happened on the way to work," Katherine lied.

Stimkin snorted. "Leave amusing anecdotes outside

the building. Here, we're concerned only with what's news. Except for some departments, of course, which waste valuable space with advice to the lovesick, fashion tips, recipes, and the like."

"You think a newspaper should be nothing but hard news?"

"Of course I do. That's why it's called a *news*paper."

Katherine had never known Stimkin so talkative. She decided to capitalize on it. "Where do I fit in? On a *news*paper, or on one of the other pages?"

"For the fortnight you've been working for me, you belong on a newspaper." While Katherine digested the grudging compliment, the news editor added, "This afternoon, you can gorge yourself on cheap English plonk and curling cucumber sandwiches at the opening of some new hotel out by Heathrow Airport. The Chiltern Towers, it's called."

"You don't sound too keen on it."

"I'm not. What's the point of another hotel? Instead of luxury accommodation, we need basic shelter for our homeless. Just be there, in case something out of the ordinary happens."

Katherine took a taxi to the Chiltern Towers, arriving there at three-thirty. Inside the hotel, burgundy-uniformed doormen guided journalists to the convention center, which was one of the features of the hotel. A public-relations person handed out press kits. Waiters offered cold champagne and hot hors d'oeuvres. Stimkin was wrong, Katherine thought with malicious pleasure—no cheap wine or curling cucumber sandwiches. The general manager of the hotel made a speech welcoming the "distinguished ladies and gentlemen" of the press. A ten-minute film about the new hotel was shown. Finally, it was time for the V.I.P. of the day—a lesser-known member of the House of Lords—to officially open Chiltern Towers.

"Make a bet with you," Katherine turned and whispered to the reporter from the *Daily Mail,* "that I junk my press kit before you throw away yours."

The lesser-known member's head snapped up as the *Mail* reporter's ribald laugh interrupted his hotel-opening speech.

As the opening ceremony finished, the supply of champagne and food dried up. With nothing left to eat or drink, the reporters lost what little interest they had in the new hotel and began to drift away. Not caring who saw, Katherine dropped her press kit into the closest garbage can. As the lid slammed shut, a hand dropped gently onto her shoulder, and a voice said, "A lot of people worked very hard to produce that press kit, you know."

Without turning around, Katherine responded, "Found a new job as a hotel clerk, Mr. Saxon?"

"If you had bothered to look inside the press kit," John Saxon said, "you would have learned that Chiltern Towers is owned by Saxon Holdings."

Katherine turned to face him. "But I didn't bother."

"Why did you even come?"

"In case someone dropped dead." Saxon's eyebrows lifted in puzzlement. "That's the only reason journalists attend these boring little happenings, Mr. Saxon, on the off chance that something unusual might happen. Sorry if that's an affront to your vanity, but it's the truth."

Saxon frowned for a moment, as though offended. "I'm still surprised to see you here. Surely a hotel opening — even one where something unusual might happen — is of little interest to your windmill-tilting brand of journalism."

"I don't tilt at windmills anymore, Mr. Saxon." She said his name with the utmost formality, as if to keep distance between them. "I work on the *Eagle*'s news desk now."

Saxon followed Katherine as she walked toward the

front lobby of the Chiltern Towers. A man in the burgundy uniform of the hotel stepped forward to hand the property developer a dark blue cashmere coat. Saxon carried it over his arm. "Writing news must be vastly different from what you were doing," Saxon said. "How difficult is such a switch?"

"A competent journalist can write any kind of story, Mr. Saxon." She passed through a revolving door into the cold outside air. Saxon came through immediately after her.

"Taxi, miss?" asked a doorman in a cape and high hat.

"Yes, please."

The doorman waved an arm. Instead of a taxi, a maroon Rolls Royce Silver Shadow glided silently to a halt in front of the hotel entrance. "My car seems to have arrived before your taxi," Saxon said. "May I give you a ride somewhere?"

"I have to get to Chalk Farm," Katherine answered, confident that destination was far enough out of the way to negate Saxon's offer. "I leave my car at the station every morning."

"William, we're taking Mrs. Kassler to Chalk Farm first," Saxon said to the chauffeur. He stepped back to allow Katherine to enter ahead of him. She sat in the corner, the armrest down to form a barrier between herself and Saxon. He noticed it, and gave the mischievous grin she remembered so well from their one lunch date. "I swear that my only intention in offering you a lift was to save you from the perils of riding in a London taxi."

"I didn't realize that riding in a taxi involved any perils, Mr. Saxon."

"Of course it does. The driver could be a homicidal maniac. He might be high on drugs or drink. He could even be a procurer for some white-slave market in Tangier."

Katherine stifled a laugh.

173

"Would you mind doing me one small favor?" Saxon asked.

"What?"

"My parents saw fit to christen me John, because they wanted people to call me by that name. In their memory, would you?"

"He wasn't one of our more illustrious monarchs, was he?"

"I would have preferred Richard, but I had to be named after some long-gone family member. Perhaps I'll put a bit of a shine back on the name."

Katherine looked out of the window, surprised to see they were well clear of the hotel, and joining the stream of traffic from Heathrow Airport. There had been no sensation of movement.

"Whatever happened to 'Satisfaction Guaranteed!'?" Saxon asked above the roar of a 747 overhead. "I haven't seen it in the *Eagle* for a month or so. Not since that retraction about the car company."

Aside from annoyance at being reminded of the Skrone Motors fiasco, Katherine felt flattered that Saxon had followed her column so closely. "Let's just say it was a thing whose time had come—and gone."

"Yes, it did seem to go downhill. Shame, actually, because I quite enjoyed some of your exposés."

"You read it regularly?"

"Wouldn't have missed it. That column was the only reason I included the *Eagle* in my daily newspaper diet." He sent a warm smile Katherine's way. "I always wanted to see who you were gunning for."

"Just to make sure it wasn't you?" Despite the smile, Katherine thought, Saxon's face never completely lost the look of arrogance. It overrode every expression with steely pride.

"I felt reasonably secure. After all, I gave you your big break, didn't I? Without me to pick on over Cadmus Court, you might never have had a column."

Katherine nodded in agreement. In some odd way,

174

she supposed, Saxon had been responsible for her fleeting success.

"How are your two small children and your large husband?"

"The children, Henry and Joanne, they're just fine. As for the large husband . . ." Katherine turned away for an instant. They were on the M4 now, speeding toward London at eighty miles an hour. "The large husband, well, he's the reason the column went downhill. No!" She caught herself quickly. How could she blame Franz for what had been no one's fault but her own? "I'm the reason it fell apart, but Franz is the reason for me being the reason . . ." Her mouth went dry. She looked across the car at Saxon, helpless, wanting his assistance.

"Franz?"

"My husband. He's German." Was that a flash of disapproval in Saxon's dark brown eyes? She recalled the way he'd spoken so fondly of the English history contained in St. James's Square.

"Would you like to tell me about your husband?"

"He had an accident a year ago. New Year's Day. Thrown from a horse and broke his neck. He's been paralyzed ever since. He has minimal use of his hands and arms, but that's all."

Saxon reached across the armrest and took Katherine's hand in his own. She did not try to resist. "I am sorry to hear that. It's a miracle you even bothered continuing with your work under such tragic circumstances."

"My work kept me sane. Until Franz came home from the hospital, and that's when everything began to fall apart." When she looked into Saxon's eyes again, she knew that she must have imagined disapproval. Only compassion was there now, and, God, she needed that more than anything else. Softly, she started to talk about the way her life had changed since Franz's return to the house in Hampstead.

"When Franz first came home, he thought the children were rejecting him. Then he blamed himself for Henry's accident. Now he thinks the best thing he can do is stay out of our lives as much as he can, because that way it's least uncomfortable for us. What it really boils down to—"

"Is that he can't cope mentally with being transformed from a fit, healthy man into a helpless cripple," Saxon said. "Have you sought help for him?"

"Psychiatric help? He wouldn't hear of it."

The Rolls Royce slowed to a crawl. The chauffeur said over his shoulder, "We're at Chalk Farm, Mr. Saxon. Where does the lady wish to be dropped?"

It was the first time Katherine had taken any notice of the chauffeur. William, that was his name. Middle-aged, with dark, wrinkled skin, and a strong Manchester accent. William would fit in well at her home, right along with German, Welsh, and cockney accents. "Over there, William." She pointed to a street lined with cars awaiting their owners' return from work. "Halfway up the street on the right-hand side, the white Stag."

The Rolls edged up the street until it was abreast of the Triumph. The chauffeur got out and walked around to Katherine's side of the car. She turned to Saxon. "Thank you for both the ride and the sympathetic audience. You just did a lot to put a shine back on the name of our former less-than-illustrious king."

The door opened, and a chill wind whipped through the Rolls. "What are you doing now?" Saxon asked.

"Going home."

"To a house where you're unhappy and confused?"

"I never said that."

"You didn't need to come right out and state it. Everything else you've told me says it for you." Saxon's brown eyes bored deeply into Katherine's blue eyes. "The only pleasure you'll get at home tonight is

176

seeing Henry and Joanne." He surprised her by remembering their names. "And how long will that last? Until they go to bed? Then what? You'll mope around the house and think about how your career has taken a nosedive."

"What are you suggesting?"

"Have dinner with me instead. Telephone home and say you've got a late assignment. You do have them sometimes, don't you?"

Katherine nodded. "You know, beneath this coat, I'm wearing one of my business outfits, not something glamorous and sexy."

Saxon laughed at having his own words of fifteen months earlier parried back at him. "I'm quite willing to be seen with you dressed like that. All I ask is that you don't interview me." He made a tiny motion with his hand. William closed the passenger door, returned to the driver's seat, and guided the Rolls back to the main road. From there, they headed toward Marble Arch.

The Rolls finally stopped midway along a narrow street, in front of a white, three-story period house fronted by black railings. The chauffeur got out and opened Saxon's door.

"William's just going off duty," Saxon said to Katherine. "Join me in the front."

She did. Saxon waited until the chauffeur entered the house before pulling away from the curb. "This is where you spend your weeks, is it?" Katherine asked.

"When you're not spending your weekends, of course, on fifteen of the most beautiful acres you've ever seen near Henley-on-Thames, with four hundred feet of river frontage."

"You have a remarkable memory, Katherine. Also a remarkable knack for pinpointing every moment I let pomposity have its way."

"I'm sorry. It must be very picturesque on the river."

"It is. Perhaps one day you'll visit me."

"I'd like to." With the chauffeur gone, she felt far more at ease. Strange; she'd never believed she'd feel that way in John Saxon's company. But then, who would have thought she'd ever be in his company again?

Saxon drove the maroon Rolls Royce with a calm precision. Much, Katherine supposed, the way a Rolls Royce was supposed to be driven. They crossed through London, from the West End to the City, eventually coming to a stop in Farringdon Street. It was now seven o'clock, and the chaos of daytime traffic had yielded to a more gentle rhythm.

"Am I getting another lesson in English history?" Katherine inquired lightly as she entered Farringdon's restaurant, situated in the original brick vaults that ran beneath Holborn Viaduct. Candles supplied illumination, and Katherine felt she was taking a ride on a time machine into Dickens's London.

"I'll keep it short," Saxon answered, smiling. "As far as I know, no prime minister ever lived here." As Katherine laughed, he added, "Don't you think you should telephone your home, to tell them you're going to be late?"

A touch of anxiety flickered through Katherine's stomach. She breathed in deeply, quelling it. There was no reason to be nervous. What was she doing that she should be ashamed of? Having dinner with someone? With a friend who had listened sympathetically to her tale of woe? No matter, when she lifted that telephone, she would be lying. Telling the truth went along with her other definitions of right and wrong: never using obscenity, and believing that divorce and desertion meant one and the same thing.

She found a public telephone and dialed her own number. The housekeeper answered. "Edna, it's me. I've run into a delay getting home, a late assignment, some rock singer giving a press conference on his latest brush with the police over drugs. Everything all right?"

"Fine. The children are getting ready for bed."

"Give them a kiss for me. What about Mr. Kassler?"

"He's with Jimmy, watching the television. What time will you be home, Mrs. Kassler?"

"I don't know. Don't bother waiting up."

Katherine replaced the receiver and joined Saxon at a table. She scanned the menu before setting it down and asking, "What do you recommend?"

"The rabbit pie; that's what I'm having."

Katherine gave a display of turning up her nose. "I've made it a point never to eat something I would like my children to have as a pet. That includes horses, cats, dogs, and rabbits."

"The fur's removed."

"Stop, before you ruin my appetite." When the waiter came, she ordered stuffed plaice.

It was after nine when they left the candle-lit atmosphere of Farringdon's and returned to the electric brightness of modern London. Katherine felt slightly tipsy; they had gone through two bottles of wine, and she'd drunk her share. It did not seem to bother Saxon, though. He was as steady on his feet as a mighty oak. He helped her into the car, climbed into the driver's side, and switched on the engine.

"God, it's freezing," Katherine suddenly complained. She flung her arms around herself and squeezed. "Don't Rolls Royce install heaters in their cars?"

"Give it a moment to warm up." Saxon leaned across, and wrapped his arms around Katherine. "Is that better?"

When was the last time she'd had a man's arms around her? Her father's hugs didn't count. She lifted her face, felt Saxon's lips brush her own. Her arms clung to his body and pulled him closer. Their lips met again, a bruising, crushing kiss that lasted for

179

fifteen seconds. And then a third time. Katherine's lips parted. Her tongue darted out and slipped between Saxon's lips to touch the smooth enamel of his teeth. Open-mouthed, tongues touching, entwining, they held together until at last they broke apart, breathless.

"I think"—Katherine breathed in deeply, fighting to control the wild beating of her heart and the frantic pumping of her lungs—"that the heater's started to work."

Saxon laughed. "Believe me, Rolls Royce was never this efficient." Slowly, he settled back into his seat, arms rigid, hands clasping the steering wheel. His face was flushed, and Katherine's lipstick was smeared across his lips and chin. She wiped the lipstick from his face with a lace handkerchief.

"Since when do you build hotels?" Katherine asked. She giggled, the moment of passion combining with the wine to make her even giddier. "That question's a non sequitur, by the way, but I can't think of anything else to say."

"When it makes financial sense, we build them. You know, if I take you back to Chalk Farm, you'll be in no shape to drive yourself home. The police would have you blowing into a plastic bag before you went a hundred yards."

"You're a very considerate man, John. First you worry about me traveling alone in a taxi, and now you're concerning yourself about me getting into trouble with the police."

"We'll go back to Marble Arch for an hour or so, give you a chance to get your breath back."

Katherine did not disagree. She sat back as Saxon guided the car across the center of London to his weekday home. They arrived at nine-forty. Saxon parked outside the house and helped Katherine from the car. Pulling a gold key chain from his trouser pocket, he unlocked the front door and swung it back. Warmth spilled out of the house. Katherine stepped into a spacious entrance hall, carpeted in sound-deadening patterned Wilton. Directly ahead, a curving staircase ascended to the other two floors. To the right, through an open door, was a formal dining room; a crystal chandelier hung over the center of a twin-pedestal mahogany table set for six places.

"How big is the house?"

"There's a two-bedroom, self-contained flat on the top floor. The housekeeper lives there. So does William, my chauffeur, when he's in town with me. Which leaves me" — he faked depression — "with just three bedrooms, two bathrooms, two reception rooms, and the dining room."

"Poor thing. It's lucky you don't have claustrophobia."

"Come in here." He led her into the front reception room. The walls were painted a pale gold, the high ceiling white, the floor was polished chestnut. Facing each other in front of the fireplace were two Chippendale sofas, covered in yellow silk; between them was a brass-topped table. Next to the window stood a pair of upholstered mahogany chairs, and a drum table with a pedestal base; Hanging from the walls were vivid paintings of historical heroes. Katherine recognized Wellington and Nelson.

"This" — Katherine spread her arms to take it all in — "is just the way I pictured you would live, everything a monument to British history, whether it's a maker of fine British furniture, or a military commander. Except for this." She indicated the long, narrow rug that covered the gleaming floor between the fireplace and the two sofas. "Where is it from?"

"France. Aubusson, from the Louis Fourteenth period."

"Shouldn't this be hanging from the wall? Surely it's priceless." Her mouth dropped as Saxon stepped onto the center of the Aubusson rug, then understanding gleamed in her eyes. "You ultranationalistic devil! Wellington and Nelson on the walls, and a French art treasure beneath your feet."

"Can you think of a better place?" He took her coat, and laid it across the back of a sofa. Walking around the room, he pulled heavy drapes across the windows. Then he locked the door. As Katherine watched, she felt an odd sensation, a fatalistic view of what was about to happen. It had been preordained, from the moment she'd first met John Saxon. Even before, from that instant when Archie Waters, the elevator operator in the Eagle building, had asked for her help.

Saxon lit the candle in one of the two Georgian silver candlesticks on the mantelpiece. Finally, he turned off the main chandelier in the center of the ceiling, leaving the room a nest of flickering shadows. Katherine slipped out of the jacket of her suit and stood waiting for him in front of the fireplace.

He slid easily into her arms. She felt his body pressing on hers, legs against legs, his chest against her breasts. Open mouths met, tongues caressed. Saxon tugged Katherine's silk blouse free of her skirt, undid buttons one by one. The blouse floated free. His slim fingers unhooked the single fastening of her delicately laced brassiere. It fell away, and Katherine's breasts dropped into Saxon's hands. His thumbs massaged her swollen nipples.

"Would you"—she pulled her mouth away from Saxon's—"like to make love to me on an Aubusson rug?" She dropped to her knees on the rug, pulling Saxon down with her. Sighing contentedly, she lay back, feeling his fingers solve the fastening of her skirt.

"How comfortable is the rug?" Saxon asked, as he flipped Katherine's skirt toward one of the sofas.

"It itches." She moved her shoulders in a circular motion. "But I like it." She watched as he removed his

182

own clothes, revealing a thin, wiry body that shimmered with energy. She kissed his lips, his chin, his neck, and then his chest. His hands ran through her hair, pressing hard against her skull as she continued. He groaned softly as her lips brushed against him with dozens of tiny kisses. "Oh, God," he whispered. "Don't stop, not now." He felt her envelop him, lips and tongue and warmth and wetness arousing all the passion that had been building steadily.

He moved his hands from Katherine's scalp to her face, pulling her upward. Her mouth retraced its journey along his body, towards his lips. As she felt him slide into her, sensations combined into an exquisite blend. The roughness of the rug on her back and buttocks, the warm weight of Saxon on top of her, and the fullness of him inside her. She gasped in pleasure at finding again feelings she had not known for more than a year.

They lay together on the rug, Saxon cradling Katherine's head on his chest. After half an hour, he said, "I think I'd better take you wherever you have to go. Do you feel up to driving yourself home from Chalk Farm?"

"It's not far."

They dressed quickly, eyes averted from each other, like two strangers sharing a changing room. In the Rolls Royce, they barely spoke a word. Only as the car crept up the street where Katherine had left her Triumph, did Saxon ask, "When can I see you again?"

"Give me a few days. I have to come to terms with what just happened."

"Katherine, when I met you at the hotel today and offered you a ride, it was never my intention that we'd sleep together. But you sounded so miserable—"

"Sounded?" She laughed dryly. "I was miserable."

"Please let me finish. When we made love, I didn't mean it to be a one-night fling. I want to see you again, Katherine. And again and again."

"I'll telephone you at St. James's Square." She kissed him quickly on the cheek and climbed out of the car. He waited until she started the Stag's engine before driving away.

Katherine drove slowly. A white sports car this late at night was a homing beacon to any cruising police car. Reaching the house, she let herself in. As she passed the door to Franz's bedroom, she felt a twinge of guilt. It lasted for a moment, until she found a way to rationalize the evening's events. If Franz were whole; if he were healthy, both physically and mentally; if she still loved him . . . then what she had done could be construed as cheating. But none of those conditions applied, so she had not cheated on anyone. She had just quenched a fiery need within herself for the affection she'd been deprived of for more than a year.

Before she went to bed, she took a long shower. Her back itched, and when she looked in the mirror she saw what looked like a rash. Saxon, with his ultranationalistic outlook, might like an antique French rug beneath his feet, but it would be the last time that Katherine made love on an Aubusson.

Her final act before leaving the bathroom was to brush her teeth. When she settled into the brass bed, the flavor of the toothpaste remained strong in her mouth. But above the minty tang, she could still taste John Saxon.

Katherine waited a week before telephoning Saxon at his office in St. James's Square. When he asked why she had allowed so long to pass before making the call, she answered, "It's taken me all this time to be sure that I wanted a relationship with you. It's very easy for you to involve yourself in an affair with me, because you only have yourself to consider. I have far more."

184

"I understand perfectly," Saxon said. "Whatever you want to do, and however long you want to take, it's fine by me."

"Are you always this obliging?"

"Only where something I want very badly is concerned."

It was the answer Katherine had hoped to hear. In the week between seeing Saxon and telephoning him, she had dissected and analyzed her feelings a hundred times or more. Each time she had reached the same conclusion. She was drawn both mentally and physically toward him. She had been, from that first proper meeting, after the publication of the Cadmus Court story. Only she had fought against it, because she had been frightened that her home life, the happiness she had already found with Franz, might be at risk. Although the circumstances were vastly different now, she needed to be sure that any involvement would be based on mutual feelings. She was sailing into uncharted waters; she was nervous, and needed assurance.

Under the pretext of another late assignment, Katherine met that evening with Saxon. They ate at a small restaurant in Chelsea. Katherine had little fear of being recognized; the most recent published photograph of her—the one that had adorned "Satisfaction Guaranteed!"—was almost eighteen months old, and she was reasonably certain that the likeness was no longer very accurate. She knew she had aged in those eighteen months. There were lines around her mouth and eyes that had not been there before, and her long blond hair no longer seemed so lustrous.

Following dinner, they returned to Saxon's house at Marble Arch to spend an hour making love, after which Katherine returned home. When she came downstairs the following morning, after a complete and restful night's sleep, there were no questions about the late assignment; no one had reason to disbelieve her.

Soon, Katherine's relationship with Saxon was down to a smooth routine. She would meet with him once or twice during the week. Sometimes for dinner, followed by an hour or two at his Marble Arch home; at other times just for a drink, a ride in the maroon Rolls Royce, and a talk. He was a wonderful listener. She could talk to him about Franz, about something that was troubling her at work, even about the children. When Joanne came down with a bad cold, Saxon listened so sympathetically over dinner to the story that Katherine was utterly amazed.

"I think you'd make some child a wonderful father." For the first time, the idea of having Henry and Joanne meet Saxon flitted through her mind. And just what, she wondered, had prompted that? Was she looking for her children's blessing of her affair with Saxon? God, next she'd be thinking of some way to arrange an accidental meeting between Franz and Saxon, to see if her husband approved of her lover.

At the end of February, after three weeks of secretive trysts, Saxon invited Katherine to his country home in Oxfordshire. "I'm giving a dinner party on Sunday night, and I would very much like you to act as hostess."

Sadly, she shook her head. "I'd love to, John, but I can't possibly go away for the weekend."

"Reporters travel, they have assignments that take them—"

She stopped him. "The weekend's the only chance I get to be with my children, and that's a treat I don't relinquish easily." That did not stop her curiosity, though, for she knew little about Saxon's personal life. "Do you do much entertaining?"

"Quite a bit. I use my London home for business entertaining, and my country home for entertaining my friends."

"Tell me about the friends who'll be there on

186

Sunday."

"There'll be a merchant banker, some lawyers, a couple of politicians—all people to whom I owe invitations. You might, quite possibly, even know some of them. They're all quite boring, really. I was hoping you'd brighten up the proceedings."

Katherine doubted if any of Saxon's friends could be boring. "If you're right, and I do know some of your guests, it wouldn't look very good for them to see me with you."

Saxon chuckled. "It certainly wouldn't harm my reputation."

"Perhaps not, but it wouldn't help mine." Still, her interest was piqued. Despite the pleasure she found with her children on the weekends, she did miss Saxon. "I could arrange to be away on Saturday night."

"And spend it with me? All of it?"

"At Marble Arch."

"Wonderful. I'll stay in town Saturday, and drive out to the country on Sunday. My guests will undoubtedly think their company is the reason for the twinkle in my eyes, but only you and I will know the truth."

"And I won't tell if you won't!" Katherine laughed and clapped her hands. She could not remember being this happy in ages. Saturday was three days in the future, and she could barely wait for its arrival.

Katherine used the annual meeting of a trade union as an excuse for going away. The meeting was at the Grand Hotel in Brighton, and she would be covering the speeches given at the wind-up dinner on Saturday evening. Edna Griffiths was the only member of the household to show interest in the Brighton assignment. Remembering how difficult it was to run a house when power strikes caused two four-hour

187

blackouts a day, she told Katherine, "Kick as many union officials up the backside as you can." Katherine promised that she would.

She left the house at four-thirty on Saturday afternoon, wearing the kind of comfortable outfit she'd choose to travel in: wool trousers, boots, cashmere sweater, and suede jacket. Fresh clothes were in the small suitcase that she placed in the Stag's trunk. Instead of driving to Brighton, though, she drove to Marble Arch, parking behind the maroon Rolls Royce. Carrying the suitcase, she rang the doorbell. Musical chimes sounded from within the house. Saxon opened the door, kissed her very hastily, and grabbed the suitcase from her hand.

"Come inside, quickly. I'm watching something very important on the news." Motioning for her to follow, he strode to the drawing room at the rear of the house.

"What is it, John?" She entered the room, furnished on an entirely different note from the front room, where they had first made love. This was like a room in her father's home: huge, comfortable floral chintz-covered chairs and sofas; tables that were meant for use, not for admiration. A large color television filled one corner. It was on, and Saxon's attention was riveted to the screen. Katherine looked at what he found so important. On the screen, she witnessed absolute chaos. Hundreds of young men fighting. Some, she swore, were no older than fourteen; many wore scarves in the colors of soccer teams. In the middle of the fracas, police tried to restore order. Even as she watched, one constable had his helmet knocked from his head. A shaven-headed youth—wearing the odd combination of heavy boots, jeans, and a doublebreasted navy blue topcoat with a red silk handkerchief showing in the breast pocket— picked up the helmet and kicked it high into the air.

"World War Three?" Katherine asked sarcastically.

"Or just another Saturday afternoon football game?"

"The game's over. This is the aftermath." He turned up the volume. Katherine listened. The scene was Highbury, in North London, where Arsenal played. The visiting team was from Liverpool. Fan trouble had erupted before the game, but police had quelled it then by separating rival supporters. Once the game was over, though, the fans had mixed, and the earlier hostilities had resumed with a vengeance.

"Turn it off, John. I see enough violence in my work every day. I don't need to see more when I'm with you." Saxon flicked the switch, and Katherine watched the mayhem fade. "It's like some barbaric lunacy has taken over the country. If you support a different team from the other chap . . . well, that's the perfect reason to beat the living daylights out of him. Now where's the sense in that?"

"There isn't any, Katherine, but you try telling that to a rampaging gang of football fans. Now let's talk about something else. What reason did you give for staying away overnight?"

She told him, and he laughed. "Can you imagine what those upright union officials would say if they knew I'd used them as an excuse for a date with a capitalist like you?" Katherine said. "What do you have planned?"

"First, I'd like to make love to you."

"And then?"

"Do it again, in case we missed anything the first time."

"Be serious."

"An early dinner, followed by a play at the Theatre Royal."

"Sounds wonderful. Let me have my case. I'll change into something more fitting." She went upstairs to the front bedroom, where Saxon slept when he was in town. The room was a mixture of antique and modern, put together so well that not a single

189

item appeared out of place. She sat on the Georgian loveseat situated at the foot of the heavily carved four-poster, and pulled off her boots. The suede jacket, jeans, and cashmere sweater followed. When she stood in just bra and panties, she set the suitcase on the bed and opened it. Inside were high-heeled shoes, an off-the-shoulder black evening dress, and a mink jacket. As she dressed, she tried to forget that the jacket had been a present from Franz. Just like the jewelry she wore, the rings on her fingers, the three-rope pearl choker around her throat, and the gold Patek Philippe on her wrist.

"I've never seen you look so beautiful," Saxon greeted her when she returned downstairs. He stepped forward, touching a fingertip to her right cheek. "What's that? A tear? Something get in your eye?"

"Just a momentary pang of guilt, that's all."

"You have nothing to feel guilty about, Katherine."

"That's what I try to tell myself. But when I wear these" — she touched a hand to the choker, showed the rings — "I get a strange feeling. Like Franz is somehow watching over me."

"Then wear this instead." Saxon removed the pearl choker from Katherine's neck. He replaced it with a platinum chain from which dropped a single pear-shaped diamond.

Katherine's hand touched the unfamiliar piece of jewelry, fingers taking the place of eyes until she could view the treasure in a mirror. "I can't possibly wear this. Franz, my entire household . . . they know what jewelry I have. They'd know it was new."

"Wear it just when you're with me."

"I will. I'll wear it tonight." She took his face and brought his lips down to hers.

Saxon parked the Rolls just off the Haymarket, close to the Theatre Royal. They ate at a nearby restaurant and got to the theater moments before the curtain rose. At the end of the first act, Saxon turned to Katherine. "Are you enjoying the play?"

"Not really. Are you?"

"No. Let's leave."

"And return to your house?"

"I didn't say that."

"I did." She leaned closer to him. "John, we've got an entire night together. Let's not waste it sitting here."

He stood up. Hand in hand, they walked out of the theater, up the Haymarket, and back to the Rolls. Saxon drove around Leicester Square, then north along Charing Cross Road, intending to cut west toward Marble Arch. Traffic was Saturday-night heavy, moving forward in fits and starts. Halfway up Charing Cross Road, traffic flow became even slower. A hundred yards ahead, blue lights flickered. Katherine rolled down her window, and the two-tone sound of klaxons drilled into her ears.

"Look at that!" Saxon pointed across the street. Running along the sidewalk, scattering pedestrians before them, came a crowd of two dozen young men. Some had long, unkempt hair; others had their hair cropped so short they could have been army recruits. A few wore the colored scarves—tied around their necks, or wound around their waists like sashes—that Katherine had seen on the news that afternoon, during the fan violence at Highbury. All of them were obviously drunk. Some had cans of beer in their hands, swilling as they ran from the dozen police officers who were giving chase.

"There's a few lads who'll miss the last train home," Saxon said. He looked on the scene as a little diversion, presented to take his mind off the traffic jam. Even when the soccer fans started to run across Charing Cross Road, weaving their way through the stationary traffic, he did not seem concerned.

Katherine could not take it so lightly. She flinched as she saw one of the youths fling his empty beer can

191

at a traffic light. Katherine turned sideways to follow the can's flight. It missed the traffic light, and caromed off the roof of a car. It could just as easily, she thought, have hit some pedestrian in the head.

Suddenly, Saxon's voice took on a sharp note. "Watch out!" Katherine's head snapped forward. The front runners were heading straight for the Rolls. The first group of youths ran past, making for Leicester Square underground station, where they hoped to lose their police pursuers.

"Get your window up!" Saxon yelled out. Katherine fumbled with the control. The window began to rise just as another group raced past. One young man, long blond hair blowing in the night breeze, swung around to face her. Their eyes met. Katherine tried to look away to avoid antagonizing him. She was too late. The youth's arm snaked through the open window.

"Stuck-up rich bitch in your bloody Rolls!" he shouted.

Instinctively, Katherine closed her eyes. She felt a hand at her neck, ice-cold, grasping. The chain ripped free, and the diamond pendant Saxon had given her hours earlier was gone.

She opened her eyes to see a group of policemen chasing the youths. One man, with an inspector's rank insignia on his uniform, stopped by the car. "Are you all right, miss?"

"Yes."

"Did he hit you?"

"No. He took something. A diamond pendant." Reaction set in, and Katherine started to shake. She clenched her teeth, balled her hands into tight fists, but the shaking did not stop.

The inspector looked past Katherine to Saxon. "We'll need a statement, sir. Could you pull over there? I'll be back with you in a minute or two."

As traffic began to move, Saxon signaled to pull

over. "What do you think you're doing?" Katherine asked him.

"What that inspector told me to."

"Keep going."

"Are you crazy? That pendant cost five thousand pounds."

"And if we stop and make a statement, a complaint, or whatever, it will mean giving our names — which will cost me even more. If you want to, John, you can go back later on. You can refer to me as Madame X. Or Lucretia Borgia, if you like. But I want nothing to do with it."

Saxon glared at Katherine, as though ready to continue the argument. At last, he continued on the journey to Marble Arch.

When they reached the house, Katherine was still shaking. Saxon helped her inside, sat her down in the drawing room, and poured her a glass of Rémy-Martin. She drank it down, but the shaking did not stop.

Saxon did his best to soothe her. "You're not hurt; that's the only thing that matters. The necklace doesn't mean a thing. You're all that concerns me."

Slowly, Katherine regained control of herself. The shaking stopped, but inside she was still in turmoil. She went upstairs with Saxon, went to bed with him in the big four-poster, but they did not make love. She was in no mood to do so, and he didn't press her. She just lay with his arms around her, staring off into the darkness.

Saxon was right, she thought. The necklace didn't mean a thing. All that mattered was the hate she'd seen in the young man's eyes. It was like nothing she had ever witnessed before, and it terrified her.

9

Sleep did little to soothe Katherine's nerves. She was still very shaken when she rose on Sunday morning. Furthermore, as if her own experience of the violence was not frightening enough, she was fated to be constantly reminded of it.

While eating breakfast with John Saxon in the kitchen of his Marble Arch home, she switched on the radio to hear the news. The main topic was the riot, and the sporadic outbreaks of violence that had occurred throughout the night. More details were available now. Sixty-four people, including eighteen police officers, had been taken to the hospital, with injuries ranging from simple cuts to broken limbs and, in two cases, knife wounds. Over two hundred people had been arrested, and were scheduled for court appearances on Monday.

Katherine and Saxon left Marble Arch together, at ten in the morning; she, once more wearing comfortable traveling clothes, to drive to Hampstead, while Saxon made the far longer journey to his weekend home in Oxfordshire. After helping her into the Triumph Stag, he stooped to kiss her. "I'm really sorry about last night. It was supposed to have been something very special between us, and it finished up as a

194

nightmare."

"John, stop apologizing. It wasn't your fault." She turned the key, and the Stag's engine burst into life. "Telephone me at the paper tomorrow?"

"I'm not sure I can wait that long."

"Try. Enjoy your dinner party tonight."

"I'd enjoy it more if you were there."

"Didn't you find another hostess?"

"There are at least a dozen young women who would jump at the opportunity. I didn't ask any of them, because you are the only young woman I wanted."

"Thank you." She kissed him again, and drove away. She'd wondered if there were other women in his life. Now she knew: at least a dozen of them. That pleased her and annoyed her all at once. She was happy that at least a dozen other women obviously found Saxon as attractive as she found him, and she was upset that he should have noticed their interest. The important thing, she supposed, was that he wanted only her.

On the way to Hampstead, she stopped off to buy a newspaper. News of the union meeting in Brighton was relegated to an inside page. Blazed across the front page were pictures of the riot, showing twisted grimaces of hatred stamped on hard, young faces.

When she arrived home, she walked right into more reminders. The sole topic of conversation was the riot. Everyone had a solution. Franz, communicative for once, said the hooligans should be forced to do community work on game days. Jimmy Phillips said it was too bad there was no longer national service, and Edna Griffiths bemoaned the passing of corporal punishment. Nowhere was there sanctuary. To get away from it, Katherine decided to make good on the promise she'd given to Erica Bentley a month earlier. She telephoned to ask if she could bring the children to the farm that afternoon. Erica's answer was "Of course!" But even in the peaceful country setting, Katherine found there was no escape.

"Don't know what this country's coming to," Cliff Bentley grumbled, as the adults sat in the farmhouse's comfortable study, having tea. "A fine thing when some decent working man can't take his son to a football game without getting set on by thugs. All the little miscreants the police caught—they should be loaded onto a ship and banished to bloody Australia."

"Cliff, dear," Erica said sweetly. "We haven't sent people to Australia for a century or more."

Henry, who was stroking a heavily striped tabby, one of the many cats the Bentleys fed, looked up at the adults. The boy had learned a new word the previous day, *riot,* and he was intent on using it at every opportunity. "Mummy didn't see the riot like we did. She had to work for the newspaper in Brighton. She missed the riot."

"Brighton," repeated his sister, who was coaxing another cat to come close enough to be stroked. "Brighton's the seaside."

"That's right, Joanne," Erica said. "Brighton's the seaside. What were you doing there, Katherine? Surely you weren't covering that stupid union meeting. That belongs to the industrial or political staff."

Katherine felt her head float off into space; if she'd drunk a pint of whiskey, she would not feel less in touch with reality. Children . . . there was no way of keeping anything secret with a couple of kids around.

"Katherine?" Erica was looking at her with a worried expression. "Are you all right?"

"Fine. You know, I think it's time I learned to ride again. Come with me, Erica? Cliff can stay and amuse the children."

The two women left the farmhouse and walked to the stable. Erica mounted a spirited chestnut gelding. Katherine took her time with a calm gray gelding, accustoming herself once more to the hardness of the saddle beneath her, the feel of her feet in stirrups.

"Everything all right?" Erica asked.

"Getting there." They walked the horses along the path leading from the stable. Katherine dug in her heels, and the gray gelding broke into a gentle canter. Erica kept pace. "Like riding a bicycle!" Katherine exclaimed. "It's something you never forget."

"Want to tell me about Brighton?" Erica asked, when they had slowed to a walk again. "The mention of it made you look sick."

Katherine knew she could lie. Put off sharing her secret for a while longer, until someone else stumbled into the tangled web she was busily weaving. Who would that be? Someone less understanding than Erica? If anyone had to find out, Katherine reasoned, she'd prefer it to be Erica.

"I haven't been to Brighton in years. I just used the union meeting as an excuse to spend the night with my lover."

Erica demonstrated no surprise, and Katherine felt vaguely disappointed. The older woman's only response was "And just how long has this been going on?"

"Since the beginning of February. Last night was the first night we'd spent together, and it was an absolute disaster. Can you believe we got caught up in the aftermath of that riot?" She told Erica about the visit to the theater, and the terrifying drive along Charing Cross Road; as she described the blond youth ripping away the pendant, she touched a hand to her throat. Finally she mentioned that morning's parting: two lovers, two different destinations.

For fully thirty seconds, Erica sat silent and still on the chestnut gelding. Then she said, "A Rolls Royce Silver Shadow . . . ? A five-thousand-pound diamond pendant that he just writes off . . . ? A *second* home in Marble Arch, not to mention an estate near Henley-on-Thames . . . ? Who the hell are we talking about here? Prince Charles, or the ghost of John Paul Getty?"

Katherine laughed at Erica's response to the casual

197

mention of so much wealth. "Neither. It's John Saxon."

"The same John Saxon you raked over the coals?"

"The very same. And not the same. That one was a pompous twerp. This one's a very lovely and considerate gentleman." She related how she had met him at the opening of the Chiltern Towers hotel, how he had offered her a ride, and what had ensued from there. "Do you think I'm doing the wrong thing?"

"That depends on whether you're asking me as a friend, or as a women's writer. Wearing my women's page editor's hat, I'd advise that no matter how loyal you are to your handicapped husband, you also have a responsibility to yourself. You have every right to give yourself some happiness, because you only travel this way once."

"And as a friend?"

"That's more difficult. Again, you owe yourself happiness, but if Franz should ever learn . . ." A wealth of expression was contained in the simple shrug of Erica's shoulders. "Franz is unbalanced now. What will happen to him if he finds out you're seeing another man?"

"He's the one who brought up the subject of divorce."

"Being divorced is one thing. Being married, even in name only, and knowing your wife is with another man—that's another matter entirely. The male ego is very fragile, easily injured, and then its owner can do strange things. Katherine, you've got to make sure Franz never learns about you and John Saxon."

"I think I'm doing a good job. I only see John twice a week, and I always have an alibi. After all, everyone knows that Lawrie Stimkin is a hard taskmaster."

Erica chuckled. "A chauvinistic pig of a taskmaster, that's what he is." She looked over her shoulder toward the farmhouse, four hundred yards away. "We'd better get back, before my husband thinks we've deserted him."

They'd covered a hundred yards when Erica called out: "Speaking as a friend again . . ."

"More advice?"

"No, a compliment. Speaking as a friend, I think you're looking better than I've seen you look in ages."

Katherine found a memorandum resting on her typewriter when she reached her desk on Monday morning. It was from the chairman of Eagle Newspapers, inviting her to a special meeting at eleven o'clock that morning in the boardroom on the executive floor. Every member of the news staff had one; those who could not make the meeting, because of prior commitments or different shifts, would receive a copy of the minutes.

As puzzled as anyone else, Katherine joined the surge of editorial people up the stairs toward the executive floor. She found herself walking next to Lawrie Stimkin. When she asked him what was going on, he shrugged his shoulders and said, "I was hoping you could tell me what the big surprise is."

"My father only lets me in on surprises that concern the Eagles family, not Eagle Newspapers."

The boardroom filled quickly. Ten chairs were placed around the long mahogany table. First come were first served. No mock chivalry existed here, where men offered seats to women. Fleet Street's gentler sex had fought too hard, too long, and too vociferously for equal rights, to be shown simple courtesies now.

At precisely eleven o'clock, Gerald Waller, the *Eagle*'s editor, walked in. Behind him came Roland Eagles, looking more serious than Katherine could recall seeing him since the day of Franz's accident. Whatever surprise he had, it was weighing visibly on him.

Waller clapped his hands to kill the expectant buzz. As it subsided, he introduced Roland. Although taller than six feet, Roland found it difficult to see over the assembled journalists well enough to address them. Waller solved the problem by jerking a thumb at the closest reporter who was comfortably ensconced in a chair. Begrudgingly, the man gave up his prize. Roland offered a cool nod of thanks before standing on the chair.

"All of you, I'm sure, are thoroughly familiar with the disgraceful exhibition of football-fan violence that took place this weekend."

Standing at the other end of the table, Katherine cupped her face in her hands. Don't tell me you're all wrapped up in this as well, she thought.

Roland ceased talking and stared down the shining table at his daughter. At the silence, she dropped her hands. Roland sent a frosty smile her way before he continued. "In the past, Eagle Newspapers has toed a very strict editorial line regarding fan violence. We have mentioned incidents as briefly as possible because, quite frankly, we did not want to give free publicity to these mindless morons whose idea of a good time is a good fight. Well, we've found out that ignoring them hasn't helped, so now we are going to publicize them to death."

Lawrie Stimkin stuck his hand in the air. Roland said he would answer any questions later, but Stimkin refused to be put off. "Just what is the reason for this change in editorial policy, Mr. Eagles?"

Roland's face soured for an instant. "Consistency, Mr. Stimkin. We have published the names of black youths who broke the law during the recent racial disturbances, but we've virtually ignored the trouble at football games, where the lawbreakers are nearly always white. Because of that, accusations of unfair practice have been forthcoming."

"I understand." Pleased with himself, Stimkin looked around the assembly. All the reporters knew it was he who had claimed unfair practice; he had done everything but come right out and accuse the group's management of pursuing a racially biased editorial policy.

"If I may continue now?" Roland asked. "Thank you. From today, we're going to find out what makes these hooligans tick. We're going to climb right into whatever minds they have and learn what motivation, what background, is responsible for such antisocial behavior."

Eager to capitalize on his moment of triumph, Stimkin handed out assignments the instant he returned to the editorial floor. Special sittings of magistrates and juvenile court had been arranged for that afternoon. Stimkin told Katherine to go along to the magistrates court, "and come back with loads of names."

Ten minutes before the court was due to convene, Katherine squeezed herself into the packed press box. Usually, three or four reporters were spread out in the box. Today, a dozen were jammed into it. At least another dozen were crowded into the public gallery at the rear of the courtroom. Members of the public who wished to view the proceedings today had to fight for the privilege with journalists. Katherine thought she recognized someone in the public gallery, a familiar-looking white-haired man. Before she could get a better view, the man was hidden from sight by two large police officers.

Katherine turned her attention to the unusually bulky court list. She was barely able to move her hands enough to turn the pages, and when she tried to force a little space for herself, she was rewarded with an angry grunt from the middle-aged *Mirror* reporter on her right.

"Would you mind keeping your lethally sharp elbows pointed toward yourself?"

"I just want a little space before I'm crushed to death."

"That's all Hitler wanted as well. Get your *Lebens-*

201

raum somewhere else."

Katherine tried the man on her left. "Do you think I could possibly get a little breathing space?"

"How's this?" The man abruptly shifted his body, and the people sitting on his left were squeezed into an even tighter area. Katherine found herself with another few precious inches.

"Thank you, Mr. . . . Mr. . . .?" Only then did she realize that the man was a total stranger. She thought she knew all the regulars, yet she'd never seen this reporter before. Come to think of it, why was she so sure he was a reporter? Just because he was sitting in the press box? He certainly did not look cynical enough to be one. Or crabby enough, like the *Mirror* man on her right. This one was young, no more than thirty-five, Katherine guessed. Thin, with a sharp, angular face, curly brown hair, and light brown eyes that seemed to be smiling at her confusion.

"My name's Barnhill. Raymond Barnhill." He made the introduction in a slow, measured voice. Katherine's ear for accents picked out the United States; somewhere in the South? "And you are?"

"Katherine Kassler, *Daily Eagle.* Which newspaper are you representing, Raymond?"

"None of them, and all of them. I'm with the London bureau of the International Press Agency."

"Oh, wire service." She took another, more critical look at him. She should not have had to wait until he opened his mouth to realize he was American. The way he dressed should have told her. An expensive gray Harris tweed sportcoat, a crisp white shirt, and maroon knitted tie — worn with a much-traveled pair of jeans, and the kind of thick-soled suede shoes her father had always referred to as "brothel creepers."

"Does the IPA always cover English magistrates' court cases?" she asked him.

"No, but this is special. My editors want all they can get. You see" — he squeezed around to face her fully;

she liked the sharply drawn, Lincolnesque lines of his face — "the British press always plays up how safe this country is compared with the States. Britain's wonderful, because you can walk the streets, that's the usual line. Now it's our turn. Our newspapers want to show how safe it is to attend a sporting event in the United States, and how dangerous it is in Britain."

Katherine felt compelled to defend the country of her birth. "That is a ridiculous and completely irresponsible attitude to take. What happened this weekend is an aberration. For heaven's sake, it's not the kind of thing you see every week."

Raymond Barnhill's brown eyes dropped to Katherine's left hand. "You married? Got any kids?" When she nodded, he said: "Would you let your kids attend a Saturday afternoon game?"

"My oldest isn't yet seven. He isn't even old enough to understand the game."

"You're evading the question."

"I just told you — this kind of violence is not a regular occurrence."

"Isn't it?" Barnhill flipped through a stenographer's pad. "Let me educate you. Three years ago, fans of Leeds United wrecked most of Paris after watching their team lose the European Cup Final to Bayern Munich. Scottish supporters, who couldn't bear the excitement of seeing their team beat England, did the same to Wembley Stadium last year. In 1974, Newcastle United fans overran the field when their team was losing to Nottingham Forest, and chased the players and officials back to the dressing rooms. And let's not forget this oldie but goodie — those hundreds of Tottenham Hotspur fans who'd just seen their team lose five nothing at Derby. They wrecked the train taking them back to London, and when they were thrown off the train in the middle of nowhere, they found the nearest peaceful village — a place called Flitwick — and leveled that, too. By the time those soccer fans finished with

Flitwick, Sherman's march through Georgia looked like a damned Sunday school picnic."

"Enough! You've made your point!"

The sharpness in Katherine's voice did not deter Barnhill. He carried right on. "Those are just some of the well-documented episodes. The smaller incidents, like the Manchester United supporters who beat up and robbed the blind program seller at Tottenham a few years back . . . well, those things are hardly worth bothering about, are they?"

"But we don't have people shooting each other on the street, do we?"

Barnhill laughed so hard that the clerk of the court, who had just taken his seat in front of the magistrates' bench, looked over crossly. "With sports fans like that, you don't need people shooting each other on the street."

Annoyed at the American wire-service journalist, and just as angry at herself for being drawn into the argument, Katherine turned away from Barnhill. The court was assembling. The three magistrates took their seats on the bench, looking down at the dock. Better skim through the court list, Katherine decided, and see if there's anything exciting. Names and addresses flew before her eyes, followed by varied charges, the lesser of which to be dealt with today by the magistrates, with the more serious being passed up to a higher court. Breach of the peace. Assault and battery. Grievous bodily harm. Assault with intent to resist arrest. The police were really going to town with these prosecutions, she thought. And so they should!

Katherine's eyes flicked on over additional pages, more charges. And then she stopped. One name and address jumped right off the page into her face. Brian Waters, an eighteen-year-old messenger of Cadmus Court, Islington, was charged with assault and battery.

Katherine's gaze flew from the court list to the public gallery. The white-haired man she'd spotted earlier, before the two policemen had blocked him from view — no wonder he'd looked so blasted familiar! It was Archie Waters, the elevator operator from the Eagle building. He had not been at work that morning, and Katherine had simply assumed he had the day off. Those two policemen had moved, and she could see Archie sitting there. His raincoat was unbuttoned. Katherine spotted a flash of color, one of the combat ribbons of which he was so rightly proud. But there was nothing proud about Archie's appearance today. His back was bent, his face gaunt, eyes hollow. He looked like an old soldier, all right, but an old soldier who had fought all of his wars this past weekend.

The court proceedings began, a massive conveyor belt of justice dispensed. There could be found among the defendants little of the fierce aggression they'd displayed two days earlier. Now, meekness was a weapon with which to beguile the magistrates; loud obscenity was replaced with overdone politeness and the contrived ending to every reply of "Sir." But the magistrates, guided by the clerk of the court, were not so gullible. The sentencing was harsh, consisting of large fines and short terms of imprisonment.

Two hours into the proceedings, Brian Waters was summoned. Wearing corduroy trousers and a brown jacket, he entered the dock. A large patch of adhesive tape covered his left cheek, and a bruise circled his eye. When he pleaded guilty to assault and battery, the American wire-service reporter on Katherine's left permitted himself a dry chuckle.

"If this is the guy being charged, can you imagine what the other fellow must look like?"

Katherine turned angrily on him. "Shut up!"

The rebuke was far louder than she had intended. In front of the bench, the clerk of the court looked at the press box over lowered glasses. "Thank you, madam, for trying to establish some decorum. Now if you would kindly heed your own good advice, we will continue."

Blushing, Katherine switched her attention back to the dock. Brian Waters was staring at her. With recognition came horror, a realization for the first time that his own name, his own misdeeds, would be made public. The charge against Brian stemmed from a fight that had taken place outside the stadium following the game. Brian pleaded guilty, but claimed in mitigation that he had been attacked first, by rival fans.

"Any assault and battery on my part," he tried to explain to the bench, "was done strictly in self-defense."

The chief magistrate was singularly unimpressed. "Assault and battery, young man, is still assault and battery. I intend for you to remember that in the future." The sentence he passed was a fine of two hundred and fifty pounds, or thirty days.

Brian's mouth dropped at the size of the fine. "I can't pay all that in one go! I'll need time. A lot of time!"

It was a perfect moment, the chief magistrate decided, to demonstrate to the larger-than-normal audience that he possessed Solomon's wisdom. "And you shall have it, young man. The same amount of time which your infernal football game takes. Ninety minutes. If the fine is not paid within ninety minutes, you will serve another kind of time."

Katherine glanced toward the rear of the court. Archie Waters was looking down, probably, she decided, at whatever money he had taken from his pockets. How much could he have, he and his grandson together? Twenty pounds? She opened her leather attache case. Inside was a purse. She counted the money there. Forty-two pounds. And no checkbook, damn it!

"The magistrate wasn't so amusing that you have to throw money," Raymond Barnhill said.

"I wasn't about to. I was trying to find the money to pay Brian's fine."

"Brian, is it? You know that little creep?"

"He works for me. For my father . . . he works for a company my father owns, that is."

"Make up your mind."

"My father owns Eagle Newspapers, and Eagle Newspapers owns Mercury Messengers. Brian works for Mercury. And he's not what you call a creep, all right?" She turned back to the dock. Brian had been led away; another defendant was firmly in the chief magistrate's sights.

"Your father . . . ?"

"Oh, shut up!" Katherine told Barnhill for the second time. Then, in a much softer voice, she asked, "How much money do you have on you?"

"Quite a bit. I just cashed my check." He pulled a large roll of bills from his trouser pocket. "See? I'm just like all Americans: overpaid, oversexed—"

"And over here. At least, your money can do some good." Before Barnhill could move, Katherine jumped to her feet, snatched the money from his hand, and darted past him.

Barnhill almost shouted, "Stop thief! Police!" Just in time he remembered that he was in a court of law. The place was full of uniforms. And what would he do once Katherine was apprehended? Press charges against her because she'd stolen the money to pay the fine of some delinquent for whom she had a soft spot? He left the press box and walked after her. She wasn't hard to catch, because she'd stopped to talk to an elderly man in a raincoat that covered some kind of uniform.

"I would have thought that with a rich daddy, you wouldn't have needed to steal from other people," Barnhill said. When Katherine refused to acknowledge him, and continued her conversation with Archie Waters, Barnhill lost his temper. He grabbed her shoulders and spun her around. "Did you hear what I just said?"

Archie bristled. "You just watch how you speak to

Miss Eagles. And take your dirty great hand off her shoulder."

Katherine stepped in between the two men. "Will you stop it, the pair of you? This is Archie Waters; he's the grandfather of Brian Waters—"

"Don't have to look far to find out where the little thug gets his aggressive nature, do we?" Barnhill gibed.

Archie tried to reach Barnhill, but Katherine stood firm. "Archie, although this American gentleman doesn't know when to keep his mouth shut, you have to believe he has a good heart. He's the one"—she held up the roll of currency—"who just lent us the money to pay Brian's fine."

"Lent you?" Barnhill laughed. "That gives it a whole new perspective. All this time, I thought you'd stolen it from me."

"Thank you," Archie said. "I promise you'll get it back."

"Very soon, I hope. I've got rent to pay."

Archie had twenty-eight pounds in his pocket. Added to Katherine's forty-two, it made seventy. She counted off one hundred and eighty pounds from Barnhill's roll and returned the remainder to him.

Archie paid the fine at the court office. Papers were signed, and Brian was released. Unlike the first time he had met Katherine, the youth needed no prompting from his grandfather. "Thanks a lot for helping me out. You as well," he added to Barnhill, as they walked out of the court. "That old scrubber of a magistrate, he had it in for me good and proper."

"Do you think you might have deserved it?" Katherine asked. "What happened on Saturday was disgraceful."

"What am I supposed to do when me and my friends get jumped by some mob from Liverpool? Stand there and let them give us a good kicking?"

They reached the street. Katherine waved down a passing taxi. As Archie held open the door for her, she

208

said to Barnhill, "This is where we part company, Raymond. If you come by the Eagle building later this evening, I'll have your money."

"I'll be there at five-thirty." He stood at the curb, watching the taxi move away before hailing one for himself.

Once the taxi containing Katherine, Archie Waters, and his grandson reached Fleet Street, the three passengers went separate ways. Archie resumed his position on the elevator, Brian went to the Mercury Messengers office, which was housed in a garage a hundred yards from the Eagle building, and Katherine visited the accounts department, where she took an advance against her monthly salary to cover the money she had borrowed from Raymond Barnhill.

When she returned to the news department, Lawrie Stimkin was waiting for her. "Got lots and lots of names, have we?"

"And sentences to go with them."

"Good. Let's pillory these antisocial monsters."

Katherine typed a lead paragraph, followed by names and charges she'd taken from the court list, and the corresponding sentences. She handed in the finished copy, stayed around long enough to see if the subeditors wanted anything clarified, then telephoned through to Gerald Waller's office.

"Tell him," she said, when the editor's secretary claimed her boss was busy, "that I need to speak to him very urgently."

Waller came on the line. "What is it, Katherine?"

"I know how to get into the minds of these football maniacs. One of them works for Mercury. Brian Waters, Archie's grandson. He got fined two hundred and fifty pounds today."

"What makes you think he'll cooperate?"

"Because I paid most of the fine for him."

"I can give you ten minutes."

"That'll be fine." She made calls to the lobby and to

209

Mercury Messengers. Five minutes later, Archie brought his grandson up to the editorial floor. Katherine was waiting by the elevator. "I don't care whether you got those cuts and bruises by defending yourself or not," she told Brian. "We're going in to see the editor, where you will sell yourself as the biggest hooligan and most violent football fan who ever lived."

Brian looked at her as though she were mad. "What on earth for? I'll lose my job."

"Remember this: right now, you owe me your job. If I hadn't paid the fine, you'd be serving the first day of a thirty-day prison term. And your job would not be waiting for you when you got out." Having put Brian in his place, she softened her tone. "I promise that you won't lose your job. You might even become something of a hero at the *Eagle,* by helping us to learn something about all this lunacy."

Katherine could see distaste on Gerald Waller's face as she accompanied Brian into his office. The editor was not accustomed to receiving visitors who had just pleaded guilty to assault and battery. Waller greeted the young messenger with "Why do you do it, Brian? What big thrill do you find in fighting?"

Brian launched into his performance. "Well, it's to prove our team, the Arsenal, is better than their team."

"Surely that's decided on the field of play."

"Our supporters, then. We prove our supporters are tougher than the pansies who follow them."

"Who's 'them'?"

"Every other team." Brian took a couple of swaggering steps around the editor's office. "Highbury's our turf. North Bank, that's where we rule."

"North Bank," Waller repeated. He'd seen the two words painted on countless walls throughout London. "The North Bank is that part of the stadium where the hard men stand, is it?"

Brian's swagger increased. "Where *we* stand."

Katherine decided it was time to take control. "Brian

210

understands that without our help today, he'd be behind bars right now. To repay us, he's willing to introduce us into his circle of friends. If we spend time with them, we'll be in the best position to do what our chairman told us to do this morning: climb right into their minds, and learn what makes them tick. At the very least, we'll get a solid human-interest series."

"You want me to pull you out of news and put you on a special assignment, is that it?"

Katherine nodded. "I won't do another Skrone Motors."

Waller glanced at Brian. "These friends of yours, how much danger will Mrs. Kassler be in?"

"Absolutely none. They'll do whatever I say."

In that moment, Katherine decided that Brian was not acting. What she saw now was him; the outraged martyr she'd seen in court had been the act. "I'll also want Sid Hall," she told Waller. "Besides being a good photographer, his presence always makes me feel safer."

Waller gave his approval to the assignment. Once outside the editor's office, Katherine turned on Brian. "So, your friends will do whatever you say, will they? What happened to the poor little lad who was only defending himself?"

"I bent the truth a little bit."

"To whom? To Mr. Waller, or to the magistrates?"

Brian flashed a devilish grin. "Surely it's less of a crime to lie to the magistrates than it is to lie to the editor of the *Daily Eagle*."

"You lied under oath. That's perjury."

"Beats going to jail."

They reached the elevator. As Brian summoned the car, Katherine said, "Count yourself lucky you're not my son. Never mind being in jail for thirty days — you wouldn't be able to sit on your moped for thirty days!"

Brian gave Katherine an even cheekier grin, and stuck out his bottom. "Go ahead, I dare you."

"Don't push your luck." She turned away as the

211

elevator door slid back. Brian Waters was as fresh as they came, but in that freshness there was something she could not help liking.

At precisely five-thirty, as Katherine was preparing to leave for the day, a shadow fell across her desk. She looked up to see Raymond Barnhill. Over his sportcoat and jeans, he wore a lined Burberry raincoat. Another part of the American uniform, Katherine reflected; where would good old Burberry's be without Americans?

"Come for your money?"

"That would be nice."

"Here." She pulled a white envelope from her desk drawer and slid it across to him. "One hundred and eighty pounds."

"That's just the principal. Where's the interest?"

"Interest on a one-hour loan?"

"I'm American, remember? We have people shooting each other on the streets, and the country's run by the Mafia. In that kind of environment, would you seriously expect there to be such a thing as an interest-free loan?"

"If I buy you a drink at El Vino's, will that be interest enough?" She had no date with John Saxon that night, nor was she in any rush to get home. That seemed to be the pattern of her life at the moment: work, a couple of secretive trysts with Saxon each week, and play with the children on the weekends. One day she'd have to get a grip on herself again, reorganize her life into a sensible routine. Only right now, there was too much flux for her to even try.

Barnhill smiled, and checked his watch. "I'd love to, Katherine, but some other time. The International Press Agency's a hard taskmaster, and I've got another assignment before I can call it quits today." Without counting the money, he slipped the envelope into his raincoat pocket. "See you around," he said with a cheerful wave, and walked quickly across the editorial floor to the elevator.

Watching him go, Katherine felt slightly disappointed. She would have enjoyed having a drink with Raymond Barnhill. He was attractive, personable, and different from the other men she knew.

Then she looked up at the gray-painted ceiling and asked God why she was even thinking such crazy thoughts. Wasn't her life complicated enough, without adding to the turmoil?

1O

Soccer specials were trains put on by British Rail to carry supporters from one city to another when their team played on the road. The round-trip fare was a fraction of the regular fare, and the original premise of such trains had been to assist genuine supporters to follow their favorites around the country without bankrupting themselves. Unfortunately, the disruptive element also appreciated cheap fares. They soon took over, and the trains became known colloquially as the skinhead specials.

The soccer special from London's Euston station to Birmingham was scheduled to leave at midday on Saturday. "No mention is ever made of the special on any of the departure boards," Sid Hall told Katherine as they parked close to the station, "because British Rail doesn't want any decent member of the public boarding the train by mistake."

"Who told you that?" Katherine asked, laughing.

"So help me, it's true," Hall said hotly, but he refused to tell where he had acquired such information. Katherine thought he was inventing it all—a joke to ease the tension before going into battle.

It was eleven-twenty when Katherine and Hall entered the station. The *Eagle* photographer wore corduroy trousers, a thick sweater, and a tweed sportcoat; a brace of Nikons hung from one shoulder. Katherine fended off the brisk early March wind with leather pants, high boots, and a sheepskin jacket over a cashmere sweater. Her silky blond hair was tucked securely into a French braid, and on her head was a red-and-white woolen hat.

The young supporters who would be riding the soccer special north to Birmingham were already gathering. Many wore the red and white of their team, rosettes and badges pinned to clothing, scarves knotted around waists. As they waited to board their own train, another soccer special arrived; this one carried northern fans come to watch their team play in London. The two sets of supporters clashed. Hall took photographs of the police moving in immediately to pick up the ringleaders.

Brian Waters arrived fifteen minutes before midday. He was accompanied by five other youths, all dressed alike in warm, zippered jackets. Brian rattled off names as though he was in a race: "Roger, Pat, Joe, Terry, Steve." While Katherine tried to join names to faces, Brian pointed to her hat and laughed. "You'd better get rid of that. Makes you a right target, it does."

"And the scarves you and your friends are wearing don't make you targets?"

"We know how to look after ourselves."

"And I can look after Mrs. Kassler," Sid Hall said.

"No." Brian shook his head vehemently. "My grandpa had a fit when he found out you were coming with us. Said he'd throw me out if anything happened to you. You're my responsibility."

Everyone was concerned about this trip, Katherine thought. Gerald Waller, Archie, and especially her father. Roland Eagles had exploded when he'd learned of the assignment. He had called Katherine into the office he used in the Eagle building, closed the door, and demanded in low but dangerous tones, "Who the hell do you think you are to request such a dangerous assignment? A war correspondent?"

"You're the one who said fan violence was a legitimate social issue, and we should find out all we could about it."

"Yes, but I never intended you to be party to this lunacy."

Then Katherine had played her trump card. "I think it's the best idea you've ever had regarding the *Eagle*. I want to do it, and if you won't let me do it for the *Eagle*, then I'll damned well do it for another paper on the street!"

The shriek of the guard's whistle split the air. "Better get on if we're going," Brian said.

Katherine turned toward the train. Every window along its entire length had someone leaning out of it. A few wolf whistles were directed at her; other window hangers were yelling to friends, or shouting abuse at regular passengers who came within hailing distance. Brian and his friends climbed into the coach, and formed a flying wedge to clear a path for Katherine and Hall.

"If you can't find a seat, darling," a fat young man with long red hair yelled at Katherine, "you can always sit here." He patted his lap. "Just watch you don't sit on my broomstick and snap it in half." He roared with laughter at his own wit; two friends, sharing the table with him, joined in, shouting, "Good one, Ginger! Good one!"

Sid Hall moved quickly, but Brian was much faster. "You apologize for that."

"I what?" Ginger looked around him. Brian and his allies formed a semicircle from which there was no escape. "Sorry, miss," he practically whispered.

"That's better. Now show some manners," Brian said, in a tone that reminded Katherine uncannily of his grandfather, "and give up your seat to the lady."

Ginger rose to his feet and walked away, motioning

with his head for his friends to follow. Brian made a sweeping gesture with his hand. Katherine and Hall sat down. Brian and his friend named Roger joined them. The remaining four members of Brian's group took the table on the other side of the aisle, after intimidating the people already sitting there into leaving.

As the train pulled out of Euston, police officers began patrolling. A red-faced sergeant stopped by the table where Katherine sat. "Are you quite certain you belong here, miss?"

Before Katherine could assure the policeman, Brian said, " 'Course she does. I take my mother to football every week."

"Your mother?" The policeman was smiling.

"And that's my dad." Brian pointed at Hall.

"And they're all your brothers, right?" The sergeant indicated Brian's friends.

"No. Those pansies are my sisters."

"Thought I spotted a family resemblance. Your sisters are all bloody ugly, just like you."

"Cheek!" Brian exclaimed.

"I'm with the *Daily Eagle,*" Katherine told the policeman. "After all the trouble last week, we're trying to learn something about the causes."

"Good luck. If you find out anything, you'll be the first." He looked down at Brian. "Seems like you've picked yourself a good guide, miss."

Katherine stretched the truth. "He's also with the *Eagle.*"

"Really? Well, be careful, all of you. And enjoy the game." He moved away, carrying on a bantering conversation with each group of fans he passed.

"He thought I was a reporter, didn't he?" Brian said, with no little pride.

"You?" Roger scoffed. "You couldn't report a flea crawling up your leg. All you do for the paper is ride around on your moped and deliver stuff."

"What work do you do?" Katherine asked Roger.

Some of Roger's cockiness disappeared. "I'm unemployed."

"Tell her how you lost your job," Brian urged.

"I was an apprentice plumber, before I got sent away for three months after some trouble at West Ham. There was no job waiting for me when I got out."

"What about your other friends?" Katherine asked.

Brian jerked a thumb across the aisle. "Pat and Joe are working, laborers on building sites. Terry and Steve, they're on the dole as well. Smile, lads," he added as he saw Hall aiming a Nikon toward the other group.

Katherine began to understand the social order that existed here. The other five youths were either unemployed or held menial jobs. Brian, who had worked continuously at Mercury Messengers for eighteen months, had established himself as their leader. And even then, what did he really have?

Accompanied by Sid Hall, and under the watchful eye of police officers, Katherine walked along the length of the train. Many of the fans were playing cards, or reading comic books and soccer magazines. She stopped to talk to several. All seemed friendly, and the moment they saw Hall's cameras, they began to ham it up. They talked willingly about their backgrounds, their work, if any, but mostly they wanted to talk about their team. Katherine just nodded as players' names were spoken with a reverence befitting royalty.

Shortly before the train reached Birmingham, Katherine and Hall returned to their seats. It was quite obvious now to Katherine that the entire train was filled with groups similar to Brian's. Some larger, some smaller, but all with the same vital ingredients. Young men sentenced to unemployment or dead-end jobs, products of poor or broken families in neighborhoods from which there was no escape. Except one, the Saturday afternoon or midweek game, when they could cheer on *their* team. Their rare chance to be a part of something exciting, to identify with a team's success, just as if they were a part of it. Bonded together by that fanatical support, these small groups formed themselves into an army few generals would have been ashamed to lead. Instead of doing battle for King and Country, they waged war on opposing supporters. Their battle flags were the scarves around their waists. Their war cry was the name of their team. And their victory was the total rout of their rivals before the police could step in and stop the flow of blood.

The train pulled into Birmingham. Doors were slammed back long before the train halted. Bodies cascaded to the platform. Within two minutes of arriving, the young fans from London had taken over the station. Numbering nearly a thousand, they marched in a tight military formation, heavy boots and shoes striking concrete with a steady, fear-inspiring cadence.

Outside the station, police waited to escort the visitors over the long walk to the stadium. Brian's group was at the head. He chatted happily with the police inspector in charge of the escort, turning on the charm at will. "We really appreciate you blokes showing us the way like this. Otherwise we might get lost, get into right trouble in a place like this. Look at them, will you . . . ?" Brian pointed with his chin toward half a dozen crop-haired youths standing on a street corner, who wore the colors of the local team. "If you and your men weren't here, superintendent, that lot would make mincemeat out of us."

"Stop promoting me, sonny. I'm just an inspector. And I don't believe for one moment that any of our home-grown tearaways could last a round with any of you London boys."

"Glory me! What do you think we are — football hooligans?" Brian affected such shock and indignation that everyone around him, including the police inspector, burst out laughing.

Katherine increased her pace to walk alongside the

inspector. She had removed her woolen hat and felt less conspicuous. She introduced herself, switched on a portable tape recorder, and held out the microphone. "How long have you had this detail, inspector?"

"Escorting the visiting fans? A few years, miss."

"Has the vandalism become worse in that time?"

The inspector scratched his chin thoughtfully. "I'd say it's become more organized. Used to be just a few hotheads blowing off steam, but now there seems to be some moving force behind it. Not with just one group of fans; with all of them. And . . . well, I may be wrong, but I think it's become more of a racial thing."

"Racial. How do you mean?"

"In the old days, the shouts and songs were obscene but harmless. Nowadays, there's a lot of picking on the colored players. Mind you, we have more colored players in the game than we used to, so that might account for it."

Another group of policemen waited at the stadium, formed into two lines between which the London fans had to pass. Spot checks were made, fans pulled out and summarily frisked. Directly in front of Katherine, a young man was searched. A metal comb was confiscated. When Katherine asked the reason, the policeman who'd made the search answered, "I've seen more of these combs used for slashing someone across the face, or gouging out an eye, than for straightening hair."

Inside the stadium, the fans who had traveled on the soccer special were steered into a small section of the main stand. A double line of policemen kept them separated from supporters of the home team. The chants began, exhortations and songs punctuated by savage clenched-fist salutes. Scarves were raised above head level to form a swaying blanket of red and white.

In the middle of this pandemonium, ears ringing, senses numbed, stood Katherine and Sid Hall. "You know . . . !" Katherine had to scream to make herself

220

heard. "Marx was wrong. Religion isn't the opium of the masses — sport is!"

Hall panned around with a telephoto lens, selecting faces that best expressed the fanatical hysteria of the occasion. He yelled back at Katherine, "You don't even need to close your eyes to make believe it's 1938, and we're at a Nazi rally in Nuremberg. It's all here — the salutes, the banners, the songs."

The game itself was anticlimactic. The movement of the crowd around them prevented all but the tallest or most determined from seeing anything that was taking place on the field; only snatches of play were visible. A few scuffles broke out, where visiting fans managed to sneak through the police line, but these were soon quelled. Brian Waters and his friends, who surrounded Katherine and Hall like an honor guard, were on their best behavior today.

Suddenly, the game was over. The visiting fans were shepherded out of the stadium, and escorted by police along the lengthy route back to the station and the soccer special that was waiting to return them to London.

"Who won?" Katherine asked Brian.

"Two-two draw. Didn't you watch the game?"

"I couldn't."

"What did you learn for your newspaper story?"

"A little," Katherine answered. "I found out what the atmosphere's like. Terrifying, to sum it up in a single word." Brian laughed at that. "And I also learned that there's a common thread among young soccer fans."

"Oh? What's that then?"

"For most of you, following a team — hoping to share in its successes — is an escape from a life that's grinding you down. Unemployment, broken homes, lousy neighborhoods."

"Not me. Maybe they're all that" — Brian indicated everyone else in the procession, including his five friends — "but not me. I've got a job. I earn. And I live in a decent place."

Katherine spotted her opening. "Then don't you think you should be doing something better with your life than causing trouble at football games?"

"Me cause trouble?" He pointed a finger at himself, the picture of injured innocence.

"Stop the act, Brian. You might be able to pull the wool over the eyes of the provincial police, but I know you better. I've seen you in court. And I saw the way you controlled the situation on the train at Euston this morning. You have leadership qualities, Brian. Now it's up to you to decide whether you use those qualities for good or bad."

The procession reached the station. An instant of chaos ensued when hundreds of exuberant passengers tried to board the train through the nearest door. Police officers, whose humor had not been dented that afternoon by any large-scale trouble, sorted out the mess goodnaturedly. The train pulled out on time.

The same playing cards and magazines came out, but the journey south was quieter than the outward trip had been. The anticipation was missing. The game was over. Now the young fans had time to recuperate. To regain their strength and vocal power for the next contest.

As the train pulled into Euston, a thin, reedy man with a bobbing Adam's apple entered the coach through the communicating door from the next coach. He walked quickly along the aisle, lips moving, right hand continually dipping into his coat pocket, flipping small packets onto the tables as he passed.

Katherine watched him approach. "Wear them at the next game, lads," the man said, tossing a packet onto the table. "Show the flag." Then he was gone.

Brian ripped open the package. Half a dozen circular badges tumbled onto the table. Katherine glanced at one. It featured the Union Jack. What had the man said — show the flag? Then Katherine saw the four words imprinted on the facsimile of the flag: "Niggers back to Africa!"

"Sid, get that fellow!" Katherine urged. She slid out of the seat to allow passage to the photographer. He lunged after the man, who, by this time, had passed into the next coach. But the train was stopping. Doors were being flung open. The man jumped off and disappeared into the crowd of fans spilling out of the train onto the platform. Hall came back, shaking his head.

"Who was he?" Katherine asked Brian.

"British Patriotic League, they call themselves. They've been passing this stuff out for the past couple of months."

"Do you wear it?" Katherine took note of the youths crowding along the aisle toward the door. Some already had the badges pinned to their clothes, sporting them as proudly as the tokens of their team.

"Not me. Stupid stuff, isn't it? I work with colored blokes. Some of them I wouldn't miss if they were shipped back to Africa or wherever, but most of them are all right. Like anyone else, right?" He looked to his friends for approval; they nodded their heads sagely.

"I'm glad to hear that."

Brian gave Katherine his cheeky grin. "Don't want to get my mum mad at me, do I? She might put me over her knee."

Katherine took a swipe at him. Laughing, he ducked back out of range.

Katherine drove from Euston station back to the Eagle building. She had arranged to share a few hours with John Saxon that night. The property developer was spending part of it in London before leaving for his country home, and Katherine had created the time for the date by telling her own family that she would be returning late from Birmingham. Before she met

Saxon, though, she wanted to do some speedy research.

The *Eagle* file on Britain's right-wing political groups was extensive. Old and new, some extinct, but more, if not actually flourishing, at least with warm blood running through their veins. And others still that were spin-offs of earlier groups, splits formed over ideological differences, schisms over hatreds that were not violent enough.

Her eyes ran through the list: the National Front, the British National Party, National Party, British Movement, Column 88 (a particularly sick group, Katherine decided upon reading that the numbers signified the corresponding letters in the alphabet — H.H., the initials for *Heil Hitler*), SS Wotan, another group steeped in Nordic superstition and the Hitler myth of Aryan supremacy, the League of St. George, Racial Preservation Society, the Northern League. The smaller, lesser-known groups that she could be forgiven for never having heard of: the Action Party, Britannia Party, the National Independence Party, the National Assembly. And even more that used the words National Socialist in their title.

Good God, she thought, just how many of these lunatic fringe organizations are out there? It was even more frightening to know that just as many must exist on the other side of the political spectrum, the fanatical left-wing crazies. But nowhere could she find any mention of the British Patriotic League. It was either too new to be included — or else it had done nothing to bring itself to the *Eagle*'s attention, yet. . . .

She turned up at John Saxon's Marble Arch home at twenty minutes after eight. He opened the door, saw the red-and-white hat perched gaily on her head, and asked, "Did your team win?"

"Never mind that. I've learned what I'm sure you'll agree is a very interesting tidbit."

"I'll agree to anything, but not on an empty stomach."

Katherine sniffed the air. "Do I smell cooking?" She followed the tantalizing aroma to the half-open kitchen door.

"I ordered dinner in, for eight o'clock. You're late. If it's ruined, it's your fault."

Katherine entered the kitchen. On a heated serving table stood a saucepan of boeuf bourguignon. "The perfect dish for a cold night," Saxon said. "The restaurant even gave me directions on how to serve it."

"Never mind," Katherine told him. "You pour the wine. I'll attend to this."

While Saxon uncorked a bottle of Chambertin, Katherine took plates, cutlery, and napkins from cupboards. She thought about using the formal dining room, but it seemed too big for just two people. Instead, she selected the drawing room at the back of the house, setting the food on a low table, and pulling up two ottomans. She lit the gas fire that had, in the name of modernization, supplanted the genuine coal fire in the hearth, and turned down the lights.

Saxon poured the burgundy into glasses. Sitting in front of the fire, they toasted each other before turning to the meal.

"Find out the name of the chef," Katherine said between delicious mouthfuls. "Put him in charge of catering at the Chiltern Towers and you'll run Hilton out of business."

Once the meal was finished, Katherine collected the dirty dishes. "Leave them," Saxon ordered. He poured more wine, then sat down on the floor, face to the fire, back against a chair.

Katherine sat next to him. "Stomach full?"

Saxon nodded sleepily. "Tell me your tidbit. See whether I agree that it's interesting."

Briefly, she described the northbound journey on the soccer special, the police-escorted march to and from the stadium, and the game itself. "On the return journey, the strangest thing happened. This odd-looking man, all skin and bone and Adam's apple, walked through the train giving these out." She reached behind for her sheepskin jacket, and pulled out the badge.

"The Union Jack? What's so strange about that? Probably some nut case who's still living in Kipling's time."

"Look closer."

Saxon squinted in the dim light. "Very nice, but then I always said that the strangest people attended football games."

She took back the badge. "Brian Waters said that the man who handed these things out belonged to something called the British Patriotic League."

"Never heard of it."

"Neither had I. I looked up the name at the *Eagle*. We have information on every bunch of right-wing lunatics except the British Patriotic League."

"That's because it's probably not worth being included. The British *Patriotic* League. God, what a joke of a name!"

"Patriotic," Katherine repeated. "Just how many rogues throughout history have hidden behind that word?"

"Precisely." He touched her thigh, running his hand down the smooth brown leather of her pants until he reached the top of her boot. "This outfit is as sexy as all hell, but aren't you baking to death in it?"

"I dressed this morning for the cold."

"Be comfortable. Take them off."

She stretched out one leg at a time. Saxon tugged off her high boots. Contented sighs escaped as he massaged her toes, then her ankles and calves. She unfastened her belt, opened the top button of her leather pants. "John, there's something I have to know."

His hands halted on her calves. "What?"

"Do you want me for my body? My mind? Or just for my interesting tidbit?"

There was something about John Saxon, Katherine decided, that inspired trust. Almost two years earlier, when Saxon's name had first surfaced, Roland Eagles had said he had the ability to sell freezers to Eskimos in midwinter. But that had been the superficial Saxon, the man Katherine had first known, and had both liked and disliked.

The real John Saxon, the man she knew now, the man to whom she regularly made exquisitely satisfying love, was a different person altogether. He was an intelligent man, sharp yet compassionate. He understood what went on around him, in his own business, and in the world in general. Which was why Katherine was especially glad to hear him downplay the importance of the British Patriotic League. That and the lack of any mention in the *Eagle* file made her confident that the League presented little or no threat.

That was on Saturday night. The blissful confidence lasted only until Tuesday. Suffering from a headache, she returned home from the *Eagle* in midafternoon. Only Edna Griffiths was in the house. Jimmy Phillips had driven Franz to the hospital for a routine examination. Joanne was playing at a friend's home, and Henry was still at school. After taking two aspirin with a strong cup of tea, Katherine went to her bedroom to lie down. After an hour, she was rudely awakened by shouting.

"Take that off at once!" Edna's angry voice carried all the way from the ground floor. "God help you if your mother sees you wearing that!"

Katherine threw on a robe and went downstairs. "God help who if I see what?"

Edna and Henry stood facing each other in the kitchen. "This," the housekeeper said, handing Katherine a dreadfully familiar badge. "Had this pinned to his lovely uniform, he did."

227

"Where did you get this badge?"

"From Alan Taylor, a big boy at school. I gave him ten pence for it."

John Saxon and the *Eagle* were both wrong. The British Patriotic League was alive and well, and doing its recruiting everywhere.

It was six o'clock in the evening when Franz returned with Jimmy Phillips from the hospital. He sensed tension the instant he entered the house.

"Where is everyone?" he asked Edna Griffiths, whom he found in the kitchen preparing dinner.

"Joanne's at a friend's house. Henry was sent to his room by Mrs. Kassler."

"Where is she?"

"She had to go to Henry's school. She should be home at any moment." Before Franz could ask more questions, Edna said, "I'll let Mrs. Kassler tell you everything when she returns."

Franz had barely settled in the television room when he heard the crunch of gravel beneath the Stag's tires. The driver's door slammed, followed by the house door. Katherine's footsteps echoed along the hall. Franz called her name.

"Why did you have to visit Henry's school?"

"I wanted to see his headmaster. I wanted to learn how something as disgusting as this" — she handed him the badge — "came to be in Henry's possession."

Franz studied the badge. "What did the headmaster say?"

"He wasn't there. I made an appointment to see him first thing tomorrow morning."

"I will come with you to the school."

Katherine saw a change sweep over Franz. The wall came tumbling down. His son had been touched by filth, and Franz would not tolerate that.

"You should not have sent Henry to his room,

Katherine. He is too young to understand the meaning of this badge. Bring him down now; let me talk to him."

Thrilled by the transformation, Katherine raced up the stairs to Henry's bedroom. "Your father wants to speak to you."

In the television room, Henry sat uncertainly in front of Franz. "What do you think this badge means?" Franz asked.

"I thought it was the British flag."

"The words — what do you think the words mean?"

"I don't know," the young boy answered.

"They are evil words, Henry, because they single out a group of people who have skins of a different color. You do not judge people by their color. You judge them by their acts. Do you understand?"

The boy nodded solemnly.

"Promise your mother and me that you will never wear anything like this again."

"I promise, Daddy."

Franz smiled, and Katherine imprinted the expression on her memory. She had waited ages for this moment of closeness. It was just too bad that something as sick as the British Patriotic League badge had to be responsible.

Early the following morning, Katherine rode with Franz and Jimmy Phillips to the school. While Phillips helped Franz from the car to the wheelchair, Katherine climbed to the second floor, where the headmaster's study was located.

Katherine had met Adrian Heath before, a tall, thin man with sandy hair and a ginger moustache. He rose from behind his desk to greet his visitor. "Good morning, Mrs. Kassler. The message I received was that you wanted to see me urgently. I trust that nothing is wrong."

"Only this, Mr. Heath. Another of your students, a boy called Alan Taylor, sold this disgusting object to my son." She showed Heath the badge. "My husband is also here, as upset about this incident as I am. He would like to see you, but unfortunately he's in a wheelchair."

"There is an office downstairs we can use."

A secretary was stationed outside the headmaster's study. Heath instructed her to locate the boy named Alan Taylor. Then he accompanied Katherine downstairs to where Franz waited. Heath led the way to a small office where, five minutes later, a fresh-faced, fair-haired boy of twelve was shown in.

"Alan, have you ever seen this before?" Heath asked.

The boy answered in tones that would have turned an elocution teacher green with envy. "Some chap gave it to me at a football game, sir. I was showing it around, and Henry Kassler offered to buy it from me."

"What game was this?" Katherine asked. She could not imagine this boy traveling on the skinhead special.

"The local amateur team. Some of us go from the school on Saturday afternoon."

"Alan's a boarder here," Heath explained.

"Could you describe the man who gave this to you?"

The boy shrugged. "He was wearing a beige raincoat, that's all I remember. What is all the fuss about?"

The answer came from Franz. "Firstly, you sold this to my son, and I do not want him to have it. Secondly, I am German. I know what happened in my country when garbage like this was circulated, when feelings were stirred up, when scapegoats were sought for national ills. It sickens me to see the same evil minds at work in this country."

The boy tried to hold the gaze of the man in the wheelchair. After five seconds, he turned away, his determination no match for those blazing blue eyes.

"You may go, Alan," Heath said softly. He watched the boy leave, then turned to his visitors. "I do apologize. I am appalled that one of my students should have been in possession of such a reprehensible object, and I will take steps to ensure that it does not happen again."

In the Jaguar on the journey home, Katherine leaned over the front passenger seat, put her arms gently around Franz's neck, and kissed him. "You were wonderful back there. I've never heard such a powerful message given in so few words."

Franz opened the glove compartment and popped up the mirror so he could see Katherine in the back of the car. "The message was also for you."

"Me?"

"This is what you should be doing on your newspaper. You should be learning what is behind this hatred."

"That's what I am doing. I've seen those badges before. I know what organization is behind them. I know how they recruit. And so help me, before all this is over, I'm going to pull back the rock they hide under and expose them for all to see."

"Brava!" Franz shouted, and burst into happy laughter.

Always accompanied by Sid Hall, Katherine visited stadiums across England. In the space of a few weeks, the *Daily Eagle* pair traveled on soccer specials to such diverse places as the port city of Southampton in the south, and Manchester, Leeds, and Newcastle in the north. The regular riders came to know them. So did the police who patrolled the specially scheduled trains.

At some of the games, Katherine spotted men she assumed were members of the British Patriotic League giving out badges that displayed the Union Jack. Once, she confronted one of them, a young, dark-haired man whose arm she grabbed as he hurried past.

"How long have you been in the BPL?" she asked.

"What's it to you?"

"What do you hope to achieve?"

"What do you think? Make it a decent country in which British people will be proud to live."

"Decent? Do you know how to spell the word?" She

231

held onto the man's arm just long enough for Hall to take his picture.

The result of Katherine's work was a series of articles in the *Eagle* on the young fans who traveled around the country. Carrying Katherine's byline, the series fell between circulation-boosting human interest and serious sociological study. She wrote about the frequently poor backgrounds of the young men, the intense loyalty to their team, and their need for an identity — to be a part of something. She finished by describing the crowds at the games as an extended family, one which the youths preferred over the broken and unhappy families from which they all too often came.

Features on the supporters, however, were not enough. When Katherine had first learned of the British Patriotic League's recruiting campaign, and had seen her own son with one of the loathsome badges, she had promised Gerald Waller that she would deliver a story connecting the League with soccer's violent fans. By mid-April, with only a few weeks remaining to the season, she was nowhere near fulfilling that promise.

On the credit side, she had learned something about the British Patriotic League, not that there was very much to learn. The League had been formed only a year earlier by three men, none of whom had any connection with the older, more established extremist parties. These three men were all newcomers. The chairman of the League was Alan Venables, a former college lecturer on government and politics. His two colleagues were men called Trevor Burns and Neville Sharpe. Burns was a free-lance writer, and Sharpe was, by profession, a chartered accountant. The League's head office — and, as far as Katherine could see, its only office at the present time — was a shopfront in the rough dockland district of West Ham.

That was all credit. On the debit side, she had nothing but her own word and her own gut feeling that this new extremist group was conducting a recruiting campaign among soccer crowds.

"Your own word," Gerald Waller told her during a meeting in his office, "and your own gut feeling are not enough to hang a story on. You, above all people, should know that you need more proof than that."

The reminder of the way she'd been duped over Skrone Motors stung Katherine. "I'll get it," she answered tartly.

"Where? And, most importantly, when? You've been on this football-violence theme for weeks, and all you've succeeded in doing is a series of features which show these young hooligans as . . . as . . ." In exasperation, Waller stubbed out a freshly lit cigarette in the ashtray on his desk. "Damn it, Katherine, you've made the bastards almost sympathetic."

"Isn't that the aim of a writer?"

"It's the aim of a fiction writer. If you're writing a novel, a sympathetic character is a top priority. But not if you're writing news. Good Lord, Katherine, we'd never have hanged Christie or Lord Haw Haw if you'd written about them."

Katherine dismissed mass murderer and wartime traitor by saying, "Before my time, Gerry. All before my time."

"But not before mine. Or before our chairman's. Who, incidentally, remarked to me only this morning that the initial rise in circulation seems to have leveled out. In other words, the readers are losing interest in your angle. Like me, he probably wants to know when we're going to hear exactly why this hate group is recruiting at the games."

"How much longer are you giving me?"

"Two weeks. After that, we're dropping the series."

And back to the news desk, Katherine thought bitterly. After enjoying this taste of freedom, she wasn't sure she would be able to tolerate Lawrie Stimkin. It might be time to decide whether to stay with

Eagle Newspapers or see who else on Fleet Street wanted her.

Fortunately, she never had to make the decision. She spent the evening at home. At ten o'clock, she heard the noisy rattle of a moped coming up the driveway. Before the visitor could ring the bell, Katherine opened the door.

"What is it, Brian?" She could only think that something had happened to his grandfather.

"I've just come from a game. The word was being put around there. The League wants as many people as possible."

"What for?"

"What for?" Brian repeated in amazement. "For the rally, of course."

"What rally?"

"The big anti-immigration rally the British Patriotic League's holding on May Day."

11

Nineteen hundred and seventy-eight was the first year that May Day was celebrated as a statutory holiday in the United Kingdom. It fell on a Monday. Rallies and demonstrations were scheduled throughout the country, some to commemorate this day of the working man, others to promote political aims and ideals. The weather chose not to cooperate. A drenching rain fell all day, causing the outright cancellation of many gatherings. At other meeting points, only the committed turned out, their sodden banners dripping rain onto bedraggled heads.

One demonstration, though, went ahead precisely as planned. In the racially tense South London suburb of Brixton, the British Patriotic league rally proceeded without a hitch. Two thousand marchers gathered at midday, all young men, all tough. All unaffected by the downpour that had ruined the assemblies of lesser men. Under a scattering of damp Union Jacks, these young members of the British Patriotic League lined up in rigid military formation. The professionally printed placards they held so defiantly against the rain called for the repatriation of immigrants. At their head, standing on a wooden platform, was a tall, thin man in a military-style raincoat. He had a gaunt, pale face with a beaky nose and stringy brown hair that the rain had plastered to his white scalp. He was flanked by two similarly dressed men. One held a large Union Jack. The other held an equally large triangular flag that depicted a flaming sword against the background of the red cross of St. George.

"The one in the middle is Alan Venables," Katherine told Sid Hall as they stood at the front of a large crowd of spectators. "The heavy man with the Union Jack, he's Trevor Burns. And the bald chap with the other flag, that's Neville Sharpe."

"Really fancy flag," Hall said. "What is it?"

A police sergeant, one of the very large police contingent on duty at the rally, identified the pennant. "That's the British Patriotic League's flag. Gaudy piece of work, isn't it?"

"Thanks." Hall raised his Nikon, looked through the telephoto lens, and captured the image of the League's leaders.

"Do you expect trouble?" Katherine asked the sergeant. She nodded toward a double police line, behind which opponents of the League had gathered.

"We always expect trouble, miss, but the rain's keeping tempers cool at the moment. Wish we'd get some thunder and lightning as well, then they might all pack up and go home."

Katherine turned back to the League rally. She had no doubt that these were the same young men she had seen at soccer stadiums, and on the special trains around the country. The League had recruited, and today the recruits had loyally answered the summons.

On the platform, flanked by the flags of his country and his extremist movement, Alan Venables began to speak. His voice was loud and clear, the delivery crisp. "All through history, great nations have been racially pure. Great white nations, great yellow nations, and" — the conjunction was weighted, pulling the listeners into the next phrase — "even great black nations. But there has never been, and there will never be, a great mongrel nation! That is what we, in Britain, are in danger of becoming! A third-rate, amoral, mongrel nation!"

On cue, the two thousand League members began to applaud. Chants of "Britain . . . white!" pierced the rain. Clenched-fist salutes speared the air.

"Our glory, our history, and our heritage have all been based on the white race," Venables continued. "Our downfall, our slump toward the garbage heap of the world, has only come about since we began diluting our purity with colored immigration! They do not belong here, and if we are to survive, they must not remain here!" Venables folded his arms across his chest and listened to the growing adulation.

At the first signs of it fading, he held up a hand. The applause stopped immediately. When he spoke again, his voice was soft, yet each word was loaded with meaning for the faithful. "The *Great* in Great Britain was never supposed to be the meaningless noun it has become. It was always intended to be a proud and true adjective. An adjective to describe Britain's place in the world. We have the opportunity now to rectify the damage committed by generations of traitorous politicians."

Venables's voice began to rise, a carefully contrived ascent toward hysteria. "We have the opportunity now to be the generation that makes *Great* an adjective once again!" The League chairman's right hand snapped into a clenched-fist salute. "We are British! We are Patriots! We are"—two thousand soaking wet young men joined in a rousing chorus—"the British Patriotic League!"

Before the roar could fade, it was eclipsed by a thunderous outpouring of rage. The double line of police broke. Hundreds of counterdemonstrators poured through the gap. The League's formation scattered. Flags became spears. Chains and brass knuckles appeared. A bottle flew through the air, trailing smoke behind it. Katherine saw the bottle smash against the side of a police car and explode in a burst of orange flame.

"Sid!" Above the tumult, she heard her own panic-stricken voice. "Let's get back to the car and get out of here!" She grabbed his arm and tried to pull him toward the white Triumph Stag parked only fifty yards away.

The photographer shrugged aside her plea with a curt "Wait a damned minute!" He had his camera up, aiming right into the middle of the battleground which the street had become. Police with dogs jumped from waiting vans, but there was nothing they could do to control a situation that had gotten out of hand with terrifying swiftness.

"For God's sake, Sid!" Katherine screamed. "How many more photographs do you need?" Two more Molotov cocktails arced through the air. One exploded harmlessly against a brick wall. The other, thrown by some herculean arm, soared over the heads of the crowd to land in the middle of a line of parked cars.

Again, Katherine tried. She knocked the camera away from Hall's face. "Come on! Let's get out of here!"

Hall swung around. The movement, possibly, saved his life. A half brick that would surely have smashed into the center of his face caught him a glancing blow on the cheek. He fell to the ground, dazed. Katherine screamed his name. She knelt beside him, trying to staunch the flow of blood with the silk scarf she had worn beneath her leather coat. Her anguished cries for help went unheeded; the police had their hands full.

A series of explosions came from the line of cars where the firebomb had landed, gas tanks erupting to fuel the inferno even more. Katherine heard sirens. Police, fire, ambulance, she had no idea. Then came another noise—the revving of a car engine, the frenzied, nonstop honking of a horn. An American-accented voice yelled, "Get in, damn it! And hurry!"

Katherine looked up to see a white BMW. "I can't move him by myself!"

The driver's door of the BMW flew open. Raymond Barnhill jumped out, ran to where Hall lay, and grabbed the semiconscious photographer under the arms to half-drag, half-carry him to the car. Katherine piled into the rear seat with Hall, pressing the blood-soaked scarf to his cheek. Barnhill slid back into the driver's seat, threw the BMW into gear, and roared away.

"What happened to your friend?" Barnhill asked.

"A brick hit him. He was lucky not to be killed." The BMW swerved to avoid a line of burning cars. Katherine's mouth dropped in shock and horror. "My car! That's my blasted car!"

"Which one?"

"The one on fire!"

"They're all on fire!"

"The Stag!" She swung around in the seat as the BMW sped past. The Stag's soft top had burned away; the interior was a mass of flame.

"Claim it on your expenses," Barnhill said, followed by a more meaningful "Just be grateful you weren't sitting in it."

Full consciousness returned to Sid Hall. He groaned loudly and clutched a hand to his face. "What happened?"

"You stayed around for one photograph too many," Katherine told him rather unsympathetically. She looked from Hall to Barnhill. "What were you doing in Brixton?"

"Covering the rally for my agency. I thought I'd seen you. When the trouble started, I legged it back to my car. Something made me come looking for you."

"Thank you. I'm glad you did."

Barnhill grinned at her in the mirror. "Quite some group back there, eh?"

Katherine said nothing. Barnhill knew about Britain's violent soccer supporters. If he read newspapers, he must also know about the series she'd been writing. She waited to see if he had come up with the same connection she had made.

"Reminded me of Klan rallies I've covered in the States," the wire-service reporter said.

"Maybe they'll dress up in bedsheets and hoods, and wave burning crosses the next time," Katherine told him. "Just so you won't feel too homesick." As the BMW approached the River Thames at Vauxhall Bridge, she asked, "Where are we going?"

"Victoria. Stop off at my apartment first. You and your photographer can get yourselves together before I drive you to the Eagle building."

Barnhill lived on a spacious fourth floor apartment in Dolphin Square, overlooking the Thames. The living room was furnished in a stark modern style. There were two bedrooms. The door of the master bedroom was closed. The second bedroom was open. Through the doorway, Katherine could see a chair, a desk, and a typewriter.

Hall went into the bathroom to clean the blood from his face. He returned five minutes later, a patch of adhesive tape stuck untidily across the wound. "I'll see a doctor after I develop my film," he said to Katherine. "Shall we thank this gentleman for his help and get back to Fleet Street?"

"Wait ten minutes and I'll take you," Barnhill said. "I just put coffee on."

"I'd rather have a double Scotch."

"Can't help you there, I'm afraid."

While Barnhill saw to the coffee, Hall sat down in the living room, eyes watering as pain asserted itself. Katherine stood in the doorway of the second bedroom, looking inside. The typewriter was a portable electric Smith-Corona, plugged into a transformer. Obviously, Katherine thought, Barnhill had brought it with him from the States. Just as obviously, he was as fussy a writer as Katherine was herself. The tall waste-basket was surrounded by crushed balls of white bond — memorials to writing that wasn't quite perfect, and aim that was even worse.

"Coffee's ready," Barnhill said.

Katherine turned around. "Doesn't the International Press Agency give you adequate office space?"

"When I'm at the IPA's Fleet Street office, on IPA time, I write copy for the IPA. Here, in Dolphin Square, where I pay the bills, I try to write the great American novel. It's a safer way of spending leisure time," he added with a quick grin, "than going to an English soccer game."

"While you're living in Britain, you're supposed to be writing the great British novel."

"Not when it's about Vietnam."

Hall and Katherine drank the coffee quickly. Afterward, Barnhill drove them back to the Eagle building, before going on to the International Press Agency office.

Katherine found the *Eagle*'s news department on full alert. The Brixton riot was headline news on every radio station, and the newspapers were playing catch-up. Before she had time to sit down, Gerald Waller sent for her. Lawrie Stimkin was also present when Katherine entered the editor's office. A shortwave radio, tuned to the police band, rattled out latest developments of the riot.

"You were there," Waller said. "How bad was it?"

"The worst thing I've ever seen. Sid was hit in the head with a brick. Thank God he's all right."

"He wasn't the only casualty. More than a hundred people have been taken to the hospital so far."

"Two dozen policemen have been injured," Stimkin added. "And there's considerable property damage."

"Not to mention my car," Katherine threw in for good measure, "which happened to be the landing zone for someone's Molotov cocktail. Look, the evening papers are going to have the latest figures in their lead paragraphs. By tomorrow, it will all be old news. Let the other mornings fill their front pages with a riot story, which they're trying frantically to freshen up with some angle or other. We can do much better than that. The *Eagle* will run the story of the recruiting campaign conducted by the British Patriotic League."

Waller looked pained. "If you could show me one positive piece of proof—"

"Once Sid Hall has today's film printed, he's going to crosscheck the Brixton photographs with photographs he took of the young fans at football games. If we find any matches . . . ?"

"If you find one match," Waller said, "we'll do it your way. If you don't, it becomes a straight news story, updated before press time. You can be sure there'll be government comments."

Katherine returned to her desk to put her notes in order. After thirty minutes, Sid Hall brought a pile of black-and-white photographs still wet from the fixer. In clear focus were the League's three leaders—Alan Venables rousing the masses, Trevor Burns and Neville Sharpe holding the Union Jack and the League pennant. Equally sharp were the pictures of the massed ranks of League supporters, and the street battle that had ensued.

Katherine began to speak. "I thought you were going to check for—"

Hall cut her off by tapping one wet picture with his index finger. "Recognize this lump of lard?"

Katherine stared along the length of Hall's finger to a picture of an overweight young man with long hair. He wore a zippered jacket, and jeans tucked into army boots.

"Pretend it's a color photograph. Give him red hair."

"Ginger!" Katherine almost shouted. "Ginger on the skinhead special at Euston. The first one we ever traveled on."

"That's him, the chivalrous young lad who invited you to sit on his lap."

Katherine closed her eyes for an instant and recalled the scene with vivid accuracy. Two friends had shared the table with him, their laughter turning to fear when challenged by Brian Waters and his little gang. When she opened her eyes again, she saw those friends — in Hall's photograph, standing beside Ginger at the League rally.

"Well?" Hall asked.

Katherine's exuberance dimmed. "Gerry Waller's not going to take my word that I saw these three louts at a football game. He'll want to see pictures of them at the game."

"And so he shall!" With a conjurer's theatrical flourish, Hall produced more photographs. "I shot this when they got up to offer you their seats, after Brian Waters *suggested* they should do so. And here's another one, of the same three characters at the stadium later that day. You can even see the playing field behind them, with the game going on."

"Sid Hall, you are a national treasure!" Katherine threw her arms around his neck and hugged and kissed him. Only when he howled in pain did she realize that, in her gratitude, she had almost ripped the tape clean off his injured cheek.

Katherine was up, showered, and dressed in cords, sweater, and boots, all before the sun had risen the following morning. She tiptoed through the silent house, opened the front door, and stepped outside. For a moment, she wondered why her car was not parked in its usual space. Then she remembered. The graceful Triumph Stag was now a burned-out hulk in Brixton.

Using the Jaguar, she drove to the nearest newspaper shop. Ten minutes later, she was back home, sitting in the breakfast room, comparing the front page of every morning newspaper with the front page of the *Daily Eagle*. Her front page!

The other mornings led with the riot story, updated with the latest details of arrests and injuries, comments from government and opposition spokesmen, and calls for a commission of inquiry. Their reporters had written exactly what Katherine had told Gerald Waller they would write: old news with new angles.

The *Eagle*'s headline, centered over a shallow page-wide picture of League supporters in their military formation, declared, "British Stormtroopers." Some of the faces were ringed and shown again—not at the rally, but at soccer games. Katherine saw the fat young man named Ginger and his two friends, along with half a dozen other matches Sid Hall had found. Even Gerry Waller, Katherine thought excitedly, could not argue with that kind of proof.

The copy was not normal news style, but folksy, chatty . . . the personal touch a teacher might use to drive a lesson home. Savoring the words, Katherine began to read aloud.

"What do football hooligans do when there are no games to watch or disrupt? Why, they attend British Patriotic League rallies to demand that all blacks and Indians and Pakistanis be sent back to where they came from. And just what is the British Patriotic League . . . ?"

"Yes . . . what is it?"

Shocked by the interruption, Katherine spun around. Franz was in his wheelchair, a dressing gown over his pajamas. Behind him was Jimmy Phillips. "I heard you go out and come in again," Franz said. "I rang for Jimmy. I wanted to know what all the excitement was about. Please continue."

Katherine resumed reading. "And just what is the British Patriotic League, this shadowy organization of the far right? It's the latest in a long line of hate groups, only it is more dangerous than some of its less-than-illustrious forerunners. Dangerous, because it has so far managed to perform its work out of the public eye. Dangerous, also, because it has chosen a new method of finding support. Not with street-corner speeches. Not with door-to-door canvassing."

She paused as her audience increased by one more person, Edna Griffiths. Then came the sound of feet hammering on the stairs. When Henry and Joanne pushed their way to the front, the entire household was hanging on Katherine's every word.

"The British Patriotic League has not sought support among traditional areas of unrest, people who fear losing their jobs to immigrants, or having blacks or Asians as neighbors. No, the League has looked among the hopeless, the devil's lost minions. Youths with no future. Young men who have nothing to lose except the chips on their shoulders. The League" — Katherine took a deep breath as she approached the climax of the story — "has sent its recruiting officers onto football-stadium terraces on Saturday afternoons, and they have found the pickings to be lush."

Five-year-old Joanne, a fingertip pressed against her chin, sought help from her seven-year-old brother. "Henry, what is Mummy saying?"

"I don't know." Equally puzzled, Henry gazed at the adults.

Franz provided the answer. "What your mother is saying, what she has written in today's newspaper, is the most important story she has ever done."

Katherine bent down to kiss him. Whoever would have thought that an organization as despicable as the British Patriotic League could have such a silver lining?

Jimmy Phillips drove Katherine to the closest underground station. Every passenger on the train into town was reading the front page of the *Daily Eagle,* and when Katherine entered the Eagle building she found herself the center of attention. Lawrie Stimkin wanted to see her; so did Gerald Waller, who had come in early. Additionally, there were messages asking her to return telephone calls from John Saxon, with whom she was having dinner that evening, and Sally Roberts. She was surprised to find no word from her father. After all, getting into the minds of the violent young supporters had been Roland Eagles's idea, and this was where it had led.

Waller came first. "Your article has stirred up a hornet's nest," the editor told Katherine. "Everyone who's got an ax to grind has been on the radio this morning to rebut your claims. This fellow Venables is being quoted everywhere. He's denying that his group has ever done any recruiting at football grounds, or that the League is actively courting young thugs."

"What about the photographs, for heaven's sake?"

"He claims they're fakes."

"He would. What else?"

"He said that if young people want to join his movement, because they agree with the League's aims, then they're welcome. And as for any newspaper that would carry such scurrilous libel, well, they're just a bunch of communists."

"If it's libel, why doesn't he sue?"

"Because he'd lose." Waller leaned back in his chair and clasped his hands across his stomach. "Katherine, you were right. What you did for the *Daily Eagle* this morning has more than made up for any egg on the face over Skrone Motors. Now, it's time to look ahead. You claimed in the story that the British Patriotic League is more dangerous than the other extremist groups. I think you're right. I want you to keep on at them. Find out what they're up to, and what makes them tick."

"May I have Heather Harvey and Derek Simon back?"

"I think we can afford that."

Next, Katherine saw Lawrie Stimkin. "You may have

noticed that I don't think highly of women reporters," the news editor said. "Real news reporters, I'm talking about, not the giggling, giddy girls who write fashion puffs for the women's pages. Now I'm not saying you've made me completely alter my position—"

Katherine spared Stimkin the pain and embarrassment of continuing. "If you're trying to give me a compliment, Lawrie, I'll take it. To tell you the truth, in the few months I worked for you, I might even have picked up a thing or two."

Stimkin absolutely beamed, and Katherine guessed she was the first woman to ever pay him a compliment.

From the news editor's office, Katherine returned to her own desk, where she telephoned Sally Roberts. "I'm taking you out to lunch," Sally said. "To celebrate your getting back into the good graces of Eagle Newspapers. Be outside at midday."

Katherine replaced the receiver, feeling a mixture of satisfaction and disappointment. Everyone but her father had told her what a great job she had done. She toyed with the idea of telephoning him at the main Adler's store in Regent Street, before deciding against it. Compliments should not have to be requested. They should be forthcoming voluntarily, like all the others had been today. Like Franz telling the children that the story was the most important article their mother had ever written. Even Lawrie Stimkin's grudging admission.

The telephone rang. "Don't you respond to messages any longer?" John Saxon asked.

"I was getting around to you."

"I thought I would have come first."

"You have to stand in line," Katherine said, a shade pompously, "to congratulate me today."

"Congratulate you for what?"

"Don't play games, John. For that story on the British Patriotic League. It's been so successful that I'm on a special assignment to find out all I can about

247

them."

"Really? In that case, the only line I'll join is the one for people who want to tell you what a damned fool you are."

"What?"

"You're a bloody little fool, and do you know why?" Without waiting for any kind of response, Saxon charged straight on. "You asked me several weeks ago if I'd ever heard of this organization. I told you no. They were too small, too insignificant, to even be listed in your file. You certainly changed all that today. What you wrote in this morning's *Eagle,* with all the print, radio, and television exposure that's going to follow . . . well, you've given the British Patriotic League more publicity than it could have got with a ten-million-pound advertising account at Saatchi and Saatchi!"

"How can you call them unimportant when they managed to draw two thousand marchers for yesterday's rally?"

"Because the next time they marched, they would have numbered one thousand, and then five hundred. Even with coverage of the riot, their support would have died. But you, with this big story, you made sure three thousand are going to turn up next time. And when you start this special assignment, and give them greater publicity, you'll have five thousand turning up. Five thousand morons looking to get their names and pictures in the *Daily Eagle.* Congratulations, Katherine."

Saxon's words hurt Katherine. Instinctively, she sought a way to lash back at him. "Damn you, John Saxon! If that's all you have to say to me, let's forget about dinner tonight!" She slammed down the receiver, and sat staring at her typewriter.

It was a childish reaction. A flash of spite, based, perhaps, on the disturbing possibility that Saxon was right. By exposing the League, had Katherine given them reams of free publicity, which might attract more troops to the cause? But there was no way Katherine was going to call Saxon back and tell him that. Tonight, she'd let him stew in his own juice.

At precisely twelve o'clock, Katherine met Sally Roberts outside the main entrance of the Eagle building. The two women walked to the corner of Fleet Street, where Sally hailed a taxi and gave instructions for Hyde Park.

"I thought we were going out for lunch," Katherine said.

Sally gave a mischievous smile. "You'll see."

In Hyde Park, the taxi followed a route that brought it to the Serpentine. A dozen cars were parked on the Serpentine's bank. Sally pointed in the direction of a gleaming silver Porsche with a black convertible top. Directly behind the sports car was a stately old limousine that was very familiar to Katherine.

"Pull up next to the Bentley," Sally told the cab driver.

Katherine spotted Arthur Parsons sitting at the wheel of the Bentley. As the taxi drew alongside, she could see her father in the rear, a fresh red rose in the lapel of his double-breasted navy suit. Leaving Sally to pay the fare, Katherine climbed into the back of the Bentley and kissed her father.

"I thought I was having lunch out with Sally."

"You are. With me as well." Roland indicated a white wicker hamper on the floor of the Bentley. "Peg Parsons was busy all morning preparing this. Arthur brought it from the house, collected me at Adler's, and drove me here."

As Sally joined father and daughter in the Bentley, Parsons opened the driver's door and stepped out. "Half an hour, sir?"

"Half an hour," Roland answered.

Katherine watched Parsons skirt the silver Porsche and begin walking along the bank of the Serpentine.

"This is a lovely surprise — a Mrs. Parsons special lunch smack in the middle of Hyde Park on a sunny spring day."

Roland opened the hamper and withdrew a chilled bottle of Dom Pérignon. Pouring champagne into three glasses, he said, "All morning long, I bet you've been muttering awful things to yourself because you thought I'd forgotten to tell you what a wonderful story you wrote, right?"

Katherine felt herself blushing. "How did you know?"

"After twenty-eight years, I think I know how your mind functions. You did something marvelous, Kathy, and you couldn't understand why I wasn't there to pat you on the back." He tipped his glass toward her. "Kathy, I'm very proud of you."

A tear burned Katherine's right eye. She blinked it back, and shone a big happy smile at her father. "Pass the food, will you? I'm absolutely starving."

Sally played hostess, distributing carefully packed china and silverware, crisp linen napkins. Finally she reached the lunch Peg Parsons had prepared. Smoked salmon, cold meats, salad, thin-sliced brown bread. All finished off with a fruit salad laced with vintage port.

"I have a special fondness for lunching in a car in Hyde Park," Roland admitted. "Mind you, this is only the second time I've ever done it."

"Tell me about the first," Katherine said.

"It was twenty-nine years ago. Your mother and I sat not fifty yards from here, sharing the back of a taxi. Our very first date, secretive as all hell . . ." Roland sighed gently. "And damned well unforgettable."

Sally patted Roland's arm. "What about the poor girl you'd stood up the night before, eh?"

Roland gave Sally a look filled with the warmth of a lengthy friendship. And something more. Katherine watched the interchange with pleasure. "I assume you

250

mean yourself."

"Was any other journalist in this car invited to Claridge's to cover Ambassador Nicanor Menéndez's ball? And did any other journalist in this car ask Roland Eagles to be her escort?"

"What Sally's tactfully trying to say," Roland broke in, "is that I went to the ball as her escort, but was both ungracious and ungrateful enough to fall hopelessly in love with a beautiful girl whose hand I shook in the receiving line."

Katherine knew the story by heart, but she loved to hear it retold like this. "From everything I've ever heard, Sally, it was your own fault. My mother's dance card was filled that night with members of the proper social set. My father would never have got a look-in if you hadn't helped him out."

"What was that artist's name?" Roland asked Sally.

"The one who was dancing with Catarina when I made us bump into them? God only knows, after all these years."

Roland turned to Katherine. "You should have seen Sally that night. She was magnificent. She made us collide with your mother and her partner. As we broke apart, Sally grabbed hold of the artist and mentioned a story she'd once written about him."

"And while the poor man tried to gather his wits, your father waltzed off with your mother," Sally finished.

"One dance, that was all it took," Roland mused. "First thing the following morning, I had roses sent to her at the embassy. She telephoned me, and I collected her for lunch. God, that was a lovely day."

"Poor Sally," Katherine said. "I'd feel sorry for you if I didn't know that helping my father meet my mother got you exclusive rights to the story of their elopement."

Sally grinned. "I made my reputation with that story. While the rest of Fleet Street had to make do with couched comments from the ambassador, I had the inside track. Not only did I know where the lovers were hiding, but I was the only journalist present at their wedding in Scotland, and I had the only photographs of the ceremony. Just like today, Katherine. The rest of Fleet Street shared a story about a riot, while the *Eagle* had an exclusive." She raised her glass. "To exclusives. Let's keep them in the family."

"You know, a friend telephoned me this morning to say I was a fool. That I'd done more harm than good by publicizing the British Patriotic League, and that the publicity would only help them get more members."

"Whoever your friend is, Kathy, he's one hundred percent mistaken. Evil is like mildew; it thrives in darkness. Expose it to bright light, and it dies."

"Gerry Waller wants me to keep on with the British Patriotic League, find out all I can about it."

"That shouldn't be too difficult," Sally said. "Like me, when your parents eloped, you have a very favorable inside track."

"I do?"

"The same inside track you've had all along."

"Brian Waters?"

"We're just suggesting it, Kathy," Roland said. "Brian, because of his background, and his criminal record, is obvious material for the League. Should anything ever come of this organization, it would give us a head start on the rest of the street if we had someone on the inside."

"I'll talk to Brian about it." Katherine looked through the driver's window to see Arthur Parsons approaching the car. Half an hour had passed already. Parsons walked around the silver Porsche that was still parked in front of the Bentley, and came to Roland's window. "Should I tell Mrs. Parsons that lunch was satisfactory, sir?"

"You may tell Mrs. Parsons that lunch was superb."

Parsons settled himself behind the wheel. "Ready to

return to Regent Street, sir?"

"I think so. Kathy, be careful how you drive Sally back to Fleet Street, there's a good girl. She's the only editorial director Eagle Newspapers has."

Katherine regarded her father as though he were mad. "Sally and I are taking a taxi back to Fleet Street. Surely you heard that my car was a casualty of the riot?"

Roland shook his head. "I knew I'd forgotten something." He reached into his jacket pocket and pulled out a key ring, which he tossed to his daughter. "Bonus for a job well done."

Katherine's face lit up. The Porsche . . . it had to be! She hugged her father and kissed him. "Thank you! If anyone ever says that your daughter's spoiled rotten, you can tell them you're to blame!" She jumped out of the Bentley and ran to the silver sports car. The engine roared into life immediately. As it settled down to a steady throb, she rolled back the top and yelled: "Come on, Sally, what are you waiting for? Let's go back to the *Eagle* in style."

Two messages awaited Katherine when she got back to her desk. One was from John Saxon, asking her to call him. The other was from Raymond Barnhill. After tearing up the piece of paper with Saxon's message, she dialed the number of the International Press Agency.

"Raymond Barnhill, please." Moments later, Barnhill came on the line. "Hello, Raymond, Katherine here. Recovered from all of yesterday's excitement yet?"

"Don't come on all chummy with me, you selfish bitch!"

Katherine nearly dropped the receiver. Who did Barnhill think was on the other end of the line? "Raymond, it's me. Katherine. Katherine Kassler."

"I know damned well who it is. Don't you believe in sharing information?"

Katherine understood. Barnhill was no different

253

from any other journalist. He'd been beaten to a story, and he didn't like it. "Don't you believe in scoops, Raymond?"

"What scoops? We don't even work the same side of the street. What harm would there have been in tipping me off to this British Patriotic League connection with the soccer hooligans? My audience isn't the same as yours. My readers are in the States. I could have arranged it so the story wouldn't have come out in American newspapers until this morning, which is anywhere from five to eight hours behind here. Now it'll get picked up in dribs and drabs, and I won't get any kind of credit for it."

Katherine was nonplussed. "You're acting as though I owe you a story, Raymond. I don't owe you anything."

"The hell you don't! You owe me for lending you the money to bail out your little thug of a friend in court. And you owe me for spiriting you and your photographer out of that riot yesterday. If I hadn't come back to look for you, you'd have been statistics."

"You're right," Katherine said, surprising both herself and Barnhill. "I do owe you something for all that. But not a share in an exclusive story I've worked on for months."

"Then what?"

Katherine remembered the broken dinner date with John Saxon. "It's worth a dinner."

"You're on."

"Good. I'll pick you up outside your block of flats at six o'clock. Give me a chance to show off my new car."

Katherine drove up to Barnhill's apartment block a few minutes after six. The American was waiting on the sidewalk. When he saw the Porsche, his eyes opened wide in admiration.

"Must be nice having a father who owns a newspaper or two."

"He also owns three department stores. And yes, it is nice. It beats waiting for the insurance company to pay

254

up. Are you going to get in, or are you going to stand ogling the car for the rest of the evening?"

Barnhill climbed in, ducking way down to avoid the convertible top that was now stretched over the soft leather interior. "Very plush," he said, settling into the contoured seat. "I wish you many years of happy driving."

"Thank you." After checking traffic, she pulled away from the curb. "Tell me something about yourself, Raymond. Which part of America are you from?"

"South Carolina. A tiny one-horse town near Columbia, the state capital."

"Do you miss it?"

"Did I make it sound like a place that anyone could miss? May I ask you a question?"

"Go ahead."

"Where are we going for this dinner you owe me?"

"Wheeler's, in Duke of York Street."

"That a fancy place?"

"A very good seafood restaurant. Would you rather go somewhere else?"

"I've been in this country for six months. I'm reaching the point where I'd kill for a good pizza."

"Is that what you eat back home in South Carolina?"

"Sure, right along with grits and collards and real pit barbecue. But you wouldn't know about such things. You were probably weaned on chauteaubriand and lobster."

"You're becoming tedious."

"Sorry. I've always had a hang-up about being around people with money."

"Me, too," Katherine surprised him by saying. "I'm perpetually suspicious about how they got it."

Barnhill roared with laughter. "Are you sure you haven't got a bit of socialism lurking beneath your veneer of opulence and sophistication?"

"I've never looked that deeply inside of myself. Mind you, our local Labour Party officials did ask me to run for office a couple of years ago. I had to turn down the offer, of course."

"Why? Did your father swear to cut you off without a cent if you brought such disgrace upon the family name?"

A light turned red. Katherine braked sharply and suddenly enough to catapult Barnhill toward the dashboard. He stuck out his hands to save himself. "You'd feel a lot safer," Katherine told him sweetly, "if you wore your seat belt." As he glared at her, she added in a sharper tone, "It might surprise you to know that I work for the *Daily Eagle* because I think it's the best newspaper on Fleet Street, not because my father is the owner. I neither ask for special treatment, nor do I expect any."

Barnhill patted the dashboard. "You've proved your point, thank you very much. I'll take your advice and make sure I'm wearing a seat belt the next time I want to make a comment you might find unwelcome."

The light turned green. Katherine let up the clutch and roared away, the instant of anger past. "Are you sure you really want a pizza?"

"Obviously, you don't. I see you looking down your nose at the very idea."

"I must admit that I would prefer something else."

"Fine! I'd say let's grab a hamburger—if only you could find a decent hamburger in this city."

"Only the best for your gourmet palate, eh? All right, pizza it is."

She drove to Soho, to a restaurant that was part of a small pizza chain. When they sat down, Katherine asked, "How's your book going? Your great American novel that's staged in Vietnam, and is being written in England."

"I'm getting close to where I write thirty."

"I beg your pardon?"

"In the States, copy ends with the figures three-zero. Once I've finished this one . . . no, let's be optimistic . . .

once I've *sold* this one, I can get going on book two."

"Two books. You are ambitious, aren't you?"

"Three books. It's a trilogy. Vietnam seen by the officers, the noncommissioned officers, and the enlisted men."

"What do you know about Vietnam?"

"Only what I learned during a thirteen-month tour of duty."

"You were there?" Katherine's interest sparked; she'd never met a veteran of that war.

"In 'seventy, 'seventy-one. Just about when we all knew that the war was a lost cause."

"Which were you? Officer, noncom, or enlisted man?"

"Officer. First lieutenant working for the public information office. I majored in journalism, worked on a daily newspaper called *The State* for a couple of years, then the nice men at the draft board remembered that they'd missed me. So long South Carolina, hello South Vietnam."

"Did you see any fighting?"

"Only by accident. I was one of many assistant public information officers at a place called Tan Son Nhut. That was an airbase just outside of Saigon, which served as headquarters for the American presence. MACV, to give it the proper title. The improper title was Pentagon East."

"What duties did you have to perform?"

"Prepare news releases for the daily press conference which took place at five every afternoon. The Five O'Clock Follies, as some wag once termed it. We had the worst public relations job in the world, trying to sell an unpopular war to journalists whose cynicism was eclipsed only by their total disbelief. When I got out, I went back to South Carolina for two years, then I got a job in New York with the International Press Agency."

"Never married?"

"I was. To my college sweetheart."

"What happened?"

Barnhill did not answer for a long time. He just sat there, chewing on his lower lip, and Katherine thought she had asked one question too many. Finally, he said, "I keep telling myself that my marriage was just another casualty of Vietnam. Mary didn't dump me while I was away, but I think that was when she started looking elsewhere for company. I used to hear things from friends I'd left behind in Carolina. When I got back home, everything was fine again. It was only when we moved up to New York City that it all seemed to go haywire. She kept complaining that she couldn't settle down in New York. She felt out of place — she belonged in the rural South, not in the big city."

"Did Mary work?"

"She was a teacher. She qualified to teach in New York, but she couldn't handle the kids. I don't think she knew what hit her the first day she walked into a New York City public school. She gave me an ultimatum: either we returned to South Carolina, or she was going to make my life a misery."

"Did she?"

Barnhill nodded. "Our working hours were so different that we might just as well have been two strangers. She worked days, and I was on the night shift. On top of that, during the long school vacations, she went back to South Carolina on her own. One night, I had a lousy cold. Before I could give it to everyone else on the night shift, I was sent home. When I let myself into the apartment, I found Mary with a friend of mine."

Katherine tried to imagine Barnhill flying into a fury, beating up the friend, and then turning on the unfaithful wife. The vision failed to materialize. "What did you do?"

"I turned around and walked out. The next day, I saw a lawyer and started divorce proceedings. Later, when I got my head together, I applied to be transferred to the London desk. And here I am."

"Has your divorce come through?"

"A few weeks ago." Barnhill stared down at the table. "And I feel more alone now than I've ever felt in my entire life. How about you?"

"Alone? No. I'm married to a man who's confined to a wheelchair, but I'm far from alone."

"That's right. You have kids who aren't old enough to understand a soccer game, and that's why you don't let them go. Not for fear of being beaten up, or recruited into a fascist organization, but because they wouldn't understand the rules."

Katherine laughed. "You could be amusing if you weren't so bloody cynical."

"What kind of a mother are you?"

"I try to be a good one, but with a journalist's hours I'm afraid that my children sometimes get ignored." She listened to what she was saying. "You know, you've got a damned nerve asking me that!"

"Why did you answer?"

"Because your question was so out-of-the-blue that it caught me right off guard."

"Mark of a good reporter," Barnhill said. "Asking questions that catch people off guard. I learned that trick from the reporters at the Five O'Clock Follies in Vietnam."

From the restaurant, Katherine returned Barnhill to his apartment. He invited her in for a cup of coffee. She shook her head and said, "Get on with your book. I want to read it."

"You have more faith than I do. Thanks for the dinner. Next time it'll be my treat."

"We'll see." She waved a hand before driving away.

It was nine-thirty when Katherine reached the street in which she lived. As she neared the house, she realized that Franz was not aware that she had a new car. He would get a big surprise when he looked out of the window and saw the sleek silver Porsche in front of the house.

She pulled into the driveway. Suddenly, the surprise was all hers. Parked next to the Jaguar sedan was a maroon Rolls Royce. Katherine braked hard, skidding the Porsche in the gravel. She fumbled with the clutch and gearshift, trying to find reverse. She had to get out of here before she came face to face with John Saxon in her own home.

Wheels spun. Gravel spat at the two parked luxury cars. Before the tires could grip, the front door of the house swung back, and Katherine knew it was too late. Edna Griffiths stood in the doorway, staring out uncertainly at the unfamiliar sports car that was trying desperately to make a getaway.

"Is that you, Mrs. Kassler?" came the singsong Welsh voice. "Oh, yes, it is. I didn't recognize the car. You have a visitor. A Mr. Saxon. He's been waiting almost an hour."

Katherine climbed out of the Porsche. She walked right past Edna Griffiths without any kind of greeting and marched along the hallway toward the television room, where she could hear voices. She did not know what had possessed Saxon to come to the house. Jealousy, because she'd stood him up this one night? Some raging macho anger that was forcing him to destroy everything? She had no idea. But now that she was in the house, she wanted to get the confrontation out of the way as quickly as possible. Face the explosion. See where all the pieces of her life fell. Then pick them up and start over again.

Her last thought, as she walked through the doorway of the television room, was: How the hell am I going to explain all this to my father?

"There she is," Saxon said. "The tabloid crusader herself."

One step inside the television room, Katherine stopped dead. Franz sat in his heavily padded chair. John Saxon sat next to him. Cups of tea were set out on the table between them, even some of Edna Griffiths's freshly baked shortbread. There was no fight. No acrimony between the man who'd stolen a wife, and the man from whom he'd stolen her. Instead, a party was taking place. A tea party. The only thing missing, as far as Katherine could see, was the Mad Hatter.

Saxon stood up, hands outspread. "A telephoned apology, even a written one, for my behavior today would never have sufficed. As rude as I was, only a personal apology would be enough. So, I apologize."

"You could have made a personal apology just as easily at the *Eagle*."

"And missed this wonderful hospitality? Your husband and I have spent the past hour, while waiting for you to return from your late assignment, by exchanging Katherine Kassler anecdotes."

"I was not aware that any existed."

"Many!" Saxon exclaimed. "The time you arrived at my office in St. James's Square, dumping photographs on my desk and claiming to be the lift operator's niece."

Katherine glanced at Franz. He was smiling. Obviously, Saxon had told the story well. He must have charmed Franz the same way he charmed everyone. Selling freezers to Eskimos in the middle of winter . . . !

Saxon checked his watch. "Regretfully, I have to leave. Again, accept my apologies for the way I jumped down your throat today. I think you're wrong to publicize lunatic organizations like the British Patriotic League, and I think this special assignment you mentioned is even more wrong—further interest by the *Eagle* will just make the League believe it is important. But I should never have told you so in the manner I did."

"I'll show you out," Katherine offered.

"Thank you." Saxon shook hands with Franz. "Good night, it was a pleasure to meet you."

Katherine saw him to the forecourt. As Saxon opened the door of the Rolls Royce, Katherine whispered, "What the hell do you think you're doing,

261

coming around to my home like this?"

"And what do you think you're doing," he responded, "by standing me up?"

"I didn't particularly like your tone of voice when you told me off. Or what you called me."

"For a journalist, you're very thin-skinned."

"I expected better from you."

"I'm sorry." She thought he was going to kiss her, and she backed away. Not here, not in front of her own home. Instead, he shook her hand formally. "I'll be speaking to you."

After watching the Rolls Royce move down the driveway, she returned to the house. Franz was no longer smiling.

"So that is the *Wunderkind*. He must know you very well to telephone you at work and yell at you."

"He thought I was wrong, but my father told me I'd done the right thing. I'd rather listen to my father."

"Is the *Wunderkind* the man you've been seeing, Katherine?"

"Pardon?" She stared at Franz. Just what had Saxon said?

"Katherine, I am not without sympathy for you. A young, attractive woman with a husband who can do little for himself."

"If I were having an affair with the man, do you seriously think he'd turn up at the house? He just disagrees with the *Eagle*'s stand on this hate group. Now if you'll excuse me, I'm going upstairs to take a shower. It's been a very tiring day."

She turned to leave. "Remember, Katherine, what we talked about once before. If you want a divorce, I would not be angry. I would understand."

"Do me a big favor and stop being so blasted understanding!"

Franz's voice followed her out into the hall. "All I ask is that you do not treat me like a fool. My body might be wrecked, but my mind still functions."

262

Upstairs, as she turned on the shower and stepped into the refreshing spray, Katherine realized exactly why John Saxon had come to the house in Hampstead. He was staking his claim to her. He was making it quite public, even to her husband, that she belonged to him.

Of all the unmitigated arrogance!

Katherine was so upset by John Saxon's action in coming to the house that she could not sleep that night. She lay on her back, looking up at the ceiling, and asking herself what she was going to do. The answer seemed blatantly obvious. She had to find the courage to give Saxon his marching orders. The relationship had been nice, but this was where it ended. Where it had to end, because one partner was placing far more emphasis on it than the other.

Edna Griffiths was serving breakfast to the children when Katherine came downstairs the following morning. A worried frown crossed the housekeeper's round face. "Are you feeling all right, Mrs. Kassler? May I get something for you?"

"If that's a nice way of saying I look bloody awful, Edna, I appreciate it." Makeup had failed to hide the dark circles beneath her eyes. "I slept badly, that's all."

When Franz entered the breakfast room, he made no mention of the previous evening. All he said was, "Does the Porsche belong to you, or did you borrow it?"

"My father gave it to me yesterday."

"Very nice. I wish" — he shrugged and glanced down at the blanket covering his legs, the hands and arms that possessed only minimal movement — "that I was able to drive it."

Katherine was glad to get out of the house. This morning, it was like a trap. The aura of John Saxon hung everywhere. Even as she walked the short distance from the front door to the Porsche, she could see the tire marks left in the gravel by Saxon's Rolls Royce.

Within a half hour of Katherine arriving at the *Eagle,* Saxon telephoned four times. Twice, Katherine explained that she did not wish to speak to him. The next two times, she replaced the receiver the instant she recognized his voice. At eleven o'clock, an enormous bunch of flowers was delivered to Katherine by one of the messengers. No card accompanied the flowers. "They were left at the front desk by a short, dark-skinned man wearing a chauffeur's uniform," the messenger told Katherine.

William, Katherine thought, Saxon's chauffeur. "There must be some mistake. Please take them away."

Ten minutes later, Saxon telephoned again. Katherine suspected he wanted to learn whether she had received the flowers. She hung up on him before he had the chance to ask.

At midday, just as Katherine was believing that Saxon had given up, came the last straw. The telephone rang again. Katherine snatched it from the hook.

"This is reception, Mrs. Kassler. There's a gentleman here wishes to see you. A Mr. — "

Katherine cut off the receptionist in mid-introduction. "I'll be down immediately!" She walked quickly to the elevator. "I've got a job for you, Archie. There's a man downstairs who's pestering me. He needs to be thrown out."

"Leave it with me, Miss Eagles," said the elevator operator.

Just before the doors opened at the ground floor, Katherine turned away, unwilling to watch. There was only one man waiting in reception. Archie recognized him instantly. "You, is it? I'll teach you to come around here bothering people."

"Get your goddamned hands off me, you superannuated King of the Khyber Rifles!"

Katherine recognized that voice. Too late, she looked out into the reception area. Despite his age, Archie was remarkably fit. He was having little trouble in forcing Raymond Barnhill toward the main door of the building.

"Archie! No!" She ran out of the elevator. "Let him go, Archie! It's not the man I thought it was!"

Just short of the door, Archie stopped. His hands opened, and Barnhill jumped free. "What do they feed you on, old man? Raw meat and jalapeño peppers?"

Katherine stepped between the two men. "I'm sorry, Archie. I thought it was someone else down here."

Archie glared at the American before executing a smart about-face and marching back to his elevator. "And just who did you think I was?" Barnhill asked Katherine. "I'd surely love to know who deserves that kind of a greeting."

"Just someone who's been making a nuisance of himself."

"I didn't come to be a nuisance. I came to thank you for dinner last night, and to return the courtesy. I know it's short notice, but how about having lunch with me today?"

"I can't. I'm busy." What was it, Katherine asked herself, about women with handicapped husbands? Did they carry a huge sign declaring that they were available? First Saxon, and now this American journalist.

"Well, what about lunch tomorrow? Or dinner, if that fits in better with your schedule."

Katherine's head spun. What had she done to deserve this? In the few hours she had spent with Barnhill, had he seen something that did not exist? Had his self-confessed loneliness prompted him to see it? She wanted to scream. When she was trying so hard to simplify her life — when she was doing her level best to find a way to end her affair with John Saxon — why did she have another man rushing in to take his place?

"Not today, Raymond! Not tomorrow! Not lunch! Not dinner! I am going on a week's holiday tonight. Now will you please leave me alone?"

She swung around and went back to the elevator. By the time she reached the third floor, her head had stopped spinning. Her mind was accepting the lie her lips had uttered so spontaneously, and she was congratulating herself. In a desperate bid to get rid of one man, she had discovered the way to lose another.

She *would* take a week off work. She would take her brand-new silver Porsche and drive around the country. Get out of London before she was suffocated by her husband's understanding, by John Saxon's arrogance, and by Raymond Barnhill's need for contact with another living soul.

"I'm going away for a week," she announced to Franz that night over dinner.

"What kind of assignment takes an entire week?"

Had his eyes narrowed just a fraction? Did he suspect that she would spend the week with Saxon? "No assignment. I'm taking a week off work and going on a thoroughly well-deserved holiday."

"Are you taking the children?"

"It's best that I don't. Henry missed a week's school at the beginning of the year when I took him and Joanne to Tenerife. He can't afford to be absent again." Besides, Katherine added silently, this time I want to be alone.

"Where will you go?"

"Lake District, then across the border country to Edinburgh. It's very pretty this time of year."

She left the house early the following morning. The roof of the Porsche was folded down, and she wore a Hermès scarf to protect herself against the wind, which whipped through the open car. In the Porsche's trunk was a Louis Vuitton suitcase that she'd bought years earlier in Paris. She had packed it hastily the previous night, with the emphasis on comfort: cashmere sweaters, woolen trousers, stout walking boots, a couple of warm, loose-fitting jackets.

It was midafternoon when Katherine reached the Lake District. She spent the night in the town of Grasmere, where the poet William Wordsworth had lived. Before sitting down for dinner, she telephoned home to speak to Henry and Joanne. She was missing them already, and regretting having left them at home. Although God alone knew there was little here for young children to do, other than admire some of the most magnificent mountain scenery in all of England.

The following morning, she visited the national park center at Brockhole on Windermere, a wisteria-covered mansion in grounds that led down to Lake Windermere. She bought postcards, mailing one to her father, one to Sally Roberts, and one to Franz and the children. Afterward, she walked for two hours along the lake bank. On the way back to the car, she bought one more postcard, which she mailed to the International Press Agency, attention Raymond Barnhill. The message read: "Sorry for biting your head off, but I really did need to get away." As she mailed the card, she decided that breathing the crisp, clean northern air was doing for her what attending church did for true believers: it was instilling in her a sense of peace and forgiveness.

She spent one more day in the Lake District before continuing north. Each night, she telephoned home to check on the children, and from each picturesque town she passed through, she sent them another postcard. At last, she reached Edinburgh, where her own parents had been married at the beginning of 1950, less than six months before her birth. She registered for two nights at the North British, the railroad hotel situated at the east end of Princes Street, in the shadow of Edinburgh Castle. In her first afternoon in Scotland's capital city, she walked the length of Princes Street, stopping to gaze into the windows of both the dignified older shops and the newer chain stores. She strolled past the Adler's department store belonging to her father, but never ventured inside.

That night, absolutely exhausted, she fell asleep the instant her head touched the pillow, and slept for eight uninterrupted hours. The following morning, thoroughly refreshed, she walked along the Royal Mile, joining Edinburgh Castle to the palace of Holyrood House. Afterward, she tagged onto a party of American tourists, curious to see what their guide would show them. The party made the long climb up Calton Hill to the Old Calton Burying Ground. Katherine wondered why this would be on any tour group's itinerary until she saw the monument to the memories of Abraham Lincoln and the Scottish-American soldiers who had died during the American Civil War.

She sought a souvenir shop that sold postcards depicting the monument, and mailed one to Raymond Barnhill. That made two postcards she'd sent to the wire-service reporter; that would show him that no ill-feeling lingered. She studied another postcard, this one showing the King Edward VII Memorial at the western end of the Royal Mile. She knew who would appreciate this little piece of British history. John Saxon, that was who.

That night, despite being as exhausted as she had been the previous night, she found it difficult to sleep. Her muscles were tired, but her brain remained alert. One message kept being repeated: she had lied to herself about John Saxon. She'd told herself that she never wanted to see him again, but she damned well did! He was arrogant, conceited, and he could be damned well rude when he felt like it. And with all that, Katherine knew that she could not just walk out on him.

God . . . ! Lying on her back, she thrust a fist into her

mouth, suddenly quite appalled. What if he had found someone else during her absence? One of those dozen other young women he'd mentioned so casually? What if she went back to him, only to learn that she was no longer wanted?

Rolling over, she lifted the receiver from the bedside telephone, and gave the switchboard operator John Saxon's unlisted London number. It was past midnight. He'd be in bed. Asleep. Alone? She heard the double ring of the telephone, then Saxon's voice, sharp and alert.

"Hello?"

Sitting up in bed, she pressed the receiver to her ear and listened. "Hello? Anyone there?"

Before Saxon could lose his patience and hang up, Katherine broke the connection. She continued to sit up in bed, tightly clasping her tucked-up knees with her arms, as if that simple action could dull the ache she felt. She missed him! She really did. And she knew that if she wanted him, she would have to go crawling back.

She looked at the telephone again, debating whether to repeat the call. No. Crawl back she might, but she'd be damned if she'd crawl all the way from Scotland.

Eyes red from lack of sleep, she left Edinburgh late the next morning, reaching London by nightfall. She had brought back presents for the children — a miniature set of bagpipes for Henry, and a Scottish doll for Joanne. Instead of going straight home, though, she drove to Marble Arch. The maroon Rolls Royce sat outside John Saxon's London home. She parked the new Porsche behind it, and knocked on the door of the house.

Saxon's chauffeur opened the door. "Good evening, William. Is Mr. Saxon home?"

"He's just preparing to go out for the evening, miss."

Had her fear been a premonition? Had Saxon already found someone else? "May I see him?"

"If you'd care to wait, I'm sure he'll be down shortly."

270

William escorted Katherine into the front reception room, with its high white ceiling and pale gold walls. She sat on one of the Chippendale sofas, feeling scruffy in her boots, trousers, and baggy jacket. Her eyes drifted from the paintings of Nelson and Wellington to the Aubusson rug on the floor. Was it already leaving a rash on some other woman's back?

The door opened. Saxon entered, adjusting the sleeves of his dinner jacket to show exactly the right amount of shirt cuff. His cuff links, Katherine noticed, were simple yet stylish gold ovals, the kind her father preferred. "When I tried to reach you at the *Eagle*," he said, "I was informed that you had gone away."

"I was touring, from the Lake District up to Edinburgh."

"Rather sudden, wasn't it?"

"I needed time alone to make some decisions."

"Oh? And what did you decide?"

"I . . ." Her mouth froze as William came into the room. He carried a clothes brush, which he used briskly on Saxon's dinner jacket. "Where are you going?"

"Opera." He moved slightly so that William could brush the front of the jacket. "Do you like opera, Katherine?"

"I have to be in the mood for it."

"You're ahead of me. I never seem to be in the mood."

"Then why do you go?"

"Noblesse oblige. Saxon Holdings has supported the arts by taking a box for the past few years, so I'm expected to show my face occasionally."

William completed his grooming, and Saxon made a gesture of dismissal. The chauffeur left the room and closed the door. "I asked what you had decided, Katherine."

"I don't want to lose what we have, John, but so help me God, if you ever come around to my home again like

271

you did last week, and present yourself to my husband . . ."

"I told you then, I don't like being stood up."

"You deserved to be stood up that night. I have never been so insulted in my life."

He gripped her arms and drew her close. "A damned fool, that's what I called you. And I was right, wasn't I?"

"How do you reach that conclusion?"

"Look what's been happening this past week, ever since you broke that story about the British Patriotic League recruiting soccer thugs as their storm troopers."

Katherine stared blankly at Saxon. "I've been away. I haven't seen a newspaper for a week."

Saxon walked to the door and called out instructions to the chauffeur. Moments later, William carried in an armful of newspapers. "These hadn't been collected yet, sir."

"Thank you." Saxon sorted through the newspapers. "Here, read this. And this." He handed pages to Katherine. She saw pictures of Alan Venables, the chairman of the British Patriotic League, news stories and features on the right-wing organization. "Wasn't just Fleet Street," Saxon said. "Venables and his two henchmen—"

"Trevor Burns and Neville Sharpe?"

"That's them. They've all been interviewed on radio and television. They're stressing that they're a legitimate political party with a legitimate platform. They claim that their membership is increasing dramatically, and they're going to be heard from in the next general election."

"And you believe I'm to blame for that?"

"You gave them aid and comfort. Before your story, barely anyone had heard of them. I certainly hadn't. Now they're frontpage news."

"You think that if I pursue this special investigation,

272

I'll help their cause even more?"

Saxon nodded. "They've already organized another rally."

"When?"

"Three weeks' time, on Spring Bank Holiday."

"We'll just have to wait and see how many marchers they attract this time, won't we?" Katherine said.

"I guess we will. By the way . . ." Saxon trapped Katherine in a candid gaze. "Where were you telephoning from last night? The Lake District, or Edinburgh?"

"I didn't speak to you last night."

"I never said you did. You telephoned me, then hung up." He smiled at the expression of innocence on her face. "My number is ex-directory, Katherine. No one who knows it would have any reason to call me so late."

"I was in Edinburgh. I missed you, and I wanted to hear your voice. But when you answered, I felt embarrassed and angry, so I put the receiver down."

"What we have, Katherine, I don't want it to end either. I was only partly honest before, when I said I came to your house because I was angry at being stood up. There's more to it. I've built up a large property business, and I've had to fight for it, building by building. Nothing ever came easy. Before I ever enter into a fight, I try to find out everything I can about the competition. That's what I was doing at your home last week."

"Franz asked if I was seeing you. He said he wouldn't be angry; he'd understand. I don't know whether he was being truthful, or just being brave. John . . ." She took Saxon's hand and gazed into his brown eyes. "As much as I don't want to lose you, I want to avoid hurting Franz even more. Life has played him a lousy trick, and I don't want to add to his suffering. Promise me you'll do nothing to hurt him."

"Katherine, I'm in love with you. I don't want to spend my life being the other man."

"I love you, too, but I also care deeply for Franz. He's

the father of my children. He's the first man I ever loved, the first man who ever made love to me. Make me that promise, John, or I'll walk out of here right now."

He stared at her. Her face had gone like stone. Her eyes were glassy, her jaw set rigidly. He knew that she meant every word of the threat.

"I promise. But remember, Katherine, should you ever need help, you turn to me."

Katherine's face relaxed. Her skin softened, and her eyes glowed with a moist warmth. "What opera are you seeing tonight?"

Saxon gave her a wide grin. *"Cavalleria Rusticana* and *Pagliacci,* a brace of operas about the mortal perils of the eternal triangle."

As she left the house, Katherine could not help thinking that no double bill could be more fitting.

Franz was still awake when Katherine returned home. He wanted a detailed account of her trip. She gave him a chronological summary. Several times he interrupted, asking questions about something she had mentioned earlier, as though trying to trap her in a lie. She went to bed certain that Franz did not believe her motoring trip had been nothing more than an innocent vacation.

Katherine gave the children their gifts over breakfast early the next morning. Joanne set the doll on the chair next to her and continued eating her cereal. Henry was not so patient. He left the table and began to play the miniature set of bagpipes. A fleshtingling, tuneless wail echoed through the house. While Katherine covered her ears with her hands, Edna Griffiths gently, but firmly, removed the bagpipes from Henry's hands.

"There are two gifts adults never give to children, Mrs. Kassler," Edna said as Katherine left the breakfast room to go upstairs. "One is a pet. The other is any kind of musical instrument."

Forty minutes later, Katherine returned downstairs, ready to go to work. As she prepared to leave the house, she was confronted by Edna and Jimmy Phillips. "Is something wrong?" Katherine asked.

Edna answered. "I'm afraid we're going to be handing in our notice, Mrs. Kassler."

"Both of you?" The prospect horrified Katherine. Without these two, where would her own family be? Aside from caring for Franz, hadn't Phillips saved Henry's life when the boy had chased the model aircraft? And hadn't Edna always been there for Katherine to fall back on? All Katherine could think of to say was "Surely you're not leaving because of those bagpipes?"

Edna looked at Phillips. "It's like this, Mrs. Kassler," the attendant began. "Edna and me, we've taken quite a liking to each other. We want to get married and set up on our own."

Katherine was touched by Phillips's quiet confession of the love he shared with Edna. It was wonderful when two people in their middle years, who must have once resigned themselves to being alone, found happiness. "That's marvelous news, Jimmy, but why should it necessitate you and Edna leaving this house?"

Phillips turned crimson. Katherine saw that Edna, too, was blushing. "Mrs. Kassler, as man and wife"— the attendant spoke with a deliberate slowness that made his cockney accent even more noticeable—"it wouldn't be the right and proper thing for us to be sleeping on different floors, would it?"

"Jimmy, Edna, you can sleep wherever you like. You can take over the top floor. I'll get builders to put in a small kitchen; it'll be like a self-contained flat up there. If you think I'm going to let you go just because you want to get married, you've got another thing coming."

"Bless you." Edna smothered Katherine with a hug. "We didn't really want to leave you, either."

275

"When will this happy occasion take place?"

"We were thinking about sometime next month," Phillips answered. With pride in his voice, he added, "Our Edna, she wants to be a June bride."

Katherine went to work in a bright mood. Edna's and Phillips's news had put the icing on her week's vacation.

"Good morning, Miss Eagles." Archie Waters touched the peak of his cap as Katherine neared his elevator. "Good holiday?"

"Excellent. Have you been well?"

"Touch of rheumatism, but I can live with that."

Katherine got out at the third floor and walked to her desk. A fully stuffed, large brown envelope rested on top of her typewriter. She opened the flap and shook the contents onto her desk—clippings from other newspapers about the British Patriotic League, similar to those John Saxon had shown her.

"Mr. Waller had those collected for you."

Katherine turned around to see the tall, thin figure of Derek Simon. "Was there a reason?"

"He wanted you to see the storm you created. If you look, I think you'll find a memo included."

Katherine sorted through the clippings to find the memo. She read it aloud. "Everyone else has jumped on *our* bandwagon. How do we regain the impetus? See me when you return."

She met with Gerald Waller that afternoon. "I read what the other papers wrote on the League, Gerry."

"What do you think?"

"They shadowboxed with them, that's all. Accepted whatever the League said. In all those interviews with Alan Venables, I doubt if one tough question was asked. Even when Venables denied that they've been recruiting a bunch of young thugs at football games, the rest of the street reported it as fact. Because by doing so, they can imply that the *Eagle* is talking nonsense. Which, of course, we're not."

"Do you want to ask Alan Venables the tough questions?"

"Interview him?" Katherine shook her head. "I've got a much better idea for getting the lowdown on the League."

Katherine met Brian Waters that evening as he left Mercury Messengers on his moped. "How would you like to make some extra money and do a good deed at the same time?" she asked.

"How?"

"Join the British Patriotic League."

Brian blanched. "My grandpa would kill me if I got myself mixed up with that lot. Nazis, he calls them."

"We'll take care of your grandfather," Katherine assured the young man. "We want you to attend the next League rally. Make friends there. Find out everything you can about the League, and report back to us."

"Be a spy?"

"That's right, be a spy."

Brian's eyes gleamed with excitement. He could already see on his chest decorations to equal those of his grandfather.

For its second rally, the British Patriotic League chose to protest immigration in the racial tinderbox of Notting Hill, the West London scene of earlier race riots. Three thousand marchers turned up. A large contingent of opponents staged an anti-League demonstration only four hundred yards away. With the Brixton riot still fresh in the country's memory, the authorities were prepared. A line of mounted police kept rival groups apart. Another three hundred police officers, including dog handlers with German shepherds, stood by.

Standing next to Sid Hall, Katherine looked around

277

the crowd of spectators, trying to spot Raymond Barnhill. He'd told her he would be covering the rally for the International Press Agency. Katherine and Barnhill had spoken several times since her return from Scotland. He had called to thank her for the postcards, first one, then the other. Somewhat hesitantly, he had asked her out to lunch, and she had accepted. Over lunch, they had agreed to be friends. It was nice, Katherine decided, having a man who was just a friend. She had not told John Saxon, though. That relationship was too recently back on an even keel to risk overturning it again.

At last, she saw Barnhill, standing on the other side of the street. She should have seen him earlier; no one else was wearing a well-cut blue blazer and faded jeans. She waved, and Barnhill waved back.

The meeting broke up without incident. The line of mounted police held. The German shepherds remained with their handlers. As Katherine and Hall walked back to where they had parked, a dozen placard-waving League supporters crowded them off the sidewalk and into the road.

"Why don't you watch where you're walking?" Hall snapped.

One of the young men — short and compact, brown eyes hard in a surly face — glared belligerently at the *Eagle* photographer. "This is a free country. We can walk wherever we want to walk."

"What would a delinquent little Nazi like you know about a free country?" Hall's camera dropped from his shoulder to his hand, dangling lazily by the strap. From a photographer's tool, it had been transformed into a weapon.

The youth gripped the pole of the placard he was holding. "Swing that camera at me, and I'll shove this straight through you." He pushed off the placard to reveal the top end of the pole, which had been sharpened to a wicked point.

Katherine grabbed the photographer's arm. "Let's go, Sid. Let's get out of here."

Eyes locked with those of the young man, Hall backed away. The instant he turned around, the League supporters burst into ribald laughter.

"Well done, my son!" one shouted, clapping Brian Waters on the back. "Made him wet himself, you did."

Brian fixed the poster back on the pole, before any police officer could spot the sharpened end. "Wasn't much of a man, was he? You'd think he'd want to impress the bit of stuff he was with, wouldn't you?"

"I'd want to impress her as well," said the youth who had clapped Brian on the back. "With this!" He patted his groin. Even Brian, who had once forced another young man to apologize to Katherine for an off-color remark, joined in the laughter.

The laughter carried to Katherine and Sid Hall, who had reached the spot where they'd left Hall's car. As they unlocked the doors, Katherine said, "I can just imagine what they're finding so amusing."

"Either skewering me on that pole, or skewering you—"

"On something else," Katherine finished.

Brian Waters had gone a long way toward establishing himself today. Katherine just hoped that the end results were worth all the bother.

A week after the Notting Hill rally, the first issue of a new magazine was mailed to Katherine at the *Eagle*. The cover showed a flaming sword set against the cross of St. George. At the top was the slogan *"Patriot,* The Magazine for a Greater Britain!"

Wondering why the magazine had been sent expressly to her, and not to the news department, Katherine started leafing through the pages. She expected the lead story to be about the latest League rally. Instead, the main news was of fast expansion. The

British Patriotic League was no longer headquartered in a shopfront in West Ham. It now had proper premises — Patriot House, in Whitechapel, in the East End of London. Katherine read on. Membership drives in the economically depressed Midlands and north of England had resulted in the establishment of League chapters in Manchester, Leicester, and Birmingham.

Before reading through the remainder of the *Patriot*, Katherine summoned her two assistants. "Check through local records," she told Derek Simon and Heather Harvey. "Find out how much the League paid for Patriot House. Find out the size of the mortgage on the property, and which financial institution supplied the money. Also find out if the League has purchased any property in Manchester, Leicester, or Birmingham."

While Derek and Heather pursued that assignment, Katherine returned to *Patriot*. It was not some cheap mimeographed journal, but a well-produced magazine, complete with halftones and artwork that would have made many trade publications envious.

Across the center spread, Katherine found a large portrait shot of Alan Venables, and an article by the League's chairman on the organization's history. "Three of us," she read, "myself, as chairman, with Trevor Burns and Neville Sharpe, formed the League a year ago, because we were tired of waiting for the established political parties to tell the truth about what is wrong with this country. None of them — Conservative, Labour, or Liberal — has the backbone to admit that immigration, above all else, has dragged this country into economic and social chaos."

Katherine moved on. Suddenly, her eyes opened wide as she saw her own picture. It was a recent photograph. Very recent. Taken at the last rally. More than the photograph, it was the accompanying copy that really stunned her.

"We Accuse!" ran the eye-catching headline. The

first lines of copy read: "We accuse Katherine Kassler and Eagle Newspapers of lying. We accuse them of distorting the facts. We accuse them of smearing the good name of the British Patriotic League." At the bottom of the article, past a hundred lines of text, was the byline of Trevor Burns, member of the League's executive committee and editor of *Patriot*.

Later in the day, Katherine showed the copy of *Patriot* to her father and Gerald Waller. Both men studied the attack on Katherine and Eagle Newspapers.

"They accuse us of forging those photographs from the Brixton rally?" Waller said. "They even claim that we produced those Union Jack badges with 'Niggers back to Africa' written on them, and tried to lay the blame on the League?" He looked at Roland Eagles. "If you want my opinion, we should sue those bastards for everything they've got."

"How much can that be? We'd just look like bullies. There must be a better way."

The deliberations were interrupted by a telephone call for Katherine. She jotted down notes, then replaced the receiver. "That was Derek Simon," she told Waller and her father. "He and Heather have unearthed some figures. Patriot House, the League's new headquarters, was purchased for seventy thousand pounds. The League has also bought properties in Birmingham, Manchester, and Leicester, the three cities where regional committees have been established. The total purchase price for those three properties is one hundred and twenty thousand pounds. No mortgages are involved. Everything was paid for in cold cash."

"A hundred and ninety thousand pounds," Roland muttered. "Never mind suing the League . . . we should be more interested in finding out where the money's coming from. Whoever puts up that kind of money must be expecting one hell of a return on his investment! But what?"

13

It was both a supreme irony and an obvious choice for the British Patriotic League to locate its new headquarters in Whitechapel. Ironic, because for hundreds of years this area of London's East End had been the welcoming point and first home for countless waves of immigrants. And obvious, because there had always existed among native East-Enders a bigoted blue-collar distrust of anything foreign, be it a dark skin, an odd accent, or a peculiar style of dress. The East End was a fertile breeding ground for extremist politics.

The single impressive feature of Patriot House was its nameplate: red letters on a white background, with the flaming sword substituting for the *i* in "Patriot." By contrast, the four-story structure itself was very ordinary. Dirty gray stone, dull windows, and an entrance framed by chipped and peeling paint. Erected after the war to fill a hole created by German bombs, Patriot House was a rundown nonentity in a row of anonymous buildings that found daily use as offices, warehouses, and factories.

Brian Waters rode a new motorcycle — bought with the money he was being paid by the *Eagle* for his undercover work — through the evening traffic until he reached Patriot House. He parked outside, chained the motorcycle to a street sign, and entered the League's new headquarters. The building smelled musty. A notice board on the wall next to a small self-service elevator listed the occupants of Patriot House. The three members of the executive committee had their own offices on the top floor of the building. The only other space so far designated for a specific purpose was the basement, which was the assembly hall. Taped to the bottom of the notice board was a handwritten announcement that tonight's meeting would take place there.

Brian joined the flow of young men to the basement. By seven-twenty, one hundred youths were gathered, waiting for something to happen. Brian joined the group he'd met at the Notting Hill rally, when he had engineered the incident with Sid Hall and Katherine.

At seven-thirty, a shrill whistle sounded. The noise of conversation stopped. One hundred pairs of eyes looked toward the raised platform at the end of the assembly hall. Alan Venables was standing there. "Welcome to Patriot House, headquarters of the struggle for a greater Britain!"

In the confined space of the assembly hall, the roar of approval was deafening. "You men have been selected as the standard-bearers of the new Britain. You will be its shock troops. While others in the British Patriotic League go about the day-to-day business of organizing the party, you men will be at the forefront of change."

Another surge of excitement ran through the gathering. Even Brian — as much as he tried to remind himself that he was only present for the *Eagle,* and not because he sympathized with Venables — could feel it. It was the same thrill you got from standing in a crowd of supporters at a soccer game, the sensation that you belonged to something that was mightier than anything else in the world.

Venables pulled a sheet of paper from the jacket of

283

his tweed sportcoat. "All of you have been chosen to be the spearhead of reforms but even among you there exists an elite corps. Men who have demonstrated extraordinary ability and leadership. These men will be your group commanders." He read ten names from the sheet of paper, motioning for the men to join him on the platform. The sixth name he read out belonged to Brian Waters.

When all ten group commanders were assembled, Venables instructed them to introduce themselves. Brian listened to those who preceded him. They all took pride in revealing criminal records. When Brian's turn came, he knew exactly what to say.

"I was fined two hundred and fifty pounds for assault and battery. I told the magistrate that Liverpool fans viciously attacked my boots with their chins, but he wouldn't believe me."

A roar of laughter swept the hall. "Don't be so modest, Brian," Venables said. "That wasn't the only reason you've been made a group commander. You're also up here because of the Notting Hill rally, where half a dozen witnesses saw you make the liars from the *Daily Eagle* back down."

After the introductions of the group commanders, Venables looked out over his audience. "You men comprise the British Brigade. You will be strong, you will be violent. Because in this world, strength and violence are the only ways to bring about change. You will act on orders you receive from your group commanders, who will, in turn, receive their orders directly from me. To the outside world, there can be no connection between the British Patriotic League and the British Brigade. Remember that." Ten seconds passed while that piece of information sank in. "Group commanders, select your men. Ten men to a group. Get to know each other."

Brian chose the young men who had been with him at the rally. He wrote down their names, addresses, and telephone numbers. When the selections had been made, Venables dismissed the gathering, but ordered the group commanders to remain. He gave them each an envelope containing fifty pounds. "For expenses. Do your jobs well, and you'll be looked after."

"What are our jobs?" Brian asked.

"Causing trouble. The British Brigade is going to stir up so much trouble for immigrants that they'll be forced to fight back. We want the streets running with blood. So much blood and so much chaos that the decent people of Britain—the white people of Britain—will demand the law and order that only the British Patriotic League can provide."

Walking up the stairs to street level, Brian decided that what he had learned tonight would not wait until he saw Katherine the following day. He had to telephone her immediately. The first pay phone he tried, close to Patriot House, was out of order. He jumped on his motorcycle and cruised along slowly, looking left and right. He spotted another pay phone, down a narrow, dimly lit side turning. This one worked. Holding his crash helmet in one hand, he dialed Katherine's home number.

"It's Brian. I've got something that won't wait."

Katherine invited him to the house. He replaced the receiver on its rest, turned around, and pushed open the door of the booth. A man stood outside, directly between Brian and his motorcycle.

"Well, well, group commander. I thought it was you up on that stage. A real comedian you were, talking about people's chins attacking your boots."

Brian could not recognize the man. The closest street lamp was twenty yards away, and while Brian's face was illuminated, the face of the man accosting him was in deep shadow.

"I saw you jump on your motorbike, and I thought I'd missed my chance. Guess I was just lucky that you stopped to make a phone call. Don't look so tough now,

285

do you, without your pals?" The man's hands came out of his pockets. Glinting dully on one hand was a set of brass knuckles.

"What pals are you talking about? I think you've got the wrong fellow." Gripping the crash helmet tightly, Brian took a step toward his motorcycle.

"You and your pals on the train to Birmingham, making me apologize to that woman. Taking our seats. Bet you thought you were hard men then, didn't you?"

Brian took another step, and the angle of the light changed. He caught a glimpse of fiery red hair. Ginger! Brian had been so intent on what Venables was saying—and then so thrilled to be chosen as a group commander—that he had not even noticed Ginger at the meeting. But Ginger had certainly seen Brian. And he believed that now was the perfect time to settle an old score.

"Strange how you should have been with that *Eagle* woman writer and her photographer on the train that time, isn't it? They got my picture that day, and they got it at the Brixton rally as well. They used both pictures in the paper." The brass knuckles came up as Ginger adopted a loose boxing stance. "Even stranger how everyone should have seen you pushing that woman and her photographer into the street. Managed to make yourself a right hero, didn't you?"

The knuckles flashed through the air. Brian ducked, and in the same movement drove hard with his head into Ginger's middle. The breath exploded out of Ginger. He doubled up. Brian lashed out with the crash helmet. It caught Ginger square in the face, splitting his lips. Brian felt warm blood spurt onto his hand as Ginger collapsed, groaning, onto the sidewalk.

Brian knelt down, his mouth inches from Ginger's ear. "You listen to me now. That woman from the *Eagle,* she made a fool of me. She used me that day on the train, tried to make it look as though she was really interested in writing about the fans, and all the time she was just using me so she could tie everyone in with the League. There's only one thing I hate worse than being made a fool of . . . and that's being reminded of it. So if you tell anyone how she made me look stupid, you're going to think what I gave you just now is a pat on the back. Understand?" He grabbed hold of Ginger's hair, lifted his head a couple of inches, and cracked it back on the sidewalk.

Fifteen minutes later, Brian was in Hampstead. Katherine, who had been listening for the motorcycle, opened the door before Brian could use the heavy knocker and disturb the children.

"My God, what happened to you?" she asked when she saw him. Spots of dried blood covered his jeans and denim jacket. He mumbled something about a fight. Katherine took him through to the television room, where she had been sitting with Franz, and sat him down with a cup of tea.

"Remember Ginger?" Brian asked. When Katherine nodded, Brian related what had happened, going right through the events of the evening, from the meeting in the basement of Patriot House to the fight with Ginger. "I told him you'd made a right fool out of me. That's why I beat him up, I said, because I didn't want him spreading it around and making me look small. But what if I haven't scared him enough? What if he talks to Venables? What if Venables puts two and two together? I mean, he's talking about us doing some terrible things."

Franz gave a faint nod. "Classic," he said. "A classic example of dual-track strategy."

"What is that?" Katherine asked him. She was glad that Brian had come around with news. The League was the only topic guaranteed to interest Franz.

"A very effective deception technique," Franz answered. "Look how well the Palestinians use it. The Palestine Liberation Organization wants to establish itself as a genuine diplomatic force, but it does not wish to give up terrorism. So it delegates the terrorism to other organizations. This allows the PLO to continue butchering civilians. Simultaneously, the world believes what the PLO wants it to believe: that these foul acts are perpetrated by renegade Palestinians. Therefore, the only Palestinian body to trust — to negotiate with — is the PLO."

Hearing Franz use the PLO as a comparison sent a shiver down Katherine's back. It was as though, for the first time, she could really understand how dangerous this latest band of lunatics really was. She turned to Brian.

"Brian, don't feel you're under any obligation. If you think you've been compromised, step back. We asked you to find out what you could about the League. We didn't ask you to put your head into a noose."

"It's just this Ginger, that's all. If I've beaten the fear of God into him, then I'm okay. But if I haven't, then it could turn very sticky. Christ help me if those madmen I saw there tonight thought I was spying for the *Daily Eagle*." He took a sip of tea. "I'll take it one day at a time. If I think I'm in trouble, I'll be on my bike so quick they won't see me for dust." A fleeting smile appeared on his face. "Make my grandpa proud of me, wouldn't it, if I helped to break up a mob like this? Have to put another display case on the wall just for my medals."

Katherine recalled the first time she had seen Brian Waters, the surly youth who had opened the door for her at Cadmus Court. She'd had no idea then just what a complicated young man he was. On the surface, he was brash, prone to find trouble without looking too hard. Beneath skin level, he was intelligent, possessing a shrewdness you learned on the streets, not in any school. He had the ability to lead, and he knew how to take care of himself, with his wits and with his fists.

But the real key to the young man, Katherine now saw, lay in his relationship with his grandfather. How proud the old man would be if Brian could help to break up the League. More than anything, Brian wanted his grandfather's approval.

Katherine realized that Brian had come to mean more to her than just an employee of her father's. He was a person she cared about very much.

Katherine felt a moment of guilt when she rode in Archie Waters's elevator the following morning. This was the nice old man whose grandson she had sent into danger. How would Archie react if, God forbid, something happened to Brian? She flushed the unwelcome notion from her mind, thinking, instead, of the display case that would be needed for Brian's commendations, and the pride his grandfather would feel.

When Gerald Waller came in at midday, Katherine was waiting. She told him of the meeting Brian had attended the previous night, the decision to form the British Brigade and go ahead with what Franz had termed the dual-track strategy.

Waller thought it over before saying, "We can write a story now, claiming that the League is following this path. They, of course, will deny it, and it'll be our word against theirs. They'll claim it's another part of a vendetta we have against them. The alternative, of which I'm more in favor, is to wait—"

"For how long? Until these lunatics hurt someone? As well as a responsibility for keeping people informed, don't we have an ethical responsibility?"

"If you're so concerned about ethics, go to the police."

"They'd laugh me out of the station," Katherine said.

"At least, you'd get a reaction. Which is more than we'd get from our readers if we printed such a weak story."

Torn two ways, Katherine returned to her desk. With a journalist's ambition, she wanted the biggest story she could get. At the same time, her conscience pricked her. Someone could be injured, or worse, and she could have avoided it. Most of all, she was still concerned about Brian Waters.

"You had a phone call," Heather Harvey told her. "Raymond Barnhill from the International Press Agency."

"Thank you." Katherine dialed the number of the IPA and asked for Barnhill.

"I wrote thirty last night," the wire-service reporter greeted Katherine. "Finished the damned book and airmailed it this morning to an agent in New York."

"Congratulations." Katherine guessed that she was the first person Barnhill had called with his good news. "Have you thought of a way to spend your millions yet?"

"Millions? If I'm lucky, it'll be thousands. And I won't get those until some publisher decides his list won't be complete without it."

"Any publisher who knows what's good for him will jump at having you as an author."

"Want to be my press agent?"

"I'd only get you mentions in the *Eagle*."

"Okay, then how about a celebration dinner tonight?"

"Sorry again, Raymond. I'm busy." She was meeting John Saxon that evening.

Barnhill's voice softened. "Guess I'll just have to do my celebrating on my own."

"Instead of sounding so mournful, why don't you start work on the second book of the trilogy, the war through the eyes of the noncommissioned officers? That way, when your agent makes a sale, you'll have the next part all ready to go."

Barnhill bucked up immediately. "You're right."

"We'll have dinner when you sell the book."

"I'm writing it in my diary now."

Smiling, Katherine hung up. When he wasn't making

her mad, Raymond Barnhill always seemed to amuse her.

It was almost seven-thirty when Katherine parked the Porsche outside John Saxon's London home. Opening the door, he kissed her and said, "Do you mind eating a little late tonight? I want to watch a television program first."

"Since when do you watch television?"

"Very infrequently. Tonight, I want to see 'Fightback.' "

The program came on. For five years, "Fightback" had been a weekly success, starting out as a half-hour consumer-action show before being expanded to an hour. Katherine had met Jeffrey Dillard, "Fightback" 's host. He was a gentleman, one of those men whose charm seems to expand as they grow older. Now in his early sixties, he had been a celebrity for as long as the country had had television, beginning as a newscaster, working his way up until he'd found a home at "Fightback." His co-host, Elaine Cowdrey, was in her twenties, an attractive redhead who had come to "Fightback" from a provincial newspaper.

As Katherine watched the tall, white-haired Jeffrey Dillard welcome viewers, an amusing idea occurred to her. "Are they pillorying you, John? Have you been an unreasonable landlord again?"

Laughing, Saxon shook his head. "I'm very choosy about whom I allow to pillory me. So far, you're the only one to qualify."

Katherine followed the entire show. The format combined live television and film clips. In folksy, conversational tones, Dillard and Elaine Cowdrey took turns in describing the problems they'd been asked to resolve. Film clips showed them reaching the solution, whether it was badgering a nationwide furniture chain to make good on shoddy work, or cutting a way through a mass of bureaucracy to learn why an abstemious seventy-year-old woman had been cited for driving under the influence.

"Well?" Saxon asked when the program finished. He stood up, ready to go out for dinner.

"Reminds me of 'Satisfaction Guaranteed!' " Katherine said.

"That's what it reminds me of as well." Saxon drove to a small Italian restaurant at the top of Regent Street. They were shown to a table at the back. Katherine sat down, straightening the skirt of the wool-and-cashmere tweed suit she'd worn to work that day. Saxon was very considerate that way. If he'd made plans to eat somewhere fancy, he would tell Katherine beforehand, and give her to opportunity to change. Tonight, they were eating at a pleasant, but really very average, Italian restaurant, where her working ensemble was not out of place.

An hour later, as they finished dinner, Katherine was wishing that she was wearing something more glamorous. For walking toward the table she shared with Saxon, wearing the same navy blue double-breasted suit he had worn two hours earlier on "Fightback" was the tall, elegant figure of Jeffrey Dillard. And Saxon, not in the least surprised, was standing, hand outstretched, to greet the television personality.

"John, how nice to see you. And Katherine too." Dillard's hand was warm and dry as it enclosed Katherine's. "If only half of what John's told me about you is true, my dear, then I want you on my show."

As Dillard sat down, Katherine caught Saxon's gaze. He grinned at her and gave a half wink. "You want me on your show as what?"

"Hasn't John told you anything?"

"Only to watch 'Fightback' tonight." Unlike most television celebrities, Katherine decided, Dillard looked as good off the set as on it. There were more lines to his face than had been noticeable during the show, but his blue eyes had the same sparkle, his hair was just as thick and snowy white.

"Elaine Cowdrey, my co-host, is leaving. She's pregnant and wants to stay home with her baby. We're going to need someone for when the next series starts in January of 'seventy-nine. John, who's been a dear friend of mine for many years, put forward your name. Of course, I'm familiar with that column you had at the *Eagle,* and I think your approach would translate very well onto the small screen."

Katherine could feel her heartbeat increase. She'd love to get back into a consumer-action role again, especially where she had the exposure of a successful television show. But there was much more to be considered. "I'm very flattered, but it's not a decision I could make immediately."

"Think about it by all means. But please, don't take too long. Unlike newspapers, television shows don't write today what you see tomorrow. We aren't that flexible. We used to be," he added with a trace of sentimentality, "but that was twenty-five years ago, when I read the news wearing a dinner jacket and bow tie, while under the desk, where viewers couldn't see, I had on gray flannel trousers and a pair of tennis shoes."

"You must have a lot of influence with Jeffrey Dillard," Katherine told Saxon as they drove back to Marble Arch.

"We're good friends, that's all. When I heard he was losing his partner, I thought you'd be an obvious replacement. After all, sticking up for the little person is your game, isn't it?"

"John, believe me, it took a lot of willpower not to jump up and kiss Jeffrey Dillard when he made the offer."

"So what's the problem?"

"I don't like leaving jobs unfinished. I've started this investigation into the British Patriotic League, and I won't quit until I've found out all there is to know. Whether you agree with my doing it or not."

"I see. There is one other thing. It's off the record,

but it bears thinking about. Elaine Cowdrey's not the only one who's leaving 'Fightback.' Jeffrey is thinking of retiring in a year or two. That would leave you with a show of your own. If you're capable of handling it, of course."

"Don't try to needle me into taking the job, John."

"Sorry."

Despite the reprimand, the extra snippet of information tantalized Katherine. To be in charge of a prime-time show like "Fightback" . . . she'd be able to redress every wrong in the whole damned world! But there was still the League. "I'll have to give it a lot of thought, John. Talk to a few people about it."

"Go ahead, but just don't take too long."

The first person Katherine spoke to was Franz. She told him that Dillard had approached her directly with an offer to work with him on "Fightback." "Stay at the *Eagle*," Franz answered without the least hesitation. "Your probe of the British Patriotic League is worth a million solutions to people's problems."

Franz's answer set the tone. When Katherine sought Sally Roberts's guidance, the older woman was frank. "You took a big fall here not long ago, Katherine. You're just getting back on track. Why in heaven's name would you want to chuck it all up?"

"Vanity? To be known wherever I go? To be a household face instead of just a household word?"

"Couldn't you continue at the *Eagle* while you worked on 'Fightback'?" Sally asked. "It certainly wouldn't hurt our circulation to have that kind of arrangement."

"No. 'Fightback' is a full-time job."

"Too bad. Don't take it."

Two votes against, and no votes for, Katherine told herself as she left Sally's office.

Soon, it was three votes against. That was after Gerald Waller arrived and spoke to Sally. He telephoned Katherine with some blunt advice. "You're a good journalist, Katherine. Don't waste your talent."

The fourth vote against was cast by Katherine's father, when he telephoned midway through the afternoon to advise her to remain with Eagle Newspapers.

The final, and most eloquent, vote belonged to Lawrie Stimkin. At five-thirty, he came by Katherine's desk and asked her to join him for a drink. They went to El Vino's. Stimkin paid for the drinks—in itself a first—and brought them to where Katherine sat. Solemnly he raised his Scotch and water. "Take it from me, Katherine, you're a good reporter. Too bloody good to be writing the kind of junk that people watch on the idiot box while they're sitting at the supper table, stuffing their faces with cod and chips and pickled onions."

Five to zero against. Katherine telephoned Jeffrey Dillard the next morning to regretfully refuse his offer.

"You're still my first choice, Katherine," Dillard told her. "Remember that in case you change your mind."

"Thank you, I will remember that." After finishing with Dillard, she dialed the number of Saxon Holdings, and told John Saxon that she was staying at the *Eagle*. "Are you going to call me a damned little fool again?"

"No. Perhaps I'll think it, but I've learned it's not wise to tell you such things to your face."

"Jeffrey Dillard did say that should I change my mind I was still his first choice."

"I hope you do change it," Saxon said. "You'd be marvelous in a show like that."

Edna Griffiths and Jimmy Phillips were married on the third Saturday in June, in a civil service at a local registry office. Katherine and Franz acted as witnesses. Henry and Joanne stood behind the wedding couple in the position of bridesmaid and pageboy, although Edna wore nothing fancier than a navy blue crepe dress, which finished, quite modestly, midway down her paddle-shaped calves. Phillips, for the first time in Katherine's memory, wore a suit. It was dark gray, the twin of fifty thousand other suits throughout the country. He had purchased it hurriedly the previous day from one of the menswear chain stores, after Edna had told him that the man she married was expected to wear a suit, a white shirt, a tie, and a carnation in his buttonhole!

Katherine had offered to host a wedding party. "Invite as many people as you like," she told the couple two weeks before the wedding. "Your family, your friends, anyone you want to share this day with."

With tears brimming in her eyes, Edna had assured Katherine that such a gesture was unnecessary. "The only people Jimmy and I have to invite to a party are right here, Mrs. Kassler."

Katherine tried another tack. "You're going away on a honeymoon, aren't you?"

"Making babies at our age? Be away with you!"

"Who said anything about that? I'm talking about a real holiday, a trip to somewhere you and Jimmy have never been. That'll be our wedding gift, Franz's and mine."

"Who'll be here, then, to look after the house?"

"Don't worry, Edna. There are agencies that specialize in temporary help, you know."

"Just as long as I get to approve, Mrs. Kassler."

"Of course," Katherine had answered, knowing it could be no other way. Edna was too jealous of her power within the house to yield it easily, even if it were only for a couple of weeks. . . .

Following the ceremony, Phillips, with a gold ring gleaming on the third finger of his left hand, helped Franz back into the silver Jaguar and folded the wheelchair into the trunk. The wedding group returned to the house in Hampstead. In the afternoon, before leaving with her new husband for the airport and a two-week honeymoon in Spain, Edna gave her replacement final instructions. "Don't forget, the children are up by six each morning, and they like their breakfast early. Mrs. Kassler works late some nights, and is not to be disturbed—"

"Edna!" shouted Katherine, who was driving Phillips and the housekeeper to the airport. "We're going to be late!"

At the front door, where Franz waited in his wheelchair, Edna did something Katherine had never seen her do before. She bent down and kissed Franz, and thanked him for the part he had played in making this day unforgettable. When the housekeeper moved on, Phillips exchanged a long handshake with Franz.

"I've left the new man a complete list of what he's got to do, Mr. Kassler. Don't worry about a thing."

"The only worry I have is that you will miss your flight. Go, Jimmy. Have a wonderful honeymoon."

The two men held the handshake a moment longer before Phillips broke it. All the way to the airport, with the newlyweds holding hands in the back of the Jaguar, Katherine replayed that parting scene in her mind. There had been emotion in Franz's voice that she did not understand. Franz was as close to Phillips as he was to anyone these days. Even to herself, Katherine admitted. So what had choked him up? Was it jealousy? That possibility intrigued her. Was Franz jealous of Edna? Katherine lifted her eyes to peek into the rearview mirror. The housekeeper sat there, eyes almost closed, moon face relaxed in a wide, contented smile. Now who could be jealous of that?

Katherine stayed at home for the remainder of the weekend, keeping a tactful eye on Anne Blyton and Harry Foster, the replacement housekeeper and attendant. Both had come highly recommended from an agency. Nonetheless, Katherine was very choosy about whom she made responsible for her invalid husband and her children.

When she left for work on Monday morning, she was no longer concerned. Anne Blyton, a middle-aged woman with a perpetual smile, had won over Henry and Joanne by giving them each a painting set, and Harry Foster had settled in quickly with Franz. Katherine was confident that the two weeks would pass without incident.

14

The group commanders of the British Brigade were summoned ten days later to an early-evening meeting. Brian Waters's stomach was trembling as he entered Patriot House. Was this a proper meeting, to discuss British Brigade business? Or was Alan Venables about to announce that they had a traitor in their midst, and throw Brian to the mercy of the men he was betraying?

Brian's worries were unfounded. Duplicity was far from Venables's mind. The chairman of the British Patriotic League had ten padded envelopes, one for each group commander.

"I want anti-immigration propaganda distributed. Each envelope contains a hundred posters. Share them among your men, ten posters each. Get them up everywhere. And tape these behind a few of the posters." Venables's thin face broke into a smirk as he handed out packets of razor blades. "These will make sure that whoever rips down our posters has something to remember."

Brian opened his envelope and looked at one of the posters. Two faces were caricatured, one Negro, the other Asian — an Indian or a Pakistani. Bold capitals announced: "Niggers and Wogs Steal British Jobs!" At the bottom of the poster, two words were printed in tiny type: "British Brigade."

Carrying the envelopes and razor blades, the ten young men filed out of the basement. Brian reached the front door of Patriot House and looked toward the street sign where he had chained his motorcycle. Leaning against the sign, waiting for him, was Ginger. Brian slipped the envelope to his weaker left hand. His strong right hand gripped the crash helmet, ready to use it as a weapon, as he had done before. He strode right up to Ginger.

"You waiting for me?"

Ginger raised his hands in front of his face. "Don't hit me, please. I don't want to be your enemy. I want to be your friend. That's why I came here tonight, when I heard there was to be a commanders' meeting. I wanted to see you."

"You want to be my friend, do you?" Brian's voice was full of mockery as he recognized the situation. He was probably the first person ever to beat the living daylights out of Ginger. In doing so, he had transformed the bully from an enemy into an ally. "And just what makes you think I need an ugly lump of blubber like you for a friend?"

Ginger's voice changed to a pleading whine. "I want to be in your group. I'm good. I won't let you down."

Brian's instincts were to lay into Ginger again, but a calm voice of reason restrained him. Ginger was the only person who could cause trouble for him. With Ginger under his supervision, the threat was removed. "All right, I'll get you switched to my group. But you'd better do right by me." Without another glance at Ginger, Brian unchained the motorcycle, kicked it into life, and roared away.

He went from the meeting to Katherine's home, arriving there at eight-fifteen. He told her about the encounter with Ginger, and Katherine agreed that Brian's wisest course was to take Ginger into his group. The matter of the booby-trapped hate posters was more difficult to resolve.

"I can take responsibility for putting out my group's quota of posters," Brian said. "That way, I can leave out the blades, and no one will ever know. But what about the other nine groups? If we don't do something, the hospitals will be running out of needles and thread."

Katherine knew exactly what to do. Perhaps Gerald Waller would not agree with her, but there were times when the public's safety was more important than an exclusive story. She addressed large envelopes to the editors of all the London dailies and to radio and television news directors. Each envelope contained one of the hate posters, a razor blade with tape covering the edges, and a note explaining the booby trap.

"Deliver these right now," Katherine told Brian. "Radio and television first, then the papers."

Brian telephoned from his grandfather's home at eleven o'clock to say that he had completed his assignment. By then, Katherine already knew. With Franz, she had watched the ten o'clock news. The second item had concerned the posters. Some had already appeared on trees and fences; so far, one man had slashed his fingers tearing them down. Holding up the flyer Brian had delivered, the newscaster said: "Police are urging everyone to use caution when removing these posters. Razor blades are taped to the back of many. Serious injuries may result." The newscaster finished off the item by saying that the posters were the responsibility of a previously unknown group called the British Brigade.

The next morning, stories of the booby-trapped posters were carried in all the London dailies. The *Eagle*'s report was no different. Like its competition, the *Eagle* could only guess at the background of the British Brigade. Brian's confrontation, and subsequent truce, with the fat young man named Ginger was too recent to risk demonstrating that the *Eagle* had an inside track.

"Your grandson's a hero," Katherine told Archie when she entered his elevator. "He tipped me off to those posters, and I passed the word to everyone else."

Archie nodded. "Sometimes, Miss Eagles, I think it's too bad that we're a civilized country. Lynch law is the only way to deal with that kind of mob. Raid their headquarters and string everyone up from the nearest lamppost."

"Sometimes, Archie, I'm horrified to find myself thinking that way as well."

Katherine lunched with her father that day at the Adler's store. Instead of eating in the crowded restaurant, they sat at a specially prepared table for two in Roland's office. Over the meal, Katherine told her father what she had not told Gerald Waller or anyone else at the *Eagle*. "I passed up an exclusive story to save a lot of pain for people."

"You did the right thing, Kathy. With Brian on the inside, you'll get other opportunities for glory."

"Just as long as Gerry never finds out that I tipped off everyone else."

Roland grimaced. Owner of the *Eagle* or not, the last thing he relished was another fight with its editor.

The telephone rang. Roland, having told his secretary that he did not want to be disturbed, glanced sharply at it. It rang again. Katherine could see the annoyance in her father's face as he lifted the receiver from the cradle.

"I thought I said I was busy." He listened for a moment. The anger softened. His forehead creased in concern. "The police? Of course I'll speak to them."

Katherine got up and walked toward her father. The look on his face worried her. So did the tone in his voice.

"Hello? Yes, this is Roland Eagles. Who am I speaking to? Inspector Ross? Yes . . . yes, that's the correct address. I see. Yes . . . just a moment." Roland turned to Katherine. He jammed the receiver to his ear

302

with his shoulder, which allowed him both hands free to hold her. "They couldn't get you at the paper, Kathy, so they rang here. Who's at the house?"

Fear gnawed at Katherine's stomach. "Franz, of course. And the temporary housekeeper and attendant. Anne Blyton and Harry Foster. Why?"

"What about Joanne and Henry?"

"They're at school. What is it?"

Roland held his daughter tightly. "The house is on fire. The police say an explosion started it."

Roland and Katherine took a taxi to Chalk Farm station, where Katherine had left the silver Porsche. From there, they zipped in and out of traffic, sometimes at speeds of twice the legal limit, until Katherine sent the Porsche flashing down the street in which she lived, screeching to a halt ten yards short of the crowd that had gathered. By the time Roland climbed out of the Porsche, Katherine was already forcing her way through the crowd, barely able to believe the scope of the disaster.

Firemen played their hoses valiantly on the house, but there was little they could do. The slate roof had collapsed. The interior of the house had fallen in on itself. Floors, ceilings, and interior walls were reduced to rubble. Only structural walls remained upright. The windows were gone, blown out by scorching heat. Flames licked hungrily around blackened window frames. In the driveway, crushed beneath a huge portion of fallen masonry, was the Jaguar sedan.

Roland caught up with Katherine as she tried to shove her way past a police constable controlling the crowd. "Let me through!" she screamed. "That's my house! My husband's in there! He's an invalid! Please let me through!"

"Sorry, miss." The constable looked around for help, before this woman with the wild blue eyes could tear herself free of his grasp and race into the smoking shell of the house.

"Kathy . . . Kathy . . . Kathy . . ." Roland took her from the policeman, and, oblivious to the ring of faces surrounding them, held her very tightly. In his comforting embrace, her rigid body turned pliant; resistance became surrender.

Another police officer approached. "Mr. Eagles? We spoke before. I'm Inspector Ross. Is this Mrs. Kassler?"

Katherine pulled her face away from her father's shoulder. "My husband . . . ?"

"I'm afraid we couldn't get him out. There must have been a tremendous explosion inside the house. Gas, perhaps. We'll know more later. By the time the alarm was given, the downstairs part of the house was an absolute inferno. Your Mr. Foster—"

"Who?" Katherine asked.

"Foster. Harry Foster. Describes himself as a temporary attendant for your husband—"

Again, Katherine cut off the inspector. "He's not inside?"

"No. Mr. Foster and a woman named Anne Blyton were out of the house when the fire started. They're standing over there." The inspector pointed a finger toward an ambulance that waited ominously on the far side of the crowd.

Katherine followed the inspector to the ambulance. Anne Blyton was sitting on a stool given to her by one of the ambulance attendants; by her feet was a shopping cart which held two bags full of groceries. Harry Foster stood next to her, one hand on her shoulder while he stared absently toward the shattered house. When Katherine stood in front of him, he shook his head slowly, like a man incapable of understanding.

"Why was Mr. Kassler left alone? You were paid to be with him the entire time. Why weren't you in the house just now?"

"Kathy . . ." Roland stepped between his daughter and Foster. "Don't blame the poor man because he wasn't burned to death."

304

"He told me to go out of the house, Mrs. Kassler," Foster said. "Your husband practically ordered me to get out."

"Why?"

"Anne here"—Foster patted Edna's replacement on the shoulder—"had gone shopping, you see. Taken the basket and gone walking to the High Street. Five minutes after she'd gone, Mr. Kassler got all panicky. He said he'd forgotten to tell Anne to buy some marmalade."

"Marmalade?"

"You'd specifically asked him to tell Anne, that's what your husband said, Mrs. Kassler. I didn't like the idea of leaving him alone, but he told me it was all right."

"I never mentioned marmalade to him," Katherine protested.

Roland took over. "Why didn't you drive? It's at least a ten-minute walk to the shops."

"I wanted to drive, sir, but Mr. Kassler told me not to. He said Mrs. Kassler had told him that the Jaguar wasn't working properly, and should be fixed before it was driven again."

Another denial came from Katherine, but her voice was little more than a whisper now, as though she understood some awful, damning truth. "I told him no such thing. . . ."

"What happened then?" Roland asked.

"I went off after Anne, like Mr. Kassler told me. It took me half an hour of looking around the shops to find her. When we got back, the fire engines were here. The house was ablaze, and there was nothing anyone could do to help poor Mr. Kassler."

Roland drew Katherine off to one side. "You'll stay with me in Stanmore. We'll go there now. Later on, I'll go with Arthur Parsons to collect the children from their schools. I'll take care of everything, Kathy."

"What about Edna and Jimmy? They're due back

305

from Spain in a couple of days. I was supposed to meet them at the airport. Who's going to meet them now? And what will they say when they hear about this?"

Roland was astounded that Katherine would even think about Edna and Phillips. Then again, perhaps it was best that her mind did jump around like that. There would be enough time later for her to dwell solely on grief.

She stepped back from Roland and ran trembling hands down the brown suede jacket and cream silk dress she wore. Voice shaking, she said: "The only clothes I have are on my back. How can I possibly wear *these* to my husband's funeral?"

Roland held her again, and kept hold of her until she stopped shivering.

Franz Kassler's badly burned body was pulled from the ruins of the house later that day. Flesh and skin were welded to the steel frame of the wheelchair which had been his prison for the final year of his life.

An inquest was held. Harry Foster gave evidence how Franz had virtually ordered him out of the house. Foster, Anne Blyton, and Katherine each testified that they had not smelled gas in the house on the morning of the fire. Nonetheless, there had been a leak; investigators had pinpointed it as causing the explosion which had led to the fierce, unquenchable blaze. The coroner summed up. A paralyzed man alone in a house, a gas leak. "The tragic finale," intoned the coroner, "of a life already heavily blighted by misfortune." He issued a verdict of accidental death, and Katherine silently thanked him for his generosity.

Roland's enormous house in Stanmore, as a rule so empty and full of echoes with just three people living there, suddenly seemed too small. Katherine slept in her old bedroom. Henry and Joanne took two more rooms. And Jimmy Phillips and Edna, when they returned from Spain, shared another.

Roland had gone with Arthur Parsons to meet the returning honeymooners. On the journey, he had told them the news. Edna had begun to sob, while Phillips sat up straight, manfully sniffing back tears. The instant they reached the house, they rushed inside to find Katherine, flinging their arms around her and crying out how sorry they were. At one point, Phillips had even blamed himself for the tragedy. "If I'd been there," he'd told Katherine, while Edna nodded her head in slow, tearful agreement, "I wouldn't have left Mr. Kassler on his own. Never!"

And Katherine, who, as the widow, was entitled to expect comfort from other people, had found herself consoling Edna and Phillips.

Roland had also been the one to inform the children. On the afternoon of the fire, Arthur Parsons had driven him in the old green Bentley first to Joanne's school, and then on to the school Henry attended. From there, Parsons was to drive to a nearby park, where Roland would tell the children about their father. Henry never gave his grandfather the opportunity to break the news in such a peaceful setting. As the limousine pulled away from his school, Henry said, "Where's the Jaguar? Where's the woman who's taken Edna's place? Why did you come for us?" And finally, the inevitable: "What's wrong?"

Parsons had stopped the car there and then. Roland sat between the two children in the back of the Bentley, arms around their shoulders.

"There's been a terrible accident," he explained as gently as he could. "A fire."

"Mummy . . . ?" Henry asked fearfully.

"Your mother is at my home. But your daddy . . ." Roland squeezed the fragile shoulders tighter, just as he had done to Katherine when the first shadow of the tragedy had fallen across them. "Your daddy could not get out of the house."

"Is he dead?" Joanne asked in a shrill voice.

"I'm afraid so." *Dead* seemed such a strange word to come from the mouth of a five-year-old. . . .

A week after the fire, Franz was buried. Katherine wore a black suit and a broad-brimmed hat with a half veil. None of the clothes were of her choosing. Sally Roberts had simply gone through the women's clothing section of Adler's and taken what she thought was necessary for the immediate future. That future included a funeral. Later, when she felt up to it, Katherine could begin to replace the extensive wardrobe that had fed the flames in Hampstead.

The funeral took place on a sunny July afternoon that was more in keeping with strawberries and cream, and Centre Court at Wimbledon, than death. Flanked by her father and Sally, Katherine stood at the graveside and listened to the priest convey Franz's immortal soul into God's hands.

After a couple of minutes, her eyes drifted from the coffin, resting on planks across the open grave, to Edna and Jimmy Phillips, who stood at the front of the large crowd attending the funeral service. Edna had a crumpled white handkerchief in her right hand, with which she kept dabbing her eyes. Next to Edna, wearing his customary black jacket and striped trousers, stood Arthur Parsons; his wife, Peg, was at Roland's home in Stanmore, caring for Henry and Joanne.

Katherine allowed her gaze to sweep on. Eagle Newspapers was well represented. In turn, she locked eyes with Erica and Cliff Bentley, Gerald Waller, and Lawrie Stimkin. Standing slightly apart from the group were Archie Waters and his grandson, Brian.

At the back of the crowd, Katherine spotted another face she knew from Fleet Street. All she could see of Raymond Barnhill was his head and shoulders. He was wearing a tie and a dark jacket. Had he accessorized it with blue jeans or corduroy trousers? Their eyes met. He sent a wan smile across the crowd and the open grave. His mouth opened and formed two silent words: "Hi, friend." Katherine read his lips and inclined her head a fraction of an inch in recognition.

Beyond the crowd was the cemetery parking lot. As Katherine looked, a chauffeur-driven maroon Rolls Royce pulled into a vacant spot. Before the chauffeur could help, John Saxon opened the rear door and stepped out. He half-walked, half-ran toward the crowd at the graveside, as though embarrassed at being late. He came to a breathless stop beside Raymond Barnhill. The two men gave each other the kind of forced smile that only total strangers at a funeral exchange.

Katherine's gaze returned to the coffin. Had she been wrong? Had Franz's death been an accident, as the coroner had decided? Or had she been right? God only knew, Franz had reason enough to end his life. How tired he must have been of the crippled body that had entrapped his active spirit.

Or had there been another reason? Had he killed himself, not because he was sick of being disabled, but to free Katherine, to allow her to enjoy a rich life without being chained to a handicapped man she refused to desert?

The service finished. People lined up to wish Katherine well for the future. Most she answered with a simple "Thank you for coming." To those who were close, she was more receptive.

Raymond Barnhill was not wearing jeans, Katherine noticed, when the American journalist stood in front of her. A dark brown suit hung well on his trim frame. "Sorry to hear about your husband, Katherine. Must have been one hell of a shock."

"It was. Do you know my father?" She introduced Barnhill to Roland. "Raymond works for IPA's London desk."

"Really?" Roland appeared interested. "Perhaps I should poach you for Eagle Newspapers."

While the two men talked, the final person in the line approached Katherine. It was John Saxon. "I'm sorry I was so late, Katherine."

"It's all right, John. You've done more than enough." He had telephoned her the instant he'd read about the fire. She had been too distressed to see him, but he had called every day to learn how she was, and to offer any help he could.

She interrupted the conversation between her father and Raymond Barnhill to introduce John Saxon. Roland already knew the property developer, but Barnhill had never met him. "John, this is Raymond Barnhill, a good friend of mine from America. Raymond, this is John Saxon, a good friend of mine from London."

"What brings you to England, Raymond?" Saxon asked.

"I'm with the IPA. What keeps you in England?"

"I'm chairman of Saxon Holdings, property developers."

Barnhill's eyes swept over Saxon, from the shining handmade shoes to the white silk handkerchief in the breast pocket of his Huntsman suit. "What kind of property do you develop?"

"Luxury residential. Luxury hotels. Office buildings in prime locations."

"Why not some unluxury residential, for the people who really need it? Or isn't there enough of a return in that kind of development to satisfy your stockholders?"

Saxon gave the American a cold smile. "You're just what the doctor ordered, another bleeding-heart liberal reporter."

Seeing Barnhill stiffen, Katherine stepped in quickly. "Don't listen to him, Raymond. John's company does cater to the residential needs of working-class people. That was how we met."

As the two men shook hands, Katherine swore she

saw sparks leap between them. Had Barnhill guessed what place Saxon held in her life? In turn, did Saxon regard Barnhill as competition? She pushed the questions from her mind; this was neither the time nor the place to worry about such things.

Late that evening, after the last of the visitors had left the house in Stanmore, Katherine sat with her father on a sofa in the drawing room. On the mantelpiece, next to the photograph of Roland and Catarina at the nightclub, the clock chimed eleven.

"Thought about what you're going to do, Kathy?"

"I'm going to do what you did when you lost my mother — throw myself so hard back into life that I won't have time to grieve."

"And work?"

"After I'm sure Henry and Joanne are all right, I'll go back to the *Eagle*."

"What about a house?"

"Do you want my menagerie of children and family retainers out of here already?"

"You know better than that. But the children will need stability in their lives. A new home will help to provide it."

Katherine nodded in agreement. She already had the staff to run a house. Edna had said that she wanted to continue working for Katherine, and she had asked if there would be room for her new husband. Katherine had answered yes. The large house she envisioned buying would need two people to run it, a husband-and-wife team, just like her father had. Besides, the familiar faces of Edna and Phillips would help to create the permanence needed by Henry and Joanne. And by herself!

She yawned. "I think it's bedtime. Good night, Daddy." She kissed her father on the cheek, and made her way up the stairs to her old room.

She undressed and slipped into a pale blue silk nightdress. As she was about to turn off the bedside lamp, she noticed a tiny photograph clipped to one of the mirrors of the dressing table. She climbed out of bed, walked across to the vanity, and removed the photograph. It was of Franz, a black-and-white passport photograph he'd given her eleven years earlier, when he had been a student in Germany. She'd put it on the dressing table then and had never removed it, not even when she'd left this house to marry Franz. Had she known that one day she would return to this room? And that this minute photograph would be one of the few pictorial memories of Franz not to be destroyed by fire?

Sitting on the edge of the bed, she held the picture under the light. He was so young, his hair so white, his eyes so full of idealism. In his most vivid nightmare, he could never have imagined the cruel fate that awaited him.

Something Franz had once said came to mind. He had accused her of trying to prove herself, of fighting to get out of her father's shadow, and she'd told him that only sons were faced with that problem, not daughters.

Franz had been right, but she'd been too stubborn to admit it at the time. At the *Eagle,* she'd had to fight constantly to prove that she was there on ability, not because of nepotism. She'd struggled to show that she was her own person, a distinct individual completely removed from her father. Yet at the same time, she was so much like him that it was uncanny. Roland had been a young widower with a child to bring up. She was a young widow, with a son and daughter to raise.

She remembered two years earlier, on her twenty-sixth birthday, looking at her reflection and seeking facial similarities between herself and Roland. She'd found them: the color of her eyes, the tough squareness of her chin.

Tough . . . that was what she had to be. Toughness tempered with compassion, just like her father. If there was ever a moment when she needed to be her father's daughter, it was now.

She got up from the bed again, walked to the dressing table, and clipped the tiny picture back to the mirror.

"*Auf wiedersehen,* Franz. Until we meet again."

Within four days of Franz's burial, Katherine took the first step back. She went out with Jimmy Phillips to purchase a metallic gold Jaguar sedan to replace the car destroyed in the fire. She used it to drive the children to and from school during the last couple of weeks before the summer break. She welcomed the trips for the opportunity to get out of the crowded house and be alone with Henry and Joanne. She thought they were accepting the situation surprisingly well, living in their grandfather's home, being surrounded by people who constantly spoiled them. They barely had time to sit around and reflect, and when they did, it was only, as children are wont to do, to think of the future.

"Will you ever marry again?" Henry asked his mother on the way home one day.

Katherine glanced in the mirror at her son sharing the back seat of the new Jaguar with his younger sister. "Why do you ask that, Henry?"

"We learned at school today about King Henry the Eighth. He was married six times, did you know that?"

"Yes, I was aware of King Henry's six marriages. And as for your question, it's not something I've thought about."

Henry refused to let go. "But if you *did* think about it, Mummy—would you get married again?"

Katherine gave the question a moment of serious thought. John Saxon popped into her mind. Although he telephoned every day, she had not seen him since the funeral. She wanted to see him, but there was so much else to be accomplished first, so many other threads of her life to be knitted back together. Saxon, despite her feelings for him, would be one of the final threads. She

313

had told him that over the telephone, and he had claimed to understand. She hoped he really did.

"Well, Mummy?" Henry pressured. "Would you?"

"If I loved someone enough, I might consider it."

Joanne piped up. "Will we have to call him daddy?"

"No." Katherine's answer was quite emphatic. "Only one person ever deserved that title. If I married a thousand more times, you'd never call anyone daddy again."

"A thousand more times . . ." Henry's voice dissolved in a fit of giggles as he and his sister curled up helplessly on the back seat of the Jaguar. Katherine smiled to herself; their laughter was a healthy sign.

She related the story of the thousand marriages that night while sitting at the long table in the dining room with her father and Sally Roberts, who had joined them for dinner. Since the funeral, Sally had become a frequent dinner guest. Katherine could never make up her mind whether the increased visits were her father's idea — that Katherine would appreciate the regular company of the woman who was the closest thing in her life to a mother — or Sally's own notion. Either way she welcomed them.

"Sounds like the children are recovering very well," Sally said. "How about yourself?"

"I'll go back to work in a few weeks. Start looking for somewhere to live as well, before my current landlord evicts me."

Through the dining-room door came the ringing of the telephone. Moments later, Arthur Parsons entered the room. "For you, Miss Katherine. The American gentleman."

"Mr. Barnhill? Thank you, Mr. Parsons." When Saxon made his daily call, Parsons always used the full name, ringing it out like a toastmaster introducing guests to a receiving line. "Mr. . . . John . . . Saxon!" But when Raymond Barnhill telephoned every few days, Parsons referred to him, in a gently disapproving

314

tone, as "the American gentleman." God, so much snobbery still existed in Britain . . . !

Excusing herself to Sally and Roland, Katherine went into the drawing room to take the call. "Raymond?"

"Didn't interrupt dinner, did I? The old boy sounded even frostier than usual."

"We were just finishing, and I do wish you'd stop referring to Mr. Parsons as 'the old boy'. He's a very sweet gentleman, who feels protective because he's known me since I was fourteen."

"I just called to see how you were bearing up."

"I'm spending a lot of time with my children, and being with them makes me feel better every day. In fact, I just decided that I'm going back to work in a couple of weeks."

"Can I have dibs on your first free lunchtime?"

"Dibs?"

"A claim. Don't you know any American slang?"

"No wonder Mr. Parsons disapproves of you."

She spent a couple of minutes on the telephone with Barnhill, talking about everything and nothing. When she said goodbye and returned to the dining room, she was smiling. The American had not lost his ability to make her laugh.

15

At the beginning of August, little more than a month after the tragic fire, Katherine returned to the *Daily Eagle*. The children seemed to have weathered the loss of their father, and she felt confident enough to leave them while she went back to work. They were in the middle of their long summer vacation, and were kept busy by constant outings with Edna and Jimmy Phillips.

Nothing had happened concerning her special assignment during the time she'd been away. The British Patriotic League had been extraordinarily quiet. Brian Waters said that he had not heard anything in his position as group commander of the British Brigade, and Gerald Waller informed Katherine that the police had drawn a complete blank in their investigation of the booby-trapped posters. The secret of the British Brigade's pedigree still belonged to Katherine.

She spent the week by catching up with people she had not seen for more than a month. On her first day back, she lunched with Erica Bentley, who brought her up to date with *Eagle* gossip. The following day, she had lunch with Raymond Barnhill. For once, the American did not amuse her. His own news was disappointing — the first two publishers to see his book had rejected it — and Katherine did her best to cheer him up. On Wednesday, she lunched with John Saxon.

"God, it's wonderful to see you again," Saxon greeted her. "How do you feel?"

"A little bit numb still, a little empty."

"Katherine, I know this has been the most miserable time of your life," Saxon said, his voice full of sympathy. "It's also been the loneliest, longest few weeks of mine."

"I missed you, too, but I couldn't bring myself to see anyone. I just wanted to be with my children."

He held her hand. "There's no need to explain. I understand perfectly. How are Henry and Joanne?"

Saxon's interest in the children he'd never seen warmed Katherine, and she leaned across the restaurant table to kiss him. "They're just fine. And so am I."

"Is there anything I can do?"

"There is. I want to start looking for a new house, and I can't think of a nicer, more knowledgeable escort than you."

"I'd be delighted to help," Saxon said. "We'll begin this weekend. Instead of going to Henley, I'll stay in town, contact a few estate agents. How does ten o'clock on Saturday sound?"

"Fine. And perhaps, if you're not busy, we could have dinner together afterward."

"I'd like that very much."

That evening, Katherine told her father of her decision to begin house-hunting. His interest sharpened when she mentioned that Saxon would be accompanying her.

"Kathy, I never did ask you why John Saxon attended the funeral. Nor did I ask why he's been telephoning so regularly since then. If it's none of my business, feel free to tell me, but does something exist between the pair of you?"

Katherine nodded. "It started soon after Franz came home." When she started to relate how she had met

317

Saxon at the hotel opening, Roland raised a hand.

"I'm only concerned about one thing, Kathy — what do you feel for him?"

"I don't know. Every other feeling has been so shaken up, that I'm not sure what any emotion means anymore."

"Kathy, you're still a very young woman. You've got all the time in the world. Don't rush into anything."

She kissed her father. "Don't worry; I won't."

Saxon was as punctual as a fine Swiss watch. At precisely ten on Saturday morning, he arrived in the maroon Rolls Royce at Roland Eagles's home. William, the dark-skinned chauffeur, remained at the wheel while Saxon rang the bell.

"I'll get it!" Katherine called out before Arthur Parsons could answer the summons. She wanted to be the one to greet Saxon, to welcome him into her father's home. This was a big day for Katherine, and starting the search for a new home was just a part of it. She wanted to see how Saxon and her father got on together. They had met before, through business, and at Franz's funeral. Today was different. They were meeting, for the first time, on a social level. And, quite possibly, on the level of a concerned father confronting his daughter's next husband . . . ! It was important for Katherine that they hit it off.

She opened the door. Saxon's fawn herringbone sportcoat and brown trousers were as exquisitely tailored as any of his suits. Katherine, in cords and a silk blouse, felt shabby by comparison.

"Good morning, madam. I have some properties in which I trust you'll be interested."

"And good morning to you. Come in and make yourself at home while I finish getting ready." She pulled him into the house, guiding him toward the drawing room. "Daddy, we have a visitor."

Roland was sitting by the bay window, reading the newspaper. He stood up as his daughter brought Saxon into the room. The two men shook hands. Katherine waited just long enough to hear Saxon say that he had learned of half a dozen properties he thought were suitable for Katherine and her family, then she left the drawing room and went upstairs to finish dressing. Ten minutes later, hair in a youthful ponytail, and an Irish fisherman's sweater covering the silk blouse, she was back in the drawing room. The scene had changed completely. Saxon was sitting down, a steaming cup of tea on the table next to his chair. A briefcase he had brought in from the Rolls Royce while Katherine was upstairs was now open on the floor. Brochures for half a dozen choice properties close to Hampstead Heath were spread out across one of the floral-print sofas. Roland, squeezed into one corner of the sofa, was examining them.

"Anything you like, Daddy?"

"I like them all."

"Thank God you're not coming with us. I'll be indecisive enough without any help from you."

"I don't think John will allow you to be indecisive."

Katherine glanced at Saxon, who gave her a slow wink. Obviously, he had used the ten minutes of Katherine's absence to charm away any doubts her father harbored.

"Shall we go?" Katherine asked.

"What about your children? Surely they're coming to look as well," Saxon said. "As they're going to be living in whatever house you choose, shouldn't their opinion also be heard?"

"Of course." Katherine tried to bite back a huge smile. She had been waiting . . . hoping that Saxon would make the suggestion. She wanted him and the children to get to know each other, but she had not felt comfortable about pushing the idea. Despite her effort to suppress it, the smile burst out. She turned it in her father's direction, and Roland nodded in understanding. "They're playing in the back garden. Come and meet them."

Katherine led Saxon through the house. Henry and Joanne were riding bicycles across the flagstone patio. Where the lawn abutted the patio, the carefully manicured grass was gouged with a crisscross of tire marks. "As much as my father loves his grandchildren," Katherine said, "I think he will be very grateful when we all pack up and leave."

The cycles stopped as the children saw the strange man with their mother. "Henry, Joanne, come here. I want you to meet a very dear friend of mine. He's going to take us all out today to look at houses. Would you like that?"

"Hello . . ." Saxon took a step toward Henry. "I'm John Saxon. You must be Henry. And you" — he turned toward the little blond girl — "have to be Joanne. I'm very pleased to meet you both."

The children shook his hand. As they stared at him, still uncertain, Saxon dipped a hand into his pocket. It came out, holding two brightly colored novelty watches. One, with a pink band, he presented to Joanne; the other, with a blue band, he gave to Henry. Hearing her children gush out their thanks, Katherine knew that Saxon had won them over as surely as he had won over her father. As the children put away their bicycles, Katherine asked Saxon how he had broken the ice with Roland.

"The moment you left the room, I told your father that I would like his opinion of the houses I was going to show you. I brought the brochures in from the car, and asked which one he thought you would like best. He was tickled pink that I would give him such a courtesy."

Katherine was filled with admiration. "John Saxon, you are a very smooth operator."

The children's excitement peaked when they saw Saxon's Rolls Royce Silver Shadow. "My grandpa's got a Bentley," Henry told William when the chauffeur opened the rear door, "but it's very old, and not as nice as this."

"I'm quite sure it's not," William answered.

Katherine sat in the rear with the children. Saxon sat in the front. As the Rolls pulled away, Katherine looked back at the house. Her father stood in the doorway, waving.

They saw two houses that morning. Neither fitted the bill. Katherine rejected the first because it was not large enough; she wanted completely separate living quarters for Edna and Jimmy Phillips. Henry and Joanne turned up their noses at the second house because the garden was all carefully cultivated flower beds and no lawn. At one-thirty, Saxon suggested they break for lunch. He had William drive to Regent's Park, where they sat down at an outdoor restaurant.

"Would you like a boat ride?" Saxon asked Henry and Joanne when lunch was finished. They accepted eagerly, and Saxon nodded at William. The chauffeur led the children toward the building where rowboats could be hired. Saxon fetched a plaid blanket from the car, then he and Katherine sat at the edge of the lake.

"They like you," Katherine said. "You really got off on the right foot when you gave them the watches."

"Right now they like William. He's rowing the boat."

Katherine heard Henry shouting. The boat was passing close to the bank where she and Saxon sat. Both children were waving, and the adults waved back. William, warm beneath the bright August sun, had his uniform jacket open; his face was glistening with the first beads of sweat.

"You know, Katherine, looking at all these houses might just be an exercise in futility."

"Am I that fussy, that choosy?"

"No. I just don't think there's any need for you to look. I already know the house where you and the children will be happiest. My house, in Henley-on-Thames."

"That's very sweet, John, but it's far too soon after Franz for me to even think about marrying someone else."

Saxon managed a weak smile. "I'll take that as a very reluctant rejection, with an invitation to try later."

"That's exactly how I meant it. In the meantime, thank you for being here."

William threw in the towel after twenty-five minutes, less than halfway through the hour for which he had hired the boat. His jacket was off, and his shirt was soaked with perspiration. Saxon told him to return to Marble Arch; for the remainder of the day, he would drive the car himself.

"Thank you for the boat ride," Henry and Joanne said.

"You're welcome," answered the disheveled chauffeur, before making his way to the park gate and a taxi.

"We could have run him home," Katherine pointed out. "Especially after he was so good with the children."

"A man that sweaty belongs in a taxi, not in a Rolls Royce."

Katherine laughed. "Snob."

Saxon checked his watch. "It's three o'clock, too late to look at any more houses today. Let's get back in the car; we'll go for a ride."

Henry and Joanne sat in the back. Katherine took the front passenger seat, wondering what surprise Saxon was hiding up his sleeve. He drove for several miles, beyond the northwest suburbs of London. At a sign that read, "Private Road, Keep Out," he stopped the Rolls and turned around to his small passengers.

"All right, who wants to learn to drive?"

"Are you mad?" Katherine asked.

"Certainly not. My company's building an estate of luxury homes on this land. The private road belongs to us."

Henry was first. He sat on Saxon's lap, small hands

322

gripping the steering wheel. Saxon's feet worked the accelerator and brake, and his hands were never more than a fraction of an inch away from Henry's, always ready to grab the wheel in case of an emergency. They drove at a steady twenty miles an hour along the private road, between the shells of luxury homes that Saxon's company was erecting. At the end of the road, Saxon swung the car around, stopped, and said, "All change." Joanne took her brother's place on Saxon's lap, her even smaller hands locked onto the wheel. This time, Katherine noticed, Saxon held the wheel as well. Something else she noticed . . . the car was filled with her children's shrieks of laughter. When was the last time she had heard them enjoying themselves so much?

They all returned to Roland's home just before six. Henry and Joanne burst into the drawing room where Roland sat. "We went for a ride on a boat in Regent's Park!" Henry told his grandfather. "Then Joanne and I learned to drive a Rolls Royce!"

Roland raised his eyes to Katherine and Saxon, who had followed the children in. "In between all this excitement, did you find time to see any houses?"

"A couple," Katherine answered.

"Anything you liked?"

"Not really. We'll look at the remainder tomorrow."

"Now, what's this about my grandchildren learning to drive?"

"They took turns sitting on my lap and holding the wheel," Saxon explained. "Rest assured that we were on a very empty and very private road."

"It's your Rolls Royce," Roland said with a laugh. "Have you made plans for tonight?"

"We were going out for dinner; that was all," Saxon replied.

"I'm dining with a friend, Sally Roberts. At Kendall's in Mount Street. Play a little roulette or blackjack afterward. Would you and Katherine care to join us?"

"We'd be very pleased to do so."

At six-thirty, Saxon left the house to return to Marble Arch and change for the evening. He promised to meet Katherine, her father, and Sally at Kendall's for dinner at eight o'clock.

"You can drive me into town now," Roland said to Katherine. "Save taking a taxi, or asking Sally to pick me up."

"That's not the reason you asked John and me to join you for dinner. You want to see how he plays the tables, don't you?"

"I do?"

"I know you, Daddy. You judge a man's character by the manner in which he gambles."

Roland laughed. It was perfectly true, a trait he had acquired many years before. How a man wagered was how he lived. An overly cautious gambler—never ask him to take a risk in anything. A reckless gambler—don't even get into a car with him. Roland had gained admiration for a lot of people after watching them at the tables, and he had lost it for just as many.

John Saxon was neither overly cautious nor reckless. After eating in Kendall's small but first-class restaurant, he and Roland moved to a blackjack table. Each man bought two hundred pounds' worth of chips. Roland kept one eye on his own cards, and one eye on Saxon. The property developer's mode of play was simple. He was not rash with his money, betting only five pounds. When he won, he doubled the bet to ten, keeping it there until he lost. Then he backed down to five, staying there until he won again. After half an hour, Roland, betting haphazardly for the fun of it, had lost all his money, while Saxon was just short of doubling his original stake.

Roland returned to the table where Katherine sat with Sally. In response to his daughter's inquisitive glance, Roland grimaced and jerked a thumb toward the cashier's cage, where Saxon was busy exchanging chips for money. Katherine laughed delightedly. Saxon had won, and her father had lost!

They returned to Sally's apartment in Curzon Street for coffee. Saxon left shortly afterward, telling Katherine that he would call for her at ten the following morning, when they would continue their house-hunting. Through the living-room window, Katherine watched the Silver Shadow glide away, then she turned to her father.

"Well, how did he play?"

"Better than your father," Sally broke in, laughing.

"I was only playing for the sheer hell of it," Roland said. "John was playing to win. He believes in streaks. When he wins he increases his stake, betting that he's in for a good streak. When he loses, he lowers his stake, because he believes that losing, too, will go in a streak. Even then, he doesn't get carried away. Win or lose, he bets sensibly. Certainly well within his pocket."

"Which makes him . . . ?" Katherine asked.

"Someone who grinds down his opponents, while keeping plenty in reserve in case he needs a big push. He's a very shrewd man, because he also knows when to walk away. He'll accept a small victory instead of risking what he's won already for a larger triumph. He is not a man," Roland said approvingly, "I would relish facing across a boardroom table."

It was almost midnight when Roland and Katherine left Sally's home. Katherine sat in the Porsche, watching fondly in the mirror as her father kissed Sally good night. When Roland climbed into the car and closed the door, Katherine asked, "When are you going to stop messing around and marry Sally?"

Roland chuckled. "Why should we ruin a good relationship?"

"You'd enhance it, not ruin it." She turned the key to start the engine. "John proposed to me today. I told him that it was too soon after Franz to even think of such a thing."

"Was that the only reason?"

"How do you mean?"

"Is it just the time factor, or aren't you sure about John?"

Twenty yards ahead, a traffic light turned amber. Katherine geared down and floored the accelerator pedal, speeding through the intersection as the light changed to red. "I feel like I'm getting to know him all over again."

"It's one thing to have an affair with someone when you know that your marriage provides a safety net, but it's something else entirely to look on that same person as a possible mate."

Katherine felt no need to reply; her father's concise summation had made a response redundant. She drove silently for two miles, every so often glancing at her passenger. Was it her imagination, or was Roland avidly watching the Porsche's dials and gauges — making believe that he was driving? She pulled into the side of the road, turned off the engine, and set the brake.

"Want to drive?"

"Don't be silly. I haven't driven since the day you were born . . . the day your mother died."

"That's not what I asked you." Katherine climbed out of the driver's seat, walked around to the passenger side, and opened the door. "You still have a license, don't you?"

"Of course. It's good until my seventieth birthday."

"So you're legal. Come on, there's no traffic on the road."

"All right." Roland switched positions and settled behind the wheel, pushing back the seat to compensate for his height. "What do I do now?"

"Start the engine."

Roland did. He flipped the gas pedal, watching, with almost childish enthusiasm, the tachometer needle rise and fall.

"People are sleeping," Katherine cautioned. Roland stopped revving the engine. He shifted into first and let out the clutch. The car jerked forward and stopped. The engine stalled.

"Take off the handbrake."

Roland felt his face beginning to burn. Clutch engaged, he selected first again, and released the brake. Slowly, he let out the clutch. The Porsche moved forward smoothly. As confidence returned, Roland turned the wheel and pulled out.

"Check what's coming!" Katherine screamed.

She was too late. A horn blasted in Roland's ear. Lights flashed. Tires squealed. Miraculously, there was no collision. Roland jammed his foot on the brake and stalled the Porsche's engine again. The white Rover, into whose path he had pulled out, was now stopped on the other side of the road, twenty yards away. Two of its wheels were up on the curb, and its two occupants were glaring ferociously at the silver sports car.

Simultaneously, father and daughter saw the lights on top of the white Rover and the reflective orange lettering on its side. "Damn!" Roland said. Katherine said nothing. She was too busy laughing. The first time in twenty-eight years that her father had tried to drive, and he had forced a police car off the road. She was still laughing when the two police officers cited her father for driving without due care and attention.

"I think I'd better drive the rest of the way," Katherine told Roland when the police had left. "You'll only get into more trouble." They swapped seats. Katherine pulled herself closer to the wheel. "Boy . . . I just can't wait to tell Sally."

Roland, embarrassed into blushing crimson, shrank down into the passenger seat. "Why don't you take a full-page ad in the *Eagle* while you're at it?"

"Don't give me any ideas." Before pulling away, Katherine leaned across the car and hugged Roland. "You might be the world's worst driver, but you're still

327

the world's best father."

John Saxon collected Katherine and the children at ten o'clock the following morning. Saxon drove himself, having given William the day off. The first three houses did little for Katherine. She went through each one quickly, eager to be on to the next.

The fourth and final house, which Katherine viewed after lunch, was an empty Edwardian residence in Frognal, on the edge of the Heath, and set in its own roomy grounds. Followed by Saxon, the children, and the estate agent, Katherine inspected the ground floor, which included a large reception hall, cloakroom, three reception rooms, playroom, breakfast room, kitchen, and laundry room. Four spacious bedrooms and two bathrooms filled the second floor. The third floor, with two more bedrooms and another bathroom, could be converted into a self-contained apartment. Although the house had been fully modernized, with gas central heating and insulated windows, its three fireplaces on the ground floor were still functional. That appealed to Katherine's traditional side; she loved nothing more than the smell of burning wood on a crisp winter's night.

Finally, she checked the grounds. The front garden was all neatly trimmed hedges and colorful rosebushes and trees. The massive back garden was nothing but lustrous green lawn, with a pond and fountain in the center. Henry and Joanne loved the house. So did Katherine. Especially when she saw the name worked into the high wrought-iron front gate; somehow, she had missed seeing that before. Kate's Haven, the house was called.

"Who was Kate?" she asked Saxon.

"The lady who's selling the house. She lived here for thirty years before moving to the coast."

"This is the house I want to buy. It makes me feel like

I've come home."

"Your father will be glad."

"Why?"

"He liked this one as well. It was his idea that I leave it until the very last."

Later that afternoon, Katherine returned to the house with her father. Standing in the front garden she spread her arms and proclaimed: "This is it. Kate's Haven. Home, sweet home."

There was a tremendous amount of decorating to be done, but one thing the builders would not touch would be that front gate.

Katherine's offer on Kate's Haven was accepted, and she made plans to move in at the end of September. She would have to put up with builders and their mess for several weeks after taking possession, but she was quite prepared for that. It was part of the price of having a home of her own again.

Excitedly, she toured stores, ordering furniture and fittings for each room. Hand-crafted kitchen cabinets in English oak, a dining-room set, easy chairs, couches, occasional tables, beds, dressers . . . everything from a cast-iron oven to a complete range of Le Creuset cookware, because that was what had been used in the old house, and she'd liked it. Katherine was starting a household from scratch, and there wasn't a single item she did not need.

John Saxon accompanied her on some of the shopping expeditions. Afterward they would go out for dinner or a drink, but Katherine never suggested that they return to Saxon's Marble Arch home, nor did he ever press her to do so. Their relationship was that of two friends catching up with one another over a meal; very similar, in fact, to the manner in which she continued her association with Raymond Barnhill, with whom she lunched whenever their schedules coincided.

Her feelings for the two men, though, were worlds apart. Barnhill was a chum, a professional colleague, really, with whom she had shared some exciting moments. Saxon was so much more. Other than Franz, he was the only man to have aroused such a mixture of feelings within her, animal hunger and loving tenderness, twisted together and inseparable. On the night before the closing of the new house, Katherine decided she had mourned for long enough. It was time to still that hunger, and, in turn, receive some tenderness and love.

After eating dinner, Katherine accompanied Saxon back to Marble Arch. He opened the door of his town house. For a full minute, Katherine remained standing in the entrance hall, becoming accustomed all over again to the surroundings. The curving staircase, the patterned Wilton, the open door of the dining room with its broad twin-pedestal table.

"Déjà vu?" Saxon asked.

"With one difference. I didn't have to invent any excuses tonight. No fake assignments, no make-believe meetings. I just said I'd be late, that I was seeing you for dinner." She removed her lightweight gabardine coat and draped it on the clothes stand in the corner of the hall. Beneath the coat she wore a bright red light wool dress, belted emphatically at her slim waist.

"Welcome back," Saxon whispered. He held her in his arms and gave her a long, bruising kiss. Her mouth opened, her tongue darted out. She dug her fingers into his back, and ground her entire body against the length of him.

At last, Saxon broke from the kiss. Holding her hand, he took a couple of steps toward the curving staircase and the upper part of the house. Katherine pulled back. "I don't want a four-poster bed. I want an Aubusson rug, with Nelson and Wellington playing Peeping Tom."

Saxon allowed himself to be led into the front room. There was none of the leisurely approach of their first encounter in this room with its pale gold walls and high white ceiling. There was no lighting of candlesticks, no slow, teasing undressing, no wonder of discovery. This time, Katherine was an aggressive initiator. As Saxon closed the door and walked around the room, drawing the heavy drapes, Katherine slipped out of her dress and tossed it onto one of the sofas, following it with her half-slip. By the time Saxon finished, she was standing on the Aubusson, completely naked, waiting for him.

She crooked a finger at him. "Come here, John Saxon."

Obediently, he stood in front of her. She started with his tie, undoing the knot and slipping it free of his collar. She tugged his jacket from his body, undid the buttons of his shirt, and pulled that off to expose his chest. While she rubbed her breasts against him, her fingers tugged at his belt, a button, the zipper. His trousers dropped around his ankles, and he kicked them away.

As she wrapped her arms around his neck, his hands gripped her sides and lifted her clear of the Aubusson. She swung her legs up and around his waist, and could feel the top of him press against her, probing, searching. Clinging tightly to him, she moved her hips back and forth, a fraction of an inch at a time. With each motion, she could feel herself opening, could feel him entering. Saxon's moan of ecstasy was drowned out by Katherine's sudden, ragged intake of breath as she slid all the way down onto him.

Balancing carefully, Saxon stepped back until he felt the edge of the sofa pressing against his legs. He lowered himself gently. Katherine sat astride him, moving up and down with tantalizing slowness, feeling him deep inside her. Swollen. Trapped, until she decided to release him. She squeezed, and heard him gasp.

"God!" Saxon cried out. "I've missed you."

They made love the second time on the Aubusson, under the watchful eyes of the heroes of Trafalgar and Waterloo. Afterward, as Katherine lay with her head on Saxon's chest, she gazed at the paintings.

"Do you think Nelson and Wellington approve?"

Saxon angled his head to peruse each painting in turn. "Wellington's got a thunderous scowl on his face—"

"They didn't call him the Iron Duke for nothing," Katherine broke in.

"But Nelson's smiling. In fact, he's winking."

Katherine began to laugh. "That's not a wink, John. The poor man only had one eye!"

"It's good to hear you laugh again."

"It sounds even better from my side. You know, tonight's like the final piece of the puzzle. Everything seems to be back together now. My relationship with my children, the new house, and my friendship with you."

"Friendship?"

"Friendship is a lovely word. I like to think that's what we have. Among"—she ran the tip of her tongue across her upper lip—"other things."

He lifted her up and buried his face in her breasts, rubbing it from side to side. She felt the finest trace of stubble—he'd shaved that evening, before their date—and the roughness spread a warmth through her. She'd have two rashes when she moved into her new home the following day, and she could think of no more welcome housewarming gift.

16

The failure of the British Brigade's initial mission, the distribution of the booby-trapped posters, did not unduly worry Alan Venables. He attributed it to bad luck, somebody ripping down one of the first posters to be put up, cutting themselves, and then calling the police; before any real damage could be done, warnings had been circulated through the media.

Nonetheless, Venables decided to wait before launching another action. After that first failed attempt, he felt his enemies would be on guard. He would let enough time pass for them to be lulled into a sense of security.

He allowed three months to elapse, until the beginning of October. Then he organized a savage campaign of harassment against immigrant organizations and sympathetic left-wing factions. In a month-long reign of terror, British Brigade members smashed the windows of homes belonging to black and Asian community leaders. Front windows of Indian restaurants had garbage cans thrown through them. A rundown house that served as headquarters for a Marxist group was set on fire late one night by Molotov cocktails thrown from a passing van. A mosque in the East End of London, which had started life seventy years earlier as a synagogue, when the immigrants had been Eastern European Jews, was daubed with hate slogans. After each incident, telephone calls were made to radio and television stations, claiming responsibility for the British Brigade.

Despite strenuous police investigation, nothing came to light about this new organization. Frustrated at being unable to hit back at the fleeting movement, victims turned to highly visible, more easily recognizable targets, such as the British Patriotic League. During the fall of 1978, the League staged well-attended anti-immigration rallies in London and in the Midlands cities of Birmingham and Leicester. An alliance of left-wing and immigrant groups disrupted the demonstrations. Rather than respond with violence of its own, the League called on the massive police presence for protection. Now that the British Brigade—the secret striking arm of his dual-track strategy—was fully operative, Alan Venables wanted the British Patriotic League to appear as the epitome of respectability. When part of the League's manifesto was law and order, how could its members act otherwise?

Brian Waters had no chance to give Katherine advance warning of these outrages. He could only tell her afterward. "Venables picks whatever group he wants," Brian explained to Katherine, "and gives them their orders right before they go out on the job." Despite this, Katherine and the *Eagle* still held an advantage over the rest of Fleet Street: they knew who controlled the Brigade.

Brian participated in one mission. The group he commanded was called upon for the mosque assignment. The entire group, including Brian's newfound ally, Ginger, met at the mosque at four-thirty in the morning. Armed with spray cans, they covered the building's walls and windows with hate. The next night, while angry headlines screamed from newspa-

334

pers, Brian met again with his subordinates to repay them the money they had laid out for the spray cans.

Ginger pocketed his expenses and asked, "Got time for a drink, then, Brian?"

Brian would have preferred to go home and sleep, but he saw the wisdom of appearing to return Ginger's offer of friendship. They went to a public house, busy with evening trade. Taking two half pints of beer to a corner table, they sat down.

"I went by that mosque today," Ginger said. "Saw what we'd done. Looked even better in daylight than it did last night."

Brian glared across the small table. "I told everyone to steer clear of that place. You think the police aren't looking for us to return to the scene of the crime?"

Ginger smiled. "Relax. I work right around the corner as a presser in a coat factory." He swallowed the beer and smacked his lips. "Drink up, Brian. I'll get us another."

"This is fine for me. Don't want to fall off my bike, do I?"

"That's a good one, Brian." Chuckling at the weak joke, Ginger walked toward the bar for a refill. Through narrow eyes, Brian watched him go. He was no longer worried about Ginger's loyalty. The fat slob practically worshipped him! Suffocated by the fawning attention, Brian decided he preferred Ginger as an enemy than as a friend.

Despite his earlier refusal to run a story on the formation of the British Brigade, and its secret link to the British Patriotic League, Gerald Waller was now becoming uneasy. He wanted to wait for the biggest possible story, but he was worried that someone might be injured or killed before the expose could be written.

"So far we've got the vandalism at the mosque,"

335

Waller said, during a meeting with Katherine, Sally Roberts, and Roland Eagles, "attacks on homes and shops, and the fire-bombing of the Marxist headquarters. It's all property damage so far, but how long will it be before these lunatics become more ambitious and start spilling blood?"

Sally's concern took a different tack. "When we break the story because of our source, can the police prosecute us?" she asked. "Can they accuse us of obstructing their investigation?"

"That's a question we should be asking our solicitors," Roland replied, "to get the legal opinion on our actions. Ethically, though, I'm becoming uncomfortable for the same reason as Gerry. If something truly tragic should happen . . ."

Katherine held up a hand to interrupt her father. "Let's hold off for one more action. We can't run the story now. The last offense—the mosque desecration—took place eight days ago. The public's memory has dimmed already. Let's wait for one more strike by the British Brigade, and then we'll print our story in the very next issue."

Sally was still concerned about police reaction when the story broke. "How are we going to explain our knowledge of the Brigade's parentage?"

"An anonymous telephone call," Katherine replied. "Our source will be a mystery caller who told us everything. Right from that very first day, when the British Brigade was formed."

Within four months of taking possession of its new headquarters, the British Patriotic League had utilized much of the space. The basement had been cleaned out and transformed into a printing center. Staff had been hired to produce *Patriot* and other propaganda literature in-house, on newly installed offset machinery. The executive committee retained offices on the top floor. The ground floor had been transformed into meeting rooms. Space on the remaining floors was assigned to various committees: recruiting, finance, public relations, and, with an optimistic flourish, even a general-election committee. Nowhere was there mention of the British Brigade. As far as the League was concerned, it did not exist.

At the beginning of November, the group commanders of the British Brigade were summoned. Alan Venables addressed them in one of the smaller meeting rooms. "I'm pleased with the work you've done. Because of you and your men, peaceful League rallies were viciously attacked. We didn't fight back. We were the injured party—assaulted by Britain's enemies, the coloreds and the communists. Believe me when I say that the League made many friends among the white people of Britain these past weeks."

The commanders' rumbling of self-approval erupted into a footstamping, hand-clapping explosion as Venables added in staccato tones, "But we haven't finished yet!"

Brian made the journey on his motorcycle from Patriot House to Katherine's new home in Frognal. The children were asleep, and Edna and Jimmy Phillips were in their self-contained flat on the top floor. Brian had to pick his way through an obstacle course of stepladders and sawhorses as he followed Katherine across the reception hall to the breakfast room that adjoined the kitchen.

"The British Brigade's planning to burn down a black social club next Saturday night," Brian reported.

"How do you know so far ahead?"

"Venables told us it's a special job, the biggest we've ever done, and he wanted us to cut cards for the honor of doing it."

"Will you be involved?"

"No, thank Christ. I got lucky and lost."

"What's the name of this club?"

"Sons of the Islands. It's in Stoke Newington, a couple of miles from where I live."

"Is the club to be burned while people are in it? Is that why it's such a special job?"

"No. You see, on Sunday night, the club's supposed to be used for some big dance. A fund raiser to fight the British Brigade. Venables wants to demonstrate that nothing can stop the Brigade, nothing can fight it."

"Except us," Katherine said. "Except the *Eagle*."

The Sons of the Islands social club was located above a West Indian grocery store. Dances were held there every Saturday night, with calypso and reggae music echoing across the street until the small hours. During the rest of the week, the club was used by its West Indian members for games of cards, snooker, and darts, or to just sit and reminisce about the Caribbean.

The dance scheduled for Sunday was something special. It was meant to raise money to fight the work of the British Brigade. The sudden upsurge in racial hatred had scared many people. The time had come to raise a war chest to fund resistance. Black celebrities from the sports and entertainment worlds had agreed to participate. Local politicians, ever aware of the need to gather votes, would be on hand. The local newspaper would give coverage.

All the grandiose planning went for nought. An hour before dawn on Sunday, a van pulled into the service road that ran behind the club. Two young men climbed out. The rear door of the club presented no problem. Carrying cans, they ran up the stairs and slopped gasoline across the club's floor and furniture. A match was struck. The two young men ran downstairs to the van, jumped in, and drove away. When the first fire engine arrived, the entire building was ablaze.

Two hours later, when the building was little more than a smoldering shell, the customary telephone call was made to the BBC, claiming that the fire was the work of the British Brigade.

Most of Fleet Street carried the story at its face value: another outrage in a long list of such outrages by the British Brigade. Some of the left-leaning newspapers used the incident to point accusing fingers at the police, who, in the opinions of the leader writers, had not done enough to discover the identity of Brigade members solely because the victims were mostly colored.

Only the *Daily Eagle* had a different slant on the story. Katherine worked late on Sunday night. So did Gerald Waller. They were both at the printing works of Eagle Newspapers when the first copy of the Monday *Eagle* rolled off the press. Waller grabbed the newspaper from the pressman and held it out. The report of the fire was on the front page, but it was part of a larger story, under the headline of "British Brigade — Who Really Pulls the Strings?"

Editor and reporter remained in the printing works for another twenty minutes, watching the machinery spew out newspapers. Then they went to their separate homes, to rest in preparation for the explosion that the morning would bring.

Katherine had barely fallen asleep when knuckles rapped on the bedroom door. She jerked awake, forcing her eyes to stare at the bedroom clock. Five minutes to six! She'd left instructions with Edna that she wanted to sleep until nine o'clock. She had even disconnected the bell of the bedroom telephone.

"Mrs. Kassler!" The housekeeper's voice came through the door. "It's the BBC!"

"Tell the BBC to buzz off! Better yet, I'll do it!" She snatched the receiver from its rest. "Hello, BBC? Buzz off and let me sleep!"

The bedroom door opened and Edna entered, a woolen dressing gown covering her from neck to feet. "Mrs. Kassler, the BBC's not on the phone. They've sent a car to take you to the studio for the morning news show on the radio."

"I'm quite capable of driving myself to the studio. Tell the driver to leave."

Edna returned two minutes later, as Katherine was stepping into the shower. "The driver says he daren't leave without you," she called out.

"Jesus Christ!" Katherine muttered, and turned the shower full on. But maybe it was just as well; as tired as she felt, she'd probably fall asleep at the wheel.

By six forty-five, Katherine was at the BBC, all business in a navy-blue suit and raspberry silk blouse. The show host spent a couple of minutes talking to her in the waiting room, going over the questions he would ask, then she was left alone to marshal her thoughts. After fifteen minutes, the program secretary approached.

"Mrs. Kassler, will you come with me, please?"

Katherine followed the woman out of the waiting room and along the corridor. As the secretary opened a door above which a red light glowed, Katherine glanced over her shoulder. Entering the waiting room, as if to take her place, was Alan Venables. Katherine opened her mouth to ask the secretary the reason for Venables's presence. The secretary's face whitened. She snapped a finger to her lips, and motioned with her head toward a round table. Six microphones were positioned at the table. The show host sat at one, and a white-haired men's fashion consultant at another, continuing their discussion as if nothing else existed. Katherine sat down and waited her turn.

The host finished his fashion interview with "Thank you, John, for another of your amusing and interesting insights into the clothes we wear." The white-haired man left the room as quietly as Katherine had entered it. "Now we have the opportunity to speak to Katherine Kassler, the *Daily Eagle* reporter whose story this morning has shaken everyone. I know it's shaken me. And like everyone else, I'm a little mystified about this dual-track strategy. It sounds like a new system of travel on British Rail. Instead, it's a particularly nasty political tactic. Is that right, Katherine?"

"A *very* nasty political tactic. Basically, you act in a civilized fashion toward a certain party, while simultaneously you are paying and instructing someone else to kick that party hard in the shins."

"When you make a claim like you've just made—that the British Patriotic League is really behind the recent attacks on minority groups—you must have some concrete evidence to back it up. Can you share this evidence with us?"

"It's the word of an unimpeachable source."

"This source has personally witnessed Alan Venables, the chairman of the British Patriotic League, giving the orders for these outrages?"

"Unimpeachable," Katherine repeated. "More detailed information than that, I am not prepared to give anyone. Suffice it to say, my source can verify that at the beginning of June, Alan Venables called one hundred of the British Patriotic League's toughest young members to Patriot House and formed them into the British Brigade, a terror organization split into ten separate squads. My source can also verify that Venables personally gave orders to these squads to carry out a terror campaign against minority and left wing groups, forcing them to retaliate.

With no idea how to strike back at the British Brigade, these groups attacked rallies of the British Patriotic League, which is precisely what Venables wanted."

"Fascinating," the host breathed. "Absolutely fascinating."

"If it's so fascinating, why do you have Venables sitting out there in the waiting room? So he can throw a few lies into this affair?"

"This is Britain, Katherine. We do have a reputation of hearing both sides of an argument."

"I'll tell you what he's going to say right now. That my newspaper is engaged in a vendetta against him."

The interview ended on that note. Katherine was escorted out by the program secretary. In the hallway, she passed Alan Venables. For the briefest moment, their eyes met, then Venables was gone.

Level with the waiting room door, Katherine stopped. "You don't have to show me out," she told the program secretary. "I'll stay and listen." She resumed her seat in the waiting room, listening as the show was piped in.

Venables wasted no time. The instant he was introduced, he branded everything that Katherine had written in the *Eagle,* and claimed on the program, as "a vicious pack of lies, invented by a woman who should be writing fiction, not news."

"Mrs. Kassler claims her source is unimpeachable."

"Nonexistent is more like it," Venables fired back.

In the waiting room, Katherine clenched her fists so tightly that her fingernails dug painfully into her hands. Tears of anger sprang to her eyes. How could a man sit in front of a live microphone and lie like this? Had he no conscience? No soul?

"What would be Mrs. Kassler's motive for lying?"

"What it's been all along, from the moment the *Daily Eagle* made its ridiculous claim that the British Patriotic League was recruiting hooligans from football games. To smear us. The *Daily Eagle,* for its own reasons, supports the people who would plunge Britain into the abyss. Not halfway into it, where we are now, but right to the very bottom of the pit. All the British Patriotic League wants to do is tell the people of this nation the truth. Rather than allow that truth to be heard, our enemies attack our peaceful rallies. And their supporters, like the *Daily Eagle,* invent these libelous stories so it would appear to the guileless that our enemies have valid reason to attack us."

Venables paused for breath before launching into his grand finale, and Katherine felt herself becoming more and more upset by his callous distortion of the truth.

"Eventually, all lies are seen for what they are. In time, everyone in this country will know the truth about slandermongers like Mrs. Kassler, and her father's newspaper, the *Daily Eagle.* The truth about the British Patriotic League. The truth about the problems our beloved country faces. And the truth shall set them free."

Katherine was waiting in the corridor when Venables was escorted from the studio. The smirk on his thin face froze as he saw her.

"You filthy, disgusting liar!" she shouted, and slapped him across the face with all her strength. Stunned, Venables staggered back into the secretary's arms. By the time he recovered enough to speak, Katherine was on her way downstairs to find a taxi that would take her to Fleet Street.

The slap haunted Katherine for the entire day. The confrontation with Venables at the BBC became a major story, aired first on the radio, then in the early racing editions of that evening's newspapers. Reporters from other papers telephoned her to learn more. Promises flowed like molasses that they would be kind to her; after all, they said, if one reporter was maligned, they were all maligned. Katherine ignored the offers of professional friendship. She simply issued the same statement to them all: she had become so distraught over Venables's lies that she had lost control of herself and hit him. End of quote, end of story.

She offered a more detailed explanation to her father, who telephoned the instant he heard the story. "Instead of relaying the news, Daddy, I lost my temper and became a part of it."

"Your temper told you to do the right thing," Roland said.

She did not go out for lunch that day for fear of becoming a target for a camera or a sharp pencil the instant her feet touched the street. She wasn't hungry anyway. She doubted that she would even be hungry by that evening, when she was supposed to have dinner with John Saxon. Seeing Venables and having to listen to his poisonous lies first thing in the morning had killed her appetite, even if slapping him hard enough to make her own hand tingle had sharpened it again for a moment.

Twice during the day, messengers brought up gifts that had been left at the downstairs reception desk. The first was a bouquet of red roses. The attached card read, "You've got your mother's temper and my right hook, and I've never been prouder of you. Roland." Katherine placed the roses in a vase on her desk, and left them, with the card, for everyone to see.

The second gift came in a brown paper bag. Boxing gloves! She knew who'd sent them even before she read the accompanying note. She telephoned the International Press Agency, and asked for Raymond Barnhill.

"What am I supposed to do with these?"

344

The American journalist roared with laughter. "They're for when you turn professional. The way I heard it on the radio, you're the next Marciano. Better looking, of course."

"Thank you." An unwelcome thought occurred. "You didn't send this story—"

"Over the wire? Damned right I did. This is human interest at its best. This time tomorrow, you'll be a household name from Blowing Rock, North Carolina, to Oshkosh, Wisconsin."

"That's what I always wanted, you louse," she said, and hung up. But she was smiling all the same.

As the afternoon drew on, she thought about her date with John Saxon. She could imagine what he'd say when they met. He would accuse her of giving even more publicity to Alan Venables and his politics of hatred. That was one thing she found so hard to understand about Saxon. How could such a successful man have such an ostrichlike mentality? How could he be so blind and timid when it came to something as important as this?

Saxon served dinner at home that evening, ordering from the same French restaurant he had used on the night Katherine had returned from her first ride on a soccer special. This time, he chose turbot fillet poached in white wine and mustard, complementing it with a bottle of Meursault from the comprehensive wine cellar he maintained at his in-town residence.

"God, that was wonderful," Katherine said as she finished the last morsel. "You may not be able to cook, but you certainly know how to order in."

"Do you know why I ordered in?"

Katherine made a noise that was half yawn, half sigh. So far, Saxon had not mentioned the day's events; she was certain that he was about to compensate for the lapse. "Because everyone would have been looking at us if we went out?"

"Your picture did appear in the newspapers."

"It was an old picture, John, the one used ages ago for 'Satisfaction Guaranteed!' I don't even look like that anymore."

Saxon split the remainder of the Meursault between the two glasses. "That was the only time you ever really used your talents, you know, when you ran 'Satisfaction Guaranteed!' What you're doing now is a shameful waste."

"Please, John, don't start that again!"

"Instead of shouting at me, you should be grateful that I care enough to worry about where your career's heading."

"And just where is my career heading?"

"Down. You're wasting yourself by fighting this bunch of fascists. Leave them alone; they'll die a natural death."

"Like hell they will. What about the disgraceful things that have been happening?"

"That's some group of monsters called the British Brigade, not Venables's British Patriotic League."

"What is it going to take for you to see they're one and the same, John? Haven't you heard of the dual-track strategy?"

"Not until this morning, when you suddenly popularized the term. Where did you get it from?"

"Does it matter?"

"Oh, I see. Your source gave it to you, did he? This unimpeachable source who's provided you with information on every move the British Brigade's ever made. Katherine, take my word for it—Frederick Forsyth doesn't need any help from you."

"You agree with Venables that I'm writing fiction?"

"I've yet to see any fact. I know, your source . . ."

"Damn it, John Saxon! My source is real! He exists!"

"Who, Brian Waters?"

Katherine's face sagged. "How did you know?"

"Who else would you know who could be mixed up in something like this? Did you pay him to be a spy?"

"Yes, we gave him something."

"Are you sure he's not earning it by telling you whatever he thinks you want to hear?"

Katherine stared stonily at Saxon, unwilling to even consider that possibility.

Saxon's voice softened. "Katherine, can't you see that even if what you claim is true, Venables's big-lie technique is still stronger? And do you know why? Because the British public does not want to hear your truth. It makes them uncomfortable to know that something could be wrong at the middle of their society."

"And just how comfortable will they feel when they finally realize how evil this man Venables is?"

"Dear, sweet, naive Katherine. It will make no difference at all. As long as it doesn't increase the price of a pint of beer or a pack of cigarettes, the British public couldn't give a tinker's cuss."

Katherine touched a hand to her face. Her cheeks were flushed, her forehead like a smooth stone in the sun. Was it the half bottle of Meursault, or the argument? "Is that how you really see my audience, John? Are they that apathetic?"

"That's how I really see them. The man in the street would rather see you tearing some department store to pieces on 'Fightback' than listen to you telling him the truth about some dangerous sociological problem."

"I don't want to believe you, John. But if I ever find out you're right, then I'll telephone Jeffrey Dillard and take that 'Fightback' job."

Detectives investigating the British Brigade attacks interviewed Katherine. They asked about her source.

She answered that the information had been given to her over the telephone by a man who identified himself each time with a prearranged codeword.

At the same time, police questioned the executive committee of the British Patriotic League. All three men — Venables, Trevor Burns, the propaganda director, and Neville Sharpe, the financial director — denied any knowledge of the British Brigade.

Despite Katherine's published allegations, and their own investigation, the police could not link the British Brigade with the quasi-respectable, if extreme, British Patriotic League. They could not even identify a single Brigade member. To provide the police with the proof they needed, Katherine would have to bring forward Brian. She would have to put him in the spotlight, and identify him as a traitor to the madmen he was pretending to support. There was no way she would do that.

For a month after the story in the *Eagle,* nothing was heard from the British Brigade. No acts of violence were perpetrated. The organization appeared to have folded in on itself. Even Brian had no information. He had not heard from Venables since the meeting to arrange the arson attack on the West Indian club.

At the beginning of December, the silence was finally broken. Venables summoned Brian late at night to Patriot House. They met in Venables's private office on the top floor, sitting on opposite sides of a gray steel desk.

"You live with your grandfather, don't you?" Venables said. "You haven't let him know of your connection to the British Brigade, have you?"

"Of course not. He knows I belong to the British Patriotic League, but that's all."

"Does he know you're out tonight on League business?"

"No. You telephoned after he'd gone to bed."

"Good." Venables rested his chin on his hands and stared across the desk at Brian. "We've learned the name of the traitor, the Brigade member whom the *Daily Eagle* calls it source."

Brian's stomach lurched; his throat constricted with fear. "Who is it?"

"Someone in your group. Michael Edwards."

"Who?" Brian asked, before remembering that Michael Edwards was Ginger's real name. "That's daft. It can't be him."

"Can't it? Think about this. The *Eagle* gets a picture of Edwards at a football game, and then they get a picture of him at the Brixton rally. Convenient, eh? That way, they can tie up their story of the League recruiting football hooligans. At the same time, they make Edwards a celebrity within the League. They arrange a cover for their own spy, don't you see?"

The tightness remained in Brian's throat. Venables could just as easily have been talking about him. Hadn't the *Eagle* arranged his cover in a similar fashion? Sid Hall, the *Eagle* photographer, appearing to pick a fight, and then backing down to make Brian look tough in front of the League supporters? But instead of choosing Brian as the spy, Venables had selected Ginger! If it weren't so serious, it would be riotously funny.

"You're his immediate superior," Venables said. "You're responsible for him. For his rewards, and for his punishments."

"What kind of punishment?"

"What's the usual punishment for high treason?"

Brian almost choked on the word. "Death?"

Venables nodded, the grim reaper with watery eyes, stringy hair, and a beaky nose.

"What's wrong with a beating?" Brian asked.

"And have him live to talk to police? To give them all our names? To tie up the loose ends for the damned *Daily Eagle?*"

Brian knew he had to get away and find a means of stopping Venables. He'd telephone Katherine the instant he left Patriot House, let her use the *Eagle*'s influence with the police. And Ginger . . . he'd call Ginger as well, put him wise so he could find somewhere to hide until it was safe to surface.

A telephone sat in the center of the desk. Venables dashed Brian's hopes when he pushed the telephone at him and said, "Call Edwards now. Have him meet us here."

Brian hesitated for an instant before lifting the receiver and dialing the number of Ginger's home. While he listened to the double ring, he offered up a silent prayer that Ginger would be out. But God was not listening. The call was answered, and Brian heard Ginger's voice.

"It's Brian. Meet me at headquarters." Suspect something, you idiot! Say you can't make it!

"Be right over," Ginger answered cheerfully, a man walking to his own execution with a spring in his step.

"He's coming," Brian told Venables.

"You wait for him outside the building," Venables said. "I'll be in my car. When he arrives, bring him to my car, then you follow on your motorbike."

Venables locked the main door of Patriot House and walked away. Brian waited on the sidewalk, an anonymous figure in his jeans and denim jacket, crash helmet covering his face. After ten minutes, a bus passed. Ginger, standing on the platform, jumped off as the bus slowed.

"What's up, then, Brian?"

"Venables wants you. He's over there, in the Austin."

"What does he want me for?"

"You'd better go ask him yourself." Brian gripped Ginger's elbow and guided him toward Venables's tiny blue Austin. Unsuspecting, Ginger climbed in. The Austin moved away, and Brian followed on the motorcycle.

He tailed the Austin for three miles, using the time to think of a way to save Ginger. No matter how big a bastard Ginger was, Brian did not want to be accessory to his murder. Or even worse, to *be* his murderer. No wonder Venables had wanted to be sure that no one knew Brian's whereabouts that night.

The Austin stopped. Brian pulled up behind it. They were in a dark, narrow street. On one side was a viaduct sheltering garages and body shops, all closed for the night. On the other side were railings, and a long grassy knoll leading down to railway lines. Over the years, some railings had been bent. Venables slipped through. Ginger followed, then came Brian. The three men walked right down to the track. Clouds covered the cold sliver of a moon; it was so black that even the rails refused to shine.

"What do you want to see me about then?" Ginger asked.

Brian could not believe Ginger's gullibility. Why did he think he'd been brought down to a railway line at the dead of night? To go train-spotting?

"Your group commander will tell you," Venables answered.

Brian stepped in between the two men. It was time to end the charade. He couldn't go through with it, not kill a man, push him onto the rails as a train went by — that was what Venables obviously had in mind. Instead of facing Ginger, Brian turned in Venables's direction. "Forget it. I'm not getting involved in anything like this. You want to kill him for being a traitor, you do it yourself."

Venables's gaunt face broke into an icy smile. The dimmest of lights bathed it, to lend the expression a ghostly perspective. On the crisp night wind came the faint rattle of a train gathering momentum as it cleared a speed zone.

From behind Brian came Ginger's voice. "He

351

doesn't want to kill me for being a traitor, Brian. It's you who's been talking his head off to the newspapers, not me."

Brian snapped his head around, fists rising in defense. Ginger swung his arm, and a steel bar smashed against Brian's left cheek. He screamed in pain as his mouth filled with blood, bone, and broken teeth. His knees buckled, and he fell to the ground. Ginger stood over him, silhouetted in the gradually increasing light from the approaching train, the bar raised to deliver the final blow.

The bar stayed raised. Venables bent over Brian, gloved hands going through the pockets of his jeans and denim jacket. Brian, too weak to resist, felt Venables remove his keys and the plastic case that held his driving license and insurance binder, the only identification he carried. Venables stood up straight. "Just as well we discovered the truth about this devious little bastard," he said to Ginger. "All right, finish him off."

Brian saw the bar twitch. His last thought was not of the pain and grief that would tear his grandfather apart. Nor was it of Katherine and the *Eagle* staff, the first classy people to ever treat him as an equal. Instead, the last thought, oddly enough, concerned Ginger. What an actor! What a bloody marvelous actor to have strung him along like this, and then turned him in. What a bloody great performance! Then all the lights went out.

Ginger grabbed Brian's hands, Venables held his feet. They flung him across the rails, gleaming dully now in the light of the train that was half a mile away and picking up speed as it swept past the fifty-mile-an-hour mark. Venables and Ginger turned and ran up the grassy bank. Venables jumped into the car. Ginger climbed on Brian's motorcycle. Both engines roared into life, drowning out the train klaxon, then the screech of brakes as the engineer spotted the untidy bundle lying on the track. By the time the train stopped — with the locomotive fifty yards beyond where Brian lay — Venables and Ginger were out of the dark street, joining traffic on the main road.

Ginger followed the blue Austin for five miles until they reached the River Lea at Tottenham. There, he pushed the motorcycle into the water, and watched the last connection to Brian Waters sink beneath the surface.

Katherine received a shock when she stepped into Archie Waters's elevator the following morning. Archie's face was a mask, with hollow eyes and sunken cheeks. Every line showed like a tiny crevice. He hadn't even shaved.

"Archie, what's the matter?"

"Brian's disappeared."

"What do you mean, disappeared?"

"He was home when I went to bed last night. I got up this morning at six, like I always do. No sign of him. No motorcycle. His bed hasn't even been slept in."

"Maybe he had a date."

"He would have told me if he was going out."

"Have you spoken to anyone?"

"I called the police to see if there's been any report of a motorcycle accident. They'd heard nothing."

"Archie, if you're so upset, why did you come in?"

"What am I going to do — stay at home by myself?"

Katherine could not argue with that.

When she reached her desk, she instructed Derek Simon and Heather Harvey to check for all incidents in London, anything where the victim could possibly be Brian Waters. Less than ten minutes passed before they brought her information about an unidentified young man being run over by the London-Glasgow night train. Derek contacted the police for further details. Although the body had been cut in half by the train's wheels, the police description left Katherine with little doubt that it was Brian.

"Oh, God." She buried her face in her hands and started to weep. Ten minutes passed before she was in control of herself. She telephoned Sally Roberts, saying she needed to see her urgently. Sally invited her up to the executive floor. Rather than risk getting into Archie's elevator, Katherine walked the two flights of stairs.

"You look terrible," Sally remarked when Katherine entered the office. "Have you been crying?"

"Yes." Katherine wiped her eyes and sat down on the sofa facing Sally's desk. "Archie Waters says that Brian disappeared last night. We've since learned that an unidentified man was run over by a train. What's left of him —" She bit back tears. "What's left of him fits Brian's description."

"Katherine, it could probably fit the description of a thousand other young men as well."

"No. Right here" — she touched the pit of her stomach — "I know it's Brian. And I put him there by having him spy on the British Patriotic League. Now how the hell do we tell Archie?"

Sally came around the desk and joined Katherine on the sofa, placing an arm around the younger woman's shoulders. "How about we tell him together?"

Sally instructed her secretary to bring Archie up to the editorial director's office. When he arrived three minutes later, he looked from Katherine's red-rimmed eyes to Sally's painfully composed face, and he knew immediately why he had been summoned. "It's Brian, isn't it? What's happened to him?"

"We don't know anything for certain, Archie," Katherine answered. "It's just . . ." She broke off and looked beseechingly at Sally.

"There was an accident sometime late last night.

On the main line. A young man was killed. He had no identification on him, but his age and appearance matched Brian's."

"My Brian run over by a bloody train?" Archie's worn face creased into a horrified grimace at the injustice.

"We don't know anything. We just picked up the report, that's all. Would you like us to call the police?"

Archie nodded. "Clear it up, would you? One way or the other, clear it up."

Sally telephoned the police station handling the incident. She spoke for a minute, then turned to Archie. "Would you be willing to look at the body? The face is recognizable."

Again, Archie nodded. He'd seen plenty of corpses during his military career, enough with faces that were unrecognizable.

Sally, Katherine, and Archie rode in a taxi to the morgue. While the two women remained in a cold waiting room that smelled of antiseptic, Archie accompanied a police officer down a long corridor. Ten minutes later, the two men returned. Archie stared straight ahead, his face set in rigid lines. His shoulders were squared, his back straight, stomach in, chest out. He was a soldier on parade once more, holding back his inner grief because he did not want to spoil the company formation.

"Archie?" Sally asked nervously.

"It's Brian. Shall we go?"

Outside, they found another taxi. "Do you want us to take you home?" Katherine asked.

"No. I want to return to the Eagle building. I need to find things out." Archie sat on one of the jumpseats, facing both women. "The police seem to think it was an accident, but it wasn't, was it?"

"What would he have been doing there to accidentally get hit by a train?" Sally asked in response.

"Nothing." For an instant, the veneer slipped. Archie leaned back, tired, eyes dropping. "I knew no good would come out of his mixing with these swine. Even if he was doing it for a good cause." His eyes opened to impale Katherine. "I'm sorry Miss Eagles. I don't mean to blame you."

Katherine reached out to pat Archie's gnarled hand. "I feel as bad about this as you do, believe me."

"I know. He liked you, Brian did. When you stayed at the flat those few evenings, and he got to know you, I think that was some kind of turning point for Brian. That, and when you helped him out in court. You opened his eyes, showed him there was more to life than what he had been satisfied with up till then." He laid his other hand on top of Katherine's, sandwiching it between his own. "Too bad it had to end like this."

"I'll speak to the police," Katherine said.

"What will you tell them?"

"That I think Brian was murdered. And about the man called Ginger, who'd seen Brian with me." Katherine told Archie of the night Brian had become a group commander of the British Brigade, the ensuing fight, and then Ginger's apparent friendship.

"And all the time he was setting up my grandson for this," Archie muttered. "What was his real name, this Ginger?"

"I never knew. I can show you what he looks like, though."

When they reached the Eagle building, Katherine took Sally and Archie down to another kind of morgue—the *Daily Eagle* morgue. There, she leafed through back issues until she found the two stories she was seeking: the first article she'd written on the soccer fans, and the report of the British Patriotic League's Brixton rally. "That's him there. Ginger."

Archie studied the pictures that accompanied both stories. "Could I get copies of these?"

"I'm sure Sid Hall would make you a print or two," Katherine answered unsuspectingly.

Katherine made her statement. She explained the undercover work Brian Waters had been performing for the *Eagle,* and she told the detectives about Brian's fear of being exposed by the young man called Ginger. "That's why I don't think his death was an accident. I think he was murdered."

"Was Waters your source?" a detective asked. "Was he the man who was supposed to have always identified himself with a prearranged codeword?"

"Yes."

"Why didn't you give us his identity in the first place?"

"I was protecting him."

"If that's the case, and he was murdered, you did a bloody awful job," the detective said callously, and guilt overwhelmed Katherine.

Detectives interviewed Ginger, real name Michael Edwards, at his place of employment, a coat manufacturer in the East End of London called Marco Modes. Ginger had a perfect alibi. He'd been in bed, asleep, in the council house he shared with his parents and younger brother.

When asked if he could prove he'd been at home, asleep, all night, Ginger snapped back, "You prove I wasn't."

When he was questioned about his membership in the British Brigade, Ginger sneered. "Not me, mate. The only thing I know about that lot is what I read in the papers."

The police also visited Patriot House to interview Alan Venables. He was ready for them. The instant Brian had been killed, Venables had contacted the remaining group commanders and issued the order to terminate the British Brigade. He was certain he had nothing to fear from the police now.

Venables freely admitted that both Ginger and Brian Waters had been associated with the League. When faced with Katherine's charge that Brian had been murdered because of his undercover work for the *Eagle,* Venables just laughed. "If Waters was the one who's been giving the *Eagle* this information, then all I can say is that he had the most fertile imagination I've ever seen. Nothing of what they printed about us was true."

The police came away from Patriot House without a single shred of evidence. It seemed that Katherine's accusation of murder was just another thrust-and-parry in the war that raged between the British Patriotic League and the *Daily Eagle.* Katherine's only victory, and a minor one at that, came during the inquest, when the coroner recorded an open verdict.

When Brian was laid to rest alongside his father, Archie Waters's late son, the majority of mourners were from Eagle Newspapers. There was even a guard of honor, six young men in motorcycle leathers and crash helmets standing by the casket — Brian's fellow workers from Mercury Messengers.

After the interment, as the crowd dispersed, Katherine and her father approached Archie. "If there's anything we can do . . .," Roland began.

Archie gave the proprietor of Eagle Newspapers an enigmatic smile. "Bring him back, can you, sir?"

"I wish I could, Archie. Everything I own, I'd give away to be able to perform that miracle."

The smile altered slightly, became warmer. "Thank you, sir, I believe you really would. Shame, isn't it? We don't have a major war for more than thirty years, and the youngsters still find ways to die. I'd like some time off, sir, if that's all right with you."

"Take as much time as you wish."

"Yes," Archie murmured as though talking to himself. "Got a few loose ends to clear up." He touched a hand to his forehead and marched briskly away.

Archie had only knowingly broken the law once in his entire life. That was in 1952, when he'd returned to England after serving in Korea. In his kit he had carried, quite illegally, an American Colt .45 automatic, which he had won in a poker game. He had considered turning it in before leaving Korea, but the explaining he'd have to do had deterred him. Back in England, the weapon became a problem. He had no firearms certificate. Without one, he was scared to take the weapon to a police station, even for a purpose as innocent as turning it in. So the Colt .45 with its magazine full of ammunition, remained in his possession.

When he returned from his grandson's funeral, Archie went into his bedroom, wheeled out the bed, and pulled back the edge of the carpet. He paused for a few seconds to gather his breath, then lifted a loose floorboard. Beneath was a large biscuit tin. Archie opened it, and took out the weapon. A fine coat of oil made it gleam dully. He dropped the magazine into his hand and worked the slide. The action was as smooth and easy as it had been that day when he'd won the weapon.

He stayed in for most of the following day, sitting around in pajamas and dressing gown. The telephone rang just once, Katherine calling to learn how he felt. He told her he was fine, and thanked her for showing concern.

At three o'clock, he began to prepare himself. He bathed and shaved. After dressing himself in his elevator operator's uniform, he stood in front of a full-length mirror to check his appearance. The brass buttons sparkled. The patent leather belt crossing from his left shoulder to his right hip shone like a black mirror; his shoes matched that gleam. He pinned his combat decorations to his chest, and snapped a sharp salute at the figure in the mirror.

At four-fifteen, he left the flat, wearing a raincoat in which he carried the Colt. He caught a bus, passing the journey to the East End by studying one of the photographs Sid Hall had provided for him. It was from the Brixton rally, cropped down to give a close-up of Ginger. Michael Edwards, as Archie now knew him to be. Katherine had passed on whatever personal information she'd learned from the police. Archie memorized every hair of Michael Edwards, every pore, every mark. He did not want to make a mistake.

At ten minutes before five, Archie was standing outside the coat factory called Marco Modes, checking the faces of everyone who went in and out of the building. At five o'clock, the movement of people quickened. There! Shoving his way through the doors, wearing corduroy trousers and a pale green bomber jacket, was the young man in the photograph. There could be no mistaking that blazing beacon of hair.

Archie stood right in Ginger's path. His voice carried the parade-ground authority of a lifetime earlier. "Are you Michael Edwards, also known as Ginger?"

Ginger stopped. Copper? No, too old. "What's it to you?"

"Don't be insubordinate!" Archie roared. The people spilling out of factories and offices stopped their homeward rush to watch. "When a sergeant asks you a question, you answer!"

"Sergeant?" The raincoat flapped open, and Ginger caught a glimpse of the uniform. "You're a bloody doorman!"

"For the last time, are you Michael Edwards?"

"Yes!" Ginger shouted back. "Now get out of my way before I give you a good kicking, you stupid old sod."

Archie reached his right hand into his raincoat pocket. It reappeared clutching the Colt. Screams of panic erupted as bystanders fled in all directions. Quite suddenly alone, Archie and Ginger faced each other.

Ginger's voice changed pitch, became the begging, snivelling whine that Brian had heard and fallen for. "Please don't shoot. What did I ever do to you, old man?"

"You piece of scum, you killed my grandson," Archie answered, and squeezed the trigger.

The bullet smashed into the bridge of Ginger's nose, ripping away the back of his head. Archie did not even look. He simply raised the weapon to his own temple, and squeezed the trigger a second time. No explosion came, no relief to the agony that had torn through him ever since the moment he had seen Brian lying in the morgue. Just a click. Unaware of the hundreds of people who had stopped their flight to watch, Archie worked the slide to eject the bullet that had fallen victim to the vagaries of time, raised the weapon to his head again, and blew his own brains out.

The earth covering Brian Waters was still fresh when the casket containing his grandfather was interred in the family plot.

A white-robed minister positioned himself at the head of the grave. Katherine, standing between her father and Sally, blotted out the minister's toneless homily of a tragedy-plagued family finding eternal peace in God's arms. If she listened to the words, she knew she would break down. Instead, she thought about herself. For the second time in less than a week, she was wearing black. A wide black hat, a black coat, sheer black stockings, and low-heeled black shoes. And all because of one lousy story she had refused to let go. All because of the *Daily Eagle*. All because of the newspaper her father had founded—the newspaper on which she had wanted to work from the very moment of its launch. In that moment, she hated everything about the newspaper.

Just what had she achieved with this vendetta against the British Patriotic League? Had she exposed its evil? Yes, she had, but she knew that wasn't the question she should really be asking herself. Had she made people believe her—that was the true test. And the true answer, she feared, was exactly what John Saxon had prophesied it would be. A loud, resounding "No!" Because people just didn't care. They didn't give a damn.

The service finished. As Arthur Parsons guided the Bentley out of the cemetery parking lot, Roland said, "I feel like we just buried part of Eagle Newspapers. Archie was there from the very beginning. The place won't be the same without him."

Perhaps it was the words her father used, perhaps it was his tone. Katherine could not be sure. All she understood was the finality of the remark. They had buried part of the company that morning, and Eagle Newspapers would never be the same again.

Katherine returned home from the cemetery. After changing into slacks, a crew-neck sweater, tweed jacket, and hiking shoes, she went walking across Hampstead Heath, needing the exercise to clear the fog that enveloped her mind. She was out for three hours. When she returned, her cheeks were red, and her mind was icily clear.

She telephoned John Saxon at his office. "John, you were perfectly right. I wrote my heart out, and no one cared. The scum at the British Patriotic League are untouched, and two people I cared for very much are dead."

"It was the old man's funeral this morning, wasn't it? I should have gone. It was because of him that I met you."

"John, would you do me a favor? Today, right now?"

"Anything."

"Tell Jeffrey Dillard that I'd like to see him. Tell him I'm very interested in working with him on 'Fightback.' "

"I'll be delighted to tell him that."

Katherine broke the connection and breathed in deeply. Then she dialed her father's number, ready to tell him that she had decided to leave the *Daily Eagle* and start a new career in television.

17

Katherine knew she should not be nervous, but she was. "I am bloody well petrified," she told Jeffrey Dillard, when, half an hour before the start of her first "Fightback," the show host visited her dressing room to ask how she was feeling.

"My dear, there's no reason for you to be so worried. You've appeared on television before. Standing in front of a camera is nothing new."

"That was almost three years ago, Jeffrey." She noticed that he held a bunch of tulips in his hand. "I was a guest speaker then, invited to participate because of 'Satisfaction Guaranteed!' This time, I'm a co-host."

"And an excellent co-host you'll be. Sit down and take a few deep breaths. You'll be surprised how those butterflies will calm down." Dillard's blue eyes twinkled merrily as he kissed Katherine on the forehead. "Before each production of 'Fightback,' I always gave flowers to Elaine Cowdrey, your predecessor. Just a silly superstition really. You see, I'd given her flowers before her debut, and that debut had been a success. So I got into the habit of giving them to her before every show. I would very much like to continue that superstition with you."

"Thank you. And it's not a silly superstition — it's a perfectly delightful tradition." As Dillard left the room, she placed his tulips on the dressing table, alongside floral tributes that had been delivered earlier. Red roses from John Saxon, who was sitting in the studio audience. An enormous orchid plant from Roland, who, with Sally Roberts, was also in the audience. And one good-luck wish that had not been formed with a florist's skill: a telegram from Raymond Barnhill urging Katherine to "Knock 'em dead!"

Four men sent me good wishes, Katherine mused. My father. My lover. My American friend. And my television mentor. All the men in my life!

She laughed, and some of the tension disappeared. Standing in front of the mirror, she checked her appearance for the umpteenth time. The cream-colored cashmere sweater dress finished just below her knees. Her hair was pulled back, and she wore beaten gold hoop earrings. The light colors were Erica Bentley's idea. "Jeffrey Dillard always wears dark suits," Katherine recalled Erica telling her. "Get out of his shadow from the very beginning, show him that you are your own person. And for God's sake, don't even think of wearing those bloody suits of yours! Burn them! Give them away to the Salvation Army! Get rid of them!"

More butterflies died. Erica was in the audience as well. Afterward, she would join in a celebration dinner at A l'Ecu de France, in Jermyn Street. Katherine hoped it would be a jollier affair than the last time they'd all been together. That had been a month earlier, just before Christmas, her farewell party at the *Eagle*. Despite the food and drink, the good wishes and merry chatter, Katherine's eyes had been brimming with tears. After ten years, she was leaving the *Eagle*, and her feelings were, understandably, mixed. As well as a career advancement, she was making an acknowledgment of failure. She'd found out, as John

365

Saxon had once so eloquently phrased it, that her readers didn't really care for much beyond the price of beer and cigarettes after all.

She had managed to keep those tears in check all through the party. She hadn't even cried at the end of it, when her father had kissed her and said, "Remember, Kathy, whenever you want to come back, the door's open." But she'd had no defense when, moments later, Lawrie Stimkin had come up to her, his lugubrious face tinged with warmth, his eyes moist.

"Don't think me daft, Kathy, but it always makes me cry to see good newspaper talent going to the flaming idiot box!"

Katherine's own tears started. She didn't object to being called Kathy; she didn't even jump back when Stimkin threw his arms around her in a bear hug. He was tipsy and sad and remorseful, and somehow it all seemed so fitting.

"You know something, Lawrie? You're not such a miserable bastard after all." Then they'd stood there, crying on each other's shoulders. . . .

By show-time, whatever butterflies weren't dead had flown away. When the call came, Katherine was ready and raring to go.

"You were marvelous, Katherine. Absolutely marvelous." Sally Roberts lifted a glass of Krug in a toast. "The *Eagle*'s loss is television's gain."

Katherine gazed around the restaurant table. Her father sat opposite, with Sally Roberts on his right. To Katherine's left sat Erica, and to her right was John Saxon. "I wish I could agree with you," she responded, "but to tell you the truth, I can't seem to recall much about it."

"Oh, come on!" Erica protested. "What were you doing out there—sleepwalking?"

Katherine shook her head. "I remember Jeffrey

366

Dillard introducing me to the audience."

"Your two audiences," Sally pointed out. "Your personal audience in the studio, and the countless millions across the country who were clustered around their television sets."

"Don't say millions; it frightens me. I remember that, but the rest of the show — the rest of my debut — is a complete blank."

Everyone tried to fill in Katherine's memory lapse. Saxon said something about a wedding. Erica drowned him out by talking loudly about men's suits. Sally mentioned the name of a clothing shop then Saxon fought his way back into the discussion by talking about bankruptcy. Roland, his hands over his ears to block out the confusing babble around him, looked at Katherine and asked, "Now do you remember?"

"Yes, yes, it's all coming back." The bad situation she'd rectified for her debut "Fightback" had concerned a wedding that had taken place the previous week. The groom, his two brothers, and the best man — all members of the same amateur rugby team, hulking brutes who could never be fitted off the rack — had ordered custom-made suits from the tailoring department of a local menswear shop. A week before the wedding, when the suits were waiting to be picked up, the shop had gone bankrupt. Immediately, a hold had been placed on the shop's assets. Those assets had included uncollected orders such as the wedding party's suits.

The wedding day had been saved by Katherine. Film clips followed her frustrating journey through the bankruptcy-court bureaucracy, waving receipts to prove the suits had been paid for. At last, she had reached an official willing to take responsibility for releasing the disputed merchandise. The final scene was of the wedding itself, to which Katherine had been invited as a guest of honor.

Katherine wound up her first "Fightback" by showing the audience a brown paper bag. "To demonstrate his appreciation, the bridegroom presented me with this." She pulled a rugby uniform—black shorts and yellow-and-black striped shirt, all caked with mud—from the bag. "I don't know whether he expects me to wear it, or to wash it."

For obvious reasons, the *Eagle*'s entertainment page made nothing more than a passing mention of "Fightback's" new co-host. Other newspapers were kinder, giving a former journalist high marks on her television debut.

After a month on "Fightback," Katherine felt as if she had been in television for as long as Jeffrey Dillard. Nerves no longer bothered her. There was really very little difference between a typewriter and a television camera in reaching people; a good story, well told, was exactly the same in any medium. And Dillard, as he came to appreciate Katherine's professionalism, gave her more and more of the show, content to let his latest discovery hog the limelight.

In March, after Katherine had been doing "Fightback" for two months, John Saxon told Katherine about a surprise party he was planning.

"In four weeks' time, on April the seventh, my friend and your colleague, Jeffrey Dillard, celebrates thirty years in television. It falls on a Saturday. I'm organizing a super surprise party for him, and I want you to be my hostess."

"Who are you inviting?"

"Jeffrey's friends, most of whom happen to be my friends as well. You know something, Katherine, in all the time we've known each other, you've never been out to my other home."

"I haven't, have I?" It seemed quite incredible, but she had never visited his home at Henley-on-Thames. She either met him at Marble Arch, or else he collected her at Kate's Haven. Nor, she thought, had she spent a complete night with him since the soccer riot that had caught them in its aftermath. She always had to be available in case her children wanted her first thing in the morning. "It's about time I did. I'd love to be your hostess, John."

The party soon took shape. Saxon gave Katherine the names of the guests who would be attending. The list read like a *Who's Who* — the director of a prestigious merchant bank, the chairman of one of the smaller breweries, an eminent surgeon, a judge, some retired high-ranking military men, and two Conservative Members of Parliament. Saxon also showed her the evening's menu — hors d'oeuvres including smoked salmon and caviar, a main course of beef Wellington, salads, and several desserts, all followed by a gigantic chocolate birthday cake. Katherine's one suggestion was that the birthday cake be made in the shape of a television set.

During the week preceding the party, cards and telegrams began arriving at the "Fightback" office for Dillard. On Thursday afternoon, while Katherine and Dillard were putting the finishing touches to that night's "Fightback," an enormous bouquet arrived.

"Is it your birthday, Jeffrey?"

"A work anniversary. Saturday makes thirty years in this daft business for me."

"That is exciting!" She kissed him on the cheek, and, acting to the full, asked, "What celebration plans do you have? Or are you leaving it to your wife?"

"Leaving it?" Dillard raised a white eyebrow. "You don't leave things to Shirley — she takes control. She's booked dinner for us at some restaurant she's discovered in the back of beyond. Won't even tell me where it is, the wretched woman."

Dillard's wife of forty years was a former actress, and she'd played this role to perfection.

Each time the telephone rang, it seemed the caller was someone else wanting to congratulate Dillard.

Finally, Katherine insisted that Dillard answer all the calls. "They're going to be for you, anyway."

The next call, of course, was not. Dillard took it, placed his hand over the mouthpiece, and called Katherine. "For you. An American."

Katherine took the receiver. "Raymond?"

"Congratulate me. I'm going to be published."

"Someone bought your book?"

"Knight and Robbins in New York. Small, independent publishers, but they put out a quality list. I got a letter from the agent this morning."

"That is wonderful news, Raymond. I'm thrilled for you." Katherine felt truly uplifted. The agent had been showing the book for nine months, and Barnhill had become more depressed with each rejection, more certain that no one would ever publish him. He had even started talking about paying to have the book published by a vanity press, if only to soothe his ego.

"Does that mean you're a millionaire now?"

Barnhill chuckled. "Far from it. Fifteen thousand up front, that's all. But that's more than enough to take you out for the slap-up, five-star, celebration dinner you promised you'd have with me tonight."

"I promised . . . ?"

"It's in my diary. Remember when I finished the manuscript and mailed it to the agent last summer? I asked you to help me celebrate then. You were busy, but you promised to have dinner with me on the day I sold it."

"I've got a show to do tonight, Raymond."

"I know, but it's over at eight o'clock. After the show we'll have dinner."

"Raymond, I always go home as soon as 'Fightback' finishes. My children are allowed to stay up late on Thursday to watch the show, and I like to hear what they have to say. Why don't we make it for tomorrow?"

"I can't." His normally easy speech turned sharp with a tone that puzzled Katherine. "I'm catching a flight to New York at midday tomorrow."

"How long will you be away?"

"Maybe a month. Some revisions need to be done. To save shuttling the manuscript back and forth across the Atlantic, I'll take care of everything over there."

"You'll finally be able to get a decent hamburger."

"You said a mouthful there."

"You are coming back, aren't you, Raymond?"

"Sure. I've written a return date in my diary, and I always keep everything I write in my diary, don't I?"

"Raymond, I think of you as a very dear friend. I don't want to lose you just because you're upset that I couldn't keep a date. That's stupid, isn't it?"

He laughed at that, but the laugh was sharp, just like his tone. "I guess it is," he said, and hung up.

For half a minute after Barnhill had broken the connection, Katherine held the receiver to her ear. He had counted on celebrating with her, because he had no one else in London he called a friend. And she'd turned him down. She'd stood him up on a date made the previous summer.

Suddenly, she understood Barnhill's odd tone of voice. Disappointment, liberally laced with petulance.

Katherine's contribution to "Fightback" that night concerned a string of odd resolutions recently passed by left-wing local councils across the country. It was a departure from the normal format, but Katherine felt some fun at the expense of what she termed the "lunatic left" was long overdue. The winter just finished had been a nightmare of industrial action as militant unions flexed their muscles. Energy strikes had led to the closure of schools and hospitals. Public transport had been paralyzed. Even gravediggers had gone out on strike . . . !

Katherine finished her piece with the most bizarre legislation of all. In one London borough, garbage collectors would no longer pick up black plastic garbage bags.

"And why is that, Katherine?" Dillard asked, in the easy, conversational tone that was the hallmark of "Fightback."

"Well, Jeffrey, the lunatic left in this instance feels that the use of black garbage bags is a deliberate and humiliating insult to black people."

"I see." Dillard nodded his head sagely, as if it all made perfect sense. "What colors are acceptable?"

"Just one. Gray. The lunatic left doesn't think any particular group will be upset by gray garbage bags."

Dillard touched his white hair. "I'm not so sure. Using the lunatic left's own yardstick, that could be taken as a deliberate and humiliating insult to the elderly."

After that, there wasn't one straight face in the audience. It was always fun, Katherine reflected as she drove home that night, to burst the bubbles of the pompous idiots who all too often filled local council seats. It was also excellent television entertainment.

Her audience at home agreed. The children had not really understood what was going on—they only stayed up in pajamas and dressing gowns to watch their mother, not to understand her—but Edna and Jimmy Phillips applauded as she entered the house.

Their weekly treat over, Henry and Joanne went to bed. Katherine tucked them in and kissed them good night. Henry fell asleep instantly, his short hair forming a blond cap around his face. Joanne was more difficult. She insisted that Katherine read her a story. Relishing one of the all too rare moments when she could be a mother, Katherine sat on the edge of Joanne's bed and told her about Goldilocks. By the time she reached the point where the three bears returned home, Joanne was asleep, her long blond hair spread across the pillow like a fan.

When Katherine returned downstairs, Edna was

busy in the kitchen, cleaning up the dinner plates she'd neglected in favor of watching "Fightback," and Phillips was in the garage, repairing a flat tire on Henry's bicycle. Katherine found herself thinking about Raymond Barnhill. He'd expected to do a lot of celebrating tonight. Instead, he was on his own, with nothing to do but pack a suitcase. Remorse got the better of Katherine. Using the telephone in the breakfast room, she dialed the home number of Raymond Barnhill. At least, she could speak to him.

Barnhill's telephone rang for two minutes before Katherine hung up. Thinking that she might have misdialed, she tried again. The telephone rang for another minute. As she was about to hang up, the ringing stopped. A voice, strangled and barely audible, said, "Hello?"

"Raymond, is that you?" Katherine pressed the receiver to her ear, then snatched it away when a crash like thunder almost deafened her. "Raymond, are you there?" She called his name several times, before hanging up and dialing the number once more. This time, she got the busy signal. She waited five minutes before trying yet again. It was still busy.

Why, she asked herself, was she even worried? She'd probably had the wrong number when that unfamiliar voice answered, and now that she'd reached the right number, Barnhill was involved in a long conversation. Nonetheless, she kept trying every fifteen minutes. By ten-thirty, she was very concerned. Barnhill's line was still busy, and no one stayed on the phone for an hour and a half. What worried her most was that strange voice . . . What if she *hadn't* reached the wrong number?

After telling Edna that she was going out, Katherine climbed into the silver Porsche and pointed it south, toward the Thames and Dolphin Square, where Barnhill lived.

All during the journey, a sense of emergency kept

373

every other thought from her mind. But the instant she entered Barnhill's apartment block, she felt foolish. What excuse was she going to give for banging on his door at eleven o'clock at night? Raymond, I had this dreadful premonition . . . ?

She rang his doorbell. After thirty seconds, she rang again. From inside, she could hear faint sounds of music. A third time she rang, then she hammered on the door with her fist. A lock snapped back. The door swung open. Barnhill, wearing only jeans, stood in front of her.

"Hey, you remembered our date after all!" Before Katherine could move, he grabbed hold of her and kissed her. Even then, it took Katherine a few seconds to comprehend the obvious: Raymond Barnhill, the American wire-service reporter, whom she had never seen take a drink, was as drunk as a lord.

She struggled free and stepped back, caught between two desires. To run, and cast Barnhill forever from her mind. Or, as a true friend, to stay and help him, and make sure he caught his plane tomorrow.

"Aren't you coming in then?"

"I will. But only if you promise to act decently."

Barnhill looked puzzled. "Decently? Sure."

Katherine entered the apartment and walked into the living room. A radio was playing at full volume. The room was a shambles. Sheets of white paper covered furniture and carpet like some gigantic snowfall. The telephone was on its side, the receiver dangling from its cord.

On a coffee table in front of the couch stood two one-liter bottles of Stolichnaya. One was unopened; the other was almost empty. Barnhill tumbled down onto the couch and reached for the open bottle. Katherine waited for him to find a glass. He didn't. He just raised the bottle to his mouth. His Adam's apple bobbed only once before Katherine ripped the bottle from his grasp. Vodka ran from his mouth, down his chin, and onto his bare chest, matting the light brown hair that covered it. He blinked at her, uncomprehending. "What the hell did you want to do that for?"

"You've drunk all you're going to drink tonight."

"I have, have I?" The words were slurred, the tone belligerent. "Says who?" He started to get up off the couch. Katherine shoved him back. He yelled in pain as his head cracked against the wall. Katherine did not turn around. Carrying both bottles, she marched to the toilet, where she flushed the vodka down the commode. When she returned to the living room, Barnhill was walking unsteadily toward the front door.

"Just where do you think you're going?" It was the tone she might have used to her children when they misbehaved.

"Buy some more vodka."

"Not like that, you won't. Apart from freezing to death, the police won't take kindly to half-naked drunks staggering around London in the middle of the night."

"Then I'll put on a damned coat and shoes."

"That won't help either. You're in Britain, not America. We have licensing laws here. Everything's closed now."

"Licensing laws!" Barnhill slammed his hands against the wall, then buried his face in his arms. "Jesus Christ, you need a license to breathe in this damned country!"

"That may very well be true, but it's still reasonably safe to walk the streets here."

Barnhill turned toward Katherine and grinned feebly. When he spoke, the words were still slurred, but the anger had gone from his voice. "I must look like a great big jerk to you, eh?"

"I've seen bigger, but not too many. Why don't you clean yourself up, and I'll make you some coffee."

Katherine watched him walk to the bathroom. Once she heard the water running, she was confident that the worst was over. She busied herself in the kitchen. When Barnhill returned, hair soaking, fully dressed, and reeking of toothpaste and aftershave, Katherine was cleaning up the living room.

"Coffee's on the table."

"I don't want coffee," he said, slipping an arm around her waist. "I want you."

"Settle for the coffee." She tried to wriggle free, but he held her tightly. When he lowered his face toward her, she said, "You promised me you'd act decently."

"And you promised me that we'd have dinner tonight. How could you stand me up tonight of all nights? Surely you know how I feel about you."

"I'm here, aren't I?"

"Sure you're here. To give me coffee and a lecture."

"I haven't lectured you."

"You will. I can see it in your eyes." He let go of her and sat down on the couch, looking around the living room. "What have you been doing in here?"

"I've been bringing some semblance of order to this chaos." She held up a handful of paper she'd collected. "What's this?"

"Book."

"What book? The sequel, the one you're writing?"

Barnhill shook his head. "The old book. The one I sold. I was reading through it. It's crap. Christ alone knows why Knight and Robbins are putting up fifteen grand. It's garbage."

"If it was garbage, they wouldn't have bought it." She collected the rest of the pages, shuffled them into a neat pile, and set the manuscript on the table. "I'll leave putting them back in the right order for you. How's the coffee?"

"Vodka would taste better."

"When did you start drinking?"

"Couple of hours ago. I began reading the manuscript, preparing for when I meet my publisher next week. It stank so much that I needed help."

"So you went out and bought two bottles worth? Why didn't you talk to a friend instead?"

"I tried to. She was busy."

Katherine felt her cheeks burning. Maybe it was the vodka telling Barnhill to blame her; perhaps it was his genuine belief. In a way, she could understand it. He was a lonely person living in a country that was not his own; the languages were almost identical, but the similarities ended there. The one friend he'd found had let him down. And in doing so, she had started a chain reaction. Barnhill had begun to question his ability, the work that meant so much to him; from there, it was only a short trip to buying a couple of bottles of vodka and locking himself away, drinking, while his life passed out of reach.

"What did you call yourself before?" she asked. "A jerk?"

"That's the word. A very descriptive piece of American slang, that."

"You're perfectly right. You are a jerk. An idiot. A bona fide, solid-gold, diamond-studded moron."

The string of insults did more to clear Barnhill's head than the coffee. "Where the hell do you come off telling me that?"

"Do you know how many aspiring writers would give ten years of their life to be able to claim they were published authors?" Katherine snapped. She was genuinely angry now. The American had a God-given talent, and he was squandering it. "Do you know how many people work themselves into the ground, deprive themselves of everything in the hope of seeing their blood, sweat, and tears in print? And look at you, who's been blessed with the natural ability to write. All you can do is drink yourself numb and say that your publisher's bought a pile of junk. For Christ's sake, Raymond, you had enough faith in yourself to write the blasted book! Now have enough faith to believe you deserve whatever success you get from it!"

Fury turned Barnhill's eyes a smoky brown. "What the hell would someone like you know about blood, sweat, and tears? About people depriving themselves of happiness to pursue a dream? You were born with a silver spoon sticking out of your mouth. No . . . a whole damned silver tea service! You don't know a damned thing about deserving success. All you've ever had to do is ask your daddy for it!"

Katherine had attacked Barnhill because she was angry at his waste of talent. Countering, he had rammed her privileged background down her throat. In doing so, he had virtually denied that she had achieved anything on her own. It was the one accusation Katherine could never accept.

"Good night, Raymond. Personally, I couldn't give a damn if you drink yourself into such a stupor that you miss your flight tomorrow." She swung around and walked out of the apartment, slamming the door behind her.

On the way home, she remembered wondering whether it was vodka or genuine conviction telling Barnhill to blame her. Now she asked the same question about his feelings for her. Was it vodka telling him that he loved her, or did he really believe it?

Either way, Katherine told herself, she didn't care. Tonight, Raymond Barnhill had drunk and misbehaved his way right out of her life.

Katherine arrived at John Saxon's country home at four o'clock on Saturday afternoon, three hours before the dinner guests. She wore tweed slacks and a loose-fitting plaid jacket over a silk shirt. In the garment bag she took from the Porsche was a backless ruched taffeta evening gown, in a vivid blue that matched her eyes.

After handing the dress and a small overnight case to a maid, Katherine was taken on a tour of the house by Saxon. "Aside from the master and guest bedroom suites, the Saxon residence has another seven bedrooms and three bathrooms. Social events of even the largest order can be handled quite adequately in the four reception rooms, while the staff have the privacy of their own flat."

"Enough, John. Enough. You sound like an estate agent making a sale. This is probably the most magnificent house I've ever seen, and I'm duly impressed."

"Katherine, I've been rehearsing this speech for ages. Please don't deny me." Saxon coughed into his hand in a theatrical clearing of his throat. "For relaxation, the house offers you an indoor heated swimming pool. There is also a games room. Now, if you'll come this way." He led her around the back of the house, across a beautifully maintained lawn that rolled on forever. At the bottom of the lawn was a boathouse and slipway, and four hundred feet of river frontage. While they stood on the dock, a yacht glided by under full sail. The scene was one of the most picturesque and peaceful that Katherine had ever beheld.

On returning from the river, Katherine and Saxon were served tea with scones and jam on an enclosed patio overlooking the lawn. Afterward, Katherine went up to the guest bedroom suite, where she found her overnight case unpacked, her evening gown lying across the bed.

At six o'clock, as she finished dressing, there was a knock on the door. "Come in."

Saxon entered, ready for the party in a beautifully tailored tuxedo. His eyes traveled from Katherine's face to her bare shoulders, then down the length of her taffeta gown. The only jewelry she wore was a simple pearl necklace. "You look very beautiful. Every other woman will be jealous of you. And every man will be jealous of me."

"Thank you."

Saxon stepped closer. "Do you remember that

dreadful night of the riot?"

"It's etched forever in my mind."

He handed her a slim package. "Please wear this tonight." Katherine opened it to find a pear-shaped diamond pendant, identical to the one she'd had snatched from her throat that night. "Just don't wear it in the middle of any football riots."

"I won't." She removed the pearl necklace and slipped on the pendant, then raised her face to kiss Saxon. "Thank you, it's magnificent."

Twenty couples were expected for dinner. The staff Saxon kept at his country home — a butler, cook, maid, and gardener — had been busy. Two long tables, arranged in a T, were set with sparkling silverware, Royal Doulton, and Waterford. Each table was decorated with exquisite floral displays. A bar had been set up, better stocked with wines and spirits than many public houses. Katherine looked at the dark-skinned middle-aged man who stood behind the bar, dressed like a guest in a tuxedo.

"Isn't that your chauffeur?"

Saxon nodded. "William is a man of diverse talents."

"Good evening, ma'am," William said. "May I get something for you?"

Saxon answered for her. "Mrs. Kassler will have a champagne cocktail, thank you."

Precisely at seven o'clock, the guests began to arrive. Cars halted along the wide circular drive in front of the house. Men and women in evening dress were announced by the butler. By seven-twenty, everyone except Jeffrey Dillard and his wife were present. Saxon introduced Katherine to each guest in turn, describing her as "our guest of honor's colleague, and my very special friend."

At seven thirty-five, Jeffrey Dillard arrived with his wife, Shirley. Seeing all the cars parked outside the house, he knew what had been planned. "Damned surprise parties!" he muttered as he entered the room where the bar had been installed. "Knew there was something odd when Shirley here kept insisting I wear this dinner jacket. Who wears a dinner jacket to go out to a restaurant, eh?" He shook hands and kissed cheeks, obviously happy, despite the protests, to have this party in his honor.

At last, he stood in front of Katherine. "You were in on this all along, weren't you? Asking what all the cards and telegrams were about. You're a damned good actress!" He gave her such a tight hug that Katherine feared she would burst out of the blue taffeta dress.

Despite the purpose of the party, the main topic of conversation was the fall that very week of the Labour government, and the upcoming general election that would, in all probability, give the country its first woman prime minister. The two Conservative MPs who'd been invited to the party — Daniel Cooper, from a mixed farming and industrial district in the Midlands, and Edwin Johnson, who represented a middle-class area in Northwest London — had to leave immediately after dinner. Bidding good night to Daniel Cooper, Katherine played the perfect hostess by asking why he could not stay longer.

"I have to start knocking on doors," the MP replied. "There is little point in doing that here. Firstly, this is not my constituency. And secondly, canvassing here would be like taking coals to Newcastle. I guarantee you that there is not a single Labour or Liberal vote in this magnificent house."

Katherine gave the perfect-hostess smile. "I was once asked to run as a Labour candidate in a local election."

"You were? Did you accept?"

"No." She swore that an expression of relief flashed across Cooper's face. "I didn't have the time."

"I'm very glad to hear that. Good night."

Katherine tugged Saxon to one side. "How do you pick your friends — by personality, or by political belief?"

"I've always found they go together, Katherine. People I like invariably vote Conservative."

They were joined by Jeffrey Dillard and Shirley, a tall, thin woman with rigid silver hair. "Super, super evening, John, old boy," Dillard enthused. "Wonderful food, wonderful company. Katherine, did you meet Air Vice Marshal Sir Donald Leslie before? Big admirer of yours."

"Mine?"

"That's right. He used to watch 'Fightback' because of me, but now he watches it to see you. Doesn't let his wife know that, of course." Dillard waved an arm, and Sir Donald Leslie joined the group. Although he had retired from the Royal Air Force eight years earlier, Sir Donald still looked very much the military man. An erect posture, a slight upward curl to the ends of his trim white moustache. His handshake was a reflection of the man himself, crisp and dry.

"Mrs. Kassler, as a woman" — the voice was clipped and upperclass; it was a voice accustomed to issuing orders, not asking questions — "as a woman, what do you think of this country having a woman prime minister?"

"As a woman . . ." She stared at the wide, livid scar that disfigured the right side of Sir Donald's face, unable to tear her eyes away. ". . . As a woman, I am interested only in whether a prime minister is capable of discharging the office to which he, *or she,* has been elected."

"Katherine's fascinated by your scar, Don," Dillard burst out. Katherine put a hand to her mouth in embarrassment, but dropped it when she saw that everyone else was laughing. "Tell her how you got it."

"Battle of Britain," Sir Donald answered proudly. "Messerschmitt pumped a burst through the cockpit of my Spitfire. Bullets missed me, but the damned glass didn't."

"Don was a squadron leader then," Dillard said. "I was a part of the squadron." He flung an affectionate arm around Sir Donald Leslie's shoulders. "Saved Britain, didn't we?"

"Some of us did. I carried on saving it, while you pursued other endeavors."

"Do you know this is the first time in fifty-five years that a prime minister's been forced out of office and into a general election?" Saxon said. "Last one was Ramsay MacDonald, back in 1924. We're witnessing history."

"Damned woman had better win, that's all I've got to say," Sir Donald muttered. "Country's rife with anarchy. Needs a firm hand. That Labour mob gave in to everyone and everything. Can't have a country in that kind of turmoil. And once she does win, she'd better show how tough she is."

"Tough with what?" Katherine asked.

"The unions, for one. Look at the winter we've just been through, for God's sake! Absolute chaos. We can't allow small groups to make life untenable for everyone else."

"Don't you believe in the right to strike? The right for a man to withdraw his labor?"

"Not when it adversely affects the welfare of the country," Sir Donald replied hotly. "If a man doesn't want his job, that's his business. But if he wants to picket, if he wants to resort to violence to stop another man from doing *his* job, then that should be the government's business!"

"But if he's only picketing to protect his job?"

"Good God! You did a program just two days ago ridiculing the Socialists in this country—the lunatic left, you called them—and now you're sounding like one of them!"

"I did not ridicule Socialists. I made fun of—"

Saxon stepped in between Katherine and Sir Donald. "As fascinating as I find this discussion, let's stop it now. I've never been partial to seeing my dinner guests resort to pistols at twenty paces. Thank you."

At eleven-thirty, the guests began to leave. Sir Donald Leslie shook Katherine's hand, and apologized. "Please excuse my earlier behavior. Sometimes I get a little irate when I consider what's happened to this country of ours. How we've slipped in the world." He touched the livid scar on his face. "I've got a personal stake in the place, you see."

"So has my father. He was evacuated from Dunkirk when he was sixteen. He won the Military Medal *and* the Military Cross. And he still manages to possess a liberal attitude."

"How long was he in the army?"

"Seven years."

"That's the blink of an eyelid, nothing more. You get a different outlook when you make a career of it, when you're responsible for the country during war and peace. Good night, pleasure meeting you."

Quite suddenly, the big house turned silent. The last car drove away, and the only noise was that of the staff cleaning up. Saxon grabbed a bottle of Rémy-Martin and two snifters from the bar before William could remove everything. He carried them to the enclosed patio that overlooked the lawn. Pouring a generous amount of cognac into each glass, he passed one to Katherine, and held his own in the air.

"Cheers. You were a wonderful hostess."

"Cheers yourself." She clinked glasses. "You weren't a bad host, but you've obviously had plenty of experience."

Saxon rolled cognac around the snifter. "You didn't think very much of some of the guests, did you?"

"Sir Donald Leslie? A bit too pompous, and a bit too much of the 'England expects every man to do his duty' for my liking."

"He's a very worried man."

"About this country?"

Saxon nodded. "Many of us are. We see it going to hell in a handcart. We hope, with the election coming up, and a probable Conservative victory, that things are about to change. They'd better change, or else we might just as well pull the plug and let the country sink."

"You agree with what Sir Donald said?"

"With his sentiments, yes. We have to stop the rot — "

"What rot?"

"The lack of ethics, the total abrogation of morality. There are far too many spongers getting a free ride in this country, and we can't damned well afford it. We have to get the work ethic back in proper focus, get everyone to accept the philosophy, old-fashioned as it may be, of a day's work for a day's pay. I don't necessarily agree with Sir Donald's desire to see everything neatly regimented by a strong government, but that's because I've spent my life building a business — being an entrepreneur, if you wish — while he spent his life in uniform."

"What about Jeffrey?"

"He feels the same way I do. Many years ago, he even ran as a Conservative candidate for Parliament, but he found out that his television fame did him more harm than good. You see, Katherine, everyone here tonight — all my friends, all Jeffrey's friends — we're people who've done well for ourselves. We've become successful, not by taking something for nothing, but through sheer hard work. We're all a little jealous of what we've achieved, and of what we own. We don't want to see it squandered. If you spoke to your father, I imagine his feelings would be very similar."

A big smile illuminated Katherine's face; her teeth shone like pearls, and bright lights danced in her blue eyes. "I can remember a few times, during my idealistic days, when I thought my father was a mile to the right of Attila the Hun. He probably does agree with you. The funny thing is, these days I regard my father as quite a liberal." She sipped the cognac, savoring both its bouquet, and the pleasant glow of the spirit down her throat. "How do you know Jeffrey?"

"I met him the same way I meet many people, including your father. On some committee or other, I forget now. In common with most of the country, I find Jeffrey vastly entertaining. Better company in the flesh, in fact, than on television. He, in turn, is fascinated by the world of business. We became friends. And through Jeffrey, of course, I met Sir Donald."

"The other people here tonight . . . the MPs, Edwin Johnson and Daniel Cooper . . ." She tried to remember the names of the other guests, but for some reason only their positions in life came to mind. ". . . The banker, the judge, the brewery chairman, the surgeon, how do you know all of them?"

"Are you writing a story on this party?"

"Of course not. I'm just curious how a man can be so politically selective in choosing his friends."

"That's simple to answer. I took out a classified ad in *The Times,* seeking friends who voted Conservative. Does that answer your question?"

She looked at him through the empty snifter. "I think you're making fun of me."

"And I think you're not fit to drive home."

"Of course I'm not; that's why I brought my toothbrush."

Saxon gave a wide grin. "You're quite drunk, aren't you?"

"I am?" She tried to recollect what she'd consumed. The champagne cocktails at the beginning of the evening, the glasses of delicately perfumed Margaux to wash down the beef Wellington, and then an after-dinner liqueur. The large Rémy-Martin had constituted a deadly overdose. "Have you ever made love to a woman who's really drunk?"

He shook his head. "Tipsy, yes. Really drunk, no. But I'd very much like to."

She held out her arms. "Carry me upstairs, and then," she added with mock resignation, "do whatever you must with me."

As she felt herself lifted up, an alarming thought occurred. "Was I drunk during the evening? Did I make a fool of myself?"

Laughing, Saxon shook his head. "You were perfect during the evening. You saved being sloshed just for me."

The alcohol ruined their lovemaking. Lying in Saxon's bed, held by his arms, and feeling him pressing hard and hot against her, Katherine found her mind wandering down a totally different path. Drunkenness focused her thoughts, for the first time in two days, on Raymond Barnhill. Instead of being angry with him, she was concerned. Had he caught his plane? He was supposed to be in New York now, preparing for his meeting, and for all Katherine knew he might have fallen in his own apartment, smacked his head on the corner of the coffee table, cut himself, and bled to death! And, she decided in a fit of tipsy moroseness, it would all be her fault for walking out on him.

"Why are you crying?" Saxon asked.

She touched her face, surprised to feel the warm wetness of tears. "I don't know. I honestly don't know."

Saxon let go of her and turned away, gazing quietly at the window and its picture of a clear spring night.

"John . . ." Wanting his warmth and comfort, she tried to draw him back. "What's the matter?"

"I told you before that I've never made love to a really drunken woman. I must admit that I was quite looking forward to it. You might have shed some inhibitions I never even realized you had. I've never made love to a woman who's crying either. That's been a very conscious choice, because I might be fooled into thinking that her tears were a reflection of the happiness she'd found in me."

They did not make love. They just lay side by side, like two strangers forced by some quirk of fate into sharing a bed. After an hour, when Saxon got up to visit the bathroom, Katherine slipped out of the bed and returned to the guest suite.

She awoke at eight the following morning with an aching head. Moving slowly, she climbed out of bed, walked into the bathroom, turned the shower full on, and stepped in. Some of the cobwebs disappeared. Afterward, she stood in front of the mirror, fixing her hair with the blow dryer she'd brought from home. Dressed in the slacks and plaid jacket she'd arrived in, and carrying the overnight bag, she went downstairs.

At the foot of the staircase, she was met by the butler. "Mr. Saxon is waiting for you on the patio, madam."

Katherine walked out to the enclosed patio. Two breakfast places were set at the table. At one, clad in blue pajamas and a blue silk robe, and reading the *Sunday Times,* was Saxon. At the other place, a copy of the *Sunday Eagle* was set out.

"Good morning, I've taken the liberty of ordering breakfast for you," Saxon greeted her, setting down his newspaper and rising to his feet. "Eggs, bacon, kidneys, grilled tomatoes, sausages, and toast."

"Don't you ever become bored with being the popular conception of the traditional English gentleman, John?"

"You have a reasonably long drive, and it's a chilly morning. You need something solid inside you."

"A cup of tea will be fine."

Breakfast was served on covered silver trays. Saxon piled his own plate high with everything, while Katherine scraped butter across a slice of toast. She did no more than glance at the frontpage headline of the *Sunday Eagle,* which referred to the upcoming election.

"I got quite a shock last night when I came back from the washroom and discovered I was alone."

"Nothing was going to happen, John. I thought it best that I returned to the guest suite. That way, we'd be able to get a good night's sleep."

"Did you manage to?"

"Yes, even if I was greeted with a hangover when I woke up."

"I didn't sleep at all. It's a type of insomnia that comes from looking forward to snuggling up all night to someone very warm and lovely, and then finishing up on my own."

"I'm sorry, John. Let's just say that last night belonged to Jeffrey Dillard, and not to us."

They finished breakfast. William carried Katherine's overnight case and garment bag to the Porsche. By the front door of the house, Katherine and Saxon kissed good-bye. "Thanks for a fabulous evening, John. All of it."

"Thank you for being such a wonderful hostess."

She ran down the steps, climbed into the Porsche, and started the engine. Saxon remained by the front door, watching as Katherine raced the Porsche around the circular drive before heading toward the small country road that ran past the estate.

Driving hard, she reached Kate's Haven by mid-morning. The children, who were riding their bicycles in the forecourt, clustered around the Porsche the instant it stopped. They wanted to know where their mother had been, and she answered that she had attended a friend's birthday party.

"Why did you stay away all night?" Henry asked.

"Because the party was held a long way away. You wouldn't want me to drive a long way late at night, would you?"

While Henry shook his head, his sister broached a more important subject. "What did you bring us from the party?"

Katherine fished into the overnight case. In a clear plastic box—specially prepared by the cook—were half a dozen petits fours. No matter where she went, she never forgot her children.

By the following Thursday, the general-election campaign was in full swing. Only three weeks remained until the country went to the polls. Every newspaper carried advertisements and editorial guidance for its readers. Television viewers were regaled by the sight of politicians telling them "what *we* have done," or "what *they* have not done."

Katherine noticed that the *Daily Eagle,* in its first pronouncement on the election, declared that it was a time for major change. She was having lunch with Sally Roberts that day, and when the two women met, Katherine asked, "Did my father lean on the leader writers to endorse Margaret Thatcher?"

"No. He leaned on me, and I leaned on Gerry Waller. Who, in turn, leaned on the leader writers. Not that any of the leaning was really necessary. I think this is the first time we've all agreed on the party we want to see in power."

After that evening's showing of "Fightback," Katherine returned home. She felt tired, and decided to stay up only long enough to watch the news. She settled in front of the television. The lead item covered the election campaign. Film clips showed the leaders of the two major parties, James Callaghan, the incumbent Labour prime minister, and his Conservative challenger, Margaret Thatcher. Then came some foreign news: South Africa had ousted three American embassy aides as spies; more executions had taken place in Iran; opponents of nuclear power were having a field day following the accident at Three Mile Island two weeks earlier.

The image on the television faded. For an instant, the screen remained blank, then a new picture appeared. Katherine sat upright. Now what had happened? Why were file pictures of the May Day Brixton riot being shown? She had no doubt it was Brixton — men fighting, cars on fire, the police powerless to restore order.

The picture froze. It wasn't a news story about a riot at all. It was a commercial. A man's voice spoke just thirteen words, but they were words that sent a chill down Katherine's back.

"Restore law and order. On May the third, elect the British Patriotic League."

18

Katherine visited the Eagle building the following afternoon, taking the elevator up to the third floor. The place was not the same without Archie Waters, she reflected. The man who had replaced him did not take the pride in his appearance that Archie had done. And Katherine missed that little half-salute, the friendly greeting, and the sound of "Miss Eagles."

Leaving the elevator, she walked to Gerald Waller's office. "Gerry, I was stunned to see a commercial last night for the British Patriotic League. How many candidates is the League running in the general election?"

"Almost a hundred. They're contesting some fifteen percent of the seats, concentrating on areas, obviously, where there's a solid core of disaffected middle-class and working-class whites."

"A hundred? My God, I feel so out of touch these days."

"That's what you get for letting the glamour of television seduce you away from the real world of Fleet Street."

"It's closer to the truth to say that I've blocked my mind to everything concerning those bags of human garbage. I didn't even realize they were putting up a

392

single candidate until I saw that commercial."

"Want to hear something funny?" Waller asked. "Yesterday evening, the agency handling the League's advertising said they wanted to buy some space in our papers. Us . . . Eagle Newspapers, who went out of our way to show up those scum for what they were! Can you imagine the nerve? We turned them down, of course, by saying that the content of the proposed ads did not meet our strict guidelines of honesty in advertising."

"What kind of platform are they running on?"

"They want to beef up the police, crush violent crime, and reintroduce capital punishment. They're vowing to get Britain out of the Common Market. They're opposed — in case you hadn't guessed — to immigration, because the structure of British society has been stretched to the breaking point by the tremendous amount of immigrants we've taken in. The League favors what it calls 'humane repatriation' of immigrants already here, with financial assistance given to the countries to which they return."

"Where's all the money to pay for this coming from?"

Waller shrugged. "I haven't the faintest idea."

"What's the *Eagle* doing about the League's campaign?"

"We'll give it the same coverage we give to the other parties' campaigns. We'll report fairly on their rallies, on their major speeches, on their platform. We will not allow them to foster publicity for themselves by claiming that Eagle Newspapers is out to destroy them. We'll let the electorate do that on May the third."

"I hope to God you're right."

As she turned to leave, Waller stopped her. "One of the contributors to the *Eagle*'s diary page turned in a piece about the party for Jeffrey Dillard. The piece claimed that the party was hosted by John Saxon and you, and hinted there was a romance between the pair

393

of you. Do you want us to use it, or spike it?"

"Thanks for the courtesy, Gerry. Do whatever you like with it. I wouldn't try to censor you, even if I wanted to."

Katherine continued to see advertisements for the British Patriotic League. Some, in a bid for the law-and-order vote, depicted scenes of riots and street fighting for which the League, itself, had been responsible. Others, aimed at women voters, centered on rising food prices, all blamed on Britain's membership in the Common Market. Women supposedly shopping for groceries were featured; without exception, they all promised to vote for the League — the party that would lower food bills by taking Britain out of Europe.

The most powerful advertisements of all pointed out how British standards had fallen. Alan Venables, the League's chairman, appeared in these. With his tweedy intellectualism, and his thin, pointed face forced into a mask of sincerity, he told viewers, "Our education system, once the envy of the world, is now the laughing stock. Our welfare system is a shambles. And ask the British workingman where he can find affordable basic housing for his family. We have taken in more immigrants than we can provide for, and they have overloaded the services that Britain provided for the British."

Venables paused, allowing his television audience to absorb the weight of this modern British tragedy. "Now is the time for courageous men to begin the process of reversal. Labour, during its years in power, welcomed more immigrants to our shores, encouraged them, because every immigrant became a Labour voter. The Conservatives will do nothing either, because they also lack the necessary backbone. Only we have the courage to do what must be done. On election day, vote for a Britain with a future. Vote for the British Patriotic League."

Not once, Katherine noticed, did Venables mention

black or Asian immigrants, but there was no doubt to which group he was referring. The appeal to whites seeking a scapegoat for their own misfortunes was ten miles high, a mile wide, and painted in blazing letters.

For the first time since starting work, Katherine followed the run-up to an election as an outsider. On the *Eagle,* she would have felt the involvement all journalists find in major events. As co-host on a television show, she was forced to do what everyone else in the country did: learn about the election from the media of which she had once been a part.

She carefully checked each opinion poll the instant it was released. Not to see how the two major parties were faring, but to learn about the British Patriotic League. If Alan Venables and his party were gaining any popularity at all, Katherine was gratified to see, it did not show up in the polls. Voters who voiced a preference for the League's divisive politics were listed in poll results as part of the minor and inconsequential "others" category, which traditionally included all kinds of outlandish candidates.

The League's campaign, however, had one noticeable side product. A dozen Conservatives — incumbent Members of Parliament defending their seats, and challengers in constituencies held by Labour — began to voice the need for far stricter immigration controls. Leading them were Edwin Johnson and Daniel Cooper, the two MPs Katherine had met at John Saxon's home on the night of Jeffrey Dillard's party.

The instant Katherine read the report, she telephoned John Saxon. "Are your friends cut from the same cloth as Alan Venables and his gang of hatemongers?"

"Most certainly not. They're stealing a little of the League's thunder, that's all, and they're doing it for a very good reason. If you look at the constituencies involved, you'll find the League is very active there. By promising to fight for a tougher immigration law — which we *do* need — these Conservatives may win votes which might otherwise go to the League."

Katherine nodded in understanding. Margaret Thatcher herself had raised a huge outcry a year earlier when, during a television news program, she had stated that many Britons were afraid of being swamped by people with a different culture, and it was the duty of the government to hold out the clear prospect of an end to immigration. "We are not in politics to ignore people's worries," Katherine recalled the Conservative leader saying. "We are in politics to deal with them." Margaret Thatcher made a strict immigration policy mean one thing, while Alan Venables twisted it into something else entirely.

The election took place on the first Thursday in May. That night's "Fightback" was preempted by an election special. Katherine was free, so she took Henry and Joanne, who had no school that day into town for lunch with their grandfather.

"Did you vote?" Roland asked his daughter.

"It was the very first thing I did."

"Would it be presumptuous to ask how you voted?"

"Conservative. I agreed with the *Eagle*'s endorsement of Maggie Thatcher." She watched her father's face light up before adding, "I would have voted for her anyway, because I'm sick and tired of the mess you men have made of this country."

Katherine returned to Frognal, ready for an evening of election fever — an evening of watching television, instead of appearing in it. The prospect was dashed even before the first results were in. She heard the telephone ring. Moments later, Edna Griffiths stuck her head around the drawing room door.

"Mrs. Kassler, there's a woman wants to speak to you."

"Who is it?"

"She wouldn't leave a name."

Annoyed, Katherine said, "Tell her that I don't speak to people who refuse to identify themselves."

"She said it was urgent, Mrs. Kassler. Concerning that story on the *Eagle*'s diary page about Mr. Dillard's party. And you and Mr. Saxon."

Katherine lifted the extension in the drawing room. "This is Katherine Kassler. May I help you?"

A high, clipped voice rapped out an order. "Meet me at the Spaniards in half an hour, Mrs. Kassler. I have some information in which you'll be interested."

"The only information I want from you is your name."

"Chalfont. Deidre Chalfont."

"Am I supposed to know you?"

"My name wasn't always Chalfont. It used to be Saxon. Deidre Saxon. Be at the Spaniards in thirty minutes. My information is very important."

The Spaniards was a three-hundred-year-old public house situated on the edge of Hampstead Heath. Even on election night it was busy, catering to its usual mixture of young and old, artist and professional, local and tourist. Katherine sat at a table tucked away in a corner, and wondered about the important information the former Mrs. John Saxon claimed to have.

Never mind the information — what would Saxon's ex-wife be like? Family-minded, Katherine decided. Had not Saxon himself admitted the marriage had failed because he'd given more time to his business than to his wife? The Saxons had been divorced for nine years. Deidre had most certainly married again. She probably had a handful of children, which was undoubtedly what she wanted out of life. Katherine resolved to look out for a middle-aged woman sensibly dressed in flat shoes and a tweedy skirt; the terse voice of command must come from continually telling the children to behave themselves.

"Good evening, Mrs. Kassler." The voice was just as curt in person as it had been over the telephone. "Thank you for seeing me at such short notice."

Katherine looked around for the sensibly attired middle-aged mother. Instead, she saw a slim brunette in her late thirties, stylishly dressed in a rust-and-black houndstooth jacket and a tight black leather skirt. Wavy hair softened a face that drew hardness from a square chin.

"Mrs. Chalfont?" Katherine asked.

"It's *Miss* Chalfont. I reverted to my single name when I got divorced."

"Excuse me. I just assumed you'd remarried."

"After John? Nothing could take his place, darling, or hasn't he told you that yet? It must have been quite a shock when I telephoned you just now."

"It was." Katherine watched Deidre sit down and cross her legs. "What is the important information?"

"We'll get to it." The two women eyed each other like boxers before the fight begins. "You're not the type of woman I thought John would get involved with," Deidre said at last.

"Then we're even. You're not exactly what I was expecting, either. I was looking for the mousy married kind."

"Sorry to disappoint you. I've seen your show several times, and I knew that Jeffrey Dillard was a friend of John's, but it never occurred to me that you and John might have something going with each other. At least, not until I saw that little diary piece in the *Eagle*. Tell me something—does my husband still use William Brown for his dirty little jobs?"

"You mean his chauffeur?"

"If you want to give him a title, fine. Why don't you ask John one day how he came to employ William? I'm sure you'll find the story quite fascinating."

Katherine glanced meaningfully at her Patek Philippe, and Deidre asked, "Are you in love with John?"

"Is it any of your business?"

Deidre nodded. "I have to know because of the information. It will only be relevant to a woman who feels quite deeply for John. Do you love him?"

"A little." Katherine wished the woman would get to the reason for this unusual meeting. Simultaneously, she could not deny that she was curious about Deidre Chalfont. "You were married to John for six years, weren't you?"

"I'm glad to see he told you about me. I was twenty-two when I met him. He was twenty-six, and already doing very well for himself. I worked as his secretary; can you believe that? It was every secretary's dream, falling in love with the bright and handsome young boss, and having him return the feeling. Only if I'd had any brains then, I would have seen that he already had three loves. Business. Himself. And his country. After six years of marriage, being a poor fourth finally got on my nerves. I told him I wanted a divorce. To be fair to the man, he treated me very well; you could never fault him for his generosity. He made a large settlement on me. A house, plenty of money. I used that to open my own secretarial agency." She looked past Katherine for a moment, as though daydreaming. "Poor dear, he's so wrapped up in himself that I sometimes wonder if he even knows I'm not there anymore . . . if he even understands I'm gone."

"Miss Chalfont, I left two children in bed, and a television screen full of election news to come here and meet you. You claimed you had some very important information for me."

"Yes, I do. I made a vow right after the divorce that if I ever heard about John remarrying—"

"I am not marrying him."

"Let me finish, darling," Deidre said with a wintry smile. "If I ever heard of him remarrying, or even being involved with someone, I'd make it my business to impart this information to the woman in question."

Katherine gritted her teeth. "I am leaving. If you have something to tell me, please do it quickly."

"Certainly. What I have to tell you is that John Saxon is the biggest bastard ever to walk this earth. I'd advise you to bear that in mind."

Deidre Chalfont's opinion of her ex-husband formed Katherine's final thought before she drifted off to sleep that night. What was behind it? Bitterness over a failed marriage? Jealousy that Saxon might have found happiness, while Deidre had not? Or was it something else entirely? Was Deidre just trying to help another woman avoid a trap into which she had once fallen? No, Katherine told herself, it couldn't be that. If John Saxon was even a tenth as bad as Deidre had tried to paint him with that single damning sentence, Katherine would have spotted some clue long ago. It had to be bitterness or jealousy. Or maybe both.

Excitement greeted Katherine when she came downstairs the next morning. In the breakfast room, a radio blared out late election results. Edna tried to serve breakfast to the children and listen at the same time. On the table was the *Daily Eagle,* its front page covered by one enormous headline: "Maggie Wins!"

"A majority of more than forty seats, Mrs. Kassler," said Edna. "That's what the experts are predicting. Tea will be up in a moment."

"Thank you." Katherine opened the paper in the middle, where polling results available at press time were listed. Both of Saxon's friends, Edwin Johnson and Daniel Cooper, had been reelected with substantially increased majorities. After years of drifting slowly to the left, the country had shifted sharply to the right.

"Bet you wish you were still on the newspaper, Mrs. Kassler," Edna said. Her face was one gigantic smile, and Katherine guessed that the housekeeper had voted for Margaret Thatcher. Phillips, too. It was some reflection on society when working people, whose traditional loyalty was supposed to be to Labour, turned around and voted Conservative.

"I do indeed, Edna. There's nowhere like Fleet Street when election results start pouring in. Especially if the paper you work for has picked the winner." Sentiment tugged and Katherine decided to pop into the *Eagle* after meeting with Jeffrey Dillard that morning to discuss the next "Fightback."

Dillard was in an expansive mood. He greeted Katherine by grasping her shoulders and kissing her on the cheek. "Did it, didn't we? Lunch is on me."

John Saxon called the "Fightback" offices within ten minutes of Katherine's arrival. She had never heard him so animated. He rambled on excitedly about "a large enough working majority for the government to push through the reforms that are necessary to turn this country around." He finished by asking, "How about a celebration lunch?"

"You're ten minutes too late. Jeffrey asked first."

Katherine finished by having lunch with both men. Even then, she felt like an outsider. They were both so busy talking about the election that they barely noticed her presence at the table. As the first course was cleared, she decided to interject herself into the discussion.

"I see your friends were reelected with larger majorities. Edwin Johnson and Daniel Cooper. Their theft of British Patriotic League thunder must have paid handsome dividends."

"Just as I told you it would," Saxon responded. "The League didn't win a single seat, did it?"

"Thank God for that." Before she could think of some way to keep their attention, Saxon and Dillard were talking between themselves again. Katherine caught a few phrases—"stronger national defense;

401

more private enterprise and a corresponding reduction in government ownership of industry; legislation against union picketing"—and then she tuned herself out.

Only when lunch was over and Saxon had gone did Katherine realize that she had neglected to tell him about meeting Deidre. Then again, did she really need to annoy him? Perhaps it was best to let sleeping dogs lie by not mentioning his ex-wife's sudden appearance.

From the restaurant, Katherine went to the Eagle building. The *Daily Eagle*'s news staff was still working at fever pitch. Lawrie Stimkin had reporters and photographers outside Buckingham Palace, where Margaret Thatcher would go to be requested by the Queen, following established ritual, to form a government. More *Eagle* reporters were among the international press legion jammed into Downing Street, where the new prime minister would be driven from the Palace, to take up her official residence at Number Ten.

Katherine stopped by Erica Bentley's office. The women's page editor was sitting at her typewriter, fingers poised like talons above the keys. "Let me guess; you're writing an open letter advising Margaret Thatcher on the way she should dress now that she's PM," Katherine said.

"Wrong. I'm writing a column on what women expect from a woman prime minister. What are you doing here?"

"Slumming."

"If you're not careful, I'll find you some work."

"I'd love to help, Erica. But working on something as mundane as a daily newspaper might harm my television career."

Erica ripped the paper from the typewriter, rolled it into a ball, and threw it at Katherine. "Remember, kid, if it weren't for me, half the television viewers in this country would think you only had one change of clothes."

As Katherine walked back toward the elevator, she heard her name being called. Lawrie Stimkin stood in the doorway of his glass-walled office. "Want an assignment?"

"I just turned one down from Erica."

"I think you'll like this one." The news editor handed Katherine a press release. At the top was a familiar triangular logo: a flaming sword against the Cross of St. George. "The British Patriotic League's holding a press conference at six o'clock tonight. They want to complain that our electoral system is grossly unfair. In some constituencies, where unemployment's high, and racial harmony's bad, they got upwards of ten percent of the vote. They think that entitles them to more than just saving their deposit."

The figure shocked Katherine. In that morning's paper, she had paid heed only to the major parties. She hadn't bothered to check the also-rans. "Ten percent? Where was this?"

"Distressed areas. Parts of Birmingham and Liverpool where a regular wage envelope is as rare as a twenty-year-old virgin. Couple of racially mixed places in London as well, where the whites don't appreciate having to learn Urdu to be able to enjoy a film at their local picture house," Stimkin added dryly.

Katherine felt the day's excitement drain from her body. "You're not sending anyone to this press conference, are you?"

"I've got no one to spare. That's why I asked you."

"Forget it. Let them tell their lies to empty walls."

She drove home quite depressed. So what if John Saxon's friends, and some of their Conservative colleagues, had stolen League thunder in their bids for votes?

The League, it appeared, had plenty of thunder to spare.

Roland Eagles thought so, too. Like Katherine, he had been fooled by the strength of the British Patriotic League. He had fully expected the League to be wiped out in the election, with every one of its candidates losing the financial deposit of one hundred and fifty pounds that was required for the privilege of running. Roland had always been realistic enough to understand that bigots abounded in Britain, the same as they did in every country, but he had never dreamed that they would proudly demonstrate that bigotry by voting so heavily for the League. If it was an omen of things to come, it was a singularly grim omen.

Since Katherine's departure from the *Eagle,* much of the sting had gone out of the campaign against the League. A feeling existed that it was best to treat the League the way the rest of Fleet Street treated it: ignore it, and hope it died on its own.

The election results destroyed that apathy. Roland summoned to the boardroom on the executive floor the three people he considered most important to the editorial side of the *Daily Eagle:* Sally Roberts, Gerald Waller, and Lawrie Stimkin.

"In the excitement of the election, we have overlooked some very important points. The British Patriotic League, with candidates running in areas where research dictated they would do well, has achieved what no other extremist group has ever managed to do in this country. It has capitalized on fear and distrust to gather a respectable number of votes. I know we did not cover the League's postelection press conference—"

"We were very thin on the ground," Stimkin said quickly.

"I'm not blaming anyone, Mr. Stimkin. I was just about to say that during the conference, their propaganda man . . . what's his name, now?"

"Burns," Stimkin responded. "Trevor Burns. He's

worked on one or two papers in the Street during his time, but I would imagine the union's pulled his card by now."

"Burns, thank you. According to reports I saw of the conference, this Burns character claimed that it would be a major mistake for anyone to regard the League as some toothless dog. I agree with him. Any extremist party that can poll ten percent in certain constituencies, needs to be taken very seriously."

Roland looked from Waller to Sally, and then to Stimkin. "The British Patriotic League has money. It purchased Patriot House in Whitechapel for cash. The same with those buildings in Birmingham, Manchester, and Leicester. The League had to lay out fifteen thousand pounds to run one hundred candidates in this election. Some of the deposits were saved because League candidates polled enough votes, but many were lost. Advertising space was bought for the election. Then there's the publication of *Patriot,* which is not some cheap mimeographed sheet. Everywhere you look, large sums of money are being spent. I want us to learn where the money is coming from. I don't, for an instant, believe sums like this could be raised from membership dues. The League is being financed. I want to know who stands to gain from any League successes."

"You sound like you're declaring total war on the British Patriotic League," Sally remarked.

"That's exactly what I am doing," Roland replied. "I am declaring war on these despicable swine. Which means that Eagle Newspapers is declaring war. I think that's the very least we can do to honor the memory of Archie Waters and his grandson."

A week after the election, Raymond Barnhill telephoned Katherine. The call came when Katherine was asleep. She snapped awake instantly, and snatched the receiver from the bedside telephone before the ringing could wake the entire household.

"How about the wild election result? Talk about the reincarnation of Boadicea . . ."

"Why are you calling me at three o'clock in the blasted morning, Raymond?"

"I really wanted to talk to you, and it's only ten o'clock over here." Katherine could feel his embarrassment. "I forgot all about the stupid time difference; can you believe that?"

"Aren't you in London?"

"No, I'm in New York. Did I disturb you?"

Katherine could not resist sarcasm. "Of course not. I'm always up this time of night, waiting for the phone to ring."

"Hey, I'm really sorry. Look, I'm booked on a flight to London tomorrow night, gets in eight-thirty Saturday morning. I wanted to call and find out if you'd see me when I got back. If you'd let me do a little bit of explaining, and one hell of a lot of apologizing."

"How did your work go?"

"Great. I locked myself away in a friend's apartment and hammered out the revisions the publisher wanted. While I was doing that, the agent was putting together a deal for the next two books."

"When do you think the first book will be published?" She tried to stifle a yawn, but failed.

"Fall of next year. I'm robbing you of your beauty sleep. I'll give you a shout when I get back to London."

"Just make sure that it's not at three o'clock in the morning," she said, and hung up.

Barnhill telephoned next at eleven o'clock on Saturday morning, the moment he reached home from Heathrow Airport. "May I see you?" he asked.

"At Dolphin Square?"

"I don't think so. This place looks like a bomb hit it."

"You sound surprised."

"Yes, well . . . I'd kind of forgotten the mess I'd left it in. Now that it's all coming back to me, I'm a bit surprised that I even made it out of here to catch my flight."

"I wondered if you had. After the way I left you, I told myself I didn't care, but I'm glad you did. I'm also glad you came back."

"Why?"

"Fleet Street has too many bombastic Brits. It needs at least one slightly touched colonial."

"I'll pretend you meant that as a compliment."

They met that afternoon in Regent's Park, shaking hands as two friends might do. Barnhill suggested hiring one of the rowboats that drifted around the lake. Katherine climbed in, grateful that she had chosen to wear cords tucked into boots instead of a skirt. She sat on the narrow bench seat and rested her hands on the sides of the small boat as Barnhill worked the oars to take them away from the bank.

"You look a lot better than the last time I saw you," she told him. "Color in your face, a shine in your eyes."

"I'd rather you forgot the last time you saw me. What I remember of that night makes me feel ashamed."

"Why?"

"I was drunk. I was as crude as all hell, pawing you like you were come cheap date. And I said some very unfair things. You told me the truth about my lack of faith in myself. It hurt. So I came right back by trying to hurt you. What I said about you being born with a silver tea service in your mouth . . . well, I'd give anything to be able to take that back."

"It's been said many times before," Katherine admitted. "From the moment I set foot in the Eagle building, I had to work twice as hard as anyone else to prove that I was half as good."

Barnhill shipped the oars, allowing the boat to drift. "That night before I left, that was the first time in ages that I'd hit the bottle. The first time since I came to this country. I thought I had it beat, and then . . . ah, you saw what happened."

"Tell me something, Raymond. If I'd had dinner with you that night, to celebrate selling your book, would you still have gone out and bought the vodka?"

"I don't know," Barnhill answered, and Katherine was grateful for his kindness.

"When did you start drinking?"

"Vietnam. There was nothing else to do. Liquor was cheap, readily available, and socially acceptable. Before that, I'd never touched a drop."

"Never?" Katherine found that hard to believe.

"I never saw it in the house when I was growing up. One, we lived in a dry county, so it required a conscious effort if you wanted a drink. Secondly, my parents were Baptists, people who believed that every evil in the world stemmed from liquor. That background kept me off it, right through college, even during the couple of years I spent working on the *State* in Columbia before the draft board caught up with me. When I first tried drinking in Vietnam, I didn't like the taste of the damned stuff, but it gave me a lift. For a few minutes, for a few hours, it got me the hell out of Vietnam. And in those days, you couldn't ask for more."

"What you told me about your wife . . . about Mary . . . was that true? That she carried on while you were away?"

Barnhill nodded. "I'd heard things, and she knew I'd heard them. Both of us worked damned hard on getting that marriage straight once I got home. It worked fine, and I stayed clean. I'd beaten it; that's what I told myself. I'd seen all those career-soldier alcoholics in Vietnam, and I'd had this terrifying fear of turning out just like that. But once I got back, I thought about them and laughed. I laughed until I got the job in New York, and that was when my world fell apart. Mary didn't like New York. The more miserable Mary became, the more I drank. When I caught her with someone else, I knew fifty percent of the blame was mine. I had the choice — either make something of my life, or quit. I tried to salvage myself by coming here."

"And you were doing so well . . ." Katherine leaned forward on the narrow bench and patted Barnhill's arm. "Going on a bender once every eighteen months or so isn't bad."

"Wrong. It's once too often."

They sat silently on the gently rocking boat until Barnhill said, "I brought you back a souvenir of New York. It's meant in a humorous vein, so don't kick me over the side of the boat."

Katherine accepted the slim box Barnhill pulled from the pocket of his brown corduroy jacket. She opened it, tore aside white tissue paper, and then started to laugh. It was a silver spoon, with a tiny enameled print of the Statue of Liberty fixed to the end of the handle.

"Thank you."

"Friends again?" Barnhill asked.

"Friends again." She leaned forward to kiss him on the cheek. The boat rocked unnervingly, and she dropped back onto the bench. "Any time I'm feeling low, I'll stick this spoon in my mouth to remind myself how privileged I am. And any time you're feeling low, call on me."

"If you're not there?"

"Keep on trying. You're too nice and too talented to waste yourself on a bottle."

Raymond Barnhill's return to London constituted a wonderful surprise for Katherine. After their explosive parting, she had not expected to see him again, and she'd told herself she didn't care. She'd been wrong on both counts, and she was happy to see him back.

She had one more surprise coming. On the morning of the last Thursday in May, she sat down with Jeffrey Dillard to make the final decisions regarding that night's "Fightback." They were finished by noon.

"Nothing to do until tonight," Dillard said. "Fancy a drink and some lunch?"

"Sounds like a wonderful idea."

They went to a private Mayfair club, of which Dillard was a member. Katherine was ready, when Dillard asked, to order a dry sherry. Dillard did not ask. Nor did he order anything. He simply sat back, smiling, as an ice bucket containing a bottle of Taittinger was set beside the table. A wine steward uncorked the bottle with barely a pop, and poured champagne into two glasses. Katherine lifted her glass to mouth level, and gazed across the bubbles at Dillard.

"Are we celebrating anything in particular, Jeffrey?"

"We've already celebrated my thirtieth anniversary in television," Dillard answered, "so I don't suppose we can commemorate it again. So why don't we celebrate my turning sixty-six later this year?"

"Couldn't we have waited until your birthday?"

"All right, then let's celebrate my retirement at the end of this year. And while we're at it — and before the bubbly goes as flat as the proverbial pancake — let us also drink a toast to the continuation of 'Fightback' after my retirement, with you as my successor."

Katherine set down the glass. "Do you mean it? You retiring, and me succeeding you?"

"You sound genuinely surprised. Didn't John Saxon ever mention anything to you? He was fully aware that I intended to retire soon, you know."

"That first night, when you came by the restaurant where we were having dinner . . . John wanted me to take Elaine Cowdrey's position, and when he saw I wasn't convinced, he mentioned that you'd be leaving soon as well. I didn't know whether to believe him or not. I thought he might be trying to sway me into taking the job." She lifted the glass. "To your retirement, Jeffrey, may it be long and happy."

"Thank you. And to your continuing triumph at 'Fightback.' "

"I'm going to miss you, Jeffrey. 'Fightback,' and the entire television industry, won't be the same without you."

"I'll be watching every Thursday night, my dear, and if I think you're letting down the side, you'll hear from me pretty quickly." Before Katherine could ask if he was serious, Dillard quickly added, "But I really don't think I'll have to bother."

19

Roland Eagles's declaration of war against the British Patriotic League began, like all well-planned campaigns, with intelligence gathering. Katherine's former assistants, Derek Simon and Heather Harvey, were assigned by Gerald Waller to find out everything they could about the League's three-man executive committee.

The two reporters backtracked through the lives of Alan Venables, Trevor Burns, and Neville Sharpe, interviewing people who had worked with the three men. After a month, they had compiled an impressive dossier. Over dinner at Roland's home one night, Sally Roberts brought Katherine up to date.

"This much you know already. Venables lectured on government and politics. Burns was a free-lance journalist, and Neville Sharpe was an accountant. Venables was highly regarded at the college by faculty members. Editors who had commissioned work from Burns all agreed he was very professional, very reliable. And the accountancy firm which employed Sharpe said the same thing. Sharpe, incidentally, was even in line for a partnership. Each man was exceptionally bright, good at his job, and respected. All three had solid futures — Venables in the educational system, Sharpe with his firm of accountants, and Burns as a journalist. And all three of them gave everything up in May 1977. Venables walked out of the college. Sharpe gave a month's notice, and Burns notified the magazines and newspapers he worked for that he was no longer accepting assignments."

"Just like that, they quit?" Katherine asked. "What about their families. How on earth did they exist?"

"There are no families," Sally answered. "Venables was divorced three years ago, and has no children. Burns and Sharpe were never married."

"They still needed money to survive," Roland pointed out. "Unless they'd put by a tidy sum in readiness for the day that they decided to form the British Patriotic League."

"On the contrary. From what Derek and Heather learned, none of the men ever gave any sign of being wealthy." Sally paused, while Arthur Parsons cleared dessert plates from the table. Roland took the opportunity to light a Davidoff. "Venables, in fact, was quite poor. He was living in a furnished room after having given his ex-wife the house they'd shared. He didn't seem to be in any shape to do without regular income."

"Does Venables still live in the furnished room?"

"No. He's in a house in East London, Leytonstone. A receptive, blue-collar area for his kind of politics. He bought the house for cash, no mortgage, nothing outstanding. Burns and Sharpe aren't short of anything, either."

"They all quit work together," Katherine mused, "and instead of being destitute, they seem to be reasonably well off. Had they known each other before?"

"There's no evidence of that. It's as though they suddenly came together for the sole purpose of forming an extremist political party."

Katherine recalled the previous year's May Day

rally, when the League had made its first public appearance. As she'd listened to Venables spout his hatred, she'd asked herself a question. Now she posed it to Sally. "Did Venables ever have any colored or Asian students in the classes he taught?"

"I was waiting for you to ask that. He had quite a few."

"How did he behave towards them?"

"In exemplary fashion. He never once gave any clue that he was racist. In fact, he even wrote glowing letters of reference for a number of Indian and Pakistani students. On top of that, he was quite friendly with colored members of the faculty. The ones Derek and Heather interviewed confessed to being very puzzled by the direction Venables has taken."

Roland studied the glowing tip of his cigar. "The same, I assume, holds true for Burns and Sharpe."

"Exactly. Not one of the men ever demonstrated any sign of being particularly bigoted."

Intrigued, Katherine stored the facts away in her memory. The following day, she met Raymond Barnhill for lunch at the Cheshire Cheese, where she told him of the previous night's discussion. "Doesn't that strike you as strange, how all three of the executive committee suddenly saw the light, as it were?"

Barnhill responded with a question of his own. "Ever hear of George Lincoln Rockwell?"

"The American Nazi leader?"

"That's him; he was shot and killed by one of his own men in 1967. When I was in Vietnam, I knew a navy captain who'd served with Rockwell in Iceland in the early fifties. This captain said that in those days, Rockwell was the greatest guy you could wish to meet, nothing like he turned out to be later on."

"What changed him?"

"The Icelanders were in the Nazi league when it

came to racial purity. Apparently, Rockwell married an Icelandic woman, and the navy captain claimed she may have messed up his mind for him." Barnhill grinned. "So all you've got to do now is find out who, or what, played around with the minds of Alan Venables, Trevor Burns, and Neville Sharpe."

"Thank you, Raymond. I'll make sure someone checks into their backgrounds for a hidden Icelandic wife."

Katherine took off all of August, reasoning that it would be the last such break she'd be able to take for a long time. Once she assumed control of "Fightback" from Jeffrey Dillard in the new year, her time would no longer be her own.

She went with Henry and Joanne on two separate vacations. A traditional sand-and-sea vacation first, at Marbella, followed by a transatlantic flight to California and a never-to-be-forgotten visit to Disneyland.

John Saxon collected Katherine and the children at Heathrow Airport when they returned from California. He laughed when he saw the big-eared Mickey Mouse hat they'd brought back for him. At Joanne's insistence, he wore it for the entire journey home.

Once they were at Kate's Haven, and Edna had taken charge of the children, Saxon took Katherine aside. "What would you do if I said I'd missed you like mad?"

She'd missed him, too. She'd asked him to come away with them, first to Marbella, then to Disneyland. Both times Saxon had found a business reason to remain in England, and Katherine had reluctantly recalled Deidre Chalfont's statement about Saxon being in love with his work. "What would you like me to do if you said you'd missed me like mad?"

"Have dinner with me tonight."

415

"And then?"

Saxon just winked.

"Let me get some sleep first. I'm suffering from a deadly combination of excitement and jet lag."

They ate at Simpson's-in-the-Strand. Replete, they returned to Marble Arch to satisfy another kind of appetite, making love on Saxon's four-poster bed. Afterward, lying securely in Saxon's embrace, Katherine talked about the impending change in her career.

"In just three months, Jeffrey won't be around for me to lean on. It's a little scary, John."

"Surely not. There are no problems, are there?"

"A couple of minor sticking points, that's all. I have to make up my mind whether to stay with the research staff Jeffrey used, or bring in my own."

"Who would you bring in?"

"I was thinking of poaching the two reporters I worked with on the *Eagle*. Derek Simon and Heather Harvey."

"Would they be interested? What are they doing now?"

"Working on a special assignment—trying to dig up dirt on the leaders of the British Patriotic League."

Saxon made a face. "Good God, hasn't the *Eagle* had its bellyful of that mob yet?"

"My father doesn't think so. He was appalled that they achieved what they did in the election. Plus, he feels that Eagle Newspapers owes a debt to the memories of Archie Waters and his grandson."

"Katherine, I am not without feeling in this matter. They were my tenants, and I was quite fond of the old man. He was a soldier who had spent his life doing his duty for his country. But there was nothing to connect the League to Brian's death."

"What about Ginger . . . Michael Edwards . . . ?"

"If it were this Ginger who killed Brian, it was a

416

personal thing. A vendetta. Twice, Brian had gotten the better of him. On the soccer special, when he'd made Ginger give up the seat to you, and the time he beat the living daylights out of him. And even if Ginger were responsible, he's been paid back in full. It's over, can't you see that? The only result your father will achieve with a continuing campaign against the British Patriotic League is the obvious result: he'll bring their existence to the attention of more maniacs, and he'll attract a few hundred more followers to their bigoted cause."

Katherine supposed Saxon was right. She was sick and tired of the whole damned business. It had cost her too much. In the loss of friends, and in the loss of faith.

"Would you be happier with Derek and Heather working for you at 'Fightback'?" Saxon asked.

"I think so. We always got along very well at the *Eagle*."

"Then do what you have to do: grab them!"

Jeffrey Dillard's final "Fightback" was shown on the first Thursday of December. Dillard bowed out with the pomp and ceremony of a royal investiture. After formally announcing his retirement as host, and Katherine's succession, he presented her with a gleaming crown, "befitting the queen of the British consumer," and a shining theatrical sword, "with which you shall slay the dragons of greed and hypocrisy." It was pure ham, and the studio audience loved it. Katherine, wearing the crown and holding the sword, wished that color television had not yet been invented; on black-and-white, her blush would be nowhere near as conspicuous!

Instead of hurrying home after the show, Katherine attended an intimate dinner party at Dillard's Mayfair club. Shirley Dillard was there, tall and thin with carefully coiffed silver hair. So was Paul Hyde, producer of "Fightback" for the many years Dillard had been with the show.

"Made any plans for Jeffrey now that he'll be home all the time?" Katherine asked Shirley. "Are you going to get him trimming hedges, weeding, and mowing the lawn?"

Shirley laughed. "I've never seen Jeffrey as the gardening type. He says he loves the smell of fresh-mown grass, but he'll be damned if he'll go out and mow it."

Paul Hyde leaned across the table. "He won't even have the time to smell it. He'll be too busy helping me at 'Fightback.' "

"I beg your pardon?" Katherine looked at Dillard, who moved uncomfortably on his seat.

"Jeffrey's staying on as executive producer," Hyde revealed. "A consultant. Going to be my right-hand man."

"We've never had an executive producer before," Katherine pointed out. "Why do we need one now?"

Dillard raised a hand, like the pope giving a blessing. Even his first words were Latin. *"Mea culpa.* My fault entirely, Katherine, but after so many years in television the old ego finds it a trifle hard to walk away completely. Paul here, bless him, understood my predicament. He invented a position for me. Nothing more than a gofer, really, but it'll keep me in touch with the show." He looked fondly at his wife. "Keep me out of Shirley's hair as well."

Shirley and Paul Hyde laughed, but Katherine did not. It was the old boys' network in operation. In his late fifties, Hyde had been in television for almost as long as Dillard. The two men were close, professionally and socially. If it had been anyone but Dillard with an ego problem, Hyde would have just shrugged his shoulders and said, "Too bad." Because it was his close friend, Hyde had made room for him.

It was not the old boys' network, though, which concerned Katherine. It was the possible erosion of her authority. "Jeffrey, I love you very dearly, and there's nothing I'd like more than for us to continue our professional association. But I'm also a little worried that I won't have complete control of what appears in my own show."

Dillard's face wore shock that Katherine could think such an unkind thought about him. Hyde was instantly conciliatory. "Katherine, I created the position of executive producer to keep an old friend from vegetating in retirement. Rest assured, the responsibility for the content of the show will be yours, and yours alone. If that were not the case, do you seriously believe I would have made room for Heather Harvey and Derek Simon, whom you asked to bring in from the *Daily Eagle?*"

Hyde's words, Katherine told herself, made perfectly logical sense. So why did she not fully believe him? And why did she feel that, no matter how much she liked, admired, and respected Jeffrey Dillard, she would never be truly free of his specter on the show?

Not only was Jeffrey Dillard true to his word, acting as a personal assistant to Paul Hyde, but Katherine was thankful for his presence in the background as executive producer. Dillard kept a tactful distance from Katherine as she finalized her first "Fightback," but when she needed advice he was more than happy to step forward and help.

"See?" he told her. "I'm a consultant. If you hit a snag, consult me."

Grateful, and just a little ashamed of herself for ever thinking that Dillard would try to butt in, Katherine kissed him on the cheek. "There's your consultancy fee. Don't forget to declare it to the taxman."

The first show, at the beginning of January, was a smash. Using Derek and Heather in a chatty question-and-answer format, Katherine exposed an expensive modeling school that, in three years of promising glamorous careers for its graduates, had failed to place even one. She followed that with a bogus clairvoyant who preyed on recently bereaved men and women, taking vast sums of money to put them in touch with the spirits of their departed loved ones. For that case, Katherine played a young widow, a role that came very naturally. And she felt more than professional pride when police initiated fraud proceedings against the alleged clairvoyant.

Two days later, on the first Saturday of the year, Katherine celebrated with a catered dinner party at Kate's Haven. The three dozen guests comprised a cross-section of her life. Family, friends, colleagues from the newspaper and from "Fightback," plus a handful of John Saxon's friends whom she had met at his home. Saxon, himself, was the very first to arrive. He entered the house staggering under an enormous box. Katherine assumed it was a gift for her. She was wrong. The box contained toboggans for Henry and Joanne to use over Hampstead Heath. It was all Katherine could do to stop the children from rushing outside to try the toboggans on the snow-covered back lawn.

"You have just been elected," Katherine told Saxon, "as the man who takes them over the heath on snowy days."

"Why do you think I chose such a gift?"

"You're a very lovely man. Thank you."

Katherine made no objection when Saxon established himself as host. As other guests arrived, he was on hand with her to welcome them. Barely anyone, Katherine noticed, appeared surprised at Saxon's forthrightness. Certainly not her father and Sally. Roland, after kissing Katherine, shook Saxon's hand warmly, as though he had already approved of the property developer as a future son-in-law. Erica Bentley, who had driven with her husband, Cliff, from their farm, gave Katherine a broad wink. A few minutes later, when Erica had Katherine alone, she asked, "How well does John get on with your children?"

"The same way he gets on with everyone—amazingly well."

"And your father?"

"Again, a hit."

"Then what are you waiting for, Katherine? Marry the man! Call a minister and tie the knot tonight. Do it right here, right now, and save yourself the expense and bother of having another party."

As more guests arrived, Katherine observed that cliques began to form. The *Eagle* people—Sally, the Bentleys, and Gerald Waller—formed one small group. Katherine thought that Waller looked tired. His face had a gaunt appearance, and his eyes seemed sunken. She found out that his temper was sharp, though, when he quietly but firmly reprimanded her for stealing two members of his staff.

"If my father didn't complain about me taking Derek and Heather for 'Fightback,' why should you?"

"Your father doesn't have to complain—he's not the one with the headache of getting the paper out each day."

Another clique was formed by the "Fightback" crew—Jeffrey and Shirley Dillard, Paul Hyde, and the two young reporters about whom Waller was so upset. Both Derek and Heather studiously avoided meeting Waller's gaze, and Katherine wondered if inviting them all had been such a tactful idea.

She pulled Sally aside. "Is it me, or is Gerry overreacting about my poaching Derek and Heather?"

"He's overreacted about a lot of things during the

past couple of weeks," Sally answered. "Perhaps it has to do with his quitting smoking."

"I didn't know he had," Katherine said quickly, before realizing that tonight was the first time she had ever seen Waller without a cigarette in his hand.

"He has, and that's what everyone in editorial claims is the reason for his change in behavior. He's hauled the subs over the coals a few times, and poor Lawrie Stimkin's been yelled at more than once because the *Eagle* didn't carry some inconsequential story that one of the other papers had."

Once, that news would have delighted Katherine, but since seeing the other, more sympathetic side of the Scottish-born news editor, she felt sorry for him. "Poor Lawrie," she said. "He must be looking gloomier than ever."

Saxon entered the room, looking for Katherine. With him was a couple in their sixties; the face of the man was disfigured by a wide scar down the right side. "Who," whispered Sally, "is that?"

"Sir Donald Leslie and his wife. They're John's friends. Come and meet them. Interesting people, even if Sir Donald does believe Maggie Thatcher's a dangerous left-winger."

The last guest to arrive was Raymond Barnhill. Katherine had told him that the party was black tie, and when she opened the front door, she was more than a little relieved to see he had remembered. Under his Burberry raincoat, he wore a tuxedo.

"Surprised to see me in a monkey suit?" he asked.

"No more surprised than you obviously are to be wearing one. Did you hire it from Moss Bros?"

"I went one better . . . I borrowed it from a guy I work with." He held out a carefully wrapped package. "A very American gift. Use it with good luck."

Katherine peeled off the wrapping to find a box containing a foot-high battery-operated slot machine. Delighted by the gift, she removed it from the box and set it on the hall table. "Where did you buy this?"

"A colleague of mine was in New York over Christmas. I asked him to bring it back for me."

"How does it work?"

"Put in a dime. Ten cents . . ."

"We're in London, Raymond. Where do I find ten cents?"

"There's a roll of dimes in the box."

Katherine pulled out the roll of money. She fed a coin into the machine, pressed the button, and watched the wheels spin.

"Two lemons and a cherry. What do I win?"

"Nothing. Check the payout chart."

She tried again, and again. On the fifth attempt, she hit three bells. To a loud peal of music, the machine churned out the five dimes Katherine had invested. She banged her fist on the table. "Cheat! It's supposed to pay out ten coins."

Barnhill was laughing. "Before you start tapping the reservoir, you have to fill it."

The noise of the machine paying out, and Katherine's cry of protest, drew people into the hall. Roland, his interest instantly piqued, studied the machine. "May I try my luck?" He took a coin from the pile of dimes. Three lemons clicked into place. He passed a coin to Sally, who met a similar fate.

John Saxon looked over Sally's shoulder. "I dare say that machine is quite illegal."

Barnhill, remembering Saxon from Franz's funeral, gave the property developer a frosty smile. "It only takes American dimes. To be illegal, I imagine it would first have to accept British currency. And as a visitor to this country, I'd be the very last person to break its laws."

"Come along, Katherine." Saxon touched her arm. "The hostess has to circulate. It's poor etiquette for her to lock herself away with a slot machine."

"Sally and I will keep it warm for you," Roland

called after his daughter.

Barnhill bowed sarcastically as Saxon led Katherine back to the other guests. "I think I'll stay with you as well. I feel most comfortable around newspaper people."

Barnhill remained with newspaper people for the rest of the evening. At dinner, he sat between Sally and Erica Bentley, relating anecdotes about his service as an information officer in Vietnam. After dinner, he became more serious, telling Sally and Gerald Waller why he believed British papers, with just a couple of exceptions, were inferior to their American counterparts.

"How can you," he demanded, "call something like the *Sun* a newspaper? Bare boobs on page three— that belongs in *Playboy,* not a daily newspaper."

"Look who owns the *Sun,*" Sally answered acidly, "and then you can understand the bad taste."

"Rupert Murdoch owns the New York *Post* as well," Barnhill countered. "That's sensational journalism, yes, but there are no bare breasts on page three."

"Yet," Waller argued.

"Never. Even in lousy newspapers, the American public's got better taste than the British public."

Overhearing the conversation, Katherine stopped to listen in. While Barnhill and Sally went at it for all they were worth, Waller remained on the periphery, as though he had something else on his mind. After a minute, she remembered Saxon's advice: she was the hostess; she had to circulate.

She approached Jeffrey Dillard, who was talking to Paul Hyde and Sir Donald Leslie, and drew him off to one side. "I never did make a proper apology to you, Jeffrey."

"How's that?"

"For my behavior when I heard you were going to remain with 'Fightback.' I was wrong to think and say what I did."

Dillard dismissed the apology with a wave of the hand. "In your place, I would probably have harbored the same suspicions."

When Katherine and Dillard rejoined the group, Sir Donald Leslie wanted to know who Barnhill was. "Heard snatches of his conversation over dinner, about Vietnam. Was he there?"

"He was an officer with the American army."

"Really? Perhaps he can answer a question that's always puzzled me — why the Yanks didn't use similar strategy to what we employed in Malaya. Fighting the same enemy, you know. Excuse me." As Sir Donald marched away in Barnhill's direction, Katherine could swear that his scar was glowing.

She heard the sound of metal striking glass. Saxon was standing on a chair. A knife was in one hand, a champagne flute in the other. Waiters walked among the guests, passing out Dom Pérignon. Only Barnhill refused, drinking, instead, soda.

"A toast!" Saxon called out. "A toast to Katherine and 'Fightback.' Health and success!"

Roland materialized beside his daughter. "I'd say that John had put his stamp on the evening rather thoroughly. You might still not be ready to make any kind of a commitment, Kathy, but he most certainly is. And he isn't embarrassed about letting everyone else know."

"I can handle him, Daddy."

As the evening petered out, and guests said goodbye, two people made completely unsolicited remarks to Katherine about Raymond Barnhill. The first comment came from Sally Roberts, who, having spent much of the evening talking with Barnhill, had formed a very favorable impression of the American. "Raymond's too bright and talented to be working for an agency. He should be on a newspaper, where his byline could become well known. Why don't you try to persuade him to join us, Katherine?"

"Us? If you want Raymond on the *Eagle,* you'll have to persuade him yourself. I'm television, Sally, not Fleet Street."

"Now, maybe, but you'll be back."

The second comment came from John Saxon, who having spent barely five seconds with Barnhill, disliked him intensely. "Why are you friends with a jackass like that in a cheap hired suit?"

"He didn't hire the suit — he borrowed it. And what business is it of yours who my friends are?"

"I just think you deserve better, Katherine."

Having seen Saxon take over the evening, and having allowed him to do so, Katherine decided it was time to take some wind out of his sails. "Thank you for your concern, but I'm quite old enough to think for myself. You're happy with your Tory friends, and I'm just as happy with my borrowed-suit friends."

Saxon was taken aback, just as Katherine had intended him to be. "I'm sorry if I offended you, but I thought we had something very special."

"We do, John. But what we have does not give you the right to criticize people with whom I wish to be friendly."

Saxon was wise enough to know when to change a subject. "If the snow's still around tomorrow afternoon, may I take Henry and Joanne over the heath?"

Having castigated Saxon, Katherine felt it was time to forgive him. "Just as long as you bring them back in one piece."

On Tuesday afternoon, just three days after the party at Kate's Haven, a tired-looking Gerald Waller walked into Sally Roberts's office on the executive floor of the Eagle building, dropped heavily into a chair, and shocked the smile of greeting right off the editorial director's face.

426

"I have to go into hospital, Sally."

"What for?"

Waller gave the crooked grin of a man trying to be brave in front of a firing squad. "I prescribed the proper treatment for myself. Unfortunately, I wrote the prescription more than thirty years too late."

"Gerry, what are you talking about?"

"Throwing away my cigarettes and lighter, that's what. Stopping smoking a fortnight ago was too little, too late, Sally. I've got cancer."

Sally sucked in her breath. She was the same age as Waller, and for a moment she caught a whiff of her own mortality. "Cancer's not the killer it used to be. Doctors can work miracles these days."

"If they catch it in time, they can. They'll need to be miracle workers with the job I'm giving them." Waller told Sally of a physical he had taken two weeks earlier. "For months it's been painful to cough, absolute bloody murder even to breathe. Knowing, I guess, what was wrong turned me into an even bigger coward than normal. Finally, I worked up enough courage to make an appointment. I quit smoking the same day, thought I could fool the doctor if my breath didn't smell like a dirty ashtray. As it turns out, I needn't have bothered. I got the results yesterday, and they want me in."

"When are you going?"

"Tomorrow. We'd better talk about a replacement editor."

"A substitute editor, Gerry, not a replacement. You'll be back at the *Eagle*."

Waller gave a slight nod of the head, too much the gentleman to disagree. "Do me a favor, Sally. Apologize to Katherine for the way I behaved the other night. She thinks I bit her head off because I was angry at her for stealing *Eagle* staff. I was just angry at myself for never paying attention to those warnings Her Majesty's Government puts on packets of cigarettes, and I was taking it out on everyone else."

In Waller's absence, Lawrie Stimkin was promoted from news editor to interim editor. On his first day in the new position, the entire *Eagle* staff waited, not on some major story, but for news from the hospital. When that news came, it was not good. Surgeons had opened Waller's chest, and closed it again. There was nothing they could do.

When he was discharged, it was with the knowledge that he had, according to the most optimistic prognosis, six months to live. Much of that time, should he want relief from pain, would be passed in a drug-induced stupor. Waller chose to spend his remaining time in the same manner he had spent most of his life: by working on a newspaper. He returned to the *Eagle* in the middle of February. Out of respect, Stimkin relinquished the editor's chair. Waller, with hangman's humor, assured the Scot that the move would be temporary.

It was obvious to everyone that Waller was in constant pain. He eased it with medication only at night. During the day, when he occupied his old office, he needed to be alert. He wanted to remain editor in function as well as in name until he could no longer physically carry out the duties.

Roland made a point of stopping by the Eagle building once a day to see Waller. Katherine was another regular visitor. She swore she could see the weight falling away from him. His once well-fitting suits now hung loosely, at least a size too large.

Waller protested the frequency of the visits. "I know you and your father have my best interests at heart," he told Katherine one afternoon, "but all these constant interruptions are stopping me from properly performing my job as editor of a daily newspaper." Then he softened the protest by adding,

"Know what I really want? To be at the helm for one more big story. After that, I'll go with no complaints."

Katherine, blinking back a tear, patted the editor gently on the shoulder. Through the padding of the jacket, she could feel bone. "We'll hire someone to create a big story for you, Gerry."

In the middle of March, a month after Waller's return to the *Eagle*, the British Patriotic League thrust its way back into the headlines. Not with a riot, or with a rally, but in a manner designed to win it support and sympathy from the white population of Britain.

In the Midlands city of Nottingham, nine white male employees of a hosiery factory had gone on strike rather than work alongside three newly hired Pakistani employees. Instead of yielding to the strikers' demand that the Pakistanis be fired, thereby leaving itself open for prosecution under the Race Relations Act, the company had threatened the nine strikers with dismissal. The union, itself a supporter of antidiscrimination legislation, had urged the strikers to return to work. When they had refused to do so, the company had fired them.

The Nottingham Nine, as the men quickly became known in the national press, soon found a champion in the British Patriotic League. The League hired lawyers to sue the hosiery company for unfair dismissal of the Nottingham Nine. As the full story unfolded, the League's lawyers emphasized that the Nottingham Nine had not refused to work with, and had not sought the dismissal of, the new employees because they were Pakistani, or because their skins were dark.

"The real reason," the League-appointed counsel told the court, "was because their sanitary habits were, to put it quite frankly, absolutely disgusting."

To a nation which had always been willing to believe the worst about its Asian citizens — from families dining on catfood because they liked the taste, to young girls being beaten and starved for refusing to marry a man chosen by their parents — the revelations of what constituted "absolutely disgusting" could not come quickly enough.

There were allegations of poor personal hygiene, of body odor strong enough to make close working contact virtually impossible. There were claims of factory toilets left in a condition that no British person would tolerate. And there was a graphic, stomach-turning description of the difference between Asian and British workers suffering from a cold. "Instead of blowing his nose into a handkerchief, as a civilized person would do," the counsel said, "the Asian employee would stand over a sink, press one nostril closed, and blow through the other. The process would then be reversed, after which the discharge would be washed down the sink. Tell me . . . would you want to wash your hands and face, or your teacup, in that particular sink?"

The response by the hosiery company's lawyer — "Since when is it so civilized and hygienic to wrap that same discharge in a square of cotton and thrust it back into your pocket?" — was lost in the collective shudder of disgust at the vision of a man blowing his nose into a sink.

The League lawyer won his case. The Nottingham Nine were reinstated. The three Pakistani workers who had caused their dismissal walked out in a protest against what they called "overt racism," but no one seemed to care. The victory against the immigrant influx was complete. In the eyes of many, the British Patriotic League was the hero of the British workingman.

The League wasted no time in cashing in on its

newfound popularity. Trevor Burns, its propaganda director, organized press conferences. Chairman Alan Venables and financial director Neville Sharpe became familiar faces on television. They answered questions freely. When an interviewer asked how much it had cost the League to represent the Nottingham Nine, Sharpe replied, "In excess of fifty thousand pounds."

"What justifies that kind of outlay?"

Venables answered. "Justice. Which is exactly what we got. Justice for nine hardworking British men. And an awakening."

"An awakening?"

"That's right. A revival of the British spirit. Starting the first Sunday in May, the British Patriotic League will hold a monthly rally. Our first one will be in London, at Hyde Park. Subsequent rallies will be staged in the provinces, a different city each time. 'Youth for Britain' will be the theme of the rallies. We're going to demonstrate how Britain's youth and the British Patriotic League can work together for this country's security and prosperity."

20

In April, halfway through the maximum of six months that doctors had given him, Gerald Waller appeared to take on a new lease of life. Gauntness was still evident in his face — sharp planes of bone structure where flesh had once filled out skin — but the loss of weight was no longer so noticeable on his body. His clothes fit better; there was no loose drape of fabric to draw attention to his thinness.

"Whatever you're doing, Gerry," Sally Roberts said to him at the beginning of an afternoon editorial meeting, "keep on with it. You're looking better than I've seen you look in ages."

"No big secret. I just went out and bought a completely new wardrobe for my new economy size. Half a dozen suits, shirts, raincoat, the works. I've spent my entire life taking a pride in my appearance, and I'll be damned if I'll let the lights be turned out on me while I'm looking like some beggar who has to wear Salvation Army hand-me-downs!"

Roland Eagles, who had traveled from the Adler's store on Regent Street to attend this meeting, clapped his hands, and cried, "Bravo!"

The purpose of the meeting was to decide the contents of the following morning's *Eagle*. One by one, department heads listed stories. Lawrie Stimkin told of an armed bank robbery that had just taken place in the West End of London. A police constable had been shot and seriously wounded. Unless an event of earth-shaking proportions happened between now and press time, the bank raid would be the lead story; police officers being shot was still front-page news in England. A much smaller story, slated for somewhere deep inside the paper, concerned permission being given by local authorities for the British Patriotic League to hold its initial "Youth for Britain" rally at Hyde Park on the first Sunday in May.

The last department head to be heard was Martin Allcock. A short, pudgy man with wire-rimmed glasses and a rumpled suit, Allcock headed the section responsible for the *Eagle*'s opinion page. "Whether or not the lead story remains the shooting of the constable, it might be timely to call for the reintroduction of capital punishment for the murder of a police officer, or for murder committed in the course of criminal activity."

Roland raised a hand. "We have supported a limited reintroduction of capital punishment in the past. To do so again, even in the light of this latest incident, would be redundant. I feel that our space and effort would be better served by publishing a denunciation of this Hyde Park rally in four weeks' time."

Sally objected instantly. "That's as redundant as any leader on capital punishment could be. Over the past couple of years, the *Eagle* has attacked the League a dozen times or more. It still exists, and after that business with the Nottingham Nine, it's enjoying unprecedented popularity."

"Then why can't we put out something that will appeal to Britain's youth—to the young people the League wants to attract with this rally?"

"To appeal to the youth, Roland, you first have to reach them," Sally said. "You won't do that on the

433

Eagle's opinion page. Britain's youth doesn't read beyond the sports and television pages, and that's if they can read at all!"

"Why not try reaching them through music?" Waller asked.

"Music?"

"That's right. Rock 'n' roll. If you want to get through to these young people, stage a free rock 'n' roll concert. See if you can get permission to hold it in Hyde Park. For every young person the League rally attracts, your concert will pull in a thousand. When you've got them there, you can brainwash them with any message you want. And you keep on doing it, all through the summer. Wherever the League gets a permit to hold one of its 'Youth for Britain' obscenities, you arrange a rock concert. Give the concerts a catchy title, something like 'Rock for Racial Harmony,' and you'll drive those bigots right out of business."

"Gerry . . ." Roland gazed at the *Eagle* editor in open admiration. "You are a bloody genius." The euphoria lasted for mere seconds, though, until Roland started to envision the problems such an undertaking would present. "It's a wonderful idea, but what can we do in just four weeks?"

Stimkin supplied Roland with the answer. "Why don't you get in touch with Sidney Glassman? If Sidney can't put a concert together in four weeks, no one can."

Sidney Emmanuel Glassman was one of that rare band of men: a self-made millionaire and a diehard Socialist.

For sixteen years, Glassman had been a Labour Member of Parliament. The constituency he represented included Stepney, a poor, rundown area of London's East End, where, sixty-five years earlier,

Glassman had been born, the ninth and final child of an immigrant cabinetmaker. This geographical accident of birth would have a profound effect on Glassman's life; much of his later philanthropy would be based on his experience of growing up in a part of London where the end of the wages always came at least a day before the end of the week.

Politics was only one of Glassman's many careers. The main one, where he had made his fortune, was show business. Starting out as a song-and-dance man before the war, right after a short and inauspicious career as a middleweight boxer with the ring name of Manny Glass, he had gone into managing other performers. By 1955, he had more than a hundred artists on his books, including top-line singers, dancers, and comedians. From there, it had been a simple step into theater ownership, buying two of the better-known houses in the West End. After going public in 1959, Glassman Entertainment expanded even further, taking over a nationwide chain of movie houses.

At forty-nine, Glassman retired from show business. That was in 1964, when the Labour Party persuaded him to stand as their candidate in the East End. Not that he required much persuasion. Although he had moved from the area before the war, along with most of his contemporaries, a strong tie remained. He could think of no nobler way to honor his birthplace — the neighborhood that had given his immigrant parents a fresh opportunity — than by representing it in Westminster.

That was not Glassman's first foray into politics. After the war, while building his business, he had been civic-minded enough to run for local councillor. He had won, and had served in the position for five years, until pressure of work had forced him to retire. In 1964, however, he had faced a far stiffer challenge. As a rule, the seat was a Labour stronghold. But the incumbent had retired, and the Conservatives, in a desperate bid to cause an upset, had put up a politically minded popular television personality to contest the seat. Labour, by using Glassman, hoped to fight fire with fire. The ploy worked, and Glassman won handily. He had retained the seat in all of the elections since. During those sixteen years, he had rejected a knighthood, because he thought of himself as a man of the people, and men of the people did not go around being called "Sir." Rumor had it that eventually he would be offered a seat in the House of Lords, and everyone who knew him expected him to respectfully reject that, too.

The day after Gerald Waller's suggestion of free rock concerts to coincide with the "Youth for Britain" rallies, Roland Eagles and Sidney Glassman met for lunch. The two men were total opposites. Roland, tall and still slim, was immaculately tailored. Glassman, overweight and bald, and wearing a badly pressed suit, looked as though he would be more comfortable at a dog track than in the House of Commons. Yet they were good friends, having cooperated frequently in the past on charitable work.

"So I asked myself after you telephoned," Glassman said as they sat down, "what could a Tory newspaper owner who endorsed Margaret Thatcher possibly want with me?"

"How about the pleasure of your company for lunch? It's been months since we've seen each other, Sidney."

Glassman gave a rich bass laugh. "I'll accept that for the time being. How's the family keeping? Katherine, the children?"

"All well." Roland was always amused by Glassman's accent. It was undiluted East End, as cockney as any costermonger selling his wares from a stall in Petticoat Lane. Unlike many who had moved to better neighborhoods, Glassman had made no attempt to alter his speech. He claimed that people understood every word he said, so what was the point of taking elocution lessons? "Your own family, Sidney, how are they?"

"My wife stays thin by hopping from one charity committee to another. As for the boys" — Roland concealed a smile; Glassman's two sons had both turned forty — "Lionel's busy with Glassman Entertainment, and Melvin . . . well, Melvin's got himself involved with the Grosvenor Sporting Club."

"Really?" Roland's curiosity was kindled at the mention of the gambling establishment off Grosvenor Square. "What's he doing there?"

Glassman shrugged. "I don't know. And to be quite honest with you, Roland, I don't wish to know."

Roland understood that he should have known better than to ask Glassman about his younger son. Ask all the questions you wanted to about Lionel, the older son. Lionel Glassman was the apple of his father's eye. Now chairman and managing director of Glassman Entertainment, he had turned out exactly as Glassman wanted him to — married, a couple of children, an honest, upright man who had brought nothing but pleasure to his father. Melvin was somewhere at the other end of the scale. He was as intelligent as his brother, but like some ancient Greek hero he carried the seeds of his own destruction. The shortcut had always appealed to Melvin more than the straight and narrow. On two occasions of which Roland knew, his father had been forced to bail him out of trouble, when a scheme on the borderline of illegality had come unraveled.

Prudently, Roland changed subjects. "What do you think about the British Patriotic League getting permission for a rally in Hyde Park?"

"Bastards," Glassman muttered. "If it was up to me, those Nazis would get a permit for the cemetery. You know, yours is the only newspaper that keeps on at those mad swine. Even the Labour papers don't bother."

"It's a personal thing with me."

"With me, too."

"I think I've found a way to beat them, Sidney. Listen to this." Roland gave details of Gerald Waller's plan. Glassman listened, totally absorbed. "Could you help to arrange such a concert? Could you line up the necessary talent in four weeks?"

"No problem. My son Lionel, he can put this together in a few hours. All the groups you want. Stage fittings. Electrical equipment, whatever you need."

"How much would this all cost?"

Glassman flapped a fat hand. "The groups will do it as a favor. My Lionel, he'll tell them they're getting a million pounds' worth of publicity out of this thing. Rock for Racial Harmony. You tell that editor of yours, Roland, that if he ever needs another job, I can help him. He's got too much imagination to be stuck in some dead-end job in Fleet Street."

Roland just smiled. There was no point in telling Glassman that if the doctors were right, Waller would not be around when the last "Rock for Racial Harmony" concert was staged.

Hyde Park had never seen anything quite like what it witnessed on that first Sunday in May. At ten o'clock in the morning, young people began to converge on the park: punks, mods, rockers, even some rock fans who looked distinctly normal, and, therefore, quite out of place. For three weeks, the word had been spread, in news stories, through advertisements in music magazines, and by posters in record shops. "Rock for Racial Harmony," a free concert featuring the best and brightest in popular music. Now they wanted to see what all the fuss was about.

At two o'clock, an estimated eighty thousand rock fans were sitting on the grass around an open-air stage.

They began to cheer when a young man with shoulder-length blond hair leaped onto the stage and lifted one of the half-dozen microphones. He wore salmon-pink jeans and a bright red shirt, with a huge silver cross hanging from his neck.

"That's right . . . you know me! I'm the Music-Maker, and I bring you the best music on radio every week." The disc jockey's voice boomed back from the trees, where speakers had been placed. "I've got a new job today. I'm master of ceremonies for the most stupendous music bargain you're ever going to find. It's all free. And it's for a very good cause. Over there"—he pointed toward the unseen northern edge of the park—"in an hour from now, a gang of real sickos called the British Patriotic League will be holding a rally. Their aim is to stir up hatred. They want to get all of us hating each other. But that isn't what we want, is it?"

Needing no amplification, the roar came back: "No!"

"What do we want?"

"We want rock!"

"What do we want?"

"We want rock!"

"And what do we want rock for?"

And it came back, just as the Music-Maker had known it would. Eighty thousand voices roared, "We want rock for racial harmony! Rock for racial harmony! Rock for racial harmony!"

A curtain dropped across the stage, cutting the Music-Maker off from the crowd. When it rose again, four young men and a girl were on the stage. Each had a hairstyle that was fifteen different shades of pink and orange. Their black leather clothing was studded with shining stars. Two of the men carried guitars, which they plugged into the amplifiers. Another sat at a piano. The fourth settled in behind drums. The girl held a microphone. The four young men started playing, and the girl began to sing in a husky, off-key voice. Another roar, louder than anything that had preceded it, swept up to the sky as the eighty thousand fans recognized the punk rock group that headed that week's hit parade.

To one side of the stage stood Roland and Gerald Waller. As the music continued, they walked right around the edge of the immense crowd. Purposely, Roland slowed his pace, so that Waller would have no trouble in keeping up. They passed several policemen, even a couple of entrepreneurs who were selling souvenir T-shirts, white with "Rock for Racial Harmony" printed in black capitals across the front. Roland did not complain; he was never against anyone making a living.

"Look over there," Waller said. *"Mirror* photographer."

The *Mirror* man was the fourth photographer Roland had seen from a major newspaper. "Marvelous, isn't it? Despite the fact that this concert has been arranged by Eagle newspapers, the other papers are covering it. Shows how fair the press can be."

"What's fair got to do with anything? They can't ignore something as big and loud as this just because another newspaper has something to do with it. Roland, you've created a major event." Waller started to laugh at what he considered Roland's naíveté. The laugh changed quickly to a deep, hacking cough. He doubled up in pain, hands clutched to his chest. Roland looked around for assistance, but Waller recovered quickly. "It's all right. I'm fine. Let's just take it easy with the walking. I've got to put in a day's work after I leave here, making sure your newspaper gets out tomorrow."

"That would be embarrassing, wouldn't it? Being responsible for such a major event, and then not having my own newspaper get out on the streets with the story."

At three-fifteen, Roland and Waller walked slowly to the northern edge of the park. The "Youth for Britain" rally was in progress. Alan Venables stood on a platform from which flew the Union Jack and the League pennant. On either side were his henchmen, Neville Sharpe and Trevor Burns. Standing fifty yards away, Roland and Waller counted the crowd. Fewer than a hundred, and of those, half a dozen were police officers, and another half dozen were press photographers. Venables's voice was lost in the sound of music coming from the concert: a reggae band now, insult added to injury.

Even as Roland and Waller watched, a group of four young skinheads broke away from the rally and headed in the direction of the concert. Minutes later, one of the souvenir salesmen walked through the sparse gathering, hawking "Rock for Racial Harmony" T-shirts. When he found a customer, it was too much for Roland. He laughed loudly. Venables swung around. When he recognized Roland, his watery eyes blazed sharp with hatred. Roland turned away, satisfied with every aspect of the day.

Roland left the park at four-thirty, ninety minutes before the scheduled end of the concert. Crossing Park Lane, he walked the half mile to Sally's apartment in Curzon Street. The music bounced off buildings, following him all the way. When Sally opened the door, she swore that through her open windows she had heard every note of every song played that afternoon.

"Was the concert a success?" she asked.

"Buy a copy of tomorrow's *Eagle*," Roland replied cockily, "and you'll know whether it was a success or not."

Roland had just finished showering when the telephone rang at seven-fifteen the next morning. While he wondered who it could be, Arthur Parsons rapped on the bathroom door.

"Sir, it's Miss Katherine."

"What?" Imagining the worst, Roland came out of the bathroom like a hurricane, a robe held about himself. Picking up the extension in the bedroom, he said, "Kathy, what is it?"

"What a fantastic front page!"

"What front page?"

"The *Eagle*. You mean you haven't seen it yet?"

"We don't get delivery until seven-thirty."

"Then ask Mr. Parsons to go out and buy one. You must see it, Daddy, it's absolutely incredible. The whole issue!" She hung up, leaving her father damp, a little confused, and full of anticipation.

Precisely at seven-thirty, the *Eagle* was delivered. Roland took it into the breakfast room, where Peg Parsons served him a cup of tea and two slices of toast. The front page comprised a two-word headline, "Racists Rocked," and an aerial photograph of Hyde Park. In the main part of the photograph, eighty thousand people mobbed tiny figures on a stage. At the very top of the picture — the northern edge of the park — another stage drew only a handful of listeners. The photograph was by Sid Hall, who had covered the concert from a helicopter.

Roland turned to the center spread. Close-ups of the concert, of the performers, of the audience. A shot of a small crowd of people, all wearing the souvenir T-shirts. And tucked away in one corner of the page, in contrast to all the fun, all the happiness and enjoyment, was a tiny photograph of British Patriotic League supporters dismantling their platform, putting away their pennants for another day.

The copy accompanying the display of photographs was factual and straightforward. Eighty thousand young people had attended a rock concert in Hyde Park, organized by Eagle Newspapers, to protest a nearby "Youth for Britain" rally by the British Patriotic League. In surprise, Roland noted that the story bore Gerald Waller's name. The editor rarely wrote anything. Even then, he never used his byline unless he was making a clear editorial statement. As major a news story as the concert was, it did not come under that classification. While he dressed, Roland made up his mind to ask Waller why he had decided to write the story and use his byline.

At eight-thirty, a company driver collected Roland and took him to the Adler's store on Regent Street. He rode the elevator to the fifth floor, walked past the restaurant, then along the row of buyers' offices toward the oak door of his own office.

"Mr. Eagles . . ." Roland turned around to see his secretary chasing him. "Miss Roberts from Eagle Newspapers just telephoned. Said she'd missed you at home. She wants to speak to you urgently." The secretary ran on ahead of Roland. By the time he entered his office, she was dialing the *Eagle* number.

"Sally, it's Roland."

"You'd better get over here, Roland. Fast. Gerry Waller's secretary has found him dead in his office."

Roland was at the newspaper fifteen minutes later. Sally met him, and took him to Waller's office. Outside, the editorial staff tried to get on with the business of filling a paper. Inside, a doctor went through the redundant motions of checking for life signs, before declaring that the *Eagle*'s editor had probably been dead for five or six hours.

Roland closed the door and leaned against it. Waller was sitting behind his desk, wearing the same clothes he had worn to the rock concert. His eyes were closed, head bent slightly, face relaxed. He could have been sleeping; instead, he was dead.

"What do you think happened?" Roland asked the doctor.

"Heart attack, I'd say. Was he ill?"

"Very. He was suffering from lung cancer, had a couple of months at the most. He had a strenuous day yesterday." Roland turned to Sally. "What was he doing here so early in the morning? Gerry never came in until midday."

"The printers said he stayed downstairs until the first issues came off the press. Then he must have brought a copy back up here, shut the door, and pulled the curtains closed. Quite probably, no one even realized he was in his office. Not until his secretary went in there when she arrived."

"I see." Roland left the office to find Lawrie Stimkin. Newspapers were like entertainment. The show had to go on.

The doctor's summary opinion on the cause of death proved to be correct. Following the exertions of attending the rock concert, Gerald Waller's heart had simply given out.

For the days preceding the funeral, Roland went around in a depressed state. More than a talented employee, he had lost a friend. And, by walking Waller around Hyde Park that Sunday, he had been responsible. That Waller's days had been numbered made little difference. Roland could not shake the feeling of guilt.

At the funeral, Roland stood between Sally Roberts and Katherine. All of Fleet Street was there, a *Who's Who* of the newspaper industry. The minister said that if any man could ever be said to have died where he wanted to die, that man was Gerald Waller. A newspaper editor dying at his desk, with the latest edition of his newspaper, hot off the press, in front of him.

"Gerry got his wish, didn't he?" Katherine whispered to her father. "He told me a couple of months ago that he would go happily if he could be at the helm for just one more big story."

The byline . . . ! Waller writing the story and using his byline, actions that had so puzzled Roland. Now he understood. "Rock for Racial Harmony" had been Waller's last major story, as editor and as a writer. Even as instigator, because the idea of a free rock concert had been his. And he had wanted the world to know about it. He had willingly run himself into the ground that Sunday, because that was the way he had wanted to go out.

Roland did not feel so guilty anymore.

Three more "Youth for Britain" rallies were held that summer by the British Patriotic League. At Birmingham, in June; at Manchester, in July; and at Leeds, in August. Each time, Eagle Newspapers, with the help of Sidney Glassman and his son Lionel, organized an admission-free "Rock for Racial Harmony" concert. Each concert drew anywhere from fifty to eighty thousand young people, while the most successful "Youth for Britain" rally attracted fewer than five hundred.

It was a summer that Roland could look back on with enormous satisfaction. He had used his newspaper company not just as a tool to bring news to the public, but as a weapon to help destroy what he saw was wrong with society. He told this to Katherine when she brought the children to Adler's one Thursday afternoon during the school summer holiday.

"Not only that, Daddy, but you provided entertainment for a few hundred thousand rock fans at the same time."

When Katherine left Adler's, heading for the "Fightback" studio and the final preparations for that night's show, Henry and Joanne remained with their grandfather. Roland would take them to Stanmore for dinner; after the show, Katherine would collect them.

Jeffrey Dillard was waiting when Katherine arrived,

his eyes shining with excitement. "Katherine, I've just picked up a marvelous item for the show."

Warning bells began to ring. "For tonight?"

"No. It needs to be researched properly, but it's hot, believe me. Almost too hot to handle."

"Tell me, Jeffrey."

"In Paul's office. He also thinks it's a splendid topic." Dillard led the way to Paul Hyde's office. The producer was sitting at his desk, checking the schedule for that night's show.

"There's a tremendous scandal about to break," Dillard said, "and we've got the inside story. One of the big London casinos has been taking down the license-plate numbers of all the fancy cars parked outside competing gaming clubs — Rolls Royces, Aston Martins, Mercedes, expensive cars like that."

"For what purpose?"

"The license-plate numbers get checked by a contact in Scotland Yard. Once the casino has the identities of the owners, it tries to persuade them to play at its tables."

"What kind of persuasion?" Katherine asked, although she could already guess. What temptation would mere money be to the owners of such cars?

It was Hyde who answered. "Women. Jeffrey's learned that the casino's offering those car owners the services of expensive prostitutes. Some of the car owners, apparently, have peculiar tastes, and these women are catering to them."

"How did you find out about all this, Jeffrey?"

"From one of the sources I used when I ran 'Fightback.' "

"Which casino is going to all this trouble? Not to mention corrupting Scotland Yard."

"The Grosvenor Sporting Club."

"I was under the impression that the Grosvenor was a very above-board establishment. They retained their license after the government inquiry into criminal infiltration of the gambling industry. Which is more than can be said for many of the clubs."

"I know, I know," Dillard said. "It seems this underhand scheme is the brainwave of the Grosvenor's newly appointed membership director." He stared straight into Katherine's blue eyes. "Melvin Glassman."

Katherine returned Dillard's gaze unflinchingly. "Forget it..I wouldn't touch a story like this with a barge-pole."

"Don't be so hasty, Katherine," Hyde said, as she started toward the office door. "Jeffrey seems to think it would be perfect for 'Fightback,' and I'm inclined to agree with him."

"I'm afraid I don't."

"What are your objections?"

"As juicy as this story might be, it is not our kind of topic. We are a prime-time family show. We come on at seven o'clock in the evening. Children watch us. What are they going to think about bribery and corruption and prostitution, especially if some of those prostitutes are catering to weird tastes? Most importantly, where is the fighting back in all of this? No one's come to us and said they've been cheated, they've been swindled, they've been run over by some massive corporation or government bureaucracy. This is something for the police to look into. It is not for us."

On top of that, she added silently, I am not going to use the show to embarrass a very dear friend of my father, who is unfortunate enough to have a crook for a son. Call it unethical, but when you've got the power in your hands, you're a damned fool if you don't use it.

"Have you quite finished?" Dillard asked.

"No. If you're still so keen on going ahead with a totally inappropriate topic, tell me. I'll step aside and make room for you; don't worry about that. I'll type my letter of resignation right now, because I will not remain in a job where I feel compromised."

Slowly, Dillard shook his head. A smile began.

"You win. I thought I might be able to go up against you, but I was wrong."

"Thank you. Now if you'll excuse me, I have a show to prepare." Katherine left Hyde's office wondering whether Dillard had been really serious about using such a topic, or just testing her resolve in case he wanted to push something through in the future.

Either way, she felt that she had come out on top. It would be a long time before he tried to test her again.

21

In the United States, Labor Day signifies the end of summer and the start of fall. August Bank Holiday, the last Monday of the month, serves the same purpose in England, ending a weekend of special summer events, such as craft and farm festivals, military musical tattoos, and regattas.

The fun fair on Hampstead Heath was one of the traditional events. Katherine and John Saxon took Henry and Joanne on Monday afternoon, watching while the children took at least one turn on every ride, and tried their luck at every stall. Henry had an uncanny aim, whether throwing a ball or a dart. He couldn't miss. Consequently, Katherine and Saxon were soon loaded down with prizes. As Katherine watched Henry pierce yet another balloon, she felt grateful that Joanne was as awkward at throwing as her brother was adept.

At five-thirty, as the sun began to dip over the western edge of the Heath, they returned to Saxon's car. When Katherine placed Henry's prizes in the trunk, Joanne began to cry.

"What's the matter, darling?" Katherine asked.

"It's sad."

"What is? Henry winning all the prizes, and you

winning nothing? Don't worry, he'll share them with you."

The young girl shook her head. "Summer ending is sad. Soon it will be cold, and we won't be able to play outside."

"Of course you will. You'll play different games; that's all." Katherine looked to her son for help.

"We'll ride the toboggans Uncle John bought for us last winter," Henry said. "Don't you remember those?"

The flow of tears lessened. Katherine looked at Saxon, who was smiling softly.

They returned to Kate's Haven. Once Henry and Joanne were having dinner, Katherine and Saxon left the house. After eating at a local restaurant, they joined the flow of traffic toward the West End.

"Fancy seeing a film?"

Katherine shook her head.

"A play, if we can still get tickets to a good one?" Another shake.

"What do you want?"

"Bed."

"Now there's a coincidence. That's what I want, too."

"Why didn't you say so, instead of beating around the bush?"

"Because you would have accused me of having only one thing on my mind."

"Like most men."

"You say that with authority. How many men have you known?"

"In the biblical sense? You're the second." She refrained from returning the question; she did not want to know how many women Saxon had slept with.

The moment they reached the house in Marble Arch, they rushed upstairs, undressed, and fell into bed like two people who had spent the entire day yearning for just this moment. Afterward, as they lay side by side, Katherine asked, "Why were you smiling before?"

"I'm smiling now."

"On the heath, I mean. When Joanne was crying."

"I was smiling at a little bit of everything. There's a certain poignancy to a child's tears at the passing of summer. And I'm very touched by the honorary title I've been given. I like the sound of 'Uncle John.' It gives me a sense of belonging."

Katherine closed her eyes and hovered on the edge of sleep. She wanted this to be her bed, her bedroom, in her home. Not Saxon's. More than anything, she wanted to spend the entire night with him. To awaken in the morning and find him next to her. Then her home would truly be Kate's Haven. But she could never do that. Not while she shared this kind of relationship with him. There would be too much explaining to do, most of all to the children.

So marry him, you fool! screamed a voice inside her head. Marry him, before another woman does. A woman less deserving than you. Then came another voice. Reasoning, cautioning. Telling her to wait, to take enough time to be really certain. And advising her to enjoy the flowers on the way.

She allowed herself to drift off to sleep. The next sensation she had was of Saxon kissing her awake, his lips brushing her forehead, her eyelids, her nose, and lastly her mouth. "It's one o'clock. I'll take you home."

The night was cool. Saxon turned on the heater. As the car's interior began to warm, he said, "I had lunch with Jeffrey the other day."

"He never mentioned it to me."

"He's probably too frightened of you right now to mention anything ever again."

"Oh, I see. He couldn't get me to agree to include some tacky little story in 'Fightback,' so now he's trying to use you to persuade me. I'd expected more of him. And of you."

"That story about the Grosvenor Sporting Club and

the chicanery with the license plates means a lot to Jeffrey, you know. He's a man who's questioning his existence at the moment. He's even thinking that perhaps he should not have retired and turned the reins over to you."

Katherine steeled herself. "I'm very sorry about Jeffrey's feelings, but I will not use that story, because it does not fit our format."

"All right. But remember this, Katherine. Paul Hyde, the producer, is Jeffrey's friend. If Jeffrey's really set on having his way, instead of asking you again, he'll simply lean on Paul."

"John, I've already told Jeffrey that I will resign if I feel that kind of pressure. I like Jeffrey an awful lot, but I will not tolerate his meddling in what is now my show. As he obviously doesn't seem to understand the message from me, perhaps you'd be good enough to repeat it to him."

"I will," Saxon said as he drove into the forecourt of Kate's Haven. "Verbatim." Katherine kissed him good night, and stood watching the Rolls glide away.

She entered the house and climbed the stairs, angry at Dillard for pursuing the idea, and more than a little mad at Saxon for allowing himself to be used as a messenger boy. As she reached the landing, she saw a sheet of paper taped to her bedroom door. The message written on it told Katherine that Raymond Barnhill had telephoned at eight that evening; would she please return his call, no matter what time she got home?

She dialed Barnhill's number. The telephone was answered almost immediately. "Katherine, is that you?"

"Yes. Are you all right?"

"Not really. May I see you?"

"Now?"

"Now. I need to talk to someone."

"Come on over." She hung up, thinking longingly of

sleep.

Barnhill arrived twenty-five minutes later. Katherine sat him down in the breakfast room and poured him a cup of coffee. "What's the matter?"

"I got my pink slip from the International Press Agency. They fired me. Happy Bank Holiday, Barnhill, you've got two minutes to empty your desk and get the hell off the premises."

"That's terrible. What reason did they give?"

Barnhill gave a bleak grin. "The best reason of all. I've been doing a lousy job for the past few months. I was giving anything but a day's work for a day's pay."

"Why?"

"Why do you think? Book Two . . . *Vietnam, the NCOs*. I've been spending every moment I can on it. The light at the end of the tunnel's beckoning brightly to me—"

"So you neglected your job? Being sacked serves you right."

"That's nice. I drive over here in the middle of the night, and you show as much sympathy as a concentration-camp guard."

"Raymond, you called me because you wanted someone to talk to. There was no guarantee that the talk would be sympathetic. What do you intend doing?"

"The first book—*Vietnam, the Officers*—is due out in October. I'd hoped to be in the States for that, the ego trip of seeing my own book in shops. Now, I'm not so sure."

"Is money a problem?"

Barnhill nodded. "I don't have much put by. That apartment in Dolphin Square costs me an arm and a leg. I inherited it from another IPA guy, who'd been assigned elsewhere. He was assistant bureau chief, making twice what I'm making. The BMW came from him as well."

"Could you"—Katherine took a deep breath before

453

sticking her foot in her mouth — "use a loan?"

"Do you think I came here to sponge off you?"

"Of course not. I'm just trying to help, that's all."

The fire left Barnhill's voice. "Thanks, but I'll make out okay. I'll get a job with one of the other agencies. Associated Press or UPI."

Barnhill began job-hunting the following morning. He applied at agencies, and at the London desks of American newspapers and news magazines. Any interest evaporated the instant he mentioned that he had a novel scheduled for publication in October.

"Your book hits big," one bureau chief told him, "and we won't see your ass for dust anymore."

"I'll make peanuts on it," Barnhill claimed. "I write for pocket money, that's all."

"Ken Follett, when he worked on Fleet Street for the *Evening News,* started out writing thrillers to pay for car repairs. One of those thrillers was a yarn called *Storm Island.* Some editor in the States changed the title to *Eye of the Needle.* Tell me something . . . you still see Follett punching a clock around here?"

Barnhill walked away, disappointed. By the end of the week, he was in despair. When he saw Katherine for lunch on Friday, he told her, "I'm beginning to think I'll never get a paycheck again as long as I live. Isn't that crazy?"

"Instead of driving yourself into the ground, why not use this free time to finish off the second book?"

"I've tried, but I haven't been able to write a word. For years I've dreamed of being able to write full-time. Now I can, I find that there's a streak of Protestant work ethic in me that says I'm worthless without a proper job."

Katherine understood perfectly. Barnhill did not have enough madness to throw everything away in order to chase a dream. He was being torn apart by the

454

desire to write and the need to have a regular income. Although she had never faced a similar dilemma—the lack of money being a barrier—she could sympathize with him. Dreams should not have a price tag.

"Despite your lowly opinions of English newspapers, would you consider working on one?"

"The *Eagle?* I'm not looking for charity."

"I'm not offering you any. It's just that you impressed Sally Roberts an awful lot during my party last January. She said you were too bright to be working for an agency, and she asked me to persuade you to go to work for the *Eagle.*"

"How come you didn't?"

"Because I knew you weren't looking for charity."

"Well, damn me," Barnhill said, and burst out laughing.

"Would you like me to speak to her?"

"Hell, no. I'm perfectly capable of speaking to the lady myself."

Which Barnhill did. That same afternoon, he met with Sally at her office in the Eagle building. She introduced him to Lawrie Stimkin, and at four-thirty, Barnhill left the building with both a proper job and the opportunity to be in New York when his first book was published. Sally had given him a temporary assignment as the *Eagle's* New York correspondent, reporting human-interest and offbeat stories on the upcoming American election under the title "Glimpses of America." When the two-month assignment was over, a decision would be made on Barnhill's future with the *Eagle.*

Barnhill spent Friday night and Saturday morning clearing out his apartment and packing. At noon on Saturday, he drove his white BMW around to Kate's Haven, where it would remain while he was away. Katherine then drove him to Heathrow Airport, to catch his afternoon TWA flight to Kennedy.

"When you get back home," he told her, "open the

trunk of the BMW. There's something there for you."

"That wasn't necessary, Raymond."

"Sorry to disagree, but it was."

She parked the silver Porsche at terminal three, and accompanied Barnhill inside. When the flight was called, she walked with him to passport control.

"Don't forget to write, Raymond."

"That's what I'm getting paid the big money for."

"Idiot. I meant letters." She stood on tiptoe and kissed him. They held tightly to each other for a couple of seconds, then Barnhill stepped back, his face flushed.

"Good-bye. I'll start writing the first letter even before the plane takes off." He passed through the barrier, turned to wave, and was then lost from sight. Feeling flat, Katherine returned to the parking lot.

When she arrived home, she opened the trunk of the BMW. Inside, a little the worse for being cooped up for half the day, was the most enormous bunch of flowers she had ever seen. Gladioli, chrysanthemums, daffodils, a blazing sunburst of color, topped off with a card that read, quite simply, "Thanks, friend." Katherine gave the display to Edna, asking her to put it in water.

When John Saxon arrived that evening to take Katherine to dinner and the theater, he spotted the flowers in a cut-glass vase in the drawing room. "Who sent you those?"

"A secret admirer."

"The same secret admirer who hands out slot machines?"

"Don't be jealous, John."

"I'm not. I might have felt a twinge if he'd sent you red roses, but that rather ostentatious offering . . . ? No, I'm not jealous at all."

In that moment, Katherine realized just how much she was going to miss Raymond Barnhill.

She heard from Raymond Barnhill midway through the following week. He telephoned her to say he had taken a short lease on a one-bedroom apartment in Manhattan, on the corner of Ninth Avenue and Forty-eighth Street.

"You can't miss it. We've got a supermarket on the ground floor, so the first ten floors are flooded with cockroaches."

"That's disgusting."

"It's okay. I'm on the fifteenth floor, too far for them to climb."

"Why don't they take the lift?"

"The elevator? They don't know about it yet. And lower your voice, will you? They might be bugging the phones."

Katherine's face creased into a huge smile.

Barnhill's first glimpse of election-mad America appeared the next week in the *Eagle*. It concerned a congressional candidate parachuting into Yankee Stadium during a televised Saturday afternoon baseball game. The candidate, trailing far behind in the polls, hoped to bring himself to the attention of the fifty thousand fans in the stadium and the millions watching on television. Badly misjudging the wind, he finished up in the Harlem River, where a police boat had to rescue him. Perversely, his rating in the polls increased. Which only went to prove, Barnhill pointed out, that Americans love a gallant loser.

The story was so successful that "Glimpses of America" was changed from weekly to twice-weekly. Barnhill had no trouble making the schedule, he wrote in a letter to Katherine; there was more than enough good copy around. Also, he had plenty of time left over to put the finishing touches to the second book.

All through September, Barnhill's letters and telephone calls continued to be upbeat. Trade reviews of *Vietnam, the Officers* were promising. Knight and

Robbins, Barnhill's publishers, continually expressed optimism. Then, in October, optimism gave way to brutal reality. *Vietnam, the Officers* was placed on the shelves of bookshops, and stayed on the shelves. Writing to Katherine, Barnhill tried to rationalize the flop. Vietnam had not been a popular war with the American public. Americans still had to come to grips with the divisiveness of Vietnam. He gave twenty reasons, but all Katherine could see was the disappointment that flowed through each word of each sentence. She telephoned immediately to tell him that the book would probably do a lot better when it came out in paperback.

Despite Barnhill's personal disappointment, his "Glimpses of America" became more and more popular, a perfect blend of the human and the zany, the tasteful and the crass, that makes America what it is. At the end of October, Sally Roberts contacted him to ask if he would be interested in staying on in New York for the *Eagle* once the election was over. He agreed. When he telephoned Katherine with the news, she asked if that was what he wanted.

"At the moment, it's comfortable," he answered. "I ready to turn in *Vietnam, the NCOs*. There'll probably be revisions to do. Then, with just 'Glimpses of America' to write, I'll be able to get on with the third book. And maybe I'll find time to get to a basketball or hockey game and know I won't get caught in the middle of a skinhead riot."

"Just be careful how you walk the streets. What about your car? Do you want me to hang onto it for you?" She hoped he would say yes, because that would mean he intended to return.

"Would you do me a favor and sell it, Katherine? I could use the money."

She masked her disappointment with a brittle laugh. "It seems to me as though you can always use the money."

"Those with it should not make fun of those without."

"All right. Send me authorization to sell the car."

Four days later, on the first Tuesday in November — Election Day in the United States — Katherine received by airmail a notarized statement from Barnhill empowering her to sell his BMW. She drove it around to half a dozen used-car dealers, and when she eventually sold it to the highest bidder, she felt quite proud of herself for having negotiated so cleverly. And a little sad. For it was the white BMW, driven by Barnhill, that had rescued her and Sid Hall from the Brixton riot two years earlier.

First thing the following morning, Katherine wired the money to Barnhill in New York. That very evening, she learned that had she waited, she could have delivered the money in person.

"I'm going to New York next week," John Saxon told her over dinner. "Closing a deal we've been putting together. Would you like to join me?"

"What kind of deal?"

"Saxon Holdings recently formed an American company to buy up desirable properties. Saxon-America, to give it the full and rather unimaginative title. We're ready to complete our first purchase, an office block on West Forty-second Street."

"How near is it to Ninth Avenue and Forty-eighth Street?"

"Not far. What interests you about that intersection?"

Katherine avoided answering. "How long is the trip for?"

"Five days. Leave here on Monday on Concorde, and fly back on Friday night."

"There's a Thursday somewhere in the middle of that. 'Fightback' day."

"Katherine, you haven't had a proper break since you took over the show. You must have some canned stories."

"Of course, there are enough stories on hold to put together a dozen shows." The trip was so appealing, but Katherine was a jealous professional, not altogether happy to leave her work in someone else's hands. "I don't know, John."

"Are you worried about the presentation of the show? Surely you have enough faith in Derek and Heather? And if they meet any difficulties, they can always fall back on Jeffrey. He's not exactly inexperienced."

The Concorde. New York. The opportunity to see Raymond Barnhill. "I'll speak to Paul Hyde about it."

Expecting opposition, Katherine met with the producer. To her surprise, Hyde raised no objections. "We've got enough to get by for one week," he told her. "It'll give your assistants a chance to shine as well."

"Just as long as they don't shine too brightly, and take away my job."

Hyde's smile declared that such a possibility was out of the question. "While you're in New York, would you like some American television exposure? I won't have any difficulty in getting you on a talk show over there."

"What would I talk about?"

"It doesn't matter, just as long as you do it with an English accent. American viewers are ravenous for anything English. 'Monty Python' and 'Upstairs, Downstairs' are two shows that spring to mind. And Benny Hill . . . for heaven's sake, you can't turn on a television set anywhere in America without seeing Benny Hill leering at large bosoms and dropping his double entendres all over the place."

"Paul, I will do anything but leer at large bosoms."

"I'll mention that when I make the arrangements."

For Katherine, her first flight on a supersonic aircraft was a revelation. Concorde was small in comparison to the other airliners that dotted the apron at Heathrow Airport. Slim and sleek, like a Morgan sports car parked in a row of comfortable but clumsy Cadillacs. Unlike in the Morgan, however, there was little sensation of speed. Only the machmeter revealed that the aircraft was flying at twice the speed of sound.

In New York, a limousine whisked Saxon and Katherine to the Sherry-Netherland. While their baggage was taken up to the suite, Saxon told Katherine that he had to go out and meet with the lawyers representing Saxon-America. "It'll probably be an all-day affair. Will you be able to keep yourself busy?"

"I think so. I'll go for a walk, look in the shops."

Katherine went up to the suite. It was on two floors, living quarters below and two bedrooms upstairs. Her baggage had been set out in one bedroom, Saxon's in another. She changed from the pants and sweater she'd worn for the flight into a figure-revealing electric-blue wool dress and black suede boots. After telephoning home — as she had promised to do — to tell her children that she'd arrived, she went downstairs. When she asked for directions to the nearest bookshop, the doorman pointed her toward Doubleday.

Katherine found four copies of *Vietnam, the Officers* in Doubleday, stacked one behind the other. The front cover depicted an army officer in dress blue uniform superimposed over a montage of war photographs. On the back was Barnhill's picture, taken in front of Buckingham Palace. The biography listed him as living in London, working as a journalist for an American wire service. Katherine bought one of the books for herself, and rearranged the remaining three so that they were prominently displayed.

Leaving Doubleday, she walked along narrow sun-starved canyons of streets until she reached the return address on Barnhill's letters, a grimy apartment building with a busy supermarket on the ground floor.

Katherine pressed the buzzer for Barnhill's apartment.

"Hello? Who's there?"

"I have a copy of *Vietnam, the Officers,* which I would like to have autographed by the author."

"Pardon?"

"Open the door and let me in. I want you to sign a copy of your book."

"Katherine!" Even the intercom's distortion failed to hide the joy in Barnhill's voice. "Are you in New York?"

"No. I took ventriloquism lessons, and now I'm throwing my voice all the way from London. Of course I'm in New York! Will you open the blasted door before the roaches get me?"

The door clicked. Katherine let herself in, and entered the elevator. When it stopped at the fifteenth floor, Barnhill was waiting, his face a mixture of utter surprise and supreme pleasure. "Hug," he said, and threw his arms around her, squeezing the breath from her body.

"Enough! I don't want to go home in a body cast."

Barnhill stepped back, amazement still glowing on his face. "I can't believe you're here. What are you doing in New York?"

"I flew over with John Saxon. He's in the middle of buying his first building here."

"Just what America needs, another real estate magnate," Barnhill muttered, parodying Saxon's greeting when the two men had first met at Franz's funeral.

"Are you going to show me where you live, or are you going to leave me out here?"

"Come on in." Barnhill led Katherine down a narrow corridor to a surprisingly bright and cheerful apartment. She was drawn to the living room window. Straight down was Ninth Avenue, a clutter of traffic punctuated by vivid flashes of yellow.

"How many taxis are there in New York?"

"Never enough."

She looked up from the street, out toward the west. Through gaps between buildings she could see water, a distant shore. "What's over there?"

"That's the Hudson. New Jersey's on the other side."

"Will you sign my book?"

Barnhill saw the Doubleday bag. "How many were there?"

"Four. Now there are only three. How many did Doubleday have when it first came out?"

"Six. One of the world's best bookstores has sold the grand total of three Raymond Barnhill books in a month."

"The other three will sell quickly now."

"How do you figure that?"

"I didn't like the way they were displayed, so I rearranged them. One has pride of place in the window now, right under the sign that reads 'Bestsellers.' "

Barnhill laughed, uncertain whether to believe her or not. "What do you want me to write in the book?"

"Don't ask me. You're the writer."

Barnhill studied a blank page for a moment, before writing, "Katherine, thank you for being my friend." When he handed the book back to her, she said, "That's very sweet. Thank you."

"How long are you here for?"

"Just until Friday night."

"When will I be able to see you?"

"During the day. I'm hoping you're going to show me New York. I want to see some real glimpses of America."

"How about starting now, with lunch? I'm feeling flushed on account of some money a kind friend sent me last week."

"It might be only one-fifteen to you, but it's six-fifteen to me. I don't want lunch; I want dinner."

Barnhill threw a herringbone jacket over his shirt. "You're going to have to settle for lunch."

463

They went downstairs and walked along Forty-eighth Street until they reached Sixth Avenue. "That's Rockefeller Center," Barnhill said. "And that"—he pointed to a cart on which was a gaudy yellow and blue umbrella—"is a genuine American hot dog stand, where we're having lunch."

"You are joking."

"I most certainly am not. You want glimpses of America? No better way to start than with a good American hot dog."

She followed him to the cart, watching as he ordered. "Doesn't the *Eagle* pay you enough to eat decently?"

He turned around, offering her one of the hot dogs. "Mustard and sauerkraut?"

She took it from him, holding it gingerly. From deep inside, a voice cautioned that she was holding a loaded gun to her head. One nibble would be like pulling the trigger. But she watched Barnhill bite into his hot dog, and he seemed none the worse for the experience.

Barnhill saw the hot dog lifted to her mouth and he understood her predicament. Raised on smoked salmon and pheasant, Katherine did not know the pleasure of lunching on the sidewalk outside Rockefeller Center. "Go on, introduce your taste buds to a whole new world."

At last, she took a bite, chewed, and had to admit that it tasted good. Three more bites, and it was gone. When Barnhill asked if she wanted another, she nodded eagerly.

"When you're dining at some gourmet restaurant with John Saxon tonight, eating off fine china, and drinking Château Latour out of high-priced crystal, you'll look back on lunchtime and wish you were eating a hot dog again."

"I bet you I don't."

"How much?"

"Five pounds . . . I mean dollars."

"You're on."

After walking a dozen blocks to the Empire State Building, they took the elevator to the observation deck. Barnhill pointed out landmarks, the Hudson and East rivers, the Statue of Liberty in the harbor, the Chrysler Building shining in the cool November sun, the twin towers of the World Trade Center. "Six hundred miles south of those towers . . . that's where I come from."

"You sound as though you're homesick for South Carolina."

"Sometimes I am. I'll take you down there. Not this time, but on another trip. In the fall. You've never seen nature in all her colorful glory until you've seen the Carolinas in the fall. New Englanders claim their fall foliage is the best, but it doesn't even come a close second to the South."

By the time they came down from the observation deck, it was almost three-thirty. They stopped in a restaurant for a cup of coffee, then Katherine said she had to return to the hotel. Barnhill flagged down a cab and stood on the sidewalk, waving, as she was driven away. While the taxi bounced its way north along Madison Avenue, Katherine sat staring at the inscription Barnhill had written into the book. "Katherine, thank you for being my friend." No other words could have meant more.

Two messages greeted Katherine at the Sherry-Netherland. The first, from Saxon, informed her that they were having dinner that evening with Frank Lane, president and chief executive officer of Saxon-America, and his wife, Alice. The second message was from a man named Larry Miller. Katherine telephoned him from the suite.

"Welcome to New York, Katherine," Miller greeted her. "Paul Hyde contacted me to say that you'd be interested in making an appearance on American television. I produce a show called 'Speak Out.' It's a

465

current-events discussion program aimed at afternoon viewers who believe there's more to life than soap operas."

"Is there?"

Miller laughed nervously. "I hope that's an example of English humor. Would Thursday be good for you to appear as a member of the 'Speak Out' panel? Our current theme concerns the election we've just had, and Thursday's show will be asking if the move to the right heralds a new, more rigid morality."

"How could I possibly contribute anything? I know nothing about American morality, rigid or otherwise."

"Your country swung to the right eighteen months before we did. Perhaps you can tell us what to expect."

"Who else will be on the panel?"

"Peg Farraday, a civil liberties attorney, Lucille Benoit, who represents the antiabortion lobby, and James Parker, an evangelist who heads the 'Glory to God' ministry in Virginia. Parker has a show every Sunday morning called 'Hour of Glory.' "

"You don't want me there for my opinion. You want me there to keep the other panelists away from each other's throats."

Miller laughed. "Ah, that English sense of humor. Save some of it for Thursday afternoon."

John Saxon returned to the Sherry-Netherland just after five, carrying a heavy briefcase, which he dropped in the center of the living room floor. Katherine, having come out of the shower ten minutes earlier, sat on a couch in a white terry robe, while she watched a television news program. Her long blond hair was wrapped, turban-style, in a towel. Saxon kissed her, senses taking in the fresh scent of the Pear's soap she always used.

"Is the building yours yet?"

"There are still details to be ironed out. Lawyers over

here must work by the minute. The longer something takes, the more they can make. How did you spend your day?"

"I went out for a walk, bought a book."

Saxon's eyes dropped to the coffee table. In the center was *Vietnam, the Officers*. He picked it up, saw Raymond Barnhill's photograph on the back, then opened it. "Was Raymond doing a signing?"

"Just one copy. Mine. I went around to see him. He lives quite close to here."

Saxon's eyebrows formed a shallow V. "Ninth Avenue and Forty-eighth Street?"

"Three cheers for your memory, John Saxon."

"Is that why you came with me to New York? So you could see Raymond Barnhill?"

"No." The instant the denial left her lips, she wondered if she had told a lie. "Just because I'm with you does not mean I can't see Raymond while I'm here. We're friends, just like he wrote in that book. Friends do not fly three thousand miles and then not see each other. Besides, Raymond works for the *Eagle*. Both Sally Roberts and Lawrie Stimkin, the *Eagle*'s new editor, asked me to pass on some messages."

Saxon replaced the book on the table. "Frank and Alice Lane are collecting us at seven-thirty. Will you be ready?"

"Of course. By the way, if you get your business finished by Thursday afternoon, you can come and lend me moral support. I'm part of a television brains trust that's trying to figure out whether or not we're entering the age of a new morality." She walked up the stairs, undoing the towel around her head, and letting the damp blond hair cascade onto her shoulders.

Frank Lane arrived at the Sherry-Netherland in a Mercedes. Five years older than Saxon, he was a tall, broad-shouldered man who had played football for Yale in his college days. Only his silvery hair gave away the fact that he had turned fifty. By contrast, Alice, his wife, was a tiny woman who seemed in danger of being eaten alive by the sable coat she wore. Katherine, wearing a Russian silver fox coat over an off-the-shoulder black dress, climbed into the back of the Mercedes with Alice. Saxon took the front passenger seat.

"Where are we going?" Saxon asked.

"I made eight o'clock reservations at Le Cirque."

"That gives us plenty of time. Let's show Katherine what all the fuss is about."

Lane drove south on Fifth Avenue, then west on Forty-second Street. Midway between Fifth and Sixth avenues, he pulled into the curb. Katherine, sitting on the right-hand side of the car, peered up at a curving tower of shimmering black glass and steel. "You're buying this?"

"Next week this time," Saxon remarked, "that building will be called Saxon Tower."

"Lawyers and their nit-picking permitting," Lane added.

"Bylines belong on books, not buildings," Katherine stated.

Saxon burst out laughing. "I'm as proud of my works as any writer is of his. Besides, buildings serve a more practical purpose than books — they provide shelter." He motioned for Lane to continue with the journey.

Midway through dinner at Le Cirque, fatigue caught up with Katherine. In New York, it might be dinnertime, but nothing could convince her body and her brain that it was not two-thirty in the morning. Saxon, noticing Katherine's head begin to nod, told the Lanes that he was feeling tired. "It's been a very long day, so I hope you'll excuse us if we make it an early night."

The short drive over bumpy roads, coupled with the brisk November night, gave Katherine a temporary burst of energy. Her eyes were wide open, her brain clear, when she entered the suite at the Sherry-Netherland. "That was very gallant of you, John, claiming you were tired when it was my face that was about to fall into the dessert."

She slipped out of the silver fox coat, and draped it over the arm of the couch. Saxon drew close to her, lowering his head to run his lips across her bare shoulders. "Tomorrow night we'll have dinner alone, I promise you."

"I'll do my best to stay awake." As if to mock her words, tiredness closed in again. She yawned, trying too late to stifle the noise with her hand.

"I think you'd better go to bed, Katherine."

"I think you'd better come with me."

The bulging briefcase was exactly where Saxon had left it six hours earlier. He tapped it with his foot. "I'd love to, but there are some papers I want to look through first. I've got to prepare for tomorrow's tussles with the lawyers."

She yawned again. "Spoilsport."

He lifted her in his arms and carried her upstairs, setting her down gently in the middle of the bed. "Katherine, whatever I said about you and Raymond before . . . I'm sorry."

"Why did you say anything?"

"Because I was tired from the journey. Because I'm very excited about this deal. And because I'm a little jealous."

"Raymond's a friend, nothing more."

"I understand. That's what he wrote in the book." He smiled down at her. "Can you manage to undress yourself?"

"I think so. If I need help, I'll call."

"I'll be listening."

Katherine undressed, removed the little makeup she wore, and slid beneath the sheets. She fell asleep quickly, but not before realizing she owed Raymond Barnhill five dollars. He had won his bet. Eating good food on fine china, and drinking vintage Bordeaux from expensive crystal, fared badly against the gourmet delight of a hot dog with mustard and sauerkraut eaten on the sidewalk outside Rockefeller Center.

Katherine gave Barnhill the five dollars the following day, when she met him again for lunch. He accepted with a smile, and a satisfied "What did I tell you?"

This time, Katherine's glimpse of America was the crowded Carnegie Deli on Seventh Avenue, just around the corner from Carnegie Hall. Barnhill ordered corned beef sandwiches — "That's what you English call salt beef," he told Katherine — and they shared a tiny table with an overweight police officer and a businessman in a Brooks Brothers suit.

No matter how wide Katherine opened her mouth, it was never wide enough to allow passage to the sandwich. In the end, she capitulated, removing half the thinly sliced meat. "This is obscene. I've never seen sandwiches like this anywhere."

"Certainly not in England."

"How many people die each year from heart attacks because of food like this?"

The fat police officer thrust himself into the conversation. "Lady, everyone's got to die from something. Personally, I can't think of a better way to go than this."

Katherine and Barnhill left the restaurant laughing. Arms linked, they crossed Central Park South. "Did I mention that I'm going to be on television in two days?" Katherine asked as they entered the park. "I'll be one of the panelists on 'Speak Out.' "

"Who else will be there?"

Katherine tried to recall the names of the other panelists. "A lawyer called Peg Farraday. Lucille Ben . . . ?"

"Benoit? The pro-life spokesperson?"

"Yes. And a television preacher called James Parker."

"Good luck. In between Parker quoting Scripture, Lucille Benoit claiming that America murders one million unborn babies every year, and Peg Farraday accusing them both of fascism, you won't get a word in edgeways."

Katherine spent the afternoon reading Barnhill's book. It was vastly different from any other war book she had ever read, an intellectual dissection of the characters rather than an action story. Katherine wondered which of the junior officers Barnhill had based on himself. Probably one of those renegades who did their military careers no good at all by arguing in the officers' club over the rights and wrongs of the war.

She finished it a few minutes before Saxon entered the suite. Asked how she had spent the day, Katherine replied that she had taken a walk and read a book. She made no mention of seeing Barnhill.

As Saxon had promised, they had the evening to themselves. After eating an early supper at the hotel, they took a taxi to Broadway's Winter Garden. "If I'm going to have my name on a building on Forty-second Street, the least we can do is see the show of the same name.

Katherine enjoyed *42nd Street*. So did Saxon. When they came out of the theater, they were both humming the music they'd just heard. "Tired?" Saxon asked.

"No. I've beaten jet lag."

"Good. Let's eat something."

They stopped off for a snack at the Café Pierre, then returned to the Sherry-Netherland. To Katherine's frustration and disappointment, Saxon did not accompany her upstairs to bed. He remained, as on the previous night, in the living room with his briefcaseful of papers, claiming he had to prepare for the following day's meetings. As she slipped into bed, alone, she puzzled over why he had asked her along. Not to be his bedmate, to spend complete nights with her as she longed to spend them with him. Had he needed her solely as an ornament on his arm for social events? She found herself looking more and more toward her next meeting with Raymond Barnhill.

On Wednesday, Katherine's glimpse of America included a visit to Bloomingdale's, a ride on the subway, and a round-trip ticket on the Staten Island Ferry. "The biggest transportation bargain in the world," Barnhill assured her.

Over lunch, Katherine mentioned that she had read the book. When Barnhill asked her opinion, she told him, truthfully, that it was too dry for her tastes. "Maybe you could add some spice for when the paperback comes out."

"There hasn't been a paperback sale. All the big houses turned it down. Now Knight and Robbins are going to the small houses, the ones that don't pay much."

"I'm sorry."

In the evening, she accompanied Saxon to Frank Lane's Westchester home for a dinner party the Saxon-America president had organized in honor of his British chairman. They returned to the Sherry-Netherland just after midnight.

"What time is your show tomorrow?" Saxon asked, as he hung up the tuxedo he had worn for the party.

"Four o'clock. Will you be able to attend?"

"I wish I could, but the lawyers aren't moving any faster. We won't get the final signing done until Friday morning. What about your friend Raymond? Won't he be there?"

Was there a special emphasis, Katherine asked herself, on *friend?* She shot Saxon a look as he was removing his gold Rolex. "Raymond said he'd try. He has an assignment tomorrow for the *Eagle*, and he isn't certain what time he'll be through."

472

"With or without moral support, Katherine, I'm confident that you'll manage just fine."

Franz came to Katherine's mind, the time his business meeting in Chicago had coincided with her first "Satisfaction Guaranteed!" She'd been angry with Franz for not being there to witness her big moment, and she felt that same anger directed toward Saxon now. Were all men so callous, putting their business commitments before anything else? Or was it just the men with whom Katherine fell in love? Was it some fatal flaw that attracted her only to men who were so business-oriented that they could see little beyond the bottom of the balance sheet?

Saxon went to bed ten minutes after Katherine. When he called her name softly, she pretended to be asleep.

At nine the next morning, after Saxon had left the hotel, Katherine telephoned home. Edna reported that the children were well, and missing their mother. Next, Katherine tried Barnhill's number. She got the answering machine, and assumed that he had already left for his assignment. She spent the morning shopping for gifts for Henry and Joanne. After searching through stores along Fifth Avenue, Katherine settled for souvenirs of New York: a Mets warm-up jacket for Henry, and a miniature New York Knicks jacket — whoever the Knicks were! — for her daughter.

She ate lunch out, and returned to the suite just after two o'clock. The telephone was ringing. Katherine answered, surprised, then instantly worried, to hear Edna's musical voice. "What's happened, Edna?"

"It's Joanne. Nothing to worry about, but Jimmy and I thought you should know. He's just taken her to hospital."

"What!"

"She and Henry were chasing each other around the house. She fell down the stairs, and we think she might have broken her arm. Jimmy's taken her to the hospital for X rays. Don't worry about a thing, Mrs. Kassler, we'll take care of everything."

Katherine stared stupidly at the receiver for a full minute after Edna had hung up. Don't worry about a thing! Joanne was her daughter; of course she was going to worry! She put through a call to the Saxon-America office. John Saxon, she was told, was in a meeting and could not be disturbed.

"Tell him this is Mrs. Kassler. He'll be disturbed for me."

Saxon came on the line. Katherine explained what had occurred. "I'm going home now. I'll cancel my appearance on 'Speak Out' and take a taxi to the airport."

"Katherine, will you slow down? A broken arm is not a serious injury."

"Not to you, it might not be. But to a seven-year-old girl, a hospital can be terrifying. Her mother should be there."

Saxon's voice was maddeningly calm. "Canceling your appearance on that show will serve no useful purpose. Go through with it, then fly out tonight. Call British Airways and change your flight. Pack before you leave the hotel for the studio. Afterward, you can take a taxi to the airport."

"Won't you be taking me to the airport?"

"Katherine, it is impossible for me to get out of here before six-thirty tonight. We want to sign tomorrow, and there are still plenty of wrinkles."

Katherine did not give a damn about Saxon's wrinkles. All she cared about was Joanne's broken arm, and the hell with anyone who accused her of overreacting. That included Saxon. "John, I have to go. I'll speak to you over the weekend, when you're back in London." Before hanging up, she said, "I hope you sign your contract on time."

She called Barnhill's apartment again. The machine was still on. She packed her two cases, and left them on the bed. Next, she telephoned British Airways and made the switch in reservations. That done, she called home. Edna answered to say that Jimmy Phillips had just telephoned from the hospital. Joanne had broken her right arm, and a cast was being applied. The little girl was in good spirits, and asking for her mother.

"Tell her I'll be there tomorrow, Edna. I'm flying home tonight. British Airways. Have Jimmy meet me, please."

She dressed in a pink wool suit for the television show. Over it, she wore the silver fox coat. She went downstairs, where the doorman hailed a taxi for her. The television studio was on Seventh Avenue, quite close to Barnhill's apartment. Katherine entered and asked for Larry Miller, the producer of "Speak Out." Miller came out to meet her, a slim, curly-haired man with warm brown eyes. She told him what had happened, and Miller promised there would be no delays with the show.

"A friend gave me the rundown on my fellow panelists," Katherine said. "It sounds as if I'll be in the middle of a war."

"Paul Hyde, when he called me from London, said you always carried a sharp pin in case you met a pompous person whose balloon needed bursting. If you feel you want to use it today, be my guest."

Miller introduced Katherine to her co-panelists. Peg Farraday, the civil-liberties lawyer, was plump and middle-aged, with unruly salt-and-pepper hair. The Reverend James Parker, head of the "Glory to God" ministry, was tall and slim, a perfect hanger for the suit he wore. Katherine knew good tailoring when she saw it, and the silver-haired television preacher with the open trust-me face was wearing a fortune on his back. The third panelist, Lucille Benoit, was a thin-lipped woman in her forties, with bleached hair and a heavily painted face.

After exchanging greetings with Katherine, the Rev-

475

erend Mr. Parker and Lucille Benoit talked to each other. Katherine saw that they made a point of ignoring Peg Farraday, and she knew that, once the show started, they would join forces against the lawyer. Katherine decided it was her duty to even up the sides.

Fifteen minutes before the show was due to start, Larry Miller's secretary approached Katherine. "There's a gentleman to see you. A Mr. Barnhill."

Katherine ran to where Barnhill waited in the auditorium. "I had to rush my work to get here on time," he told Katherine. "If Lawrie Stimkin complains, I'm pointing him in your direction."

"Am I glad to see you, Raymond!" In half a minute, she told him everything that had happened.

"I'll take you out to Kennedy," he promised.

She kissed him in front of everyone.

The host of "Speak Out" was a man named Victor Fisher. He introduced the panelists, who sat in easy chairs around a low glass table, Katherine and Peg Farraday on one side, and Lucille Benoit and the Reverend James Parker on the other. Fisher explained the show's theme, before throwing it open to the panel with the question "Are we entering the age of a new morality?"

Parker grabbed the initiative. "I pray that we are. If ever a country was in need of a new morality, it is the United States. We have fallen so far from God's law that we may well be too late in trying to make the return journey."

As Parker spoke, Katherine found herself being reminded of Jeffrey Dillard's old squadron leader, Sir Donald Leslie. When he paused, Victor Fisher, the show's host, turned to Katherine. "Would you say there's been any noticeable change in British morality since Mrs. Thatcher's victory last year?"

Katherine shook her head. "I don't see how a change in government can alter morality. Unless, of course, the incoming government is the Inquisition."

476

"Which is precisely," interjected Peg Farraday, "the kind of government Reverend Parker and Mrs. Benoit would like to inflict upon us. Thought police, spies in the bedroom."

Katherine looked up at the ceiling. Two minutes old, and the discussion was going exactly the way Barnhill had predicted it would.

The first half of the show developed into a battle between Parker and Peg Farraday. Every so often, as though obeying some unseen cue, Lucille Benoit chipped in a few words of support for Parker. When the show broke for commercials, the producer hurried onto the set.

"Could you get yourself more involved, Katherine?"

"I'm sorry," she answered, knowing she had been little more than a spectator. "My mind must be on my daughter."

Miller patted her encouragingly on the arm. "Try using that pomposity-pricking pin. Lord knows," he dropped his voice to a whisper, "you've got enough targets here."

Within seconds of the restart, Lucille Benoit took over the spotlight with a plea for the government to legislate against abortion, "the willful murder of millions of unborn children every year." The Reverend Mr. Parker nodded his head back and forth in total agreement. Peg Farraday started to speak, but Katherine held up a hand. She had no strong feelings on abortion, believing in individual choice, but she was becoming angry at the way Parker and Lucille Benoit were using the show to push their own hardline views, instead of openly addressing the question of whether the country was entering into a new era of morality.

"I might be exhibiting ignorance, Lucille," she said, "but if something is unborn, how can it be murdered?"

"Life begins with conception, not with birth."

"Why don't we have conception days instead of birthdays then?" Katherine heard muted applause from the audience, and when she turned to look at Farraday, the attorney gave her a tight-lipped smile.

"Britain's demise in the world," Parker chimed in, "can probably be traced directly to the flippancy with which its subjects treat God's work."

Katherine's voice turned icy. "Britain is probably closer to God than America is, because our monarch is Defender of the Faith, and we don't have a constitution separating church from state. Something else we don't have are sanctimonious scoundrels on television who hold a crucifix in one hand and a gigantic begging bowl in the other, with the implied threat that you'll go to hell in a handcart if you don't cough up!"

This time, there was nothing muted about the applause. Mixed with laughter, it rocked the studio.

Parker turned scarlet, speechless. Lucille Benoit tried to regain some control of the show. "We were talking about abortion. You are deliberately changing the subject because you understand that abortion is indefensible."

"Indefensible? Not at all. I don't believe it should be used as a substitute for birth control, but there are situations where it's the only proper course."

"Abortion is never the proper course."

"What about when the mother's health is at stake? When a woman is made pregnant by a rapist? Or when amniocentesis determines the presence of a diseased embryo?"

"You're wasting your time, Katherine," Peg Farraday said. "Mrs. Benoit and her whiter-than-white good Christian friends want amniocentesis banned right along with abortion. That way, if no one knows an embryo is diseased, there'll be no temptation to have an abortion. Wonderful logic, eh?"

Katherine glared at Benoit and Parker. "Just where does it say that being a good Christian means you have to turn the clock back a thousand years?"

Instead of answering the question, Benoit looked at

Victor Fisher, the host. "May I set the record straight? Miss Farraday and Mrs. Kassler are under the misapprehension that only white Christians are against the slaughter of abortion, and the meddling with God's work by amniocentesis. The pro-life movement is supported by decent people from all groups, from all races, and all religions."

Katherine had her pin out now, ready to burst every bubble in sight. "In that case, Mrs. Benoit, I hope that every black pro-lifer has a child born with sickle-cell anemia. I hope that every Jewish pro-lifer has a child born with Tay-Sachs. And I hope that every white Catholic and Protestant pro-lifer"—she dreamed up a scenario that would really throw a scare into the likes of Lucille Benoit and the Reverend Mr. Parker—"has a daughter made pregnant through being raped by a black man. Preferably a black man with a disease or a drug dependency that can be passed on to the child. Then let those pro-lifers speak out against the evils of abortion and amniocentesis!"

The show ended in total uproar. Larry Miller grasped her hand and said she'd been fantastic. She found Raymond Barnhill, who got her out of the building and into a taxi.

"What made you come out with a line like that?" he asked.

"It seemed the right thing to say. I couldn't let them think I was there as a backdrop, could I?"

The taxi took them to the Sherry-Netherland, where Katherine had her suitcases loaded into the trunk, and from there they went to the airport. Barnhill waited at the British Airways terminal until she boarded the flight. At the gate, he held her hands. "Thanks for a great week, Katherine."

"Raymond . . ." She looked into his light brown eyes. "Don't get too despondent about the book. The second one will do better, you'll see. And in the meantime, 'Glimpses of America' is making you as well known as Alistair Cooke."

They kissed, and Katherine walked toward the waiting 747.

Pushing a cart that held her two cases, Katherine passed unchecked through customs at Heathrow, and out into the arrivals area. She surveyed the waiting people, seeking Jimmy Phillips's comfortable face. To her shock, her eyes met those of her father. Joanne was with him, her right arm encased in a white cast that was already covered with signatures.

"Look, Mummy!" Released by Roland, the little girl ran to Katherine. "I've got a cast, just like Henry had."

Amazed that Joanne could remember back so far, Katherine lifted her up, kissed her, and set her on the cart. "Did you leave room for my name?"

"Of course. There." She pointed to a space on her wrist, "You can write there."

Katherine pushed baggage and daughter toward her father. She kissed him on the cheek. "I hope you didn't drive here."

"Arthur Parsons is waiting outside." Taking the cart from Katherine, Roland pushed it toward the parking lot. The green Bentley was positioned by the entrance. Roland ushered Joanne into the front with Parsons, before sitting in the back with Katherine. Once the Bentley had cleared the airport, Roland asked, "Do you know why I came to meet you?"

"To show me that Joanne was all right?"

"No." Roland reached into the door pocket and withdrew that morning's copy of the *Daily Eagle*. "What do you have to say about this, Kathy?"

She gulped. Sidney Glassman's face leaped off the front page. His younger son, Melvin, was also pictured.

"Sidney Glassman resigned his seat in the House of Commons at nine o'clock last night, exactly one hour after 'Fightback' did a major exposé on the crooked dealings of his son, Melvin, at the Grosvenor Sporting Club."

"I don't know a thing about it," Katherine protested.

There was anger in Roland's voice; a dear friend had been hurt, and he wanted to know why. "What do you mean, you don't know anything? That's your show, isn't it? How on earth could something like this happen without your knowledge, Katherine?"

"I don't know," she repeated, painfully aware that her father had used her full name. "But I'm bloody well going to find out!"

22

When the green Bentley pulled into the forecourt of Kate's Haven, Katherine jumped out and ran into the house. She stayed there just long enough to grab the keys to the Porsche from the key caddy in the downstairs hall. Moments later, she sent the Porsche accelerating out of the forecourt and onto the street, heading for the center of town and the "Fightback" offices.

Her father had called her Katherine! That alone disclosed just how upset he was with her. When was the last time he had used her full name instead of the diminutive, affectionate "Kathy"? Racking her brains, Katherine could not recall a single instance.

The inside of the Porsche grew warm. She opened the window and flicked off the heater, not needing it with the silver fox coat. She felt grubby wearing the same clothes since the previous afternoon, but a shower and a change would have to wait.

Both Derek Simon and Heather Harvey were in the office when Katherine swept in like a destroyer at flank speed. She cut off any greeting, any surprise at her early return, with a curt "Would someone mind telling me what the hell happened last night? Why the scheduled program did not go out on the air? Why it was replaced by utter trash that had no business being on 'Fightback'?"

"Where were you yesterday when we tried to reach you?" Heather demanded. "We called your hotel in New York, but you weren't there."

"Never mind where I was. All I'm concerned about is what happened here."

"If you'll allow us to," Derek said, "we'll tell you. At six-thirty last night, half an hour before we were due to go on the air, Jeffrey Dillard informed us that the content of the program was being changed. He had a major story which he was going to present himself. He had film clips of Melvin Glassman, the membership director of the Grosvenor Sporting Club. He had taped interviews with clients who had been persuaded by sexual lures to switch their gambling business to the Grosvenor."

"You should have seen who some of those clients were," Heather broke in. "Directors of major companies, foreign diplomats, a couple of Saudi Arabian princes."

"Dillard even had the name of Melvin Glassman's contact at Scotland Yard, who checked out the license-plate numbers of the luxury cars and furnished the owners' names and addresses. When we questioned Dillard's authority to make the change, he brought Paul Hyde in as an ally. Hyde said he was in full agreement."

"I tried to telephone you at your hotel," Heather said. "For a solid half hour I tried, but each time the switchboard operator rang your suite, there was no answer."

Six-thirty? That had been one-thirty in the afternoon in New York. She'd been out shopping, having lunch. And when she'd returned to the suite at two o'clock, she'd kept the telephone busy on her own. "Is Jeffrey Dillard coming in today?"

"He said he'd be here at eleven," Derek replied.

Katherine sat at her own desk to wait out the fifteen minutes until Dillard's arrival.

Jeffrey Dillard entered the office at two minutes before eleven, accompanied by Paul Hyde. "Katherine!" A bright, professional smile lit Dillard's face. "This is a nice surprise. I didn't think you were coming home until tomorrow."

"What right did you have to alter last night's show?"

Paul Hyde stepped between Katherine and Dillard. "Let's talk about this in my office. In private."

"I don't mind Heather and Derek hearing what I've got to say. Or don't you and Jeffrey want them to hear your excuses?"

"Very well," Hyde said. "Let them hear. Jeffrey came to me yesterday, to complain that the content of 'Fightback' wasn't worth a damn. He also questioned your judgment, and your ability to control the show."

"Why? Because I would not touch the Melvin Glassman story? It was not our kind of piece."

"Jeffrey did not agree with you. Now that I know the facts, neither do I. You were being too soft, Katherine. You were allowing your father's friendship with Melvin Glassman's father to influence an issue. Jeffrey first told you about the story at the end of the summer. When you turned him down, he carried on researching it alone. Yesterday, when he had the entire story ready to go, and 'Fightback' was set to run with a handful of third-rate pieces, I gave my approval for the change. Obviously we were right, because this morning is the first time that 'Fightback' has ever made the front pages of the national press."

"How dare you alter the show without consulting me? Without . . . without even informing me?" The question died on Katherine's lips as the truth asserted itself. "You didn't decide all this yesterday, did you? You've been planning to do it for ages, and you were seeking an opportunity. No wonder you didn't object to my taking a few days off. You and Jeffrey must have seen it as the perfect opportunity to slip in the Glassman piece." She shook her head in mock admiration. "No wonder the pair of you are such good friends. You deserve each other . . . !"

Without another word, she stormed out. As she started the engine of the Porsche, sending the tachometer needle swinging into the red, she thought about John Saxon, another of Dillard's good friends. Had Saxon, also, been part of this plot? It had been his idea that she accompany him to New York. And hadn't Saxon, after she had rejected Dillard's first proposal, tried to persuade her to change her mind? Hadn't he told her how important the story was to his dear friend?

No! She thrust that idea from her mind. Whatever else John Saxon might be—arrogant, inconsiderate, even, by his own admission, jealous—he was not underhanded. What did it matter anyway? After the way she'd left him in New York, she'd probably lost him. Lost him, and lost the damned show!

Exhausted physically from the overnight flight, and mentally drained by the confrontation with Jeffrey Dillard, Katherine went to bed that evening within an hour of kissing the children good night. Her bedroom was in the front of the house, overlooking the forecourt. She always slept with the window slightly open, and some nights she drifted off to the modern lullaby of passing cars, reflections of their lights casting tiny patterns across the ceiling. Tonight, she needed no such help. She was asleep within thirty seconds of her head touching the satin pillow.

She slept right through until nine o'clock, when Edna, who had kept Henry and Joanne from disturbing their mother, brought her in a cup of tea and the newspaper. Katherine sat up against the headboard, a bedjacket covering her shoulders. "No noise from the

485

children, tea and the paper in bed . . . why is everyone being especially nice to me today, Edna?"

The housekeeper, who had been told the previous night of the trouble at "Fightback," fussed over Katherine. "You stay in bed as long as you like, Mrs. Kassler. Jimmy and I have some errands to run. We'll take the children with us.

"Thank you." Drinking the tea, Katherine skimmed through the newspaper. There was an article on Sidney Glassman, in which the elderly politician said he had been thinking of retiring anyway. His son's troubles had just accelerated that decision. Katherine did not believe it for a second; shame and embarrassment had forced Sidney Glassman's hand. Dropping the newspaper onto the carpet, she rolled onto her side and went back to sleep.

Her eyes opened again at ten-thirty. She heard a car door close, and assumed that Edna and Jimmy Phillips had returned with the children. When she looked out of the window, she saw, instead of the Jaguar sedan, a maroon Rolls Royce Silver Shadow. Moments later, the doorbell's chimes echoed through the house.

Quite unhurriedly, Katherine slipped into a woolen robe, walked down the stairs, crossed the entrance hall, and unlocked the front door. Saxon, normally so well groomed, looked tired and rumpled. His clothes were creased. He needed a shave, and dark shadows underlined his eyes.

"Hello, John. Did you sign all the contracts that needed signing? Do you own the building now?"

"Don't be facetious. I didn't come here straight from the airport to be ridiculed. I came to see you, to talk about what happened in New York."

She looked past him. William, who had been waiting for Saxon at Heathrow, sat behind the steering wheel, watching. "I just discovered where I belong in your life, that's all."

Saxon ignored the gibe. "How's Joanne?"

"Her arm's in a cast, but she's all right."

"And you got to Kennedy Airport all right?"

"Yes. After the show, I returned to the Sherry-Netherland for my baggage, and took a taxi to the airport." She didn't tell him that Raymond Barnhill had accompanied her. Let Saxon think she had done it all on her own. "Did you hear about the show?"

"Everyone in New York heard about the show, Katherine. It sounded like you were mad at the entire world, and that preacher and the antiabortion woman provided convenient targets at which to discharge all your anger."

Katherine considered that. Was Saxon right? When she had attacked the Reverend James Parker and Lucille Benoit, had she just been substituting them for Saxon? "Did you hear about the other show? About 'Fightback'? Did you hear what your friend Jeffrey Dillard got up to while I was away?" Her earlier suspicion resurfaced. "Or was Thursday's 'Fightback' topic old news to you?"

"I have no idea what you're talking about, Katherine."

For the first time, Katherine noticed the cold. She invited Saxon into the house, leading him through to the kitchen, where she put the kettle on the gas. While she made a pot of tea, she filled Saxon in on what had happened at "Fightback" while she'd been away.

When she finished, Saxon said, "I asked you to New York simply because I wanted your company. I thought we would enjoy ourselves together. There was no ulterior motive."

Katherine poured two cups of tea. "The fact that I believe you doesn't make Jeffrey any less of a slimy swine."

Saxon winced. "I don't like hearing someone I love rip apart one of my best friends."

"Someone you love?"

"That's right. And that smart remark about where

487

you belong in my life was totally uncalled for. If I had thought there was a real emergency, I would have walked right out of the most important meeting to be by your side. For a real emergency, I would have chartered a plane to get us back to England immediately. But a broken arm, Katherine . . . ?"

She stared down at the cup of tea in front of her. While she had been frantic, Saxon had been reasonable. He had tried to calm her down. He had persuaded her not to cancel her appearance on the talk show. While she had acted with her heart, Saxon had thought clearly with his head.

"I never thought I'd see you again," she said at last.

"You were upset. I took that into account. All you've got to do now is resolve your differences with Jeffrey."

Katherine shook her head vehemently. "He compromised me by what he did. My name headed the credits, but I had nothing to do with the subject matter. As far as I am concerned, I'm finished with the show. I'll take in a letter of resignation first thing on Monday morning."

Once more, Saxon pitted calm reason against Katherine's heated action. "Before you sever the connection, why not talk with Jeffrey? He may have had what he considered a very good reason for what he did."

"How do you know what reason he might have had?"

"Just talk to him. Then decide."

Katherine talked to Dillard that evening, in a strained meeting that took place at Saxon's London home in Marble Arch. When Dillard entered the formal front reception room, with its paintings of historical heroes, Katherine regarded him stonily.

Saxon broke the ice. "Do you remember my telling

you some time ago that Jeffrey had once run for Parliament?"

When Katherine nodded, Dillard took up the story. "It was 1964, Katherine, the year Labour defeated the Tories by just four seats. Both sides knew it would be a close race, and all the stops were pulled out. A constituency in the East End of London was vacant — it was a Labour stronghold, but the incumbent wasn't standing again. The Conservatives persuaded me, as a well-known television figure, to contest the seat. Labour, seeking to fight fire with fire — or show business with show business, if you prefer — put up Sidney Glassman, who, although a very wealthy man, had grown up in that district. It was a fight worthy of any American political contest, with mud slung in all directions. Sidney Glassman was better at it than I was. He painted me as a television creation, a man playing a role, who spoke lines he'd learned by heart. The voters believed him, and I was defeated by an embarrassingly large margin."

"You waited all this time for revenge?"

"Sidney Glassman is a hero. His constituents idolize him. Anyone who attacked him personally would have risked being lynched. No, Katherine, I never planned revenge, but when a source told me of his son's chicanery . . . well, it was too sweet an opportunity to pass up."

Katherine looked at Saxon. "You knew this all the time, didn't you? You told me this morning that Jeffrey may have had good reason for what he did, so you were obviously aware of the background. And at the end of summer, you even tried to persuade me to accommodate Jeffrey on the Glassman story, didn't you? You said he was questioning his existence."

"I knew, and I did try to influence you once, yes. When I saw how firm you were, I dropped it. But I did warn you that Jeffrey might use his friendship with Paul Hyde."

"You did." She could forgive Saxon for trying to help his friend, but she could not forgive Dillard. "There is no way I could have reached where I am without your help. You got me onto 'Fightback,' and you guided me along. Without you, I would never have made it past my debut. But everything you've done for me does not excuse what happened on Thursday. If a libel action should be forthcoming—"

"It won't be," Dillard interrupted. "The facts I presented are verifiable."

"Please allow me to finish. If a libel suit were to be brought, I might be liable because the content of the show is my responsibility. You placed me in an untenable position. But most of all, you used your power to shatter the life of a man who has done a tremendous amount of good. Sidney Glassman is a friend of my father, and a very decent man. You have ruined his remaining years."

"Are you saying you wouldn't use any power you have to gain revenge on someone who'd got the better of you?"

"That's exactly what I'm saying, Jeffrey. A journalist's power is supposed to be used for rectifying wrongs. It is not for pursuing vendettas." She turned to Saxon, who had adopted the role of spectator. "I talked to him, all right? And my decision remains the same."

Dillard stood up, ready to leave. "I'm sorry that our association has to end this way, Katherine."

"So am I. But only one of us is to blame."

Saxon saw Dillard to the front door. When he returned, Katherine was staring at the painting of Wellington. "I hope this unfortunate incident has no effect on us, Katherine."

She turned away from the Iron Duke. "I don't hold you responsible, John. You tried to help a friend, that's all. But I'd never be able to face myself if I returned to 'Fightback.' I would not be able to face my

490

father, either."

"That's not an answer to the question I asked. Will what happened affect us?"

"Why should it? But please don't invite Jeffrey and me to the same party. I'm going home now. It's been a very hectic week, and I need some rest if I'm to start looking for a new job on Monday. Good night."

As she walked toward the door, she realized that this was the first time she'd been in the front reception room without gazing nostalgically at the Aubusson rug in front of the hearth.

On Sunday morning, Katherine drove Henry and Joanne to Stanmore to visit their grandfather. The four of them went for a walk on the common, and while the children ran on ahead, Katherine told Roland of her decision to leave "Fightback."

"How do you feel about that?" Roland asked.

"Self-satisfied. Righteous. And inordinately proud of myself. That's today, of course. Tomorrow, when all the fleeting glory has faded, I'll probably start worrying myself sick about being unemployed."

"Are you short of a bob or two?"

"Would you help me out if I were?"

"I'd offer to buy the children from you."

"Henry . . . ! Joanne . . . !" The children stopped at the sound of their mother's voice. "Your grandfather has just offered to buy you from me. How much are you worth?"

"A billion pounds!" Henry shouted back.

"We live in inflationary times," Roland lamented.

In the afternoon, Katherine typed out a formal letter of resignation, addressed to Paul Hyde. She hand-delivered it that evening to the "Fightback" offices. Afterward, she drove to Fleet Street, where she explained the reasons for her resignation to Lawrie Stimkin, who filled two pages of a notepad with shorthand symbols. It was not normal procedure for the editor to conduct an interview, but neither was it normal for the proprietor's daughter to be the subject of a major story.

The news of Katherine's resignation from one of the country's most popular television shows came out the next morning. No punches were pulled. She explained exactly why she had left the show "As much as I respect Jeffrey Dillard professionally," she was quoted as saying, "I cannot work with a man who uses his power to pursue a personal vendetta for something that happened sixteen years before. My integrity is worth more to me than any position."

At midday, Sally Roberts telephoned Katherine at home. "Heather Harvey and Derek Simon walked in ten minutes ago to ask Lawrie Stimkin for their old jobs back."

Katherine had hoped her assistants would quit the show and return to the *Eagle*. "I hope he said yes."

"Of course he did. We don't like seeing good talent go elsewhere. Now what about yourself?"

"I'd like some time to myself to think about it, Sally."

Other newspapers supported Katherine's stance. Not because they were particularly sympathetic to her, but because Sidney Glassman had been a popular politician, who had done a lot of good in his sixteen years in Westminster. One editorial opinion described Dillard's use of his media position as "a despicable example of absolute power corrupting absolutely."

Under the barrage of bad publicity, and the loss of its staff, there was no way for "Fightback" to continue. The announcement was made on Thursday morning that the show was canceled from that night. Katherine received the news with sadness. Not for the people involved, but for the show itself. For almost two years, "Fightback" had been an important part of her life, what Thursday evenings were all about. Now it was gone, just a step in her career. A memory.

Out of curiosity, she watched television that evening to see what replaced "Fightback." The station ran a special feature on actor Steve McQueen, who had died earlier that month. Katherine switched off, and went out for a walk, hoping the cold night air would dispel the depression she felt forming.

It did not. By the time she returned home, she was feeling quite maudlin. She went upstairs to her bedroom, looked at her address book, and dialed the fourteen-digit telephone number of the man who always managed to amuse her.

"Raymond, it's Katherine. I'm miserable. Cheer me up."

"What's got you down in the mouth?"

She told him. He already knew about the Glassman story and Katherine's resignation—he'd read that in the airmailed edition of the *Eagle* he bought each day from the Hotalings shop in Times Square—but the closure of "Fightback" was news.

"You're creating upheavals in television on both sides of the Atlantic, Katherine. You're a one-woman wrecking crew."

"Not funny, Raymond."

"But it is. Remember Larry Miller, the former producer of 'Speak Out'?"

"Former?" What trouble had she caused for the poor man?

"He got fired after that show. A couple of major advertisers blame him for your being so insulting—"

"Whom did I insult?"

"With that closing comment? Everyone except the American Indian. Anyway, Miller got fired, but the next thing you know, another station offered him a new show—because he'd had the brains to use someone as outrageous and controversial as you."

"I don't believe it," Katherine said, her own dejection forgotten. "The television world's crazy."

493

"That's right. Aren't you glad you're out of it?"

"I think I am. Raymond, you're not using that story for your column, are you?"

She expected him to say yes. Instead he said, "I'm using my powers of censorship to kill it because it might upset someone I like very much."

"Thank you."

When she replaced the receiver and lay back on the bed, the depression had lifted. A conversation with Raymond Barnhill was good medicine. The hours she'd spent with him in New York had been a real tonic. Without seeing him, she realized, the New York trip would have been the most tedious week she'd ever spent.

Despite Katherine's assurance to Saxon that the argument with Jeffrey Dillard would have no effect on their relationship, an awkwardness grew between them. Perhaps it was because Saxon continued to maintain his friendship with Dillard, and Katherine felt uncomfortable about it. Not that she would ever dream of telling Saxon whom he could, and could not, have for friends. Saxon had once done that to her, on the night of the party at Kate's Haven. He had questioned her friendship with Raymond Barnhill, who had worn a borrowed tuxedo to the party, and Katherine had cut him down instantly.

Whatever the reason, in the weeks leading up to Christmas, she and Saxon saw each other no more than once a week, for polite conversation over dinner. There were no visits by Katherine to Saxon's Marble Arch home, no journeys back to Kate's Haven late at night, with her hair and makeup disarranged. From lovers, she and Saxon had metamorphosed into acquaintances.

Two weeks before the holidays, Saxon asked Katherine if she would be his guest at a Christmas Day dinner party given by Sir Donald Leslie. "I'd love to, John," she told him, "but Christmas is very special. The family gets together at my father's home." Despite the rejection, Saxon turned up at Kate's Haven on Christmas Eve with gifts to be placed beneath the tree.

Early Christmas morning, Raymond Barnhill called from New York to wish her a happy holiday. As a rule, he wrote, claiming he could express himself better on paper than through any other medium. A telephone call was something special, and Katherine, still snuggled up in bed, cradled the receiver to her ear.

"How's New York?"

"Damned cold."

"How's the Staten Island Ferry, the subway, and gigantic corned-beef sandwiches — all those wonderful glimpses of America you showed me? Not to mention the ones I found for myself, like television preachers and fanatical pro-lifers."

"All missing you. When are you coming over again?"

"I've no idea."

"Are you looking for a job yet? No, of course not — you don't have to worry about your next meal."

"Only if you're buying it."

"When you make fun of hot dogs and sauerkraut" — Barnhill impersonated John Wayne — "you're making fun of everything the United States of America stands for."

"You make me laugh."

"Your father's going to cry when the *Eagle* accounts office gets my next telephone bill."

"Let him cry. If an employer won't let you make personal telephone calls at Christmastime, then he's a rotten employer."

For a minute after the conversation ended, Katherine lay with the receiver pressed between the pillow and her ear. Damn, she missed Raymond Barnhill. Even more so now that she and Saxon were just friends.

Christmas Day followed the set routine. The five members of the household drove to Stanmore, where Roland and Sally Roberts waited. Gifts were exchanged, then the family sat down to enjoy Peg Parsons's traditional Christmas fare.

During the following week, Katherine took the children on the usual round of pantomimes and seasonal treats. They enjoyed themselves, but Katherine felt empty. She knew why. There was nothing special about the holidays for her. Without a job to return to, one day was much the same as the other.

After the children returned to school at the beginning of January, Katherine went to see Sally Roberts at the Eagle building. "I'd like a job, please."

Sally smiled triumphantly. "I told you that you'd be back. Are you looking for anything in particular?"

"What's open?"

"Feature writer on the *Eagle*'s color supplement. That's the only senior position available."

The color supplement, published every Wednesday, dealt with a mixed bag: the arts, leisure activities, real estate. "I'll take it," Katherine said, with barely a moment's hesitation.

Katherine began working the very next day, making the familiar journey each morning to the *Eagle*. It was harder than she remembered to find a parking space close to Chalk Farm Station, and the trains seemed less frequent and more crowded, but she was glad to be back. The *Eagle* was her home—the people there were family—and she'd been away for too long.

That evening, she telephoned Raymond Barnhill in New York to tell him they were coworkers. When he asked what she was doing, she replied, "Editing your 'Glimpses of America' columns."

There was a long pause from the other end, then Barnhill said, "Tell me you're joking. Please."

"I'm joking. I'm working on the color supplement."

Barnhill's sigh of relief was audible from three thousand miles away.

Two days later, Katherine received a bunch of red roses, ordered by Barnhill from New York, and an accompanying card that wished her luck.

At the end of the first week, she had one of her infrequent dinner dates with John Saxon. He arrived at Kate's Haven at six-thirty. When she went outside, Katherine's eyes sought the familiar Rolls Royce. Instead, she saw the sleek, powerful shape of an Aston Martin. "Bought a new toy for yourself?"

"Psychologists contend that it's a way of fending off approaching middle age. I thought I'd try it." He helped her in, settled himself behind the steering wheel, and started the engine. "Want to see how quickly she reaches a hundred?"

"Not really. I don't encourage people to break the law."

Over dinner, Katherine asked about William. "Surely you don't need a chauffeur to drive an Aston Martin?"

"He looks after the Rolls. I kept it."

"Two cars; I am impressed."

"Why? You own two cars."

"John, by no stretch of the imagination does a Porsche and a Jag equal an Aston Martin and a Rolls Royce. There's something particularly decadent about your combination."

"Perhaps that's because I am decadent."

When they left the restaurant, Saxon took the Aston Martin onto the motorway. His behavior until this moment gave Katherine no clue as to what would happen next. Twenty miles north of London, when traffic became sparse, Saxon slammed his foot down on the gas pedal. The speedometer needle rocketed from the legal seventy to one hundred and twenty.

"Slow down!" Katherine cried out. "You'll get us killed!"

497

Saxon's response was to increase the speed to one hundred and forty. "Don't tell me you're scared, Katherine."

She tore her gaze away from the white lane markings being gobbled up by the Aston Martin's headlights, and looked at Saxon. His face was taut with the concentration of keeping under control a car that was covering a mile every twenty-six seconds. His eyes were slits, his lips drawn back from gleaming teeth.

Katherine had to shout to make herself heard over the wind and road noise. "What is the matter with you, John Saxon?"

"I'm angry!" he shouted back.

"At what?"

"At myself. And at you. What went wrong, Katherine?"

"Stop driving like a maniac, and we'll talk about it!"

Saxon lifted his foot, and the Aston Martin slowed. Half a mile ahead was a service area. Saxon pulled into it, and killed the engine. "Is it that American you saw while you were in New York with me? Were you carrying on with him there? Or was it that business with Jeffrey? You said that it wouldn't affect us, but that's when you started to draw away from me."

"Maybe whatever there was between us had just about run its course." Katherine unfastened her seat belt and swung around to face Saxon. "John, when we first met, Franz was healthy. I brushed you off then, remember?"

"The large husband and the two small children. Of course I remember."

"When we met again, at the opening of your hotel out by Heathrow Airport, my situation was entirely different. Franz was crippled, and I was going crazy both at home and at work. I needed something—affection, sympathy, a shoulder to cry on. You provided all those things for me."

"I see. I filled a need. And now that you've got your

life all straight again, the need's no longer there, and I'm excess baggage. Is that what you're saying?"

"I was trying to make it sound less cold and cruel."

"You succeeded in sounding like a first-class bitch. Besides, I don't agree that we have run our course. I think we're as good for each other as we ever were."

He restarted the Aston Martin's engine and gave the gas pedal a couple of sharp jabs. Katherine touched his arm. "If you're planning on driving back the same way you drove out here, you can drop me off right now. I'll take my chances on thumbing a ride home."

"Don't worry." Back on the motorway, Saxon kept the speedometer needle fixed at the legal limit. Instead of driving to Kate's Haven, he headed right into town. When he pulled up outside his home in Marble Arch, he switched off the engine and swung around to face Katherine. "Would you like to come inside?"

"If I say no?"

"I'll take you home. And"—he gave a philosophical shrug of the shoulders—"perhaps I'll agree with you that we're all washed up. But I don't think you really believe that."

Katherine felt torn. Earlier, she had seen this as the night she finished with John Saxon. He had started out by making it so easy, tearing up the motorway in his new Aston Martin, shouting, even offering her reasons for the break-up. Now it was different. He was asking her to make the decision, a firm yes or no, and while her brain could form the words, her mouth was unable to speak them. Despite the denials of her mind, her body yearned for him.

"Well, Katherine?"

Instead of answering, she opened the passenger door, stepped out, and walked toward the house.

It was midnight when Saxon drove her home. Katherine sat contentedly, one hand resting on Saxon's shoulder, her fingers curling the ends of his hair. Out of the blue, she said, "How did you come to hire

499

William as your chauffeur?"

"Why do you ask that?"

"Deidre told me to."

"My ex-wife? When did you meet her?"

"On election night, two years ago. She telephoned me, and we met at the Spaniards. She'd seen our names linked in that gossip piece about Jeffrey's party, and she wanted to pour a pint of poison in my ear. She said, and I quote, that you were the biggest bastard ever to walk this earth."

Saxon chuckled, as though proud of the description. "Did you believe her?"

"Would I have just made love with you if I had done?"

"You could be the kind of woman who likes loving a bastard."

Katherine did not respond, because she suddenly had the unnerving thought that Saxon might be right. She searched for another topic, one that would take her mind off that particular doubt. "Tell me about William. Deidre made him sound far more interesting than I've ever found him to be. Without going into all the gory details, she said he did all your dirty jobs."

Saxon gave Katherine a querying glance, as though wondering exactly what she had been told. "When Deidre and I were married, I caught William trying to steal my car. He was broke and hungry, and I felt sorry for him. Instead of calling the police, I gave him work."

"That was very charitable of you."

"Deidre didn't think so. She wanted, and I quote, 'the despicable little swine locked up for the rest of his miserable life.' As for all the dirty jobs, he does whatever chauffeurs and general factotums normally do." He looked at Katherine again, trying to see how she was accepting the story. Her face gave no clue to her feelings. "Why did you never mention meeting Deidre before?"

"I didn't want to upset you."

"And now you don't mind?"

"I just feel we've found a different level tonight, John. A new, more open plane."

Saxon swung the Aston Martin into the forecourt of Kate's Haven. "Where do we go from here?"

"Can we leave things as they are, John?"

"Until when?"

"I don't know." She kissed him good night and entered the house. Everything had gone a little crazy tonight. She had thought, for an instant, that her limping relationship with John Saxon was coming to an end. Instead, they had revived it.

There was only one problem. For a moment, as she had lain in his arms, in her mind's eye she had seen Raymond Barnhill.

23

Raymond Barnhill wrote at least one letter a week to Katherine. She responded by telephoning him just as frequently, always happy to hear his voice, and glad to learn that he had finished the second book and was outlining the third. The poor reception encountered by the first book had not destroyed his enthusiasm.

In the middle of March, he was brought over to London by the *Eagle* for two days of meetings. He stayed at the Mayfair Hotel. The first night, he took Katherine out to eat. The second night, she invited him to Kate's Haven for a rack-of-lamb dinner. He came by taxi, bringing gifts for Henry and Joanne.

"Why don't you stay in England longer?" Katherine asked.

"I'd love to, but who's going to write the column? On top of that, I'll have the galleys for *Vietnam, the NCOs* to check soon. That book's scheduled to be out in the late summer. I'm also breaking my back to get ahead with the third book of the trilogy, about the enlisted men. That's supposed to be completed by the beginning of August. Why don't you" — he looked at Katherine, then the children — "all come over to the States this summer for a couple of weeks?"

"Can we, Mummy?" Henry and Joanne chorused.

Katherine spread her hands to show surrender. "Why not?" After dinner, when the children had gone to bed, Katherine and Barnhill went for a walk. Wrapped up warmly—Katherine in a sheepskin coat, and Barnhill in the ever-present lined Burberry—they strolled arm in arm. A bright, cold moon shone through the branches of the oak and horse chestnut trees that lined the avenue where Katherine lived.

"What happened at your meetings today?" Katherine asked.

"I signed a new contract for 'Glimpses of America.' That takes me through to the end of next year."

"You grew to really like it, didn't you?"

"It's a lot of fun, and it's a healthy contrast to books. I think a column like that needs a solid couple of years from one person before another writer can take it over." He paused for several seconds, before asking, "Did you mean what you said before, about coming over in the summer?"

"Of course. It'll be exciting for the children. The only glimpse of America they've had was Disneyland. Will you take off some time to show us around?"

"I'd be delighted to." He switched subjects suddenly. "How's your friend John Saxon?"

"As arrogant as ever," Katherine answered with a laugh.

"That's a good description. You still see him, though?"

"Once a week or so."

"May I ask why?"

"Because he makes me appreciate quiet, unassuming men like you." She stopped beneath a street light and looked at him. "Why have you never made a pass at me, Raymond?"

"I did once."

"When you were drunk? That wasn't a pass—that was a wild lunge and a grab."

"I thought it was a pass."

"Take my word for it, Raymond, it wasn't. Why didn't you make one during those few days in New York?"

Barnhill chewed his lip. "To begin with, I was too embarrassed and too mortified over that other time. I still am. I cringe whenever I think of it. And secondly, it isn't good strategy to make a pass at the boss's daughter."

"Even if she wants you to?"

"I thought you were well set up with Saxon in New York."

"He was well set up with his briefcase and his papers. He took me along, I suspect, as companion, an ornament for when he had a business dinner."

"Then why do you still see him?"

"You asked me that before."

"I know. This time I'd like a different answer."

"Because, for all his arrogance and his occasional insensitivity, John Saxon is a very hard habit to break."

At nine-thirty, Barnhill asked Katherine to telephone for a taxi to take him back to the Mayfair. He had one more meeting at the *Eagle* early in the morning, before catching an afternoon flight home.

"I'll drive you."

She parked the Porsche a couple of hundred yards from the Mayfair, and they walked the rest of the way. Two couples in evening dress passed them in the lobby, and Katherine noticed a sign giving information about the annual dinner and dance of something called the "B.O.B. Association."

"What do you think that is?" Barnhill asked. "A fraternal society for men named Bob?"

"I haven't the foggiest idea."

"Coming upstairs?"

"Yes. I think I should see what kind of accommodation Eagle Newspapers affords its foreign staff."

"In case it's too opulent? So you can make cuts once

you're on the board of Eagle Newspapers?"

She smiled at the thought of herself on the board. "Just the opposite, in fact. Journalists are the heart and soul of newspapers . . . we deserve the very best."

Once they entered the room, Katherine removed her sheepskin coat and sat on the edge of the bed, bouncing up and down. "Does it meet with your approval?" Barnhill asked.

"Come and test it with me."

The mattress sagged as Barnhill joined her. "I think we'd be doing the bed a favor if we sat in the middle, and not on the edge," Barnhill said, grinning broadly. "Is that a pass?"

"That is most definitely a pass." She moved a couple of inches closer, took one of Barnhill's hands and held it to her lips. His fingers were long and slim, flattening slightly at the tips. The nails were carefully filed, the cuticles pushed back to show white halfmoons. Katherine felt an involuntary shudder as she anticipated those fingers discovering her body.

She lay back on the bed, arms outstretched. He lowered himself until his face was an inch above hers. Katherine's mouth opened, her tongue drew a glistening circle across her own lips, then darted out to meet him.

"You taste of mint sauce," she said.

"It went well with the lamb."

"Mmmm . . . It's wonderful. Please, sir, may I have some more?" While Barnhill laughed, she clutched him tightly. Through their clothing, she could feel him digging into her. His long fingers worked at her dress. Her own hands slid beneath his shirt to caress a body that lacked a single ounce of spare flesh.

"Katherine, I think I've been in love with you from that day we first met, at the magistrates court."

"Show me," she whispered. "Show me just how much."

It was eleven-thirty when they returned downstairs.

The annual dinner of the B.O.B. Association had just finished. The lobby was full of men and women in evening dress, waiting for their cars to be brought to the front of the hotel.

"I'll walk you to your car," Barnhill said, "if we can get past all these men named Bob."

"Thanks. I don't want to let go of you just yet." She held his arm tightly, as if to emphasize her words. Making love with Barnhill had been a vastly different experience from making love with Saxon. No matter how much she had enjoyed her lovemaking with Saxon, she had always had the feeling that he was an athlete on display, a man justifiably proud of his prowess and determined to show it off to perfection. Barnhill possessed a tenderness that Saxon lacked.

"Katherine . . . !" a man's voice barked. "What a surprise to see you here."

She turned around to see a white-haired man with a slightly curling moustache, and a livid scar down his right cheek. Now she knew what the B.O.B. Association was: not a society for men called Bob, but a group of Battle of Britain veterans.

"Sir Donald, how nice to see you. You know Raymond Barnhill, don't you?"

"Yes, yes, of course I do, from your party. There are some people here you know as well. My guests for the association's annual bash. Always take a table, got to keep up the standards, eh?" He looked around, and Katherine tugged Barnhill's arm for them to escape. She knew the retired air vice marshal meant Jeffrey Dillard, and she had no wish to see him.

She was too late. Dillard appeared, with his wife, Shirley. Behind them came two more couples. One couple Katherine did not recognize. The second couple comprised John Saxon and a tall brunette in a shimmering gown of black and gold. They were holding hands and laughing, and then the woman kissed Saxon on the cheek with the fondness of long familiarity.

Katherine's eyes moved from the woman to Saxon. "Hello, John. Did you enjoy your dinner?"

He seemed surprised to see her, but he recovered quickly. "Yes, thank you." He turned his gaze to Barnhill. "I didn't realize you were back in the country."

Barnhill answered, "I'm a guest at the hotel."

"Really?" Saxon whispered something to the brunette, and a smile crossed her face. "Are they your own clothes you're wearing, or did you have to borrow some again?"

Barnhill tugged Katherine's arm. She could feel him shaking with barely suppressed fury. "I'll see you to your car."

From the corner of her eye, Katherine saw Saxon leave the woman in the black and gold dress and come after her. He caught up just as she and Barnhill stepped out into the street.

"Katherine, I want to talk to you."

Barnhill stepped between Katherine and Saxon. "She doesn't wish to talk to you."

"No one asked for your opinion, my friend."

"I am not your friend, and I am giving you my opinion whether you want it or not."

Katherine pushed her way past Barnhill. Two men fighting over a woman may have been fine in King Arthur's day, but not in Mayfair in 1981. "What do you want, John?"

"The woman I was with . . . I needed a date for tonight, and there was no point in asking you. Not with Jeffrey Dillard being at the same table as a guest of Sir Donald."

"You don't have to explain anything to me, John. You can do whatever you want. We're all adults, and we don't have to rationalize our actions to anyone." She turned around and walked to the car, with Barnhill one step behind. Saxon watched them for a few seconds before going back into the hotel.

"Are you all right?" Barnhill asked as Katherine settled into the Porsche.

"I'm fine. I'm not letting a scene like that upset me."

When Barnhill leaned over to kiss her good night, he said: "This is good-bye until you come to the States in the summer. Can't you make it before then?"

"I'm one of the slaves of Eagle Newspapers, just like you. I can't take time off whenever I feel like it."

"You could."

"But I won't, and you know the reason why."

Barnhill nodded. "Yes, I know. You've got to work twice as hard to prove you're half as good as anyone else on the paper." He stood up, hands in his raincoat pockets. "I'll stroll around the block. I don't want to meet our friend again, because I have the overwhelming desire to punch him in the mouth."

Katherine gave the lightest beep of the horn as she passed, and he blew her a kiss.

All the way home, she thought about the woman on Saxon's arm. There had been an intimacy between them that spoke of more than just a convenient dinner date. Had Saxon been sleeping with this woman while he had been seeing Katherine? For two months after the showdown with Dillard, their affair had been platonic. Then Saxon had talked his way back into Katherine's affections, and talked her into his bed. Had he been making love to this woman at the same time?

Saxon telephoned her at the *Eagle* the following morning. "About last night, Katherine . . ."

"John, you don't have to explain a thing. I told you two months ago that our relationship had run its course. I was right. Let's just call it quits, and leave it at that."

"That's not what I want at all."

"What is it, John? Pride? Is pride not letting you accept that it's over?"

"What do you mean?"

"Your ego's so big that you believe a relationship's not over unless you say it is. You can't accept anyone else telling you." While he pondered that, she hung up.

He made three more calls to her that morning. The first two times, she asked again why he couldn't understand that it was finished. The third time, she lost her temper. "John, I don't want to see you! Can't you get that through your arrogant, conceited head?"

This time the message got through. Saxon did not telephone again. And Katherine was pleasantly surprised to find that he had not been as hard a habit to break as she had thought.

The weekly letters and telephone calls between Katherine and Barnhill continued. He sent her a copy of the cover of the new book. She thought it was very similar to the first one, except that the figure superimposed over the montage of war photographs was a sergeant in fatigues, instead of an officer in dress blues.

In the last two weeks of August, with two excited children in tow, Katherine boarded a British Airways flight for New York. Barnhill met them at the airport, and took them out for dinner that night. It was a celebration dinner, he explained; days earlier, he had delivered the manuscript for the third book to his publisher.

The following morning, Katherine hired a car, and began a tour of the Northeast with Henry and Joanne, starting and ending with boat rides — from the *Maid of the Mist* beneath Niagara Falls, to a Circle Line trip around Manhattan. The only complaint came from Henry, who kept asking when they were going to see a cowboy; he had to be satisfied in the end with the promise to visit a dude ranch on his next trip to America.

The second week, they were joined by Raymond Barnhill, who guided them across the Middle Atlantic states, from the District of Columbia, through Virginia and the Carolinas, to Savannah. At night, Katherine stayed in one hotel suite with the children, while Barnhill slept next door. Only when she was convinced that the children were asleep did she pass through the communicating door to where Barnhill waited.

Barnhill was more familiar with the South than any tour guide, keeping Katherine and the children interested with stories about the sites they passed. Katherine was amused at how his accent deepened the farther south they went.

On the return journey to New York, Barnhill drove through the small South Carolina town where he'd been born and raised. It was little more than a handful of shops and gas stations, a couple of churches, a few dozen houses, and a scattering of rusty barns on the farms that spread out from the town. Barnhill's parents were dead. He had no family or friends in the town, and he did not stop.

The car was silent. The children, sitting in the back, stared through the windows at farmland. Katherine could sense the emotional turmoil this dot on the map caused Barnhill. She tried to help him over it. "You've come a long way, Raymond. All the way from nowhere to somewhere."

"How do you know when you've reached somewhere?"

"That's easy. When you see the friends you've made, the life you've created, the accomplishments you've achieved."

Taking a hand off the steering wheel, Barnhill placed it on Katherine's arm. "If that's what it takes, I guess I have made it to somewhere. Thanks."

"You're welcome."

On the day Katherine and the children left New

York for London, Barnhill received copies of *Vietnam, the NCOs*. He gave one to Katherine. The biography on the inside flap now had him listed as writing the "Glimpses of America" column for London's *Daily Eagle*.

The parting at Kennedy Airport was emotional. The children had grown attached to Barnhill. Joanne even clung to his legs, claiming that she wanted to stay in America. Katherine, also, had to fight back tears. What distressed her most was the new contract Barnhill had signed with the *Eagle*. Until the end of 1982 . . . that was sixteen months in the future!

"Will you come to London for Christmas?" Katherine asked Barnhill, as they prepared to say good-bye.

"Do you want me to bring the turkey?"

"Just bring yourself." She threw her arms around his neck and hugged him tightly. "Thank you for a wonderful time. You keep writing, and I'll keep telephoning."

The British Airways 747 took off on time. Once dinner was served, the children fell asleep. Katherine watched the in-flight movie before turning to Barnhill's book. She read it right through, thinking it was a clone of the first book—too much character analysis, and not enough plot or action. The NCOs in the second book were interchangeable with the officers in the first. There were those who blindly followed orders, and those who questioned. She considered *Vietnam, the NCOs* apologist in tone, just as its predecessor had been, as though the author was using it as a vehicle to express his anguish for ever having been to Vietnam. When she put the book down, just as the first streaks of dawn showed through the cabin window, she felt very disappointed.

She did not pass on her feelings to Barnhill when she next spoke to him. She just hoped she might be wrong, and the book would be successful despite her misgiv-

511

ings.

For a month, there was nothing to indicate in Barnhill's letters that Katherine's view was shared. He wrote that he had seen the book in shops, and early reviews had been promising. Then, on the first Monday in October, Barnhill telephoned Katherine at home.

She knew it was trouble the instant she recognized his voice. He sounded stunned as he told Katherine of the letter he had received that morning from Knight and Robbins, his publishers. "They said that *Vietnam, the Officers* was a commercial flop, and they're claiming that the second book's showing every sign of following suit. They've returned the manuscript for the third book on the grounds that it's unsatisfactory, and I should feel free to approach other publishers with the work, as the contract is now canceled."

Katherine sucked in her breath. That was a body blow, to Barnhill and herself. There was no point now in telling him that she hadn't thought much of the second book. He wanted support, not more criticism, even if it was constructive.

"What are you going to do?"

"Now? Throw the manuscript down the incinerator."

She did not know whether he was joking or being serious. "Don't you dare!"

"What should I do with it, then?"

"Send it to me. Airmail express. Let me have a look."

He did not ask why. He just said, "Watch your mailbox."

The manuscript arrived four days later. Katherine started to read it that evening, after dinner. Sitting cross-legged on her bed, she flipped through the first hundred pages, then reached for the telephone.

"Raymond, I've read a hundred pages. I don't need to read any more to know what's wrong with it."

Barnhill, in the middle of writing his column for the *Eagle,* reacted strongly. "What do you mean—wrong with it?"

Katherine took a deep breath. "Your publishers sent it back, so there can't be much right with it, can there?"

"Go on." Barnhill's voice was like ice.

"Vietnam finished six years ago, Raymond, and you're still apologizing for it. When I read the first book, about the officers, I thought it was fair to have some of the younger men questioning their government's policy. When I read the second book, about the noncommissioned officers, I felt I was reading the same book again, only you'd changed the names and ranks. And now this! You've got privates, most of whom are conscripts—"

"Draftees."

"Whatever . . . but they're still suffering from the same angst, still wondering why they're in Vietnam, still saying that they have no business there. My God, Raymond, you haven't written a trilogy. You've written ten one book and given it three different titles."

"But that's the way I felt."

"Don't you see? Your own feelings were important enough to be included in only one book. Now do something else." She stared at the manuscript, thinking. "The way you're writing it, the Americans in Vietnam were about the most pitiful excuse for a military force that ever existed. Surely there was some fighting instinct . . . what's that phrase . . . ?"

"Gung ho?"

"That's it. Surely there were some gung ho soldiers who felt proud enough, or crazy enough, to give a good account of themselves. Weren't there any men who said, 'While we're in this damned hellhole, let's do all we can to win this war'?"

"But it wasn't winnable."

"To you, perhaps. But to other men it might have

been. At least, their own little war, their own battle, their own piece of the front line, might have been winnable. Let's hear about them, Raymond, because I think America is just about ready to stop listening to apologies for Vietnam."

Katherine heard the rustle of pages turning. "You know, you might have something."

"I might?"

"Okay, you do have something. Satisfied? What'll we call it? *Vietnam, the Enlisted Men* is all finished with as a title now, I guess."

"Why not use a military term? *Brigade, regiment,* something like that?"

"Too big. Vietnam was a war of small units. A title, come on, damn it! A title!" Katherine could hear him becoming excited over the new idea. "Company? No. What about squad? That's it! I'll call it *The Squad.* Draftees, furious at being in Vietnam in the first place . . . a bunch of reprobates, and they come home as heroes. Those who come home, anyway. Katherine, if you were here right now, I'd hug you so tightly you wouldn't be able to breathe. *The Squad!* You're a genius."

"Not me, Raymond. You did it all by yourself."

"I did?" He sounded surprised, then pleased. "I did, didn't I? But I'd still hug you if you were here."

"Save it until you come over at Christmastime. And I expect you to bring whatever you've done with you."

"You won't have to wait until then. I'll mail you pages every week."

Barnhill kept his promise. At the end of October, the first seventy-five pages arrived in a large brown envelope, accompanied by a note that read, "Find an apologist — show me someone suffering from angst — anywhere in these pages!"

Katherine could not. Barnhill had invented as wild a

group of characters as she had ever seen in a book. *The Squad* was nowhere near as literate or sensitive as his previous two novels, but its commercial appeal seemed far greater.

Another fifty pages followed quickly, and Katherine could picture Barnhill sitting at his desk, the sheets just flying out of the typewriter. She would bet that he was having far more fun writing this than the other two.

Barnhill arrived in London on the morning of Christmas Eve. As he cleared customs, he saw Katherine leaning over the barrier. Not caring who saw, he rushed over to her and kissed her.

"You look marvelous!" he exclaimed. "Even better than when I last saw you."

"You as well." There was a gleam in his eyes. Katherine hoped it was because of her, but she wouldn't mind if some of it was due to the new book. She was a part of that as well.

"What's happening with *The Squad?*" Katherine asked as she drove away from the airport.

"I sent a few chapters and the outline last week to an agent who specializes in suspense and war novels. Now I've got to wait and see if he wants to represent me."

"He will," Katherine said. She stopped at a traffic light, drumming her fingertips on the steering wheel while she waited for the green. "What do you want to do today?"

"I'd like to go shopping. I've been working so hard on *The Squad,* I didn't get time to pick up anything for the kids."

They spent the afternoon battling the crowds of last-minute shoppers in the West End. "My God!" Barnhill exclaimed, as he and Katherine staggered out of Hamleys toy store on Regent Street. "I'd forgotten how rude Londoners can be. They're even worse than those monsters in New York."

"Nonsense!" Katherine told him, ready to defend

her town. "The British have bonier elbows, that's all. Comes from having less to eat than New Yorkers."

They ate dinner at Kate's Haven. Later, when Henry and Joanne had gone to bed, Katherine and Barnhill set gifts beneath the Christmas tree which Jimmy Phillips had erected in the front room. When they finished, Phillips and Edna added their own gifts to the pile. The housekeeper had expressed pleasure when Katherine had told her that Barnhill would be a guest for the Christmas week. A house the size of Kate's Haven needed lots of people, otherwise it was in danger of becoming an echo chamber.

At eleven o'clock, after Edna and Phillips had retired to their self-contained flat on the top floor, Katherine saw Barnhill to the door of the guest bedroom. "Should you need anything during the night, Raymond, my room's there." She pointed across the wide hall. "Can you remember that?"

"I think so."

"Good." She kissed him quickly, then again, more slowly. "Sleep well."

"I'm three-quarters of the way there already."

"I should warn you. My children are notoriously early risers, especially on Christmas morning. I hope they don't disturb you." She stayed for one more lingering kiss before going to her own room.

The kisses lit a slow fire within her. She lay in bed, anticipating the sound at her door. When half an hour had passed, she grew impatient. Throwing a robe over her satin nightdress, she crossed the hall to the guest bedroom. The door swung back quietly. Moonlight covering the queen-sized bed showed Barnhill to be asleep.

Katherine hesitated. What if one of the children chose this moment to wake up and wander into the hall? She backed away from the guest room, and looked first into Henry's room, then Joanne's. Both children slept soundly. She returned to the guest room.

This time, she walked straight in, dropped her robe and nightdress onto the carpet, and slid beneath the quilt that covered Barnhill.

He woke up when Katherine's fingernails teased his flat stomach. "I thought you might be lonely," she whispered.

"You're a very considerate hostess."

"I hope you're an appreciative guest."

He laughed. She killed the sound by kissing him. Hungry for each other, they made love quickly. Afterward, Katherine rested her head on Barnhill's chest, listening to his steady heartbeat.

"Don't let me fall asleep, Raymond. I have to get back to my own room."

"There's time." He ran fingers through her long blond hair. "Plenty of time."

Katherine's eyes began to close. Twice she snapped them open, each time asking, "Are you awake, Raymond?"

"Awake, and alert."

A third time she let her eyelids drop. When she opened them again, the moonlight had gone. The sky was a dirty gray, and the sharp and happy sound of children's voices rang throughout the house. Barnhill's wristwatch, sitting on the edge of the bedside table, read six-forty.

"Damn!" Katherine sat up, throwing back the quilt. Barnhill was still asleep. She slapped his chest. "Wake up!"

"What is it?"

"You let me sleep. Now everyone's up. How on earth do I get back to my own room?"

"Check that the coast is clear, then make a dash for it."

After putting on her nightdress and robe, she cracked open the door. "It's clear."

"Move out!"

Taking a deep breath, Katherine opened the door

wide and stepped out into the hall. As she did so, Joanne came flying up the stairs, chased by Henry. Behind them, trying valiantly to preserve the early-morning peace and quiet, was Edna. Katherine, half in and half out of the guest bedroom, turned to stone.

Seeing their mother, the children stopped. Edna summed up the situation in an instant. "Good morning, Mrs. Kassler. Did you find out if Mr. Barnhill prefers tea or coffee with his breakfast?"

"Coffee," Katherine answered as she closed the door to the guest room. "Americans don't drink tea." She crossed the hall to her own room, closed the door and leaned against it. She could kiss Edna. The housekeeper was worth her considerable weight in gold.

Following tradition, the family traveled to Roland Eagles's home for Christmas lunch; this year, the group included Barnhill. Sally Roberts was also there, and much of the conversation centered on the work Barnhill had done for the *Eagle*. As the day drew to a close, Roland extended an invitation to Barnhill.

"Would you and Katherine care to join Sally and me for dinner tomorrow night? A club I belong to in Mount Street. Kendall's. They have a particularly fine restaurant."

"Thank you, sir. That sounds very nice."

"Afterward, perhaps, we'll have time to play the tables."

Barnhill made no response to that suggestion.

On the way home, Katherine asked Barnhill if he realized he was being tested. "My father has his own aptitude and character tests. They concern how people gamble."

"In that case, I'll be a major disappointment to him."

Katherine found out what Barnhill meant the following evening at Kendall's. After dinner, Roland inclined his head toward a blackjack table. "Care to try your luck, Raymond?"

518

"No, thank you, sir."

"No?" Roland appeared startled. He was unaccustomed to his invitation being rejected. "Why on earth not?"

"I don't make so much money that I can afford to fritter it away on games of chance. Even if I did, I would rather donate it to charity than risk losing it on the turn of a card."

Sally, sitting on Barnhill's right, clapped her hands loudly, crying, "Well said! Now where does that put all your ridiculous theories about gambling and life, Roland Eagles?"

Roland wasn't through yet. "Call it a gambler's silly superstition, Raymond, but I hate to play alone. I'll stake you. Just play alongside me."

"No, thank you, sir. I do not play."

"But you gave Katherine a slot machine as a present once," Roland protested.

"That was a gag, sir. Your daughter suffered from certain misconceptions about the United States, and I was merely accommodating her."

"Would you do me one favor?" Roland asked. "Stop calling me 'sir'. It makes me feel very, very old. You wouldn't mind, I take it, if I tried my luck?"

"Not at all. Your money is your own, to use wisely or to waste as you wish."

While Roland played blackjack, Sally said to Barnhill, "You've impressed him more by refusing to gamble than you could ever have done by winning."

Sally was correct. Watching the cards being dealt, Roland felt nothing but admiration for Raymond Barnhill. The American held strong convictions from which he refused to be swayed. Even to humor his employer.

In the days before the new year, Barnhill joined Katherine and the children on visits to circuses and pantomimes, Disney movies and ice spectaculars. Joanne, captivated by the stream of entertainment, was

519

too busy enjoying herself to ask any questions. But Henry, at ten, two years wiser than his sister, needed explanations for the changes he had witnessed in his mother's life. He wanted to know why Uncle John had not come to the house for so long.

"Aren't you friends with him anymore?" Henry pressed.

"We're just interested in different things, darling."

"What about Raymond?"

"Raymond?" Katherine wished that Barnhill had not been so informal with Henry and Joanne during the previous summer's vacation. Claiming to dislike honorary titles, he had told the children from the start to call him Raymond. They had been thrilled to do so, even if their mother hadn't been certain at the time that she liked such familiarity. Now it was too late to change. "Raymond and I are interested in similar things."

"You mean newspapers and writing?"

"That's right, Henry." Katherine hid a smile from her son. "Newspapers and writing."

Barnhill flew back to New York on New Year's Day. A week later, he was on the telephone, voice brimming with excitement. "That agent I sent *The Squad* to . . . he just called me. He read the stuff I sent him and he wants to handle it for me."

"When will you know anything?"

"He wants a few more chapters before he shows it around. What do you think I should put in the dedication?"

"Never mind the dedication. Write the book."

"How about 'For Katherine, the prettiest Kate in Christendom'?"

Katherine laughed.

Barnhill sounded annoyed. "Hey, I think that deserves something better than a hearty guffaw. I was being poetic, showing off my Shakespeare."

"I know it's Shakespeare. *The Taming of the Shrew.*

520

I'm laughing at the coincidence, that's all. My mother's name was Catarina, and the morning after my father met her, he sent her a bunch of roses with those words on the card."

Knowing the tragic story, Barnhill said, "Perhaps the Bard isn't so appropriate. I'll come up with something else."

"The Bard is very appropriate, and I think it's a beautiful dedication. Thank you. But remember what I said—get the book written before you worry about anything else."

Barnhill worked at it. Each week, more pages came through Katherine's mailbox, and each time she spoke to him, they discussed how the latest scenes could be improved. By the middle of February, Barnhill had written almost half of *The Squad*, enough for the agent to show around.

"He's sent it out to nine publishers," Barnhill told Katherine. "Those who are interested will have the opportunity to bid in an auction on the last day of March."

"Are you nervous?"

"Petrified. What if no one bids?"

"Don't be such a pessimist. Do you think the agent would waste his time and effort unless he thought he could make some money out of it?"

"He could be crazy . . . New York's full of crazy people."

Beneath the banter, Katherine could feel Barnhill's anxiety. The disaster of the last two books was haunting him, and the next six weeks, especially the actual time of the auction, would be pure hell for him. Katherine made up her mind to help.

"Raymond, I can take a few days off at the end of March. Would you like me to come over?"

"Would you?" He sounded like he'd just been offered the keys to Fort Knox.

"Of course."

521

The auction was set for a Wednesday. Katherine flew out on the Monday, with a homeward reservation for the Thursday evening, April 1. She carried an assortment of reading material that included the latest pages of *The Squad,* which had arrived two days earlier, and a copy of the *Eagle.* She put the newspaper down within a couple of minutes, depressed by the front-page news of saber-rattling between Britain and Argentina over the Falkland Islands. She hoped it was just press talk to sell more papers.

Barnhill met her at the airport and took her to the Carlyle. They went out for dinner that night to the Four Seasons. Barnhill just pecked at his food, and Katherine could see the tension working on him. By Wednesday, the date of the auction, he would be a nervous wreck, either ready to jump clear over the moon, or dig himself a hole into which to crawl.

On Tuesday, Barnhill was even more agitated. Katherine spent the entire day with him, constantly trying to find new things to do. They visited the zoo, and in the evening they saw a movie.

Wednesday, auction day, was pure murder. When Katherine arrived at the apartment at ten o'clock, Barnhill was standing by the telephone, ready to spring the moment it rang.

"As well as driving yourself crazy, Raymond, you're driving me mad. Will you just relax? The agent will contact you when he has some news."

Barnhill didn't move.

Katherine left the apartment. When she returned twenty minutes later, she was carrying a game of Scrabble. "Sit down and play," she ordered Barnhill.

The game of Scrabble occupied Barnhill's interest until lunchtime. After turning on the answering machine, they went out for lunch, walking from the apartment to a busy Italian restaurant on Seventh

522

Avenue, close to Central Park. A man at another table was reading a newspaper while he ate. The headline caught Katherine's eye: "War Imminent over Falklands."

They returned to the apartment at two-thirty. The light on the answering machine was flashing. Barnhill replayed the tape. There had been two calls: a hangup, and a message from Lawrie Stimkin, of all people, asking for a story on American reaction to the growing tension in the South Atlantic. Barnhill went back to watching the telephone, and Katherine could do nothing but watch Barnhill.

The telephone rang three times during the afternoon. Barnhill got rid of each caller as quickly as possible; he didn't even bother telling Katherine who it was.

At four-thirty, Katherine suggested he call the agent.

"And show him just how nervous I am?"

"What's wrong with that? If he knows you're really anxious, he might work harder and push some of the fence-sitters into action."

"Katherine, maybe no one's sitting on the fence."

She almost told him not to be so bloody pessimistic. Instead, she phrased it differently. "You know, if you ever want to write about a real down-in-the-mouth worry wart, you can base the character on yourself."

That drew a rare laugh from Barnhill.

At five o'clock, the telephone rang again. By this time, nervous energy had deserted Barnhill. There was fatigue in his voice as he answered. He listened, spoke a few words, then listened again. When he replaced the receiver and turned toward Katherine, his face was expressionless.

"That was the agent."

"And . . . ?" Katherine feared the worst.

"You're going to have a dedication in a hundred-thousand-dollar book. That's what *The Squad* sold

523

for. One hundred thousand dollars."

The news took time to sink in. "Raymond, it would mean just as much if you gave me the dedication in a book of stamps."

"I know," he said, and reached out his arms to hug her. "That's one of things I love about you."

By the following day, as Katherine prepared to return to London, the storm clouds gathering over the South Atlantic had grown blacker. Barnhill used the situation to try to persuade Katherine to stay on in New York.

"Your country's going to be at war with Argentina in a few days. Why go back to a country at war? Bring Henry and Joanne over here."

"There won't be any trouble over the Falklands. It's just rhetoric. President Galtieri has a mess of trouble at home, so he's distracting his people by reviving the age-old controversy over ownership of the Falklands. Cooler heads will prevail."

"The cooler heads will be British, like yours. I'm afraid they won't be Argentinian."

Katherine flashed a triumphant smile. "You're forgetting that my mother came from there. I'm half Argentine."

"Do you have any family over there?"

"No. My grandfather, the old ambassador, and my grandmother are both dead. My mother had an older brother, but I know nothing about him."

"So you really won't feel too upset if the Brits have to kick a few Argentinian butts."

"I'll feel very upset. Most wars are senseless, and the Falklands seems a pitiful reason to fight."

That evening, when Barnhill escorted her to Kennedy Airport, the air of impending trouble was even more apparent. The British Airways terminal, normally a hive of activity, was strangely silent. Katherine found a copy of that morning's *Eagle,* which a passenger had brought over on the earlier west-bound flight. The headlines were ominous. Britain was to request action by the United Nations Security Council to restrain Argentina from any aggressive action aimed at the Falkland Islands; simultaneously, Argentina was seeking support from the Organization of American States. Inside, on the *Eagle*'s opinion page, was a plea for patience and moderation. Katherine saw her father's hand there.

"I really wish you weren't going back," Barnhill said.

"Stop worrying. The Falklands are eight thousand miles from Britain. I promise you that the moment an Argentine plane flies over Kate's Haven, I'll come right back with Henry and Joanne."

Despite his concern, Barnhill smiled.

When the flight was called, they kissed good-bye. "Thanks for coming over and holding my hand."

"Thank you for the dedication in a hundred-thousand-dollar book."

"I'm going to write to you every day."

"Save some of those written words for the book. You haven't finished it yet." She wrapped her arms around him and held on tightly, suddenly afraid to let go.

"Give the kids a hug for me."

"I will." At last, she released him. "Go back to your book. Just because I'm not here, it doesn't mean you can slack off." She passed through the gate, turned once to wave, and carried on toward the aircraft.

The next day, while Katherine's body caught up to English time, Barnhill's bleak scenario came true. A huge Argentine force seized the Falkland Islands, South Georgia, and the South Sandwich Islands. The Royal Navy prepared to regain the dependencies. And in the war fever that swept Britain, Roland Eagles's pleas for moderation were to make him a marked man.

24

Roland Eagles had never visited Argentina, nor was he enamored with the military junta that gripped its populace in a fist of iron. Despite that, he possessed a certain warmth of feeling toward the South American country, which had, quite suddenly, become the enemy of his own. His beloved Catarina had come from Argentina, brought to England as an eighteen-year-old girl by her father, the Ambassador to the Court of St. James's. Because of the blissful year he had spent with her, and the daughter she had given him as a tangible memory of their love, Roland was prepared to regard the country of her birth with more tolerance than the average Englishman.

When news of the invasion flashed across the world, Roland's initial feeling was not anger, but disappointment. He understood that the junta was seeking to quell domestic strife by focusing attention on the popular Falklands (or Malvinas, as the Argentines called them) issue. British intelligence appeared to have been taken woefully by surprise, and the handful of Royal Marines garrisoned on the Falklands had been no match for the force Argentina threw at them. If anything, Roland believed that the fault lay almost as much with Britain as it did with Argentina. The thief had made off with the valuables only because the householder had left the door wide open. If you were going to claim some barren rocks eight thousand miles away, right on the enemy's doorstep, at least protect them adequately.

That was the tone of the *Eagle*'s leader on the day after the invasion. Calmness, read the final paragraph, was needed now. A death-before-dishonor attitude would serve no purpose, except to make widows out of young women in both Britain and Argentina. The problem should be solved not through force of arms, but through negotiation.

When most of the country was demanding a military strike that would teach Argentina a lesson it would never forget, the *Eagle*'s message was not popular. Thousands of letters poured into the newspaper. For every one that agreed with the *Eagle*'s stand, twenty disagreed. Many people wrote that they would no longer buy the *Eagle*. Some queried the patriotism of a newspaper owner who could allow such anti-British drivel to appear in his publication. One retired colonel even offered to start a fund for buying Roland a one-way ticket to Buenos Aires, where he obviously belonged.

Roland showed Katherine what he considered the cream of the crop. "Aren't you frightened?" she asked him, after reading just a couple.

"Why should I be? Letters can't harm me. We'll publish the ones that argue cogently against our position. I was even thinking of replying to some of the really abusive ones. Writing M.C. after my name, to show I'm a holder of the Military Cross."

"I don't think it would carry much weight, Daddy. Some of the letter-writers sound like the very men you won your medals fighting. How damaging is all this to Eagle Newspapers?"

"We'll lose a few customers, that's all. Unpopularity is sometimes the price you have to pay for being right."

Katherine glanced at another letter, one that labeled the *Eagle* staff as traitors, and was illustrated with a drawing of a hangman's noose. It all she could do to suppress a shudder. The fleet was little more than a week out of port, and Britain had declared a two-hundred mile war zone around the Falklands. If her father was getting hate mail like this when nothing had really happened yet, what would he receive when the bullets and bombs, heaven forbid, started to fly?

When Raymond Barnhill saw the letters in the *Eagle,* he telephoned Katherine immediately. "Were those the letters that were fit to print? If so, I can just imagine what garbage was in the rest."

She tried to calm him. "Raymond, I really appreciate your concern, but there's no need to worry. I still say this is going to blow itself out before any real damage is done."

"Do you really?" he asked sarcastically. "Argentina has backed itself into a corner from which it can't escape. Two days ago, the Brits retook the Port of Grytviken on South Georgia, and yesterday Margaret Thatcher told the Commons that further combat appears inevitable. On top of that, the Argies suggested Alexander Haig go jump in the lake, and take his ideas for a peaceful solution with him. And you think it's going to blow over before real damage is done? Katherine, it won't be long before Britain launches a full-scale offensive on the remaining territories. Then you're going to have an all-out war on your hands, and the *Eagle*'s moderate position will make it the target for every flag-waving lunatic with a grudge."

Frightened by such a scenario, Katherine tried to dismiss it with humor. "Will you fly over to protect me?"

"I'd rather you came here. Bring the kids until this mess is resolved."

"And leave my father to face trouble on his own? Never."

Bullets and bombs began to fly in earnest four days later. Carrier-based British planes attacked Argentine airstrips on the Falklands, and at sea each side claimed hits on the other's ships. Theaters and restaurants in the West End of London were empty — unheard-of for a Saturday night — as anxious people stayed at home, waiting for the latest reports.

The first decisive blow was struck when a British submarine sunk the Argentine cruiser *General Belgrano,* inflicting heavy loss of life. While most of the country cheered the event with the enthusiasm of a sports crowd, the *Eagle*'s opinion page lamented the hundreds of fatalities, and questioned the wisdom of the sinking. "Before *Belgrano,*" ran the editorial comment, "there was still the possibility, no matter how remote, of a negotiated settlement. Now, Argentina will make certain that any solution costs British blood and British lives."

The statement proved to be an uncanny forecast. Two days later, front pages of newspapers across the world carried the picture of the Royal Navy destroyer H.M.S. *Sheffield* being struck by an Exocet missile. Blood had now been drawn on both sides, and the only thing left was a bitter fight to the death.

Two days after the Sheffield incident, Sally Roberts invited Katherine to lunch. Erica Bentley was also present, and Katherine soon learned the reason why.

"You've been working on the color magazine for more than a year," Sally said. "Would you like to do something different?"

"Such as?"

"How about doing some work for me?" Erica asked. "An assignment that you're particularly qualified to handle."

"Erica wants to run a series on the women left behind by the war," Sally said. "The wives who wait and pray for their men to come home, and especially those who now understand that all the waiting and praying in the world won't help."

"Young widow interviewing other young widows?"

"Precisely."

Katherine began the assignment early the following morning, driving to the naval town of Portsmouth with Sid Hall, her favorite *Eagle* photographer. By midafternoon, they were back at Fleet Street without a story.

"I spoke to some navy public affairs officer," Katherine told Sally. "The instant I identified myself, I was given a stiff lecture on being associated with a newspaper that provides aid and comfort to the enemy, and then Sid and I were escorted out. The *Eagle*'s absolute poison to those people."

"I'd have thought someone with your experience would have talked her way around any obstacles."

"I had the distinct feeling that if Sid and I had stayed to argue the point, we'd have ended up swinging from the yardarm." Katherine dropped into one of the chairs facing the desk. "Sally, I'm worried about my father. Do you think he's taken his stand on the war too far?"

Sally took her time answering, as though she, too, had pondered the same question. "Katherine, every editorial comment in the *Eagle* about the Falklands has been prompted by what your father believes is best for this country. He wanted to see the problem resolved without anyone being killed. So did I. So did anyone with an ounce of brains. Unfortunately, when wartime hysteria runs riot, as it is doing, a single voice of sanity all too often becomes confused with enemy propaganda. Right now, the *Eagle*'s banner might just as well be the Argentine flag. It's a crying shame, because all your father wants to do is avoid bloodshed."

Over the next few days, Katherine saw more evidence of the *Eagle*'s low standing. On one instance, she passed a shop that sold televisions. Display units in the front window were turned on, and a small crowd had gathered to learn the latest news from the war zone. Katherine stopped to watch. A ragged cheer went up at the report of the sinking of an Argentine ship by a British frigate in the waters between the East and West Falklands. As the cheer died away, Katherine heard a woman say: "Too bad someone doesn't drop a bomb on the bloody *Eagle!* Our boys are dying out there, and all those swine can say is that they've got no business being there!"

Face burning, Katherine turned and walked away. There was no point arguing with the woman, explaining that the *Eagle* had been trying to avoid casualties, not cause them. Logic and truth would be wasted on a lynch mob.

Katherine quickly learned that the lynch-mob mentality went far beyond the man in the street. In the House of Commons, a motion was put forward to censure the *Eagle* for activities prejudicial to the country's welfare. The motion was proposed and seconded by two Conservative Members of Parliament. The men belonged to a right-wing clique that had advocated the bombing of Buenos Aires; they were also the two MPs Katherine had met at John Saxon's home, Daniel Cooper and Edwin Johnson.

The instant Katherine learned of the censure motion, she telephoned Saxon at his office in St. James's Square. They had not seen or spoken to each other for more than a year. She did not ask how he was, or what he had been doing. She just blasted him. "Who the hell do your friends think they are to stand up in Parliament and accuse my father of treason?"

"I didn't read of that word being used."

"How else would you define 'activities prejudicial to the country's welfare'?"

"Daniel and Edwin might ask who your father thinks he is to use his newspaper to question the actions of the government in a time of national crisis."

"My father is entitled to criticize. We're living in a free country. At least, we were the last time I looked."

There was a lengthy pause. Katherine wondered if Saxon had hung up, until he said, "You're right, Katherine, we do live in a free country. And the laws that permit your father to criticize elected officials give those same officials the right to question your father's motives."

"For God's sake, John, the *Eagle* wept far more editorial tears for the *Sheffield* than it did for the *Belgrano*. My father was never trying to aid the enemy. He was trying to stop blood being spilled. He was trying to point out that war is not an acceptable means of solving problems."

Katherine's arguments scratched Saxon's smooth veneer. His voice turned sharp with anger and impatience. "Why can't you understand, Katherine, that when the country is at war, any show of understanding toward the enemy is liable to be treated as high treason? Maybe it's about time your father stopped worrying about his principles, and started worrying about his family."

"What does that mean?" The question was redundant, because Raymond Barnhill had already given her the answer. They would all be the target for every flag-waving lunatic with a grudge!

"See if you can get your father to publish a statement of support for the government, Katherine. Persuade him to get off his high horse before his obstinacy endangers himself and everyone around him."

"I happen to like my father's obstinacy, John Saxon. I think it's one of his most admirable traits!" She slammed down the receiver. Saxon was no different from his friends in Parliament, a staunch nationalist who viewed every slight to Britain as a personal insult, and every person who made such a slight as a traitor.

Still, Katherine told herself, she'd known that all along. Why should she be so surprised by it now?

The flood of letters protesting the *Eagle*'s antiwar position, the navy's refusal to cooperate with Katherine, and, finally, the attack on the *Eagle* in Parliament, were little more than heralds of the trouble that was to come.

On the night of May 13, as British troops expanded the beachhead they had gained two days earlier on East Falkland Island, another army was active. Eight thousand miles away, its soldiers moved unnoticed through London, advancing, stopping, advancing again. With the gray light of dawn, Londoners caught their first view of this phantom army's achievements.

"Mrs. Kassler, take a look at this!" Jimmy Phillips entered Kate's Haven clutching a piece of paper in his hand. "I took the Jag to the garage to fill her up, and I saw this stuck on a telephone pole."

Katherine, having her early morning cup of tea in the breakfast room, took the paper from Phillips. At first, she thought it was a poster advertising a romance movie, because the black-and-white picture depicted a smiling, hand-holding couple. Why on earth had Phillips found this important enough to remove from the pole and bring back to the house? Suddenly, her heart leaped into her mouth and nearly choked her. She knew the picture! It was more than thirty years old, taken by a newspaper photographer five months before her own birth, but Katherine recognized it — her father and mother returning to London after their publicized elopement and marriage at the start of 1950.

"You found this on a telephone pole, Jimmy?"

"Have you read what's written there, Mrs. Kassler?"

Katherine dropped her eyes to words she hadn't even

noticed in the shock of seeing the old picture. A caption identified Roland Eagles and his young wife, Catarina, who was described as the only daughter of multimillionaire Argentine businessman Nicanor Menéndez. Centered above the picture, in block capitals, was the question: "If you stood to lose millions on the Buenos Aires stock exchange, wouldn't you be against the war as well?"

No credit was taken for the poster, but Katherine saw the British Patriotic League all over it.

She snatched the telephone receiver from its rest and dialed her father's number. Arthur Parsons answered. "May I speak to my father, please?"

"Just a moment, Miss Katherine."

Katherine glanced at the clock on the wall. Seven-thirty, and the day was ruined already. She heard her father's voice asking if everything was all right. "No, it's damned well not. Jimmy just brought back a libelous poster he found tacked to a telephone pole." She described it to her father, and heard his intake of breath.

"I'll get dressed and bring it over to you. Then you can decide what to do." She ran up to her room, threw off her robe, and dressed hastily in slacks and a cashmere sweater. Ten minutes after making the call, she was swinging the silver Porsche out of the forecourt of Kate's Haven, and pointing it north toward her father's home in Stanmore.

Two hundred yards along the road, she stamped on the brakes. There was a poster, tacked to a garden fence. She jumped out of the car to grab it, only to see another, affixed to an oak tree. Wherever she looked, she saw the damned things. If she stopped to take down every one, she'd never get to her father's home.

When she reached Stanmore, her father opened the door. Seeing the posters clutched in her hand, he said, "You needn't have bothered, Kathy. Sally telephoned five minutes after you did. She looked out of her bedroom window and saw one pasted to a traffic sign not twenty feet away."

"They're everywhere, Daddy."

"I know. Arthur Parsons just drove down the hill to see how many he could find." Even as he spoke, the green Bentley glided between the red brick pillars. Parsons carried three of the posters, which he handed silently to Roland. They were all torn, as though Parsons had vented his fury by ripping them down.

Katherine followed her father into the drawing room. "Are we in any doubt who's behind all this?"

"Of course not. It's the League. They have the printing facilities, and they can call on a few hundred people to work through the night distributing these things."

The telephone rang. It was Lawrie Stimkin, calling from home. He had heard that the posters were everywhere across London, tens of thousands of them. Just what was going on? "I'll be at the Eagle building in two hours," Roland said. "I'll tell you exactly what's happening, and then I'll hold a press conference and tell the same thing to everyone else."

A press conference was scheduled for three that afternoon in the boardroom of Eagle Newspapers. Roland sat at the head of the long mahogany table, with Katherine and Sally Roberts next to him. Holding up a copy of the poster, Roland started to talk.

"You've all come this afternoon because you want to know if there's any truth to what's printed here, right? Well, some of it is true." He waited for the flutter of excitement to subside before continuing. "This is me in the picture. And this is my late wife, Catarina, who, as it says in the caption, was the only daughter of Nicanor Menéndez. That is the truth. The rest—this preposterous accusation that I opposed the war because I stood to lose money on the Buenos Aires stock

535

exchange—is nothing but libelous garbage."

"Who do you think is responsible for circulating these posters, Mr. Eagles?" an agency reporter asked. "The whole city's covered with them, you know."

"We're looking very hard at the British Patriotic League."

"Why?"

"You might remember that two summers ago, Eagle Newspapers staged free rock concerts as an alternative to the 'Youth for Britain' rallies organized by the British Patriotic League. We proved beyond any shadow of a doubt that Britain's youth would rather listen to music than bigotry, and the League has not forgiven us for that."

Beyond denying the allegations, and identifying the revenge motive, there was little else that could be done. The press conference ended, leaving Roland alone with Sally and his daughter.

"How did we do?" Roland asked.

"We'll know tonight," Sally answered.

Katherine invited her father and Sally for dinner. Later, they watched the evening news. As usual, the fighting took up the major portion. Afterward, the newscaster related the poster campaign, mentioning Roland's refutation of the allegations, and his accusation against the British Patriotic League.

The newscaster finished with "A spokesman for the League, Mr. Trevor Burns, has denied all knowledge of the origins of these posters."

The picture changed, and there was the overweight figure of Trevor Burns, the former journalist who was now a member of the League's executive committee and its public-relations director. "We are too busy raising money for the families of the brave men lost in this war to waste time sticking posters all over town."

Again, the picture altered. "Christ almighty!" Sally yelled. "Will you just look at that?"

On the screen was a gigantic rummage sale. Dozens

of tables were stacked with assorted goods that had been donated to the League. The camera panned across the helpers. In the middle of them, working at a stand that sold secondhand clothing, was Alan Venables, his thin face breaking into a fawning smile as he accepted money from a customer. Positioned strategically behind him was a huge placard with the League's crest and the message "The Falklands Are British!"

Roland shook his head in sadness and frustration. He was witnessing a public-relations coup. All anyone would remember of this evening's news was that the British Patriotic League had actively helped the families of fallen soldiers. How much more patriotic could they be than that? Simultaneously, the League had squared accounts with the *Eagle,* for Roland had no doubt that the League was behind the paper blitz. Just as he was certain that the insinuations made against him, as groundless as they were, would cause business and personal hardship.

For Alan Venables, the war with Argentina could not have occurred at a more opportune moment. At a time when the British Patriotic League had been slipping out of the public eye, the conflict in the South Atlantic had thrust a two-edged sword into Venables's hands. With one stroke, he had wreaked a long-awaited vengeance on Roland Eagles, a man he hated; simultaneously, he had demonstrated how solidly the League supported the British effort to regain the Falklands.

The picture of Roland and Catarina had come from Trevor Burns. Still with many contacts in Fleet Street, he had acquired it from an agency file. A plate had been made, type set, and fifty thousand copies of the poster had been printed on the equipment in the basement of Patriot House, the League's headquarters. On Sunday night, two hundred members of the

League, each armed with two hundred and fifty copies, had spread out through the capital city, from its center to its suburbs. As an added touch, Venables had organized a rummage sale in aid of the Falkland widows for the following day, when he knew that reporters would be questioning the League's executive committee for a response to Roland Eagles's accusations.

Venables felt even more pleased the next morning when he met with Burns and Neville Sharpe, the League's financial director, at Patriot House. Sharpe had a check for more than two thousand pounds, the proceeds of the rummage sale, which would be given to the Falklands widows.

"You're arranging for a photographer to cover the check presentation, aren't you?" Venables asked Burns.

"Of course." One picture would appear in the League's own publication; others would be sent to newspapers. "Shall I send a copy to the *Eagle?*"

"I've got other plans for those people."

Neville Sharpe spoke with all the gravity of the accountant he was. "Alan, the distribution of the posters was already stepping well outside our brief."

"Not when it was tied in with the column inches and television time our rummage sale received."

"Instead of satisfying some personal vendetta, we should be concentrating on our primary function, which is preparing for the next general election. It could come very soon. Once the Union Jack flies over the Falklands again, Thatcher will have tremendous popularity. She'll be able to call an election whenever she feels the Tories will win the biggest majority."

Venables shook his head. "I am not letting Eagles off the hook. Him and his damned newspaper have been a thorn in our sides ever since we started the League. They exposed our recruiting scheme at the football games, they planted the Waters boy on us—

and you both know what had to be done to recover that situation — and they damn near tied the British Brigade into us. Not to mention ruining the 'Youth for Britain' rallies two years ago. And don't think for a moment that I've forgotten that slap in the face Eagles's daughter gave me at the BBC that morning."

Sharpe tried again. "Our brief is to run at least one hundred and fifty candidates at the next general election. A lot of money has been invested to make sure that happens."

"Forget you're an accountant for once. Act like the leader of an emergent political party, not some pencil-pusher who's forever checking expenses."

"At least one hundred and fifty candidates, that is what our instructions call for."

"And we'll have them, Neville. But first, I'm going to use some of the power we have at our fingertips. Christ alone knows that we won't have it forever. After the next election, it might be time for us to fade away like three old soldiers and enjoy our retirement."

"Pity," Trevor Burns said. "I think I could grow accustomed to being a political big shot."

Venables looked at the former journalist, and smiled. "You're only a big shot if you get elected. And that was never in our plans, was it?"

The day after the press conference, Roland scrutinized every newspaper. His denial of interests in Argentina was given adequate space. All he wanted was fair treatment, and that was what he had been accorded. It was gratifying to know that dog did not eat dog after all.

Fair treatment proved to be of little help. Within a day, several advertisers canceled contracts with Eagle Newspapers. The reasons were as diverse as a car dealership that expected an immediate weakening of the economy to a furniture store's failure to obtain enough merchandise to make a special sale feasible after all. Roland noticed that the advertisements continued to run in other newspapers. The insinuation that he was dealing with the enemy was a poison for which there was no antidote.

The feeling against Roland soon moved from his newspaper group to his retail business. Roland arrived at the main Adler's store in Regent Street on Friday morning to find a demonstration taking place. Two dozen young men marched in a circle on the wide sidewalk, just far enough away from the store entrance to avoid interfering with people entering and leaving — but close enough to make them stop and stare. One marcher waved the pennant of the British Patriotic League; the rest carried placards. Roland saw the words "Buy British, not Argentine!" as he crossed the sidewalk to the entrance.

When he reached his own office, his secretary was waiting with news that similar demonstrations were occurring outside the Manchester and Edinburgh stores. The demonstrations lasted all day in London and Edinburgh. Only Manchester provided a respite; there, a driving rainstorm forced the League's protesters from the streets at midday. Activity in all three stores was way down, with the traditionally busy Friday yielding fewer sales than a wet Monday.

There were no demonstrations the following week. An injunction taken out by Roland's lawyers against the League saw to that. The lack of protesters failed to ease the situation, though. As May turned to June, and the Falklands conflict entered its third month, store business continued to dip. Likewise, the *Daily* and *Sunday Eagle* went to press with a minimum of advertisements.

Sally Roberts acquainted Roland with a new problem. Over dinner at her Curzon Street flat, to which she had also invited Katherine, Sally said, "I'm seeing more and more copies of *UK Press Gazette* and

540

Campaign around the building these days. I think that editorial and advertising people are worrying how long it will be before layoffs begin."

"First thing tomorrow, I will send a memo to every staff member at Eagle Newspapers and Adler's. No one should fear losing his or her job." Roland fixed a smile on his face. "Besides, if what I read in my own newspapers is to be believed, this nasty little war should be over quite soon."

"And when they all shake hands, does that mean our lives will return to normal?" Katherine asked. "The British forgive their enemies a lot quicker than they pardon a traitor — even a man who has been falsely accused of treason."

"Once this rush of public-spirited blood to the head calms down," Roland answered, "reason might prevail."

"If it doesn't?"

Roland's voice was strained. "I am praying that it will."

Katherine recalled John Saxon's idea — a statement of support for the Falklands venture. She'd slammed the receiver down on him; her father would never accept such an about-face! But a lot had happened since then. Saxon's prophesies had come true. Now, a derivative of his idea might work. "When this war is over, perhaps the *Eagle* can put one of those blank advertising pages to good use. Not to celebrate victory, but to commemorate peace. To explain that freedom cannot be taken for granted. Like everything, it has a price, and sometimes that price is blood."

Sally gave Katherine a cool, admiring glance, but Roland contradicted her. "That's nothing but a transparent political ploy. It's asking to be pardoned, when I've done nothing to be pardoned for."

"It's better than being forced out of business, isn't it?"

"Since the day I got out of the army in 1947, I have

been in business. Kathy, I don't want to be remembered for being a magnate, a tycoon, or whatever the current phrase is. I want to be remembered as a decent man who stood by his principles, no matter what it cost him."

Katherine blinked away the sudden tears in her eyes. Her father's principles were his most precious possessions. He would die with them intact. But if he refused to help himself, he would have to be helped. It was as simple as that.

Any doubts Katherine had about going over her father's head were swept away that weekend. On Saturday night, a fire broke out in the menswear department on the second floor of the Adler's store in Manchester. By the time firemen controlled the blaze, the second floor was gutted. Much of the merchandise on the other floors was ruined by smoke and water damage.

Investigators pinpointed three separate hot spots. The burned but still identifiable remains of timing mechanisms were found. The scene was reconstructed: small but powerful firebombs had been slipped into the pockets of three pieces of clothing, probably just before closing on Saturday evening to eliminate the possibility of being found by accident. Police interviewed the sales clerks on the floor. Could they recall the last customers? The last browsers? Had they noticed anything suspicious? No one remembered a thing.

Roland spent two days in Manchester promising everyone from the lowliest porter right up the store manager that they would continue being paid until the store was operational again. He also met with the police. When the chief inspector in charge of the arson investigation asked who might want to harm him, Roland grabbed the telephone directory, and flung it open to the B's.

"Look there for your arsonist—the Manchester office of the British Patriotic League. Those madmen aren't short of a motive. They've been libeling and harassing me for the past week."

The chief inspector was unimpressed by Roland's outburst. Motive was one thing; finding witnesses was something else.

When Roland returned by train to London, Katherine met him. His face was one big scowl, and as he climbed into the Porsche he gave vent to the fury that had been building all the way down from Manchester. "Those bastards burned me down, and there's not a damned thing I can do about it."

"What about the police?"

"The police? They treated me like I was the accused, not the injured party. I told them who was responsible, and they replied that they could not go out and arrest someone on my word. What was that supposed to mean . . . that my word wasn't worth a damn? That I'm not to be believed because I might have business interests in the Argentine? The police believe those lies about me more than they believe me."

"That's not what they meant at all. They need witnesses and evidence before they can arrest anyone." All the same, Katherine could not help wondering whether her father was right. Were the police being deliberately unhelpful because they felt there was some truth in the allegations? It was crazy. A reputation took a lifetime to build, and only a couple of hours and some clever lies to destroy.

More than ever, Katherine knew she had to help her father.

On the morning of Monday, June 14, ten weeks after the Argentine invasion, a white flag was seen flying over Port Stanley, the capital of the Falkland Islands. The next morning, Argentine forces formally surrendered. The fighting, at last, was over.

Across Britain, public houses were full at lunchtime, and again in the evening. The country was witnessing an outpouring of pride, pleasure, and relief that had not been seen since the spring of 1945.

When the pubs disgorged their celebrants at closing time, Fleet Street was moving into full stride. Presses rolled on early forms, compositors labored over late pages. A party atmosphere prevailed, joy over triumph's headlines.

At the *Eagle,* Lawrie Stimkin made the final check of the front page. Block capitals screamed "Victory!" Beneath the headline was a photograph of the surrender. The story itself, with other details of the war's final moments, was carried on pages two and three. Satisfied, the editor passed the page to Roland, who, with Katherine and Sally Roberts, had made a special trip to see the paper put to bed on this momentous occasion.

The one-word headline, and the stark picture of triumph and defeat, jumped right off the page into Roland's face. It was the most eye-catching *Eagle* front page he had ever seen. So it should be, considering the importance of the occasion. But all Roland could say was "About blasted time. How many men had to die so this picture could be taken?"

No one answered, because it was obvious that the question was rhetorical. Katherine studied her father as he looked at the front page. The tension of the past few weeks—the personal attacks, the harassment, the arson at the Manchester store—had taken its toll. Roland's eyes looked sunken. Deep lines were etched around his mouth. And his shoulders, Katherine noticed, seemed bent, taking two or three inches off his six-foot-plus frame. For the first time in her life, Katherine applied an adjective to her father that she'd never dreamed she'd use. He looked old.

"If you've seen enough," Katherine said, "I'll take

you home. Then I'll be able to get some sleep."

Roland nodded in agreement. Sally walked with them to the street. When they reached the Porsche, Sally wrapped her arms around Roland's neck and kissed him. "When you wake up tomorrow, Roland Eagles, the world's going to be a much better place. You wait and see."

"I believe you're right." He bent to enter the Porsche. Over his head, Katherine flashed the quickest of winks at Sally.

As the Porsche roared away, Sally walked quickly into the Eagle building and rejoined Lawrie Stimkin. "Ready?"

"Ready." Stimkin rapped out orders, and compositors who had been sworn to secrecy went about their special work.

Despite staying up to watch the *Eagle* put to bed, Roland rose at eight o'clock the following morning. He showered and shaved, and came downstairs in a shirt and the trousers of the blue suit he would wear to work that day. A place was set for him in the breakfast room. A steaming cup of tea waited, set out by Peg Parsons, who had heard his footsteps on the stairs. Next to the tea was a copy of the *Eagle*.

Roland picked up the newspaper and held it at arm's length to get the full impact of that graphic front page. His mouth dropped. His hands gripped the paper fiercely enough to tear it. This was not the front page he had seen at press time. The layout was similar. It was just as graphic, just as startling, but it was not the same page!

Instead of "Victory!," the headline read "Freedom!" The picture of the surrender was replaced by a photograph that burned its way into the brain. A weary British paratrooper sat on the ground, his back against a tree. A bandage covered his forehead, and the eyes

545

that squinted at the camera described the pain and suffering of every war that has ever been fought. Beneath the picture, in bold type surrounded by a black box, was the simple message: "Freedom, like everything we hold precious, is not free. It must be paid for. With determination. With vigilance. And sometimes, unfortunately, with blood. Thank you."

The front-page message of gratitude to the troops who had recovered the Falkland Islands and rescued the eighteen hundred residents from a government and culture under which they did not wish to live, was attributed to the proprietor, management, and staff of Eagle Newspapers Limited.

Peg Parsons chose that moment to come in from the kitchen, carrying a plate of buttered toast. She saw Roland sitting rigidly in the chair, his mouth open, the paper torn, and she feared that he was suffering a stroke.

"Mr. Eagles, what is it?"

Roland recovered quickly. "Nothing, Mrs. Parsons. Nothing that a telephone call will not cure." He left the table and dialed Sally's number from the extension in the drawing room.

Sally, voice thick with sleep, answered on the fourth ring. "Yes, Roland."

"How did you know it was me?"

"Who else would ring so early to moan about the front page?"

Anger surged over Roland. Sally was patronizing him. They all were, damn it! Gently poking fun at him while they went over his head. "Is this what you meant by the world being a better place this morning? How dare you make this gesture of apology on my behalf? I will be at the *Eagle* at ten o'clock. I want to see you when I arrive. I want to see Lawrie Stimkin as well."

Sally let Roland run out of steam before saying, "Lawrie won't be in until midday, and after last night, neither will I. I am utterly exhausted."

"Yes, I can see where all this playing charades could be exhausting."

"Roland?"

"Yes."

"Buzz off!" And the telephone went dead in his ear.

Roland was in his office on the executive floor of the Eagle building by ten o'clock. There was no sign of Sally or Stimkin. He sat in the office for two hours, but he was not bored. The switchboard put through one telephone call after another. Readers, advertisers, half a dozen Members of Parliament, even military people. Each caller was full of praise for the dramatic front page, and the moving tribute to the men who had fought for freedom. Faced with the choice of accepting the praise, or denying any knowledge of the page, Roland took the easy route. He accepted the praise.

At ten minutes after twelve, as Roland replaced the receiver on what he estimated was the fiftieth call, Sally walked into the office. With her were Lawrie Stimkin and Katherine. They looked as if they were going to a funeral. Katherine was dressed in a navy blue suit and white silk blouse. Sally wore a black dress, with a tiny emerald pin. Stimkin, his gloomy air complemented by a dark brown suit, could have been the undertaker.

"You wanted to see us?" Sally asked in a voice that was icily sweet.

"I wanted to see you and him. Why is Katherine here?"

"Because it was her idea to switch the front page."

"I see. Would you mind telling me why you went to the trouble of staging this elaborate confidence trick?"

Stimkin answered first. "As editor, that was the front page I wanted. I felt everyone else would have front pages depicting victory and surrender. I wanted ours to be more meaningful."

Roland looked at Sally. "And you?"

"I'm editorial director. I obviously wanted what was

547

best for the *Eagle,* and that page was it."

At last, Roland turned to his daughter. "I suppose you're also going to claim this undying allegiance to the *Eagle.*"

"No. I'm going to claim allegiance to my father. I was fed up with watching him make a fool of himself. You talked about Mrs. Thatcher and the Argentines painting themselves into corners. You did the same thing. And the only way to get you out was to offer you the route you couldn't see for yourself."

"Arguing with you was impossible," Sally broke in. "And if we hadn't done anything, your own stubbornness would have caused a catastrophe. The way advertising was going, the paper would have had to close. We had hundreds of jobs to protect. Not to mention lives and property, with all the animosity your stand was causing. That was why we took matters into our own hands."

"The switchboard operator said that you've had dozens of complimentary calls on the front page," Stimkin said.

"A few," Roland admitted.

"I think," Katherine said, "that you owe the three of us an apology, and a thank you."

"We'll forgo the apology," Sally added, "but we would like to hear a thank you."

"I came here this morning to . . . to . . ." Roland spread his hands helplessly. "I don't know what I was going to do. But I was certainly not planning to thank you for anything." He paused. "Thank you. Thank you for going over my head. Thank you for making a conciliatory statement on my behalf."

"Lunch would be a nice show of gratitude," Sally said.

Stimkin passed; he had work to do, but Katherine eagerly backed Sally's proposal. They went to a restaurant overlooking Tower Bridge and the Thames. Roland traveled in Sally's sports car, while Katherine rode alone in the Porsche. While the wine was being poured, Roland said, "I'm glad Lawrie didn't come, because I could never have made this toast with him here." He raised his glass. "To two of the three most important women in my life. I love you both very dearly."

Sally gave Katherine a querying look. "Should we tell him how we feel about him?"

"I don't know. Lunch is just the start. Let's see what else we can take him for first."

"No. Put him out of his misery."

Katherine turned to her father. "You're obstinate, obstreporous, cantankerous, and bloody-minded to the core. Notwithstanding all that, we still love you."

Roland beamed. The years Katherine had seen imprinted on his face fell away. His back straightened; sparkle returned to his eyes. He was her father again, middle-aged and vibrant.

They left the restaurant just before three. Sally sped away, leaving Katherine caught at lights. When she cleared them, Sally's car was nowhere in sight. Katherine took her time, thinking over what had happened that day. Her father angry at first over the way he had been duped, and then coming around to admit they'd done the right thing. She smiled . . . just because Roland owned the paper didn't mean that they'd let him run it.

A demonstration was taking place outside the Eagle building. Katherine saw flags and placards being waved as she turned onto the street. She read one slogan—"Saying Sorry Is Not Enough"—before her eyes picked up something else. Crossing the street from the parking-lot to the building entrance were Roland and Sally. Their stride was purposeful; they had no intention of being deterred by the twenty young pickets.

"It's him!" yelled a youth in jeans and denim jacket. "It's Eagles!"

549

Other demonstrators took up the cry, turning it into a parody of a soccer-crowd chant. "Eagles for Argentina! Eagles for Argentina!"

Katherine saw her father and Sally push through the mob. The uniformed doorman came out to lend assistance. Behind him were two maintenance men; one swung a length of pipe, the other carried an adjustable wrench. For a few steps, the crowd gave. Then Katherine watched it swallow Sally and Roland. She pressed down on the horn, floored the Porsche's gas pedal, and aimed for the edge of the mob, where it had spilled into the road.

The crowd disintegrated like bomb fragments. Placards were dropped as their owners ran from the car. Roland and Sally were pulled into the building by the doorman and the maintenance workers. Hurtling at forty miles an hour down the narrow street, Katherine saw two of the demonstrators right in front of her, arms and legs pumping as if they could outrun the Porsche. At the very last moment, when it seemed that nothing could prevent the car from smashing the two youths aside, Katherine jerked the steering wheel to the left. The car slewed across the road and smashed into a lamppost. The seat belt kept Katherine from being thrown through the windshield, but it did not save her from injury. Her knees cracked against the bottom of the dashboard; her head slammed into the steering wheel. She managed to unfasten the seat belt, open the door, and stagger out of the car before collapsing, unconscious, onto the road.

Katherine came to in a hospital bed. She ached from head to foot. Her forehead was bandaged, her ribs strapped, her left leg immobilized. Every breath sent painful spasms rocketing through her chest.

A nurse entered the private room and gave Katherine a smile. "You're very lucky to be here. Your seat belt saved your life."

"What did I break?" Even whispered speech hurt.

"A couple of ribs. Your left knee's badly bruised and twisted, and you dented your skull. Other than that, you're in great shape. Feel up to seeing visitors?"

"Yes, please."

Roland and Sally entered the ward. Roland tried to hide his concern with a joke. "I'm not buying you any more cars if you're going to drive them like that."

"I was worried about you and Sally."

"Of course. So, quite naturally, you drove straight into a lamp-post."

Katherine started to laugh, then stopped as pain tore through her chest. "I was trying to run down a couple of those louts. At the very last moment, sanity prevailed, and I took evasive action. Who were they, the League?"

"Who else?" Roland retorted.

"How long will I be here?"

"A couple of days for observation. The doctors are having difficulty in believing that anyone got out of that car alive."

"It's not a complete write-off," Sally said cheerfully. "They can probably save the rear bumper."

Roland nodded. "Even I don't drive like that on purpose."

Katherine screwed her eyes shut, the first movement that did not cause pain. She was going to take a lot of teasing about this accident, but she didn't care. She had wrecked the Porsche because it was the only way to save Roland and Sally from the mob. On any balance sheet, that was a worthwhile trade.

The following afternoon, Jimmy Phillips and Edna came to see her bringing with them enough fruit and candy to open a store. She gave them the good news that she would be discharged the next day. Erica Bentley and a crowd of people from the *Eagle* also visited, eating most of the fruit and candy while they sat around the bed and gossiped about the newspaper. In the late afternoon, Roland and Sally returned. When they left at seven-thirty, Katherine, expecting no more visitors, closed her eyes and wished for sleep. Two minutes later, she opened them with a start. Raymond Barnhill stood in the doorway. He was breathing heavily, and appeared disoriented. In his hand was a small suitcase, and pasted across his face was a big grin.

"Made it, by damn!" he burst out, and practically fell into the room.

Katherine stared at him in amazement. "Have you just come from New York?"

"You bet. Concorde."

"Concorde? That's expensive."

Barnhill waved off Katherine's protest. "I'll worry about it when American Express bills me next month. You should have seen it — we landed at ten after six, I got through immigration and customs, and the guy who taught Jackie Stewart to drive was behind the wheel of the cab that brought me here." Dropping the suitcase onto the floor, he leaned over the bed and kissed Katherine. "How the hell are you?"

The concern in his drawn face brought tears to Katherine's eyes. "God, I've missed you," she whispered into his chest. "But how did you know I was here?"

"Edna, when I called last night. She said you'd been injured in an accident. I was first in line at Kennedy Airport this morning. What happened?"

"I tried to run down a couple of young Nazis from the British Patriotic League. They were assaulting my father and Sally outside the Eagle building, all to do with this business over the Falklands war. I missed them both, but I did score a bull's eye on a lamppost."

"You wear out cars like other people go through socks. Are you going to ask your father for another one out of petty cash?"

"You are lucky that I'm flat on my back."

"I wouldn't have said it if you were on your feet. How long are you going to be stuck here?"

"Until tomorrow. Are you moving in with me?"

Barnhill tapped the suitcase with his foot. "Think they'd let me?"

"No. You'd better telephone Edna and let her know you're in town. She'll prepare a room for you."

"She already knows. I told her last night that I'd fly to see you."

"She never mentioned a word to me."

"I asked her not to say anything. I wanted to surprise you." He hopped from one foot to the other. "I got through the airport so fast, I didn't have time to—"

"Turn left and straight down the hall."

"Thanks," Barnhill said as he bolted from the room.

Little more than a minute later, the door opened. "That was quick," Katherine started to say, and then she stopped. It was not Barnhill who stood there.

"That was a wild piece of driving," John Saxon said as he walked into the room and sat down next to Katherine's bed. "Were you trying to kill yourself?"

Saxon was the last person Katherine expected to see, and the very last person she wanted to see. But short of asking him to leave, there was little she could do but be polite. "On the contrary, John, I was trying to save a couple of people from being killed."

"According to newspaper reports, that was a very nasty demonstration."

"It was the grand finale of ten weeks of very nasty demonstrations, ranging from abusive letters to libel, arson, and assault and battery."

Saxon gave a disarming shrug of the shoulders, a tight little smile. "Katherine, you can't say that no one warned you and your father what might happen."

"Why did you come here, John? To visit me, or to gloat?" Over Saxon's shoulder, she saw Barnhill take one step into the small room, then freeze when he

553

recognized the visitor.

"It was your father's obstinacy that stirred up all this trouble."

"My father's courage in sticking to his beliefs was only partly responsible."

"Oh? What was primarily responsible?"

"Your right-wing friends in Parliament. People like Daniel Cooper and Edwin Johnson give a mantle of respectability to hate groups like the League."

Saxon, still unaware of Barnhill's presence, smiled patronizingly. "Do you really believe that?"

"Of course I do. When politicians start wrapping themselves in the flag, they give bigots the green light to do the same thing. You can hide an awful lot of hate behind a waving flag."

"Katherine, that is a ridiculous claim to make."

Barnhill came right into the room. "Like hell it is. I've seen it happen in the States often enough. Whenever the right's in power, Klan activity increases. So does acceptance of them."

"I was wondering who owned this suitcase," Saxon said. He stood up to face Barnhill, running his eyes over the rumpled sportcoat and trousers, the scuffed loafers.

Saxon's steady, appraising gaze made Barnhill uncomfortable. "Are you looking for anything in particular?"

"Not really. I'm just trying to understand what attracted Katherine to an unkempt clown like you."

"John!" A stab of pain seared Katherine's chest as she fairly shouted his name. "You have no call to speak to Raymond like that."

Saxon, keeping his eyes on Barnhill, ignored Katherine's objections. "What's that word they use in your part of the world? A wonderfully descriptive word. Oh, yes. *Redneck.*"

Again Katherine protested. "John! Apologize to Raymond at once!" Her voice changed to a shriek.

"No . . . !"

She was too late. Barnhill bunched his right hand into a fist, drew it back with methodical slowness, then launched it in the general direction of Saxon's face. Saxon tried to duck. The punch caught him a glancing blow on the cheek, and sent him stumbling back to the wall. Before he could recover, Barnhill grabbed him by the collar of his jacket, held open the door, and shoved him through it.

"Get out and don't bother coming back."

Saxon regained his balance in the hallway. He stared at Katherine through watery eyes, undecided whether to speak. Barnhill denied him the chance by closing the door in his face.

Breathing heavily, Barnhill sat down in the chair Saxon had been using. He opened and closed his right hand tentatively, as though checking for broken bones. "I'm sorry, Katherine, but I've wanted to do that from the moment I met him. Your husband's funeral wasn't the right place; neither was that party at your house. Or that time at the hotel. So I figured, what better place to give that arrogant jerk a fat lip than a hospital?"

She offered him a hand to hold. "That doesn't answer why."

"I like being called a redneck about as much as you like being accused of having been born with a silver spoon in your mouth. I put up with enough of it when I was with IPA, all those northern hotshots who thought there was nothing but tobacco farms and white-lightning stills below the Mason-Dixon line."

"If I hadn't been stuck in this bed, I'd have hit him for what he said to you."

Although he shrugged off Katherine's confession, Barnhill felt relieved. Saxon had always made him unsure of himself. Saxon's wealth, position, but most of all what he had meant to Katherine, all combined to make Barnhill feel at a disadvantage. He had never been able to shed the anxiety that Katherine might still feel something for the property developer.

Until now.

Katherine returned home the following day with nothing to do but wait for bones to knit and cuts and bruises to heal. Barnhill stayed the weekend before flying back to New York on the Monday.

Two months later, when Katherine had recovered fully from the accident, Barnhill returned for a surprise ten-day visit. When Katherine asked the reason, he gave her three.

"The *Eagle* owed me vacation time. Secondly, I'm done with *The Squad*, and that entitles me to a vacation with all the trimmings. And I wanted to see how well you were mending."

For five days, Barnhill devoted himself to Henry and Joanne, who were in the middle of their summer break. He took them cruising along the Thames and sightseeing in a helicopter. In turn, Joanne made him go riding with her, and Henry persuaded him to sit through a cricket match.

The remaining five days were reserved for Katherine. Barnhill hired a car, and they drove west, staying at small hotels in picturesque areas of Devon and Cornwall. In Plymouth, while sitting where Sir Francis Drake had played bowls before setting sail to defeat the Spanish Armada, Katherine asked Barnhill about his plans.

"Once your contract for 'Glimpses of America' is up, and you come back to England, will you devote yourself full-time to writing?"

"No. That's too much like solitary confinement. I'll need a job, something to keep me in touch with sanity. I'll ask Sally or Lawrie Stimkin if they can use another hand at the *Eagle*."

In Bath, on the return journey, Katherine made a

confession. "The day after you took the children on the Thames, Joanne asked if I was going to marry you."

"What did you tell her?"

"That you hadn't asked me."

Barnhill's head moved up and down in understanding. "That explains the question Henry asked me the very next day, when I went to the cricket game with him. He wanted to know if I was going to ask you to marry me."

"What answer did you give him?"

"I didn't. I told him to watch the game and explain to me what was going on, because I couldn't make head or tail of it."

Katherine was quite satisfied with that. She would consider marriage when she was ready to do so, not when her children pushed her into it.

When Barnhill's vacation was over, Katherine took Henry and Joanne to Heathrow to see him off. As they waited for the flight to be called, Katherine found herself wishing away the next few months. She yearned for it to be the end of the year already, when Barnhill would return to London.

She wanted it to be Christmas, and she wanted to find Raymond Barnhill beneath her tree.

25

Raymond Barnhill wrote his final "Glimpses of America" in the third week of December. It was a bittersweet moment. "Glimpses" was his personal creation. Despite the time and effort he had invested in his fiction writing, he had never neglected the column during its more than two years of life. When he passed responsibility for it to his successor, he felt as though he were handing his own child into the care of a foster parent.

Two evenings later, Barnhill was strapped into the seat of a London-bound British Airways 747. The briefcase by his feet contained his passport, travelers' checks, and the galleys for *The Squad*. The two suitcases in the aircraft's hold held the rest of his possessions. Thirty-seven years old, and all his worldly goods — his clothes, a camera, a new portable electric typewriter, a couple of copies of the two books he'd published, and some personal effects — fitted neatly into two cases. There was a lot of truth to the old proverb about rolling stones.

After eating, he turned on the reading light and read through the galleys for *The Squad*. Immediately, he noticed a difference between these and the galleys for his earlier books. Reading those had been a chore.

This story, as familiar as it was, carried him through for three and a half hours of solid reading. By then, the in-flight movie was finished, and most of the passengers were sleeping. Barnhill was wide awake. He looked out of the tiny window at the star-sprinkled sky, too excited to sleep. This was the second time he was leaving the United States to work in England. Five years earlier he had been running away from a bad marriage, and from his own problems. This time, he was running toward something.

When Barnhill passed through customs, Katherine was waiting. Other people held small signs with the names of arriving passengers on them. Katherine held a two-foot-high placard, on which was printed, "Welcome Home, Barnhill!"

"Put that down, or I'll turn around and get on the first flight back."

"Give me a kiss in front of all these people, and I'll put it down."

He did. Holding her tightly, he gave her a long, slow kiss that left them both breathless. She abandoned the placard in a trash can.

Pushing the trolley that held his worldly goods, Barnhill followed Katherine to the parking lot. "One word about my father paying for this out of petty cash," she said as they stopped by a gleaming white Lotus, "and you will be walking from here."

"When did you get this exotic piece of machinery?"

"After you went back in August. I kept it as a surprise."

"That makes us even. I've got one for you." When she looked inquisitively at him, he laughed and shook his head. "It'll hold until Christmas. Just make sure you keep this car away from British Patriotic League demonstrations."

"There haven't been any. At least, not against my father. They've just had routine protests, to stir up trouble for colored immigrants."

They joined the heavy morning traffic. "I hope you like the place I rented for you," Katherine said.

"The apartment?"

"Not apartment. Flat. You're back in England now."

Katherine pulled into the forecourt of an apartment block in Swiss Cottage, less than a mile from Kate's Haven. On the second floor, they walked along the hallway to a door at the very end. Katherine handed Barnhill a key.

Barnhill inspected the furnished apartment. Two bedrooms, one fitted out as a den with an old-fashioned desk. The refrigerator in the kitchen was fully stocked. "I'll take it."

"How about my finder's fee?"

"How much?"

Katherine shrugged herself out of her three-quarter-length cashmere coat. Holding her arms toward Barnhill, she said, "I'll give you three guesses."

For the second straight year, Barnhill was invited to spend Christmas at Roland Eagles's home. After lunch, and before the traditional walk over the common, Barnhill asked if he could propose a toast. No one made any comment when he filled his own glass with apple juice instead of wine.

"Technically, I'm unemployed. I finished working for the *Eagle* in New York last week, and I don't start working for the *Eagle* in London until the beginning of January. Because of that, I could be forgiven for feeling out of place here. The truth is, I have a greater sense of belonging right now than I've ever had in my entire life, and I want to thank all of you for that."

"That's not a toast," Roland grumbled lightly. "It's a vote of thanks."

"And you're very welcome," Sally said with a warm smile.

When they went walking over the common, Katherine, bundled up in a sheepskin coat, clung to Barnhill's arm. "Was the toast the big Christmas Day surprise?" she asked.

"No. That'll come later." He pulled her closer, dragging her bare hand into the pocket of his coat.

"I love you," Katherine said.

"I love you, too."

"Is that the surprise?"

"Not to me it isn't."

Katherine looked ahead. She was surrounded by love. Her father and Sally were walking arm-in-arm, heads together as though engaged in some intimate conversation. Leading the procession were Henry and Joanne, chasing each other in a wild game of tag. Even that was a sign of love, Katherine reflected, as she watched Joanne slap her brother across the back of the head before running away.

Her mind went back six years. Christmas 1976, taking this walk with Franz. She could even remember what she'd been thinking at the time. About the end of a marvelous year, and how the following one would be even better. She felt the same way now. With the exception of the Falklands, 1982 had been a super year. And 1983 would eclipse even that. But she'd be damned if she'd dwell on how much better it would be. That would be tempting fate again, and one shattered life was more than enough for anyone to bear.

When they returned to the house, Katherine waited to learn of Barnhill's surprise. Instead, the bombshell came from another quarter completely. Roland invited Katherine and Barnhill to join him and Sally in the drawing room, then closed the door.

"Sally has an important announcement to make." He glanced at Barnhill. "You're here, Raymond, because this concerns you as well — as both a former and future member of the Eagle Newspapers staff. Sally . . . ?"

561

"This past year has made me realize I'm no longer a spring chicken. I'm sixty-one, and that entitles me not to have to battle my way through hostile mobs, or help to formulate an editorial policy that has most of the country wanting to burn me in effigy. So I'm hereby giving six months' notice of my decision to retire."

"That's ridiculous!" Katherine burst out. "Doing nothing will drive you mad!"

Roland shook his head sadly. "Kathy, please don't speak in that tone of voice to your future stepmother."

"Stepmother!" Sally was genuinely offended. "Don't call me that. It makes me sound like some wicked old witch in one of the Grimm Brothers' fairy tales."

Katherine ran up to Sally and hugged her. "I always dreamed of calling you 'Mum' in front of poor old Gerry Waller, just to see the look on his face." Still holding onto Sally, Katherine turned to her father. "What took you so long?"

Before Roland could answer, Sally said, "Your father's very old-fashioned. He did not want to marry a career woman, so he waited until I decided to retire."

"And you let him wait? The pair of you are crazy. You've wasted years and years."

"Not at all," Roland said. "We couldn't have been any happier with each other than we have been. In fact, if we'd lived together and worked together, we probably would have fallen out long ago."

Sally winked at Katherine and Barnhill. "He'd never put up with me telling him what to do at home as well as at board meetings of Eagle Newspapers."

Barnhill shook Roland's hand. "Congratulations."

"Thank you, but we aren't finished with the announcements."

Sally took the floor again. "Your father agreed to accept my resignation only on the condition that I recommended my own replacement. And"—she looked directly at Katherine—"I recommended you."

"I'm only thirty-two."

"So? Do you feel that's too young to be sitting comfortably on the top floor instead of being out there writing? I'm confident you can fill the position." Sally turned to Barnhill. "How do you feel about it, Raymond? You're on the *Eagle*'s editorial staff, even if you are between jobs."

"I've seen Katherine handle herself like a champion on both sides of the Atlantic."

Katherine started to laugh. "I'm being coerced here. Unless I say yes, you two won't get married. All right, if that's what it takes. Yes. I will accept the appointment. And now"—she swung around to face Barnhill—"what's the big surprise you've been holding back?"

She expected Barnhill's revelation to be along the same lines. Was he carrying an engagement ring he'd bought for her in New York? She hoped it wasn't too big, too flashy. Even diamonds could be overdone.

Barnhill reached into his jacket pocket, but he did not bring out a jewelry box. He withdrew an envelope containing several sheets of paper stapled together. "I want you to be a witness, Katherine."

"To what?"

"To my signature on this contract."

"What contract?"

He looked in amazement at Sally and Roland. "Can you believe she's asking what contract? The one for the movie that's going to be made out of *The Squad,* of course."

Sally's retirement, the talk of marriage, and her own impending appointment to the board of Eagle Newspapers flashed out of Katherine's mind. Her voice jumped several octaves. "How could you keep such wonderful news to yourself all this time?" She snatched the three copies of the contract from Barnhill, and plucked the gold pen from the inside pocket of her father's jacket. "Where do I sign?"

563

"As witness, Kathy, you're supposed to let Raymond sign first." Roland smiled at Barnhill. "I think it's my turn to offer congratulations to you."

"Thank you. I feel that I owe you all a piece of this good fortune. Katherine was the one who spotted where I was going wrong with my writing. You and Sally, if you hadn't created that job for me in New York—"

"Created?" Sally queried. "We created nothing. You went out there and did some very valuable work."

Barnhill raised a hand. "Please let me finish. If you hadn't offered me that job in New York after I'd been canned by IPA, I don't know how I would have managed. That was the turning point in my life."

Katherine handed the contracts and her father's pen to Barnhill. "I've witnessed your signature. Now sign."

He glanced at the contracts. "I hope this is no indication of how you'll fill that slot on the board of Eagle Newspapers."

"What do you mean?"

"Darling, you've witnessed my signature in the very space where I'm supposed to sign."

Katherine thrust a hand to her mouth. "At least I'm consistent. I made the same mistake on all three copies." Then she joined in the laughter which surrounded her. . . .

They returned to Kate's Haven in the evening. After the children were in bed, and Edna and Phillips had retired to their apartment on the third floor of the house, Katherine and Barnhill sat in the breakfast room, drinking hot chocolate. Soon she would take Barnhill home—he had not shopped for a car yet—but before she did so, she wanted to talk about Christmas Day.

"Raymond, I didn't know whether to laugh or cry in the middle of all those surprises. I was happy and sad all at the same time. It was the strangest feeling."

"What was there to be sad about?"

564

"Sally. When she leaves Eagle Newspapers, an era will be over. It'll be the end of a chapter in her life, and in mine."

"So a new one will start."

"I suppose you're right. It's just that changes of this magnitude take a long time to get used to. And, somehow, you never feel that they're happening for the best."

"If you're taking Sally's place, they can't be happening for any reason but the best." He took a sip from the hot chocolate, then pushed the mug away. "I've got a confession to make. When I told your father and Sally about 'Glimpses of America' being a turning point in my life . . . that wasn't really true. The turning point was that day in court when I met you."

"When I stole the money from you to pay Brian's fine? Poor devil, it didn't help him very much." A look of sadness passed across her face, immediately replaced by a smile. "And I asked you out for a drink, remember? That was a turning point in my life as well, because I'd never asked a strange man out for a drink before. Or since."

"Why did you?"

"I thought you were attractive, different. And my life was so messed up at the time, I decided I'd confuse it a bit more. But you weren't playing along, and you turned me down."

"So that's why you never shared that story with me, about the British Patriotic League recruiting young thugs at football games. Hell hath no fury like a woman reporter scorned, eh?"

"Just wait until you've seen a woman editorial director scorned." She put the two mugs in the dishwasher, and wiped the table. "I'll take you home. If you don't scorn me too much, I'll even tuck you in."

Nine days later, Raymond Barnhill resumed his

Fleet Street career. News of his success with fiction had preceded him, and he took great delight in coming face-to-face with those people who had turned him down more than two years earlier, when he had needed both a job and emotional support.

At the beginning of April, *The Squad* was released in the States. Copies were mailed to Barnhill in London. Over dinner at Kate's Haven, he gave one to Katherine. Looking at the dedication, she said: "So you decided against using Shakespeare after all."

"I thought I should be more original."

She read the dedication aloud. " 'For Katherine, who adds luster to an already regal name.' It's original and very lovely. Thank you."

Reviews of *The Squad* soon followed. Without exception, the book was panned. Critics called it insensitive, graceless, heavyhanded. "And those are the kinder adjectives," Barnhill told Katherine, after showing her some of the reviews.

"Then why on earth are you smiling?" Her own face wore shock and dismay.

"Because the other two books got great reviews, and look what happened to them. They dropped right off the end of the shelf." He crushed the reviews into a ball and tossed them into the wastebasket. "Those reviewers must be afflicted with the same apologist mentality, the same Vietnam angst that I was suffering from. That's why they can't accept this book. You wait and see, it'll hit really big."

The wait was short. By the middle of May, *The Squad* was creeping into best-seller lists across North America. In London, half a dozen publishing houses were after British rights, and in California, the complicated process of transferring a story from paper to film was slowly getting under way. But by then, Barnhill's interest in the book was of secondary importance. First and foremost, he was a news reporter, and the year's big story was beginning to break. Buoyed by successes in local elections and a marked reduction in inflation, interest rates, and taxes, the ruling Conservative Party had called a general election for June 9.

Within twenty-four hours of the election announcement, the British Patriotic League held a press conference at Patriot House in Whitechapel. The *Eagle* was represented by Derek Simon, Katherine's former research assistant. Twenty minutes after he wrote up his story, he was called to the editor's office.

Lawrie Stimkin was sitting at his desk, the story in front of him. "Are you certain about these figures?"

"Absolutely certain."

"Thank you." When the reporter left, Stimkin picked up the telephone and called Sally Roberts. "The British Patriotic League has just announced that it will be contesting one hundred and eighty-two seats in the coming election."

Sally gasped. "That's thirty percent of the total seats."

"That's right. What are we going to do?"

"Come up in half an hour."

Thirty minutes later, Stimkin entered Sally's office. Katherine was present, as was her father, who had been summoned from the Adler's store. Roland greeted Stimkin with the same question the editor had asked Derek Simon. "Are you quite certain about this figure of one hundred and eighty-two seats?"

"It was on the radio news not ten minutes ago. Alan Venables sounded damned sure of himself. He said that this time the League would have the added financial benefit of saving most of its deposits."

Roland smacked his fist into the palm of his hand. "We owe those bastards for so much. The deaths of Archie and his grandson, the Manchester store fire, the poster campaign. None of it could we ever prove in a court of law, but we know in our hearts they were responsible for everything."

"Don't forget my accident," Katherine said. "That

was my fault, but it was still caused by them. Our present priority, however, is deciding how to deal with their election campaign. I suggest we begin by adopting a strong editorial position against proportional representation."

"The Liberal-Social Democratic Alliance won't like that," Stimkin argued. "They feel that the current winner-take-all system is unfair to smaller parties."

"It is, which is why it prevents extremists like the League from sneaking into minor positions of power just because they polled a small percentage of the overall vote."

Sally nodded approval. Since the beginning of the year, Katherine had been working on the executive floor, sitting in on meetings, and working with Sally and other members of the Eagle Newspapers board of directors. Katherine's ability to grasp problems and wrest solutions from them came as no surprise to Sally. "That's a solid start. Beyond that . . .?"

Roland sighed. "I feel like I'm playing some old and cracked record. Cover their campaign the same way we cover everyone else's. Publicize every lousy, stinking idea they have. Give them enough rope to hang themselves, and maybe the electorate will finally recognize them for the scum they are, and send them packing. We're supposed to be better off now than we were in 1979, so logic dictates that the base of support for extremists like the League should have shrunk. Let's hope that logic, for once, is right."

Reporters were assigned to cover the League's campaign. They brought back news of a manifesto that was little changed from 1979. Law and order. A strong military. Opposition to immigration. A crackdown on welfare cheats. Outlawing of strikes that threatened the public interest.

"Simplistic programs," commented the *Eagle's*

568

opinion page, "guaranteed to appeal to simple-minded voters who believe that simple solutions exist to complex problems."

A week into the campaign, another similarity to the previous election emerged. A handful of Conservative MPs, all representing constituencies where opinion polls had shown the League to be particularly active, began to push a line that was far to the right of the official party platform. Leading them, as in 1979, were the two politicians Katherine had met at John Saxon's home, the two who had sponsored the censure of her father: Daniel Cooper and Edwin Johnson. Both men were tipped for possible cabinet positions in any new Tory government.

When Lawrie Stimkin mentioned this maneuver at an editorial meeting, Katherine offered the explanation Saxon had given her four years earlier. "They're stealing some of the League's thunder, Lawrie. By doing so, they're hoping to steal votes that would otherwise go to the League."

Stimkin snorted. "This particular group of MPs doesn't need to steal thunder from the League. They're already so far to the right, they're an embarrassment to their own party."

Raymond Barnhill was one of the reporters covering the League's campaign. He attended press conferences, accompanied candidates canvassing for votes, and listened to hours of wholly predictable speeches. The assignment was a stark example of journalism's tedious side, and Barnhill quickly became bored with it.

"Some junior reporter could adequately handle what you have me doing," Barnhill complained to Lawrie Stimkin. "I feel like Van Gogh being asked to draw cartoons."

Stimkin's face broke into a rare smile at the analogy.

He quite liked the American journalist who had decided to make England his home. And he respected him, because he had not let success with a book turn his head away from his newspaper roots. "What do you think you should be doing?"

"What I'd be doing if I were in the States. I'd take a photographer and sniff around. I'd dig up some dirt, see what was underneath. And then I'd splash it across the front page."

Stimkin's smile grew even broader. "Why not? We already have McDonald's and Burger King in the High Street, and Pizza Hut and Wendy's on every corner, so what harm can it do to try American-style news coverage? I'll give you until Thursday. Don't bring me home any libel suits."

Barnhill sought out Sid Hall. "Grab your long lenses and plenty of film, Sid. We're going hunting."

"What's in season?"

"The head honchos of the British Patriotic League."

Hall needed no second bidding. He still wore a scar where his cheek had been torn by a flying brick.

Barnhill signed out a company car for three days, then he and the photographer headed toward Patriot House. Instead of entering, Barnhill parked a hundred yards away, with a clear view of the entrance. Hall focused the five-hundred-millimeter lens of his motor-driven Nikon on the entrance, firing off shot after shot of the people who came and went. After half an hour, a short, dumpy man in a brown corduroy jacket and flannel trousers came hurrying out of the building. Hall tapped Barnhill's arm.

"There goes Trevor Burns."

The League's publicity director drove off in a blue van. Barnhill followed. Burns's journey took him to a large building on which was a sign: "Blackford Printing Company." He backed up to a loading dock. Through the long lens, Hall took photographs of Burns supervising the loading of four dozen cardboard boxes.

"I thought they had their own press," Hall said, as Barnhill followed the van back to Patriot House.

"They're running nearly two hundred candidates in a general election, Sid. The League's press probably can't handle the necessary volume."

The van stopped in front of Patriot House. Half a dozen young men came running out to unload the boxes and take them inside. Burns opened one of the boxes, pulled out a handful of magazines, and began passing them out to pedestrians. An elderly man took one, glancing through it as he walked toward where Barnhill and Hall were parked. He dropped it into a trash can not five yards from the car. Barnhill waited a minute before leaving the car to retrieve it.

The magazine was a special pre-election edition of *Patriot*. The front cover showed a color photograph of 10 Downing Street, with the Union Jack and the League pennant superimposed across the door. Block capitals declared: "You can make it happen!"

Barnhill skimmed through the magazine. It contained pictures and biographies of the League's candidates, a slanted history of the organization, and an interview with Alan Venables on why the League was Britain's last remaining hope. "Check this out, Sid," Barnhill said. "Sixty-four pages, and four-color all the way through."

"Even some advertising," Hall said, studying a full-page ad for a building supply company. "Must have cost a pretty penny to put this together, but the advertising sure didn't pay for it."

Reporter and photographer remained in the car until seven-thirty that evening. Although hundreds of people passed in and out of Patriot House, they saw no more of the executive committee. They drove back to Fleet Street, stopping on the way for a sandwich and a cup of tea. While Hall developed the eight rolls of film he had shot that day, Barnhill took the copy of *Patriot* to his desk. A message in his typewriter asked him to telephone Katherine at home.

"Did you find any real dirt?" she asked him.

"I see you spoke to Lawrie Stimkin."

"He told me you gave him a lecture on how things were done on *The New York Times* and the *Washington Post*."

"I wasn't that aggressive. I made suggestions."

"What did you get?"

"Just a super-glossy commemorative edition of the League's rag, with enough four-color in it to sink a battleship. Sid and I will try again tomorrow."

"Good luck."

Barnhill went back to reading the magazine. An hour later, Sid Hall appeared with contact sheets and a magnifier. A dozen frames were of Trevor Burns. The remainder showed visitors to Patriot House. Barnhill sifted through them. Men, women, young, old. The only common denominator was that they were all white, but he had not expected anything different.

"Recognize anyone?" Hall asked.

"Not a soul. We'll try again tomorrow."

Early the next morning, they were parked in the same place, in time to see all three members of the executive committee arrive at campaign headquarters. Alan Venables was first, at eight-thirty. Pinned to his tweed jacket was a red, white, and gold rosette. He stopped to shake hands with several passersby, and posed for a press photograph before entering the building.

Trevor Burns was next, wearing the same clothes as the previous day, a rosette pinned to his corduroy jacket. No one shook Burns's hand, or asked for his picture. Neville Sharpe, the League's financial director, arrived just before nine o'clock, tall and somber in a dark blue suit with the inevitable rosette.

Burns came out again fifteen minutes later, carrying a dozen buff envelopes. He stepped into a white

Vauxhall driven by another man. Barnhill started his own car, and the tail began again. The white Vauxhall headed west. After a mile, Sid Hall let out a painful groan.

"What's the matter with you?" Barnhill asked.

"I bet I know where they're going."

"Where?"

The photographer did not answer. Barnhill continued to follow the Vauxhall, and soon he knew. Where else did a man seeking publicity go? Trevor Burns was leading them home to Fleet Street.

Burns went from one newspaper to the next, delivering the buff envelopes. He did not neglect the *Eagle;* he left an envelope there as well, addressed to the editor. Barnhill entered the Eagle building long enough to find out that the envelope contained a copy of the speech Alan Venables would give that evening to a meeting of electrical trade union members.

"Not much of a hunting season so far, is it?" Hall remarked on the journey back to Patriot House.

Barnhill shrugged. "You don't hit a bird with every shot. We'll get our chance yet, you'll see."

In the afternoon, they followed Venables as the League chairman lent his personal support to candidates in East London. In the evening, when Venables kept his appointment with the union members, Barnhill and Hall returned to the *Eagle.* Again, there was a message in Barnhill's typewriter. He telephoned Kate's Haven, ready for some more teasing.

Katherine did not disappoint him. "How did the American plan go today?"

"You keep riding me, and I'll find another job."

"Don't do that. But I did hear that you and Sid were shown the way back to Fleet Street this morning."

"Tomorrow," Barnhill vowed. "Tomorrow we're going to come up with a story that will win the Pulitzer Prize, or whatever they award over here."

Katherine blew a kiss into the telephone. "I'll give

you a prize whether you find anything or not."

An hour later, Sid Hall brought that day's collection of photographs. More faces going in and out of Patriot House. Burns delivering press releases in Fleet Street. Venables canvassing. "All we need now," Barnhill said sourly, "are pictures of Neville Sharpe engaged in some thoroughly useless pursuit, and we'll have the complete set."

Shortly before noon the following day, they got the complete set. Neville Sharpe emerged from Patriot House, smart and businesslike in a dark gray pinstripe suit, with a large briefcase swinging from his hand. The League's financial director climbed into a yellow Ford and pulled away. Barnhill followed.

"Where do you think this one's going to lead us, Sid?"

"I'm paid to take photographs, not think."

Barnhill tailed Sharpe across the Thames at London Bridge, past the Elephant and Castle, and all the way to Kennington. The yellow Ford signaled a right turn, and Hall began to laugh.

"What the hell's so funny?" asked Barnhill, who was quite unfamiliar with south London.

"He's going to the Oval. The cricket ground. In the middle of an election campaign, he's going to sit on his arse and watch a bloody cricket match!"

"No offense, Sid, but you English are an unfathomable lot."

"Maybe we're just more civilized than you Yanks." Barnhill grinned. "Please don't call me a Yank."

A minute after Sharpe had entered the stadium, still carrying the briefcase, Barnhill and Hall followed. The photographer panned the crowd with the powerful telephoto lens. Barnhill heard the motorized film advance whir into action.

"Where is he?"

Hall passed him the camera. Barnhill looked across the vast playing field, beyond the white-clad cricketers to the crowd on the far side. In a sea of casual clothing, Sharpe's pinstripe suit was easy to spot. Barnhill returned the camera and wondered how he would explain this to Lawrie Stimkin. Other reporters were busy following election campaigns, and Barnhill was wasting time at a cricket game! So much for sniffing around and digging up some dirt.

Something was happening on the field. Barnhill watched. A ball hit into the air, a barehanded fielder hauling it in, the umpire raising his index finger magisterially into the air. Despite his irritation, Barnhill had to smile. In baseball, the umpire would have signaled the out with a snarling, arm-snapping, thumb-jerking, foot-dragging performance deserving of an Oscar. Here, the man simply held up his index finger. Perhaps Sid Hall was right, and the English were more civilized. They were certainly more restrained.

"He's going."

"Huh?"

"Sharpe. He's getting up and leaving."

"He's only been here fifteen minutes. What can he possibly see in fifteen minutes? For crying out loud, the games sometimes last three days, don't they?" Still complaining, Barnhill followed Hall toward the exit. They reached their car first and waited. Sharpe headed back the way he had come. Before reaching London Bridge, he pulled into the curb. Barnhill drove past, looking for a parking spot.

Hall swung his head around. "He's going into a bank."

Alarm bells rang in Barnhill's head. "Sid, check it out!" He stopped just long enough to allow the photographer to jump out of the car, then pulled into an empty space fifty yards on.

Sharpe came out of the bank five minutes later and drove away. Hall was a minute behind him. "What happened, Sid?"

"While I asked for information about opening an account, I managed to overhear Sharpe's transaction. He was making a deposit. A bundle of money he had, took it out of that briefcase he's been lugging around all day. All fifty-pound notes it looked like, as well. Hundreds of them, maybe even a thousand."

"Was it to his own account? To a League account?"

"I don't know. I couldn't very well look over his shoulder, could I?"

"No, I guess not." Barnhill pulled out into the traffic. There was no hurry now. Sharpe had gone. They'd just head back to Fleet Street, and wonder about all that money. "Why a cricket match, Sid? Why did he go to a cricket match at the Oval?"

"Maybe the man just likes cricket. Some people do, you know," Hall said in a voice which implied he did not.

"I suppose so." Would he ever understand the English, Barnhill wondered. Sir Francis Drake played bowls before defeating the Spanish Armada, and Neville Sharpe punctuated an election campaign with a quick visit to a county cricket game.

Sid Hall went straight to the darkroom to develop his film. Barnhill stayed out for an hour, eating lunch. He wanted to defer seeing the other reporters for as long as possible. When he eventually showed his face, the visit to the Oval was common knowledge. Sid Hall had told a couple of people that he'd watched a cricket game, and the word had spread. Barnhill just smiled and nodded as he was ribbed about lazing around while everyone else worked.

Lawrie Stimkin, however, seemed sympathetic. Standing by Barnhill's desk, he said, "American ideas just don't work over here, that's all. Maybe it has to do with us using two hundred and forty volts instead of one-ten, or perhaps it's because we drive on the other side of the road."

"Don't forget the money Sid saw Neville Sharpe

deposit. Sid's sure it was a big bundle."

"So?"

"Well, where does it come from?"

"It could have been membership dues from the cretins who belong to the British Patriotic League."

Before Barnhill could think of an answer, Sid Hall's voice roared across the editorial floor. "Raymond . . . ! There is a Santa Claus after all!"

The photographer spread prints over the desk top. Much had been cropped out. Gone was the field of play which had been between camera and subject. Gone was most of the crowd. All that remained was the area where Sharpe had been sitting.

Two dozen spectators were in each picture. Most were staring straight out, intent upon the game. Only Sharpe and the man seated next to him had other interests. In some prints, Sharpe could be seen talking to his neighbor, a fat man stuffed into an open-necked shirt and a sportcoat. He could have been anywhere between forty and fifty, with dark, curly hair that was going gray at the sides, and thick horn-rimmed glasses that gave him the appearance of an obese owl.

And in a series of three pictures, clearly shown, was the fat man passing four bulging envelopes to Sharpe, and Sharpe slipping them into the large briefcase.

Barnhill turned triumphantly to Stimkin. "Now what have you got to say?"

"How much was it, Sid?" the editor asked.

"A lot. All fifties. A real bundle."

"Telephone the bank. Find out—"

Barnhill was far ahead of the editor. He opened a telephone directory, looked up the bank and the branch, and dialed the number. "May I speak to the manager, please?" His voice took on a plum-in-the-mouth English stage accent. "My name is Raymond Lloyd, sales director of Blackford Printing Company."

The manager came on the line. "We are doing some printing work for the British Patriotic League,"

Barnhill explained. "Their Mr. Neville Sharpe wishes to pay by a check drawn on your bank, and as it's for a rather large amount, we're understandably cautious. He claims he has just made a deposit that will cover the check, and he has advised us to contact you to put our minds at rest."

"How much is the check for?" the manager asked.

Barnhill took a deep breath and played Sid Hall's words over in his mind. All fifties, maybe even a thousand of them . . . "Forty-eight thousand pounds."

"You may accept Mr. Sharpe's check with confidence, Mr. Lloyd. Fifty thousand pounds was deposited a short while ago."

"Thank you." Barnhill replaced the receiver and dropped the false accent. "Fifty grand, that's what our fat boy in the picture passed to Sharpe."

Stimkin stared thoughtfully at the photograph. "You know, for years we've been trying to find out where the League gets its money. This could be the first worthwhile clue."

"If we can find out who fat boy is," Barnhill said soberly.

Hall took a grease pencil and drew a circle around the fat man's face. "The *Sunday Eagle* runs a competition during the football season—a crowd shot from one of the games, with half a dozen faces ringed like this. Whoever comes forward wins a prize. Why don't we do something similar here, run this picture and offer a prize for anyone who can identify this man?"

"That's not a bad idea. Let me check with upstairs and see how much of a bounty we're willing to pay." Stimkin rang through to Sally Roberts. After he'd explained about the picture and the hefty bank deposit, Sally told him to come up.

Accompanied by Barnhill and Hall, Stimkin rode the elevator to the executive floor. Katherine was with Sally when they entered the office. The two women had been going over budgets; computer printout covered the desk. Sally cleared a space, and Hall set out his pictures.

Stimkin jabbed a finger at the circled face. "You can see him handing over the envelopes to Sharpe, and Sid Hall here witnessed Sharpe making a bank deposit with money that was in the envelopes."

"And you've since found out that the deposit was for fifty thousand pounds?" Sally asked.

"Right." Stimkin stepped back as Katherine bent low over the picture. "How much can we offer?"

"One thousand pounds," Sally answered immediately.

Katherine snapped her fingers. "Give it to me, then. I'm sure I know that man, or I once did."

"What?" Sally and the three men joined Katherine in bending over the picture. "Who is he?"

Katherine could feel her heart pounding. Blood rushed to her head. She had to steady herself against the desk as solutions to a thousand riddles pounded her brain.

Her answer, when it came, contained all the vehemence she could muster. "He's a fat bullying pig called Nigel Hawtrey."

26

At five in the afternoon, Oxford Street was awash with a tidal wave of people rushing home. Katherine elbowed her way through the crowd, looking from the piece of paper in her hand to the numbers on the buildings. At last, she spotted the one she wanted. Veering to her right, she navigated the stream of human traffic, and pushed open a heavy glass door. She crossed a small lobby to the elevator. A directory board informed her that the Chalfont Office Bureau was on the third floor.

The elevator opened into a spacious reception area. Three young women sat filling out forms to register for temporary secretarial work with the agency. At a desk facing the elevator sat another young woman wearing a blue dress with a white collar.

"Welcome to the Chalfont Office Bureau," the receptionist greeted Katherine. Her right hand moved toward a tray full of application forms. "Have you worked with us before?"

"I'm afraid I'm not looking for a job. I'd like to see Deidre Chalfont."

"Do you have an appointment?"

"No. But if you tell her Katherine Kassler is here, I think you'll find that she'll be willing to see me."

The receptionist dialed an internal number. "Ask Miss Chalfont if she'll see a Katherine Kassler." A pause was followed by "She will? I'll send her along." Replacing the receiver, she looked at Katherine. "Go to the end of the corridor and turn right. Miss Chalfont's personal assistant will be waiting for you."

"Thank you." Katherine followed the directions. On the walls she passed were blown-up advertisements for the bureau. She remembered seeing them in newspapers and in trains. Until now she had never connected the name.

"Mrs. Kassler?" A redhead in a plum trouser suit was waiting. "Miss Chalfont's waiting for you." She opened a door behind her desk. "Please go in."

Deidre Chalfont was as Katherine remembered her from election night in 1979. Slender, smartly dressed in a red skirt, a double-breasted blue-on-blue striped blazer, and a white silk blouse. Thick dark hair was waved around her face to soften the firmness of her jaw.

"I've been waiting four years for this moment," Deidre said. "Ever since that night in the Spaniards."

"Your wait's over."

"Please sit down." She waved toward a couch against the wall. Katherine dropped onto it. Deidre pulled up a chair. "Four years ago, you thought I was a bitter, jealous bitch, didn't you?" Seeing the embarrassment on Katherine's face, Deidre smiled. "You were tactful enough not to come right out and say it, but it was obvious that you were thinking it. So why have you come to see me now?"

Katherine was not about to share her blackest doubts with Deidre. They were too horrible to be true, yet the more she considered them, the stronger they became. She was so horrified that she had not even confided in her colleagues and friends at the *Eagle*. After her outburst earlier that afternoon on recognizing Nigel Hawtrey, she'd put a clamp on her tongue.

581

Sid Hall, certainly; remembered who Hawtrey was—the villain of Cadmus Court, when poor old Archie Waters and his grandson had been victimized. Sally must remember him, too. But neither had recognized the ominous significance that had leaped in front of Katherine's eyes.

Katherine did not even let on to Deidre that she and Saxon were no longer together. "You suggested four years ago that I ask John how he came to employ William Brown. I did. He told me that he'd caught William trying to steal his car. John took pity on him, because he was penniless and starving. Instead of calling the police—which is what you wanted him to do—he offered William a job. Is that how it really happened?" Katherine was counting on Deidre's loathing of her former husband being as strong as it ever was. She was hoping that the woman would not even need a solid reason to spew hatred about John Saxon, and she was not disappointed.

"You're making him sound like a damned philanthropist, darling. He caught William trying to steal his car, all right. But he didn't take pity on him. He gave William a choice: do a nasty little chore for John, or be turned over to the police."

"What kind of chore?"

"John had an old friend with whom he'd fallen out over some trifling business affair. From there, it had gone completely out of hand. The ex-friend's pride and joy was an absolutely irreplaceable vintage Rolls Royce, which he drove every Sunday morning to a public house a couple of miles away. So all the lesser mortals could admire it, I suppose. Anyway, William's chore was to steal the Roller from outside the pub, and wreck it. Which he did. He jumped out at the top of a hill, and let the car smash itself to pieces at the bottom. John was so thrilled that he gave William a bonus of one hundred pounds, a lot of money in those days. Then, when they realized how suited they were to each other, he offered William full-time employment."

"What other dirty work did William do for John?"

"While I was in the picture?" Deidre closed her eyes as she tried to remember, and Katherine could see that Saxon's former wife was enjoying the opportunity to wash the dirty linen in public. "A couple of times, John had business deals going sour on him, like someone else offering more money for a piece of property than he was prepared to pay. William had a lot of friends on the seamy side of the street, and if there was any dirt to be learned about these business rivals, anything worth blackmailing them over, William's friends could come up with it pretty quickly."

"I'd never have guessed that John could have been involved in anything so shady."

"You should have been more attentive to me four years ago."

"You're right, I should have." Katherine gave Deidre an apologetic smile, and segued into the real reason for her visit. William had just been a preamble to loosen Deidre up. "Did he meet Nigel Hawtrey the same way?"

Deidre shuddered. "That one! He must have been born on Halloween, with a vulture for a father and a snake for a mother. That swine deserves a place of honor in the *Guinness Book of Records* as the biggest rogue who never went to jail."

Elated by the reaction, Katherine asked, "What did he do?"

"He was John's silent partner. You see, in the early days, John was involved in two distinctly different types of property. There were the expensive office buildings that he moved around with such razzle-dazzle, but there was also some very cheap and nasty property that he kept close to his chest. John would buy houses in poor areas that he thought would improve. That way, he'd get growth. And for quick income, he rented them out and gouged the tenants."

"John was a slumlord?"

"Through Nigel Hawtrey he was. Nigel ran that side of the business for John. Ran it very efficiently, and kept it well insulated from the main company. More than once, when John got into financial difficulty with the main business, the steady income from Nigel kept the boat from sinking. Then Nigel got bigger ideas. Instead of buying more houses, he persuaded John to buy up blocks of flats in improving areas. The plan was to get rid of the sitting tenants, decorate the flats, and sell the building for a good profit. One of Nigel's jobs, of course, was *persuading* the tenants to leave. They even formed a company called Cadmus Property Company, but by then my marriage to John was on the rocks, and I was on the way out. I seem to remember that John was forced to get rid of Nigel some six or seven years ago—some scandal over Nigel's methods of getting tenants to leave. But I doubt very much if he really severed the cord. Nigel was too valuable a rogue to lose so easily."

"So the brigadier did know what every corporal in the brigade was up to," Katherine murmured.

"I beg your pardon?"

"Just thinking aloud." Katherine made a show of glancing at the clock on the wall. "Five-thirty already! I have to fly. Thank you for the information." She rushed out before Deidre could remember the exact circumstances in which Saxon had been forced to get rid of Nigel Hawtrey, because then she might start asking questions of her own.

Outside, surrounded by the swirling rush of Oxford Street, Katherine paused long enough to gather her thoughts. Although Deidre Chalfont had just dropped a few more pegs into the proper holes, Katherine still had little more than hearsay to go on. Hearsay, circumstantial evidence, and her own gut feeling. No court of law would accept that. More was required. She needed some corroborating testimony, the gospel from someone who'd been involved. She rang home to tell Edna that she would be working late. After that, she returned to the *Eagle*.

Seven years earlier, when writing the Cadmus Court story, Katherine had learned Nigel Hawtrey's unlisted home number by bribing an *Eagle* contact at the Post Office. This time, she did not have to go to those lengths. No longer in the business of property management, Hawtrey let himself be listed. Katherine found him in the directory, with an address in Kensington.

Next, she went looking for Raymond Barnhill and Sid Hall. They were both about to leave for the night. After telling them to wait, she sought Lawrie Stimkin. He was in a discussion with the *Eagle*'s political editor. Apologizing, Katherine pulled him to one side. "Lawrie, I want Raymond and Sid for an assignment which could involve some serious flirting with the law."

"Does it have anything to do with that fat man whose picture Sid took at the Oval?" When Katherine said yes, Stimkin nodded. "You're the editorial director-designate; why are you even bothering to ask me?"

"Because you, Lawrie dear, are the editor."

Stimkin, his ego tickled, smiled. "Take them, but do me a favor and keep them out of jail. We'll need everyone for the final runup to the election."

First, Katherine bought both men dinner. Over the meal, she said, "I've got a special job. It doesn't require you to bring a camera, Sid. And Raymond, you won't need a notebook or a pen. You might have to babysit someone all night, though."

They listened as Katherine outlined her plan. When she finished, the only comment came from Barnhill. "This sounds like another of your schemes to get an exclusive story for yourself."

Across the table, in Hall's view, Katherine's reply was all sweetness. "Sally retires in a little over four weeks, and I move into her office. Would you begrudge me one final exclusive?" Beneath the table, where the photographer's eyes could not follow, she kicked Barnhill in the ankle. He trapped her foot between his legs, grinning widely as she struggled to free herself.

At eight-thirty, they drove to Kensington, Katherine leading the way in the white Lotus, with Barnhill and Hall following in a company car. The address in the telephone directory turned out to be a new apartment block called the Terrace Tower. In the lobby, buttons and mailboxes were lined up along one wall. Next to Nigel Hawtrey's name on the directory board was the number 410. Katherine pressed the corresponding button.

After thirty seconds, a loud voice yelled, "Who is it?"

"Mr. Hawtrey?" Katherine asked.

"Yes."

"Neville Sharpe sent me. He said you gave him two hundred and fifty pounds too much, and I'm returning it."

"Come up."

The security door clicked, and Katherine led the way into the building. In the elevator, she noticed a sign stating that the building was owned and managed by Saxon Holdings. Now why, she asked herself, shouldn't that surprise her? They got out at the fourth floor and walked along a wide, carpeted hall. At 410, Katherine motioned for Barnhill and Hall to stand off to one side, then she gave the door buzzer three sharp jabs.

"All right, all right!" a voice yelled from inside the apartment. "I'm coming!" Katherine felt herself being inspected through the peephole. She pulled five fifty-pound notes from her bag and waved them.

The door swung back. Hawtrey stood there, a bright red silk robe over his shirt and trousers. The instant he saw the two men, he stepped back and tried to slam the door. Hall was far too quick. He jammed his foot into the opening, and smashed through with his shoulder. The door flew back into Hawtrey's face. The three intruders piled into the apartment and closed the door.

"We want to talk to you, Mr. Hawtrey," Hall said. He grabbed Hawtrey by the shoulders and shoved him into the living room, pushing him down into an imitation leather recliner.

"I know you!" Hawtrey pointed a finger at Katherine, and began to get up. "You're that bitch—"

The words were cut off by Hall's beefy hand slapping Hawtrey across the mouth. His head snapped around and his glasses went flying onto the carpet. Barnhill picked them up and stuck them back on Hawtrey's face.

Katherine took Hall's photographs from her handbag. "This is you, Mr. Hawtrey, isn't it? You giving fifty thousand pounds to Neville Sharpe of the British Patriotic League."

"Are you asking me, or are you telling me?"

This time Hall waited for Hawtrey to finish the sentence before hitting him. A sharp, clubbing blow with the side of the hand against the back of the neck sent Hawtrey flying forward.

Katherine waited for him to recover. In a level voice, she said, "Mr. Hawtrey, please listen to me. We need some answers, and you are going to supply them. How you do so is up to you. We would prefer you gave them to us willingly, but if you want us to force them out of you, we'll do so."

Hawtrey stared up into Katherine's face. Her lips were compressed into a thin line, and her blue eyes had all the warmth of an Arctic blizzard. "I gave Neville Sharpe fifty thousand."

"Thank you." As hard as she'd made herself sound, Katherine had to fight down nausea as she forced herself to look at Hawtrey. Blood trickled from his mouth, and his eyes were misty from the rabbit punch.

"What was the fifty thousand pounds for?"

"Campaign expenses."

"Why was it cash, not a check?"

"It was always cash. That way there was no chance of its origin being traced."

"On whose instructions did you give the money to Sharpe? Was it on John Saxon's instructions?"

Hawtrey let out a deep breath with agonizing slowness. Betrayal was a painful process, even when there seemed little left to betray. "Yes, John instructed me to do it."

"Seven years ago," Katherine said, "John Saxon, in order to protect his own reputation, dismissed you over the Cadmus Court scandal. He pretended, and we all believed him, that you alone had been responsible for the disgraceful events at Cadmus Court. How did you go from there to the British Patriotic League?"

Hawtrey found the courage to answer the question with one of his own. "What do I get out of helping you?"

Hall grabbed a handful of hair. Hawtrey started to rise from the chair. Katherine waved a hand, and Hall released his grip. "You know me, Mr. Hawtrey. I'm not the police. I'm just a reporter after a story, the same as last time. I know most of the story already. If you help me fill in the last couple of squares, I promise that we'll let you go before the story comes out. Then you can find your own hole to crawl into."

Whether Hawtrey got away or not was of little concern to Katherine. At Cadmus Court she had unwittingly settled for a minnow and only half the story. This time she wanted the entire story and all the big sharks.

"John and his right-wing friends had figured out a way to save the country—"

"Right-wing friends?"

"Those MPs, Cooper and Johnson. Sir Donald Leslie, Jeffrey Dillard, that whole crowd John was friendly with. They were always discussing ways to bring Britain around to their way of thinking. They played politics like other people play chess or Monopoly. Finally, they came up with one idea they thought would work. It was as complicated as hell, and it was a long-term project, but they were all for it. They put a proposition to me. They wanted me to organize an extremist party for them, a hate group. They wanted me to find the leaders for it, then they wanted to channel funds through me to get it going."

"So you went out and found Alan Venables, Neville Sharpe, and Trevor Burns. How did you get them interested?"

"With money, how else? John and his friends are loaded. Some of them can cough up a million pounds and not miss it."

"Why Venables, Sharpe, and Burns?"

"We wanted an intellectual who could speak, who could really work people into a frenzy like Hitler used to do. That was Venables. We needed a communicator; that was Burns. And we needed a man who was good with finances to cover everything up, and that was Neville Sharpe."

Katherine looked up at Barnhill standing behind her. "Remember telling me about the navy captain you met in Vietnam?"

Barnhill nodded. "The guy who'd served with George Rockwell? Looks like you've found your Icelandic wife."

Katherine returned her attention to Hawtrey. "Venables, Sharpe, and Burns, they don't have any strong political feelings, do they?"

"They learned to have them. Take Venables, for instance. He was as liberal as anyone when I first met him. He could afford to be—he was broke and living in a furnished room. I gave him a few right-wing ideas when I waved a bundle of money under his nose."

"And the others? Burns and Sharpe?"

589

"For the right amount of money, they all became supporters of the master-race theory."

"How long was this charade supposed to last?"

"Until next week."

"Next week?"

"That's right, election time. Edwin Johnson and Daniel Cooper head a clique of a dozen or so right-wing Conservative MPs. Four years ago . . ."

Hawtrey talked on and on, from the British Patriotic League's initial recruiting campaign — "getting together a group of tough young thugs who'd punch and kick their way into the headlines" — to the League's ultimate objectives. As she listened to the low monotone, Katherine saw more pieces of the puzzle falling into place.

Just after ten o'clock, Hawtrey stopped talking. Katherine turned away and gazed at the window. What had Deidre said four years earlier? Yes, that was it — before marrying John Saxon, she should have seen that he already had three loves: his business, his country, and himself. Especially his country, Katherine reflected. Deidre's biggest bastard ever to walk this earth was looking more the part with every passing minute.

There was a telephone in the living room. Katherine dialed the number of Saxon's London home. The call was answered on the second ring, and Katherine recognized William's voice.

"Is Mr. Saxon there, William? This is Katherine Kassler."

If the chauffeur was surprised at the caller, he showed no sign of it. "I'm afraid not, miss."

"Do you know what time he'll be in?" She looked at Hawtrey sitting in the chair. Sid Hall had a hand pressed to the fat man's mouth in case he tried to shout a warning. "It's urgent that I speak to him, William."

"You might catch him at Saxon House. He said he'd be working late tonight."

"Thank you." She pressed the receiver rest, then dialed another number. "Lawrie, what have you got for the front page?"

"Campaign news. It's becoming a real mudslinging fight. A Labour MP started a riot by accusing the prime minister tonight of glorying in the slaughter of the Falklands war, and seeking votes on the backs of dead and injured British troops."

"Cut it to a paragraph and stick it inside. Then get file photographs of John Saxon, Sir Donald Leslie, Jeffrey Dillard, Edwin Johnson, Daniel Cooper . . ." She ran through the list of every notable she had ever met through Saxon. "Also photographs of the British Patriotic League executive committee. And some graphic shots of the riots they were involved in. I am going to give you a front page, and a turn to pages two and three, that will make the rest of the street throw their typewriters out of the window in absolute despair."

Stimkin's response to this news was a gruff "When?"

"Soon. I need to see just one more person."

"One o'clock, Katherine. That's as long as I'll give you."

Hanging up, she turned to Barnhill and Hall. "I'm driving to St. James's Square. After that, I'll return to the *Eagle*. Once I've got my story written, and it's too late for anyone else to get wind of it, I'll telephone you here to release Hawtrey."

"If you think I'm going to let you see Saxon on your own," Barnhill said, "you'd better think again."

"Your job is to stay here and guard Hawtrey."

"Sid can take care of him. I'm coming with you."

Barnhill took two steps in Katherine's direction. She speared his chest with a rigid index finger. She started to say "I can do this by myself," before changing it to "This is something I have to do by myself."

"Because of what you and —"

"Precisely. Make yourselves comfortable and listen

591

for my phone call. I'll ring twice, then hang up and ring again. Don't answer for anyone else." She hurried downstairs, climbed into the Lotus, and sped away.

As she wove in and out of the heavy traffic, her mind raced. God, how could she have been so naive? How could she have missed all the clues, all the coincidences that had punctuated her life since meeting John Saxon? She'd been so infatuated with him and so confused with everything else, that she'd been unable to see. And even when the infatuation had worn off, had changed to irritation as she recognized his arrogance, she'd remained blind.

She slotted the Lotus into a parking spot on the east side of St. James's Square, got out, and walked across the road to Saxon House. Looking up, she saw lights in Saxon's top-floor office. The windows to the balcony were open. Did he admire his front garden at nighttime as well?

A night doorman was on duty. "May I help you, miss?" he asked, as Katherine sailed through the revolving door.

"I'm going to see Mr. Saxon."

"Is he expecting you?"

"Yes." She walked across the lobby to the elevator. Waiting for the door to open, she saw the doorman fiddling with his telephone. On the sixth floor, the elevator opened out into the reception area Katherine remembered so well, with its proud paintings of properties owned by Saxon Holdings. She recognized a new one: Saxon Tower in New York City, the curving black glass edifice on West Forty-second Street.

At this time of night, there was no receptionist to guide Katherine to Saxon's office. She didn't need one. She marched along the corridor flanked by glass-fronted offices and pushed back the heavy oak door. Saxon was sitting at his desk. A gold fountain pen was poised in his hand as he studied a set of blueprints.

"Hello, Katherine," he said without looking up.

"William phoned to say you were asking for me. The doorman also warned me that a young woman was on the way up. What can I do for you?"

She opened her handbag and pulled out the photographs she had shown Hawtrey. "What do you have to say about this, you despicable bastard?"

The pen dropped from Saxon's hand. His head shot up from the blueprints. His astonishment at being addressed so rudely was nothing compared to his shock at seeing the photographs. He picked them up. Eyes wide in stunned surprise, he looked at Katherine.

"It's you, isn't it, John? You and your friends. You're the ones behind the British Patriotic League. All those clues you gave me, and I was too stupid to see them. Remember the night the pendant was stolen? When I got to your home in Marble Arch, you were watching the football riot on television. You never watched television as a rule, but you were watching that! Something important, that's how you described it. Damn right it was important. It was the start of the League's campaign to kick its way into the public eye."

Saxon regained some composure. "Are these photographs supposed to signify something to me, Katherine?"

She ignored his question. "The *Eagle* started its probe of soccer hooliganism. We made the link between the thugs and the League. That's when you started criticizing the work I was doing. You said by publicizing the League I'd only help them get more recruits. And when you saw you couldn't stop me, you tried to persuade me to quit the *Eagle* altogether, remember? I thought you were genuinely concerned about my career, but all you were doing was trying to stop me digging further. Your friend Jeffrey Dillard, he was in on it, wasn't he? He's a part of this, so it was easy to offer me a job on 'Fightback'. Then later, when I was taking over the show from Jeffrey, and I was dithering about poaching Derek Simon and Heather

Harvey from the *Eagle* to be my research assistants, you urged me to go ahead. And why? Because you knew Derek and Heather had taken up where I'd left off on the League investigation. Congratulations, John! I took your advice, and the investigation was sabotaged again."

Katherine rested her hands on the edge of the desk and leaned over Saxon. "And what you did to Sidney Glassman was shameful. He was a good man, and you helped to ruin him. Who gave Jeffrey the information about Sidney Glassman's son Melvin? Was it William, who made a science of discovering blackmail secrets among your business competitors?" She saw Saxon flinch at that, and she smiled coldly. "Oh, yes, I spoke to Deidre again. This time I picked her memory clean, and I believed every detestable thing she had to say about you. It wasn't a case of Jeffrey wanting revenge on Glassman for some election defeat back in 1964, was it? You all wanted the total destruction of Glassman because he'd helped my father organize those rock concerts to combat the League's 'Youth for Britain' rallies. After I'd turned down Jeffrey's original suggestion for the Glassman story, you made damned sure he got the opportunity to run it by persuading me to go to New York with you!"

Katherine stepped back a pace, and caught her breath. "And the worst thing of all, you swine, was Brian Waters. Why did Brian die, John? Was it because of his feud with Ginger, like you tried to convince me it was? Or did he die because you knew he was my source within the League, within the British Brigade?"

She did not expect Saxon to answer, but he did. "Ginger warned Venables that Brian wasn't to be trusted. Venables had to be sure, though. I found out the truth for him. From you."

"Who decided Brian had to die?"

"We all did, Katherine," Saxon stated in a remarkably calm voice. "My associates and the League's executive committee. Each of us had as much to lose as the other. Venables and Ginger saw to it. Then, while we were thinking of a way to make sure Ginger never talked, old Archie Waters obligingly helped us out."

"What about the personal attacks on my father? Were they joint decisions as well?"

"That was Venables's doing. He wanted revenge on you for the way you made him look a fool that morning at the BBC. And he wanted revenge on your father because of the manner in which the *Eagle* had hounded him. I tried to warn you during the Falklands business, only you weren't in the mood to take advice. But that's all in the past now, isn't it?" Saxon said as he stood up. "What we have to concern ourselves with now is how you intend to use all this information."

"How do you think I'm going to use it? In a front-page story, of course! But first, let me make sure I've got it all straight. I wouldn't want to damage your reputation by libeling you, would I?" she asked sarcastically. "Those bigots who actually support the British Patriotic League—all the candidates for the election, and the morons who'll vote for them—they don't realize that they're being used. They think they're part of a genuine political movement, when really it's nothing more than a carefully constructed charade. A prop to help a clique of reactionary Conservative MPs, led by Edwin Johnson and Daniel Cooper, gain influence within the party. The League was never supposed to win any seats, was it? It was just meant to indicate a groundswell extremist support, so that the Johnson/Cooper clique could push Conservative policy and thinking further and further to the right. Just how far to the right did you and your friends intend to take the Conservative Party, John?"

Saxon made no attempts at denial. "Until supreme power rests in the hands of the industrialists. Until the unions are abolished. Until we have a productive country where able-bodied people work, and where only the sick and helpless are given a free ride."

"That's classic Fascism. The corporate state."

"Give it any name you like, Katherine, but it's the only chance this country has." Saxon's voice turned sharp. "For God's sake, you should be able to understand that. Look at your father, and look at me. We're two very similar men. We built something, and we have to protect it constantly against those who would steal it from us."

Outrage flared within Katherine. "Don't you dare compare yourself to my father! He would never dream of doing the things you've done." She forced herself to be calm again. She wanted all the answers before she could afford herself the luxury of anger. "Tell me something, John. All those times you said you loved me — was that the truth, or were you using our relationship as yet another method of throwing a spanner into the *Eagle*'s investigation?"

"I did love you, Katherine. If you hadn't been so damned loyal to a handicapped husband, I would have married you. But you wanted to stand by that cripple, didn't you? You spent all your time dreaming up alibis for the evenings you were with me, events you needed to cover for the newspaper so Franz's feelings would not be hurt. You cared more about sparing his feelings than you ever damn well cared about mine! That was why I came to the house. I wanted him to see me, because I wanted him to think that you and I were having an affair. Then he might do the decent thing and kill himself. Did he, Katherine? Did Franz somehow set that fire, or did we just get lucky?"

"You bastard!"

She jumped at him. He shoved her back, sending her crashing to the floor. "You've done enough talking; now it's my turn."

As Katherine struggled to get up, Saxon reached into the center drawer of his desk. His hand came out holding a small automatic pistol. "I'd give anything to turn back the clock, Katherine, but we both know that can't be done. And we also know that I can't afford to allow you to walk out of here to publish your story. There's far too much at stake."

In the brown eyes that had once expressed compassion, Katherine now saw only madness. "You'd kill me?"

Saxon nodded slowly.

Stunned by the sight of the gun, Katherine forced her mind to function. "And how would you get rid of me, John? Throw me over the balcony into your front garden, and hope the police are stupid enough to think I fell from a different floor? And what about the gun? Do you think the police couldn't match up the bullets from it? They'll know within five minutes that any bullets in me"—she felt herself shiver—"would have come from your gun."

The telephone on Saxon's desk began to ring. He ignored it. "Do you take me for a total idiot, Katherine? This gun doesn't belong to me. It's yours."

"Mine?"

He kept the gun pointed unwaveringly at her chest. "It's not registered to me. I don't have a certificate for it. It was something William came by one day. He thought I should keep it here, in case something happened on one of the nights that I worked late. Like tonight, for instance. But it was you who came up here with this gun, wasn't it, Katherine? You came with the gun looking to kill me. I tried to wrest it away from you, and in the ensuing struggle, the gun went off. Unfortunately, it was pointed in your direction at the time."

Katherine kept her eyes fastened on the weapon. The moment it moved, the instant Saxon's hand trembled, she'd leap for it. Try to knock it away from him and hope that in the time it took him to recover, she could run or scream for help. Until then, keep him talking.

"Why would I have come looking to kill you? What motive would I have had?"

"Jealousy, of course. The curse of the rejected woman."

Despite the terrifying predicament, Katherine laughed. "I threw you out, John, don't you remember? How could you possibly convince even the most naive police investigator that I was jealous of you?"

He stepped back to the desk, felt behind him until he found what he wanted. "Here." He flipped a white card to Katherine. "Read what's on there, and you'll see why you're jealous."

Very slowly, she picked up the card. It was a wedding announcement. John Saxon to Susan Beasley. "You met her once, Katherine. At the Mayfair Hotel, when you were with that American. We're getting married next month. Aren't you going to wish me good luck? No, of course you wouldn't wish me good luck. You're jealous, you're mad at me for marrying another woman, and that's why you came up here with this gun. To kill me. If you couldn't have me, then no woman could."

The telephone continued to ring as Katherine desperately sought to stall for time. "I'm happy to see your ego hasn't shrunk at all, John. That was what I liked most about you, your ego. It was big enough for both of us, with enough left over for the rest of the country."

"I'm glad, Katherine, because you'll have all eternity in which to remember it." He stepped toward her, the gun held like a rigid extension of his hand. Katherine knew what he was doing; she'd read enough books, seen enough films. If she were shot during a struggle over the gun, there would be powder burns. Saxon was coming close enough to be sure he left some.

She never took her eyes off the gun. She would have done better to watch Saxon's free hand, which came sweeping around to knock her off her feet again. As

598

she fell, Saxon jumped on top of her. She felt the muzzle of the gun jam into her ribs, just below her heart, and she waited for eternity to begin.

A man's voice yelled, "You son of a bitch!" The pressure of the gun in her side lessened, then the wind was knocked clean out of her body as Raymond Barnhill flung himself on top of Saxon. The gun went off with a loud roar close by Katherine's head. Big Ben chimed twelve o'clock in her ears, but she wasn't hurt. Neither was Barnhill or Saxon. She lay on the floor, watching as the American lifted Saxon to his feet, held him by his tie and swung a huge roundhouse right that landed with a sickening thud. Saxon's head snapped back, his eyes rolled up in his head. Barnhill opened his hand and Saxon fell to the floor.

"Katherine . . . Katherine . . . are you all right?" Barnhill knelt on the floor beside her, a hand cradling her head.

"I'm dazed, that's all, and bells won't stop ringing in my ears. Why . . . how . . . ?" She shook her head, unable to phrase the question.

"I left Hawtrey's place right after you did. There was no way I was going to let you come up here by yourself. But you drove like a lunatic. I lost you at the first set of lights. The doorman tried to stop me when I came running into the building, but I just pushed him away. I think he called up here to warn Saxon."

"The phone rang while he was telling me how he was going to kill me. But he never answered it." She held Barnhill tightly.

"If that . . ." The American looked at Saxon, who was showing the first signs of regaining consciousness. "If he'd harmed you, I'd have torn him to pieces."

Footsteps sounded. The doorman entered the office. "Mr. Saxon, are you all right?" He looked at Barnhill and Katherine. "What's going on here? I'm going to ring the police."

"Please do," Barnhill said. "The phone's on the

desk."

Katherine stood up, breathing deeply. "Walk me down to my car, Raymond. I have to go. I have a story to write."

"What about the police?"

"Tell them they can reach me at the *Eagle*. Let me write my last exclusive."

On the way out of the office, Barnhill scooped up the gun in his handkerchief. The doorman called after them. "Don't worry," Barnhill said. "I'll be back in a minute."

By the time they reached the white Lotus in St. James's Square, Katherine's breathing was normal. Her ribs ached where Barnhill and Saxon had landed on her, but she'd be able to drive back to Fleet Street. Before she climbed into the car, she gave Barnhill a long kiss.

"You're a lifesaver, Raymond, and I really mean that."

Barnhill cut the sentimentality with a joke. "You saved my life when I was down. Now I've saved yours. We're even. Go and write your exclusive, before someone else gets wind of it."

She got into the car and started the engine. Barnhill watched her drive away before he returned to Saxon House. A police car pulled up outside as he entered the elevator, and he held the door for the two police officers who got out of it.

"I can tell you everything you need to know, gentlemen." He pressed the button for the sixth floor, and winced. He'd hit Saxon so hard that he'd broken his hand.

It was just before midnight when Katherine arrived back at the *Eagle*. Lawrie Stimkin had all the photographs she had asked for. Waiting with him was a copy editor to go over the story as Katherine wrote it.

She sat at a typewriter, inserted a sheet of paper, and stared at it for almost a minute. Looking over her shoulder was Stimkin. At the adjacent desk sat the copy editor, ready to prepare the story for press. Katherine refused to be hurried. This was the most important story of her life, and, quite possibly, the last story she would ever write. After this, managerial decisions would be her forte. Before she wrote the first word, she wanted time to think.

John Saxon was in custody. And Katherine's last meeting with him had commenced in the same manner as her first. Photographs shoved in front of his face, and explanations demanded. He would not be visiting the *Eagle* or sending roses after this story was published; that was for sure!

Recalling that first time she'd had lunch with him, at The Anchor, on the south bank of the Thames, Katherine yielded to a trace of nostalgia. She'd enjoyed that lunch, sitting there among the memories of the Globe Theater, swapping Samuel Johnson quotations with a handsome, charming man.

One such quotation came to mind right now. Not one she had exchanged with Saxon over lunch that day, but a piece of Dr. Johnson's wisdom that seemed particularly fitting to this moment. Her fingers flew over the typewriter to create the opening words of her story:

"Patriotism is the last refuge of a scoundrel."

The police were waiting for Katherine when she finished the story. She gave them a statement, telling how she had confronted Saxon with her discovery, and how he had tried to kill her. Her voice softened as she described Raymond Barnhill rescuing her with no time left on the clock.

Barnhill returned to the *Eagle* after the police had gone. Only after ascertaining that Katherine was all right did he agree to go to the hospital to have his broken hand attended to.

Katherine was still at the *Eagle* when the presses began to roll with her exclusive. From the telephone in Sally's office, she dialed Nigel Hawtrey's number. Sid Hall answered.

"You can stop your babysitting job now, Sid. Hawtrey's in the paper along with everyone else. He won't get very far if he tries to run."

She kicked off her shoes, stretched out on Sally's couch, and closed her eyes. She'd grab a few minutes rest before driving home.

She was still fast asleep on the couch when Sally came in at nine-fifteen.

27

The British Patriotic League's election campaign collapsed. Within a day of the *Eagle* story, every candidate withdrew from the race; instead of heralding in a political upheaval, they had been sacrificial pawns in a higher power play.

The three members of the League's executive committee were arrested. Alan Venables was charged with the murder of Brian Waters. Neville Sharpe and Trevor Burns were charged with conspiracy to murder, as was John Saxon. Saxon was also charged with attempting to murder Katherine. A police spokesman told eager reporters that further charges were pending.

Arrest warrants on conspiracy charges were also issued for two Conservative MPs, Edwin Johnson and Daniel Cooper, as well as Sir Donald Leslie, Jeffrey Dillard, William Brown, Nigel Hawtrey, and everyone Katherine could remember meeting through John Saxon. Hawtrey, living up to the image of a sharp rogue that Deidre Chalfont had ascribed to him, saved police the bother of searching for him. Once he saw the extent of the damage, he surrendered himself at London's West End Central police station. With him was a top criminal lawyer, who stated that his client, in return for favorable treatment, would testify for the

Crown.

In the general election on June 9, the Conservative government was returned to power with a landslide victory. The reactionary wing, stripped of its two leaders and ripped apart by the scandal, fell to pieces. Despite the scope of victory, not one of the Johnson/Cooper followers held his seat.

At the end of June, Sally Roberts retired from the position of editorial director of *Eagle* Newspapers Limited. Katherine succeeded her, maintaining the office on the executive floor in the same bright and cheerful decor that Sally had chosen. Although there had been a change, there was still a woman on the board of directors

Two weeks later, on a Saturday morning in the middle of July, Sally and Roland were married in a civil ceremony. Henry and Joanne were pageboy and bridesmaid, and Katherine filled the role of matron of honor. "Remember today," she told her son and daughter as she checked their appearance before the ceremony. "Only very lucky boys and girls have the opportunity to be pageboy and bridesmaid at their grandfather's wedding."

After the ceremony, a party was held under a green-and-white striped marquee erected in Roland's back garden. More than two hundred people attended, and uniformed waitresses had to fight their way through a solid mass of people to serve champagne and hors d'oeuvres. Only when all the guests sat down for lunch did the chaos cease.

Roland and Sally shared a small top table with Katherine and Raymond Barnhill and Henry and Joanne. As lunch was served, Katherine took a white envelope from her bag. Smiling, she handed it to her father.

"A special wedding gift. You'll find it very useful."

Roland hesitated to open the envelope. He saw the wide grin on Sally's face and knew that she was a party to whatever the joke was. "Does it go bang?"

"Open the envelope and find out."

Slitting the flap, Roland pulled out a gift voucher for a dozen driving lessons. He raised an eyebrow at his daughter. "To suggest a man's driving is poor can be taken as an attack upon his very virility."

"No one's questioning your virility, Roland darling," Sally said. "Just your driving." She turned to Katherine. "Don't worry, I'll make sure he takes the lessons. I won't drive him anywhere, and I won't let Arthur Parsons behind the wheel either. He'll get the message."

Katherine threw her arms around Sally's neck and kissed her. "I always knew you'd make a great mum!"

In the evening, Katherine and Barnhill returned to Kate's Haven with the children. Henry and Joanne, tired from the day's excitement, needed little urging to go to bed.

The night was clear and mild. Katherine and Barnhill watched the moon come up from the back patio, where they shared an upholstered swing chair. Like the children, they were comfortably exhausted, content to hold hands and swing gently back and forth.

After fifteen minutes, Barnhill broke the silence. "These last couple of weeks, I've been thinking about starting on a new book."

"Is that a tactful way of saying you're handing in your notice? We won't accept it, you know."

"Don't worry. I need the stability of a regular job at the *Eagle* more than the *Eagle* needs me."

"What will the book be about? Vietnam again?"

"No. I'm cured of that hang-up. I'm cured of a few things," he said, and Katherine knew exactly what he meant. "I was thinking of doing a roman à clef on what happened with the British Patriotic League and the influential businessmen who were the brains behind it."

"Am I going to be in it?"

"Do you want to be?"

"Only if you make me very beautiful and very intelligent. And only if I can suggest my own happy ending. After all, it's my hard work that's given you the idea."

Barnhill leaned back, smiling. "I'm damned glad you quit writing and moved up to the executive floor."

"Why? Frightened of a little competition?"

"No. I'm frightened of the confusion."

"What does that mean?"

"Say a woman writer with an established byline gets married. What happens—does she have to alter her byline?"

"Of course not. She keeps her byline the way it is. She has a dual identity; that's all."

Barnhill wrapped his arms around her, pulled her close, and kissed her. "But since you've been appointed editorial director of Eagle Newspapers—which, by the way, would have happened even if you weren't the proprietor's daughter—the question of dual identity is academic."

Understanding came. "Is that a proposal?"

"Didn't I make it clear enough?"

"Not really."

"Let's try again. What would you say to marrying me?"

"I'd say wonderful. But the children have a vote in this as well. I'll ask them first thing tomorrow morning."

"Ask them now."

"They're asleep."

"Wake them."

"You're cruel."

"Is it kind to keep me in suspense until the morning?"

"Very well." Katherine led the way into the house and up to her daughter's bedroom. Joanne blinked in the sudden light, but she never really came to. When Katherine asked, "Would you like me to marry Raymond?" Joanne gave a sleepy smile and closed her eyes again.

"That was a definite yes," Barnhill said.

"Can you read children's minds?"

"I can read their smiles."

They were more fortunate with Henry. He sat up in bed, fully awake, the instant his door was opened. "What is it?"

Katherine sat on the edge of her son's bed, while Barnhill stood on the other side. "Henry, Raymond has asked me to marry him. What do you think about that?"

The boy's clear blue eyes flicked to Barnhill, then back to his mother. "Would I become Henry Barnhill?"

"No, darling, you'll always remain Henry Kassler, after your father." She glanced up at Barnhill, who nodded in agreement. He had no problem with Katherine and the children maintaining strong memories of Franz.

"Then I think that would be super," Henry said. "Will we have another wedding like today? I might be the only boy ever to be a pageboy at the weddings of his mother and his grandfather."

They were both smiling when they left Henry's room and returned downstairs. Katherine made hot chocolate, which they took out to the patio. The moon was high, and as they watched, a shooting star streaked down from the sky.

"Make a wish," Barnhill said.

"No need. Everything I want has already come true."

Barnhill gazed at the point where the shooting star had disappeared. "I don't mind if you want to remain

607

Katherine Kassler."

"No, I'll change. I'll be Katherine Barnhill."

"It might not be such a good idea after all. Could be confusing with two people named Barnhill."

"Don't argue with me. I'll be Katherine Barnhill, and that way every woman at Eagle Newspapers will know you belong to me. You won't be distracted from your work by other women making eyes at you."

Barnhill whistled through his teeth. "Boy, you marry a woman you work for, and straightaway she starts laying down the law."

But Katherine was not listening. She was running the new name over in her mind and deciding she liked it more and more.